THE

LYLE
OFFICIAL
ANTIQUES
REVIEW 1994

$8 200

THE LYLE OFFICIAL ANTIQUES REVIEW 1994

A PERIGEE BOOK

Perigee Books
are published by
The Putnam Publishing Group
200 Madison Avenue
New York, NY 10016

ISBN 0-399-51833-9
LC 74-640592

Cover design by Jack Ribik

Printed in the United States of America
2   3   4   5   6   7   8   9   10

This book is printed on acid-free paper.

INTRODUCTION

This year over 100,000 Antique Dealers and Collectors will make full and profitable use of their Lyle Antiques Price Guide. They know that only in this one volume will they find the widest possible variety of goods – illustrated, described and given a current market value to assist them to BUY RIGHT AND SELL RIGHT throughout the year of issue.

They know, too, that by building a collection of these immensely valuable volumes year by year, they will equip themselves with an unparalleled reference library of facts, figures and illustrations which, properly used, cannot fail to help them keep one step ahead of the market.

In its twenty four years of publication, Lyle has gone from strength to strength and has become without doubt the pre-eminent book of reference for the antique trade throughout the world. Each of its fact filled pages are packed with precisely the kind of profitable information the professional Dealer needs – including descriptions, illustrations and values of thousands and thousands of individual items carefully selected to give a representative picture of the current market in antiques and collectables – and remember all values are prices actually paid, based on accurate sales records in the twelve months prior to publication from the best established and most highly respected auction houses and retail outlets in Europe and America.

This is THE book for the Professional Antiques Dealer. 'The Lyle Book' – we've even heard it called 'The Dealer's Bible'.

Compiled and published afresh each year, the Lyle Antiques Price Guide is the most comprehensive up-to-date antiques price guide available. THIS COULD BE YOUR WISEST INVESTMENT OF THE YEAR!

Anthony Curtis

The publishers wish to express their sincere thanks to the following for their involvement and assistance in the production of this volume:

EELIN MCIVOR (Sub Editor)
ANNETTE CURTIS (Editorial)
CATRIONA DAY (Art Production)
DONNA CRUICKSHANK (Art Production)
ANGIE DE MARCO (Art Production)
JAMES BROWN (Graphics)
DONNA RUTHERFORD
JACQUELINE LEDDY

CONTENTS

Advertising 16
Aeronautical Items 20
Alabaster 24
Americana 25
Amusement Machines 27
Antiquities 28
Architectural Fittings 30
Arms & Armor 32
    Armor 32
    Bowie Knives 34
    Cased Sets 36
    Daggers 38
    Flint Lock Guns 40
    Flint Lock Pistols 42
    Helmets 44
    Militaria 48
    Percussion Carbines 50
    Percussion Revolvers 52
    Powder Flasks 54
    Swords 56
    Tsubas 58
    Wakizashi 60
Autographed Documents 62
Automatons 66
Barometers 70
Baskets 72
Blue John 73
Bronze 74
Buckets 79
Caddies & Boxes 80
Cameras 87
Car Mascots 92
Carousel Figures 93
Chandeliers 94
China 96
    American 96
    Arita 98
    Berlin 99
    Bow 100
    British 102
    Canton 106
    Cardew 106
    Caughley 107
    Chelsea 108

Chinese 110
Clarice Cliff 113
Coper 115
Delft 116
De Morgan 119
Derby 120
Doulton 122
Dresden 126
European 127
French 130
Gardner 133
George Jones 134
German 135
Grueby 138
Hamada 139
Italian 140
Japanese 142
Leach 143
Liverpool 144
Longton Hall 145
Lucie Rie 146
Martinware 148
Meissen 149
Minton 152
Moorcroft 154
Pearlware 156
Prattware 157
Rockingham 157
Rookwood 158
Rosenthal 158
Royal Dux 159
Ruskin 160
Satsuma 160
Sevres 164
Spode 166
Staffordshire 167
Vienna 171
Wedgwood 172
Wemyss 174
Westerwald 175
Worcester 176
Clocks & Watches 180
    Bracket Clocks 180
    Carriage Clocks 182

Clock Sets 184
Lantern Clocks 187
Longcase Clocks 188
Mantel Clocks 192
Skeleton Clocks 201
Wall Clocks 202
Watches 206
Wrist Watches 210
Copper & Brass 212
Costume 216
Dolls 218
Domestic Equipment 224
Enamel 228
Fans 229
Film Star Autographs 230
Firegrates 236
Fireplace Furniture 238
Fireplaces 240
Fishing Equipment 243
Furniture 244
    Beds 244
    Bookcases 246
    Bureau 248
    Bureau Bookcases 252
    Cabinets 254
    Canterburys 259
    Chairs, Dining 260
            Easy Chairs 266
            Elbow Chairs 272
    Chests of Drawers 278
    Chests on Chests 284
    Chests on Stands 286
    Chiffoniers 288
    Commode Chests 289
    Commode & Pot Cupboards 292
    Corner Cupboards 294
    Cupboards 297
    Davenports 300
    Display Cabinets 302
    Dressers 306
    Kneehole Desks 308
    Linen Presses 311
    Lowboys 312
    Screens 314
    Secretaire Bookcases 316
    Secretaires 318
    Settees & Couches 322
Sideboards 330
Stands 333
Stools 336
Suites 340
Tables 344
    Breakfast Tables 344
    Card & Tea Tables 346
    Center Tables 350
    Console Tables 354
    Dining Tables 356
    Dressing Tables 359
    Drop Leaf Tables 363
    Drum Tables 366
    Dumb Waiters 367
    Gateleg Tables 368
    Large Tables 370
    Occasional Tables 372
    Pembroke Tables 376
    Side Tables 378
    Sofa Tables 382
    Workboxes & Games Tables 384
    Writing Tables & Desks 386
Trunks & Coffers 392
Wardrobes & Armoires 396
Washstands 398
Whatnots 399
Wine Coolers 402
Garden Statuary & Furniture 404
Gas Appliances 410
Glass 412
    Ashtrays 412
    Baskets 412
    Beakers 413
    Bottles 414
    Bowls 417
    Candlesticks 420
    Decanters 421
    Dishes 422
    Drinking Glasses 424
    Flasks 426
    Goblets 428
    Jugs & Pitchers 430
    Miscellaneous Glass 432
    Paperweights 434
    Shades 438
    Stained Glass 439
    Vases 440

Wine Glasses 446
Golfing Items 450
Hollywood Posters 458
Icons 466
Jewelry 468
Lacquer 477
Lamps 478
Marble 486
Mechanical Music 488
Miniature Furniture 495
Mirrors 496
Models 504
Model Ships 505
Model Trains 508
Musical Instruments 510
Optical Instruments 511
Pewter 514
Photographs 516
Pianos 520
Plaster 521
Portrait Miniatures 522
Prints 528
Quilts 530
Radios & T.V.'s 536
Robots 539
Rock 'n' Roll 540
Rugs 548
Samplers 554
Scent Bottles 556
Scientific Instruments 558
Scrimshaw 571
Sewing Machines 573
Signed Photographs 574
Silhouettes 577
Silver 578
    Baskets 578
    Beakers 579
    Bowls 580
    Boxes 582
    Candelabra 583
    Candlesticks 584
    Casters 586
    Centerpieces 587
    Chambersticks 588
    Cigar Boxes 589
    Cigarette Cases 589
    Claret Jugs 590

Coasters 591
Coffee Pots 592
Cream Jugs 594
Cruets 595
Cups 596
Dishes 597
Flatware 598
Goblets 600
Inkstands 601
Jugs 602
Miscellaneous Silver 603
Mugs & Canns 606
Mustards 607
Pitchers & Ewers 608
Plates 609
Porringers 609
Salts & Peppers 610
Sauceboats 611
Tankards 612
Tea & Coffee Sets 614
Tea Caddies 618
Tea Kettles 619
Teapots 620
Toast Racks 622
Trays & Salvers 623
Tureens 624
Urns 625
Vases 626
Vesta Cases 627
Vinaigrettes 628
Wine Coolers 629
Snuff Boxes 630
Spectacles 632
Sporting Items 633
Steel & Iron 634
Tapestries 638
Teddy Bears 640
Terracotta 642
Textiles 644
Toasters 646
Toys 647
Travel Requisites 652
Trays 653
Tunbridge Ware 654
Typewriters 656
Weathervanes 657
Wood 660

ACKNOWLEDGEMENTS

AB Stockholms Auktionsverk, Box 16256, 103 25 Stockholm, Sweden

Abbotts Auction Rooms, The Auction Rooms, Campsea Ash, Woodbridge, Suffolk

Abridge Auction Rooms, Market Place, Abridge, Essex RM4 1UA

Allen & Harris, St Johns Place, Whiteladies Road, Clifton, Bristol BS8 2ST

Jean Claude Anaf, Lyon Brotteaux, 13 bis place Jules Ferry, 69456 Lyon, France

Anderson & Garland, Marlborough House, Marlborough Crescent, Newcastle upon Tyne NE1 4EE

Antique Collectors Club & Co. Ltd, 5 Church Street, Woodbridge, Suffolk IP 12 1DS

Auction Team Köln, Postfach 50 11 68, D-5000 Köln 50 Germany

Auktionshaus Arnold, Bleichstr. 42, 6000 Frankfurt a/M, Germany

Barber's Auctions, Woking, Surrey

Bearnes, Rainbow, Avenue Road, Torquay TQ2 5TG

Biddle & Webb, Ladywood Middleway, Birmingham B16 0PP

Bigwood, The Old School, Tiddington, Stratford upon Avon

Black Horse Agencies, Locke & England, 18 Guy Street, Leamington Spa

Boardman Fine Art Auctioneers, Station Road Corner, Haverhill, Suffolk CB9 0EY

Bonhams, Montpelier Street, Knightsbridge, London SW7 1HH

Bonhams Chelsea, 65–69 Lots Road, London SW10 0RN

Bonhams West Country, Dowell Street, Honiton, Devon

British Antique Exporters, School Close, Queen Elizabeth Avenue, Burgess Hill, Sussex

William H Brown, The Warner Auction Rooms, 16–18, Halford Street, Leicester LE1 1JB

Butterfield & Butterfield, 220 San Bruno Avenue, San Francisco CA 94103, USA

Butterfield & Butterfield, 7601 Sunset Boulevard, Los Angeles CA 90046, USA

Canterbury Auction Galleries, 40 Station Road West, Canterbury CT2 8AN

Central Motor Auctions, Barfield House, Britannia Road, Morley, Leeds, LS27 0HN

H.C. Chapman & Son, The Auction Mart, North Street, Scarborough.

Christie's (International) SA, 8 place de la Taconnerie, 1204 Genève, Switzerland

Christie's Monaco, S.A.M, Park Palace 98000 Monte Carlo, Monaco

Christie's Scotland, 164–166 Bath Street Glasgow G2 4TG

Christie's South Kensington Ltd., 85 Old Brompton Road, London SW7 3LD

Christie's, 8 King Street, London SW1Y 6QT

Christie's East, 219 East 67th Street, New York, NY 10021, USA

Christie's, 502 Park Avenue, New York, NY 10022, USA

Christie's, Cornelis Schuytstraat 57, 1071 JG Amsterdam, Netherlands

Christie's SA Roma, 114 Piazza Navona, 00186 Rome, Italy

Christie's Swire, 1202 Alexandra House, 16–20 Chater Road, Hong Kong

Christie's Australia Pty Ltd., 1 Darling Street, South Yarra, Melbourne, Victoria 3141, Australia

A J Cobern, The Grosvenor Sales Rooms, 93b Eastbank Street, Southport PR8 1DG

Cooper Hirst Auctions, The Granary Saleroom, Victoria Road, Chelmsford, Essex CM2 6LH

The Crested China Co., Station House, Driffield, E. Yorks YO25 7PY

Clifford Dann, 20/21 High Street, Lewes, Sussex

Julian Dawson, Lewes Auction Rooms, 56 High Street, Lewes BN7 1XE

Dee & Atkinson, 8 Harrisen, The Exchange Saleroom, Driffield, Nth Humberside YO25 7LJ

Garth Denham & Assocs. Horsham Auction Galleries, Warnsham, Nr. Horsham, Sussex

Diamond Mills & Co., 117 Hamilton Road, Felixstowe, Suffolk

David Dockree Fine Art, 224 Moss Lane, Bramhall, Stockport SK7 1BD

Dowell Lloyd & Co. Ltd, 118 Putney Bridge Road, London SW15 2NQ

Downer Ross, Charter House, 42 Avebury Boulevard, Central Milton Keynes MK9 2HS

Hy. Duke & Son, 40 South Street, Dorchester, Dorset

Du Mouchelles Art Galleries Co., 409 E. Jefferson Avenue, Detroit, Michigan 48226, USA

Duncan Vincent, 105 London Street, Reading RG1 4LF

Sala de Artes y Subastas Durán, Serrano 12, 28001 Madrid, Spain

Eldred's, Box 796, E. Dennis, MA 02641, USA

R H Ellis & Sons, 44/46 High St., Worthing, BN11 1LL

ANTIQUES REVIEW

Ewbanks, Welbeck House, High Street, Guildford, Surrey, GU1 3JF
Fellows & Son, Augusta House, 19 Augusta Street, Hockley, Birmingham
Finarte, 20121 Milano, Piazzetta Bossi 4, Italy
John D Fleming & Co., 8 Fore Street, Dulverton, Somerset
Peter Francis, 19 King Street, Carmarthen, Dyfed
G A Property Services, Canterbury Auction Galleries, Canterbury, Kent
Galerie Koller, Rämistr. 8, CH 8024 Zürich, Switzerland
Galerie Moderne, 3 rue du Parnasse, 1040 Bruxelles, Belgium
Geering & Colyer (Black Horse Agencies) Highgate, Hawkhurst, Kent
Glerum Auctioneers, Westeinde 12, 2512 HD's Gravenhage, Netherlands
The Goss and Crested China Co., 62 Murray Road, Horndean, Hants PO8 9JL
Graves Son & Pilcher, 71 Church Road, Hove, East Sussex, BN3 2GL
Greenslade Hunt, 13 Hammet Street, Taunton, Somerset, TA1 1RN
Peter Günnemann, Ehrenberg Str. 57, 2000 Hamburg 50, Germany
Halifax Property Services, 53 High Street, Tenterden, Kent
Halifax Property Services, 15 Cattle Market, Sandwich, Kent CT13 9AW
Hampton's Fine Art, 93 High Street, Godalming, Surrey
Hanseatisches Auktionshaus für Historica, Neuer Wall 57, 2000 Hamburg 36, Germany
William Hardie Ltd., 141 West Regent Street, Glasgow G2 2SG
Andrew Hartley Fine Arts, Victoria Hall, Little Lane, Ilkely
Hauswedell & Nolte, D-2000 Hamburg 13, Pöseldorfer Weg 1, Germany
Giles Haywood, The Auction House, St John's Road, Stourbridge, West Midlands, DY8 1EW
Heatheringtons Nationwide Anglia, The Amersham Auction Rooms, 125 Station Road, Amersham,
    Bucks
Muir Hewitt, Halifax Antiques Centre, Queens Road/Gibbet Street, Halifax HX1 4LR
Hobbs & Chambers, 'At the Sign of the Bell', Market Place, Cirencester, Glos
Hobbs Parker, Romney House, Ashford, Ashford, Kent
Holloways, 49 Parsons Street, Banbury OX16 8PF
Hotel de Ventes Horta, 390 Chaussée de Waterloo (Ma Campagne), 1060 Bruxelles, Belgium
Jacobs & Hunt, Lavant Street, Petersfield, Hants. GU33 3EF
James of Norwich, 33 Timberhill, Norwich NR1 3LA
P Herholdt Jensens Auktioner, Rundforbivej 188, 2850 Nerum, Denmark
Kennedy & Wolfenden, 218 Lisburn Rd, Belfast BT9 6GD
G A Key, Aylsham Saleroom, Palmers Lane, Aylsham, Norfolk, NR11 6EH
Kunsthaus am Museum, Drususgasse 1–5, 5000 Köln 1, Germany
Kunsthaus Lempertz, Neumarkt 3, 5000 Köln 1, Germany
Lambert & Foster (County Group), The Auction Sales Room, 102 High Street, Tenterden, Kent
W.H. Lane & Son, 64 Morrab Road, Penzance, Cornwall, TR18 2QT
Langlois Ltd., Westway Rooms, Don Street, St Helier, Channel Islands
Lawrence Butler Fine Art Salerooms, Marine Walk, Hythe, Kent, CT21 5AJ
Lawrence Fine Art, South Street, Crewkerne, Somerset TA18 8AB
Lawrence's Fine Art Auctioneers, Norfolk House, 80 High Street, Bletchingley, Surrey
David Lay, The Penzance Auction House, Alverton, Penzance, Cornwall TA18 4KE
Brian Loomes, Calf Haugh Farm, Pateley Bridge, North Yorks
Lots Road Chelsea Auction Galleries, 71 Lots Road, Chelsea, London SW10 0RN
R K Lucas & Son, Tithe Exchange, 9 Victoria Place, Haverfordwest, SA61 2JX
Duncan McAlpine, Stateside Comics plc, 125 East Barnet Road, London EN4 8RF
McCartneys, Portcullis Salerooms, Ludlow, Shropshire
Christopher Matthews, 23 Mount Street, Harrogate HG2 8DG
John Maxwell, 75 Hawthorn Street, Wilmslow, Cheshire
May & Son, 18 Bridge Street, Andover, Hants
Morphets, 4–6 Albert Street, Harrogate, North Yorks HG1 1JL
D M Nesbit & Co, 7 Clarendon Road, Southsea, Hants PO5 2ED
John Nicholson, 1 Crossways Court, Fernhurst, Haslemere, Surrey GU27 3EP
Onslow's, Metrostore, Townmead Road, London SW6 2RZ

ANTIQUES REVIEW

Outhwaite & Litherland, Kingsley Galleries, Fontenoy Street, Liverpool, Merseyside L3 2BE
J R Parkinson Son & Hamer Auctions, The Auction Rooms, Rochdale, Bury, Lancs
Phillips Manchester, Trinity House, 114 Northenden Road, Sale, Manchester M33 3HD
Phillips Son & Neale SA, 10 rue des Chaudronniers, 1204 Genève, Switzerland
Phillips West Two, 10 Salem Road, London W2 4BL
Phillips, 11 Bayle Parade, Folkestone, Kent CT20 1SQ
Phillips, 49 London Road, Sevenoaks, Kent TN13 1UU
Phillips, 65 George Street, Edinburgh EH2 2JL
Phillips, Blenstock House, 7 Blenheim Street, New Bond Street, London W1Y 0AS
Phillips Marylebone, Hayes Place, Lisson Grove, London NW1 6UA
Phillips, New House, 150 Christleton Road, Chester CH3 5TD
Andrew Pickford, 42 St Andrew Street, Hertford SG14 1JA
Pinney's, 5627 Ferrier, Montreal, Quebec, Canada H4P 2M4
Pooley & Rogers, Regent Auction Rooms, Abbey Street, Penzance
Pretty & Ellis, Amersham Auction Rooms, Station Road, Amersham, Bucks
Peter M Raw, Thornfield, Hurdle Way, Compton Down, Winchester, Hants SC21 2AN
Harry Ray & Co, Lloyds Bank Chambers, Welshpool, Montgomery SY21 7RR
Rennie's, 1 Agincourt Street, Monmouth
Riddetts, Richmond Hill, Bournemouth
Ritchie's, 429 Richmond Street East, Toronto, Canada M5A 1R1
Derek Roberts Antiques, 24–25 Shipbourne Road, Tonbridge, Kent TN10 3DN
Rogers de Rin, 79 Royal Hospital Road, London SW3 4HN
Russell, Baldwin & Bright, The Fine Art Saleroom, Ryelands Road, Leominster HR6 8JG
Sandoes Nationwide Anglia, Tabernacle Road, Wotton under Edge, Glos GL12 7EB
Selkirk's, 4166 Olive Street, St Louis, Missouri 63108, USA
Skinner Inc., Bolton Gallery, Route 117, Bolton MA, USA
Sotheby's, 34–35 New Bond Street, London W1A 2AF
Sotheby's, 1334 York Avenue, New York NY 10021
Sotheby's, 112 George Street, Edinburgh EH2 4LH
Sotheby's, Sommers Place, Billingshurst, West Sussex RH14 9AD
Sotheby's Monaco, BP 45, 98001 Monte Carlo
Southgate Auction Rooms, 55 High St, Southgate, London N14 6LD
Henry Spencer, 40 The Square, Retford, Notts. DN22 6DJ
Spink & Son Ltd, 5-7 King St., St James's, London SW1Y 6QS
Street Jewellery, 16 Eastcliffe Avenue, Newcastle upon Tyne NE3 4SN
Stride & Son, Southdown House, St John's St., Chichester, Sussex
G E Sworder & Son, Northgate End Salerooms, 15 Northgate End, Bishop Stortford, Herts
Taviner's of Bristol, Prewett Street, Redcliffe, Bristol BS1 6PB
Tennants, 27 Market Place, Leyburn, Yorkshire
Thomson Roddick & Laurie, 24 Lowther Street, Carlisle
Thomson Roddick & Laurie, 60 Whitesands, Dumfries
Timbleby & Shorland, 31 Gt Knollys St, Reading RG1 7HU
Venator & Hanstein, Cäcilienstr. 48, 5000 Köln 1, Germany
T Vennett Smith, 11 Nottingham Road, Gotham, Nottingham NG11 0HE
Duncan Vincent, 105 London Road, Reading RG1 4LF
Wallis & Wallis, West Street Auction Galleries, West Street, Lewes, E. Sussex BN7 2NJ
Walter's, 1 Mint Lane, Lincoln LN1 1UD
Ward & Morris, Stuart House, 18 Gloucester Road, Ross on Wye HR9 5BN
Warren & Wignall Ltd, The Mill, Earnshaw Bridge, Leyland Lane, Leyland PR5 3PH
Dominique Watine-Arnault, 11 rue François 1er, 75008 Paris, France
Wells Cundall Nationwide Anglia, Staffordshire House, 27 Flowergate, Whitby YO21 3AX
Woltons, 6 Whiting Street, Bury St Edmunds, Suffolk IP33 1PB
Peter Wilson, Victoria Gallery, Market Street, Nantwich, Cheshire CW5 5DG
Woolley & Wallis, The Castle Auction Mart, Salisbury, Wilts SP1 3SU
Austin Wyatt Nationwide Anglia, Emsworth Road, Lymington, Hants SO41 9BL

AMERICAN PERIODS

PILGRIM STYLE – 17TH CENTURY

This earliest distinguishable American style was derived from Renaissance and 17th century English models. Items were massive, rectilinear and of simple basic construction. Tables were mainly trestle based or gateleg; chairs were comprised often of posts and spindles with rush seats or had hard slat backs. Typical was the Wainscot chair, which, with its solid back and columnar turned legs, was based on Elizabethan models.

WILLIAM & MARY 1690–1725

This style was introduced into America at the end of the 17th century, and was essentially a New World version of the baroque. Chairs had scroll, spiral and columnar legs, surfaces were richly decorated, painted or veneered, and walnut and maple replaced oak as the major working media. Innovations at this time included the butterfly table, and tea and dressing tables also became popular.

QUEEN ANNE 1725–50

This followed the English Queen Anne style, with elegant curving forms. Walnut, cherry and maple were the most popular woods, and mahogany began to be imported from around 1750. Finely decorated candlestands and tea-tables with tripod, cabriole bases are typical of this period, and folding games tables and large, drop-leaf tables also emerged at this time.

Chippendale maple stand front desk, 1750. (Christie's)

CHIPPENDALE 1750–80

This was more conservative than its English counterpart and reflected earlier 18th century trends such as ball and claw feet, which were already démodé in London. Designs were much lighter than those of the Queen Anne period and forms became more ornamental. Intricate chair backs, including the ladder back, now became popular. Mahogany was by now the favored wood.

During this period different regional preferences became apparent. Craftsmen in Newport, Rhode Island, for example, followed the classical style more closely, with fluted and reeded columns and legs, whereas their Philadelphia counterparts produced more elaborately carved rococo pieces.

FEDERAL 1780–1820

This was the American answer to neoclassicism. Most furniture of the period will be described as either Sheraton or Hepplewhite, although it is difficult to establish how much American craftsmen actually depended on their designs. In any case, the suggestion that there is a vast difference between them is also somewhat spurious.

The later Federal period saw a much more literal borrowing of Greco-Roman motifs, and the French influence of the Empire style, whether it came direct or filtered through England, is also apparent. New forms, such as the work table, appeared. Side tables too became popular as did chair backs with a center splat carved with classical motifs such as urn and feather or a series of columns. After 1800, however, chair designs became heavier, while sofa designs became simpler. The Grecian couch found its modern counterpart as a daybed. Duncan Phyfe was one of the best and most sought after exponents of the Federal style.

EMPIRE 1815–40

The delicacy of early neo-classicism gave way now to heavier classical forms with more emphasis on outline than on carved detail. In the Empire style, undulating scrolls typically balanced heavy geometric shapes with ornamentation carved in high relief. Mahogany, rosewood veneers and marble were common materials. A French emigré, Charles Henri Lannuier, was among the first to introduce the style to America in the first years of the 19th century. His work combined late Louis XVI and Empire designs and was characterised by the use of gilded caryatids on tables and chairs.

COUNTRY 1690–1850

This term is used to describe most simple furniture made between the late 17th and late 19th centuries, which combined both fashionable and more conservative features. As the name suggests, it was supposed to be made by rural artisans, who modified more sophisticated designs to suit rural homes, but some was also made in cities. Pine and maple were the principal woods and surfaces were often painted, with very sparse decoration. Often, features of various styles were combined, those being chosen for ease of crafting. Thus turned William & Mary legs persisted long after they were no longer fashionable elsewhere, and cabriole legs are very rare. Windsor and slat back chairs are perhaps two of the most characteristic products of the Country style.

SHAKER FURNITURE 1790–1900

This furniture was made by the Shaker religious sect living in Massachusetts, New York and a few other states, and was in the finest tradition of country design. Its heyday lasted from 1820–70 and the furniture is characterised by its simplicity and utility. Form was subsidiary to function. Many pieces reflect the agricultural nature of the Shaker communities, such as tables for sorting seeds. Pine and maple were again the principal woods. Surfaces were unadorned and painted, legs were turned and slender.

Gothic stiple dresser with decorative panels, 1870's. (Sotheby's)

19TH CENTURY REVIVAL STYLES
GOTHIC REVIVAL 1840–1890

In its early stages the Gothic Revival was mainly expressed in decoration, with the use of details imitating historical ornament, such as quatrefoils, trefoils, tracery etc. Designs tended to be extravagant and florid and by the 1850s designers were turning rather towards Norman, Romanesque and Elizabethan models.

A further surge of neo-Gothicism came in the 1870s. This took a much simpler and functional form, and followed the purist theories of William Morris in trying to return to genuinely medieval designs. Walnut, oak and cherry were the woods most used, and decoration consisted of simple turned or cut out elements.

ROCOCO REVIVAL 1840–70

The Rococo Revival, also referred to at the time as the Louis XIV style, reached America around 1840 and persisted for about thirty years. It took a much bolder form than the 18th century style on which it was based, with ornament carved in very high relief on forms which were very 19th century in taste. Ornamentation consisted of florid roses, leaves, vines scrolls and shells, all richly carved on curving forms, with mahogany, rosewood and walnut as the preferred media. The main output of pieces in this style was concentrated in New York, Boston and Philadelphia, though there were makers all over the States. It was a style favored for 'Social' furniture, such as sofas, the newly introduced tête à têtes, center tables etc. The period too saw an increasing use of upholstery as techniques advanced and comfort became all important.

RENAISSANCE REVIVAL 1850–90

While it began as early as 1850, this is often looked on as a reaction to rococo. Features of both Renaissance and 18th century neoclassical style were combined on straight rectilinear forms. Porcelain and bronze plaques were often incorporated as embellishments, and popular motifs included flowers, medallions, classical busts, caryatids etc, combined with architecturally derived features such as pediments and columns. Light woods, such as walnut, were favored. Pieces were produced both by skilled craftsmen in New York, and mass produced in midwest factories, notably Grand Rapids.

EASTLAKE STYLE 1870–90

This was one of the styles conceived as a rejection of the flamboyance of most of the preceding 'revivals'. It was named for Charles Lock Eastlake, an influential English architect who advocated a return to simple, honest furniture, where there was a basic relationship between form and function.

17th century forms were recalled, and to avoid the simple repetition of classical motifs, new inspiration was sought for decoration from Middle Eastern and Far Eastern sources. Eastlake believed in letting the natural wood grain speak for itself and preferred oak, cherry and rosewood and walnut when not heavily varnished. Later, however, the movement fell away from his high standards, and a great deal of poor quality furniture was produced.

L. & J.G. Stickley mantle clock, Fayetteville, 1910. (Skinner)

MISSION, AND ARTS & CRAFTS 1900–1925

These again were reactions against much of the design of the 19th century. The Mission style purported to be based on the furniture supposedly found in the old Franciscan Missions in California and was seen as a revival of medieval and other functional designs. It was, broadly speaking, the American expression of the British Arts & Crafts Movement.

Most pieces were executed in oak, forms were rectilinear and functional, the construction simple, often with obvious signs of handwork, such as exposed mortice and tenon joints. Chair backs consisted chiefly of flat vertical or horizontal splats. One of the most important proponents of the style was Gustav Stickley, who was uncompromising in the austerity of his pieces. His brothers, working in Grand Rapids, turned out pieces in a similar style, though they were more flexible in their approach to decoration.

ANTIQUES
REVIEW 1994

T HE Lyle Antiques Price Guide is compiled and published with completely fresh information annually, enabling you to begin each new year with an up-to-date knowledge of the current trends, together with the verified values of antiques of all descriptions.

We have endeavored to obtain a balance between the more expensive collector's items and those which, although not in their true sense antiques, are handled daily by the antiques trade.

The illustrations and prices in the following sections have been arranged to make it easy for the reader to assess the period and value of all items with speed.

You will find illustrations for almost every category of antique and curio, together with a corresponding price collated during the last twelve months, from the auction rooms and retail outlets of the major trading countries.

When dealing with the more popular trade pieces, in some instances, a calculation of an average price has been estimated from the varying accounts researched.

As regards prices, when 'one of a pair' is given in the description the price quoted is for a pair and so that we can make maximum use of the available space it is generally considered that one illustration is sufficient.

It will be noted that in some descriptions taken directly from sales catalogues originating from many different countries, terms such as bureau, secretary and davenport are used in a broader sense than is customary, but in all cases the term used is self explanatory.

An amusing carved and painted pine circus advertising figure of a tiger, Cole Brothers Circus, Indiana, circa 1920, height 59in. (Sotheby's) $4,313

A painted wooden and wrought-iron barber shop trade sign, American, 19th century, with three shaped panels inscribed *Ladies Barber and Gents* in red letters on blue and white grounds, 35¹/₂in. wide. (Christie's) $1,650

A painted composition and zinc Indian scout cigar store figure, W. Demuth & Co., 501 Broadway, New York, circa 1870, 77in. high. (Sotheby's) $26,400

An Elgin advertising display, a driver standing cranking his vintage car before an Elgin billboard on which lights flash on and off, clock attachment above, 42cm. high, circa 1920. (Auction Team Köln) $195

An advertising clock for Busch Light Beer, 110v electric, unused and in original packing with operating instructions, 35cm. diameter. (Auction Team Köln) $117

An amusing carved and painted pine circus advertising figure of a zebra, Cole Brothers Circus, Indiana, circa 1920, height 59in. (Sotheby's) $5,175

A carved and painted pine and gesso 'pig' butcher's trade sign, American, 20th century, carved in the round, length 30in. (Sotheby's) $3,450

An Ever Ready Safety Razor advertising clock, made of wood with American 8 day movement, the price of 12 blades on the pendulum. (Auction Team Köln) $2,064

Chas. Wilson & Sons, Leeds, cataloge of gas cooking and heating stoves, two color plates, 1898. (Christie's) $302

A carved and painted pine fish trade sign, American, late 19th/early 20th century, the solid, boxy fish with open jaws and carved fin, length 32in.
(Sotheby's) $4,313

Gilt zinc apothecary trade sign, America, 19th century, 40in. high.
(Skinner) $468

Equestrian breeder's advertisement, *Malcolm Forbes*, Ohio, 20th century, centering an oval reserve containing the full-standing portrait of the horse 'Malcolm Forbes', 75½in. wide.
(Christie's) $5,280

A Pan American Exposition 1901, Buffalo, USA advertising clock in the form of a frying pan, signed on reverse, *Mfd by C F Chouffet Jeweler – Buffalo NY*, 29cm. high.
(Auction Team Köln) $120

A Coca Cola neon advertising clock with second hand and surrounding neon tube with typical Coco Cola Stop Sign symbol, in green hammered casing, 40 x 39cm, 1942.
(Auction Team Köln) $463

A Telechrom electric advertising clock, with drum under the dial for six advertising signs which change automatically every 5 minutes, painted silvered dial, 54cm. high, 1910.
(Auction Team Köln) $225

A painted sheet-iron blacksmith sign, American, late 19th/early 20th century, painted black, 36in. high.
(Sotheby's) $2,310

A Corgi Toys shop display stand, circa 1960's, with seven cream and blue metal shelves, 20in. wide, 34in. high.
(Bearne's) $2,980

Victorian six-drawer spool cabinet by J. P. Coates, paneled ends, flanking columns, 20½in. high.
(Eldred's) $385

ADVERTISING

'J. Marston, Thompson & Son Ltd., ... Brewery, Burton on Trent', a comprehensive view of the factory, reverse printed on glass by Barclay & Fry Ltd., London, 50 x 62cm.
(Phillips) $312

Robin Starch, enamel sign, pictorial bird on basket of washing, 88 x 74cm., framed.
(Onslow's) $669

James Buchanan & Co. Ltd, 'Buchanan's Special Red Seal' a view of the Discovery in the ice, titled on mount, in original gilt frame, 44 x 59cm.
(Phillips) $320

K. Kunik, West Germany, a 16mm. red-body Mickey Mouse camera with paper Mickey laid on to shaped metal advertising stand.
(Christie's) $388

J. Buchanan & Co. Ltd., 'Best of Spirits' four white terriers in a cartouche, 'Finest Quality In Scotch, Black & White Whisky' in original oak frame, 49.5 x 37cm.
(Phillips) $464

A nickel-plated seated figure of Bibendum with Michelin sash, 4³/₄in. high.
(Christie's) $745

Johnnie Walker Red Label The Whisky That Goes With A Swing Born 1820 Still Going Strong, color lithographic showcard, 44 x 39cm.
(Onslow's) $652

Carved and painted watchmaker's sign, New England, late 19th century, 29in. high.
(Skinner) $1,540

Farmers Glory Toasted Wheat Flakes My Favourite Breakfast, shaped 3-D standing showcard, 72cm. high.
(Onslow's) $117

18

Komo Metal Paste enamel sign
'Komo For Metals', pictorial elf
holding tin lid with blue
background, some damage to
border, 76 x 61cm.
(Onslow's) $184

Nestle's Milk For All Time
Richest In Cream, circular
printed tin simulated wood wall
clock, 48cm. diameter.
(Onslow's) $502

'Christie's' ash cookie case,
America, circa 1900, 54in. high.
(Skinner) $1,210

A Carlton Ware Guinness
'Toucan' table lamp, with
original printed shade, painted
in colors, printed factory marks,
16¼in. high.
(Christie's) $533

All Colman's, three sided 3-D
standing display woman and
child at cupboard of Colman's
products, 86cm. high, circa
1935.
(Onslow's) $686

Art Deco period pottery flat
backed bust of a sailor,
advertising 'Senior Service
Cigarettes', 14in. high.
(G. A. Key) $106

Oxo Makes It Rich and Beefy by
Edwin Byatt, original artwork
for showcard, 76 x 51cm.
(Onslow's) $309

Georg Jensen display plaque,
with company New York logo, in
characteristic Jensen surround,
not marked, 5 x 4½in.
(Skinner) $220

'John Dewar & Sons Ltd', a
butler carrying a flask of
Dewar's Whisky on a serving
tray, in black glass mount, 60 x
49cm.
(Phillips) $256

A Tippco clockwork lithographed tinplate high-wing bomber, with operating **propeller,** undercarriage and bomb-dropping action, circa 1936.
(Christie's) **$695**

A silk Union Jack inscribed in ink *Flown on Apollo 15 26th July–7th Aug 1971* and signed by the astronaut Al Worden.
(Christie's) **$3,476**

A fine and detailed flying scale model of the Bristol Bulldog, with fabric covered wooden **airframe, finished in the colors** of No. 3 Sqn. R.A.F., wingspan 64in.
(Christie's) **$869**

A commemorative paper napkin printed *A Souvenir in Commemorative of the FIRST FLYING WEEK IN ENGLAND held on Doncaster Racecourse from Friday Oct. 15 to 23, 1909,* 14 x 14³/₄in.
(Christie's) **$239**

A 1:144 scale aluminium model of the Hawker Hurricane Ser. Letters LK-A, mounted by D. Vann, wingspan 6³/₄in.
(Christie's) **$217**

H. S. Williamson, Imperial Airways, London, Scylla, **lithograph in colors, 1934,** backed on linen, 20 x 25in.
(Christie's) **$1,195**

A detailed static display model of the Sopwith Pup, the cockpit with flying and engine controls, windscreen, machine gun, 9-cylinder rotary engine, propeller, undercarriage and other details, 9¹/₂in. long.
(Christie's) **$543**

An unusual and detailed flying scale model of the Junkers D1 single seat fighter, the wooden airframe covered with simulated corrugated aluminium with working control surfaces, wingspan 76in.
(Christie's) **$2,172**

An unusual flying scale model of the Hansa Brandenburg float plane with fabric covered wooden airframe, working control surfaces, finished in Finnish Air Force livery and markings, wingspan 78in.
(Christie's) **$1,521**

AERONAUTICAL ITEMS

A finely detailed flying scale model of de Havilland Mosquito FB.VI Ser. No. NS850 Sqn letters TH-M with wooden airframe, finished in R.C.A.F. camouflage of 418 (City of Edmonton), wingspan 72in. (Christie's) **$2,824**

A Lehmann Ikarus 653 **motorized monoplane with pilot,** tinplate lithographed in yellow and red, 1920s, in original box. (Auktionsverket) **$2,907**

A detailed flying scale model of the Curtis Owl with wooden airframe, working elevators, rudder ailerons and flaps, finished in USAAF camouflage, wingspan 82in. (Christie's) **$760**

A menu card, The Graf Zeppelin over New York from the first Europe Pan-American flight, issued by the Louis Sherry Hotel N.Y., 1929.

A 19th century board game 'Aviation' with original pieces, and board in original box, instructions. (Christie's) **$152**

(Christie's) **$478**

A fine R.A.F. operations room sector clock with painted dial **divided into colored triangles** of red, yellow and blue for 2½ minute periods, made by W. Elliott Ltd., 1941. (Christie's) **$2,607**

A Meccano biplane No. 2 from kit assembly, painted in silver and red, with original box and two pilots, 1930s, 52cm. long. (Auktionsverket) **$536**

A fine laminated mahogany four-blade propeller, built in two sections and with brass leading edges, 107in. diameter. (Christie's) **$1,781**

A Günthermann lithograph aeroplane, marked *1425* on the wings, the open cockpit with two pilots and three clockwork driven propellers, 1930s, 47cm. long. (Auktionsverket) **$1,073**

A detailed and finely finished flying scale model of a Fokker DVI Ser. Letter 'A' single seat fighter with fabric covered wooden airframe, wingspan 73in.
(Christie's) $2,172

Bachem Ba 349 Natter (Viper) replica, wood and metal construction with engine and rocket propulsion units constructed from non-contemporary parts so as to appear as near as possible to the original, length 20ft.
(Christie's) $8,256

A fine flying scale model of the Hawker Fury, with fabric covered wooden airframe, finished in the colors of No. 43 Sqn. R.A.F., the famous 'Fighting Cocks', wingspan 60in.
(Christie's) $869

An R.A.F. 2nd World War period sector clock, the dial sectors in colors with R.A.F. crest, 17¼in. diameter overall.
(Christie's) $3,476

A Gloster Meteor control column handgrip with firing buttons in as new condition, 8in. wide.
(Christie's) $239

A gilt-bronze medallion, the obverse embossed with a pilot's head and shoulders, in flying dress, embossed *Lindbergh Medal of the Congress of the United States of America, Act May 4 1928*, 2³⁄₄in. diameter.
(Christie's) $145

Anonymous, Imperial Airways, lithograph in colors, circa 1936, backed on linen, 38 x 25in.
(Christie's) $1,412

A gilt-bronze and enamel commemorative plaque inscribed *ZIELFAHRT ZUR ZEPPELIN – LANDUNG Autom. CL. Meiningen Ortsgr.d.A.D.A.C. MEININGEN 1931*, 3¹⁄₄in. wide.
(Christie's) $413

Veedol, lithograph in colors, backed on linen, 50 x 29¹⁄₂in.
(Christie's) $1,086

A fine and detailed flying scale model of the Bucker Bu131 Jungmann with fabric covered wooden airframe with working control surfaces, finished in Luftwaffe markings and camouflage, wingspan 72in.
(Christie's)   **$1,260**

An unusual and detailed flying scale model of the Sparmann P-1 with fabric covered wooden airframe, working control surfaces, finished in Swedish Air Force silver livery, wingspan 82in.
(Christie's)   **$1,086**

A detailed flying scale model of the Gloster Gladiator, with wooden airframe, working control surfaces, rubber tired undercarriage, glazed cockpit canopy, finished in the colors of No. 43 Sqn. R.A.F., wingspan 56in.
(Christie's)   **$869**

A USAAF issue silk lined leather flying jacket, size 30, the back decorated with an F86 Saber surrounded by stars.
(Christie's)   **$369**

A bronze medallion commemorating the Montgolfier brothers' ascent, with molded signature *N. Galteaux*, 1⁵/₈in. diameter.
(Christie's)   **$304**

A four-bladed laminated mahogany aircraft propeller, the boss stamped *G64N51, D2366P3340, T28096 LH, 200HP, HISPANO SUIZA, SE5*, 94in. diameter.
(Christie's)   **$1,260**

A leatherette and silk lined correspondence folder, the cover embossed in gilt *Graf Zeppelin*, with a pictorial representation of LZ 127, 17¹/₂in. wide opened.
(Christie's)   **$1,043**

A Supermarine Spitfire blind flying panel, comprising air speed indicator, artificial horizon, climb and descent indicator, 14in. wide.
(Christie's)   **$869**

A rare LZ 130 'Graf Zeppelin', folding broadsheet with detailed cut-away and publicity information for this, the last Zeppelin built, dated 5/39.
(Christie's)   **$326**

ALABASTER

One of a pair of late 19th
century French alabaster and
ormolu mounted urns, the
covers with pineapple finials,
18in. high.
(Christie's)
(Two) $1,500

A painted and molded
composition bust portrait of
George Washington, American,
20th century, height 23¼in.
(Sotheby's) $1,035

One of a pair of carved
alabaster and ormolu mounted
figural wall brackets, each in the
form of satyrs holding twin
cornucopiae branches, 32cm.
wide.
(Phillips)(Two) $3,363

A Greek alabaster figure of a
maiden, shown standing beside a
well, her robe falling loosely
from one shoulder, holding a
ewer attached to a rope in her
right hand, late 19th century,
23¼in. high.
(Christie's) $1,899

Two early 17th century
alabaster sculptures in high
relief of the Crucifixion and the
Compassion of Christ, the
figures still with traces of
gilding, monogramed *IDH*,
Malines, 24 x 19cm.
(Finarte) $12,988

A late Victorian alabaster and
gilt metal mounted pedestal, the
rectangular revolving top above
a Corinthian style column, 12in.
wide.
(Christie's) $924

A carved alabaster figure of a
dancer, after Canova, wearing a
classical gown, her head tipped
to one side and her legs crossed,
late 19th/20th century, 21in.
high.
(Christie's) $1,444

Polychrome alabaster group of
the Nativity, Venice, 17th
century, 44 x 42cm.
(Finarte) $11,290

A late 19th century sculpted
alabaster group, after the
Antique, of Cupid and Psyche,
on a circular integral plinth,
29in. high.
(Christie's) $1,236

Cased painted and decorated wood, metal and fabric model of 'Diamond Tally-Ho' coach, America, circa 1930, 22in. wide.
(Skinner) $1,100

An International Order of Odd-Fellows painted and decorated fire ax, Myerstown, Pennsylvania, 19th century, 33¹/₂in. long.
(Christie's) $1,100

An unusual carved and painted pine house model, American, early 20th century, in the form of a circa 1920 frame house with red shingled roof, length 35in.
(Sotheby's) $2,185

Certificate of seven years service in the Fire Department of the City of Boston, issued to James F. Marston, 1859, 17¹/₂ x 12¹/₂in.
(Skinner) $165

Painted silk military band banner, America, first half 19th century, painted in sienna and gilt, 29 x 23¹/₂in.
(Skinner) $275

Arnold Schwarzenegger's black leather jacket from 'Terminator 2: Judgment Day', 1991, with bullet holes, traces of 'blood' and heavy scuffing.
(Sotheby's) $13,068

Harrison Ford's hat from 'Indiana Jones and the Raiders of the Lost Ark', 1980, together with a Continuity Script, issued 28th May, 1980.
(Sotheby's) $1,416

Painted staved 'Boston Oyster Company' covered bucket, New England, early 20th century, 12¹/₄in. high.
(Skinner) $302

A rare hand-painted ceremonial parade fire hat: Vigilant, initialed *J.W.W.*, probably Pennsylvania, mid-19th century, 7in. high.
(Sotheby's) $14,850

Polychrome printed silk commemorative handkerchief, America, circa 1866, 32 x 30in. (Skinner) **$1,320**

Membership certificate in The Society of The Cincinnati for Otho Holland Williams, signed by Washington and Henry Knox, New York, August 7, 1790. (Eldred's) **$12,650**

Certificate for Joseph Chadwick to serve as Fireman in the City of New York, 1807, 14 x 10¼in. (Skinner) **$357**

Carved, gilt and painted alarm list, Massachusetts, late 19th century, the applied tin roster board with printed paper squad names for North Chelmsford, Chelmsford Center, Carlisle and Westford, 36 x 28in. (Skinner) **$440**

A Victorian painted and carved birdhouse, American, late 19th century, the clapboard house green-painted with shingled roof and rear turret and two fenced porches and the third level with dormer windows, 21in. high. (Christie's) **$1,210**

Declaration of the Independence of the United States of America, July 1776, a printed cotton handkerchief depicting the scene with the protagonists listed, 30 x 31in., circa 1840. (Christie's) **$911**

Alert Eagle Fire Society invitation, dated *Boston Feb. 25, 1800*, signed in plate *D. Staniford del* and *S. Hill SC 1800*, 7⅝ x 6½in. (Skinner) **$880**

A fine hand-painted leatherboard ceremonial parade firehat: The Independence Hose Company, initialed *A.R.R.*, probably Pennsylvania, mid 19th century, height 7in. (Sotheby's) **$5,750**

A political campaign banner, Kentucky, third quarter 19th century, the red-painted cylindrical valance with gilt acorn finials above a flag banner inscribed *Kentucky*, 64½in. high. (Christie's) **$1,650**

AMUSEMENT MACHINES

A three drum coin operated Rotomat amusement machine. (Auction Team Köln)

$501

A Jokers Wild poker dice coin machine for 5 cent pieces by the Von Star Amusement Co., Columbia SC, USA, circa 1930. (Auction Team Köln)

$405

American coin operated Baseball Machine pinball machine set for US 1 cent pieces, circa 1935. (Auction Team Köln)

$463

A coin operated Rotomat Super Krone wall-hanging amusement machine by Günter Wulff Apparatebau, Berlin, in working order, circa 1970. (Auction Team Köln) $77

A German 3 drum Omega amusement machine with four peppermint roll dispensers and three brake buttons, by Max Jentzsch & Meerz, Leipzig, restored and in working order, circa 1931. (Auction Team Köln)

$578

A Fayre Win pinball amusement machine, set for old one penny pieces, in working order, American, circa 1930. (Auction Team Köln)

$463

The Governor, a three drum amusement machine by Jennings, USA, with original key, set for US 10 cent pieces, original condition, 1964. (Auction Team Köln)

$1,158

A Yankee Trade Stimulator cigarette promoting amusement machine for Wings shop counters, a five-drum machine for 1 cent coins. (Auction Team Köln)

$254

A Mill's Stars three-drum amusement machine with jackpot, set for 5 cent pieces, with key and coins, circa 1958, unrestored, in full working order. (Auction Team Köln)

$1,389

A Cypriot black-topped red polished ware bowl, with simple pierced lug, circa Z500 B.C., 6in. diameter, chips to the rim.
(Bonhams) $143

An Egyptian fragmentary painted cartonnage mummy mask of a child, late period, after 600 B.C., 7¹/₂in.
(Bonhams) $979

A small near Eastern schematic terracotta of a piebald horse with harness, 3in. high.
(Bonhams) $127

A twin-handled bichrome ware Cypriot amphora on a pedestaled foot, Cypro-Geometric period, circa 1050–750 B.C., 8¹/₄in. high.
(Bonhams) $349

A North Iranian sea-green glazed deep cylindrical pottery beaker, with horizontal lug handles and five yellow wheel-sunbursts around the exterior, 4in. high.
(Bonhams) $286

An Apulian red-figure volute krater, with white painted masks instead of volutes on the handles, Greek, South Italy, 4th century B.C., 24¹/₂in.
(Bonhams) $6,530

A fine Etruscan full-bodied handled olpe with trefoil lip and spur red handle, 7¹/₄in. high.
(Bonhams) $477

A Viking whalebone plaque with openwork and incised ornamentation, 15¹/₄ x 9³/₄in., 9th-10th century A.D.
(Bonhams) $2,612

A large Canaanite duck-bill fenestrated bronze socketed axhead, 8th-7th century B.C., 3¹/₂in.
(Bonhams) $392

An Egyptian white stone torso of a standing male figure, wearing a shenty kilt, Ptolemaic, probably a trial piece, 6in. high. (Bonhams) $875

An ancient near Eastern terracotta chariot, in the form of a ram, circa 2nd Millennium B.C., 6³/₄in. (Bonhams) $2,122

A Roman style metallic gray terracotta comic actor's mask, wearing the skin of Herakles, 3¹/₂in. (Bonhams) $238

A pottery seated 'Mother Goddess' figurine, her arms curved beneath prominent breasts, 3¹/₂in., Tel-Halaf, 6th Millennium B.C. (Bonhams) $2,612

An Egyptian limestone relief fragment with the cartouches of the Pharoah Ptolemy V, 205–180 B.C., 11 x 9¹/₂in. (Bonhams) $986

A buff pottery near Eastern twin-handled tripod vessel, with painted umber decoration of four armed warriors, early 1st Millennium B.C., 5¹/₂in. high. (Bonhams) $445

An uninscribed light green composition Ushabti figure, with finely detailed face and wig, hoe, pick and seed basket, late period, circa 500 B.C., 5in. high. (Bonhams) $349

A white limestone plaque with strongly modeled figure of the dwarf god Bes in high relief, Roman Egypt, 1st-2nd century A.D., 7³/₄in. high. (Bonhams) $731

A large Minoan terracotta fragment of a wide-eyed bull's head with flaring nostrils, mid 2nd Millennium B.C., 5in. high. (Bonhams) $604

A stone keystone, carved with a
female mask, 13½in. wide,
17¾in. high.
(Christie's) $258

A modern set of pine double
doors and door surround, in the
Adam style, with a breakfront
molded cornice carved with
egg-and-dart and dentil
ornament, 92in. wide.
(Christie's) $13,475

A stone keystone, carved with a
bearded mask, 19th century,
13½in. wide, 17¾in. high.
(Christie's) $483

A modern pine door and carved
door surround, the surround
with a broken, scrolling
pediment supported by two
volutes, the frieze and jambs
decorated with drapery swags,
71½in. wide.
(Christie's) $6,738

A pair of Vicenza stone fruit
baskets and a pair of pineapple
finials, the baskets: 17½in., the
finials: 25in. high.
(Christie's) $1,293

A pair of French oak door
surrounds with double doors, of
Louis XV style, the arched
frames with molded edges
carved with foliate scrolls,
enclosing a pair of arched
paneled doors, the doors:
52½in. wide.
(Christie's) $2,695

Two mahogany doors, each with
six inset panels to both sides the
fielding carved with leaves and
flower heads, late 18th century,
42 x 83in.
(Christie's) $1,552

A set of eight stone columns,
each with an Ionic capital, the
column formed from six
tapering sections, with a stepped
base, 19th century, 173½in.
high, approximately.
(Christie's) $29,325

A set of mahogany and bird's
eye maple double doors, each
with three recessed panels to
both sides, 19th/early 20th
century, 21⅞in. wide.
(Christie's) $2,888

A George II carved pine door surround, with a broken pediment above a frieze elaborately carved with acanthus leaves, 18th century. (Christie's) $2,888

An unusual and rare molded copper canopy corbel, Clinton and Russell, New York, circa 1900, in Renaissance style, height 33in. (Sotheby's) $2,645

A carved pine door surround, with repeating foliate and fluted borders, embellished at the upper corners with paterae, on block feet, 55in. wide. (Christie's) $963

An elaborately carved set of oak double doors and door surround, the surround with a broken, arched pediment with repeating foliate and rosette borders, 19th/early 20th century, 80³/₄in. wide. (Christie's) $6,160

A quantity of George III green and parcel-gilt paneling, including a chimney-breast flank with an architectural molded pediment, and two door surrounds, height: 142¹/₂in. including the cornice. (Christie's) $25,240

One of a pair of mahogany doors, each with six plain molded panels to one side, and six plain molded panels with ebony and boxwood stringing on the other, first half 19th century, 34in. wide. (Christie's) (Two) $2,118

A cream-painted wooded door and door surround, of George I style, the pediment supported by two scrolls, the entablature with dentil, triglyphs and foliate borders, 87in. wide. (Christie's) $7,378

Finely carved marble base, mid-19th century, relief decoration depicting Diana, the goddess of the hunt, 30 x 26in. (Eldred's) $825

A George II carved pine door surround, with a molded and carved cornice and dentil ornament, the frieze with foliate scrolls, late 18th century, 69³/₄in. wide. (Christie's) $3,273

ARMOR

A two piece gorget, probably 17th century, front plate with roped edge and later riveted border.
(Wallis & Wallis) $239

An English Civil War period steel hat liner 'secret' of simple skull cap form.
(Wallis & Wallis) $448

An iron mempo, Edo period, 17th century, the plain iron mask set with two 'S' cheek flanges and with a separate nosepiece.
(Christie's) $1,760

A kon-ito-odoshi mogami haramaki, the kabuto comprising a fine sixty-two plate russet-iron sujibachi with gilt and silvered five-stage yukimochi.
(Christie's) $14,119

An English Civil War period breastplate, four brass rosettes to base rim, two buckle fastenings to top, two musket ball proof marks.
(Wallis & Wallis) $643

A composite cuirassier armour of bright steel, studded with rivets and with turned edges, early 17th century, probably German.
(Christie's) $11,253

A fine kon-ito-shira odoshi domar, comprising a kabuto with a sixty-two plate russet-iron sujibachi with iron mabizashi.
(Christie's) $13,288

A decorative Italian armour, comprising close helmet, gorget of four plates, breast plate, backplate, front to skirt with tassels of three plates, late 16th century.
(John Nicholson) $8,505

ARMOR

A World War I tank driver's anti shrapnel mask, leather covered with eye slits, chain mail skirt, securing ribbons and original label.
(Wallis & Wallis) **$231**

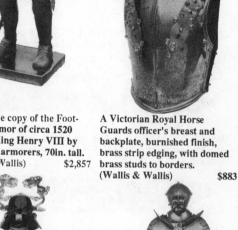

A pair of bridle-gauntlets of bright steel, each comprising an elbow-length cuff made in two pieces engraved with two lines and with roped edges, early 17th century, probably English, 20in.
(Christie's) **$5,483**

A European mail shirt entirely of riveted steel rings, with elbow-length sleeves, probably 15th century, 34in. long.
(Christie's) **$3,084**

A well made copy of the Foot-Combat armor of circa 1520 made for King Henry VIII by his Almain armorers, 70in. tall.
(Wallis & Wallis) **$2,857**

A Victorian Royal Horse Guards officer's breast and backplate, burnished finish, brass strip edging, with domed brass studs to borders.
(Wallis & Wallis) **$883**

A curassier's armor, comprising close helmet, gorget, breast plate and backplate, tassets to the knee and full arms with gauntlets, 17th century.
(John Nicholson) **$11,340**

A shira-ito-ni-odoshi kebiki laced tosei-gusoku, the hotoke-do covered with shohei-gawa (stencilled buckskin).
(Christie's) **$15,780**

A German fluted 'Maximilian' full armor in early 16th century style, of bright steel, on wooden figure mounted on an octagonal wooden base.
(Christie's) **$19,705**

BOWIE KNIVES

Large Bowie knife by Booth, Sheffield, circa 1850, 10³/₄in. spear point blade bearing engraved and etched panels on left side with deep serrations on the obverse and reverse, with horn and mother-of-pearl scales and two piece silver plated crossguard, 16⁷/₈in. overall.
(Butterfield & Butterfield) $6,600

Bowie knife by T. Ellin, Sheffield, circa 1845, 8¹³/₁₆in. clip point blade etched *Prarie Knife*, German silver and ivory hilt set with German silver bands, 13⁵/₈in. overall.
(Butterfield & Butterfield) $5,225

Bowie knife by Fisher, Sheffield, circa 1860, 10¹/₂in. spear point blade marked *George Fisher, Sheffield*, the ricasso stamped *S.D.*, stag handle with German silver crossguard, 15¹/₄in. overall.
(Butterfield & Butterfield) $1,100

English style Bowie knife, unmarked, circa 1880, 11¹/₂in. spear point blade, coin silver mounted hilt with celluloid grip, 17¹/₈in. overall.
(Butterfield & Butterfield) $385

Bowie knife by C. Congreve, Sheffield, circa 1835, 9¹¹/₁₆in. clip point blade with Spanish notch marked *CELEBRATED AMERICAN BOWIE KNIFE*, German silver and ivory hilt, 14¹/₄in. overall.
(Butterfield & Butterfield) $17,600

Large Bowie knife by Greaves, Sheffield, circa 1840, 11⁵/₈in. double edged spear point blade, German silver mounted hilt with ivory grip scales bearing escutcheon plates on either side, 16¹/₂in. overall.
(Butterfield & Butterfield) $8,250

Bowie knife by Thompson, Sheffield, circa 1850, 12¹/₁₆in. blade, German silver crossguard with checkered ebony handle, 17⁵/₁₆in. overall.
(Butterfield & Butterfield) $715

Bowie knife by Lingard, Sheffield, circa 1850, 8⁷/₈in. clip point blade etched with 8 florals, eagle carrying bag of gold in beak and clutching riband displaying *Draw me not in haste*, 14¹/₈in. overall.
(Butterfield & Butterfield) $550

Bowie knife by Samuel Robinson, Sheffield, circa 1840, 11¹/₁₆in. clip point blade stamped with scenes of early trains and hounds chasing deer, ornate copper plated base metal handle and crossguard, 17³/₈in. overall.
(Butterfield & Butterfield) $1,430

Bowie knife by Tillotson, Sheffield, circa 1850, 9⁷/₈in. clip point blade etched *Hunters Companion*, German silver mounted hilt, oval crossguard and horn grip scales, 17¹/₂in. overall.
(Butterfield & Butterfield) $2,475

Rare alligator hilt Bowie knife by Woodhead and Hartley, Sheffield, circa 1845, 7³/₁₆in. clip point blade etched and stamped *American Hunting Knife*, German silver and ivory hilt set with German silver medallion plaque, 12¹/₄in. overall.
(Butterfield & Butterfield) $4,400

Bowie knife by Wragg, Sheffield, circa 1845, 7⁵/₈in. clip point blade marked *Alabama Hunting Knife, For Use, Surpass All Try Me*, with figures of hound, buffalo, sphinx, soldier and centaur, ornate cutlery hilt.
(Butterfield & Butterfield) $935

CASED SETS

A good 5 shot 120 bore Tranter's patent self cocking percussion revolver, 8in., barrel 3³/₄in., Birmingham proved, engraved with retailer *Thos Williams, South Castle St. Liverpool*, spring stud retains arbor pin, sliding safety bolt locks cylinder.
(Wallis & Wallis) $2,612

Cased Nimschke engraved presentation Smith & Wesson Second model double action revolver, **serial No. 15362, .32 caliber, 3¹/₂in. barrel**, profusely scroll engraved on barrel, frame and cylinder, the backstrap engraved *L.V. Sone/From/N.Y. Rifle Club*, mother-of-pearl grips.
(Butterfield & Butterfield) $6,600

Cased Colt second model 1855 Root sidehammer percussion revolver, factory engraved and presentation inscribed, serial No. 6707, .265 calibre, 3¹/₂in. octagon barrel marked *Colt's Pt. 1855 and Address Col Colt Hartford, Ct. U.S.A.*, finely scroll engraved frame, hammer, barrel and loading lever.
(Butterfield & Butterfield) $17,600

Deluxe cased presentation pair of Colt model 1895 double action revolvers gold and silver inlaid and engraved by Cuno Helfricht, serial numbers 88566 and 88567 hand engraved, **.38 caliber, 6in. barrels with gold band inlays at** breech and muzzle, engraved overall in tight floral-scroll motifs.
(Butterfield & Butterfield) $44,000

Cased Colt Bisley flattop single action army revolver, engraved with pearl grips, serial No. **326568, .44 Russian caliber, 7¹/₂in. barrel** stamped on left side *Bisley Model 44 Russian Ctg*, engraved by Cuno Helfricht with scroll engraved frame, barrel, gripstraps and both cylinders on a punched ground.
(Butterfield & Butterfield) $71,500

Cased Colt factory engraved single action army revolver, English proofed, serial No. 53441, .450 Eley caliber, 5¹/₂in. barrel marked *Colt's Pt. Mfg. Co. Hartford Ct. U.S.A. Depot 14 Pall Mall London*, profusely factory scroll engraved with nickel plated finish, blued screws and mother-of-pearl grips.
(Butterfield & Butterfield) $49,500

CASED SETS

Deluxe cased and engraved Colt model 1851 navy percussion revolver with attachable shoulder stock, serial No. 90140, .36 caliber, 7¹/₂in. barrel marked *Address Col. Colt London*.
(Butterfield & Butterfield) $121,000

Cased Colt model 1851 navy revolver, serial No. 198817, .36 caliber, standard model, the modern red velvet lined case containing *Colt's Patent* flask and mold and two cap tins.
(Butterfield & Butterfield) $2,475

A rare 6-shot 54-bore Pennell's patent open-frame self-cocking percussion revolver, 13¹/₂in. overall, detachable barrel 7in. engraved *Clark, Lynn*, Birmingham proved, totally enclosed action with half-cock button on left of scroll-engraved frame.
(Wallis & Wallis) $2,696

A 5-shot .31in. Colt model 1849 pocket percussion revolver, 10in. overall, barrel 5in., number *6347* on all parts, London address and proofs, stage coach scene on cylinder, steel trigger guard with traces of plating, plain polished walnut grips.
(Wallis & Wallis) $2,190

Special issue Buffalo Bill Historical Center Winchester Museum 1 of 250 Colt Frontier revolver, serial No. 1BB, 44–40 calibre, 7¹/₂in. barrel marked *Colt's P.T.F.A. Mfg. Co. Hartford, Ct. U.S.A.* and at the muzzle *Buffalo Bill Historical Center/Winchester Museum/1 of 250* with scroll engraving featuring panel of Buffalo Bill as a Pony Express rider.
(Butterfield & Butterfield) $8,800

Unique deluxe cased engraved and inscribed pair of Colt model 1851 navy percussion revolvers with attachable shoulder stock, serial numbers **88066 and 88067**, .36 caliber, 7¹/₂in. barrels marked *Address Sam's Colt Hartford Ct.*, frames, hammers, recoil shields, loading levers and iron grip straps profusely scroll engraved by the shop of Gustave Young.
(Butterfield & Butterfield) $165,000

A good scarce late 17th century hunting dagger, slightly curved bifullered single edged blade 19¹/₂in., brass stirrup hilt and **ferrule chiseled overall with foliage pierced knucklebow.** (Wallis & Wallis)

$592

Southeast Asian dagger, having a 9in. undulating blade, the low grade silver hilt with ivory pistol grip, with silver mounted wood scabbard, length overall 13in. (Butterfield & Butterfield)

$220

A World War II 'Smatchet', leaf blade 10in., oval metal guard, squared brass pommel with WD arrow and 5, wood grips, in its canvas sheath. (Wallis & Wallis)

$388

A large 19th century Indian silver mounted dagger, 17¹/₄in. broad straight single edged blade 9¹/₂in., nicely engraved with scrolling palmettes, in its green velvet covered sheath with silver mounts. (Wallis & Wallis)

$488

A Soviet army officer's dagger, blade 7¹/₂in., lacquered brass hilt, reversed crosspiece, octagonal yellow composition grip, star to pommel, spring catch, in its leatherette covered metal sheath. (Wallis & Wallis)

$137

A scarce 19th century Burmese dagger, straight single edged blade 9¹/₄in., brass crosspiece with **nicely chiseled and chased lion's head finials, two piece checkered ivory grips.** (Wallis & Wallis)

$175

DAGGERS

A good early 19th century Persian dagger, 12³/₄in., finely watered single edged blade 6³/₄in., with chiseled ribs along back edge, floral and foliate engraved silver bolster, one piece walrus ivory hilt.
(Wallis & Wallis) $1,053

An unusual 19th century Ottoman enameled Qama, 22¹/₂in., broad double-edged fullered blade 13³/₄in., thickly silver damascened at forte with foliage, copper hilt and sheath.
(Wallis & Wallis) $414

Silver mounted dagger, probably late 18th/early 19th century, the 7in. sharply tapered blade with false edge and serrated back, the tapered silver hilt with plain fluted channels alternating with repoussé floral panels.
(Butterfield & Butterfield) $605

A 19th century Tibetan silver mount dagger, pattern welded straight single edged blade 11¹/₄in., fluted sharkskin covered grip, pommel pierced with foliage and set with 2 turquoise.
(Wallis & Wallis) $250

European dagger, early 18th century, the 9¹/₂in. double edged blade with double fullers flanked by pierced sections, the ricasso with chiseled panel of a mounted warrior à la Antique on one side and seated Victory on the obverse.
(Butterfield & Butterfield) $770

An unusual Bosnian dagger with bird shaped hilt, 12³/₄in., bi-fullered single edged blade 7in. with bird shaped brass forte, one piece horn hilt carved in the form of a bird, with inlaid ivory eyes.
(Wallis & Wallis) $143

A rare dagger of a member of the French Mameluk Guard, imitating a jambiya, the slender curved double-edged blade of hollow triangular section, etched *Coulaux Frères* on one face and *Mfture de Klingenthal* on the other, 1801–4, 21in.
(Christie's) $3,490

ARMS & ARMOR

Kentucky flintlock rifle, the 48in. part-round/part-octagon barrel engraved on top flat *D. Christ*, the lock marked *T./Ketland/& Co.*, the full stock with incised lines framing the ramrod trough and relief carved scrolls framing the bottom thimble.
(Butterfield & Butterfield) $14,300

French flintlock coach gun, the 25½in. two stage barrel slightly flared at muzzle and mounted on the underside with a 12in. spring bayonet, the half-stock with iron fittings.
(Butterfield & Butterfield) $660

A .62in. Baker's Volunteer flintlock rifle, 49in., barrel 30in., Tower proved, 2 leaf rearsight, bayonet bar to muzzle, fullstocked, regulation lock stamped *W. Ketland* with crowned *GR*.
(Wallis & Wallis) $2,527

Fine flintlock Indian trade gun, having a 36in part-round/part-octagon barrel marked *H.E. Leman Lancaster, Pa.* with proof marks, plain pinned full stock with brass dragon sideplate.
(Butterfield & Butterfield) $7,700

A .62in. Baker flintlock rifle, 46in., barrel 30in., fullstocked, lock engraved with crowned *GR* with inspector's stamp, regulation brass mounts, buttcap spur stamped *G/65*.
(Wallis & Wallis) $1,854

A German flintlock wall-piece, with earlier heavy two-stage sighted barrel dated *1612* at the breech and struck with two **indistinct marks, earlier plain rounded lock, molded figured** walnut half-stock carved with foliage in relief behind the barrel tang, early 18th century, 58¾in. barrel.
(Christie's) $3,307

A 60 bore Kentucky flintlock rifle, 56½in., octagonal barrel 40¼in., fullstocked, adjustable double set triggers, brass furniture comprising trigger guard with finger rest, hinged patchbox, engraved buttcap spur.
(Wallis & Wallis) $885

Kentucky flintlock rifle, the 43in. octagon barrel with inlaid silver plaque engraved *J. Bean*, striped maple full stock with brass fittings, the pierced brass patchbox with bird terminal.
(Butterfield & Butterfield) $990

A .68in. Volunteer flintlock rifle by Probin circa 1790, 45³/₄in. overall, octagonal barrel 30¹/₂in. with 8 groove rifling, flat lock with swan neck cock, fullstocked, regulation pattern brass mounts.
(Wallis & Wallis) $799

Indo-Persian flintlock rifle, the 32in. octagon barrel with swamped muzzle and integral rear peep sight, the engraved lock, with frizzen spring roller, marked *W. Parker*, the oval butt with silver inlays and checkered wrist.
(Butterfield & Butterfield) $770

French double barrel flintlock shotgun, the 35in. Damascus barrels with maker's stamps at breech, the double cheekpieces terminating in relief carved roundels inlaid with German silver game birds.
(Butterfield & Butterfield) $1,100

U.S. model 1819 Hall hook lever flintlock rifle, the lockplate marked *J.H.Hall/H. Ferry/U.S./1838*, with associated socket bayonet.
(Butterfield & Butterfield) $2,750

A German flintlock gun, of finer quality, with straight-groove rifled two-stage barrel struck with the dagger mark of Essen, with pierced brass saddle back-sight and retained by a brass band pierced with a rosette, engraved signed flat beveled lock, engraved brass mounts cast and chased with masks, foliage and profile busts, by Dörman, Essen, circa 1720, 42¹/₂in. barrel.
(Christie's) $2,204

A very scarce 32 bore breech loading flintlock rifle by Durs Egg circa 1785, built according to Patrick Ferguson's patent of 1776, 46in., browned octagonal barrel 29in., London proved.
(Wallis & Wallis) $12,300

FLINTLOCK PISTOLS

A .56in. long flintlock Sea Service pistol, 18½in. overall, barrel 12in. with Tower proofs, flat lock with line-engraved borders, stamped with crowned *GR* and *Tower*, fullstocked with 1806 storekeeper's mark.
(Wallis & Wallis) $1,011

English flintlock pistol, the 8in. two stage brass barrel with octagonal breech engraved *Staton London*, the lock marked *Henry Richards*, full stock with checkered bag shaped grip, length overall 13in.
(Butterfield & Butterfield) $990

A 16 bore flintlock trade pistol of military style, 14½in., barrel 8½in. Birmingham proved, fullstocked, lock stamped with an elephant and howdah.
(Wallis & Wallis) $342

English flintlock pistol, the 5in. large caliber octagonal barrel marked *London* with top mounted 4in. spring bayonet, full stock with bag shaped grip and silver escutcheon.
(Butterfield & Butterfield) $825

An all-steel flintlock pistol of unusually small size, with two-stage barrel engraved with a band of flowers, flattened hollow iron butt with separate pommel engraved with foliage and a grotesque mask on each side, by Jan Cloeter à Grevenbroch (sic), circa 1660, 10¼in.
(Christie's) $6,981

FLINTLOCK PISTOLS

A German flintlock pistol with sighted barrel inlaid with silver strapwork, the top flat signed in silver, carved figured walnut full stock, by Johann Andreas Kuchenreuter, Steinweg bei Regensburg, third quarter of the 18th century, 14½in.
(Christie's) $2,204

Scottish flintlock pistol, the 2¾in. round rifled barrel with engraved leaf panel at muzzle and fitted with 3½ triangular spring bayonet secured by sliding trigger guard, flat sided bag shaped grip with silver escutcheon.
(Butterfield & Butterfield) $770

Middle Eastern flintlock pistol, the 10¼in. barrel with punched decoration at breech centred by maker's stamp, the barrel tang with silver overlay, large brass buttcap, brass trigger guard and Middle Eastern style brass barrel bands.
(Butterfield & Butterfield) $330

Italian flintlock pistol, the 7¾in. barrel with banded breech, brass plated bust and marked *Pie Gatelli* on top flat, stock with relief carving at tang, trigger guard, ramrod thimbles and lock.
(Butterfield & Butterfield) $880

A very rare Bohemian flintlock three-shot revolving pistol with sighted barrel, three hand-rotated steel chambers each fitted with a pan and steel, and locked by a spring-catch with trigger-guard release, unsigned, circa 1740, 19in. long.
(Christie's) $4,748

HELMETS

A Victorian officer's green cloth spiked helmet of The Prince Albert's (Somersetshire Light Infantry), gilt mounts and white leather backed chinchain and ear rosettes.
(Wallis & Wallis) $843

A Cromwellian trooper's 'lobster tailed' helmet, two piece skull with low raised comb, pierced ear flaps, hinged visor with triple bar face guard.
(Wallis & Wallis) $2,009

An officer's fine helmet of the 2nd Life Guards complete with chin-chain and plume, the elaborate plate having the white metal field to the enamel cross within the Garter.
(Christie's) $4,147

A trooper's helmet of French Cuirassiers circa 1870, steel skull with brass front plate and comb and ear bosses with slightly defective chin-chain.
(Christie's) $1,348

An extremely fine 1843 pattern officer's helmet of the 3rd Dragoon Guards, plain burnished gilt skull, ornate rayed plate mounted with Royal Arms and the battle-honors.
(Christie's) $6,220

An 1818–34 officer's pattern helmet of the Royal Dragoons with black japanned skull of 'Roman' form decorated with gilt laurel leaf ornaments.
(Christie's) $8,294

A Victorian black cloth plumed helmet of the 3rd Devon Light Horse, having Queens Crown badge with garter and oak leaf border.
(Bearne's) $1,937

An Austrian Dragoons officer's helmet circa 1860 of black finished metal with gilt ornaments including the front plate mounted with Franz-Josef I cypher.
(Christie's) $1,555

A trooper's brass 1843 pattern helmet of the 2nd The Queen's Dragoon Guards with ornate brass comb and mounted helmet plate.
(Christie's) $2,592

HELMETS

An Austrian Dragoons officer's helmet, circa 1850, with gilt ornament.
(Christie's) $2,073

A Cromwellian trooper's lobster tail helmet, the skull formed in two halves with overlapping join, hinged peak stamped with initials *IH*.
(Wallis & Wallis) $2,317

A fine helmet of the 1st Oxfordshire Light Horse Volunteers, of black cloth with red horsehair mane and tuft to the white metal comb.
(Christie's) $1,866

An officer's rare helmet circa 1820, of the East Devon Volunteer Cavalry: being an 1812 pattern black leather helmet of Heavy Cavalry.
(Christie's) $3,940

A Prussian infantryman's ersatz pressed tin Pickelhaube, brass helmet plate, spike and mounts, leather lining and chinstrap.
(Wallis & Wallis) $387

A trooper's 1871 pattern helmet of the 3rd (Prince of Wales's) Dragoon Guards with black and red plume.
(Christie's) $726

An Austrian Dragoons officer's helmet with the sides of the gilt comb unpainted and lacking its chinscales and lining.
(Christie's) $995

An officer's pattern Second Empire chapka of the French 7th Lancers with blue cloth top, chin-chain and a crimson hair plume.
(Christie's) $933

A rare Georgian officer's Tarleton helmet of the Abingdon Volunteer Cavalry, black leather skull and peak with silver plated binding.
(Wallis & Wallis) $6,572

ARMS & ARMOR

An interesting Victorian officer's blue cloth spiked helmet of The Cheshire Regt., gilt mounts, velvet backed chinchain and ear rosettes.
(Wallis & Wallis) $706

An officer's 1847 (Albert) pattern helmet of The 5th (Princess Charlotte of Wales's) Dragoon Guards, gilt skull with oak and acanthus ornaments and top mount.
(Wallis & Wallis) $1,487

A Victorian officer's blue cloth spike helmet of The Bedfordshire Regt., gilt mounts, velvet backed chinchain and ear rosettes.
(Wallis & Wallis) $666

An 1897 other rank's Pickelhaube of the 25th Hessian Train Battalion No. 25, brass helmet plate, fluted spike, leather backed chinscales, both cockades.
(Wallis & Wallis) $588

A cuirassier helmet with rounded one-piece skull and low file-roped comb, domed steel lining rivets throughout, circa 1600, probably Italian, 11in. high.
(Christie's) $3,770

An officer's feather bonnet of The Argyll and Sutherland Highlanders, red and white diced wool headband, white feather plume, leather chinstrap, leather and silk lining.
(Wallis & Wallis) $628

An Imperial Bavarian trooper's M 1842–79 helmet as worn by the Kurassier Regiment No. 2, steel skull, brass raised comb with black horsehair crest.
(Wallis & Wallis) $1,190

An Imperial German Prussian M 1897 Pickelhaube as worn by Guard Infantry or Railway Battalions, removeable spike and mounts.
(Wallis & Wallis) $387

A good Royal Horse Artillery other rank's busby, scarlet cloth bag, yellow cords and acorns, white hair plume in flame socket.
(Wallis & Wallis) $245

A Prussian Infantry Reserve Senior NCO's Pickelhaube, brass eagle helmet plate with white metal Landwehr cross, leather backed chinscales and mounts.
(Wallis & Wallis) $387

An officer's chapka of Austrian Uhlans circa 1880 with crimson cloth top, ornate chinscales, and falling hair plume with cockade.
(Christie's) $788

A Victorian officer's blue cloth spiked helmet of the 3rd Lanarkshire Rifle Volunteers, silver plated mounts, leather backed chinchain and ear rosettes.
(Wallis & Wallis) $625

A mid 17th century pikeman's pot, the skull formed in two halves with raised comb and recessed border to brim.
(Wallis & Wallis) $1,794

A German burgonet of bright steel, the one-piece skull with prominent comb and fixed fall pierced for a nasal secured by a wing screw, late 16th century, 11in. high.
(Christie's) $5,483

A Belgian cuirassier's silver plated helmet, brass peak binding, high ornamental comb with white metal grenade finial.
(Wallis & Wallis) $937

A 1915 pattern infantryman's Pickelhaube of Mecklenburg Schwerin, as worn by the 1st or 3rd Battalions of the 89th Grenadier Regiment.
(Wallis & Wallis) $568

A scarce 1902–8 other rank's gray cloth busby of the Queen's Westminster Rifle Volunteers, scarlet piping to top, gray cord and plaited loop trim.
(Wallis & Wallis) $372

A post 1902 officer's blue cloth spike helmet of The Worcestershire Regt., gilt mounts, velvet backed chinchain and ear rosettes.
(Wallis & Wallis) $745

MILITARIA

A post 1902 heavy gilt crown Household Cavalry standard top, 4¼in., with base screw stud.
(Wallis & Wallis) $118

A late 18th century model of a **bronze barreled field gun, 21in.** overall, bronze barrel 9in. with turned reinforces, swollen muzzle and cascabel.
(Wallis & Wallis) $653

Civil War Ketcham hand grenade, marked *Patented Aug. 20, 1861*, mounted on a wood plaque.
(Butterfield & Butterfield) $440

A German cartridge-holder, comprising wooden body drilled for five cartridges and inlaid on either side,blackened iron frame with bright lines, circa 1570, 4¼in. high.
(Christie's) $1,456

The embroidered devices from an early Victorian Household Cavalry trumpet banner, double sided, laid down on pink damask, with original gilt cords and tassels, 26 x 24in.
(Wallis & Wallis) $69

A massive brass shell case, 16 x 31in., engraved *Jokobynessen Battery (Deutschland)* headstamped *Polte Magdeburg X–17–1679*.
(Wallis & Wallis) $371

A leather, brass & steel MacArthur & Prain 1905 patent 'Gannochy rapid load' cartridge-dispenser, for one hundred 12-bore cartridges.
(Christie's) $794

A silver bugle of the London Rifle Brigade, engraved with Regimental Badge, and, around the mouth, *Presented by Captain G. R. Reeve, M.C., and Lieutenant R. R. Reeve 6th May 1935*.
(Wallis & Wallis) $674

A rare Accles Positive feed magazine, for the Model 1883 Gatling gun, the hollow drum with internal spiral guides and rotating cartridge propeller.
(Christie's) $973

MILITARIA

A massive brass shell case, 48in. in length, engraved *Knocke Battery (Kaiser Wilhelm II)* on wooden stand.
(Wallis & Wallis) $635

A good .56in. Colt bullet mould for the percussion revolving rifle, 8in., for ball and bullet, body stamped *.56 S*, cut off stamped *Colts Patent*.
(Wallis & Wallis) $238

A scarce Victorian embroidered buff silk pipe banner of the 1st Bn The Seaforth Highlanders, **gilt tasseled border.**
(Wallis & Wallis) $446

A remarkable 1890 halfpenny coin, the obverse stamped *Oakley*, the edge deformed by shot or bullet strike.
(Christie's) $2,125

An Imperial Chemical Industries Eley & Kynoch cartridge-board with metallic and paper dummy-cartridges and components arranged radially around an *I.C.I* medallion, 31 x 25in. overall.
(Christie's) $2,508

An interesting 18th century turned wood ramrod head, for a 32pr gun, diameter 6in., stamped on rear flat *32*.
(Wallis & Wallis) $180

A large, well produced Italian Fascist Party calendar for 1933 bearing a portrait of Mussolini, in unused state.
(Wallis & Wallis) $211

A rare Imperial German Leib Gendarmerie helmet Parade Eagle, gilt finish, screw-nut attachment, 7in. high.
(Wallis & Wallis) $1,095

An interesting 18th century gunpowder barrel, height 21in., diameter 18in., bound with four copper bands and remains of split willow binding.
(Wallis & Wallis) $78

PERCUSSION CARBINES

Marlin model 1894 saddle ring carbine, serial No. 442849, .25–20 **caliber, 20in. round barrel with full magazine, blued finish, plain** straight stock, saddle ring in place.
(Butterfield & Butterfield) $1,650

Winchester model 1866 saddle ring carbine, serial No. 21953, .44 **caliber, standard model with 20in. Henry marked barrel, saddle** ring in place.
(Butterfield & Butterfield) $12,100

Fine German percussion sporting carbine, the 23in. large caliber octagon barrel with swamped muzzle, folding leaf rear sight and brass front sight, checkered wrist, brass tipped ramrod.
(Butterfield & Butterfield) $4,125

Rare Henry marked first model flatside Winchester model 1866 saddle ring carbine, serial No. 13865, .44 caliber, having the flat gate with rare detent hold-open.
(Butterfield & Butterfield) $19,800

Winchester model 1894 saddle ring carbine, serial No. 924180, **.30 W.C.F. caliber, standard model with blued finish and plain** straight stock, with Winchester hang tag.
(Butterfield & Butterfield) $4,950

Rare Winchester model 1873 saddle ring carbine with saber bayonet, serial No. 107951A, .44 caliber, 20in. round barrel with full magazine, the front barrel band with factory lug for saber bayonet, plain straight stock.
(Butterfield & Butterfield) $14,300

PERCUSSION CARBINES

Spencer model 1865 U.S. saddle ring carbine, serial No. 13517, **.50 caliber, frame marked *Model 1865/Spencer Repeating Rifle/** *Pat'd March 6 1860/Manuf'd at Prov. R.I./By Burnside Rifle Co.,* stock with inspector's cartouche.
(Butterfield & Butterfield) $3,575

Ball Civil War carbine, .52 caliber, the casehardened frame marked *E. G. Lamson & Co./Windsor, Vt./U.S./Ball's Patent/June 23, 1863/Mar. 15, 1864,* inspector's cartouche *GGS* on left of stock.
(Butterfield & Butterfield) $4,125

Factory engraved Volcanic carbine, serial No. 284, .38 caliber, 21in. octagon barrel marked *New Haven Conn. Patent Feb. 14, 1854,* scroll engraved silver plated brass frame, blued barrel, varnished stock, silver plated buttplate.
(Butterfield & Butterfield) $30,250

Winchester model 1873 saddle ring carbine, serial No. 156644A, **.44 caliber, 20in. round barrel, blued finish with casehardened** hammer, lever and buttplate, saddle ring in place, plain straight stock.
(Butterfield & Butterfield) $11,000

U.S. model 1884 trapdoor Springfield carbine, serial No. 126601, **.45–70 caliber, sling ring in place.**
(Butterfield & Butterfield) $1,210

Winchester model 1886 saddle ring carbine, serial No. 40400, **.45–90 caliber, 22in. round barrel with full magazine, blue and** casehardened finish, saddle ring in place, oil finished walnut stock and forend.
(Butterfield & Butterfield) $24,750

PERCUSSION REVOLVERS

A 6 shot 60 bore self cocking transitional percussion revolver, 12in., octagonal barrel 5½in., London proved, engraved *Smith & Co, London*, foliate engraved round frame.
(Wallis & Wallis) $290

Massachusetts Arms Co. Maynard primed pocket revolver, serial no. 145/407, .28 caliber, 3in. round barrel, automatically revolved cylinder.
(Butterfield & Butterfield) $550

Massachusetts Arms Co. Maynard primed pocket revolver, serial No. 242, .28 caliber, 3in. round barrel, automatically revolved cylinder.
(Butterfield & Butterfield) $1,760

A .38 single-action second model revolver by Smith & Wesson, No. 97634, the checkered hard rubber grip-scales impressed with the Smith & Wesson monogram, sighted rifled barrel, 3¼in. barrel, circa 1877–1891.
(Christie's) $86

A 6 shot 60 bore self cocking bar hammer transitional percussion revolver, 12in. overall, barrel 5½in. with Birmingham proofs, engraved *Bentley & Son, Liverpool*, checkered wood grips.
(Wallis & Wallis) $463

A 6 shot 80 bore self cocking transitional percussion revolver,
11in., octagonal barrel 5¼in., Birmingham proved, foliate
engraved rounded frame, steel furniture and bar hammer.
(Wallis & Wallis) $265

A .38 double-action fourth model revolver by Smith & Wesson,
No. 406863, the backstrap stamped *Am. Ex. Co. 906*, the right-
hand side of the frame impressed with the Smith & Wesson
monogram, pearl grip-scales, sighted rifled barrel, 3¼in. barrel,
circa 1889–1909.
(Christie's) $121

A 6 shot Baker's patent 80 bore single action transitional
percussion revolver, 11½in., half octagonal barrel 5½in.,
Birmingham proved, foliate engraved rounded frame stamped
Registered April 24 1852, two piece varnished walnut grips.
(Wallis & Wallis) $404

Rare factory engraved Smith & Wesson first
model 'Baby Russian' revolver, serial No. 8669,
.38 caliber, 4in. barrel, scroll engraved on frame
and barrel with a circular panel on the left side
showing a bearded man in a Roman style helmet.
(Butterfield & Butterfield) $3,025

A scarce Belgian 4 shot .36in. hammerless ring trigger
transitional percussion revolver of Collère type, 11½in. overall,
octagonal barrel 5½in. with loading groove below, plain walnut
grips.
(Wallis & Wallis) $370

POWDER FLASKS

A large German cow-horn gunner's powder-flask finely engraved with the figure of Mars within martial trophies and with two cannon, all within a landscape, dated *1615*, 21½in.
(Christie's) $3,674

A German powder-flask of flattened cow-horn incised on the front with three figures in a procession, and on the back with patterns of concentric circles and semi-circles, early 17th century, 12¼in.
(Christie's) $771

A brass mounted powder horn for the Baker flintlock rifle, made for the Percy Tenantry Volunteers, 13¾in., cow horn body, brass end cap.
(Wallis & Wallis) $459

A German powder-flask in the manner of Johann Michael Maucher of Schwäbish-Gmünd, carved in high relief with two hounds attacking a boar, late 17th century, 4¼in. diameter.
(Christie's) $14,696

A German gilt-brass powder-flask, the front of the body cast and chased after Jost Amman with a landscape inhabited by figures engaged in different forms of the chase, perhaps late 16th century, 7¼in.
(Christie's) $1,713

A German circular powder-flask, of wood with a horn-lined hole in center, iron nozzle and tap, and two rings for suspension, 17th century, 5½in.
(Christie's) $1,627

A German combined powder-flask, wheel-lock spanner and turnscrew, with tapering reeded horn body of circular section with wooden base-plate, second half of the 17th century, 8¼in.
(Christie's) $918

A German circular powder-flask with turned wooden body encircled by a thin steel band carrying the nozzle, late 17th century, 5¾in. diameter.
(Christie's) $1,378

A scarce embossed copper powder flask, 8in. in the form of two entwined dolphins, common top stamped *Bartram & Co*.
(Wallis & Wallis) $429

POWDER FLASKS

An interesting American powder horn inscribed with scrimshaw work depicting an Indian hunting an officer on horseback, inscribed *Made in Hez'ah, Calvin Aitchpillake AD 1785*, 12½in. wide.
(Bearne's) **$4,766**

A scarce embossed copper powder flask of curved shape embossed on one side *Rifle Horn* in rayed panel.
(Wallis & Wallis) **$183**

An eastern European powder-flask with forked body of natural staghorn, the outer side engraved with geometric designs, Carpathian Basin, 18th century, 13¼in.
(Christie's) **$1,371**

An embossed copper 3 way powder flask, 5in., fixed nozzle with common lever charger, base cap with 2 swivel covers.
(Wallis & Wallis) **$180**

A German circular powder-flask in the manner of Hans Schmidt of Ferlach, with turned rootwood body inlaid on the front with scenes of the chase in engraved silver sheet, third quarter of the 17th century, 5½in. diameter.
(Christie's) **$7,715**

An Italian powder-flask, entirely of steel, with fluted triangular body of plano-convex section engraved with bands of running foliage, 17th century, 7¾in. high.
(Christie's) **$942**

An embossed copper powder flask, 8in. overall, embossed with oak leaves, acorns, stag's heads and foxes' masks, stamped *G&JW Hawksley.*
(Wallis & Wallis) **$104**

A triangular musketeer's powder-flask with cloth-covered wooden body mounted in iron, the back with a pierced design, late 16th/early 17th century, probably German, 10in. high.
(Christie's) **$1,885**

A good plain tinned metal gun size powder flask by James Dixon & Sons, Sheffield, 8¼in. overall, charger from 3 to 4½ drams.
(Wallis & Wallis) **$111**

SWORDS

A late Victorian naval flag officer's sword, blade 30in., by John Adams, Devonport, etched with crown, fouled anchor, Royal **Arms and foliage, copper gilt hilt, guard chiseled with crown,** fouled anchor and laurel sprays.
(Wallis & Wallis) $329

Confederate staff and field officer's sword, 30in. slightly curved blade with shallow 22in. fuller showing slight traces of etched floral decoration, brass hilt with pierced florals and cast on the interior *C S*.
(Butterfield & Butterfield)   **$2,200**

A Dragoon trooper's sword circa 1780, straight single edged blade 35in., iron slotted guard, small side loop to each side of knucklebow, cloth bound spiral grip, egg shaped pommel.
(Wallis & Wallis) $286

A French Cuirassier's M 1816 sword, double fullered blade 38in., spear point, trace of engraving to rounded backstrap date *1831*, brass hilt, in its steel scabbard.
(Wallis & Wallis) $365

Confederate foot officer's sword by Boyle, Gamble and Macfee, 30in. straight single edge blade with shallow 22in. fullers, brass hilt with two side branches.
(Butterfield & Butterfield)   **$5,225**

A George V RASC officer's prize sword, blade 33in., by Wilkinson Sword, retaining some original polish, etched with crown, Royal cypher, regimental badge, foliage, and presentation inscription, wire bound fishskin covered grip.
(Wallis & Wallis) $172

SWORDS

A Georgian 1796 infantry officer's sword, straight single edged
blade 32in., retaining approximately 60% original gilt and 40%
original blued etched decoration, copper gilt hilt, double shell
guard, one folding.
(Wallis & Wallis) $239

A French Napoleonic officer's sword circa 1800, straight single
edge blade 32in., by *SH*, etched with military trophies and foliage
with traces of gilding, copper gilt hilt with guard.
(Wallis & Wallis) $490

An Imperial German artillery officer's sword, slightly curved
plated blade 33in., etched upon blued back panel *Feld Art Regt
Konig Karl (Wurtt) Nr 13*, plain plated stirrup hilt.
(Wallis & Wallis) $229

A scarce 1822 infantry pattern Brazilian officer's sword of the
reign of the Emperor Pedro II, slightly curved, pipe back clipped
backed blade 28in. etched with Brazilian arms.
(Wallis & Wallis) $222

A late 18th century Continental cavalry officer's sword, long,
slim, slightly curved blade 40in., with narrow back fuller, copper
gilt hilt with heart shaped guard, fluted ebony grip.
(Wallis & Wallis) $340

A Georgian officer's sword spadroon circa 1765, broad straight
single edged fullered blade 34in., etched at forte with garter
motto *Honi Soit Qui Mal Y Pense* with foliage and traces of
gilding.
(Wallis & Wallis) $266

An iron tsuba, Edo period (circa 1700), signed *Shushin Saku*, pierced to form two interlocking jewels (tama), width 7.3cm.
(Christie's)   **$1,870**

An 18th century mokkogata shakudo-nanakoji tsuba, Mino-Goto style, 7.1cm.
(Christie's)   **$860**

A Higo school tsuba, Edo period (circa 1700), with openwork design of four family crests, width 7cm.
(Christie's)   **$1,320**

A Mino school tsuba, Edo period (circa 1750), signed *Mino ju Nakanaga*, decorated with flowers and insects in high relief and finished in gold and silver, width 6.6cm.
(Christie's)   **$2,750**

A rare Iyo Shoami tsuba, mid-Edo period (circa 1750), signed *Yoshu Matsuyama ju Shoami Hidetsugu* (Shoami Hidetsugu [fl. circa 1750]), the plate with heart-shaped (inome-bori) openings at the indentations, width 7.8cm.
(Christie's)   **$7,150**

An Akasaka Nobuie tsuba, Edo period (circa 1750), slightly dished to the centre with openwork design of an adze, a plum blossom, and a melon, width 7.6cm.
(Christie's)   **$880**

A Choshu style tsuba, Edo period (circa 1750), pierced in a design of two peony blooms and a bud caught in a web of scrolling stems, width 7.8cm.
(Christie's)   **$770**

A Hizen school tsuba, Edo period (circa 1750), the web decorated in scroll work with two dragons pursuing the celestial pearl, width 6.8cm.
(Christie's)   **$286**

A Kyoto school tsuba, Edo period (circa 1700), carved in an openwork design of linked scrolls (karakusa), width 8.2cm.
(Christie's)   **$1,430**

A Tokyo Art School tsuba, Meiji era (circa 1875), the left half carved as rocky hills with a clump of shakudo pine trees and a silver moon, width 7.7cm.
(Christie's) $308

A Hagiya school tsuba, Edo period (circa 1875), signed *Hagiya Katsuhira*, inlaid with two finely carved gold dragons, width 7.8cm.
(Christie's) $6,050

A Kano Natsuo school tsuba, Meiji era (circa 1900), inscribed *Iwamoto Konkan*, the iron plate with two carp carved in high relief from the plate, width 8cm.
(Christie's) $2,750

A Yoshioka style tsuba, Edo period (circa 1800), inscribed *Yoshioka Inaba No Suke*, the right side decorated with chrysanthemums on water, in gold, shakudo and silver inlay, width 6.7cm.
(Christie's) $2,420

A Yokoya school tsuba, Edo period (circa 1800), inscribed *Yokoya Tomotsune* with kao, the shakudo plate decorated in gold carved with a shishi, two peony blooms, three buds and two leaves, width 6.7cm.
(Christie's) $5,500

A Kinko tsuba, Edo period (circa 1800), inscribed *Iwamoto Konkan* with kao, the shakudo nanako plate inlaid with a bonsai plant in a shakudo and gold large rectangular tub, width 7cm.
(Christie's) $2,860

A Kato school tsuba, Edo period, dated *Sei* (Ansei) *Kinoe Tora Moshun* (early spring 1859), decorated with lily flowers in shakudo and gold relief, width 7.5cm.
(Christie's) $1,045

A Teimei school tsuba, Edo period (circa 1800), signed on the face *Kishu Ju Teimei* and on the reverse *Goshu Ju Namitoshi*, decorated with a pierced design of eggplants, width 7.8cm.
(Christie's) $1,320

A Hirata school tsuba, Edo period (circa 1800), signed *Hirata Naritsuke* with kao, the face inlaid with three butterflies in clear and opaque (white) cloisonné, width 7.2cm.
(Christie's) $4,180

ARMS & ARMOR

An Osaka Ikkanshi style wakizashi, Edo period, dated *Genroku 5* (1692), inscribed *Awataguchi Ikkanshi Tadatsuna*, with longitudinal ridge line (shinogi-zukuri), shallow peaked back (iori-mune) and large point (o-kissaki); length (nagasa): 1 shaku, 2 sun, 8 bu (38.7cm.); curvature (sori): torii-zori of 1cm.
(Christie's) $9,350

An Osaka Gassan school ko-wakizashi after Yasutsugu, dated *1968*, signed *Yasutsugu (no) Hoto(o) Utsushi Tatematsuru/Ryuoji Sadatsugu, kao/(Aoi-mon) Hono Bishu Atsuta Daimyojin*, of flat, wedge section (hira-zukuri) with tri-beveled back (mitsu-mune); length (nagasa): 1 shaku, 1 sun, 8bu (35.8cm.).
(Christie's) $28,600

A Shinshinto Kii wakizashi, Edo period (circa 1805), signed *Kishu To Yoshikawa Minamoto Toshiyuki*, with longitudinal ridge line (shinogi-zukuri), shallow peaked back (iori-mune) and medium point (chu-kissaki); length (nagasa): 1 shaku, 6 sun, 3 bu (49.6cm.).
(Christie's) $6,600

A Shinshinto Edo Suishinshi ko-wakizashi, Edo period, dated *Tempo 8* (1837), signed *Fujiwara Masatsugu* with kao, with longitudinal ridge line (shinogi-zukuri), shallow peaked back (iori-mune) and large point (o-kissaki); length (nagasa): 1 shaku, 5 sun, 4 bu (46.7cm.); curvature (sori): torii-zori of 1.2cm.
(Christie's) $9,900

An Echizen Seki wakizashi, Edo period (circa 1600–15), signed *Oite Namban Tetsu Esshu Sukemune*, with longitudinal ridge line (shinogi-zukuri), shallow peaked back (iori-mune) and medium point (chu-kissaki); length (nagasa): 1 shaku, 8 sun, 3 bu (55.6cm.); curvature (sori): torii-zori of 1.3cm.
(Christie's) $8,800

An Osaka Inoue wakizashi, Edo period, dated *Kanbun 6* (1666), signed *Inoue Izumi (no) Kami Kunisada* (Inoue Shinkai), with longitudinal ridge line (shinogi-zukuri), shallow peaked back (iori-mune) and medium point (chu-kissaki); length (nagasa): 1 shaku, 5 sun, 3 bu (46.4cm.); curvature (sori): koshi-zori of 0.9cm.
(Christie's) $41,800

WAKIZASHI

A later Satsuma Masafusa wakizashi, Edo period (circa 1715), signed *(Aoimon) Mondo (no) Sho Masakiyo* (attributed to Masakiyo I), with longitudinal ridge line (shinogi-zukuri), and large point (o-gissaki); length (nagasa): 1 shaku, 2 sun, 9 bu (39.3cm.).
(Christie's) $4,400

A Hizen Tadayoshi wakizashi, Momoyama period (circa 1600), signed *Hi Tadayoshi* (Tadayoshi I), outside (omote): hira-zukuri; inside (ura): shobu-zukuri; tri-beveled back (mitsu-mune); length (nagasa): 1 shaku, 2 sun, 9 bu (39.2cm.); curvature (sori): rather strong (0.6cm.).
(Christie's) $24,200

An Echizen ko-wakizashi, Edo period (first half 17th century), attributed to Shigetaka, of deep, flat, wedge section (ohira-zukuri) with tri-beveled back (mitsu-mune); length (nagasa): 1 shaku, 3 sun, 5 bu (41cm.).
(Christie's) $13,200

An o-wakizashi, the blade honzukuri and torii-zori, ihorimune and chugissaki, with mokume hada with wild midare hamon, with tobiyaki, hakkakeru boshi, ubu nakago with one mekugi-ana, inscribed *Hizen Kuni ju Tadayoshi* (possibly made at Kuwana in Ise Province), early 17th century, 20³/₄in.
(Christie's) $4,284

Cloisonné mounted Japanese wakazashi, having a 15in. slightly curved blade having a single fuller at back edge extending from hilt to 3in. from tip, the grip of cloisonné decorated with dragons and peonies on a beige ground.
(Butterfield & Butterfield) $3,575

A Bizen wakizashi in full Mino style mounts, the blade, Muromachi period (circa 1500), with longitudinal ridge line (shinogi-zukuri), shallow peaked back (iori-mune) and medium point (chu-kissaki); length 45.6cm.
(Christie's) $4,620

William Makepeace Thackeray, autographed letter, in his sloping hand, one page, 26th April, to *My dear Young*, listing **his programe of lectures in Oxford.**
(Vennett-Smith) $192

King George IV, signed document at head, as Prince Regent, given at the Court of Carlton House, 11th May 1815 being a military Commission appointing W. J. Gregory an ensign in the 14th Buckinghamshire Regiment of Foot.
(Vennett-Smith) $136

General Ernst Udet, Luftwaffe General, shot himself to death on 17th November 1941, signed postcard.
(Vennett-Smith) $320

Charles Dickens, brief autographed letter, in the third person, one page, 25th August 1868, in full Mr. Charles Dickens begs Messrs Sparks & Son to be so good as make and send him 2 pairs of elastic stockings.
(Vennett-Smith) $328

Ulysses S. Grant, signed document, one page, Washington, 3rd Fenruary 1873, partially printed and completed in ink in another hand.
(Vennett-Smith) $480

Queen Victoria, signed document, at head, given at the Court of Saint James's, 1st January 1900, granting the dignity of a Companion of the Most Distinguished Order of Saint Michael and Saint George to Colonel Trevor Patrick Breffnay Ternan.
(Vennett-Smith) $179

Gaetano Donizetti, autographed letter ('Donizetti', in the third person), one page, n.d., in Italian, to an un-named female correspondent.
(Vennett-Smith) $1,088

Irving Berlin, color songsheet cover for 'Alexander's Ragtime Band', signed in green ink by Irving Berlin.
(Vennett-Smith) $200

William S. Hart, autographed letter, two pages, 9th September 1942, in pencil, to Mr. Harwood, regretting to say that he is not returning to the screen.
(Vennett-Smith) $96

Duke of Wellington, signed letter, one and a half pages, London, 5th May 1829, to E. B. Portman, stating that he had received his letter and asking him to call upon him.
(Vennett-Smith) $128

King George III, signed document at head, given at the Court of Saint James's, 20th May 1794, being a military Commission appointing Gregory an ensign in the 106th Regiment of Foot.
(Vennett-Smith) $208

Sir Ernest Shackleton, signed menu card, for the visit of Shackleton and company of the 'Quest' to Rio de Janeiro, 7th December 1921.
(Vennett-Smith) $272

Nureyev and Fonteyn, a cast list from a Covent Garden **programe for 'Marguerite and** Armand' signed by Rudolf Nureyev and Margot Fonteyn individually.
(Vennett-Smith) $152

Virginia Woolf, signed piece, beneath an attractive small printed sketch.
(Vennett-Smith) $320

Dwight D. Eisenhower, typed letter, one page, 24th May 1944, on Office of the Supreme Commander Allied Expeditionary Force notepaper.
(Vennett-Smith) $176

Herbert Hoover, typed letter, one page, 31st March 1943, to John H. Weichert, thanking him for his letter and adding *Many of the States are organising the High Schools.*
(Vennett-Smith) $128

William Randolph Hearst, typed letter, one page, September 1933, being a letter of reference for Mr. George R. Britton.
(Vennett-Smith) $144

Bela Bartok, a good boldly signed postcard, to white border, half length showing Bartok alongside, but not signed by, William Mengelberg.
(Vennett-Smith) $720

AUTOGRAPHED DOCUMENTS

W. F. Cody, signed 2.25 x 3.5 card, also signed *Buffalo Bill*, rare, very slight smudging. (Vennett-Smith) $512

Robert Browning, portion of an autograph envelope signed, with complete address and signature, addressed to Sir George Grove, 1867. (Vennett-Smith) $96

Sir Winston S. Churchill, signed album page, full signature. (Vennett-Smith) $656

King George III, bold signature on piece, probably cut from a document. (Vennett-Smith) $51

Rutherford B. Hayes, brief autographed note, with initial *H*, on Executive Mansion card, Washington, 7th May 1878 (whilst President). (Vennett-Smith) $96

Anna Pavlova, signed album page, 1929. (Vennett-Smith) $88

Queen Elizabeth II, signed document, at head, two pages, given at the Court at St. James's, 26th August 1955, being a remission document addressed to the Governor of Wakefield Prison. (Vennett-Smith) $384

A drawing of Mickey Mouse by Walt Disney, executed in gray crayon, signed and dedicated by the artist, 7½ x 4¾in. (Sotheby's) $5,227

Noel Coward, a hardback edition of 'The Noel Coward Song Book', signed and inscribed to front title page, First Edition, 1953. (Vennett-Smith) $72

Admiral Karl Donitz, 6 x 4 printed card in German, giving thanks for birthday greetings, signed in ink by Donitz. (Vennett-Smith) $96

Sir William Russell Flint, autographed letter, on one side of a correspondence card, 22nd June 1952, to Mrs. Hodges. (Vennett-Smith) $67

Albert Schweitzer, signed 6 x 4 photograph to lower white border, being a photo of one of Schweitzer's hospitals. (Vennett-Smith) $216

Oscar Hammerstein, signed album page, annotated in ink in another hand to lower border.
(Vennett-Smith) $40

Sean O'Casey, autographed letter, one page, 1st November 1953, to Don Burke, stating that a mutual friend has received the record safely.
(Vennett-Smith) $114

Douglas Haig, signed document, one page, 1st May 1900, written in pencil entirely in Haig's hand, being a trench order addressed to the 4th Brigade.
(Vennett-Smith) $64

Andrew Carnegie, signed document, one page, 14th May 1902, being a document of application *to be admitted to the Freedom of the City of London*.
(Vennett-Smith) $168

Sir Edward Elgar, signed piece, closely cut from the end of a letter.
(Vennett-Smith) $72

Richard Strauss, signed piece, tear to fold, not affecting signature.
(Vennett-Smith) $160

King William IV, a fine and boldly signed document, one page, 5th March 1835, approving leave of absence to Major Waller for twelve months.
(Vennett-Smith) $120

Laura Knight, autographed letter, on one side of a correspondence card, 6th May 1954, to Mrs. Hodge.
(Vennett-Smith) $61

Enrico Caruso, signed piece, together with an unsigned color cigarette card of Caruso, slight smudge.
(Vennett-Smith) $104

Joe Louis, signed album page, annotated in ink in another hand *Heavyweight Champion of the World 1948*.
(Vennett-Smith) $42

Neville Chamberlain, typed letter, one page, 14th May 1940, to Captain Sir William Brass, *My dear Willie*, thanking him for his letter.
(Vennett-Smith) $352

Charles M. Schulz, signed color 8 x 10 of Snoopy and friends from 'Snoopy Come Home'.
(Vennett-Smith) $160

A Leopold Lambert musical automaton of a girl with an Easter egg, French, 1890, 19in. high.
(Sotheby's) $1,528

A Roullet et Decamps musical automaton of a knitting woman, French, circa 1900, 26in. high.
(Sotheby's) $2,430

A Gustave Vichy musical automaton of a moresque harpist, French, circa 1870, 31in. high.
(Sotheby's) $13,023

A Renou musical automaton of a mouse trapper, French, circa 1900, the Gaultier bisque head impressed *F.G.* in a scroll, 17in. high.
(Sotheby's) $7,809

A Renou musical automaton of a magic baker, French, circa 1900, the Jumeau head stamped in red *DÉPOSÉ TÊTE JUMEAU B^{TE} S.G.D.G.*, with open mouth and upper teeth, 17in. high.
(Sotheby's) $6,941

A composition-headed character banjo player, with straw hat, original shirt, glass eyes, bamboo stool, movements to head, hand, chest, feet and eyelids, 35in. high, circa 1920.
(Christie's) $3,366

Nègre Fumeur, a composition-headed figure, with glass eyes, lorgnette, cigarette holder, and spring movement in body, 23½in. high.
(Christie's) $3,564

A cylinder musical box with musical automaton doll, Swiss, circa 1880, the Jumeau bisque head with open mouth and articulated tongue, 47in. high.
(Sotheby's) $24,293

A Decamp clockwork bear automaton, in his papier mäché paws he holds a bottle and a beaker which he fills and drinks, 1900–10, 33cm. high.
(Auktionsverket) $864

A musical Palais Royal figure of a cupid playing a harp, of typical gilt metal and mother-of-pearl construction, 9in. high.
(Christie's) $1,954

A Leopold Lambert musical automaton of a tambourine player, French, circa 1880, in red and yellow net dress, 16½in. high.
(Sotheby's) $4,512

A Michel Bertrand musical automaton of a clown acrobat, after a Gustave Vichy design and using many original Vichy parts, 20th century, 37in. high.
(Sotheby's) $15,617

A Roullet & Decamps musical waltzing cat automaton, French, circa 1890, the furry cat with green glass eyes and wearing a plumed hat, 20in. high.
(Sotheby's) $6,941

A Gustave Vichy musical automaton of Pierrot serenading the moon, French, circa 1890, the painted papier-mâché crescent moon with rolling brown glass eye and articulated lower jaw, 21in. high.
(Sotheby's) $41,646

A rare Roullet et Decamps musical automaton of a mask seller, French, circa 1910, 41in. high.
(Sotheby's) $101,925

A good French singing bird automaton with coin operated mechanism, late 19th century, 23in. high.
(Bearne's) $2,160

A Michel Bertrand musical automaton of a clown artist, after a Gustave Vichy design and using many original Vichy parts, 20th century, 36in. high.
(Sotheby's) $15,617

A late 19th century French musical automaton diorama, the double sided display depicting Summer and Winter scenes, 22½in. high.
(Bearne's) $626

A snuff box with singing bird automaton, the brass box with enamel decoration, 6cm. high, circa 1955.
(Auction Team Köln)
$3,010

A Roullet et Decamps musical drinking bear, French, circa 1910, the fur covered bear with glass eyes, lifting and pouring liquid from a metal bottle, 15³/₄in. high.
(Sotheby's) $1,388

An automaton cart with two bisque headed dolls, French, circa 1910, one head impressed *Limoges*, the doll seated in the wooden cart stamped *Savon* on the side, 16in. high.
(Sotheby's) $1,128

A Théroude clockwork doll on a three-wheeled platform, French, circa 1880, with a bisque head and closed mouth, in cream and rose satin outfit, 12¹/₂in. high.
(Sotheby's) $2,256

A color lithographed clockwork moving picture of a cooper's workshop, 11 x 9in., German, circa 1880.
(Christie's) $950

A bisque shoulder-headed automaton figure of an organ-grinder, with closed mouth, fixed blue eyes and wooden base, 17in. high, French, circa 1880.
(Christie's) $2,747

Grandmother with coffee grinder electric advertising figure for cafes and coffee houses, circa 1955.
(Auction Team Köln)
$540

A shop display of two gnomes peeping from behind a toadstool, felt on papier mâché, electrics in working order, 1955, 70cm. high.
(Auction Team Köln) $117

A clockwork nodding cobbler figure, French, circa 1915, the seated figure with black painted composition head and well defined features, 17¹/₄in. high.
(Sotheby's) $1,128

An early rocking ship automaton clock, the gilt bronze clock case with marine motifs, with two-train movement signed *Berthon*, 21¹/₂in. high.
(Christie's) $2,043

A pull along with two bisque headed clowns, German, circa 1900, each clown with open mouth and fixed blue glass eyes, 11³/₄in. long.
(Sotheby's) $868

A clockwork smoking nodding Negro figure, French, circa 1910, the papier-mâché face with open mouth and glass eyes, 17¹/₄in. high.
(Sotheby's) $1,562

A musical manivelle of two dolls, German, circa 1880, one watching a bisque doll inside a barrel on base containing the keywind musical movement, 9¹/₂in. high.
(Sotheby's) $1,562

A clockwork automaton of a coolie pulling a rickshaw, probably by Decamps, circa 1910, the Simon and Halbig dolls with bisque heads, 41in. long.
(Sotheby's) $3,498

A Roullet et Decamps musical knitting doll, French, circa 1890, the bisque head stamped in red *Deposé Tête Jumeau Bte S.G.D.G.5* with red check mark, 17in. high.
(Sotheby's) $4,338

A Black Forest cased singing bird automaton by Karl Griesbaum, the black and yellow bird with moving head, beak and tail, 25cm. high.
(Auction Team Köln)
                    $772

A Lambert automaton of a lady combing her hair, French, circa 1890, in taupe figured silk dress, overall height 23¹/₄in.
(Sotheby's) $1,388

A Roullet et Decamps automaton doll in chair, with open mouth and trembling tongue with blue glass eyes, domed head and composition body, 17in. high.
(Sotheby's) $1,301

A George IV mahogany wheel barometer, 12in. silvered dial with subsidiary hygrometer dial, 47in. high. (Bonhams)

$2,261

A mahogany stick barometer, the register with vernier scale and signed *Jo. Smith, Royal Exchange, London*. (Lawrence)

$1,648

Georgian mahogany banjo barometer with satinwood crossbandings, signed *Potts, London*. (G. A. Key)

$828

Stick type barometer with thermometer, having an improved sumpiesometer by W. F. Fisher of Great Yarmouth. (G. A. Key)

$674

A George III mahogany bowfronted stick barometer, silvered scales signed *Geo Tickell, Dublin*, with Vernier and trunk set thermometer, 39¹/₂in. high. (Bonhams)

$3,553

A George IV mahogany wheel barometer, 9¹/₂in. silvered engraved dial, signed spirit level below, *G. Dotty, Braintree*, 44in. high. (Bonhams)

$1,292

Dutch neoclassical mahogany barometer, signed *JAM Bekking, Rotterdam*, early 19th century. (Skinner)

$3,300

An early Victorian rosewood wheel barometer, lower half spirit level signed *J. Spelzini, 11 Beauchamp St., Holborn*, 37¹/₂in. high. (Bonhams)

$1,324

An early 19th century rosewood wheel barometer/thermometer by Aronsberg & Co., 44in. high.
(Spencer's) $660

A Victorian carved oak stick barometer, bone scales, signed *E. W. Bachmann, Guernsey*, twin Verniers trunk set with thermometer, 3ft. 9in.
(Bonhams) $926

A George III wheel barometer/thermometer/timepiece by F. Faveria & Co., 46in. high.
(Spencer's) $1,815

A 19th century mahogany stick barometer, bone scales, signed *J. Jenkins, Swansea*, and tube flanked by a thermometer, 3ft. 1in.
(Bonhams) $868

A Victorian stick barometer, the white opaline glass scales inscribed *Yates & Son, Opticians, Dublin*, in heavily carved oak case, 44in. high.
(Christie's) $1,251

A Victorian walnut wheel barometer, 12in. silvered circular dial, *L. Casartelli, 20 Duke St., Liverpool*, trunk with thermometer, 3ft. 9in.
(Bonhams) $694

Early 19th century mahogany and boxwood angle barometer, boxwood thermometer scale signed *Charles Howard Fecit*, 37in. high.
(Bonhams) $3,876

A French ormolu-mounted and kingwood barometer, with the printed label of *L. Couturier, 39 rue de la Paroisse*, late 19th/early 20th century, 14in. wide.
(Christie's) $2,590

Nantucket basket, Nantucket Island, Massachusetts, early 20th century, with swing handle, incised base, 5in. high.
(Skinner) $605

Four Shaker splint baskets, 11 to 22in. wide.
(Skinner) $2,860

A fine cut-tin reticulated basket filled with an assortment of painted stone fruit, American, 19th century, height 10in.
(Sotheby's) $2,300

An unusual woven splint oval basket, American, late 19th/ early 20th century, the tightly woven basket in Nantucket-style with scalloped rim, height 9¹/₂in.
(Sotheby's) $1,265

Splintwork handled basket painted green, 19in. diameter.
(Eldred's) $237

Nantucket basket, Nantucket Island, Massachusetts, early 20th century, swing handle, incised base, 4¹/₂in. high.
(Skinner) $550

Nantucket basket, signed *Stanley Roop*, Nantucket Island, Massachusetts, cover with carved ivory plaque of a dolphin, 8in. high.
(Skinner) $1,100

A wooden basket, American, 19th century, circular with finger molding and handle for carrying, stamped on the lid and bottom *J. DYER*, 13¹/₄in. diameter.
(Christie's) $110

A woven splint basket, American, late 19th century, with square base and circular rim with stationary split ash handle, diameter 15in.
(Sotheby's) $173

A Regency blue john and bronze mounted urn, the ovoid body raised on an acanthine chased square tapering plinth, 12in. high overall.
(Christie's) $1,500

A brass-mounted Derbyshire bluejohn and alabaster wall bracket, the plateau with cast-leaf chased border, late 18th/early 19th century, 10¹/₂in. wide.
(Christie's) $6,545

A Derbyshire bluejohn ovoid urn, the riveted, reeded body with lotus leaf cast finial, on square carrara marble base, late 18th century, 12¹/₄in. high, overall.
(Christie's) $1,348

A pair of George III ormolu-mounted blue john twin-branch candelabra by Matthew Boulton, each with removable stepped turned fluted domed foliate finial issuing stylized Greek-key pattern scrolled acanthus-cast branches, 12in. wide.
(Christie's) $75,735

A large Derbyshire bluejohn urn, the 'fine vein' body with gadrooned top and pineapple finial, the carrara marble and black slate stand with flaming torch amidst foliage, late 18th century, 20in. high.
(Christie's) $12,513

A pair of George III ormolu-mounted blue john cassolettes by Matthew Boulton, each with domed reversible top with acanthus finial and guilloche frieze enclosing a nozzle, 7¹/₂in. high.
(Christie's) $15,989

A 19th century blue john urn, mounted on a fleur-de-pêche marble plinth, 10³/₄in. high.
(Bonhams) $1,800

A pair of George III turned blue john ovoid urns, with stepped surmounts and cylindrical socles, 7¹/₄in. high.
(Christie's) $1,050

A fine George III blue john urn of large size with heavily veined body of good color, 13in. high.
(Bonhams) $3,000

BRONZE

A patinated bronze model of a hound branded *W*, on naturalistic base, signed *P. J. Mene*, 1843, 9¼in. wide.
(Christie's) $703

A Continental cold painted bronze figure of an Arab praying, kneeling on a rug, 6½in. high.
(Christie's) $1,001

A gilt bronze spread-winged American eagle, American, 20th century, with head turned left grasping the United States shield in its talons, 34½in. long.
(Sotheby's) $550

A bronze statue of Narcissus, after the Antique, his right hand containing a candle holder, converted to electricity, 27½in. high.
(Christie's) $693

A pair of Napoleon III brass and bronzed models of the Marly horses, on spreading rectangular contre-partie boulle bases, one indistinctly signed *Coustou*, 27in. wide.
(Christie's) $11,709

An English bronze figure of 'The Sluggard', cast from a model by Frederic, Lord Leighton, the naked youth with his arms raised as he stretches, late 19th century, 20½in. high.
(Christie's) $10,164

A bronze bust cast from a model by Charles Vyse, of an Army Officer, on a tapering square section stepped base, circa 1918, 34.5cm. high.
(Christie's) $861

An Art Deco bronze sculpture, of a lady kneeling, one arm resting on her knee, the other outstretched, mounted on a black and white marble base, 36cm. high.
(Christie's) $1,053

A bronze portrait head of Albert Einstein on black plinth, signed, circa 1950, total height 59cm.
(Auction Team Köln) $521

BRONZE

A bronze figure, cast from a model by Raymonde Guerbe, of a nude maiden sitting poised with a flowing drape decorated with silver stars, 39cm. high.
(Christie's)   **$3,828**

An English bronze bust of 'La Boulonnaise', cast from a model Aimé-Jules Dalou, wearing traditional hooded cloak fastened at the neck with a decorative clasp, 19th century, 18¼in. high.
(Christie's)   **$1,863**

A French bronze model of a walking lion, cast from a model by Antoine-Louis Barye, his right foreleg forward and his mouth open in a roar, signed *BARYE*, mid 19th century, 9⅛ x 16⅛in.
(Christie's)   **$5,421**

French bronze figure, 19th century, 'Mousse Siffleur' (Whistling boy), by V. Szczeblewski, French foundry marks, 17¼in. high.
(Eldred's)   **$1,980**

Two bronze Art Nouveau relief sculptures, France, 1900, women with flowing dresses, unsigned, 23in. high.
(Skinner)   **$1,980**

'Dancing Girl' a bronze and ivory figure, carved and cast from a model by Bruno Zach, of a young lady wearing a crinoline dress and long gloves, 39cm. high.
(Christie's)   **$5,359**

A massive cold painted spelter group, cast as a native dancing girl leaning languidly against a baluster vase, 36in. high.
(Lawrence)   **$1,562**

A bronze model of a goat, on a naturalistic base, signed *P. J. Mene*, 5½in. wide.
(Christie's)   **$1,087**

A Continental cold painted bronze figure of an Arab carpet seller, 7in. high.
(Christie's)   **$1,059**

A 19th century bronze group of a stag and a hind, signed *Alfred Dubucand? Paris 1828*, 42cm. high.
(Arnold) $851

A French bronze animalier inkstand, cast from a model by P. J. Mêne, the group entitled Chasse à la Perdrix depicting a setter and a pointer pursuing a gamebird, inscribed *P.J. MÊNE 1847*, second half 19th century, 20¹/₂in. wide.
(Christie's) $4,317

Tiffany Studios bronze marsh marigold planter, heavy walled cast bronze dish with separate copper liner, 10³/₄in. diameter.
(Skinner) $3,740

One of a 19th century pair of gilt bronze and silver colored metal candlesticks, supported by a naturalistic stem flanked by three swans, on a shaped triform base, 21cm. high.
(Phillips)(Two) $3,363

A pair of bronze reliefs of Greek warriors, each wearing a large plumed helmet and with one foot resting on a pedestal, 19th century, 36⁵/₈ x 22³/₄in. the frames.
(Christie's) $5,082

A French silvered bronze group of Hebe and Jupiter's eagle, cast from a model by Albert-Ernest Carrier-Belleuse, Hebe shown seated on the eagle, pouring ambrosia from her ewer into the cup, circa 1858, 19³/₄in. high.
(Christie's) $11,858

A bronze equestrian group by Arno Breker (1900–91), 75cm. high.
(Kunsthaus am Museum) $1,362

Pair of 19th century Oriental bronze vases of baluster form, with applied bird and foliage decoration, 18in. high.
(G. A. Key) $502

E. A. Lanceray, a bronze group of a mounted Tartar with a lasso in his right hand signed in Cyrillic, 8¹/₄in. high.
(Woolley & Wallis) $773

'A Dancer', a bronze and ivory figure, carved and cast from a model by Claire J. R. Colinet, of a dancing girl poised on one foot, her arms outstretched, 32.4cm. high.
(Christie's) $2,680

Hermann Georg Hasse, a bronze equestrian group of a naked maiden sitting on a horse and reaching down to a young girl standing beside her, 25in. high.
(Bearne's) $1,117

A gilt bronze and marble sculpture, carved and cast from a model by A. Gori, of a dancing girl poised on one foot, her arms outstretched, 93cm. high.
(Christie's) $5,359

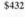

A bronze group of a young satyr with a dog, by August Sommer (1839–1921), signed, 72cm. high.
(Finarte) $3,202

A pair of bronze Marly horses, after the Antique, on shaped oval naturalistic bases, 19th century, 23in. high.
(Christie's) $1,444

A Japanese bronze vase, the neck, body and foot with shaped panels of various birds, animals and foliage, 1ft. 10in. high.
(Russell Baldwin & Bright) $432

Lord Kitchener by Sydney March, 1915, inscribed *Sydney March, Elkington & Co.*, 1915, bronze, mid brown patination, 18½in. high.
(Sotheby's) $7,672

A pair of French bronze figures, depicting Venus and Cupid, each shown partially clad, both standing by a tree trunk on naturalistic bases inscribed *SEVRES*, on circular stepped black marble feet, 12¾in. high.
(Christie's) $1,727

A bronze equestrian group by Otto Richter (b. 1867), signed and dated *1910*, 85cm. high.
(Kunsthaus am Museum) $2,290

A bronze and ivory figure of a dancer by Ernst Seger (1868–1939), on rectangular marble base, signed, 14cm. high. (Kunsthaus am Museum) $1,362

A pair of 19th century painted metal and gilt bronze mounted bread coasters with scrolling leaf decorated handles, 31cm. wide. (Phillips) $508

A Continental cold painted bronze of an Arab, kneeling on a prayer mat, 4³/₄in. high. (Christie's) $1,300

An English bronze figure of a cowboy on horseback, cast from a model by Walter Winans, the horse jumping over a tree trunk, late 19th century, 15³/₄in. high. (Christie's) $3,312

Paul Philippe, group of three dancers, 1930s, cold painted bronze, tinted ivory, onyx, 18¹/₂in. high. (Sotheby's) $11,583

Prof. Otto Poertzel, 'Medieval lady with two hounds', 1930's, cold painted bronze, ivory, onyx, marble, 19¹/₂in. high. (Sotheby's) $25,559

A bronze figure, cast from a model by Lorenzl, of a nude female standing on one leg, 30.2cm. overall height. (Bonhams) $468

A pair of French parcel-gilt-bronze vases, Louis-Philippe, Paris, 1840, each finely cast with grape, vine and classical figures, 32cm. high. (Sotheby's) $11,194

A chryselephantine group by Ernst Jaeger (b. 1880) of a page with a hawk, painted in silver and red, 23.5cm. high, on round marble base. (Kunsthaus am Museum) $805

A Georgian brass-mounted
mahogany plate bucket of
conventional form with swing
handle and slatted sides, 14in.
high.
(Bearne's) $1,377

A pair of late Victorian black-
painted and parcel-gilt leather
fire-buckets each with later loop
handle and green-painted
interior, 12in. high.
(Christie's) $420

A small mahogany brass bound
bucket of oval shape with three
brass bands, brass liner and
swing handle, 9in. high.
(Lawrence Fine Art) $517

Antique leather fire bucket with
coat of arms.
(G. A. Key) $237

A George III mahogany plate
bucket with brass rim and swing
handle, vertical pierced pale
sides, 11³/₄in. diameter.
(Lawrence) $1,475

A George III brass-bound
mahogany oval bucket, with
arched handle and later drop-in
brass lining, 15¹/₂in. wide.
(Christie's) $2,449

A fine painted pine and sheet-
iron bucket, Joseph Lehn, Lititz,
Pennsylvania, circa 1860, bound
with three sheet-iron bands
painted with a running rosebud
motif, height 9¹/₄in.
(Sotheby's) $4,025

A pair of George III Irish brass-
bound mahogany plate buckets,
each with a brass swing handle
above a spirally-turned body,
24¹/₂in. high.
(Christie's) $12,547

A George III Irish brass-bound
mahogany plate bucket, one side
with an opening and a later tin
liner, 24¹/₂in. high.
(Christie's) $2,342

An unusual stenciled and painted 'Theorem' box, American, probably New England, mid 19th century, with hinged lid opening to a compartmented interior with slide, 9³/₄in. wide.
(Sotheby's) $2,200

A pine hinged-box, American, 19th century, oval with iron sliding lock and bracket front, 17¹/₄in. wide.
(Christie's) $220

An early 19th century papier mâché tea caddy decorated with scrolled flowers, mother of pearl inlay, highlighted with rose motifs, supported on ball feet, 9in. wide.
(Locke & England) $480

A rare William and Mary walnut spice box, Pennsylvania, 1720–60, the hinged door with inset molded geometric panel, 17¹/₂in. wide.
(Sotheby's) $14,300

An early 19th century French mahogany and gilt mounted nécessaire and musical box in the form of a piano, with extensively fitted velvet-lined interior, 30cm. wide.
(Phillips) $1,062

A brown oak letter box either by George Bullock or George Morant, banded overall in holly, first half 19th century, 8³/₄in. wide.
(Christie's) $588

A cherry and mahogany cigar box designed by David Joel, with three bar curved chrome handles, the top with medallion inlaid with *RJWP* monogram, 50cm. wide.
(Christie's) $766

A Victorian coromandel toilet box, having the complete fitted interior and assorted mother of pearl handled and silver mounted requisites.
(Locke & England) $1,120

An early 19th century serpentine front tortoiseshell veneered tea caddy, opening to reveal two lidded zinc lined compartments, 20cm. wide.
(Spencer's) $410

An unusual painted chip-carved box, American, probably Pennsylvania, early 20th century, the rectangular top with hinged lid opening to a compartmented interior, 19¹/₂in. wide.
(Sotheby's) $1,650

A mahogany veneered miniature sideboard tea chest, inlaid brass stringing with a fitted interior, 13in. wide.
(Woolley & Wallis) $1,265

A painted and stenciled pine box, American, 1844, oval, vinegar painted, 11¹/₂in. diameter.
(Christie's) $220

A Chippendale brass-mounted mahogany serpentine-front letter box, probably American, circa 1785, the sloped lid opening to a divided well, 13in. high.
(Sotheby's) $1,430

A George III sycamore and inlaid tea caddy of rectangular form with canted corners, the oval inlaid panels within foliate surrounds, 20cm. wide.
(Phillips) $637

A George III satinwood knife box, with tulipwood crossbanding, the lid inlaid with a shell medallion, 9in. wide.
(Lawrence) $1,006

A Victorian coromandel writing slope, the interior in unused state with tooled green velvet and glass ink bottles with engraved gilded coves.
(Locke & England) $896

A George III marquetry and satinwood tea-caddy, the hinged rectangular top centered by a shell motif, the front with two oval floral marquetry panels above a pin-locked drawer, 13¹/₂in. wide.
(Christie's) $1,051

A George III mahogany veneered tea caddy, inlaid satinwood and floral marquetry with canted corners, 4¹/₂in. high.
(Woolley & Wallis) $500

A Regency ormolu-mounted penwork and painted tea-caddy of sarcophagus form, with hinged domed lid decorated with a chinoiserie pastoral scene, 7¼in. wide.
(Christie's) $1,681

A hardwood tea caddy in the form of an aubergine, 5¼in. high.
(Woolley & Wallis) $533

A fine George III inlaid satinwood lap desk, circa 1795, the rectangular hinged top centering an oval reserve inlaid with a conch and beetle, 20in. wide.
(Sotheby's) $2,750

A pine pipe box, American, dated *1723*, with upswept cresting centered by a flowerhead above a rectangular box with shaped top carved with a flowerhead, 12½in. high.
(Christie's) $1,980

An early Victorian tortoiseshell veneered and mother-of-pearl inlaid tea caddy of oblong form, the lid and front panel decorated with trailing thistle and flower motifs, 16.5cm. wide.
(Phillips) $900

A black-painted pipe-box, American, 18th century, with recessed carved heart and pierced C-scrolling crest, 20in. high.
(Christie's) $4,400

A fine painted and decorated pine utility box, New York, early 19th century, the rectangular top painted with a view of St. Stephen's Park, 12¾in. wide.
(Sotheby's) $2,090

A 20th century mahogany 'Country House' table letterbox of hexagonal form with domed lid and acorn finial, 48cm. high.
(Phillips) $2,301

A Regency octagonal work box finely painted with putti, masks, birds, urns, flowers and foliage, the interior divided into compartments with similarly-decorated covers.
(Bearne's) $512

Patriotic inlaid mahogany box, dated *1864*, 9¼in. wide. (Skinner) **$2,090**

A 19th century large fruitwood pear caddy, (side with crack and stalk missing), 6¼in. high. (Woolley & Wallis) **$1,299**

Shaker-type oval covered box in pine and maple, 6in. wide. (Eldred's) **$303**

A Chippendale pine tricorn hat box, late 18th century, the triangular top with hinged front over a rectangular case with two thumbmolded short drawers and a long drawer, 31in. high. (Christie's) **$3,080**

A Federal inlaid mahogany tea-caddy, New York, 1790–1810, the rectangular hinged top with rounded recessed corners with inlaid fluting centering an inlaid conch, 6in. wide. (Christie's) **$1,650**

A Regency mahogany and foliate inlaid sewing box, the interior with tray, 9¼in. wide. (Christie's) **$867**

A Victor – HMV tin with 4-color illustration of Nipper, 18cm. diameter. (Auction Team Köln) **$101**

A 17th century Dutch painted box of oblong form with sliding carved lid, with pierced arched hanging backplate, 36cm. high. (Phillips) **$540**

An early Victorian tortoiseshell veneered rectangular bow fronted tea chest, on copper ball feet, 8in. wide. (Woolley & Wallis) **$1,137**

Small Victorian figured walnut lap desk, brass bound and having fitted interior, 11in. wide.
(G. A. Key) $294

Large early 19th century figured walnut tea caddy with sarcophagus formed lid, ring handles and squat circular feet, 15 x 9in.
(G. A. Key) $536

Fine Victorian walnut sewing box with Tunbridgeware crossbanding.
(G. A. Key) $169

A George III ivory and tortoiseshell tea caddy of decagonal form with silver **monogramed plaque and escutcheon**, 5in.
(Bearne's) $1,788

An unusual painted metal figural cigar box, American, late 19th century, height 9¾in.
(Sotheby's) $3,220

A good George III rolled paperwork tea caddy of octagonal form, the front panel inset with an oval silk portrait plaque, 7in. wide.
(Bearne's) $1,937

Late 19th century rosewood coal box with marquetry inlays, brass carrying handle, complete with shovel.
(G. A. Key) $236

A fine painted and decorated document box, initialed *EMD*, probably New England, 19th century, with a white-painted heart escutcheon, the sides with two white houses, height 6¼in.
(Sotheby's) $1,265

A fine mahogany ballot box, circa 1840, with yes and no drawers with ivory plaques, 12in. high.
(Sotheby's) $8,496

A rare Chippendale walnut spice chest, Pennsylvania, late 18th century, the door opening to an arrangement of fifteen small drawers fitted with brass pulls, 15¼in. wide.
(Sotheby's) $9,900

Fine Victorian walnut dome lidded tea caddy, inlaid with Tunbridgeware decoration, interior of two small boxes and a glass mixing bowl, 12in. wide.
(G. A. Key) $536

Fine Victorian rosewood and brass banded vanity box with several plated and glass interior fittings, 9 x 12in.
(G. A. Key) $317

A painted and decorated pine bride's ribbon box, probably Continental, late 18th/early 19th century, decorated on the top with the figures of an amorous couple, 19¼in. long.
(Sotheby's) $3,300

A pair of George III mahogany urn-shaped cutlery-boxes, inlaid overall with satinwood and ebonized lines, each with acorn finial and domed rising cover, 30½in. high.
(Christie's) $3,323

A fine mahogany domestic medicine chest, compartments for twelve bottles and glass preparation slide, above a single drawer with lift out tray, 8¼in. high.
(Christie's) $1,301

Late 19th century oak stationery cabinet/writing box with fitted interior, 12in. wide.
(G. A. Key) $445

Fine Victorian figured walnut games compendium containing chessmen, checkers and various card games, 14½in. wide.
(G. A. Key) $1,447

Early 19th century rosewood vanity box with fitted interior and plated tops.
(G. A. Key) $204

A Regency leather workbox, the hinged rectangular top enclosing an interior fitted with various ivory sewing implements, 9in. wide.
(Christie's) $581

An early 19th century navette shaped giltwood and paper scroll tea caddy, with brass swing handle to the cover, 7³/₄in. wide.
(Christie's) $1,361

A tortoiseshell veneered dressing table box and cover, the hinged cover stamped and applied with a silver fascia depicting a polar bear and her two cubs, 9cm. wide.
(Spencer's) $165

Cased set of six blown glass liquor bottles, 18th century, in a mahogany case, one bottle not original.
(Eldred's) $110

A Dutch oak foot warmer, the pierced and foliate carved rectangular top fitted with iron swing handle, 18th century, 8¹/₂in. wide.
(Christie's) $1,452

A fine early Victorian toilet case, veneered in coromandel, brass bound and inlaid stringing, maker Francis Douglas London 1845/46.
(Woolley & Wallis) $1,089

An Anglo-Indian Vizagapatam ebony and ivory games board in the form of two volumes, 19th century, 18¹/₄in. wide.
(Christie's) $1,953

A James II oak spice box, opening to reveal an interior fitted with four variously sized drawers, 14¹/₂in. wide.
(Christie's) $1,996

A painted and decorated hanging watch-holder, the rectangular crest centering a pierced heart, with hinged door centering a glazed bull's eye, 10¹/₂in. high.
(Christie's) $660

R. and J. Beck, London, a 6.5 x 9cm. Presentation Frena camera no. 13017 with pigskin covered body, gilt metal fittings, lens and rotary shutter.
(Christie's) $790

A 35mm. Leica Luxus camera with gilt metal-finished body, brown snakeskin body covering, shutter speed to 1/500, mushroom release and a gilt-barrel Leitz Elmar f/3.5 50mm. lens.
(Christie's) $6,237

Thornton-Pickard Mfg. Co. Ltd., Altrincham, a 5 x 4 inch mahogany and brass bound Type C aerial camera No. 67, internal roller blind shutter.
(Christie's) $2,825

A Rolleiflex Number 1 original model with 75mm. F3.5 Tessar lens, cased.
(Spencer's) $82

Thomas Sutton/A. Ross, London, a 10 x 5½ inch mahogany-body Sutton Panoramic camera with lacquered brass fittings, rear focusing screw, top-mounted locking screw.
(Christie's) $45,903

A 35mm. Sico camera no. 38 with polished teak body, brass fittings and a Rüdersdorf A. G. Sico Anastigmat f/3.5 6cm. lens, in a leather case.
(Christie's) $4,466

A whole-plate brass and mahogany field camera with red square-cut bellows, maker's label *George Hare*.
(Christie's) $666

A 4.5 x 6cm. miniature falling plate camera.
(Christie's) $312

J. Lancaster & Son, Birmingham, a 1½ x 2 inch Improved-pattern patent watch camera with nickel-plated body.
(Christie's) $21,186

Eastman Kodak Co., Rochester, NY, a 127-rollfilm blue-coloured 'flash pattern' Kodak Petite camera with original blue colored bellows.
(Christie's) $490

A 4.5 x 6cm. Monocular disguised camera with reflecting viewfinder, magazine back and a H. Roussell Stylor f/6.3 25mm lens.
(Christie's) $2,452

A 35mm. Peggy I camera no. M.165/3 with a Carl Zeiss Jena Tessar f/3.5 5cm. lens no. 1292504 in a Compur shutter, in maker's leather ever ready case.
(Christie's) $447

A 35mm. black Leica M4 camera no. 1207276 with a Leitz Summicron f/2 50mm. lens no. 2340225 and 12585 lenshood.
(Christie's) $2,079

A 35mm. Zi Jin Shan [Purple Mountain] camera with a f/3.5 50mm. lens no. 5900374.
(Christie's) $357

A 35mm. Weltini camera with a Leitz Elmar 5cm. f/3.5 lens in a rimset Compur Rapid shutter, in maker's leather ever ready case.
(Christie's) $290

A 35mm. black Nikon SP camera 6219041 with a Nippon Kogaku W-Nikkor f/2.5 3.5cm. lens no. 244179 and related accessories.
(Christie's) $1,767

Canon Camera Co., Japan, a 35mm. Bell and Howell/Canon 7 camera no. 840105 with a Canon 50mm. f/0.95 lens no. 13017.
(Christie's) $998

Zeiss Ikon, Germany, a 35mm. Nettax 538/24 camera no. A.47738 with a Carl Zeiss Jena Tessar f/2.8 5cm. lens no. 1551159, in maker's leather ever ready case.
(Christie's) $790

A half-plate tropical Vaido camera model B with polished teak and brass bound body, tan leather bellows and viewing hood.
(Christie's) $1,752

C. P. Goerz, Germany, a 45 x 107mm. Photo-Stereo-Binocle camera no. 233 with two sets of rotating lenses, in maker's fitted case.
(Christie's) $2,079

Eastman Dry Plate & Film Co., Rochester, NY, a rollfilm No. 1 Kodak camera no. 13199 with winding key, shutter, lens and felt lens plug.
(Christie's) $2,978

Nippon Kogaku, Japan, a 35mm. chrome Nikon S2 camera no. 6147510 with a Nippon-Kogaku Nikkor-S.C f/1.4 5cm. lens no. 359858.
(Christie's) $1,081

A rollfilm tropical The King's Own De Luxe Model B camera no. B.407 with polished teak body, brass binding.
(Christie's) $1,489

Eastman Kodak Co., Rochester, NY, a 127-rollfilm lavender-colored 'step pattern' Kodak Petite camera with black bellows.
(Christie's) $210

A 35mm. Witness camera no. 5010 with a Dallmeyer Super-Six anastigmat f/1.9 2 inch lens no. 383472, lenshood, guarantee sheet and original instruction booklet.
(Christie's) $2,079

A Ticka watch pocket camera with swinging viewfinder lens and lens cap, in slip case, in maker's box, and a Wynne's Infallible Exposure meter in maker's tin.
(Christie's) $1,143

A 35mm. 'no name' Contax camera no. 6306372 with a Carl Zeiss Sonnar f/2 50mm. lens no. 1733933, in maker's leather ever ready case.
(Christie's) $1,340

A 35mm. black Leicaflex SL2 camera no. 1424093.
(Christie's) $790

A Leica Flex SLII black with 50mm. F2 Summicron R lens.
(Spencer's) $907

A 35mm. black paint Nikon S3M camera no. 6600056 with a Nikon Nikkor-H f/2 5cm. lens.
(Christie's) $45,545

Asahi Optical Co., Japan, a 35mm. Asahiflex IIb camera no. 79334 with an Asahi-Kogaku Takumar f/2.4 58mm. lens no. 88310, in maker's ever ready case.
(Christie's) $541

A 9 x 12cm. Universal Juwel 275/7 camera no. P.90770 with a Carl Zeiss, Jena Tessar f/4.5 15cm. lens.
(Christie's) $841

A 35mm. black-paint Nikon S3M camera no. 6600090 with rear-mounted sliding viewfinder frame adjuster.
(Christie's) $32,407

A 45 x 107mm. Stereo Mentor camera no. 12444 with a pair of Carl Zeiss Jena Tessar f/4.5 9cm. lenses, three double darkslides and a Mentor filmpack, in maker's leather case.
(Christie's) $424

A 4.5 x 6cm. baby Deckrullo camera no. 641700 with a Carl Zeiss Jena Tessar f/2.7 8cm. lens no. 659881 and twelve single metal slides, in maker's leather case.
(Christie's) $873

A 35mm. Sept camera with a Roussel, Paris Stylor f/3.5 50mm. lens no. 42725 and three Sept film cassettes, in maker's fitted leather cae.
(Christie's) $458

C. P. Stirn, Germany, a 4 inch diameter Concealed Vest No. 1 camera no. 7158 with lens and front panel engraved *Patentees Agents J. Robinson & Sons*.
(Christie's) $1,247

The Griffiths Camera Co. Ltd., a double quarter-plate boxform falling plate camera with shutter, wheel stops, independent plate changing mechanisms, and maker's label.
(Christie's) $623

A 4.5 x 6cm. Ermanox camera no. 1185290 with an Ernemann Anastigmat Ernostar f/2 10cm. lens no. 150548, film pack adapter and single metal side, in maker's leather case.
(Christie's) $1,559

A 35mm. Mecaflex camera no. A-288 with Type-R-Seroa Anastigmat 4mm. f/3.5 lens, in maker's case.
(Christie's) $938

S. J. Levi & Co., London, a quarter-plate The Pullman detective camera with tan leather covered body and a brass bound lens in a rolled blind shutter.
(Christie's) $1,247

A 6 x 9cm. tropical Minex camera Folding Model no. 8090 with polished teak body, tan leather focusing hood and bellows.
(Christie's) $10,718

A 35mm. walnut-body cinematographic camera/projector no. 130 with brass-body direct vision finder, a walnut film magazine, maker's plate *Cinématographe, Auguste et Louis Lumière*.
(Christie's) $23,901

A 6 x 13cm. Heidoscop camera no. 9596 with a Carl Zeiss Jena Sucher-Triplet f/4.2 7.5cm. viewing lens no. 714362, in maker's fitted case.
(Christie's) $790

A quarter-plate brass and mahogany tailboard camera with a brass bound Ross, London 5 x 4 Rapid Symmetrical lens no. 34554, Waterhouse stops, double darkslide and plaque *Newton & Co.*
(Christie's) $624

Thornton-Pickard Mfg. Co. Ltd., Altrincham, a 16mm. black-crackle finished Ruby cinematographic camera with direct vision finder, the film gate stamped, *39*, a Dallmeyer 1 inch f/1.9 lens no. 121480 and front panel marked *The Ruby*.
(Christie's) $936

Eastman Kodak Co., Rochester, NY, a 120-rollfilm cardboard-body George Washington Kodak camera with blue star-patterned body covering, the front section with center-set waistlevel viewfinder.
(Christie's) $29,029

A 120-rollfilm tele-Rolleiflex camera no. S.2303308 with light meter, a Heidosmat f/4 135mm. viewing lens no. 2719888 and a Carl Zeiss Sonnar f/4 135mm. taking lens, in maker's ever ready case.
(Christie's) $1,663

A 35mm. Leica R4 camera no. 1608360 with a Leitz Summicron-R f/2 50mm. lens no. 3083797, in maker's ever ready case.
(Christie's) $830

A Presentation Leica outfit containing a 35mm. black Leica II camera, a nickel Hektor 5cm. f/2.5 lens with button release and front cap, in maker's fitted leather outfit case.
(Christie's) $12,890

A 35mm. chrome Nikon F camera no. 6732600 with a Nikon Motordrive F36 unit no. 87071.
(Christie's) $624

A nickel-plated bulldog wearing goggles, 3¹/₂in. high.
(Christie's) $355

'Cinq Chevaux', a Lalique lightly tinted amethyst glass mascot, with chromed metal part fitting, 11.5cm. high.
(Christie's) $3,678

Darel, Indian head Mohican, circa 1930, chromium-plated bronze, mounted on wooden base, 4³/₄in. high.
(Christie's) $391

A monkey mascot, with an elongated mouth, brass, circa 1920, mounted on a brass base, 4in. high.
(Christie's) $239

A bronze nickel-plated head of a retriever carrying a pheasant, signed on the collar *Ch. Paillet*, 3³/₄in. high.
(Christie's) $319

A Lalique car mascot, modeled in satin glass as a Siren thrust forward on the crest of a wave, 18cm. high.
(Bearne's) $4,350

René Lalique, mascot, 'Cinq Chevaux', after 1925, clear glass, wood mount, 6¹/₂in. high.
(Sotheby's) $5,702

A nickel-plated Radial Aero Engine, the rotating propeller stamped *Robt. Beney & Co*, 5in. high.
(Christie's) $603

A circus bear, brass, circa 1930, seated on a column and holding a pole, 6in. high.
(Christie's) $261

A carved second row Dentzel jumper, circa 1908, in the Philadelphia style, with original dappled body paint, 52in. wide. (Sotheby's) **$8,250**

A carved and painted wooden carousel horse, with mane to right, hole for pole and iron strengthening straps, circa 1900. (Christie's) **$471**

A rare carved carousel frog, Herschell-Spillman Co., North Tonawanda, New York, circa 1914, 42in. long. (Sotheby's) **$19,800**

Centre row carousel horse, circa 1900, 47in. long, carved by Herschel Speilman, peg construction, on brass pole. (Du Mouchelles) **$2,250**

An unusual pair of carved pine miniature carousel horses, Muller-style, American, late 19th/early 20th century, carved in the round, overall height 13½in. (Butterfield & Butterfield) **$3,850**

Carved polychrome horse carousel figure, America, late 19th century, old repaint, 37in. high. (Skinner) **$1,650**

A carved and painted wood 'Prancer' carousel horse, Looff or Dentzel, New York or Philadelphia, circa 1895, 62in. long. (Sotheby's) **$6,900**

A fine carved and painted pine outside row carousel horse jumper, Gustav Dentzel & Co., Philadelphia, circa 1880. (Sotheby's) **$14,950**

A fine carved and painted pine outside row standing carousel horse, Gustav Dentzel & Co., Germantown, Philadelphia, circa 1895. (Sotheby's) **$23,000**

Steuben three light chandelier, rib molded trumpet form gold Aurene shades affixed to vasiform hanger, total height 22¹/₂in.
(Skinner) $715

Daum Art glass chandelier, three-socket ceiling light with oval gilt metal drop supporting orange and amethyst glass bell shades, 20in. high.
(Skinner) $605

An Empire chandelier in the form of an oil lamp suspended by chains, in bronze and ormolu, with pineapple finial, 110cm. high.
(Finarte) $6,048

Quezal two-tier chandelier, designed by Martin Boch, five elongated bell-form opal, green and gold pulled feather shades, 46in. high.
(Skinner) $4,125

A Venetian glass twelve-light chandelier, the urn shaped sconces with alternate colored glass petal liner, supported by barley-twist upswept arms, 1.5m. diameter approx.
(Phillips) $720

A George IV large ormolu colza-oil hanging-light possibly by William Collins, the central shaft cast with layers of lotus-leaf divided by balls, above three addorsed eagles with outstretched wings, 99¹/₂in. high.
(Christie's) $47,124

Quezal three light chandelier, shoulder flared opal shades with rib mold design, height below chain 16in.
(Skinner) $440

Leaded glass hanging lantern lamp, two-part fixture composed of caramel slag brickwork pagoda top, widest diameter 21in.
(Skinner) $1,870

Chandelier with Tiffany acorn shades, suspended from elaborate metal cased light bowl with cast butterflies, women and Art Nouveau floral elements.
(Skinner) $5,170

CHANDELIERS

An ormolu and cut-glass eight-light chandelier, the circular corona and circlet hung with icicle drops, the circlet hung with four diminishing tiers, second quarter, 19th century. (Christie's) $3,425

A Gallé carved and acid-etched, triple-overlay hanging light, with elaborate copper fitting in the form of plane-tree leaves and branches with fruits, 52cm. diameter. (Christie's) $13,398

An ormolu and green-painted eight-light chandelier, of Empire style, the scroll branches arranged about a circular well, 26in. wide. (Christie's) $5,390

An ormolu and blue-painted six-light chandelier, the bifurcating branches surmounted by goat head masks, modeled with birds with outstretched wings supporting riband floral swags, 40¹/₂in. high. (Christie's) $5,775

An ormolu twelve-light chandelier, the central baluster stem with an acanthus corona above a fluted 'vase' with spreading base, late 19th/20th century, 48in. wide. (Christie's) $7,253

A fine cut-glass sixteen-light chandelier, the drip pans and shaped sconces supported by scroll arms, hung with chains of faceted beads and lusters, second quarter 19th century, 64in. high. (Christie's) $25,025

An ormolu nine-light chandelier, the open superstructure with chased acanthus scroll arms arranged about a central urn with a flaming finial, 19th century, 30¹/₂in. high. (Christie's) $6,738

A brass six-light chandelier, the baluster shaft with ring finial and six S-scroll branches, each with circular dished drip-pan and turned nozzle, 17³/₄in. high. (Christie's) $2,731

A Bohemian ruby glass chandelier, circa 1870, the six lights with trumpet shades painted with white and blue foliage, 120cm. high. (Sotheby's) $5,422

AMERICAN

Van Briggle pottery vase, caramel glaze with moss green mottling, inscribed mark and *1913*, 6in. high.
(Skinner) $467

Buffalo pottery Deldareware water pitcher, *Ye Old English Village*, 10in. high.
(Eldred's) $523

A green-glazed incised earthenware pickle jar, attributed to Lucius Jordan, Washington County, Georgia, late 19th century, 15in. high.
(Sotheby's) $1,100

A rare slip-decorated glazed redware large pie plate, Pennsylvania, 19th century, the interior with yellow slip inscription *G. W. Rhoads Dealer in Dry goods groceries & cc also Schwitzer Kase*, diameter 13½in.
(Sotheby's) $3,738

Pairpoint Limoges Garden of Allah vase, porcelain blank, exquisitely decorated in the Crown Milano manner, handpainted and enameled with Far Eastern merchants and camels, 13¼in. high.
(Skinner) $1,650

Scheier pottery charger, hand-thrown plate glazed mauve and brown with central geometric panels, 14½in. diameter.
(Skinner) $880

Teco floor vase, Gates Potteries, Terra Cotta, Illinois, circa 1906, green glazed with rolled rim continuing into four squared vertical strap handles, 20⅝in. high.
(Skinner) $7,150

Paul Revere Pottery Saturday Evening Girl tile, incised Boston street scene, colored pink, blue, brown, white and grey with black outlines, 3¾ x 3¾in.
(Skinner) $385

A glazed earthenware 'Face-jug', attributed to Norman Smith, Bibb County, Lawley, Alabama, circa 1930, with strap handle, 10in. high.
(Sotheby's) $2,640

AMERICAN

Van Briggle Lorelei vase, dark Persian rose baluster-form with hand modeled face of Lorelei inside rim, 9¹/₂in. high. (Skinner) $468

Polychrome chalkware reclining stag, America, 19th century, 16in. wide. (Skinner) $935

A fine and rare glazed stoneware night owl whistle, signed *Anna, Illinois*, dated *1890*, the molded hollow figure with details picked out in yellow and brown glaze, 5¹/₂in. high. (Sotheby's) $3,300

Glazed stoneware grotesque jug, circa 1980, Burlon Craig, Lincoln County, North Carolina, impressed mark at base, 16¹/₂in. high. (Skinner) $330

Adelaide Robineau porcelain vase, Syracuse, New York, circa 1912, spherical form with white crystalline glaze, 4³/₄in. high. (Skinner) $5,500

A rare incised and cobalt blue-decorated salt-glazed stoneware crock, Nathan Clark & Co., Lyons, New York, circa 1845, 14¹/₂in. high. (Sotheby's) $16,500

Marblehead Pottery decorated vase, Arthur Baggs, 1913, hand-thrown cylinder with subtle repeating decoration of five conventionalized tree clusters, 9³/₄in. high. (Skinner) $5,500

A very rare slip-decorated glazed redware large pie plate, Pennsylvania, mid 19th century, of circular form with crimped edge, 14³/₄in. diameter. (Sotheby's) $3,850

Chelsea Keramic Art Works elephant vase, Hugh C. Robertson, circa 1880, angular 'metal shape' octagonal body with applied elephant head handles, 6¹/₂in. high. (Skinner) $495

ARITA

A rare Arita octagonal blue and white vase decorated with scholars and attendants in a boat on a river, late 17th century, 52cm. high.
(Christie's) $12,000

A pair of large Arita porcelain vases, painted with various shaped panels of birds, flowers and landscapes, 141.5cm. high.
(Bearne's) $2,025

A large Arita blue and white tankard finely painted with butterflies, a bird and ducks among peonies, late 17th century, 25cm. high.
(Christie's) $2,990

A Japanese Arita porcelain vase and cover, the domed cover surmounted by a shi-shi dog, 15½in. high, circa 1720.
(Tennants) $1,377

Two rare Arita blue and white ewers in the Kakiemon manner of Islamic form, each decorated with birds among branches of bamboo, late 17th century, 28.5cm. high.
(Christie's) $31,559

An Arita blue and white coffee urn with elaborate engraved Dutch silver mounts, the urn decorated with a ho-o bird on rockwork, late 17th/early 18th century, 33cm. high.
(Christie's) $6,975

An Arita blue and white tureen and cover decorated with six shaped panels depicting sprays of peony and chrysanthemum among rockwork, late 17th century, 31cm. diameter.
(Christie's) $12,000

A fine Arita blue and white charger, the central roundel with a lady fanning herself, late 17th century, 59cm. diameter.
(Christie's) $12,458

A large rare Arita octagonal tureen and cover decorated with a continuous clouded landscape, surmounted by a large knop finial, late 17th century, 32cm. wide.
(Christie's) $16,610

A Berlin rectangular plaque painted by R. Dittrich with a portrait of Ruth in the cornfield's, artist's signature, circa 1880, 19 x 11¹/₂in.
(Christie's) $9,200

A Berlin ruby luster two-handled campana vase, finely painted in colors with an elaborate family tree of the House of Hohenzollern, circa 1820, 43cm. high.
(Christie's) $17,700

A K.P.M. rectangular plaque of 'Clementine', late 19th century, signed *Von L. Schunzel* and *C. Kiesel*, 12⁵/₈ x 10³/₈in.
(Christie's) $7,000

A Berlin rectangular plaque painted by Back with a portrait of a young girl, artist's signature, impressed KPM and scepter mark, circa 1880, 9¹/₂ x 6¹/₄in.
(Christie's) $8,500

A pair of Berlin two-handled porcelain vases and covers, of inverted baluster form, each painted with scenes of lovers in 18th century costume, late 19th century, 15in. high.
(Christie's) $1,450

A Berlin rectangular plaque painted in Vienna by Fr. Wagner with Gute Nacht, a young girl holding a pewter chamberstick and shading the glow of the candle with her left hand, circa 1880, 13 x 7³/₄in.
(Christie's) $4,145

A very good Berlin porcelain plaque, depicting courtiers in a garden setting, possibly Mary Antoinette, 13³/₄in. diameter.
(John Nicholson) $4,500

A K.P.M. plaque of Christ in the Temple, late 19th century, impressed marks, 17 x 14¹/₂in.
(Christie's) $4,000

A K.P.M. plaque of Königin Luisa, late 19th century, impressed marks, signed *Karu*, 11¹/₂ x 10in.
(Christie's) $6,000

BOW

A pair of Bow porcelain figures modeled as a lady and gentleman in exotic costume, circa 1760, 5³/₄in. high. (Christie's) $898

A Bow triple-shell sweetmeat stand modeled as three shells resting on a bed of shells and seaweed, 6³/₄in. wide. (Bonhams) $1,200

A pair of Bow porcelain tubs filled with bouquets of flowers painted in a bright palette, circa 1760, 8¹/₄in. high. (Christie's) $1,980

A Bow mug of cylindrical shape with a grooved loop handle and heart-shaped terminal, 5⁵/₈in. high, circa 1770. (Bonhams) $750

Two rare Bow models of kestrels perched on flower-encrusted tree trunks, the birds with red heads, and mostly green plumage with touches of blue, purple and red, 14.5cm. (Phillips) $3,680

A Bow model of a cockerel standing on a mound base, with red comb and wattles, 11cm. high. (Phillips) $576

A Bow saucer painted in blue with a heron by a bridge in an Oriental-style landscape, 4⁵/₈in. wide. (Bonhams) $375

A pair of Bow figures of Harlequin and Columbine, after the Meissen Commedia dell'Arte originals, both standing in dancing attitude, 13.5cm. high. (Phillips) $2,240

A Bow botanical octagonal plate painted with a specimen spray of pink flowers and buds and with scattered butterflies and insects, circa 1758, 23cm. wide. (Christie's) $4,145

BOW

A Bow botanical octagonal plate painted with a spray of guava and with a caterpillar, scattered butterflies and insects, circa 1758, 24cm. wide.
(Christie's) $3,454

A pair of Bow figures of Harlequin and Columbine, after the Meissen Commedia dell'Arte models, 11.5cm. high.
(Phillips) $1,440

A rare Bow star-shaped dish painted in blue with floral sprays within a jagged blue border, 6in. wide.
(Bonhams) $360

A pair of Bow porcelain candlestick bases modeled as seated cherubs beside bocages, circa 1760, 5¼in. high.
(Christie's) $518

A rare Bow Commedia dell' arte group of Scaramouche and Isabella seated side by side beneath a flowering tree, 29.5cm.
(Phillips) $4,500

A pair of rare Bow models of small green parrots perched on flower-encrusted cross boughs, the green plumage with black markings and orange patches on the wings, 11.4cm.
(Phillips) $2,720

A small Bow model of a monkey, also an adaptation from the chinoiserie group, holding a flower in its paw, 5.7cm.
(Phillips) $448

A pair of Bow white models of birds, perched on conical bases applied with leafy branches, the birds with long tail feathers, 10.8cm.
(Phillips) $1,600

An attractive Bow group of a monkey with young, the mother seated and eating a fruit, 6.8cm.
(Phillips) $1,280

BRITISH

A Bursley Ware vase designed
by Frederick Rhead, decorated
in the 'Trellis' design, 31cm.
high.
(Christie's) $251

A Pountney's 'The Fiscal
Pottery' commemorative bowl,
17cm. diameter.
(Allen & Harris) $62

A Della Robbia twin-handled
terracotta vase by John Shirley,
decorated on both sides with
confronted peacocks, dated
1898, 41.5cm. high.
(Christie's) $1,421

A tin glazed pottery spouted
posset pot and cover, the
bulbous vessel with two strap
handles supporting perched
birds, 11in. high, English, early
18th century.
(Tennants) $32,400

A pair of Carlton Ware book
ends, each modeled with a
Britannia figure standing with
shield and serpent against a
triangular back, 18.5cm. high.
(Christie's) $184

A Walton type group of lovers
standing before a flowering
bocage, the man wearing a
brown cap, the woman wearing
a plumed hat, circa 1820, 7in.
high.
(Christie's) $447

A Gray's Pottery plate painted
with a stylized spray of flowers,
in orange, green, yellow, blue
and black, 26.5cm. diameter.
(Christie's) $301

A Wileman & Co 'Intarsio' vase,
designed by Frederick Rhead,
Celtic style foliate bands, the
neck with flowers, 8³/₄in. high.
(Bonhams) $598

A rare Thackeray Turner bowl,
the interior with three entwined
mythical beasts in the center,
14¹/₂in. diameter.
(Bonhams) $747

BRITISH

A Louis Wain 'Haw Haw' cat,
the pottery spill holder modeled
as a caricature of Lord Haw
Haw, 13.5cm. high.
(Christie's) $502

A Yorkshire or possibly Scottish
pottery plaque molded with a
ram to the left with trees in the
distance, circa 1790, 13in. wide.
(Christie's) $1,072

A Maw yellow and green luster
baluster vase painted with
flowers and foliage, dated *1899*,
31cm. high.
(Christie's) $167

A Della Robbia terracotta vase,
incised with stylized flowers and
foliage painted in brown, green
and yellow, dated *1896*, 23cm.
high.
(Christie's) $251

A pair of Herculaneum urn
shaped vases, having caryatid
winged handles, printed
Herculaneum and Liverpool
ribbon mark, circa 1835, 12in.
high.
(Woolley & Wallis)

$1,970

A rare Vauxhall vase, painted in
colors with a bouquet of
flowers and smaller sprays, gilt
foot rim, 4¹/₈in. high.
(Bonhams) $1,440

A Gray's Pottery circular wall
plaque, painted with large
flowerheads in shades of blue,
green and gilt, 33.5cm. diameter.
(Christie's) $251

A Crown Devon coffee pot and
cover painted with a geometric
pattern of overlapping circles
and diamonds, 19.5cm. high.
(Christie's) $117

A Susie Cooper Crown Works
plate, painted in silver luster
with stylized tulips, with lime
green border, 28cm. diameter.
(Christie's) $251

BRITISH

A Christian sauceboat with scroll handle, painted in blue with chinoiserie landscape panels, 8cm.
(Phillips) $475

An A. J. Wilkinson toby jug of Neville Chamberlain, his hands folded in front of him, the chamfered base inscribed *Justice, Peace, Truth, Happiness*, 29.5cm.
(Phillips) $384

Charlotte Rhead Crown Ducal pottery charger, decorated with flowers and foliage, on speckled brown ground, green rim, 14¹/₂in. diameter.
(G. A. Key) $491

An early earthenware jug by David Leach, with ocher glaze over dark brown slip decoration, impressed *DL* seal, 7³/₄in. high.
(Bonhams) $184

An unusual Chaffers octagonal dish painted in blue with the 'Jumping Boy' pattern, within an alternating border of diaper and floral panels, 10.5cm.
(Phillips) $2,233

Mochaware pitcher, England, 19th century, with incised green bands enclosing central bands of butternut, brown and white with twig, wave and cat's eye decoration, 8in. high.
(Skinner) $2,750

A rare Davenport 'Drunken Sal' jug, the obese lady in green dress spotted in black and red and a blue shawl, 32cm. high.
(Phillips) $1,120

A remarkable Coalport trompe l'oeil plate decorated in London in red, brown, gold and platinum luster, on a solid gilt ground, 23.5cm.
(Phillips) $1,200

A rare Limehouse model of a dog with upturned pointed face and seated on a rectangular mound base, its eyes, nose and paws picked out in blue, 4.5cm.
(Phillips) $4,263

Victorian stoneware teapot and cover of globular form, inscribed in black *What About A Dish of Tea*, 7in. high. (G. A. Key) $42

A rare and large lustered and colored figure of Peace as a classical lady, wearing a purple luster cloak and diadem, 63cm. (Phillips) $1,440

A creamware teapot and cover, unusually decorated with a chintz design in polychrome printing heightened in colored enamels, 16cm. (Phillips) $640

A very interesting bell-shaped mug, painted in blue with a Chinese fenced landscape incorporating a small house, 13cm., probably Vauxhall or Gilbody. (Phillips) $576

An attractive and unusual Belleek porcelain coffee service, the shell molded body painted in polychrome enamels with a landscape. (Spencer's) $1,216

A Watcombe pitcher, attributed to Christopher Dresser, circa 1875, glazed terracotta, stamped on underside *WATCOMBE PORCELAIN*, 10in. high. (Sotheby's) $682

Brannum pottery floor vase, having peacock and butterfly decoration on green ground, signed *John Dewdney* (circa 1882–1910), 2ft. 5in. high. (Lawrences) $900

A rare and interesting Absolon-decorated double-handled cup and cover titled *A Trifle from Yarmouth* in puce above a vignette of two ladies in a governess cart drawn by a spirited horse, 10cm. (Phillips) $1,522

A very finely painted Lowestoft covered jug, painted in blue with two Chinese figures discussing a small vase, 26cm. high. (Phillips) $2,400

CANTON

19th century Cantonese toilet jug with brilliant enamel decoration in the famille-rose palette, 11in. high.
(G. A. Key) $147

Antique Canton rectangular serving dish, 8½in. square.
(Eldred's) $165

A pair of unusual Canton vases, applied with writhing dragons below an everted rim, the body brightly painted with processions, 63.5cm. high.
(Bearne's) $1,500

CARDEW

A Wenford Bridge stoneware tea-pot by Michael Cardew, unglazed, red-brown brushwork decoration of pairs of fish within linear bands, 15cm. high.
(Christie's) $383

An early earthenware Winchcombe jug by Michael Cardew, with a band of painted swirls, ocher and brown, 9in. high.
(Bonhams) $587

An earthenware cider jar by Michael Cardew, the top half with green slip drawn through to brown, Winchcombe Pottery seals, 14½in. high.
(Bonhams) $568

An earthenware bowl by Michael Cardew, cream with brown slip-trailed lines, impressed *MC* and Winchcombe Pottery seals, 10½in.
(Bonhams) $710

A fine Winchcombe Pottery earthenware cider flagon by Michael Cardew, covered in a mottled dark olive-green glaze with bands and panels of pale brushwork decoration of a deer and foliage, 39cm. high.
(Christie's) $689

An earthenware open bowl by Michael Cardew, with trailed dark brown slip over a vivid green and ocher glaze, circa 1930, 13¾in. diameter.
(Bonhams) $2,202

CAUGHLEY

A Caughley custard cup, with a scrolled loop handle, printed in blue with the 'Willow Nankeen' pattern, 2in. high.
(Bonhams) $300

A Caughley asparagus server, printed in blue with the 'Fisherman' pattern, 2³/₄in. long.
(Bonhams) $375

Fluted porcelain Caughley teapot and cover, printed in blue with a temple pattern, circa 1790, 5¹/₄in. high.
(G. A. Key) $373

Caughley porcelain dessert dish of square form, decorated with a blue weir pattern, circa 1790, 8in. wide.
(G. A. Key) $361

A Caughley royal cabbage-leaf-molded mask-jug painted in blue and puce and richly gilt, probably in the Chamberlain's workshop, circa 1785, 26cm. high.
(Christie's) $1,470

A Caughley egg drainer, printed in blue with the 'Fisherman' pattern, leafy handle, 3⁷/₈in. long.
(Bonhams) $330

A Caughley trefoil dessert dish, with a scroll molded handle, painted in blue with 'chantilly sprigs', 7¹/₂in. diameter.
(Bonhams) $180

A Caughley leaf-molded inverted baluster mask-jug painted with sprays of flowers amongst scattered sprigs, circa 1785, 7¹/₂in. high.
(Christie's) $1,122

A Caughley 'pickle' leaf, printed in blue with the 'Fisherman' pattern, 3¹/₂in. long.
(Bonhams) $300

CHELSEA

A Chelsea cup and saucer with a pale yellow ground painted with purple tulips and green leaves.
(Bonhams) $928

'The Balloon Woman', Chelsea pottery figure designed by Charles Vyse, painted in colors, painted factory mark, dated *1922*, 22cm. high.
(Christie's) $502

A Chelsea Red Anchor period cauliflower tureen and cover, decorated in shades of green, 4½in. high, circa 1755.
(Tennants) $2,511

A pair of Chelsea sweetmeat-figures modeled as a lady holding a fan and a gentleman, their clothes elaborately painted and enriched in gilding, circa 1760, 19.5cm. high.
(Christie's) $5,526

A Chelsea architectural watch-stand representing the Dawn of Day, modeled as a rococo fountain, circa 1758, 27.5cm. high.
(Christie's) $6,563

A pair of Chelsea groups of gallants and companions emblematic of the Seasons, Winter and Spring, circa 1765, about 35.5cm. high.
(Christie's) $13,816

A Chelsea 'Hans Sloane' botanical soup-plate painted in a vibrant palette with a large puce fritillary and a spray of small blue flowers, circa 1756, 23cm. diameter.
(Christie's) $15,543

'The Lavender Girl', a Chelsea Cheyne pottery figure by Charles Vyse, painted in colors, 22cm. high.
(Christie's) $468

A Chelsea 'Hans Sloane' botanical soup-plate painted in a vibrant palette with a spray of magnolia and with scattered butterflies and insects, circa 1756, 23.5cm. diameter.
(Christie's) $12,953

CHINESE

A Chinese blue and white porcelain tureen and cover, with paired animal mask handles, 13in. wide, Qianlong, circa 1760. (Tennants) **$1,377**

A Chinese Export figure of a seated rabbit, late 18th/early 19th century, naturalistically modeled with ears pricked back, height 5¼in. (Sotheby's) **$3,450**

A Chinese blue and white porcelain platter, centrally painted with a busy lakeland scene, 14½in. wide, Qianlong, circa 1760. (Tennants) **$259**

A large Chinese blue-glazed vase, Kangxi, early 18th century, of baluster form, with trumpet neck, 80cm. high. (Sotheby's) **$6,996**

A matched pair of 18th century Chinese porcelain wine pots adapted with French ormolu mounts as pot pourri vases, on later oval bases, 14cm. high. (Phillips) **$4,760**

A Chinese flambé baluster vase, with French gilt-bronze mounts, Paris, circa 1860, 76cm. high. (Sotheby's) **$6,296**

A Chinese Export circular soup tureen and cover, 1765–75, each piece painted in rose, iron-red, yellow and shades of green, width 11¼in. (Sotheby's) **$1,610**

A Chinese Dehua figure of Hsi Wang-Mu, the goddess standing full length in robes carrying a basket of flowers, 15¾in. high. (Tennants) **$1,004**

A Chinese Export 'Tobacco leaf' pattern plate, 1770–85, painted with a green-centered rose and purple and yellow tobacco blossom, diameter 8¹⁵⁄₁₆in. (Sotheby's) **$1,725**

A Chinese Export 'Rose-verte' large platter, 1725–30, the oval center painted with a lady holding a peony, length 19¹/₂in. (Sotheby's) $2,070

A late 18th century Chinese Export porcelain famille rose decorated tureen, cover and stand, 40cm. wide. (Spencer's) $4,662

A fine Chinese Export famille-rose charger, circa 1740, painted in the center with a basket of peonies, diameter 14¹/₈in. (Sotheby's) $1,840

A Chinese blue and white bottle-shaped crocus vase painted with dragons and exotic birds among clouds and flames, 18th century, 9¹/₄in. high. (Christie's) $1,361

A fine Chinese Export mythological plate, circa 1745, painted en grisaille in the center with Juno seated in her chariot, diameter 9in. (Sotheby's) $920

A Chinese earthenware bottle vase decorated in a mottled purple and red glaze, 41cm. high. (Spencer's) $354

One of a pair of Chinese silver-shaped octagonal dishes, each painted in iron red and gilt, with peonies and chrysanthemums, 18th century, 12¹/₄in. wide. (Christie's)
(Two) $1,004

A Chinese blue and white Fitzhugh-pattern barrel-shaped water jug and cover, with buddhistic lion finial, 18th century, 8in. high. (Christie's) $1,089

A Chinese Export circular basin, mid-18th century, painted with a brown-delineated gold crane perched on an underglaze-blue rock, diameter 15⁹/₁₆in. (Sotheby's) $690

CHINESE

A Chinese armorial oval plate, the centre painted in famille rose enamels with the coat of arms for John Rowsewell impaling Colthurst, 26.4cm. wide, Qianlong.
(Bearne's) $1,162

A Chinese Export famille-rose bidet with a Chippendale-style mahogany stand, the bidet circa 1745, length 23¹¹/₁₆in.
(Sotheby's) $3,450

A rare Chinese Export 'Washington Memorial' large platter, 1800–02, painted in brown monochrome in the center with a spread-winged eagle perched on a monument, length 18¹/₂in.
(Sotheby's) $6,900

A pair of Chinese baluster jars, each brightly painted with birds, chrysanthemums and peonies in a rocky garden, 30.5cm. high, Qianlong, covers missing.
(Bearne's) $1,401

A Chinese Export barrel-shaped toddy jug, circa 1795, painted on either side with a gilt floral sprig, height 8⁹/₁₆in.
(Sotheby's) $460

A pair of Chinese floor vases in blue and white, decorated with figures of exotic birds in landscapes, four square character marks, 2ft. 7in. high.
(Russell Baldwin & Bright) $662

An 18th century Chinese porcelain tankard, decorated in polychrome enamels with flowers and fruit beneath a scroll and diapered border, 19.5cm. high.
(Spencer's) $573

A Chinese Export blue and white circular soup tureen and cover, circa 1760, each with a whorl-patterned ground decorated with lotus blossoms, width 10¹¹/₁₆in.
(Sotheby's) $2,300

A Chinese Export blue and white small cruet pot and cover, mid-18th century, painted with flowering plants growing from the footrim, height 5¹/₄in.
(Sotheby's) $920

CHINESE

A Chinese famille rose Jacobite punch-bowl, the exterior painted with a rifleman and a piper, Qianlong, 11¼in. diameter.
(Christie's) $41,745

Turquoise ground Export porcelain basin painted in the 'Famille Rose' palette, 15⅝in. diameter.
(Butterfield & Butterfield) $990

An exceedingly fine, very large christening bowl, early Qianlong, painted in overglaze enamels of rose, jaune, vermilion, aubergine, blue, iron red and orange, 22in.
(Greenslade Hunt) $18,420

Sancai glazed vase, Tang Dynasty, the high-shouldered ovoid body curving inward to the small mouth and tapering to a flat foot, 10¼in. high.
(Butterfield & Butterfield) $1,210

Pair of 'Famille Rose' double vases, circa 1900, each two-sectioned vase of baluster form, with a four-character Qianlong mark in iron red to the base, 9¾in. high.
(Butterfield & Butterfield) $7,150

A Chinese porcelain vase decorated in underglaze blue and overglaze polychrome enamel colors, 6¾in. high. Kangxi 1675–1690.
(Tennants) $1,004

One of a pair of Chinese blue and white porcelain circular plates, each centered by a pagoda lakeland landscape, 18in. diameter, Qianlong, circa 1760.
(Tennants) (Two) $454

A pair of Chinese Export white-painted Chinese geese, each with repaired break to neck, 19th century, 25¾in. high.
(Christie's) $95,150

A Chinese Export armorial charger, circa 1745, painted in the center with the arms of Willey, diameter 16⁷⁄₁₆in.
(Sotheby's) $3,450

CLARICE CLIFF

A 'Bizarre' Chester fern pot in the 'Swirls' pattern, painted in colors, 4in. diameter.
(Christie's) $416

A 'Bizarre' double bonjour candlestick in the 'Green Bridgewater' pattern, painted in colors, 5in. high.
(Christie's) $868

A 'Fantasque Bizarre' plate in the 'Farmhouse' pattern, painted in colors, 9in. diameter.
(Christie's) $521

A 'Latona Bizarre' stepped circular vase in the 'Red Roses' pattern, painted in red and black, 18in. high.
(Christie's) $4,859

A pair of 'Bizarre' cottage book ends painted with orange roof to cottage, green and yellow base, 5¹/₂in. high.
(Christie's) $2,603

A 'Bizarre' isis vase in the 'Diamonds' pattern, painted in colors between contrasting striped borders, 9³/₄in. high.
(Christie's) $1,909

A 'Bizarre' wall mask modeled as the head of an exotic woman with blue ringlets and a cap of green foliage, 9in. long.
(Christie's) $521

A 'Bizarre' Chippendale jardinière in the 'Crocus' pattern, painted in colors, 9¹/₄in. diameter.
(Christie's) $416

A 'Bizarre' grotesque mask designed by Ron Birks, painted in orange, red, yelow and black, 10¹/₂in. long.
(Christie's) $868

CLARICE CLIFF

A Clarice Cliff comical figure of a fish on rectangular base, painted in shades of green and brown, 21cm. long.
(Christie's) $251

A Wilkinson Ltd. toby jug of Winston Churchill, modeled by Clarice Cliff, wearing the uniform of an Admiral of the Fleet, 30.5cm. high.
(Phillips) $800

A Clarice Cliff 'Bizarre' bowl in the 'Woodland' pattern, painted in colors, 19cm. diameter.
(Christie's) $468

A Clarice Cliff 'Fantasque Bizarre' vase, decorated in the 'Orange House' pattern, painted in colors, 20cm. high.
(Christie's) $752

A Clarice Cliff Fantasque pair of inverted baluster vases, painted with bands of orange flowers, cream fruit and green leaves, 30cm. high.
(Allen & Harris) $953

Clarice Cliff Bizarre Newport pottery jug, 'Floreat' pattern, 11in. high.
(G. A. Key) $522

Clarice Cliff Bizarre Newport pottery biscuit barrel and cover, 'Fantasque Gibraltar' pattern, with cane handle, 7in.
(G. A. Key) $371

A Clarice Cliff 'Bizarre' tankard coffee set for six in the 'Crocus' pattern, printed factory marks, height of coffee pot 18cm.
(Christie's) $535

Clarice Cliff Bizarre Honolulu patterned jug, hand painted by Newport pottery company, 11½in. high.
(G. A. Key) $2,196

COPER

A stoneware bulbous form on a stem by Hans Coper, surmounted with a two-tone brown disc, circa 1965, 4¹/₂in. high.
(Bonhams) $4,037

A superb cycladic arrowhead form by Hans Coper, mounted on a cylindrical mottled base, 1975, 10³/₄in. high.
(Bonhams) $17,433

A magnificent spade form by Hans Coper, the buff body with inlaid horizontal and spiraling lines, the whole surface varied in tones, circa 1972, 13³/₄in. high.
(Bonhams) $17,433

A tall black cycladic standing form by Hans Coper, the round base rising to an oval rim and distinguished by a raised spiral of lines at the center, circa 1975, 8³/₄in. high.
(Bonhams) $12,845

A beautiful round white pot by Hans Coper, the subtle variations of white varied by fine lines, 1966, 7³/₈in. high.
(Bonhams) $16,515

An exceedingly rare white oval bud form on a tall carved stem by Hans Coper, the buff body whitened with several slips, 1979, 7³/₄in. high.
(Bonhams) $17,433

A wonderful oval cup form by Hans Coper, the upper part mottled with dark brown and deep orange, the cup mounted on a cylindrical base which rises to a point, circa 1972, 6¹/₄in. high.
(Bonhams) $27,525

A handsome sack form by Hans Coper, with wide brown disc rim on circular neck, the buff body accentuated with brown texturing, circa 1974, 9³/₈in. high.
(Bonhams) $16,515

A fine stoneware 'Spade' form by Hans Coper, covered in a buff slip glaze with areas of blue glaze burnished to reveal matt manganese beneath, 31cm. high.
(Christie's) $6,690

A Bristol delft plate, circa 1740, decorated with a manganese sponged plant in a blue pot, 8³/₄in. diameter. (Christie's) $495

A Lambeth delft dated armorial caudle-cup, dated 1657, decorated with the arms of the Bakers' Company beneath the initials M/AR. (Christie's) $71,500

A Dutch delft blue and white fluted dish, circa 1690, the center with a half portrait of William of Orange in crown and ermine robes, 9⁵/₈in. diameter. (Christie's) $4,400

An English delft plate painted in colors with a central roundel incorporating a flower spray, 22.5cm. (Phillips) $487

A pair of Liverpool delft wall-pockets, circa 1770, modeled as fish in blue and green with iron-red spines, 8in. high. (Christie's) $8,800

A Lambeth delft blue and white bowl, circa 1740, with stylized floral decoration beneath a band of blue stylized leaves, 9in. diameter. (Christie's) $2,860

An English delft blue and white royal portrait plate, circa 1690, the center with half-length portraits of William and Mary in crowns and court robes, 8¹/₈in. diameter. (Christie's) $3,300

A Lambeth delft blue and white posset-pot and cover, circa 1690, decorated in the 'Transitional' style with Chinamen seated in landscapes, 6³/₄in. high. (Christie's) $6,600

A London delft ballooning plate painted in blue, green and manganese with a balloon above a fenced terrace of a house, 23cm. (Phillips) $974

DELFT

A London delft plate painted in the center with a tree with sponged-manganese foliage, flanked by a tree on each side in blue and green, 22cm.
(Phillips) $487

A pair of Lambeth delft cups, circa 1700, decorated in iron-red, blue, green and ocher with a dancing Chinaman.
(Christie's) $4,180

A Bristol delft blue-dash Adam and Eve charger, circa 1670, both figures holding yellow fig leaves, 13in. diameter.
(Christie's) $4,950

A Bristol delft blue and white octagonal plate, circa 1770, decorated with a couple taking tea in a garden within a circular reserve, 8½in. diameter.
(Christie's) $3,850

A pair of Liverpool delft wall-pockets, circa 1760, each decorated in the Fazackerly palette with a yellow-breasted green bird perched in flowering branches, 8½in. high.
(Christie's) $4,180

A Liverpool delft plate, circa 1760, of Fazackerly type decorated in colors with a yellow and blue bird, 9in. diameter.
(Christie's) $1,650

A massive Liverpool delft punch-bowl, circa 1760, the interior decorated in colors with a ship flying the Union Jack within a Fitzhugh-type border, 20in. diameter.
(Christie's) $10,450

A Lambeth delft salt, circa 1680, modeled as a seated boy with yellow hair, blue robe, yellow shirt, stockings and buckles holding an oval basin in his lap, 7¾in. high.
(Christie's) $165,000

A Lambeth delft blue-dash portrait charger, circa 1640, painted with Charles I in blue armor astride a manganese rearing war horse, 16¼in. diameter.
(Christie's) $99,000

DELFT

A Dublin delft blue and white reticulated oval dish, circa 1760, the center with flowers in vases and issuing from rockwork, 11¹/₂in. wide.
(Christie's) $2,090

A Brislington delft portrait charger boldly painted in blue, manganese and yellow with a portrait of a gentleman, probably King William III, 34cm.
(Phillips) $6,916

An English delft large bowl, circa 1740, probably Bristol, decorated in blue, iron-red and green with leafy foliage, 12in. diameter.
(Christie's) $3,520

A delft charger, the central dished circular section painted in underglaze blue with a European couple in a landscape, 34.5cm. diameter.
(Spencer's) $314

A Bristol delft blue and white two-handled double-lipped sauceboat, circa 1760, decorated with stylized flowering branches, 8⁷/₈in. wide.
(Christie's) $2,860

A delft plaque, painted in blue, green, brown and ocher with a chinoiserie figure standing, holding a bunch of flowers, 24cm. high.
(Spencer's) $322

An 18th century English delft small charger, with Fazackerly type decoration, the central circular panel painted with flowers and leaves, 31cm. diameter.
(Spencer's) $450

A Dutch blue and white delft cabinet in the form of a miniature armoire, the sides and doors painted with figures in gardens, 44cm. high.
(Bearne's) $954

One of a pair of attractive English delft 'bird' plates, boldly painted in the centers with a yellow and blue crane-like bird with red head, 22.5cm.
(Phillips)(Two) $1,920

DE MORGAN

A William De Morgan twin-handled vase, the cream ground painted in shades of red and pink, 16.5cm. high.
(Christie's) $1,200

A William De Morgan vase, decorated in 'Persian colors' with scrolling foliage below a geometrically banded neck, circa 1890, 74cm. high.
(Christie's) $5,347

A Craven Dunhill yellow luster charger decorated with a design by William De Morgan, 38cm. diameter.
(Christie's) $1,380

A William De Morgan ruby luster vase, decorated with a young boy attacking a winged dragon, impressed *J. H. Davies*, 46.6cm. high.
(Christie's) $3,000

A William De Morgan two-handled vase, Merton Abbey Period, circa 1882–1888, painted with peacocks and Iznik flowers bordered with fish on a blue scale ground, 13³/₈in. high.
(Sotheby's) $6,820

A large William De Morgan vase, Merton Abbey Period, circa 1882–1888, painted with mythical sea serpents and dragons in bright colors, 39³/₄in. high.
(Sotheby's) $7,672

A William De Morgan 'Rose trellis' tile, painted with two yellow, brown and red flowers, 15.2cm. square, and three similar.
(Bonhams) $517

A William De Morgan bottle vase decorated in the Persian manner, with cranes walking in a pool laden with fish, 26.5cm. high.
(Christie's) $318

One of a set of eight William De Morgan tiles, painted with blue cornflowers atop tall leafy stems in green, 15.3cm. square.
(Bonhams) (Eight) $824

DERBY

A Derby figure of Minerva standing before flowering bocage, wearing a plumed helmet and a gilt cuirass, circa 1765, 12½in. high. (Christie's) **$280**

A Derby, Duesbury & Kean semi-circular section bough-pot and pierced cover with richly gilt ram's head handles, circa 1800, 10in. wide. (Christie's) **$907**

A Derby figure of Britannia, painted in colors and enriched in gilt, on a scroll-molded base, circa 1770, 10in. high. (Christie's) **$525**

A Derby composite part tea-service painted in the Imari palette with stylized foliate panels on scrolling and cell-pattern grounds below blue bands, circa 1810–1825. (Christie's) **$660**

A Duesbury & Kean Derby porcelain porter mug of cylindrical form, with 'S' shape handle, richly gilded with scrolls and anthemion, 4½in. high, circa 1810. (Tennants) **$1,620**

A pair of Derby figures of a sportsman and companion holding guns and with satchels slung from their shoulders, Wm. Duesbury & Co., circa 1770, about 16cm. high. (Christie's) **$4,935**

A Bloor Derby porcelain jug, richly gilded with feathered scrolls and anthemion, possibly by Thomas Steel, 6¼in. high, circa 1820. (Tennants) **$1,004**

A Derby heart shaped dish, the center decorated with a kangaroo beetle and moths within three gilt bands, circa 1810, 9³/₄in. across.
(Woolley & Wallis) $533

A pair of Derby Mansion House dwarfs, one with puce-flower decorated tunic and yellow breeches, 18.5cm. high.
(Phillips) $1,040

A rare and early white Derby model of a pug dog, scratching its left ear with its hind leg, 9.5cm.
(Phillips) $1,440

A fine Royal Crown Derby dessert dish, the center painted by Albert Gregory, 22.3cm. diameter, date code for 1905.
(Bearne's) $1,341

A pair of impressive Derby ice pails and covers painted possibly by Robert Brewer, 24.1cm.
(Phillips) $3,040

Derby porcelain chocolate mug and cover, decorated in Imari style enamels, red painted mark, circa 1825, 4¹/₂in. high.
(G. A. Key) $340

A rare dated Nottingham or Derby 'Weather House' incised with the initials SS and the date 1790, 32.5cm. high.
(Phillips) $480

A magnificent pair of Derby campana-shaped vases, probably painted by W. 'Quaker' Pegg, with a profusion of flowers, 33.3cm.
(Phillips) $6,902

A Derby coffee pot and cover, painted in colors with flower sprays and scattered sprigs, 23cm.
(Phillips) $1,040

DOULTON

An unusual Royal Doulton Flambé ware model of a goblin, seated with his legs drawn up to his chest clasped by his hands, 10cm. high.
(Spencer's) $659

Royal Doulton figure 'First step', HN 2242, 6¼in. high.
(Eldred's) $248

Royal Doulton pottery parrot, formed with a parrot seated on a dome formed rock base, 15in. high.
(G. A. Key) $169

Doulton Lambeth earthenware jug, two tone brown, mask top and plated lip, 7in. high.
(G. A. Key) $67

Pair of Doulton pottery vases, brown ground raised with blue and light brown floral and leaf pattern, 12½in. high.
(G. A. Key) $261

Royal Doulton slater patent jug, designed in the 'Black Jack' style and inscribed with Landlords Caution, 7in. high
(G. A. Key) $59

A Royal Doulton stoneware tyg, the body applied and molded with flowerheads, leaves and foliate rosettes, in mottled green, brown and blue glazes, 18cm. high.
(Spencer's) $152

A good and large Doulton Lambeth stoneware clock case, the whole incised with flowers and molded with husks, dated 1882.
(Spencer's) $997

A Doulton Lambeth art stoneware ink pot, cover and liner, with incised stiff leaf border over a column molded body and bead stamped base, dated 1877, 12cm. high.
(Spencer's) $220

DOULTON

Doulton stoneware ornament, a suffragette figured ink well, 3in. high.
(G. A. Key) $491

Royal Doulton luster glazed vase depicting storks and foliage, ovoid formed, 8in. high.
(G. A. Key) $74

Royal Doulton figure 'Top of the Hill', HN 1849, 7¹/₂in. high.
(Eldred's) $121

A large Royal Doulton pottery jug commemorating Sir Francis Drake, No. 129 of an edition limited to 500 copies.
(Bearne's) $507

A pair of Doulton Lambeth art stoneware candlesticks, with stiff leaf molded circular drip pans issuing from gilt whorl decorated incised stems, 17cm. high.
(Spencer's) $251

Royal Doulton 'Nelson' commemorative loving cup, number 245 of an edition of 600, signed by *H Fenton*, 10in. tall.
(G. A. Key) $608

Royal Doulton figure 'Sweet Anne', HN 1496, 7¹/₄in. high.
(Eldred's) $132

Royal Doulton pottery jardinière, 'The Gallant Fishers', 9in. high.
(G. A. Key) $352

Doulton porcelain pitcher with gilt decoration and red glaze, 9¹/₄in. high.
(Eldred's) $154

DOULTON

A Doulton Lambeth salt-glazed stoneware figure of a Boer War soldier, modeled by John Broad, 12½in. high.
(Christie's) **$497**

A Doulton pottery model of a Elizabethan house, naturalistically painted, printed factory marks, 9in. high.
(Christie's) **$449**

A Royal Doulton pottery figure in the form of a Mandarin dressed in a gold decorated brown under garment.
(Bearne's) **$1,110**

'The Mikado' D.6501, a'Royal Doulton character jug, printed factory marks, 6¾in. high.
(Christie's) **$301**

'Old Salt' D.6110, a Doulton wall pocket, printed and painted marks, 7¼in. high.
(Christie's) **$719**

'Billy Bunnykin', the seated Doulton figure wearing orange pantaloons and blue jacket, 4in. high.
(Christie's) **$899**

A Doulton Blue Children ware vase, on pedestal foot, the spherical body flanked by reeded loop handles, 23¾in. high.
(Christie's) **$719**

'Patricia' H.N.1462, a Royal Doulton bone china figure, printed and painted marks.
(Christie's) **$284**

'Smuts' D.6198, a Royal Doulton character jug, printed factory marks.
(Christie's) **$746**

'Calumet' H.N.1689, printed and painted marks, 6¹/₂in. high. (Christie's) $202

Doulton figure 'Spook', H.N.625, printed and painted marks, 7¹/₄in. high. (Christie's) $2,920

'Punch and Judy Man', a Royal Doulton character jug, printed factory marks, 7¹/₂in. high. (Christie's) $401

'Ugly Duchess' D.6599, a Royal Doulton character jug, printed factory marks, 7in. high. (Christie's) $201

Royal Doulton 'Chang' baluster vase, the blue iridescent glazed lower body with off-white neck, 15in. high. (Canterbury) $3,675

'The Pied Piper', a limited edition Doulton loving cup, painted in colors, printed factory marks, 10¹/₄in. high. (Christie's) $786

A Royal Doulton stoneware vase, by Frank Butler, incised with cartouches of scrolling foliage, 14in. high. (Christie's) $231

Unmarked Royal Doulton figure inscribed to the base *Tunisian Scholar of Law by The Studio Potter R Johnson*, 6in. high. (G. A. Key) $191

A Doulton stoneware silver mounted cracker barrel and cover, decorated by Florence E. Barlow, height 17.5cm., dated *1881*. (Bearne's) $659

DRESDEN

A Dresden model of a crouching rabbit with white and gray-brown fur, its nose, mouth and inner ears painted in pink, circa 1880, 11¼in. long.
(Christie's) $3,281

A Dresden center-dish for a table modeled as a pierced rectangular balustrade with rectangular columns, painted on the interiors with figures and on the exteriors with bouquets, circa 1880, 22 x 16in.
(Christie's) $660

Two Dresden white-glazed models of bulls, their muscular frames with visible ribcages and their necks with pendent dewlaps, circa 1880, 15in. long.
(Christie's) $1,240

An impressive pair of Dresden Helena Wolfsohn porcelain large vases and covers, of ovoid form, painted in colors with courtiers and peasants seated in open landscapes, 50cm. high.
(Spencer's) $1,538

A Dresden porcelain figure group modeled as a courting couple, the gentleman embracing the lady from behind as a young man looks on, circa 1900, 12½in. high.
(Christie's) $2,274

A pair of Dresden claret-ground bottle-vases and flat covers, painted predominantly in shades of pink, yellow and gray with Watteauesque scenes, 20th century, 19¾in. high.
(Christie's) $1,159

A Dresden center-piece formed as a young man and a woman wearing striped and flowered 18th century-style rustic dress, playing hide-and-seek around a tree, circa 1880, 28½in. high.
(Christie's) $2,815

Dresden porcelain figure group, two children with bird and lamb, oval formed base, early 20th century, 5in. high.
(G. A. Key) $141

A Dresden rectangular mirror-frame, the arched surmount modeled with two cherubs flanking a medallion painted with a portrait-medallion of an 18th century lady, circa 1880, 36½in. high.
(Christie's) $2,590

EUROPEAN

A Goldscheider polychrome painted pottery figure of a young girl, wearing pleated sleeveless dress with butterfly patterned split skirt, 23cm. high.
(Christie's) $1,170

A Creil oval creamware bowl printed in black with a scene of Cupid at play, circa 1810, 12¹/₂in. wide.
(Christie's) $315

A Goldscheider figure, after a design by Laurenzl, modeled as a woman in Eastern dress, 46cm. high.
(Bonhams) $4,522

A Rosenburg Juliana pottery vase, painted with a milkmaid surrounded by panels and cartouches of flowers and foliage, 13¹/₂in. high.
(Christie's) $853

A pair of Continental porcelain oviform vases each painted with a girl, one playing with a kitten, the other with a puppy on her lap, 19th century, 16in. high.
(Christie's) $2,298

Reissner Stellmacher and Kessel for Amphora, portrait vase, circa 1900, 10⁵/₈in. high.
(Sotheby's) $2,851

A Zurich arched rectangular tea-caddy and cover painted in iron-red monochrome with stylized trees on fenced terraces, circa 1770, 15cm. high.
(Christie's) $6,308

A Continental porcelain cup and saucer painted with a mermaid emerging from the sea to embrace her lover seated on the rocky shore, circa 1850, 5in. high.
(Christie's) $227

A Gustavberg Argenta, with a spray of white metal honeysuckle and lily of the valley on a mottled green ground, 5in. high.
(Christie's) $100

Austrian Amphora Art Pottery planter, figural depiction of gilded male and female lions on rocky outcropping, 10¹/₂in. high. (Skinner) **$550**

A large and colorful matched pair of portrait busts, probably representing King Leopold of Belgium and Princess Charlotte, 50cm. and 52cm. high. (Bearne's) **$11,026**

Art Deco pottery ornament by Vago-Weiss of a leaping ibis, 18in. wide. (G. A. Key) **$151**

A tin-glazed earthenware maskhead jug of Hamburg-type, probably Portuguese, inscribed in blue *Ag. Tusiliaginini*, within an elaborate scrollwork cartouche, 23cm. (Phillips) **$893**

A reduction ware ceramic sculpture, 'Red Sacred Cow' by Rosa Nguyen, the head covered **with a running translucent gray** glaze, 18in. long. (Bonhams) **$440**

An enameled stoneware ovoid vase decorated with a frieze band of a stag and five hinds in a clearing, signed *Ch. Catteau*. (Galerie Moderne) **$1,715**

An Hispano-Moresque copper-luster dish, the center with a displayed bird and a stylized foliage roundel on a ground of berried foliage and tendrils, early 17th century, 40cm. diameter. (Christie's) **$1,294**

A pair of Continental majolica olive-green-ground jardiniéres and pedestals, the bulbous **bodies modeled with large** satyr's mask handles enriched in a dull gilding, circa 1900, 38in. high. (Christie's) **$2,418**

A Spanish faience blue and white baluster vase boldly painted with three panels, two with figures and one with a stylized monkey, late 17th century, perhaps Catalan, 17.5cm. high. (Christie's) **$1,016**

EUROPEAN

Continental bisque model of a boxer dog, 18in. high.
(G. A. Key) $675

A Royal Copenhagen oval terrine in the Flora Danica pattern.
(Herholdt Jensen)
                                    $2,696

Lladro porcelain ornament of an elephant and her baby, 14in. high.
(G. A. Key) $139

Royal Copenhagen figure in the form of one child reading a book to another child, 7¹/₂in. high.
(Eldred's) $165

A pair of treacle glaze pottery tobacco jars and covers in the form of pug dogs, 22cm. high.
(Spencer's) $438

An outstanding burnished earthenware vase by Gabriele Koch, with flared rim, deep red and brown, 13⁵/₈in. high.
(Bonhams) $826

Continental pottery wall plaque, **brightly enameled in the** Persian manner, 19in. diameter.
(G. A. Key) $254

A Dahl Jensen porcelain figure of a harnessed horse, design No. 1252.
(Herholdt Jensen) $186

Large Continental pottery wall plaque, **gray, blue and white** decoration with figure on a trellis, 19in. diameter.
(G. A. Key) $131

FRENCH

A Paris porcelain cabinet cup painted with a female gardener with a watering can, 19th century.
(Christie's) $246

A Vincennes ewer and basin, after a design by Jean-Claude Duplessis, the pear-shaped jug with gilt and blue rocaille scrolls, circa 1752, the jug 24.5cm. high.
(Christie's) $50,715

A Paris porcelain inkstand, painted with bouquets of flowers and applied with a seated model of a hound, blue mark for Jacob Petit, 19th century.
(Christie's) $665

A French faience jardinière or ice pail, possibly Sceaux, finely painted in colors with exotic birds, 7in. high.
(Bonhams) $80

A large pair of Samson famille rose baluster jars and domed covers, each painted with shaped panels of figures in fenced gardens, 25in. high.
(Christie's) $3,358

A French gilt-bronze mounted vase with cover, Napoléon III, by Sampson of Paris, circa 1870, 52cm. high.
(Sotheby's) $9,620

A pair of French porcelain vases, decorated in Naples, the handles in the form of female terms, painted with Neapolitan views, 42.2cm. high, circa 1830.
(Finarte) $7,462

A Samson armorial plate in the Compagnie des Indes style, painted with a central coat-of-arms, circa 1880, 16¼in. diameter.
(Christie's) $497

A pair of French porcelain metal-mounted oviform vases, the porcelain painted in colors by Collot, late 19th century, 12¾in. high.
(Christie's) $2,627

FRENCH

Samson porcelain teapot and cover with fluted molded body, domed lid, shaped handle and spout.
(G. A. Key) $131

A Gallé tin glazed faience cat, the white and blue ground polychrome painted and gilded with flowers and a locket and chain, 33.3cm. high.
(Christie's) $8,039

A Paris Flamen-Fleury porcelain cup and saucer, the cup modeled as a shell with coral branch handle, early 19th century.
(Christie's) $460

A Paris porcelain cabinet cup and saucer painted with geometric panels of stylized flowers and foliage, circa 1820, 2³/₄in. high.
(Christie's) $296

A pair of French Art Deco pottery book ends modeled as Pierrot and Columbine, painted in colors, 19cm. high.
(Christie's) $635

A Paris porcelain vase of baluster form, painted with a bouquet of garden flowers and grapes, early 20th century, 15¹/₂in. high.
(Christie's) $1,281

Handpainted Limoges flagon decorated with the figure of a monk in a wine cellar, 14¹/₂in. high.
(Eldred's) $165

A pair of unusual French flambé porcelain vases, Paris, circa 1880, in 18th century manner, 68.5cm. high.
(Sotheby's) $27,984

Emile Gallé, cat, circa 1875, tin glazed earthenware, 12¹/₂in. high.
(Sotheby's) $3,920

FRENCH

A Gallé tin glazed faience cat, the yellow and white ground polychrome painted and gilded with flowers and a chain and locket, 33.5cm. high.
(Christie's) $3,062

A Paris porcelain plate, finely painted with a grayhound and his catch, 9¹/₂in. diameter.
(Bonhams) $320

A French faience pot pourri vase and 'crown' cover, the ovoid body molded with mask handles, 12¹/₄in. high, circa 1800.
(Bonhams) $224

An early French harvest flask of Palissy-type, the body molded in relief with a crowned head and one side molded with a crowned coat of arms incorporating three fleur-de-lys, 20cm.
(Phillips) $406

A Vincennes two-handled seau à verre painted en camaieu rose one side with a boy flying a kite before a thatched cottage in a pastoral scene, circa 1752, 11cm. high.
(Christie's) $5,914

Pair of Massier Art Pottery scenic vases, realistically handpainted fall wooded landscapes, signed at side *Narbon d'Honre*, 7in. high.
(Skinner) $550

A Strasbourg figure of a huntress after the model by J. W. Lanz, in a large green tricorn hat with a gilt rim and white fringe, 1752–55, 18cm. high.
(Christie's) $3,326

An attractive Guerhard & Dihl (Duc d'Angoulême's factory) teapot and cover, probably painted by Salembier with a scene of a young woman spinning cotton, 13.5cm.
(Phillips) $1,522

A French model of a cockerel standing in crowing attitude, with brown, yellow, white and black plumage, 72cm.
(Phillips) $1,116

GARDNER

A Gardner biscuit figure of a peasant woman dancing, in ocher scarf, pink dress and white apron, 21cm.
(Phillips) $528

A Gardner biscuit figure of an old peasant seated barefoot on a bench and sprinkling salt on a piece of brown bread, 13.5cm.
(Phillips) $447

A Gardner porcelain figure of a pilgrim, with a walking stick in one hand and carrying a bag over his back and a pair of shoes strapped to his belt, 20cm.
(Phillips) $264

A Gardner biscuit figure of a pedlar warmly dressed in fur trimmed coat and mitts, carrying a tray on his head with its contents covered by a white cloth, 21cm.
(Phillips) $528

A Gardner biscuit figure of a peasant, reputedly Tolstoy, seated on logs and wearing a pink tunic, pale blue breeches and boots, 17cm.
(Phillips) $528

A Gardner biscuit figure of a young woman playing Blindman's Buff, holding a white scarf before her, in turquoise scarf, pink dress and blue apron, on a square base, 26cm.
(Phillips) $406

A Gardner biscuit figure of a mother holding a child wrapped in gray cloth, the woman standing barefoot dressed in gray and blue, 25cm.
(Phillips) $447

A Gardner biscuit group of two peasant children cracking Easter eggs, both in tunics and breeches, on a rectangular base, 16cm.
(Phillips) $731

A Gardner biscuit figure of a peasant in white shirt, pale blue breeches and black boots, on a circular base, 26.5cm.
(Phillips) $609

GEORGE JONES

A George Jones rectangular sardine-box and cover with a pink-glazed interior, the sides molded in relief with fish swimming among seaweed on a turquoise ground, printed registration mark for 1874, 6in. wide.
(Christie's) $1,209

A George Jones majolica dark-blue-ground drum cabaret, the globular forms bound with molded brown buckled straps and with yellow rope secured with white staples, the interiors glazed in turquoise, registration marks for 1877, tray 15¹/₂in. wide.
(Christie's) $8,289

A George Jones majolica chamber-stick with a branch-molded loop handle and blossoming terminals, circa 1870, 6¹/₄in. diameter.
(Christie's) $622

A George Jones majolica cheese-dish and cylindrical cover molded to simulate a barrel with yellow bands entwined with blossoming bramble leaves, circa 1873, 11¹/₄in. high.
(Christie's) $1,122

A George Jones majolica sweetmeat-dish with two faun vintner supporters, both with wreaths of fruiting vine adorning their hair, one standing wearing a lion-pelt around his thighs, the other kneeling holding a bunch of grapes, circa 1870, 9¹/₄in. high.
(Christie's) $1,727

A George Jones model of a camel, partially glazed on a dark-brown parian body, supported on a cluster of green leaves with two turquoise saddle-bags bound with gilt and black cord suspended from its back, circa 1868, 8¹/₂in. high.
(Christie's) $2,072

A George Jones dark-blue-ground majolica jug and hinged cover, with an angular handle, the cylindrical body molded in relief with a hound chasing a game-bird through grass, printed registration mark for 1872, 11³/₄in. high.
(Christie's) $1,122

Three George Jones majolica baluster lotus jugs in graduated sizes, the sides molded in relief with clumps of bulrushes dividing large stylized green leaves, circa 1865, 6¹/₄, 7¹/₄ and 8¹/₄in. high.
(Christie's) $2,418

A George Jones majolica sweetmeat-dish formed as a young faun kneeling on a mound before a hollow cluster of fern leaves, supporting a turquoise and pink nautilus shell swathed in white drapery on his knee, circa 1865, 9in. high.
(Christie's) $1,295

GERMAN

A Documentary slop-basin, the shaped rectangular cartouches containing a stag hunt crossing a river, a boar hunt in a rocky wooded glade, Dreher's three circles for Künnel, circa 1730, 15.5cm. diameter.
(Christie's) $48,048

A Nymphenburg figure of Cupid as Vulcan from the series of Ovidian Gods modeled by Franz Anton Bustelli, circa 1757, 11cm. high.
(Christie's) $9,012

A German porcelain architectural cabinet cup, cover and saucer, of square section molded with Corinthian columns, 4³/₄in.
(Bonhams) $640

A Nymphenburg two-handled tapering oval pail and domed cover in the Frankenthal style, with a striped multiple leaf finial, the pail painted with a magnificent pheasant spreading its tail-feathers, perched on a grassy bank beside rocks and shrubs, circa 1860, 20³/₄in. high.
(Christie's) $7,771

A pair of Ludwigsburg miniature masked figures from the Carnival de Venise series after models by Johann Jakob Louis, circa 1765, 6.8cm. high.
(Christie's) $13,518

A Bayreuth glazed red-stoneware coffee-pot and cover, the curved square spout issuing from a dolphin's-head mask and joined to the body by a convex bridge, circa 1725, 18.5cm. high.
(Christie's) $12,936

A Hanau pewter-mounted Enghalskrug painted in blue and yellow and outlined in manganese with an Oriental seated among flowering shrubs, circa 1700, 27.5cm. high.
(Christie's) $3,326

A Höchst pug dog naturally modeled and seated on his haunches to the right and scratching his chin, circa 1755, 10cm. high.
(Christie's) $4,435

A Frankfurt blue and white paneled baluster vase and domed cover painted with fruiting flowering branches issuing from rockwork, circa 1700, 35cm. high.
(Christie's) $2,957

GERMAN

A German faience bottle vase, painted in blue with an Oriental style river landscape with Chinamen, 13¹/₂in., possibly Frankfurt.
(Bonhams) $448

A German porcelain oval plaque, finely painted with two young women, 22 x 16.5cm., set in a carved and gilded wood frame.
(Bearne's) $2,533

'Lulu', a Volkstedt porcelain figure of a female nude, standing in a provocative pose, printed mark in blue, 36cm. high.
(Spencer's) $570

A Höchst cylindrical tea-caddy and cover, the sides painted with two gilt scroll cartouches with a couple of peasants on a bridge in a landscape, circa 1765, 11.5cm. high.
(Christie's) $2,402

Pair of 19th century German porcelain cherub candle holders, 7in. high.
(G. A. Key) $550

A German faience Stein, probably Bayreuth, pewter mounts inscribed *AFW* and *CCW*, 1773, ball finial, 11in. overall.
(Bonhams) $720

Fine porcelain double master salt with surmounting figure of Cupid, bears the mark of the Royal Porcelain Manufactory, Berlin, circa 1820, 5in. high.
(Eldred's) $363

A German candlestick figure of a young man in the Meissen style, wearing flowered dress and his hair loosely tied en queue, holding a spray of flowers and a basket, circa 1880, 29¹/₄in. high.
(Christie's) $691

A German porcelain group of a sculptor kneeling before his muse at a sacrificial ceremony, the muse wearing flowered robes and standing on a marbled pedestal attended by cherubs, circa 1910, 14in. high.
(Christie's) $604

GERMAN

German porcelain comport, the top of circular form with pierced detail and painted and encrusted roses, 15in. tall.
(G. A. Key) $549

German Villeroy & Boch pottery punch bowl in blue and white, 14¹/₂in. diameter.
(Eldred's) $99

A faience portrait plaque, probably South German, painted on a deep puce ground, 13¹/₂ x 11in.
(Bonhams) $8,800

A blue painted gray stoneware cylindrical jug, decorated in relief with berries and leaves in diamond shapes, with metal cover, German, Höhr-Frenzhausen, circa 1910, 34cm. high.
(Kunsthaus am Museum)
                               $558

A pair of R. M. Krause majolica figural candlesticks, modeled as a man, standing wearing a Romanesque tunic, his female companion wearing a head dress, 54cm. and 52.5cm. high.
(Spencer's) $809

A Nuremberg fayence (Kordenbusch Workshop) Walzenkrug of cylindrical shape, painted in blue with St. Francis receiving the stigmata, 18.6cm. high.
(Phillips) $2,233

A Biedermeier centerpiece set with finely painted miniature cartouches, 20.5cm. high.
(Arnold) $794

A German topographical circular plaque painted with a view of Dresden from the banks of the Elbe, circa 1810, 16.5cm. diameter.
(Christie's) $4,435

19th century German porcelain figure group of a seated lady with cherub, 9in. high.
(G. A. Key) $714

GRUEBY

Grueby faience pumpkin vase, squat melon-ribbed organic body with autumn harvest yellow matt glaze, 9in. high. (Skinner) $2,310

Grueby pottery bowl, Boston, Wilhemina Post, bisque form with carved and incised overlapping leaves, 8¹/₂in. diameter. (Skinner) $825

Important Grueby pottery vase, Boston, attributed to Wilhelmina Post, matt green glaze, 11¹/₄in. high. (Skinner) $7,150

Grueby pottery vase, Boston, Gertrude Stanwood, matt navy blue glaze with incised alternating floral and leaf decoration, 5⁷/₈in. high. (Skinner) $990

Grueby Pottery two-color vase, leaf-carved jardinière form with textured butterscotch yellow matt glaze decorated by eight white matt enamel flower buds, 7in. high. (Skinner) $4,400

Grueby pottery lotus bulb vase, heavy walled sphere with seven broad green leaf forms around central light blue matt bottle-top, 8¹/₂in. high. (Skinner) $3,190

Grueby pottery vase, Boston, matt green glaze, impressed mark, 12¹/₂in. high. (Skinner) $1,760

Grueby Pottery Eros tile, red clay square decorated by raised cupid with bow against matt black background, 6 x 6in. (Skinner) $165

Grueby pottery vase, Boston, matt dark green glaze, impressed mark, 13in. high. (Skinner) $605

A stoneware teabowl by Shoji Hamada, browns and orange, circa 1940, 5in. diameter. (Bonhams) $768

A stoneware bottle vase by Shoji Hamada, covered in a running brown glaze, circa 1940, 7³/₄in. high. (Bonhams) $642

A fine stoneware bowl by Shoji Hamada, olive-green with three beige splashes merging into deep green in the well, 6in. diameter. (Bonhams) $1,183

A fine stoneware bottle vase by Shoji Hamada, covered in a tenmoku and olive-green glaze, each face quartered by white and blue green vertical and horizontal divisions, 23.6cm. high. (Christie's) $3,828

A stoneware square dish by Shoji Hamada, kaki, the upper surface with resist stepped cross pattern, 10¹/₂in. square. (Bonhams) $2,840

A fine stoneware bottle vase by Shoji Hamada, covered in a brown glaze beneath bands of matt pale sage-green, khaki green and tenmoku, 22.5cm. high. (Christie's) $3,828

A hexagonal stoneware vase by Shoji Hamada, kaki glaze with three floral motifs, circa 1965, 7³/₄in. high. (Bonhams) $2,840

A stoneware teapot by Shoji Hamada, with floral decoration, orange, buff and brown, circa 1942, 7in. wide. (Bonhams) $514

An important stoneware cut sided bottle by Shoji Hamada, tenmoku glaze over red body, circa 1951, 11in. high. (Bonhams) $5,995

ITALIAN

A Sicilian albarello of waisted cylindrical form, painted in blue and manganese with circular panels enclosing trees on a diaper ground, 26cm.
(Phillips) $812

A Doccia rectangular snuff box, relief-decorated with sprays of fruiting strawberry plants, gilt metal mounts, 6.5cm.
(Phillips) $1,440

A Doccia giltmetal-mounted oval snuff-box con basso relievo istoriato, the cover with Mars and Venus before a ruin and Time in flight above, circa 1750, 8cm. wide.
(Christie's) $4,066

An Urbino deep dish painted in the center with a winged putto in running attitude and holding a flaming torch, 26.5cm., probably Fontana workshop.
(Phillips) $5,120

A Tuscan armorial baluster jug, painted in ocher and blue with a coat-of-arms flanked by scrolling tendrils within an ocher, blue and yellow cartouche, early 16th century, probably Cafaggiolo or Montelupo, 25cm. high.
(Christie's) $1,571

An Italian maiolica tazza painted in the martyrdom of St. Barbara kneeling in the center and her executioner, 24.5cm., possibly Paduan.
(Phillips) $800

A Sicilian waisted broad albarello boldly painted in ocher with a draped bust within an oval cartouche, late 17th century, probably Caltagirone, 22cm. high.
(Christie's) $2,033

An Italian maiolica footed dish of Bianchi di Faenza class, the center painted with a coat of arms within blue and yellow leaf scrolls and surmounted by a crowned head, 27.5cm.
(Phillips) $1,177

A small Pesaro albarello of dumb-bell form, painted with the drug name SEM. DI IVSQVI (Seeds of Henbane) between bands of birds, 12.5cm.
(Phillips) $386

ITALIAN

A Bassano shaped-oval dish, the center painted in ocher with a gallant and companion in a wooded glade, circa 1770, 39cm. wide.
(Christie's) $3,696

A Faenza compendiario pierced tazza, the center painted in blue and pale manganese with Cupid leaning against a slender jar, circa 1600, 20.5cm. diameter.
(Christie's) $1,016

Fornasetti figural cat, white porcelain whimsically decorated with black splotches, circular blue mark on base, 12in. long.
(Skinner) $275

An Urbino tazza on low foot, painted in the center with a figure of Medusa standing and wearing a green and amber dress, 26cm., probably Fontana workshop.
(Phillips) $1,920

An 18th century Italian albarello, with griffin handles and blue and yellow decoration of foliage and painted figures, 36cm. high.
(Arnold) $3,118

An 18th century South Italian maiolica dish painted with the Sacrifice of Isaac in turquoise, yellow, ocher, green and manganese, 46.5cm. diameter.
(Finarte) $3,731

A massive 'Talavera' faience vase, decorated in typical blues, greens and yellows with an oval panel depicting a bacchanalian scene, 61cm. high.
(Spencer's) $723

A Castelli oval dish painted by Ed. Foiviteau with a fierce Roman battle scene with combatants attempting to cross a river by an arched bridge with a burning town in the distance, perhaps 1857, 19¾in. wide.
(Christie's) $1,899

An 18th century maiolica jug, the handle with serpentiform attachment, decorated with a two headed eagle in black, green, yellow and turquoise, Pesaro, 22cm. high.
(Finarte) $1,017

JAPANESE

Handpainted Nippon porcelain vase with landscape scene and Moriage-style trees, 8¹/₄in. high. (Eldred's) **$77**

Large 19th century Imari salver, traditional blue, rust and green palette, scalloped border, 17in. wide. (G. A. Key) **$457**

Handpainted Nippon porcelain vase with relief floral design and upswept handles, 9¹/₂in. high. (Eldred's) **$50**

An unusual Japanese pierced porcelain bowl, late 17th/early 18th century, with French Napoléon III gilt-bronze figures, circa 1870, 27cm. high. (Sotheby's) **$5,072**

A large Japanese Imari urn molded and painted in underglazed blue and enameled in iron red, lilac, turquoise and puce, late 17th/early 18th century, later carved and pierced wood cover, 18in. high. (Christie's) **$2,007**

A pair of late 19th century Japanese porcelain chargers, the borders with diaper, floret and triangular patterning, 18¹/₄in. diameter, circa 1890. (Tennants) **$972**

An inlaid stoneware oviform vase by Tatsuzo Shimaoka, the exterior inlaid in white slip with a cell pattern against a celadon ground, 19.5cm. high. (Christie's) **$574**

A Japanese Imari barber's bowl painted in underglazed blue and iron-red with a central vase of flowers, late 17th/early 18th century, 10¹/₂in. diameter. (Christie's) **$1,452**

An early 20th century Japanese earthenware vase, decorated in gilt and colored enamels with seated grim faced immortals, with pagodas and mountains beyond, 31cm. high. (Spencer's) **$1,318**

LEACH

A St. Ives stoneware bottle vase by Bernard Leach, covered in a translucent crackled cream-white glaze stopping short of the foot, circa 1950, 26.8cm. high.
(Christie's) $574

An outstanding stoneware dish, 'The Pilgrim', by Bernard Leach, with stencils of a pilgrim against mountains and sky, circa 1965, 12$\frac{1}{2}$in. diameter.
(Bonhams) $6,423

A fine white stoneware vase by Bernard Leach, with narrow neck and vertical indentations, impressed *BL* and *St. Ives* seals, circa 1960, 10$\frac{3}{4}$in. high.
(Bonhams) $1,468

A large stoneware vase by Bernard Leach, covered in a speckled pale buff colored glaze beneath white, stopping short of the foot, circa 1955, 32.6cm. high.
(Christie's) $3,828

A St. Ives stoneware jar and cover by Bernard Leach, with domed cover, covered in a pale mushroom colored glaze, two sides with blue panels and iron-brown brushwork, circa 1970, 16.5cm. high.
(Christie's) $1,531

A St. Ives stoneware vase by Bernard Leach, with incised decoration, covered in a thick matt pale yellow green glaze running and pooling at the foot, circa 1960, 34.2cm. high.
(Christie's) $2,871

A superb stoneware vase by Bernard Leach, with incised mountain design, glazed brown above gray, 9$\frac{1}{2}$in. high.
(Bonhams) $10,093

A large stoneware charger by Bernard Leach, with decoration of a bird in flight, wax resist, covered with tenmoku rust glaze, circa 1970, 13$\frac{1}{2}$in. diameter.
(Bonhams) $5,872

A tall stoneware fish vase by Bernard Leach, covered with a rust wax resist glaze revealing four vertical bands of aquatic forms, circa 1970, 16in. high.
(Bonhams) $1,652

LIVERPOOL

A Liverpool coffee cup, with a plain loop handle, painted in colors with flower sprays, 2³/₈in. high.
(Bonhams) $210

A Liverpool teapot and cover, probably Chaffers, with flattened ball finial and loop handle, 5¹/₂in. high.
(Bonhams) $225

One of a pair of Liverpool teabowls and saucers transfer-printed in black with The Rock Garden or Rural Conversations, Philip Christian's factory, circa 1766.
(Christie's) (Two) $541

Liverpool transfer-printed creamware jug, circa 1800, printed in black on one side with a three-masted ship in full sail, the hull highlighted in yellow, 10in. high.
(Butterfield & Butterfield) $6,000

Liverpool transfer printed creamware pitcher, circa 1790, with L'Enfant's *Plan of the City of Washington*, the reverse with *Peace, Plenty and Independence*, 9¹/₈in. high.
(Skinner) $2,860

Liverpool transfer-printed creamware jug, circa 1800, transfer-printed in black on one side with a three-masted ship flying the American flag, 10³/₄in. high.
(Butterfield & Butterfield) $1,200

Liverpool creamware pitcher, England, circa 1790, black transfer printed with Boston Fusilier (McCauley 251) enhanced with red, yellow and blue enamels, 11¹/₂in. high.
(Skinner) $5,225

A Liverpool plate, circa 1760, decorated in colors with orange and yellow flowering branch issuing from blue rockwork beside a fence, 8⁷/₈in. diameter.
(Christie's) $935

Liverpool transfer-printed creamware masonic large jug, probably Herculaneum, early 19th century, 13in. high.
(Butterfield & Butterfield) $1,500

LONGTON HALL

A rare Longton Hall figure of a Turk standing with his right hand on the hilt of his dagger, 18.5cm.
(Phillips) $6,080

A very rare Longton Hall model of a pointer, his mouth and eyes picked out in red, standing before a tree stump on an irregular-shaped base, 6cm.
(Phillips) $2,560

A Longton Hall figure emblematic of Winter in a brown overcoat and lime green lining and buttoned cuffs, circa 1755, 4¹/₂in. high.
(Christie's S. Ken) $635

A Longton Hall cream jug molded with vine leaves, the twisted stems as a handle, 7.7cm. high, late 18th century.
(Bearne's) $2,025

A Longton Hall figure of a seated flower seller on a rococo scroll base, 4⁷/₈in. high.
(Bonhams) $375

A Longton Hall paeony dish, modeled as a pale purple flower between two green leaves, 7in. wide.
(Bonhams) $1,200

A rare Longton Hall 'snowman' figure of 'Arlecchino', standing in dancing attitude, with right arm raised, 14.5cm. high.
(Phillips) $1,500

A Longton Hall rococo scroll molded vase and flower encrusted cover, the vase with two oval panels, 23cm. high.
(Spencer's) $450

A Longton Hall porcelain figure, of a young lady, wearing a lemon hat, puce jacket over iron red buttoned lemon waistcoat, 18cm. high.
(Spencer's) $334

LUCIE RIE

A lovely oval earthenware bowl by Dame Lucie Rie, the exterior burnished, the interior white with painted brown lines and a yellow band, circa 1947, 8¼in. wide.
(Bonhams) $5,505

A lime-yellow stoneware bowl by Dame Lucie Rie, with feathered bronzed band, impressed *LR* seal, circa 1975, 5¾in. diameter.
(Bonhams) $2,753

A cobalt blue stoneware bowl by Dame Lucie Rie, the rim speckled with a darker blue, impressed *LR* seal, circa 1970, 8¼in. diameter.
(Bonhams) $4,037

A white stoneware milk jug by Dame Lucie Rie, with bronzed feathered rim, impressed *LR* seal, circa 1958, 3⅝in. high.
(Bonhams) $404

A superb stoneware vase by Dame Lucie Rie, of different clays forming a spiral of white with pink, brown and green, 14½in.
(Bonhams) $14,986

An outstanding oval vessel by Dame Lucie Rie, the shoulder with a band of impressed hollows heightened turquoise, impressed *LR* seal, 7in. wide.
(Bonhams) $14,986

A fine stoneware pot by Dame Lucie Rie, beige and blue, with fine inlaid lines accentuating the squeezed form, circa 1960, 6¾in. high.
(Bonhams) $1,835

A white stoneware teapot by Dame Lucie Rie, the lid with brown rim, the tip of spout repaired, circa 1957, 9in. wide.
(Bonhams) $1,376

A fine early red earthenware vase by Dame Lucie Rie, glazed beige to interior, circa 1948, 9¼in. high.
(Bonhams) $3,471

LUCIE RIE

A fine bronze and white porcelain bowl by **Dame Lucie Rie**, sgraffito radiating lines inside and contrasting inlaid lines to exterior, circa 1980, 8in. diameter.
(Bonhams)   **$5,505**

A fine stoneware bowl by **Dame Lucie Rie**, on shallow foot, slate-gray ground covered in thick white pitted glaze, circa 1960, 24cm. diameter.
(Christie's)   **$10,527**

A rare stoneware 'spinach' bowl by **Dame Lucie Rie**, covered in a thick cratered glaze with a golden bronze band at the rim, circa 1986, 7in. diameter.
(Bonhams)   **$4,037**

A fine stoneware vase by **Dame Lucie Rie**, the body with diagonal fluting, covered by a lightly pitted mustard glaze with a bluish hue, 8in. high.
(Bonhams)   **$4,771**

An impressive stoneware jardinière by **Dame Lucie Rie**, yellow and beige pitted glaze, impressed *LR* seal, circa 1960, 8¹/₂in. high.
(Bonhams)   **$4,771**

A stoneware bottle vase by **Dame Lucie Rie**, pink, brown and white culminating in a spiral on the flared rim, circa 1968, 8³/₈in. high.
(Bonhams)   **$3,120**

An exquisite white porcelain vase by **Dame Lucie Rie**, with inlaid lines running around the body, impressed *LR* seal, circa 1980, 7in. high.
(Bonhams)   **$3,670**

A dramatic stoneware open bowl by **Dame Lucie Rie**, the white bowl flecked with dark brown, circa 1960, 12⁵/₈in. diameter.
(Bonhams)   **$7,707**

A pink porcelain vase by **Dame Lucie Rie**, the round form squeezed to form an oval rim, a darker pink spiral and white rim adds to its individuality, circa 1975, 5¹/₂in. high.
(Bonhams)   **$1,376**

MARTINWARE

A rare Martin Brothers dog and cover, grotesque figure of a seated bulldog, 1895, 28.5cm. high.
(Christie's) $9,487

A Martin Brothers stoneware rectangular plaque modeled in relief with a scene depicting all three brothers at work in the Southall studio, dated 1904, 17in. wide.
(Christie's) $622

A Martin Brothers stoneware tobacco jar and cover modeled as a comical grotesque bird with elongated beak, dated 1883, 12¹/₂in. high.
(Christie's) $4,797

A Martin Brothers 'monk' bird and cover, circa 1894, with broad smile and balding head, 7¹/₂in. high.
(Sotheby's) $5,456

A rare Martin Brothers triple bird group of 'Two's company, three's none', circa 1906, modeled as a central, complacently smirking male bird with his wings about two females, 7¹/₂in. high.
(Sotheby's) $14,492

A Martin Brothers vase, incised with two panels decorated with insects and foliage, 24.2cm. high.
(Bonhams) $678

A Martin Brothers square stoneware flask with lug handle on the shoulder, incised with comical fish, dated 1898, 10in. high.
(Christie's) $533

A pair of Martin Brothers stoneware candlesticks, incised with panels of water birds, 8in. high.
(Christie's) $391

A Martin Brothers bird and cover, circa 1897, the plump bird with balding head, resembling a monk, 9in. high.
(Sotheby's) $5,967

MEISSEN

19th century Meissen porcelain ornament, 'The Tailor's Wife, 6in. high.
(G. A. Key) $1,073

Two unusual late Meissen models of Bolognese hounds, their faces, ears and patches of their coats picked out in brown, 26cm.
(Phillips) $3,451

A Meissen style porcelain wall sconce supporting three candle branches and a cherub painted central floral bouquet.
(Russell Baldwin & Bright) $604

A late Meissen topographical cup and a saucer, the cup painted with 'Der grosse Garten bei Dresden' in colors, within gilt line borders.
(Phillips) $568

A Meissen ewer in the form of a monkey with her young, after the model by Johann Joachim Kändler, circa 1740, 18.5cm. high.
(Christie's) $7,608

A Meissen model of a green woodpecker perched on a tree stump, underglazed blue crossed swords mark, impressed number *144*, 10³/₄in. high.
(Christie's) $635

A late Meissen pot pourri vase, cover and stand, after the model by Kaendler, of ogee rococo shape, with naturalistic applied flowers, 28in. high.
(Bonhams) $8,000

A pair of late Meissen vases, finely painted with panels of Venus and Cupid after Boucher, 53cm. high.
(Phillips) $10,400

A Meissen figure of a fruit-vendor after the model by J. J. Kändler as an old woman in **gray scarf, turquoise and black bodice**, circa 1745, 17.5cm. high.
(Christie's) $2,033

MEISSEN

A Meissen model of three hounds attacking a bull, indistinctly marked, 6⅝in. wide. (Christie's) **$1,255**

A late Meissen 'Bottger Steinzeug' bust of a woman with negroid features, the head held up and the eyes open, 27.5cm. (Phillips) **$800**

A fine Meissen teabowl, the exterior with gilt quatrelobed panels painted in colors in the manner of J. G. Hoeroldt with two Chinese figures at various pursuits in a garden, 7.5cm. (Phillips) **$731**

A Meissen group modeled by J. J. Kändler of a gallant and his companion beneath a tree, he wearing a red coat and black boots, leaning over and offering her snuff, 11in. high. (Christie's) **$1,505**

A Meissen model of a mallard probably after a model by Johann Joachim Kändler, on a circular green-washed base, circa 1750, 28cm. high. (Christie's) **$28,028**

A Meissen group of Phoebus Apollo in the Chariot of the Sun after an original model by J. J. Kändler, the young god seated in glory wearing a purple robe and brandishing a torch, circa 1875–76, 11¾in. high. (Christie's) **$6,563**

A Meissen group in the manner of J. J. Kändler, with a young boy removing eggs from bird's nest, with his mother seated by the base, 8¼in. high. (Christie's) **$4,349**

A Meissen tea canister and cover, painted in colors with sprays of flowers and scattered sprigs, the cover with flower finial, 13.5cm. (Phillips) **$832**

A late Meissen model of the 'Padua Rooster', after a model by Kaendler, the plumage in shades of brown, gray and yellow with red wattles, 77cm. (Phillips) **$1,624**

MEISSEN

A Meissen water goddess, scantily clad and reclining on a rococo scroll base encrusted with flowers, 6¹/₂in. high overall.
(Bonhams) $1,120

A late Meissen group emblematic of Literature modeled as three putti with one holding a scroll, 23cm.
(Phillips) $893

A late Meissen crinoline group, after the model by Kaendler, usually said to be Augustus III of Saxony, 21.5cm.
(Phillips) $1,218

A Meissen group of a sportsman and his companion seated beneath a tree, he dressed in a red coat and black breeches, offering her a duck, 12¹/₄in. wide.
(Christie's) $1,505

A pair of Meissen figures of a gardener and companion wearing flowered 18th century dress and holding baskets of flowers, she with Pressnummer 74, blue crossed swords marks, circa 1880, 19³/₄in. high.
(Christie's) $3,799

Fine antique German Meissen figure group, early 19th century, in the form of four children, 6in. high.
(Eldred's) $715

A Meissen baluster coffee-pot and cover with S-scroll handle and richly gilt spout, painted with extensive harbor scenes, circa 1735, 21.5cm. high.
(Christie's) $28,838

A late 19th century Meissen porcelain figure group 'The Quack Dentist', cross swords mark in blue, 20.5cm. high.
(Spencer's) $1,647

Fine Meissen porcelain figure of Cupid holding a garland of flowers beside a pedestal with Greek key and ram's head decoration, 5¹/₂in. high.
(Eldred's) $605

MINTON

A rare Minton majolica ware pigeon salad bowl, on a base of twining oak branches and leaves and three fantail pigeon supports in pale blue and white, 32.5cm., date code for 1873.
(Phillips)   **$3,857**

Mintons pâte sur pâte small plaque by Alboine Birks, signed, with a figure of a goddess in windblown dress, in a chariot drawn by putti, 9.5 x 13cm.
(Phillips)   **$1,522**

A Minton Lazy Susan (revolving tray on foot) of circular form of lobed outline, painted by William Wagstaff, signed, 47.5cm., code for 1869.
(Phillips)   **$812**

A Minton majolica dark-blue-ground marine vase, the amphora-shaped body molded as interlocking scallop-shells with laurel-wreaths pendent from the crests, date code for 1869, 16in. high.
(Christie's)   **$2,418**

A pair of Minton vases modeled as putti, scantily clad in manganese drapes, each straining to support a fluted vase formed as a rhyton with a goat's head, date codes for 1868, 14³/₄in. high.
(Christie's)   **$4,145**

A Minton majolica tower jug and cover, the tapering cylindrical body molded in relief with a frieze of medieval figures dancing around a tower, date code for 1870, 13in. high.
(Christie's)   **$1,122**

A Minton majolica triform vase modeled as three bulbous radishes, their white skins shading to pink at the shoulders and with a ring of everted green leaves forming the necks, date code for 1866, 4in. high.
(Christie's)   **$1,727**

A Minton majolica dark-blue-ground vase and cover of waisted campana shape, the handles formed as winged putto caryatids and the finial of compressed baluster form, circa 1860, 13¹/₂in. high.
(Christie's)   **$484**

A Minton majolica pigeon-pie tureen and cover, the circular body molded and colored to simulate yellow wicker-work, impressed date code for 1859, 12¹/₂in. diameter.
(Christie's)   **$3,809**

MINTON

A Minton double dahlia inkstand modeled as a green leaf with a pink and white dahlia inkpot, 21.5cm.
(Phillips) $650

A Minton majolica center tablepiece, a pierced trellis bowl with floral banding raised on three feet molded as doves, 15cm. high.
(Bonhams) $1,534

A colorful Minton 'perforated plate' of fruit and flowers, the fruit almost completely covered by a profusion of flowers including dahlias, morning glories and tulips, 21cm.
(Phillips) $2,030

One of a pair of Minton majolica celadon-ground oyster-plates, with marbled brown centers imitating porphyry and with nine wedge-shaped dishes forming the borders, registration marks and date codes for 1867, 9³/₄in. diameter.
(Christie's)
(Two) $1,554

A Minton majolica bottle-cooler of campana shape with a scroll and acanthus-leaf-molded rim and two goat's mask handles, the pale-turquoise ground molded in white relief with a woman and child on a goat, impressed date code for 1859, 9³/₄in. high.
(Christie's) $1,554

A Minton majolica tazza, the shallow shell-molded dish glazed in turquoise on the upper surface and in shaded ocher below, supported on the entwined tails of three dolphins, date code for 1871, 8in. high.
(Christie's) $449

A Minton majolica floor vase, with a putto riding a dolphin before fluted cornucopia, on a rectangular base, impressed Minton mark, 27¹/₂in. high.
(Christie's) $3,345

A Minton vase and cover of double ogee form, with double acanthus molded handles, painted with fancy birds, 34cm. high.
(Phillips) $736

A Minton majolica ware Christmas dish made for the Crystal Palace Art Union, molded in relief in the center with a white rose within a garland of mistletoe, 39cm., date code for 1859.
(Phillips) $1,928

MOORCROFT

A Moorcroft 'Moonlit blue' plate, the obverse tube-lined with trees in a landscape, 21.9cm. diameter.
(Bonhams) $614

A William Moorcroft Liberty & Co. 'Pomegranate' pewter mounted trumpet vase, tube-lined with a band of large fruits amongst berries, 6³/₈in. high.
(Bonhams) $508

An attractive Moorcroft Florian ware vase, slip trailed in white and decorated in shades of blue with a flower pattern.
(Spencer's) $380

A William Moorcroft 'Pomegranate' tobacco jar and cover, tube-lined with a band of large fruits, berries and foliage, 7¹/₂in. high.
(Bonhams) $568

An attractive pair of early 20th century James Macintyre & Co., Moorcroft Florian ware cornflower pattern vases, 16cm. high.
(Spencer's) $1,254

A Moorcroft 'Liberty & Co.' Florian ware vase, tube-lined with poppies in blue and green, on a yellow ground, 12.4cm. high.
(Bonhams) $807

A Moorcroft shouldered oviform vase, with a band of leaf and berry design in shades of pink and green on a deep blue ground, 27cm. high.
(Christie's) $702

A Moorcroft 'Willow Tree' vase, footed ovoid, tube-lined with weeping willows in pink and green, 16cm. high.
(Bonhams) $1,292

A William Moorcroft Liberty & Co. pewter mounted 'Claremont' jar and cover, 8¹/₄in. high.
(Bonhams) $1,495

MOORCROFT

A William Moorcroft 'Pansy' vase, tube-lined with purple, yellow, mauve and pink open flowerheads, 5in. high. (Bonhams) $478

A miniature William Moorcroft vase, tube-lined with pommels of forget-me-nots on a powder-blue ground, 3³/₈in. high. (Bonhams) $329

A Macintyre 'Claremont' pattern bowl designed by William Moorcroft, with decoration of crimson, blue and green mushrooms, printed marks Made for Liberty & Co, circa 1903, 21.5cm. diameter. (Christie's) $1,914

A Moorcroft 'Claremont' pattern vase designed by William Moorcroft, blue and green mottled ground with yellow, pink, green and blue mushrooms, circa 1920, 17cm. high. (Christie's) $574

A Moorcroft Macintyre Florian ware vase, tube-lined with poppies, in blue and green on a cream ground, 10cm. high. (Bonhams) $307

A good William Moorcroft Liberty & Co. 'Poppies' flambé cookie barrel and pewter cover, 6¹/₂in. high. (Bonhams) $1,495

An early 20th century Macintyre Moorcroft Florian ware poppy pattern jug, with simulated bamboo molded handle, 22cm. high. (Spencer's) $533

A pair of Moorcroft Florian ware vases, tube-lined with iris and leafy flowers, in shades of blue, 20.2cm. high. (Bonhams) $969

A Moorcroft jug, tube-lined with fish amongst weeds, in gray/blue and brown on a matt cream ground, 13.1cm. high. (Bonhams) $678

PEARLWARE

A pearlware portrait bust of a gentleman looking to the right, in full wig, painted in colors on square socle, 9in. high.
(Christie's) $107

A pearlware figure of a fishwife wearing a white hat, with fish cradled in her apron, 6³/₄in. high, and similar figure.
(Christie's) $286

A pearlware portrait bust of John Wesley, painted in colors, on a shaped socle, inscribed to the reverse *W. L., Oct. 26 1822*, 12in. high.
(Christie's) $751

A pearlware portrait bust of the Duke of York modeled in full military uniform above the socle molded with the Prince of Wales feathers, circa 1820, 5³/₄in. high.
(Christie's) $447

A pearlware model of Obadiah Sherratt type of The Flight into Egypt, the Virgin Mary modeled seated on a donkey, circa 1820, 7³/₄in. high.
(Christie's) $626

A pearlware portrait bust of a male child, his head turned to the right, mounted on a gray marbelised socle, circa 1830, 10in. high.
(Christie's) $268

A pearlware figure group of a woman scything corn, a child gathering the sheaves at her side, possibly Yorkshire, circa 1810.
(Christie's) $500

Two pearlware figures emblematic of Hope and Charity modeled as women, circa 1820, 8in. high.
(Christie's) $500

A pearlware model of a girl cradling a cat in her arms, in mob cap, jacket and apron, circa 1790, 6¹/₄in. high.
(Christie's) $232

PEARLWARE

A pearlware figure of Jupiter standing, lightning bolts in upraised hand, in crown and flowing robes, circa 1800, 10¹/₄in. high.
(Christie's) $447

An Astbury 'Fair Hebe' pearlware loop-handled jug molded in relief with a young man offering his sweetheart a bird's nest, circa 1790, 5¹/₂in. high.
(Christie's) $1,162

A pearlware portrait bust of Nelson modeled in full naval uniform, painted in colors, circa 1800, 6in. high.
(Christie's) $500

PRATTWARE

A Pratt-type portrait bust modeled as a bearded man looking to the right, fur-lined robes about him, circa 1780, 7¹/₄in. high.
(Christie's) $393

A Prattware cider jug, circa 1880, molded with exotic barnyard fowl within an oval reserve edged with stiff leaf-tips, 7³/₄in. high.
(Christie's) $1,430

A creamware model of an owl, circa 1785, of Pratt type, with alert expression and incised plumage and splashed in ocher, green and brown spots, 5¹/₂in. high.
(Christie's) $5,280

ROCKINGHAM

A very large Rockingham armorial soup tureen, cover and stand, painted with fruit, probably by Thomas Steele, and exotic birds and butterflies, 43cm.
(Phillips) $4,000

A pair of Rockingham porcelain small spill vases, each decorated with a continuous scene of a spoonbill and other birds, 3¹/₄in. high, circa 1830.
(Tennants) $3,726

An important Rockingham Royal Service plate, from the service made for William IV, the light blue border gilt with oak leaves with acorns, 24cm.
(Phillips) $5,760

ROOKWOOD

Rookwood scenic vellum vase, Fred Rothenbusch, 1914, extensive blue green pastoral scene with brook and pathway, 12in. high.
(Skinner) $2,420

Rookwood bookends, William P. MacDonald, 1922, Art Deco Oriental figural, with black comb highlighted in red, 8in. high.
(Skinner) $825

Rookwood large corn jug, Sallie Toohey, 1896, standard glaze with four ears of corn, conforming stopper with cork insert, impressed marks, total height 13in.
(Skinner) $1,210

Rookwood butterfly handle goose vase, 1891, standard glaze with three geese in flight, blue green areas, impressed marks, 6¹/₂in. high.
(Skinner) $825

Rookwood scenic vellum plaque, Sara Sax, 1916, 'The Top of the Hill', snow covered landscape, impressed marks, 7³/₈ x 9³/₈in.
(Skinner) $4,070

Pair of Rookwood crow bookends, 1926, oversize weighted set of mauve molded rooks in William McDonald's design, 6¹/₂in. high.
(Skinner) $413

ROSENTHAL

A Rosenthal figure of a female tennis player, striding out on an oval base, by Fritz Klimsch, 1936, 51cm. high.
(Kunsthaus am Museum)
                              $743

A Rosenthal guitar playing pierrot with poodle, seated on a mound, by Rudolf Marcuse, 1913, 33cm. high.
(Kunsthaus am Museum)
                              $805

A Rosenthal figure of a crouching nude, by Fritz Kilmsch (1870–1960), matt, 1936, 36cm. high.
(Kunsthaus am Museum)
                              $433

ROYAL DUX

A Royal Dux figure group, boy in tunic and breeches with setter type dog, on rustic plinth, 13in. wide, pink triangle mark.
(Russell Baldwin & Bright)
$931

A Royal Dux figural lamp, **realistically modeled as a Turkish dancer, in naturalistic colors, 31.5cm. high.**
(Bonhams)
$840

A Royal Dux figure group, standing cloaked shepherd with sheep and dog, on rustic **modeled plinth, 18^{1}/$_{2}$in. long.**
(Russell Baldwin & Bright)
$1,031

An attractive Royal Dux figure **group modeled by Hampel, as a** young goat herder, standing on a rocky outcrop holding a scantily draped maiden, 55cm. high.
(Spencer's)
$1,318

A pair of Royal Dux figures of harvesters, the young man standing wearing a sou'wester, pink patch marks, 54.5cm. and 52cm. high.
(Spencer's)
$1,483

A Royal Dux figure group, as classical potters, standing and seated on a rocky outcrop on a **naturalistically molded base,** pink patch mark, 53cm. high.
(Spencer's)
$927

Royal Dux porcelain ornament of a conch shell with a nymph attendant, on a rock formed and lily leaf base, 15in. tall.
(G. A. Key)
$600

A Royal Dux figure of an Eastern female water carrier, wearing a green turban and blue dress tied at the waist with a shawl, 47cm. high.
(Spencer's)
$514

Royal Dux, Art Nouveau centrepiece, circa 1900, porcelain glazed in shades of green, brown and rust, 13^{1}/$_{2}$in. high.
(Sotheby's)
$1,278

RUSKIN

A Ruskin high fired stoneware bottle vase covered in a mottled pink glaze flecked with blue and jade green, 1924, 6¹/₂in. high.
(Christie's) $497

A Ruskin high fired lamp base, of tapering cylindrical form with bulbous neck, impressed factory marks, 8³/₄in. high.
(Christie's) $763

A Ruskin Pottery high-fired vase, cylindrical with flared foot and rim, incised *W Howson Taylor*, 1932, 29.7cm. high.
(Christie's) $1,050

A Ruskin Pottery high-fired stoneware vase, tall tapering form with bulbous foot, white ground with speckled liver-red, purple and mauve, 1925, 20cm. high.
(Christie's) $574

A Ruskin Pottery high-fired stoneware vase, with tall cylindrical neck, gray ground with mottled liver-red and mauve, 1924, 29cm. high.
(Christie's) $766

A fine monumental Ruskin Pottery stoneware vase, with tall neck and slightly flared rim, cream gray ground with mottled liver red beneath mauve blue, 1925, 59.5cm. high.
(Christie's) $2,680

SATSUMA

A globular jar painted and heavily gilt with three roundels enclosing a shishi lion above waves and peonies, 11in. high.
(Christie's) $15,286

Satsuma style lidded vase, Meiji Period, finely painted in gilt and polychrome enamels with a kikko-diaper ground, 11¹/₂in. high.
(Butterfield & Butterfield) $1,100

A bowl painted and heavily gilt to the interior with a central roundel of peonies attached to canes, 5in. diameter, signed *Kinkozan*.
(Christie's) $2,548

SATSUMA

An ovoid ewer and domed cover with a dragon spout, handle and finial, painted and gilt with chrysanthemums, 7¹/₄in. high.
(Christie's) $3,821

Pair of large Satsuma style vases, Meiji Period, signed *Taizan*, each with everted rim and pear-shape body, 13¹/₄in. high.
(Butterfield & Butterfield)
                    $1,210

A large reticulated koro and pierced domed cover modeled as a kiku head with upright square handles, 14¹/₂in. high.
(Christie's) $13,800

A square dish with canted corners painted and heavily gilt with numerous figures and children, 7¹/₂in. wide.
(Christie's) $8,067

A pair of ovoid vases painted and gilt with tapering rectangular panels of butterflies amongst chrysanthemums, 9³/₄in. high.
(Christie's) $5,308

A good small Japanese Satsuma square dish, with floral gold painted border, the center painted with a lakeland landscape, 6in. wide.
(John Nicholson) $2,325

A good Japanese Satsuma cricket basket and cover, with looped handle and pierced sides, painted with floral panels, 7in. high.
(John Nicholson) $1,950

A good small pair of Japanese Satsuma vases, with lion ring handles, the body painted with birds and flowers, 7¹/₂in. high.
(John Nicholson) $630

A vase painted and gilt with a cockerel, hen and chicks beside a river bank in a landscape, 8¹/₄in. high.
(Christie's) $2,760

SATSUMA

A lobed rectangular koro and pierced domed cover with mask handles, 4in. high, signed *Satsuma yaki Hogetsu*.
(Christie's) $3,609

A standing figure of Kannon on a tripod double lotus base wearing robes and a celestial scarf, 12¹/₂in. high.
(Christie's) $3,185

A tripod flattened globular koro and pierced silver and enamel domed cover modeled as a kiku head, 4in. high.
(Christie's) $2,760

An ovoid vase painted and heavily gilt with a broad band of birds amongst peonies and chrysanthemums, 14¹/₂in. high.
(Christie's) $8,067

A pair of ovoid vases painted and gilt with tapering rectangular panels of ladies and children in pavilions, 8in. high.
(Christie's) $8,917

An ovoid vase painted and gilt with a panel of Buddhist figures and a tiger, 18¹/₂in. high.
(Christie's) $1,592

A Satsuma jar, the globular body painted with chrysanthemums below a flower decorated lappet shoulder, 13.3cm.
(Bearne's) $2,160

Massive Satsuma style pottery vase, Meiji Period, with wide waisted neck above an octagonal-sectioned shoulder supporting two karako, 46in. high.
(Butterfield & Butterfield)
          $9,900

A tripod flaring cylindrical koro painted and gilt with chrysanthemums issuing from behind wicker fences, 5¹/₂in. high.
(Christie's) $2,548

A deep bowl painted and gilt to the interior with a roundel of dense kiku heads within a continuous band of ladies and children, 4³/₄in. diameter.
(Christie's) $6,369

A vase with flattened shoulder painted and heavily gilt with a continuous scene of chrysanthemums, 12¹/₄in. high, signed *Dai Nihon*.
(Christie's) $5,308

A shell-shaped dish molded, painted and heavily gilt with a female immortal in flight above Buddhist sages, 12¹/₂in. wide.
(Christie's) $679

A teapot and domed cover with snake finial and dragon spout, painted and heavily gilt with fan-shaped panels of warriors, 7¹/₂in. high.
(Christie's) $1,274

A pair of ovoid vases with short flaring necks, painted and heavily gilt with scenes of the Immortals, 17¹/₂in. high.
(Christie's) $17,409

A box and cover modeled as a hokkai box, painted and heavily gilt with panels of warriors in landscapes, 4¹/₂in. high, signed *Kinkozan*.
(Christie's) $955

A dish painted and heavily gilt with Kannon and arhats holding various attributes, 10¹/₂in. diameter.
(Christie's) $594

A tapering square vase painted and gilt with alternating panels of pavilions in mountainous river landscapes, 6¹/₂in. high.
(Christie's) $5,308

A combination Satsuma mask and bowl, the mask in the form of a chubby face, the jet black hair decorated with flowers, 22.3cm. high.
(Bearne's) $2,309

SEVRES

A Sèvres two-handled bleu nouveau écuelle, cover and stand painted with bouquets of full-blown garden flowers and fruit, 1772, 22.5cm. wide.
(Christie's) $5,410

A Sèvres bleu nouveau ewer and basin, the ewer of pear-shape with a helmet-shaped lip and foliage-molded handles, date letters *CC* for 1780.
(Christie's) $43,953

A Sèvres tray from the Duchess of Bedford service, of lozenge shape, the center painted with fruit and flowers within an oval reserve, 1762, 30cm. wide.
(Christie's) $8,114

An ormolu-mounted Sèvres **Vase de Rhodes modeled in** three sections, the white body of tapering oviform and painted by Jules-Eugène Humbert in a muted pastel palette with figures of young girls allegorical of Spring and Autumn, iron-red and green printed marks and date codes for 1862, 39in. high.
(Christie's) $9,498

A pair of Sèvres plates from the service given by Louis XVI to Archduke Ferdinand of Austria, the centers painted with sprays of pink roses on a purple ground, date letters for 1785, 24cm. diameter.
(Christie's) $7,607

A gilt-metal-mounted Sèvres-pattern tapering oviform vase and domed cover, painted by E. Parot with a young man courting a lady by offering her a rose, circa 1900, 38³/₄in. high.
(Christie's) $4,140

A Sèvres two-handled écuelle, cover and stand painted with alternate garlands of pink roses and berried laurel, date letter *r* for 1770, 26.5cm. wide.
(Christie's) $5,917

A Sèvres armorial bleu nouveau dessert-plate from the Sudell service, the center painted with a yellow and black bird, 1793, 20.7cm. diameter.
(Christie's) $5,410

A Sèvres vase, 'Cuvette à Fleurs à Tombeau', and brass liner, finely painted with a panel by Bouchet, 7¹/₄in. high.
(Bonhams) $2,560

SEVRES

A Sèvres circular two-handled écuelle, cover and stand, the kidney-shaped panels painted with pastoral landscapes, circa 1765, the stand 19cm. diameter.
(Christie's) $10,143

A Sèvres cuvette à fleurs Courteille of bombé form with two concave aubergine-ground pilasters gilt with entwined trailing foliage, circa 1765, 25cm. wide.
(Christie's) $12,679

A Sèvres Empire coffee-cup and saucer painted with bands of full-blown garden flowers, date code for 1829.
(Christie's) $4,066

A pair of metal-mounted Sèvres-pattern tapering oviform vases and domed covers painted by Tisserand with scenes of Napoléon engaged in his campaigns, imitation Sèvres marks, late 19th century, 44½in. high.
(Christie's) $16,560

A Sèvres rose Dèjeuner en Porte-Huilier comprising a Porte Huilier, a teapot and cover and a cup and saucer, date letter H for 1760.
(Christie's) $5,071

A pair of Louis XVI ormolu-mounted Sèvres hard-paste porcelain vases, each painted on one side with Chinese musicians within a drapery cartouche, possibly for Nicolas Schadre, 15½in. high.
(Christie's) $71,060

A Sèvres plate, finely painted with a central spray of summer flowers within a bleu celeste border, 9¼in. diameter.
(Bonhams) $480

A pair of gilt-metal-mounted Sèvres-patten dark-blue-ground vases and covers with drum-shaped bodies and tall trumpet necks, circa 1880, 22in. high.
(Christie's) $4,968

A Sèvres plate, painted with Tapisseries des Gobelins/Haute-lice, with men at looms weaving tapestries, finished examples on the walls, 1820–35, 23.5cm. diameter.
(Christie's) $35,500

SPODE

A Spode Felspar porcelain regimental plate, second quarter 19th century, 9¼in. wide. (Bonhams) $210

A rare pair of Spode tapersticks, brightly decorated with the popular Japan pattern, No. 967, on circular bases, 3¹/sin. high. (Bonhams) $640

A Spode blue and white oval shaped dish from the Caramanian series printed with the Triumphal Arch of Tripoli, circa 1800, 21in. wide. (Christie's) $815

A Spode flared vase, painted with oval panels of roses and other flowers on a lilac blue and gilt cell pattern ground, 6¹/₄in. high. (Christie's) $836

A Spode garniture of three green-ground campana-shaped vases, the seeded green grounds reserved and gilt with stylized foliage, circa 1810, 16cm. and 13.5cm. high. (Christie's) $1,267

A Spode miniature watering-can painted in an Imari palette with flower-sprays within shaped gilt cartouches, circa 1815, 10cm. high. (Christie's) $1,436

A Spode blue and white plate painted with the DEATH OF THE BEAR within a border of wild animals, circa 1800, 9⁷/sin. wide. (Christie's) $807

A pair of Spode matchpots, circa 1820, each gently flaring cylindrical form finely painted with a continuous arrangement of colorful summer flowers, 4¹/₂in. high. (Sotheby's) $3,406

A Spode blue and white plate with a shaped rim from the Caramanian series printed with Sarcophaga and Sepulchres, circa 1800, 10in. wide. (Christie's) $450

STAFFORDSHIRE

Staffordshire pottery figure group, 'The Gardeners', with stream and bocage back, 8in. high.
(G. A. Key) $745

An attractive pair of Staffordshire pottery models of grayhounds, seated with fully modeled fore-legs, the base molded with a dead hare, 21cm. high.
(Spencer's) $472

Staffordshire pottery character jug 'Doctor Johnson', seated 8¹/₂in. high.
(G. A. Key) $137

Large Staffordshire figure of a huntsman on horse with hounds chasing fox, approximately 9in. high.
(G. A. Key) $393

A 19th century Staffordshire figure of a standing elephant in brown shades with oblong white base, 8in. long.
(Russell Baldwin & Bright) $509

A rare Staffordshire group of boxers 'Heenan. Sayers' with painted details and molded title, 9¹/₂in. high, First Heavyweight Boxing Championship.
(Russell Baldwin & Bright) $1,000

Staffordshire figure of Queen Victoria and a young princess, 10in. high.
(G. A. Key) $231

Pair of Staffordshire pottery dogs with molded bodies, painted eyes and noses, 12in. high.
(G. A. Key) $205

Staffordshire toby jug, 19th century, red, green and yellow sponged hat and base, 9³/₄in. high.
(G. A. Key) $132

STAFFORDSHIRE

A Staffordshire solid-agate pectin-shell molded teapot and cover, circa 1760, with dolphin handle, lion finial and serpent spout, 5¹/₂in. high.
(Christie's) **$6,600**

A Staffordshire saltglaze two-handled cup, circa 1765, **enameled in colors with a Chinaman seated in a garden and a Turk seated at a table,** 4³/₄in. high.
(Christie's) **$2,420**

A Staffordshire creamware figure of William III or the Duke of Cumberland, circa 1785, in blue cloak, green and **blue armor astride a rearing brown charger,** 14³/₄in. high.
(Christie's) **$13,200**

A Staffordshire creamware dated cider jug, printed in red with *The World in Planisphere* the reverse with *The Tythe Pig* and inscribed and dated *John Smallwood 1790,* 11in. high.
(Christie's) **$2,640**

A Staffordshire slipware dish, second quarter 18th century, the center with a four-petaled brown flower with blue edging, 15³/₄in. diameter.
(Christie's) **$11,000**

A Staffordshire saltglaze solid-agate model of a seated cat, circa 1745, in dark-brown and buff clays with blue ears and splashed in blue, 4in. high.
(Christie's) **$4,950**

A Staffordshire saltglaze arbor group, circa 1760, modeled as a couple seated beneath an arbor, his hands on her bare knee, 6in. high.
(Christie's) **$60,500**

A Staffordshire glazed redware small teapot and cover, circa 1745, of Astbury type, with applied white slip flowering branches, 3¹/₄in. high.
(Christie's) **$880**

A Staffordshire creamware toasting cup, circa 1770, of **Ralph Wood type, modeled as with the faces of Dr. Johnson and Boswell,** 4in. high.
(Christie's) **$3,300**

STAFFORDSHIRE

A Staffordshire glazed redware small teapot and cover, circa 1745, of Astbury type, with dolphin handle and serpent spout, 4¼in. high.
(Christie's) $3,520

A Staffordshire creamware teapot and cover, circa 1785, of **Ralph Wood type, modeled as a** brown elephant surmounted by a monkey seated in a green crenellated howdah, 11in. high.
(Christie's) $28,600

A Staffordshire creamware punch-pot and cover, circa 1760, with strap handle, Buddhistic lion finial and crabstock spout, 8½in. high.
(Christie's) $9,350

A Staffordshire solid-agate cylindrical tankard, circa 1755, with strap handle and mottled **brown, ocher, blue and buff** clays, 5⅛in. high.
(Christie's) $935

A Staffordshire creamware **arbor group, circa 1765, modeled as a couple in a covered arbor splashed in ocher, brown and green, 6in. high.**
(Christie's) $71,500

A Staffordshire creamware 'Fair Hebe' jug, circa 1788, signed and dated *I. Voyez 1788*, 9½in. high.
(Christie's) $1,540

A Staffordshire creamware oval two-handled reticulated basket and stand, circa 1760, of Whieldon type, 9⅝in. wide.
(Christie's) $6,050

A Staffordshire creamware model of a swan, circa 1800, splashed in blue with brown beak and feathers, 3½in. high.
(Christie's) $660

A Staffordshire saltglaze Jacobite quatrefoil teapot and cover, circa 1760, enameled in colors with Charles II in the branches above the shells, 5¼in. high.
(Christie's) $8,250

STAFFORDSHIRE

A Staffordshire saltglaze sauceboat, circa 1760, the spout molded with a leaf and enameled in colors with a lady playing the harpsichord, 7⁷/₈in. wide.
(Christie's) $3,850

A Staffordshire pearlware model of two lovers seated beneath a tree beside a stream, painted in light colors, circa 1790, 11in. high.
(Christie's) $643

A Staffordshire creamware hexagonal teapot and a cover, circa 1755, with green crabstock handle and finial, 4in. high.
(Christie's) $5,500

A large Staffordshire saltglaze candlestick group, circa 1755, modeled as two cranes, each standing on either side of a bamboo candle-holder, 11³/₄in. high.
(Christie's) $110,000

A Staffordshire creamware model of a parrot of Whieldon type covered in a bright-green glaze and with blue/gray beak, circa 1760, 16.5cm. high.
(Christie's) $9,499

A Staffordshire pearlware coffee-pot and cover modeled as a muzzled bear seated on his haunches, the spout formed by a dog held between his forepaws, impressed *J. Morris Store*, circa 1820, 12¹/₂in. high.
(Christie's) $12,512

A Staffordshire creamware figure 'The Lost Sheep', circa **1780**, modeled as a shepherd in black hat, green coat and breeches, 8⁵/₈in. high.
(Christie's) $990

A Staffordshire slipware press-molded dated 'Man within the Cumpas' charger by Samuel Malkin, 1726, 35cm. diameter.
(Christie's) $14,680

A Staffordshire creamware toby-jug, circa 1780, of Ralph Wood type, modeled seated holding a frothing jug of ale and a beaker with a pipe between his feet, 9¹/₄in. high.
(Christie's) $1,100

A Vienna figure of a dwarf 'Die Walper Hollriglin' modeled by J. L. C. Lück, advancing, her arms outstretched and her mouth open, circa 1755, 11cm. high.
(Christie's) **$18,925**

A Vienna circular wall plaque, painted by H. Reldas, signed, after Rubens, with 'The Rape of the Sabine Women', 45.5cm.
(Phillips) **$2,400**

A Vienna group of two children, he in brown jacket and green breeches proffering a bunch of grapes to a seated girl with grapes in her apron, 17cm.
(Phillips) **$731**

A Vienna-style circular dish painted with Esther seated on red drapery beside a banquet-table before a sacrificial urn among columns, King Ahaseurus standing beside her ordering the seizure of Haman, circa 1880, 21¹/₄in. diameter.
(Christie's) **$6,044**

A Vienna-style claret-ground two-handled baluster vase, painted by Wagner with Schmiede des Vulcan, the god seated among clouds, draped in a red robe and with his sword swathed in green ribbon, France mark, circa 1900, 13in. high.
(Christie's) **$2,418**

A gilt-metal-mounted Vienna (Franz Dörfl) tea-kettle and cover of globular form, the burnished gilt ground tooled with C-scrolls and painted by A. Wenz with two scenes of classical figures, circa 1900, 8¹/₄in. high.
(Christie's) **$2,763**

A pair of large Vienna vases on square bases, finely painted with panels of classical figures, 30in. high.
(Bonhams) **$12,800**

A Vienna pear-shaped hot-water jug, painted on one side with two hearts tied with ribbon to a tree above the inscription *Toujours en vigueur*, 7¹/₂in. high.
(Christie's) **$804**

A pair of Vienna-style two-handled tapering oviform vases, covers and square stands, painted by Wagner, late 19th century, 30in. high.
(Christie's) **$8,289**

WEDGWOOD

Wedgwood jasperware bowl on standard with raised figures on an olive green ground, 5¹/₂in. high.
(Eldred's) $77

A Wedgwood white-jasper anti-slavery medallion, relief decorated in black with a kneeling figure of a black slave, beneath the words *Am I not a man and a brother*, 3.5cm.
(Phillips) $832

A Wedgwood Fairyland lustre octagonal bowl decorated with 'Dana' pattern, the interior with fairies, rainbows and long-tailed birds, 18cm., Portland Vase mark and no. Z5125.
(Phillips) $1,827

A late 18th century Wedgwood porcelain bust of Mercury, 45cm. high.
(Finarte) $2,705

A good and unusual EPNS mounted Wedgwood tortoiseshell majolica three piece tea service, of tapering cylindrical form.
(Spencer's) $506

A Wedgwood bust of G. Stephenson, the reverse inscribed *Josiah Wedgwood & Sons, Published, July 12, 1858, E. W. Wyon.F.*, on socle, 15¹/₂in. high.
(Christie's) $577

A rare Wedgwood flame Fairyland luster 'Fairy Slide' Malfrey pot and cover, 7¹/₈in. high.
(Bonhams) $14,950

A fine and rare Wedgwood Fairyland luster 'Ghostly Wood' ginger jar and cover, designed by Daisy Makeig-Jones, 12³/₄in. high.
(Bonhams) $24,667

A rare Wedgwood Fairyland luster 'White Pagodas' Daventry bowl, designed by Daisy Makeig-Jones, 10¹/₈in. diameter.
(Bonhams) $7,475

WEDGWOOD

A Wedgwood black basalt coffee biggin and cover enameled in famille-rose style enamels with sprays of chrysanthemums and paeonies, 18.5cm.
(Phillips) $512

A Wedgwood majolica teapot and cover of squat bulbous form and with an overhead loop handle, the body glazed in mottled manganese, date code for 1872, 6in. high.
(Christie's) $415

A Wedgwood Fairyland luster bowl, the exterior decorated with a midnight-blue ground gilt with trees and flowerheads flanking panels of flying fairies against a flame sky, 27cm.
(Phillips) $4,699

A tall Wedgwood Fairyland luster 'Imps on a Bridge and Tree House' vase, designed by Daisy Makeig-Jones, 16⁷/₈in. high.
(Bonhams) $8,222

A pair of Wedgwood black-and-white jasper two-handled urns, each molded in high relief with classical figures above a fluted tapering stem and square-shaped foot, 11in. high.
(Christie's) $753

A rare Wedgwood Fairyland luster 'Sycamore tree' variation vase, 8in. high, gilt printed Portland vase mark.
(Bonhams) $2,990

A Wedgwood encaustic decorated basalt vase, decorated with a classical figure of a winged maiden, above a band of anthemion leaves, 23cm.
(Phillips) $1,218

An unusual Wedgwood Baguley type three piece coffee service, each piece 'incised' with ferns and flowers.
(Spencer's) $354

Wedgwood pottery jug, cream glazed, commemorating Thomas Carlysle with portrait and verse, dated for the 30th April, 1881, 9in. high.
(G. A. Key) $228

WEMYSS

A Wemyss Ware pig painted with clover leaves (repair to one ear), impressed *Wemyss*, circa 1900, 6in. wide.
(Christie's) $270

A Wemyss Ware rectangular pin tray painted with a terrier looking at a grasshopper, circa 1900, 5³/₄in. wide.
(Christie's) $1,636

A Wemyss Ware dog bowl painted with roses and the inscription *Love me, Love my Dog*, impressed mark *Wemyss*, circa 1900, 6¹/₂in. diameter.
(Christie's) $616

A Wemyss Ware preserve jar and cover painted with pink roses and foliage within green dentil rims, circa 1900, 4³/₄in. high.
(Christie's) $154

Wemyss china tankard, decorated with flowering tulips, 5¹/₂in. high.
(G. A. Key) $442

A Wemyss Ware slop-bucket painted with two black cocks and five black hens, impressed Wemyss mark and printed T. Goode & Co. mark, 11¹/₈in. high.
(Christie's) $1,815

A Wemyss Ware ewer and basin painted with cabbage roses, impressed Wemyss Ware R, H & S marks, the basin 15¹/₂in. diameter.
(Christie's) $1,270

A Wemyss Ware Bovey Tracey model of a smiling cat, painted with pink roses, 31.5cm. high.
(Christie's) $3,010

A Wemyss Ware pink-glazed model of a pig, impressed *Wemyss Ware R.H.&S.*, circa 1900, 6in. wide.
(Christie's) $616

CHINA

WESTERWALD

A Westerwald jug, the body with three rows of double-headed eagle motifs and a grotesque mask under the spout, 18cm., pewter hinged cover.
(Phillips) $528

A Westerwald salt modeled as a roaring lion, clasping a shallow bowl in its fore-paws, on a heart-shaped foliage base, early 18th century, 17cm. high.
(Christie's) $2,033

A Westerwald Krug, the short cylindrical neck applied with masks and birds, the globular body with The Crucifixion, 17th/18th century, 22.5cm. high.
(Christie's) $2,772

A Westerwald grey stoneware oviform armorial jug applied with molded crowned coat-of-arms accollé on an octagonal panel, late 17th century, 17.5cm. high.
(Christie's) $845

A Westerwald desk-set modeled as two gallants in incised perukes, their companion holding a shallow circular container and wearing a pleated dress, early 18th century, 23cm. high.
(Christie's) $5,544

A Westerwald Enghalskanne with loop handle, the oviform body with incised and applied scrolling foliage on a blue ground, late 17th century, 24.5cm. high.
(Christie's) $1,016

A Westerwald stoneware Schraubflasche (screw-neck flask) of square shape, molded with horned ogre masks on the shoulders, 30cm.
(Phillips) $512

A Westerwald salt modeled as a gentleman in an elaborate peruke, his pleated frock-coat with flared sleeves, holding a shallow bowl before him, early 18th century, 22cm. high.
(Christie's) $2,772

A Westerwald globular jug glazed in blue and manganese and molded with a royal equestrian portrait medallion, circa 1690, 28cm. high.
(Christie's) $2,367

175

WORCESTER

A Worcester 'Japan pattern' teapot stand of lobed hexagonal shape, 5³/₄in. high.
(Bonhams) $240

A Worcester hop-trellis fluted teapot, cover and stand of barrel shape, painted with red berried foliage-swags, circa 1770, the teapot 12.5cm. high.
(Christie's) $7,253

A Worcester shaped square dish painted in the atelier of James Giles, with a gilt dentil rim, circa 1770, 21.5cm. wide.
(Christie's) $2,418

A Worcester hop-trellis fluted baluster hot milk jug and cover, circa 1770, 13cm. high.
(Christie's) $1,900

A Grainger Lee & Co. garniture of three campana pot-pourri vases, finely painted with titled views, 13¹/₂in, and 11¹/₄in. high.
(Bonhams) $4,000

A very rare and fine Royal Worcester reticulated presentation ewer, 18cm., date code for 1913, incised signature G. Owen.
(Phillips) $5,280

A Worcester tankard of cylindrical 'Scratch Cross' form, with grooved strap handle, painted in blue with the 'Prunus Root' pattern, 11.5cm.
(Phillips) $4,263

A Worcester cauliflower tureen and cover naturally modeled with white florettes and green foliage, circa 1758, 11cm. long.
(Christie's) $3,454

A Royal Worcester 'Aesthetic' teapot and cover, circa 1882, polychrome decorated in 'greenery yallery' colors, 6¹/₈in. high.
(Sotheby's) $3,410

WORCESTER

A Worcester outside-decorated globular teapot and cover painted in black with two quail flanked by a brightly colored flower-spray, circa 1770, 13.5cm. high.
(Christie's) $2,418

A Flight & Barr inkwell and cover, the front panel finely painted with a variety of feathers, 14cm. wide.
(Phillips) $3,200

A Worcester barrel-shaped teapot and cover with curved spout and lightly ribbed loop handle, circa 1760, 12.5cm. high.
(Christie's) $4,490

A rare Chamberlain's Worcester lilac-ground jug, with a large oblong octagonal panel painted in the manner of Humphrey Chamberlain, 10in. high.
(Christie's) $8,364

A pair of Royal Worcester vases and covers painted with swans by C. H. C. Baldwyn, signed, 12½in. high, 1903.
(Tennants) $2,456

A magnificent Barr, Flight & Barr vase, the full front panel painted with a study of tropical shells including a glorious strombus, a murex and limpet, 33cm.
(Phillips) $16,000

A fine and early Worcester tankard of cylindrical 'Scratch Cross' form, with grooved strap handle, painted in vivid palette with the 'Beckoning Chinaman' pattern, 9cm.
(Phillips) $8,526

A Worcester blue-ground fable-decorated plate painted in the manner of Jefferyes Hammett O'Neale, circa 1768, 19cm. diameter.
(Christie's) $4,836

A Worcester coffee pot and domed cover of slender baluster form with scroll handle, painted in blue with the 'Gazebo' pattern, 19.5cm.
(Phillips) $5,887

A Worcester leaf-shaped dish brightly painted in colors with the 'Chinese Magician' pattern, 21cm.
(Phillips) $2,190

A Worcester partridge tureen and cover sitting on a rest, with natural colored plumage in shades of brown, red and black, the head in red, 14.5cm.
(Phillips) $2,639

A rare Worcester serving dish with molded strap flute border, painted in blue with the 'Two-Level Fence and Rock' pattern, 30.5cm.
(Phillips) $5,481

A Worcester ovoid tea canister painted in colors with two Chinese figures beside a table, 13.5cm.
(Phillips) $365

A pair of rare Worcester scale pink vases, each painted with Chinese figures in fenced gardens, 21cm., the porcelain circa 1770, the decoration probably later.
(Phillips) $4,060

A very rare Worcester white figure of the Sportsman's Companion, standing and holding a bird in one hand and a flask in the other, 17.8cm.
(Phillips) $11,200

A Worcester pierced circular basket painted in colors in the center with a bouquet and scattered sprigs, 17cm.
(Phillips) $2,008

A Worcester egg cup painted in blue with the 'Egg Cup Floral Sprays' pattern, 6.5cm.
(Phillips) $949

A Worcester saucer dish painted in blue with the 'Fisherman and Willow Pavilion', 19cm., workman's mark.
(Phillips) $448

178

WORCESTER

A Worcester pierced oval basket with twig handles and floral terminals, printed and colored in the centre with the 'Chinese Family' pattern, 20cm.
(Phillips) **$1,928**

A Worcester strap-flute sauceboat painted in famille-verte enamels with Chinese figures and landscape panels, 7cm.
(Phillips) **$704**

A Worcester leaf-shaped dish, painted in colors with a bouquet and scattered sprigs, two veins picked out in puce, 26cm.
(Phillips) **$1,460**

A Royal Worcester two handled porcelain vase, painted with sprays of pink and crimson roses by W. Austin, dated *1904*, 27.5cm. high.
(Spencer's) **$570**

Three Royal Worcester wall-brackets allegorical of the Seasons after models by James Hadley and formed as maidens seated in grottoes, pierced for suspension, circa 1870, 9¹/₂in. high.
(Christie's) **$949**

A Royal Worcester vase with slender ovoid body painted with nasturtium-like flowers in bold colors, 26.5cm., date code for 1903.
(Phillips) **$893**

A richly decorated Worcester scale blue dish, painted in the center with butterflies and insects and on the rim with exotic birds in colors, 24.5cm.
(Phillips) **$3,857**

William Ricketts, a Royal Worcester pot pourri vase and pierced cover, painted in colors with a cluster of ripe fruits, 17cm., date code for 1926.
(Phillips) **$853**

A very rare Worcester leaf dish, the center molded with an open Oriental scroll painted in blue with a bird perched on a slender leaf, 18.6cm.
(Phillips) **$5,684**

BRACKET CLOCKS

Regency period bracket clock, the striking mechanism housed in an ebonized and brass inlaid case, inscribed *Henry Ellis of Exeter*.
(G. A. Key) $1,517

A 19th century ornately carved neo-Renaissance bracket clock, the silvered dial with applied gilt **moldings, playing two melodies** on 8 bells, English, 70cm. high.
(Duran) $1,779

Regency mahogany cased bracket clock with brass inlay and mounts, the striking movement inscribed *E Watson, King Street, Cheapside*, 18in. tall.
(G. A. Key) $1,517

George III mahogany striking bracket clock, the case with handle to the arched top and on brass bracket feet, the painted dial signed *John Hardy Preston*, 15in. high.
(Christie's) $1,724

Tho: Tompion Londini Fecit, a Charles II ebony striking early miniature bracket clock, unnumbered, circa 1675–80, the well-molded plinth-form case with later bun feet and side frets, 9³/₄in. high.
(Christie's) $58,625

An ebonized and brass-mounted bracket clock with pierced brass caddy top hood and scrolled carrying handle, inscribed *Jo. Buckingham, London*, 19in. high overall, 17th century.
(Christie's) $9,982

A rare Chippendale brass-mounted mahogany bracket clock, signed *Leslie & Price, Philadelphia*, 1793–1799, 17¹/₄in. high.
(Sotheby's) $7,150

A George III mahogany striking bracket clock, the 8in. arch dial signed on a silvered plaque *George Norris, London*, with strike-silent in the arch, 21in. high.
(Bonhams) $2,745

A George III mahogany bracket clock, silvered arch dial, signed *Willm. Dorrel, London*, Roman numeral dial, strike/silent in the arch, 17¹/₂in.
(Bonhams) $2,509

BRACKET CLOCKS

Victorian ebonized ormolu mounted chiming bracket clock, the case on foliate paw feet with detached fluted Corinthian columns to the sides, 26in. high.
(Christie's) $2,586

19th century bracket clock with silvered brass dial, the black lacquered case decorated with a polychrome chinoiserie pattern, 14in. high.
(G. A. Key) $502

A George II mahogany striking bracket clock, the 6in. dial signed *Delander, London*, on a brass plaque to the matted center, with false pendulum aperture and date, 16in.
(Bonhams) $11,580

A George III faded mahogany striking bracket clock, the seven-inch dial signed on a silvered plaque, *John Rycutt, London*, matted center with false pendulum aperture and date, 18in.
(Bonhams) $5,790

A fine George III bracket clock, in a mahogany case, the lunette inscribed *John Scott, London*, the center with bob aperture and calendar, 15½in. high.
(Woolley & Wallis) $6,660

A George III ormolu mounted ebonized musical bracket clock for the Turkish market, the case with pineapple finials to bell top applied with ormolu floral mounts, 28½in. high.
(Christie's) $4,138

A Victorian English walnut veneer chiming bracket clock, white painted dial signed *F. Dent, 61 Strand, London*, triple fusée, signed anchor movement chiming on eight bells, 31in.
(Bonhams) $1,640

An 18th century ebonized bracket clock, the 17cm. square brass dial inscribed *Jonathan Lowndes, Pall Mall, London*, 16in. high.
(Spencer's) $3,900

A George III black lacquer striking bracket clock with alarm, 6¾in. dial signed in the silvered aperture *Ralph Goat, London*, on cast bracket feet, 21in. high.
(Bonhams) $3,230

CARRIAGE CLOCKS

A French 19th century carriage clock, silvered dial mask, gong strike/repeat movement marked with Margaine stamp, 6¹/₂in. including handle.
(Bonhams) **$1,130**

An early French 19th century alarm carriage clock, by Paul Garnier, with a silvered engine-turned dial and Roman chapter ring, 6³/₄in.
(Bonhams) **$2,261**

Good quality French gilt brass and enamel carriage clock, silvered dial, MacKay & Chisholm, Edinburgh Retailer's mark, 6³/₄in. high.
(G. A. Key) **$1,146**

An English repeating double fusée carriage clock with thermometer and calendar, by Nicole Nielsen & Co. Limd., 6in. high.
(Lawrence) **$8,329**

A late 19th century French carriage clock, 2in. silvered annular chapter ring, set within a pierced bird and foliate and polished gilt background, signed *EGLG Paris*, 6¹/₄in.
(Bonhams) **$733**

A gilt brass striking calendar carriage clock, with bi-metallic balance to silvered lever platform, strike/repeat/alarm on gong on backplate with stamp for Margaine, 6³/₄in. high.
(Christie's) **$2,242**

A carriage-style clock, the movement striking on coiled gong, with white enamel dial in beveled-glazed brass-framed case, 8in. high.
(Christie's) **$424**

French brass and crystal carriage clock in a wooden carrying case, with quarter hour repeater and alarm, 7in. high.
(Eldred's) **$743**

A French 19th century carriage clock, engraved foliate mask, repeating gong striking movement by R & Cº, Paris, 7¹/₂in.
(Bonhams) **$727**

CARRIAGE CLOCKS

A French 19th century carriage clock, the gong striking movement, No. 1933, marked with the 'B' trademark, 6³/₄in. (Bonhams) $646

An attractive French gilt brass grande sonnerie alarm carriage clock, together with key, 8in. high over handle. (Spencer's) $2,535

A French striking carriage clock, movement with lever escapement and gong strike, in a gilt corniche case, 6³/₄in. (Bonhams) $517

A gilt brass grande sonnerie carriage clock with cut bi-metallic balance to silvered lever platform, strike on two gongs with three-position selection lever in the base, 5³/₄in. high. (Christie's) $6,897

Gilt brass porcelain mounted miniature carriage timepiece with bi-metallic balance to lever platform, the blue porcelain dial with Roman chapter ring and pierced gilt hands, 3in. high. (Christie's) $2,586

An attractive French gilt brass repeating carriage clock by F. L. Hausburg of Paris, the white enameled dial with black Roman numerals, 6in. high. (Spencer's) $1,014

A late 19th century grand sonnerie carriage clock, with repeat and alarm, the gilt brass dial inscribed *E. Gubelin, Lucerne*, 7¹/₂in. high. (Bearne's) $1,447

An English carriage timepiece, in the manner of Thomas Cole, silver engraved dial with Roman chapter, signed *Hunt & Roskell*, 4³/₈in. (Bonhams) $3,474

Fine Victorian brass and glass cased carriage clock with Corinthian column supports and similar carrying handle, 6in. high. (G. A. Key) $785

CLOCK SETS

French three-piece brass clock/garniture set, the clock with two cherubs supporting a flower basket, 12in. high.
(Eldred's) $303

Victorian spelter and gilt metal clock garniture, the French drum cased clock having striking movement and surmounted by an angelic figure.
(G. A. Key) $287

An Art Nouveau-style mantel clock, with cream enamel dial in gilt brass-mounted green onyx architectural case, surmounted by a spelter figure of a female mandolin player, 31½in. high, and a pair of side ornaments ensuite.
(Christie's) $1,155

A French 19th century porcelain and ormolu clock garniture, painted dial, black Roman numeral reserves, colorful center scene below figures looking into a pond, bell striking movement signed *Japy Freres*, 20in.
(Bonhams) $2,316

An impressive French ormolu mounted and Sèvres style porcelain clock garniture, the clock with Japy Frères movement, 23in. high.
(G. A. Key) $5,292

An attractive French gilt metal and pink and gray striated marble garniture de cheminée, the clock with convex circular white enameled dial and black Arabic numerals, 24in. high.
(Spencer's) $792

CLOCK SETS

A Victorian mantel clock, with gilt-embellished black slate dial, in gilt brass-mounted black slate architectural case, 16½in. wide, and a pair of five-branch candelabra ensuite, 21½in. high. (Christie's) **$1,251**

A 19th century French porcelain and ormolu clock garniture, with two Imari vases on ormolu bases holding candelabra, the clock face set in a similar vase, flanked by putti. (Finarte) **$3,416**

An Austrian porcelain three-piece clock set, the clock case molded with arches and painted with classical figures, 47cm. high, a two-handled pedestal jar and cover on either side. (Bearne's) **$954**

A French 19th century fine porcelain mounted and ormolu mantel clock, the porcelain dial signed *Le Roy e fil, Paris*, together with a pair of matched jeweled porcelain urns, 17in. (Bonhams) **$4,037**

A black marble French clock garniture, the black enamel dial ring with gold Roman numerals, signed *Requier a Lisieux*, the decorated brass chapter ring with beveled glazing, circa 1880, 42cm. high. (Auction Team Köln) **$525**

A Louis XV-style mantel clock, in lacquered brass balloon-shaped case cast with acanthus scrolls and flowering foliage, on paw feet, 19½in., and a pair of five branch candelabra ensuite. (Christie's) **$1,155**

CLOCK SETS

A 19th century French black and red marble garniture de cheminée, the 8 day Paris movement sounding the half hours on a bell, with porcelain dial, 47cm. high.
(Duran) $890

A 19th century French clock garniture in black and white marble, the clock in architectural style housing, surmounted by a sphinx and flanked by winged tigers, obelisks, 78cm. high.
(Duran) $1,872

A 19th century Empire style French clock garniture, the clock and matching urns of ormolu mounted Sèvres type porcelain, the 8 day movement striking the half hours on a bell.
(Duran) $2,575

A 19th century Napoléon III clock garniture, the clock in the form of a neoclassical temple, surmounted by an urn, flanked by two four light candelabra.
(Duran) $2,809

A French porcelain and gilt-bronze small clock garniture, Paris, circa 1900, in Louis XVI style, the clock 37cm. high.
(Sotheby's) $4,897

A French 'silver'-mounted turquoise porcelain clock garniture, Napoléon III, Paris, circa 1870, the movement in a four-column temple case, clock 40cm. high.
(Sotheby's) $4,897

LANTERN CLOCKS

A brass lantern clock, the posted frame surmounted by a bell, the engraved brass dial signed *Peter Amyot, Norwich*, 24cm. high. (Phillips) $450

A brass lantern clock by William Selwood, the circular foliate cast dial with Roman numerals, inscribed *William Selwood at ye Maremaid in Louthbury*, 15in. high. (Christie's) $4,719

Reproduction brass mantel clock in the form of a lantern clock, striking movement, 15in. high. (G. A. Key) $659

Late 19th century English lantern clock, the 8 day Vicentini movement striking the half hours on a bell, signed *Rt Evens Halstead*, 40cm. high. (Duran) $1,124

A Charles II brass lantern clock, Charles Fox at the Fox in Lothbury, London, the bell surmounted by an urn finial over pierced frets, circa 1670, 14¹/₂in. high. (Christie's) $5,500

Brass lantern clock by J. Windmills, London, with silvered chapter ring, Roman numerals and anchor escapement, early 18th century, 36cm. high. (Auktionsverket) $385

A brass lantern clock, the case of typical form, the twin fusée movement striking the quarters on two bells, 41cm. high. (Phillips) $1,200

A brass lantern clock, signed in the arch *Jos. Hocker, Reading*, with a French twin train carriage clock movement, 21.5cm. high. (Phillips) $450

Henry Ireland, Londini (circa 1654–75), a brass cased lantern clock, converted to anchor escapement, 38cm. high. (Bearne's) $2,850

An early 19th century Scottish longcase clock, inscribed *Geo. White, Glasgow,* 7ft. 2in. high. (Woolley & Wallis)
$1,073

An 18th century Dutch walnut and marquetry musical longcase clock, Jan Bernink, Amsterdam, 7ft. 4in. high. (Spencer's)
$4,485

A Chippendale carved walnut tall case clock, Pennsylvania, circa 1770, 8ft. 1¹/₄in. high. (Sotheby's)
$4,400

A George III black and gold lacquer longcase clock, inscribed *Frances Durrell, London,* the hood with brass finials, 7ft. 8in. high. (Woolley & Wallis)
$3,663

A Chippendale mahogany tall-case clock, dial engraved *Benjamin Morris, Hill Town,* Bucks County, Pennsylvania, 1760–1780, the hood with molded swan's-neck pediment terminating in carved rosettes, 92¹/₂in. high (Christie's)
$13,200

Henry Sanderson, London, a fine George III longcase clock, the eight-day movement striking on a bell, with foliate engraved arched brass and silvered dial, 106¹/₂in. high. (Bearne's)
$5,825

An oak and mahogany veneer eight-day longcase clock, 11¹/₂in. arched brass dial signed John Safley, Nicolson's Street, matted center, silvered chapter, seconds dial with masonic engraving, 7ft. 4in. high. (Bonhams)
$1,544

A Chippendale carved cherrywood tall-case clock, dial signed *Isaac Brokaw,* case attributed to Matthew Egerton, New Brunswick, New Jersey, circa 1790–1810. (Christie's)
$24,200

A George III
mahogany and oak
longcase clock, with a
12¹/₂in. arched dial
signed in the engraved
center *N. Davidson*, 7ft.
high. (Bonhams)
$1,615

A George III
mahogany musical
longcase clock, Robert
Wood, London, 8ft.
5in. high (Spencer's)
$6,630

A mid 18th century
Provençal walnut
longcase clock, the lyre
shaped case carved
with foliate and shell
motifs, 267cm. high.
(Finarte)
$1,993

Antique American tall
case clock in pine with
wood works, by Riley
Whiting of Winchester,
Connecticut, 82in.
high.
(Eldred's) $990

A Dent Victorian oak
cased railway longcase
regulator clock, the
12¹/₂in. engraved
silvered dial signed
*Dent, London,
Clockmaker to the
Queen*, date circa 1855.
(Bonhams)
$3,553

A Federal mahogany
tall-case clock, by
Benjamin Willard,
Roxbury,
Massachusetts, circa
1775, the hood with
pierced fretwork
centering three brass
ball-and-spire finials,
93in. high.
(Christie's)
$8,800

An early 19th century
eight-day longcase
clock, the 12in. enamel
square dial with
painted shell
spandrels, 199cm.
high.
(Allen & Harris)
$707

A George III
mahogany and oak
longcase clock, 12in.
painted dial, faded
signature *Barry,
Lichfield*, with seconds
dial, calendar
aperture, painted
floral spandrels and
arch, 7ft. 2in. high.
(Bonhams)
$2,123

LONGCASE CLOCKS

Bertler & Eggert, Bristol, an unusual George III longcase clock, the eight-day movement striking on a bell, 87in. high. (Bearne's)

$2,824

A Chippendale walnut tall-case clock, Pennsylvania, dated 1804, the base with applied shell-carved 'turtle' panel, 7ft. 8¹/₂in. high. (Sotheby's)

$12,100

A Federal inlaid mahogany tall-case clock, Baltimore, Maryland, early 19th century, 8ft. 6in. high. (Sotheby's)

$6,050

A Federal ivory-inlaid mahogany bow-front tall case clock, John Esterlie, Maytown, Pennsylvania, circa 1815, 8ft. 4¹/₄in. high. (Sotheby's)

$9,900

William Webster, Exchange Alley, London, an 18th century chinoiserie lacquer longcase clock with eight-day movement striking on a bell, 104in. high. (Bearne's)

$2,648

Henry Pearce, Grantham, a mid-19th century eight-day regulator longcase clock with circular silvered minutes dial, 83in. high. (Bearne's)

$2,824

John Skyner, Exon, a George III longcase clock, the arched brass and silvered dial with subsidiary dials for 'High Water at Topsham Bar', 102in. high. (Bearne's)

$3,696

A fine Federal inlaid and figured cherrywood tall case clock, Elisha Cheney, Middletown, Connecticut, circa 1800, 7ft. 5¹/₄in. high. (Sotheby's)

$34,100

LONGCASE CLOCKS

Federal mahogany
inlaid tall case clock,
Massachusetts, circa
1797, overall 96³/₄in.
high.
(Skinner)

$9,350

A mahogany long case
clock, with 12¹/₄in.
arched brass dial,
signed in the center
Brand & Hine/Exon,
95in. high. (Lawrence)

$3,644

Queen Anne maple tall
clock, Benjamin
Cheney, East Hartford,
Connecticut, circa
1760, 89¹/₂in. high.
(Skinner)

$15,400

A Chippendale carved
walnut tall case clock,
Pennsylvania, 1870–
1890, the hood with
carved swan's neck
pediment, 92in. high.
(Christie's)

$4,180

A George III
mahogany and oak
longcase clock, 14in.
painted dial signed *W.
Nicholas, Birmingham*,
with seconds and
calendar dials, 7ft. 5in.
high.
(Bonhams)

$1,351

A fine Chippendale
carved cherrywood
tall-case clock, Stephen
Sibley, Great
Barrington,
Massachusetts, circa
1795, 7ft. 7in. high.
(Sotheby's)

$7,700

A Federal inlaid
mahogany tall-case
clock, Aaron Willard,
Roxbury,
Massachusetts, circa
1805, the hood with
three brass ball-and-
spire finials, 91in. high.
(Christie's)

$24,200

A late Victorian
mahogany longcase
clock, the broken
pediment above an
arched and glazed
hood enclosing a brass
dial, 93in. high.
(Christie's)

$3,561

MANTEL CLOCKS

An unusual gilt metal mariner's mantel timepiece, the circular white enamel dial with black Roman numerals, 20in. high overall.
(Spencer's) $546

A Heller musical chalet clock, Swiss, circa 1880, the carved wood case with stairs, balconies, beehives, doghouse and two train clock striking on bell, 18in. wide.
(Sotheby's) $1,180

A German oak and walnut cased desk clock with calendar automaton, the 8-day movement with half hour striking on a gong, circa 1890, 51cm. high.
(Auction Team Köln) $2,623

American 'Beehive' desk clock, the mahogany case in the form of a beehive, the door with glazed Spanish landscape scene, 8 day movement by the Waterbury Clock Co. striking on a gong, 48cm. high, circa 1880.
(Auction Team Köln) $210

French ormolu clock, the 8-day movement striking the half hours on a bell, the movement signed *Pierre LeRoy*, the white enamel dial with Roman numerals and minutes in Arabic numerals, 43cm. high, circa 1770.
(Auction Team Köln) $3,448

A walnut musical alarm clock, the movement signed *Made in Wurttemberg*, circa 1920, 21cm. high.
(Auction Team Köln) $337

A brass digital desk clock with calendar attachment, the American movement signed *The Plato Clock*, 15cm. high, circa 1900.
(Auction Team Köln) $225

A large free standing mantle clock with Ship's Bell strike on gong, silvered dial with raised Arabic hour numerals signed *Chelsea Ship's Bell*, 14in. wide.
(Christie's) $1,051

A French 19th century white marble and bronze table clock, trumpet playing winged putto carrying a drum incorporating an eight day cylinder movement, signed *Falconnet*, 9in.
(Bonhams) $926

MANTEL CLOCKS

German cast metal desk clock with a hunter and his bag, German 1-day movement, silvered dial, 30cm. high, circa 1930.
(Auction Team Köln) $150

Bungalow Clock, a colored wooden and papier mâché country house with red roof and incorporating a clock, made in the half round by the Lux Clock Mfg. Co., New York, 15cm. high.
(Auction Team Köln) $50

A French 19th century ormolu and porcelain mounted clock, painted dial with Roman chapter, bell striking movement, signed *R. and C.*, 14¹/₂in.
(Bonhams) $1,254

An early Victorian mantel clock, the movement striking on a carillon of eight bells and a coiled gong, the cream enamel dial inscribed *Viner, Bond St., London*, 21¹/₂in. high.
(Christie's) $962

An Empire-style French gilt bronze mantel clock, decorated with a mythological goddess, the 8-day movement with half-hour strike on a bell, with gilt dial and Roman numerals, 1860, 36cm. high.
(Auction Team Köln) $727

A Hiller talking clock, with single-train timepiece movement connected to the speaking movement, in oak case with full-height dial, 16¹/₂in. high, circa 1911.
(Christie's) $4,558

An attractive 19th century gilt brass and champlevé enamel mantel clock, the circular gilt dial with black Roman numerals, the movement striking the hours and half hours on a gong, 35cm. high.
(Spencer's) $660

A Royal Worcester clock case, colored in ivory and gold and encrusted with flowers, containing a French circular eight-day striking movement, 29cm., date code for 1887.
(Phillips) $1,421

Fine Austrian automatic repeating mantel clock, 19th century, the ormolu face with two cherubs below a mask which has movable eyes, 27¹/₂in. high.
(Eldred's) $2,090

MANTEL CLOCKS

An ormolu mantel timepiece, round silvered Roman dial and anchor movement stamped *Silvani*, 11in.
(Bonhams) $646

A 19th century ormolu mantel clock, 3in. enamel dial with Roman numerals, bell striking movement with silk suspension, 17in.
(Bonhams) $452

Fine Regency period satinwood balloon cased mantel clock with sunburst inlay, and pineapple finial, 17in. high.
(G. A. Key) $1,474

An American Sambo figural clock, the cast iron colored figure of a Negro playing his banjo, with American 30-hour movement, 39cm. high, circa 1875.
(Auction Team Köln)
$1,649

Gustav Stickley mantel clock, circa 1902, overhanging top above single door with copper hardware, Seth Thomas works, 21in. high
(Skinner) $6,600

A Junghans Mysterieuse pendulum clock with a cast pewter female figure on a black wooden base, the white enamel dial with Arabic numerals, 35cm. high, circa 1900.
(Auction Team Köln)
$675

Antique American pillar and scroll shelf clock in mahogany with brass finials, painted dial, 31in. high.
(Eldred's) $495

Early 19th century long cased striking mantel clock by J. R. Chapman, two train movement with circular dial enameled, 17½in. tall.
(G. A. Key) $1,224

French Empire ormolu and black lacquer mantel clock, early 19th century, under a glass dome, 19½in. high.
(Eldred's) $413

MANTEL CLOCKS

19th century French ormolu and gilt metal mantel clock with Sèvres porcelain plaques at face, striking movement.
(G. A. Key) $707

A late 19th century French burnished gilt metal mantel clock by Henri Marc of Paris, 16in. high.
(Spencer's) $1,170

A French gilt-metal and white marble mantel clock with circular white enamel dial and Roman numerals, late 19th century, 16in. high.
(Bearne's) $715

19th century brass framed and **cloisonné paneled striking** mantel clock, the French movement of drum case design, 11in. tall.
(G. A. Key) $726

E. F. Caldwell brass and champlevé enamel mantel timepiece, New York, 8^1/₁₆in. high.
(Skinner) $2,200

Mid 20th century mahogany cased mantel clock with a German chiming and striking movement, 18in. tall.
(G. A. Key) $296

French brass mantel clock, 19th century, decorated with butterflies and flowers, Japy Frères gong striking movement, 13^1/₂in. high.
(G. A. Key) $648

An oak cased railway station clock, the white 14in. dial with black Roman numerals, **initialed B.R. (W)**, 23in. high.
(Bonhams) $404

Carved oak cased chiming mantel clock, German movement, square dial with brass spandrels, 17^1/₂in. high.
(G. A. Key) $473

MANTEL CLOCKS

A French 19th century porcelain and ormolu clock, dial signed *Chancellor & Son*, bell striking movement signed *Japy Freres*, 18in.
(Bonhams) $1,544

An attractive late 19th century French black slate mantel clock/ perpetual calendar/aneroid barometer, 18in. high.
(Spencer's) $1,485

A finely decorated and cast gilt French desk clock with hand painted porcelain inlay, the 8 day non striking movement signed *Japy Freres, France*, 45cm. diameter, circa 1890.
(Auction Team Köln)
                    $247

Hand painted, floral decorated Ansonia porcelain desk clock, signed *La Savoie von F M, Bonn, Germany*, the American 8 day movement striking the half hours on a gong, 29cm. high, circa 1900.
(Auction Team Köln)
                    $300

A Liberty & Co. lightly hammered silver mantel clock, with panels of repoussé decoration, the circular clock face with Arabic chapters, stamped *L&Co* with Birmingham hallmarks for 1911, 14.5cm. high, 760 grams gross.
(Christie's) $1,723

A mahogany Steeple table clock, the American 8 day movement by the Gilbert Clock Co. Winsted CT, striking on a gong, the painted metal dial with Roman numerals, 43cm. high, circa 1850.
(Auction Team Köln)
                    $202

A Japanese gilt-brass and padouk wood striking mantle clock of standard form with four baluster pillar movement, 5¼in. high.
(Christie's) $3,234

A Bulle Clockette electric desk clock in red-brown bakelite case, the silvered dial behind arched glass door, 21cm. high, 1910/20.
(Auction Team Köln) $150

An unusual 19th century ebonized mantel clock, with perpetual calendar and equation of time by William Jones, Gloucester, painted white dial with Roman numerals.
(Bonhams) $3,667

196

MANTEL CLOCKS

An attractive late 19th century French gilt metal mantel clock, the circular white enameled dial with black Roman numerals, inscribed *Hry Marc a Paris*, 19in. high.
(Spencer's) $594

A French 19th century gilt metal and porcelain mantel clock, painted dial, signed *Archer Jack, Paris & Cheltenham*, 10in.
(Bonhams) $1,004

A wooden Ansonia child's clock, with pointed roof and painted with fairy tale characters, with American 30-hour movement, 23cm. high.
(Auction Team Köln) $45

An owl desk clock with blinking eyes, in wooden case with pewter and silvered front, the 1 day movement by Junghans, the paper numeral ring with Arabic numerals, 17cm. high, circa 1900.
(Auction Team Köln) $562

A late French 19th century four glass regulator clock, 4in. white enamel dial signed, *L. Leroy & Cie H^{GERS} Dela Marine, Paris 7 Boul^D De La Madeleine*, 13in.
(Bonhams) $772

A Seth Thomas American desk clock, the 8-day movement striking on a gong, in walnut case with galleried pediment, the painted metal dial with Roman numerals, circa 1880/90.
(Auction Team Köln) $270

A French 19th century boulle clock, gilt dial with white enamel chapter and blue Roman numerals, bell striking movement marked *Vincente Cie*, 16in.
(Bonhams) $965

A French Empire mantel clock, the eight-day movement striking the hours and half-hours and with white enamel dial, 16in. high.
(Bearne's) $2,736

A French 19th century gilt ormolu portico clock, engine-turned gilt dial, putto on a swing pendulum, 18in.
(Bonhams) $1,447

MANTEL CLOCKS

An Arts and Crafts pewter
mantle clock, cast in relief with
a tall stemmed rose tree
enclosing circular dial, 33.5cm.
high.
(Christie's)   **$1,421**

A late 19th century mahogany
night watchman's clock, 5in.
engraved silvered dial inscribed
H. H. Plante, 15in. high.
(Bonhams) $614

A Louis Philippe ormolu and
porcelain-mounted striking
mantle clock, the foliate-cast
case with Sèvres-style panels,
stamped *Lagarde á Paris*, 18¹/₂in.
high.
(Christie's)   **$3,404**

An 18th century French
ebonized and ormolu mantel
clock, the dial with Roman
numerals in enamel cartouches,
above an applied bronze scene
of the Banquet of the Gods,
38cm. high.
(Finarte) $2,565

A Black Forest clock automaton,
the brightly painted limewood
figure of a clockmaker moves
his head and whistles a tune,
while carrying under his arm a
small Black Forest clock with
pendulum and key, circa 1950.
(Auction Team Köln)
                          $974

A 19th century French bronze
and glass mantel clock, 8 day
Paris movement sounding the
half hours on a bell and with
Brocot escapement, 30cm. high.
(Duran) $703

An Empire mahogany and
ormolu pendulum mantel clock
of architectural design, the
circular dial with Roman
numerals on a white enamel
face, 53cm. wide
(Finarte) $3,202

A Swiss hexagonal silver 8-day
desk clock, enameled in blue,
signed on box *St. Pauls Lodge
num. 43, Ladies Night 1928*, 9cm.
high.
(Duran) $374

A French 19th century ormolu
bracket clock, the elaborate
rococo style case cast with
scrolls, flowers, and seated
satyrs, on low matching plinth,
3ft. high.
(Russell Baldwin & Bright)
                          $892

CLOCKS & WATCHES

A Louis XVI style French mantel clock, the silvered rectangular dial with porcelain cartouches for the Roman numerals, 19th century, 39cm. high.
(Duran) $1,591

An Empire ormolu mantel clock flanked by the figures of Apollo and Venus, the rectangular base applied with a mythological scene in bas relief, 54cm. high.
(Finarte) $5,693

A George V silver and tortoiseshell-mounted dressing table clock, 14cm. high, William Comyns, London 1910.
(Bearne's) $2,682

An unusual Continental musical portico clock, the circular white enamel dial with black Roman numerals indistinctly inscribed with maker's name, 20in. high overall.
(Spencer's) $2,438

A black wood rectangular mantel clock by Ehrhardt & Söhne Schwäbisch Gmünd, with brass and marquetry dial, circa 1910, 20cm. high.
(Kunsthaus am Museum) $588

A 19th century ormolu mantel clock, the base decorated with putti in a palm leaf border, surmounted by a female figure holding a cornucopia, 68cm. high.
(Finarte) $1,853

A gilt and ormolu French mantel clock, with a female figure leaning on a rocky mound, the dial with Roman numerals and signed *Bioula a Amien*, mid 19th century.
(Herholdt Jensen) $661

1950s round Cartier desk clock, with lapis and gold face and gold and green enamel hands, signed *Cartier nn 8364–5728*.
(Finarte) $7,138

Rare Federal mahogany inlaid shelf timepiece, John Gains, Portsmouth, New Hampshire, circa 1800, eight-day weight driven brass movement, 41in. high.
(Skinner) $22,000

MANTEL CLOCKS

A Victorian gilt-metal mounted porcelain mantel clock with circular white enamel dial inscribed *Hewell and James & Co.*, the case surmounted by two birds resting on stylized cloud bands, 13in. high.
(Christie's) $1,270

A George III mahogany striking clock, the case on gilt brass ball feet with fish-scale sound frets to sides and front door, chapter disc signed *Gravel & Son, London*, 16³/₄in. high.
(Christie's) $1,379

A Victorian helical-geared small skeleton timepiece, the silvered frame with double-screwed pillars, single chain fusée with helical gearing to the anchor escapement, 10in. high.
(Christie's) $2,759

Napoléon III bronze and ormolu mantle clock with automaton rocking ship, the case of naturalistic form with the ormolu figure of Neptune, 21in. high.
(Christie's) $1,725

An early Georgian ebonized mantel clock, by William Webster, the brass dial with silvered chapter ring, inscribed *William Webster, Exchange Alley, London*, 14¹/₂in. high.
(Christie's) $2,904

A Napoléon III ormolu and porcelain mounted striking mantle clock, the oval case draped with ribbon-tied oak leaves, the porcelain panels below painted with cherubs, 18¹/₂in. high.
(Christie's) $2,414

'Sirènes', a Lalique frosted opalescent glass desk clock, the square frame molded in relief with sea sprites, 11.5cm. high.
(Christie's) $2,257

A Napoléon III bronze and ormolu singing bird mantle clock, the glazed case applied with trailing foliage and with acanthus leaf moldings, 16¹/₂in. high.
(Christie's) $4,138

A Vitascope bakelite clock, the pink body enclosing a marine scene of a ship on rough seas, 32cm. high.
(Bonhams) $388

SKELETON CLOCKS

A 19th century English cathedral skeleton clock, with pierced chapter ring and Graham escapement, 40cm. high.
(Duran) $1,030

A 19th century skeleton timepiece, pierced silvered chapter ring, single fusée movement with passing bell strike and dead beat escapement, 14in. high.
(Bonhams) $646

A Victorian skeleton clock with passing strike, the 7in. elaborately pierced silvered dial with Roman numerals, 17in. high.
(Bonhams) $888

A Victorian skeleton timepiece, 5in. pierced silvered dial and Roman numerals, the movement with shaped polished scroll plates, single fusée with chain and half dead beat escapement, 16in. high.
(Bonhams) $775

An unusual English skeleton clock, the movement placed between two C-scrolls, anchor escapement, based on the famous model by William Strutt, 29cm. high.
(Duran) $890

A Victorian skeleton timepiece, the unusual scroll frame surmounted by two crosses, the arcaded Roman chapter ring signed *J. Burton. Bradford*, 16½in. over dome.
(Christie's) $1,106

Single train brass striking skeleton clock by Thwaites, eight day warranted movement, under brass dome, 18in. tall.
(G. A. Key) $1,012

A gilt-brass rolling ball clock of standard form, the posted fusée movement with silvered annular dials, signed *Dent*, 17¾in. high.
(Christie's) $3,404

Brass skeleton clock, spring-driven pendulum striking movement, probably English, 20th century, 16in. high.
(Eldred's) $440

201

WALL CLOCKS

A small tower clock movement, cast iron with brass wheels, anchor escapement, with large black copper dial with gold Roman numerals and hands, dial 105cm. diameter.
(Auction Team Köln)

$2,248

An early 19th century thirty-hour wall alarm timepiece, the 6in. brass dial signed *Whitehurst Derby*.
(Bonhams) $646

Fine custom-made banjo clock by Foster S. Campos of Pembroke, Mass., inlaid mahogany case with presentation bracket, 41¹/₂in. high.
(Eldred's) $1,265

A French Art Deco wall regulator in walnut casing with octagonal silvered metal dial signed *MF Manufacture Francaise d'armes et cycles, Saint Etienne*, circa 1920, 74cm. high.
(Auction Team Köln)

$404

French 'Ox-eye' musical clock in walnut case inlaid with brass and mother of pearl, the marble dial with enamel cartouches, signed *Larroumets à St Palais*, the 43 tooth comb musical movement sounding just before the hour, circa 1860.
(Auction Team Köln)

$3,148

A Junghans wall regulator in carved walnut casing with half columns, the dial with brass chapter ring and Roman numerals, 70cm. high, circa 1890.
(Auction Team Köln)

$337

A fine early Victorian mahogany railway drop-dial clock, by Vulliamy, the 12in. painted mahogany dial with *G.W.R.* logo, 23¹/₂in. high.
(Bonhams) $5,168

A mahogany and eglomise gallery clock, Crosby & Vosburgh, New York, circa 1850, the octagonal surround centering a glazed door, 25ft. ¹/₂in. high.
(Sotheby's) $1,540

A mahogany railway drop-dial clock, 12in. white dial with Roman numerals and initialed *G.W.R.*, 27in. high.
(Bonhams) $614

WALL CLOCKS

CLOCKS & WATCHES

A South German wall timepiece, with a repoussé brass surround and silvered Roman chapter ring, 13¹/₂in. high.
(Bonhams) $614

Federal gilt and mahogany banjo timepiece, attributed to Aaron Willard, Boston, circa 1815, dial inscribed *A. A. Cheney Brookline, Mass*, 42¹/₂in. high.
(Skinner) $6,820

An early Victorian mahogany drop-dial railway clock, the restored 12in. white dial with Roman numerals and initialed *G.W.R.*, 23in. high.
(Bonhams) $888

A late 19th century French wall clock, the 8 day movement striking on a bell, in bronze casing with red latticework under, signed *Philippe FT 66 Paris Royal 67*.
(Auction Team Köln) $712

A Glasgow style wall clock, pewter covered curved triangular form with chased Arabic numerals, the hands set with abalone, 27.4cm. high.
(Christie's) $3,062

A fine Federal mahogany and eglomisé panel banjo clock, Lemuel Curtis, Massachusetts, circa 1815, the circular glazed dial door with brass bezel enclosing a white-painted dial with Roman numeral chapter ring, 33¹/₂in. high.
(Christie's) $20,900

Giltwood mirror wall timepiece, A. Chandler, Concord, New Hampshire, circa 1830, 30in. high.
(Skinner) $1,870

A Big Ben musical picture clock in black wooden case, the melody playing every quarter, or on pulling the cord, 70cm. high.
(Auction Team Köln) $487

A mid 18th century Amsterdam oak hooded Friesland clock, the repeat alarm movement with an anchor escapement.
(Woolley & Wallis) $4,496

WALL CLOCKS

Victorian Vienna wall clock, with a striking movement to an **enameled and brass dial, glazed door and side panels to a walnut case.**
(G. A. Key) $573

An Art Deco theater clock, cast iron, with the current time on the left and the end of the programe on the right, circa 1920.
(Auction Team Köln)
                $170

A fine Caledonian Railway signal box wall regulator clock, in truncated mahogany wall case with circular sliding hood, 62in. high.
(Christie's) $3,259

A Comtoise longcase clock movement, the white enamel dial with Roman numerals and quarters in Arabic numerals, signed *Lafabrie Hger a Nogaro*, the cast brass face with sun and putti, 1810–20.
(Auction Team Köln)
                $2,173

A Viennese quarter striking picture clock, the painting on copper depicting a harvest scene with the sea and mountains in the background, circa 1860, 35^1/$_4$ x 36^1/$_2$in.
(Christie's) $3,449

A Louis XV ormolu cartel clock with circular glazed enamel Roman-chaptered dial and movement signed *Etienne Le Noir A Paris*, in a raised rockwork and scroll cartouche, 22in. high.
(Christie's) $7,994

A German ISGUS time-clock in oak case with brass mountings, the metal dial with Arabic numerals, with two-color stamping mechanism, 108cm. high, circa 1930–5.
(Auction Team Köln)
                $824

A Regency mahogany wall timepiece, the silvered engraved dial signed *Edw. Tutet London*, Roman and Arabic chapters, 15^3/$_4$in. diameter.
(Christie's) $1,293

A classical carved mahogany and eglomisé eight-day wall clock, labeled *Eli Terry, Jr.*, Connecticut, circa 1835, height 36in.
(Sotheby's) $1,955

WALL CLOCKS

A late 18th century French cartel clock, urn shaped and festooned with laurels, with a female face above the dial and pineapple finial, the white enamel face signed *Hartingue, Paris.* (Finarte) $4,070

A rare French automaton clock picture, Napoléon III, Paris, circa 1851, depicting the Crystal Palace, Hyde Park, with two rows of automated figures, 122cm. wide. (Sotheby's) $11,543

Victorian Vienna wall clock with striking movement, the mahogany case with fluted detail, glazed door and side panels. (G. A. Key) $653

An imposing late 19th century shop interior wall clock and bracket, the 17¹/₂in. cream painted dial with black Roman numerals inscribed *Fredjohns Ltd, Jewellers, Wimbledon*, total height 62in. (Bearne's) $1,371

English station clock, in mahogany casing, striking on the hour, the white metal dial with large black Roman numerals, signed *T Barton & Sons*, 64cm. high, first half 19th century. (Auction Team Köln) $375

A George II black lacquered striking Act of Parliament clock, the dial of typical cartouche outline with ogee-moulded frame surmounted by two gilt-wood flambeau finials, 61in. high. (Christie's) $12,765

A Victorian mahogany wall regulator, signed *Jas. Gowland, London Wall*, 12in. painted dial, concentric minute ring, subsidiary seconds and hour dial, 3ft. 8in. high. (Bonhams) $3,474

A musical clock set into the frame of a Bavarian landscape picture, with Roman numerals and playing two melodies. (Herholdt Jensen) $770

Howard banjo clock in rosewood veneers, black, dark red and gilt reverse-painted tablet with throat glass, 28¹/₂in. high. (Eldred's) $1,375

WATCHES

Vacheron Constantin, a German issue Luftwaffe watch, the silvered dial with Arabic numerals and subsidiary dials for seconds, 60mm.
(Bonhams) **$2,422**

A nickel cased railway watch, cracked white enamel dial with Roman numerals, inscribed *G.W.R.*
(Bonhams) **$210**

A gold French verge pocket watch, by Le Roy A Paris, white enamel dial with Roman numerals and outer Arabic minute ring, 40mm.
(Bonhams) **$618**

A silver repoussé pair cased verge watch, signed *T. May*, pierced bridge balance cock, plain pillars, white enamel dial border with black Roman numerals, London 1796, 52mm.
(Bonhams) **$733**

A silver pair cased verge pocket watch, square baluster pillar movement signed *Jmᵗ Robinson*, in an outer shagreen covered case, London 1745, 50mm.
(Bonhams) **$888**

Rolex, 9ct. gold two-tone dress watch, silver dial, signed *Rolex Prince Imperial*, concentric chapter ring at 12 o'clock and subsidiary seconds below, H.M. Glasgow 1931, 42mm.
(Bonhams) **$1,197**

An 8 day pocket watch by Wyss Freres, Switzerland, in nickel steel case, the white enamel **decentralized dial with black** Arabic numerals and engraved, 5cm. diameter, circa 1910.
(Auction Team Köln)
$225

A silver pocket watch by the Cortebert Watch Mfg Co, with Swiss anchor escapement, the **two colored enamel dial with** windows for hours and minutes and seconds dial below, 5.5cm. diameter, circa 1900.
(Auction Team Köln)
$525

A silver verge pocket watch, the white enamel face signed *Gabriel Mansion a Huy* and with Arabic numerals, 5.5cm. diameter, 1800–50.
(Auction Team Köln)
$225

WATCHES

An English 18ct. gold open faced fusée pocket watch, the gilt dial with checker pattern center and Roman chapter with subsidiary seconds, Chester 1871, 52mm.
(Bonhams) $646

A Hamilton American gold watch, the Swiss anchor movement with Breguet escapement and compensation balance, the silvered dial with Arabic numerals, 4.5cm. diameter, circa 1920.
(Auction Team Köln) $323

A silver pair cased verge watch, signed *Alfred Heald Wisbech*, white enamel dial with painted center of a rural scene of a man ploughing the land, London 1860, 55mm.
(Bonhams) $367

A silver, part-gilt watch with white enamel dial, the movement signed *Le Fleuron, Beaucort*, the back with floral relief decoration, circa 1900, 4cm. diameter.
(Auction Team Köln) $210

An Elgin watch in very narrow 14ct gold case, Swiss anchor movement, the dial with gilt Arab numerals, 17 jewels, 4.5cm. diameter, circa 1920.
(Auction Team Köln) $127

A silvered Arnex pocket watch with the profiles of John and Robert Kennedy in relief on the back, the white enamel dial with the American eagle and Stars and Stripes in the center, circa 1970.
(Auction Team Köln) $127

A silver pair cased verge watch, signed *Geo Robinson*, white enamel dial with the name *John Robinson* written around the inside of the border, H.M. London 1789, 60mm.
(Bonhams) $579

A digital pocket watch, in brass case, the white enamel dial with apertures for the hours and minutes, with seconds dial under, 5cm. diameter, circa 1900.
(Auction Team Köln) $501

An open faced silver verge watch, signed *Robt. Neill Belfast*, silver dial with applied gilt Roman numbers with subsidiary second dial and foliage border, hallmark, London 1820, 55mm.
(Bonhams) $270

WATCHES

A skeleton pocket watch in octagonal faceted rock crystal case, with plain Roman numerals and steel hand.
(Christie's) $4,719

Russells Ltd., Liverpool, an 18ct. gold minute repeating keyless hunter pocketwatch in plain case with engraved monogram to the front cover and armorial crest to the reverse, hallmarked *London 1920*, 53mm. diameter.
(Christie's) $4,655

A gold openface quarter repeating pocketwatch in engine turned drum case, the white enamel dial with Arabic numerals signed at VI *Breguet et Fils*, 54mm. diameter.
(Christie's) $12,070

An English silver pocket watch, the porcelain dial with a shield flanked by two females and marked *Amicitia Amor et Veritas* beneath the letter *G*, by P. R. J. Ness, marks for Birmingham 1838, 55mm. diameter.
(Duran) $450

An English silver verge pocket watch, the movement signed *London Nr 525*, the enamel face painted with a castle motif, the centralized dial with Arabic numerals and gilt hands, 5.5cm. diameter, circa 1850.
(Auction Team Köln) $1,874

A 10 carat gold plated railwayman's pocket watch, the bar movement signed *Made in USA*, with white enamel dial signed *Hamilton* and black Arabic numerals, 5cm. diameter, circa 1905.
(Auction Team Köln) $330

An early 20th century gold pocket watch, the case set with black enamel with a swallow in rose diamonds on one side and a flower in rose diamonds on the other.
(Finarte) $1,020

Dunhill, an 18ct. white gold, diamond and emerald-set petrol burning lighter with watch inset to the hinged front cover, 43 x 38mm.
(Christie's) $5,518

Cartier, a King George VI £5 coin containing a watch, with concealed catch in the rim, the matt silvered dial with Roman numerals and blued steel moon hands, 36mm. diameter.
(Christie's) $4,138

WATCHES

An 18th century French ladies' watch hanging from a brooch, the gold case with a double secret back opening to reveal an erotic scene.
(Duran) $7,488

An open-faced pocket watch with gilt dial and serpentine hands, with engine-turned and reeded case.
(Christie's) $871

An 18ct. gold pair-cased pocket watch with repoussé decoration by Porthouse, Penrith 1766.
(Christie's) $2,359

An 18th century Swiss gold repeating pocket watch, the white porcelain dial signed *Jn Chaponniere à Genève*, the case **enameled with figures and musical symbols**, 50mm. diameter.
(Duran) $8,425

A French gold quarter repeating pocket watch, the face with Roman numerals and guilloché border.
(Finarte) $3,319

A gold enamel and stone-set minute repeating keyless hunter pocketwatch for the Eastern market, the covers decorated with translucent green enamel on guilloche background, 55mm. diameter.
(Christie's) $7,242

A calendar watch with anchor escapement, the white enamel dial with Roman and Arabic numerals and subsidiary dials for seconds, date, weekdays and moonphases, 67mm. diameter.
(Auktionsverket) $554

Swiss desk watch in large black metal case, gilt and enamel dial with minute and hour hand, leather case, 3³/₄in. diameter.
(Eldred's) $523

A 14ct. gold double dial calendar watch with anchor escapement, the rear dial showing the date and day of the week, 53mm. diameter.
(Auktionsverket) $1,340

WRIST WATCHES

A 1920's gold curvex tonneau
wristwatch, the matt white dial
with gilt Arabic numerals,
signed *Tiffany & Co.*, 35 x
26mm.
(Christie's) $1,983

A large 1930s Longines aviator's
hour angle watch, the enamel
chapter ring signed *A. Cairelli,
Roma*, 46mm. diameter.
(Bonhams) $3,876

Rolex Oyster, chrome plated
wristwatch, white enamel dial,
black Roman figures, nickel
lever movement, in a cushion
shaped case, 32mm.
(Bonhams) $405

A gold chronograph wristwatch
in circular case, the silvered dial
with outer tachymetric scale,
Arabic numerals, subsidiary
dials for running seconds,
elapsed minutes, hours and date,
31mm. diameter.
(Christie's) $1,724

A gentleman's 9ct. gold Oyster
wristwatch, the two-tone
silvered dial inscribed *Rolex
Oyster*, subsidiary seconds,
Glasgow 1934.
(Bonhams) $1,615

A steel automatic Voyager
calendar wristwatch in typical
case, the rotating bezel inscribed
with various capital cities, the
white dial with outer 24 hour
ring, 37mm. diameter.
(Christie's) $1,724

Rolex, a gold steel Oyster
perpetual chronometer
wristwatch in tonneau case with
pink gold bezel and winder,
31mm. diameter.
(Christie's) $1,552

A 'Rolex Oyster Perpetual
Submariner' wristwatch in
stainless steel case.
(Bearne's) $805

An 18ct. pink gold Rolex Oyster-
perpetual 'day-date' wristwatch
in tonneau shaped case.
(Bearne's) $2,160

WRIST WATCHES

Rolex, gentleman's 18ct. rose gold round cased wristwatch, nickel seventeen jewel chronometer, hand wound movement with center seconds, circa 1960, 35mm.
(Bonhams) $849

A gentleman's stainless steel chronograph wristwatch, the silvered dial inscribed *Breitling Premier*, Arabic numerals, 35mm.
(Bonhams) $565

A gentleman's 1960's period Rolex Oyster Perpetual wristwatch, the circular silvered dial inscribed *Rolex Oyster Perpetual – Officially Certified Chronometer*.
(Spencer's) $645

Vacheron & Constantin, Genève, an 18ct. gold perpetual calendar and moonphase automatic wristwatch, cream dial with raised baton numerals, 35mm. diameter.
(Christie's) $11,725

Patek Philippe, a 1960's white gold automatic perpetual calendar wristwatch, the matt gilt dial with raised baton numerals, subsidiary date ring with sector for the moon, apertures for day and month, 37mm. diameter.
(Christie's) $24,140

Patek Phillipe, a late 1940's gold wristwatch in circular case with fluted lugs, the silvered dial with raised dagger numerals and sweep center seconds, 32mm. diameter.
(Christie's) $4,483

A gentleman's stainless steel cased Rolex wristwatch, the champagne dial with luminous Arabic numerals, in a case of plain circular form.
(Spencer's) $419

Patek Philippe, Genève, an 18ct. gold and diamond-set ladies wristwatch in circular shaped case, the bezel and dial set with diamonds, 30mm. diameter.
(Christie's) $5,690

A stainless steel Mickey Mouse wristwatch, the dial signed *Disney Watch, Made in France*, the seconds in inset dial shown by a small red globe with Mickey Mouse ears.
(Auction Team Köln) $90

A Hagenauer brass bowl, the cylindrical foot pierced with stylized golfing scenes, 20cm. diameter.
(Christie's) $669

19th century helmet shaped embossed brass coal scuttle, 19in. high.
(G. A. Key) $126

An early 18th century brass upright scissor snuffer and holder, of urn shape with an octagonal base.
(Lawrence) $434

A Siebe, Gorman & Co. brass and copper diver's helmet, 50cm. high, and a 1916 Admiralty Diving manual.
(Bearne's) $2,025

A pair of W. A. S. Benson chamber sticks, copper and brass, each on flared stepped base with curved up-turned handles, the sconce in the form of a lotus flower, 13.8cm. high.
(Christie's) $383

A miner's brass safety lamp by the Koehler Mfg. Co., Marlboro, MA, USA, with original key, circa 1910.
(Auction Team Köln) $101

Medium size 19th century oval copper kettle and lid.
(G. A. Key) $151

A set of six brass drum measures, stamped *FAIRBANKS*, 1 gal-1 gill.
(Christie's) $378

Large early 19th century globular formed copper samovar with lid, ring handles, brass tap and rectangular base, 16in. high.
(G. A. Key) $179

Eight-piece Chester Billings & Son beverage set, circa 1910, round tray of hammered brass with applied hammered silver rim, 9¹/₂in. high.
(Skinner) $2,310

Large Georgian brass footman on cabriole front legs with carrying handles.
(G. A. Key) $530

A copper oil can of squat round bombé form, with spiral handle and slender curving spout, circa 1800, 28cm. high.
(Auktionsverket) $198

Art Nouveau copper fire screen, England, circa 1900, framed in wrought iron, central ceramic insert with blue glaze, unsigned, 28¹/₂in. high.
(Skinner) $330

A pair of Georgian brass candlesticks, second quarter, 19th century, each with molded flaring bobèche and turned stem with push-up mechanism over a beaded baluster, 8¹/₂in. high.
(Christie's) $462

A Dutch brass and copper jardinière, the open circular top above bombé sides with lion-mask and ring-handles, on studded plinth base, 20¹/₄in. high.
(Christie's) $2,274

A yellow copper collection plate with a central repoussé medallion surrounded by inscriptions, 17th century German.
(Galerie Moderne) $1,058

A Regency gilt-copper and ebonized inkstand, the rectangular top with molded bead-and-laurel edge with two dished pen-trays, centered by a chamber candlestick with gadrooned edge and turned shaft, 13¹/₄in. wide.
(Christie's) $8,752

A brass bucket, with a swing handle and incised ribbing, 9¹/₂in. diameter.
(Lawrence) $607

Gebelein hammered copper bowl, circa 1915, repeating foliate band with copper finish rim and stepped disc base, 8¹/₂in. diameter.
(Skinner) $330

A George III copper plate warmer, of cylindrical helmet shape, on three cabriole feet, 20in. high.
(Lawrence) $729

A brass jardinière with rounded rectangular open top above a studded frieze, the sides with lion-mask and ring-handles, on paw feet, 19th century, 26¹/₂in. wide.
(Christie's) $2,731

Pair of Jarvie style copper candlesticks, bulbous candle nozzle on tapering stem on disc base, bronze patina, unsigned, 14¹/₂in. high.
(Skinner) $550

Three brass candlesticks, early 18th century, with short faceted tapering stems above a circular stem over a circular dish drip pan, 6¹/₂in. high.
(Christie's) $2,860

Jarvie brass three-branch candelabra, circa 1905, three removable trumpet bobeches supported by coiling arms mounted on central shaft, 10¹/₄in. high.
(Skinner) $1,210

A John Pearson repoussé charger, 1903, hand wrought copper, the underside engraved *J.P. 1903*, 12³/₈in. diameter.
(Sotheby's) $648

Two rare large brass candlesticks, Continental, 17th century, 11¹/₂ and 11⁵/₈in. high.
(Sotheby's) $1,760

An Artificers Guild hammered brass bowl designed by Edward Spencer, supported on six-shaped feet with pierced openwork decoration of stylized foliage, 19.7cm. high.
(Christie's) $1,244

A ship's external lantern of copper and brass with red glass for the stern, fitted for electricity, 'Red Light', Japan. (Auction Team Köln)

$117

A brass fireplace jamb hook, possibly American, circa 1800, the bifurcated C-scroll support with two ball-and-steeple finials, 4¼in. wide. (Christie's)

$440

A Wiener Werkstätte brass five-piece coffee service, designed by Josef Hoffmann, each piece stamped with designer's monogram, *Made in Austria*, 22.6cm. height of coffee pot. (Christie's)

$7,656

A Glasgow style copper wall sconce, rectangular, with repoussé decoration of peacocks amid stylized honesty, 36.5cm. high. (Christie's)

$479

A pair of Georgian brass candlesticks, 18th century, each with cylindrical stem with a low drip cup, 8in. high. (Christie's)

$4,400

One of a pair of 18th century Dutch embossed copper wall sconces, decorated with two seated cherubs above an oval shield, with scrolling upswept arms, 31cm. wide. (Phillips) (Two)

$1,260

Gustav Stickley copper serving tray, no. 274 variant, circa 1907, wide rim with riveted handles and hammered finish, 16⅞in. diameter. (Skinner)

$550

A pair of Georgian brass candlesticks, stamped *Geo. Grove*, each with flaring bobèche above a molded candlecup and knopped stem, 7¼in. high. (Christie's)

$1,540

A Dinanderie brass alms dish embossed with the Paschal lamb, with everted rim and geometric decoration, 16in. diameter. (Christie's)

$586

A pair of embroidered gauntlet gloves, English, early 17th century, of white kid leather, embroidered in raised work gold purl wire, 13¼in. long overall. (Sotheby's) $1,215

A pair of ladies' shoes of pale blue moiré grosgrain silk with ivory satin covered 2¼in. heels and straps, 1782. (Christie's) $911

A pair of rare young girl's hoops composed of an oval hoop with two supporting bands, covered with padded glazed linen, mid 18th century. (Christie's) $8,635

A gentleman's waistcoat of ivory satin, woven à disposition with chocolate cut and ciselé velvet floral border and pockets, 1740s. (Christie's) $695

A doublet of black wool with small ball buttons possibly made of horsehair, early 17th entury. (Christie's) $7,378

A Royal Company of Archers uniform comprising a coat of tartan trimmed with green braid, mid 18th century. (Christie's) $17,138

An Indian chintz open robe, circa 1780, the Indian cotton printed with rosebriars, stylized blue and red flowerheads, original linen lining. (Sotheby's) $1,735

A pair of kid gloves, the ivory silk gauntlets embroidered in coloured silks, gilt threads and spangles, English, circa 1610. (Christie's) $2,524

A gentleman's suit of pale green silk with a figured pin stripe, faced and lined with pink silk, 1770s. (Christie's) $5,960

A printed silk gentleman's morning-gown, circa 1830–40, the yellow ground printed with brown stripes of angular foliage and black spots.
(Sotheby's) $607

A Jeanne Lanvin embroidered evening jacket, Paris, autumn-winter, 1925–26, with large woven satin label.
(Sotheby's) $625

A Jeanne Lanvin printed chiffon summer dress, Paris, summer 1931, with large woven silk label.
(Sotheby's) $434

An open robe of chintz printed with exotic scrolling flowers in red, blue and purple, circa 1780.
(Christie's) $29,123

Gentleman's embroidered silk waistcoat, circa 1820, embroidered with silk threads, chenille yarns and ribbon in shades of blue, yellow, taupe.
(Skinner) $468

An evening coat of deep brown wool, the vermilion velvet collar heavily embroidered with gilt leather flowers, labeled *Schiaparelli, London*, 1937.
(Christie's) $8,635

A sack-backed open robe and petticoat of pink silk brocaded with sprays of orange and pink flowers, circa 1755–60.
(Christie's) $13,530

A fine pair of Woodlands tanned skin moccasins, the brown velvet cuffs sewn with flowers and leaves in colored and transparent beads.
(Christie's) $3,993

An open robe of dark ground chintz, printed with lily of the valley and other flowers, late 1790s.
(Christie's) $2,418

A Belton-type bisque doll, French, circa 1880, the domed head with fair mohair wig and ball jointed wood and composition body, 11in. high. (Sotheby's) $1,487

A Catterfelder Puppenfabrik bisque doll, German, circa 1910, with open/closed mouth, painted brown eyes, and curved limb composition body, 14½in. high. (Sotheby's) $735

A bisque-headed character doll modeled as an Oriental, with dark eyes, pierced ears, and jointed wood and composition body, 14½in. high. (Christie's) $1,584

A wax-over composition headed doll, with blue eyes, blonde mohair wig, stuffed body with wax limbs, 17in. high. (Christie's) $1,089

A Rohmer shoulder-china fashion doll and her trunk, French, circa 1865, with closed mouth, fixed blue glass eyes, together with her trunk of studded black rexine, 13¾in. high. (Sotheby's) $2,623

A Simon & Halbig three faced bisque doll, German, circa 1890, the faces turning by means of a ring in the cardboard cowl, 13in. high. (Sotheby's) $787

A DEP bisque musical doll, French, circa 1900, with open mouth and upper teeth, fixed blue glass eyes, and jointed wood and composition body, 18in. high. (Sotheby's) $1,749

A shoulder china pedlar doll, German, circa 1870, the face with painted features and center parted black hair, 9in. high. (Sotheby's) $5,247

A Heubach Koppelsdorf painted black bisque doll, German, circa 1926, with open mouth and two lower teeth, fixed brown glass eyes, and five piece composition body, 16in. high. (Sotheby's) $612

A Rabery & Delphieu bisque doll, French, circa 1890, with fair real hair wig and jointed wood and composition body, 13in. high.
(Sotheby's) $1,137

A shoulder-Parian bisque doll, German, circa 1850, with painted features and blue eyes, the cloth body with bisque lower limbs, 15in. high.
(Sotheby's) $1,224

A bisque-headed character doll, with dark sleeping eyes, blonde wig, jointed wood and composition toddler body, 17½in. high.
(Christie's) $1,584

A poured wax-headed doll, with blue inset eyes, light brown hair inset in ringlets, stuffed body with wax limbs, 24in. high.
(Christie's) $2,376

A rare Lenci pressed felt 'Bersagliere' soldier doll, Italian, circa 1920, with painted face and brown eyes, in original Lenci box.
(Sotheby's) $1,399

A bisque-headed three-faced doll, smiling, sleeping and crying, the stuffed body with jointed limbs, 14in. high.
(Christie's) $1,287

An Armand Marseille bisque googly doll, German, circa 1914, with closed smiling mouth, weighted blue glass eyes, and five piece composition body, 9in. high.
(Sotheby's) $787

A bisque-headed character doll, with closed pouty mouth, painted features, fair mohair wig, and jointed wood and composition toddler body, 13in. high.
(Christie's) $2,178

A Simon and Halbig bisque Oriental doll, German, circa 1895, with open mouth and upper teeth, weighted brown glass eyes, and jointed wood and composition body, 15in. high.
(Sotheby's) $874

DOLLS

A Bruno Schmidt bisque Oriental doll, German, circa 1905, with open mouth and upper teeth, weighted brown glass eyes, and jointed wood and composition body, 13³/₄in. high. (Sotheby's) $1,049

A Tête Jumeau molded bisque doll, French, circa 1895, with red real hair wig and jointed wood and composition body in white muslin dress with navy wool coat, 18in. high. (Sotheby's) $5,247

A Delcroix molded bisque doll, French, circa 1897, with well painted eyebrows, pierced ears, brown real hair wig and eight ball jointed wood and composition body, 19³/₄in. high. (Sotheby's) $10,494

An Henri Alexandre Bébé Phénix pressed bisque doll, French, 1889, with blonde mohair wig and jointed wood and composition body in red gingham dress, 15³/₄in. high. (Sotheby's) $3,498

A Bru Jeune pressed bisque doll, French, circa 1885, with open/closed mouth showing white between lips, together with a trunk in red, banded and studded, 15in. high. (Sotheby's) $8,745

An E.D., for Jumeau moulded bisque doll, French, circa 1890, with fixed blue glass paperweight eyes, pierced ears and red real hair wig over cork pate, 19in. high. (Sotheby's) $1,137

A Kämmer & Reinhardt/Simon & Halbig bisque character doll, German, circa 1911, with closed pouty mouth, in original navy spotted white sailor dress and straw bonnet, 16¹/₂in. high. (Sotheby's) $4,722

A Kämmer & Reinhardt bisque character doll, German, circa 1909, with closed pouty mouth, and jointed wood and composition body, 19in. high. (Sotheby's) $3,148

An A. Thuillier pressed bisque doll, French, circa 1875, with open/closed mouth, fixed blue glass paperweight eyes, and jointed wood and composition body, 13¹/₂in. high. (Sotheby's) $22,737

A fine Casimir Bru circle and dot pressed bisque doll, French, circa 1875, in eau-de-nil brocaded satin dress with aubergine satin edging and silk bows, 20½in. high.
(Sotheby's) $24,486

A Jumeau pressed bisque portrait doll, French, circa 1870, with fixed blue glass paperweight eyes, pierced ears, blonde mohair wig and a jointed wood body, 18½in. high.
(Sotheby's) $11,368

A Danel et Cie molded bisque doll, French, 1891, with red check marks, closed mouth, fixed blue glass eyes, and jointed wood and composition body, 15¾in. high.
(Sotheby's) $5,597

A Bru pressed bisque swivel head fashion doll, French, circa 1875, with closed mouth, fixed blue glass eyes, pierced ears, brown real hair wig and jointed wood body, 15¾in. high.
(Sotheby's) $4,897

A Bähr & Pröschild bisque Oriental doll, German, circa 1888, with closed mouth, fixed black glass eyes, with wooden composition body in original green and polychrome patterned dress, 13¼in. high.
(Sotheby's) $1,836

An 'H' pressed bisque doll, French, circa 1880, impressed 2/0 H, with open/closed mouth, fixed blue glass eyes, and jointed wood and composition body, 15in. high.
(Sotheby's) $73,458

A painted felt-headed doll by Lenci, with brown side-glancing eyes, original felt-trimmed organdy dress, green felt bolero, shoes and hair ribbon, 16in. high.
(Christie's) $376

A Kämmer & Reinhardt/Simon & Halbig bisque character doll, German, circa 1912, with open mouth and two upper teeth, 17¾in. high.
(Sotheby's) $1,049

A Jumeau molded bisque doll, French, circa 1880, with jointed wood and composition body with bisque hands in original red white and blue spotted dress with red sash, 25½in. high.
(Sotheby's) $4,897

A bisque headed key-wind walking doll, German, circa 1905, the wood and composition body with jointed arms and straight walking legs, activated by a key-wind mechanism in the body, 16¹/₂in. high.
(Sotheby's) $840

A Huret shoulder-china doll, French, circa 1860, with closed mouth, painted blue eyes, blonde lambswool wig over cork pate and jointed wood body, 17¹/₄in. high.
(Sotheby's) $7,171

A mechanical walking/talking bisque doll, German head on French body, circa 1910, the head impressed *DEP*, with open mouth and molded upper teeth, 23¹/₂in. high.
(Sotheby's) $1,224

A Bru pressed bisque bébé, French, circa 1880, with open/closed mouth and simulated tongue, in checked pink, brown and beige silk dress and broderie-anglaise bonnet, 15³/₄in. high.
(Sotheby's) $19,239

A Jumeau triste pressed bisque doll, French, circa 1875, in apricot silk dress with embroidered white muslin overdress and pintucked cotton petticoats, 28in. high.
(Sotheby's) $8,745

A J. D. Kestner shoulder-bisque doll, German, circa 1880, with closed smiling mouth, dimple in chin, fixed blue glass eyes, the kid body with ne plus ultra hip joints and Universal knee joints, 24in. high.
(Sotheby's) $1,836

A Simon & Halbig Gr 46 bisque-headed doll, open mouth, blue sleeping eyes, pierced ears, wig replaced, 46cm. long, circa 1910.
(Auction Team Köln)
     $695

Sailor doll with composition head and cloth body, sewn-on hands and feet, circa 1940, 46cm. long.
(Auction Team Köln) $58

A bisque swivel-headed doll, with closed mouth and pale blue wool sailor suit, tucked underclothes, shoes and socks, 14in. high.
(Christie's) $1,584

A Bru two faced bisque doll, French, circa 1880, with painted blue eyes, the other face laughing with similar mouth and eyes, 15³/₄in. high.
(Sotheby's) $6,121

Bähr and Proschild type bisque head doll with wooden jointed arms and legs, painted features with open mouth and six upper teeth.
(Eldred's) $275

A Petit et Dumontier pressed bisque doll, French, circa 1880, the eight ball jointed wood and composition body with metal hands in cream satin lace paneled dress and black velvet and straw bonnet, 18in. high.
(Sotheby's) $12,243

A fine pale pressed bisque Jumeau portrait doll, French, circa 1875, with blonde curly mohair wig over cork pate and the eight ball jointed wood and composition body with straight wrists, 24¹/₂in. high.
(Sotheby's) $20,988

A fine large Bru Jeune pressed bisque doll, French, circa 1875, with open/closed mouth, dimple in chin, large blue glass paperweight eyes with well painted lashes, 35¹/₂in. high.
(Sotheby's) $26,235

A François Gaultier pressed bisque doll, French, circa 1880, with auburn real hair wig and gusseted kid body with bisque forearms in beige velvet and rose pink moiré paneled dress, 24in. high.
(Sotheby's) $6,996

An S.F.B.J. black bisque character doll, French, circa 1910, with jointed wood and composition body in striped velvet trousers and rust velvet waistcoat over cream shirt, 13³/₄in. high.
(Sotheby's) $1,662

A François Gaultier pressed bisque swivel head doll, French, circa 1870, with separately stitched fingers in brown velvet lace edged dress and brown shoes incised 7, 21¹/₄in. high.
(Sotheby's) $2,798

A François Gaultier swivel head bisque fashion doll, French, circa 1865, with closed mouth, fixed pale blue glass eyes, and gusseted kid body, 20in. high.
(Sotheby's) $1,749

A patented American cast iron Enterprise coffee grinder on wooden base, US patent dated *21 October 1873*, 32cm. high. (Auction Team Köln)

$271

A Fletcher Russell 'Celebrity' **copper disk hot water heater** with bracket, circa 1905. (Christie's) $107

A Philips speaker with original flex and plug, 1928. (Auction Team Köln) $308

Crescent electric fire on a cast Art Nouveau base, circa 1920. (Auction Team Köln) $109

Ericsson skeleton desk telephone with magneto and enclosed mouth-piece, circa 1910. (Auction Team Köln) $1,543

An American automatic mouse trap with guillotine action, circa 1905. (Auction Team Köln) $77

Cigarette dispenser in the form of a church tower, cast iron, Russian. (Auction Team Köln) $16

Wooden 12 litre butter churner, the 'New style white cedar', almost unused. (Auction Team Köln) $85

An unusual automatic butter slicer by Strite-Anderson Mfg. Co., Minneapolis, with **enameled base, circa 1920.** (Auction Team Köln) $139

An Ericsson wall telephone with fixed mouthpiece and bell shaped ear piece, black metal housing and plated double bell, circa 1915.
(Auction Team Köln)
$346

A Bernhardiner nutcracker of cast iron in the form of a dog, on a chromed base.
(Auction Team Köln) $85

An early patented plated American desk telephone by the Western Electric Company, of candlestick form, 1904.
(Auction Team Köln)
$293

An early General Electric fan in an unusually decorative 'Industry-Design', detachable, motor with rotor, circa 1925.
(Auction Team Köln) $131

Cast iron American 'Sensible Press' winepress, complete with seive, by N. R. Streeter & Co., Rochester, New York, 42cm. high, circa 1920.
(Auction Team Köln) $54

A Fitzgerald Model 430 electric fan, gold-brown, with designer stand, circa 1955.
(Auction Team Köln) $85

An Original Edison Hotpoint Automatic percolator, plated housing, possibly unused, with original 110v flex, 1924.
(Auction Team Köln) $154

A Western Electric magneto telephone with japanned finish, splayed feet and Bell Telephone Mfg. Co. handset, circa 1906.
(Christie's) $817

Yellow cast samovar with original tray, circa 1880, 56cm. high.
(Auction Team Köln) $77

IRONS

A Beefall early English cast iron gas iron with front flue turned sideways, 1896.
(Auction Team Köln)
$339

A 19th century Egyptian foot iron, 75cm. long.
(Auction Team Köln)
$617

An English patented Salter's gas iron with air regulator, circa 1910.
(Auction Team Köln)
$117

East Frisian charcoal iron, an early brass iron with cold tip for ironing ruches and bands, 19.5cm. long, circa 1800.
(Auction Team Köln)
$254

An early cast tailor's iron, with handle support and original brass mounted wooden handle, 19cm. long.
(Auction Team Köln)
$232

An early American flat iron No. 3, of unusual rounded shape, cast iron with wooden handle, 18cm. long, circa 1870.
(Auction Team Köln)
$540

An Omega spirit iron, a pointed nickeled iron with transverse barrel-like tank, 20cm. long, circa 1905.
(Auction Team Köln)
$139

A brass box iron with horn handle and hinged closure, imprinted *Heinrich Thomsen, Boholzau* and dated *1876*.
(Auction Team Köln)
$77

An American Steam-o-Matic Model B-300 early electric steam iron made by Waverly Prod. Inc in cast aluminium housing, 1944.
(Auction Team Köln)
$27

IRONS

The American Fluter pleating iron by the American Machine Co., Philadelphia, the heated plate hinged for inserting the heating iron, 1895.
(Auction Team Köln) $123

An English The Rhythm No. 375 U Radiation gas iron, enameled in black and green, complete with enameled stand.
(Auction Team Köln) $69

An American Crown pleating iron by the American Machine Co., Philadelphia, with table clamp and brass rollers, 1880.
(Auction Team Köln)
$216

An early Diamond Self Heating Iron gas iron with 45° calibrated nickeled tank, wooden handle and inscribed *Patented 27 Oct, 1914.*
(Auction Team Köln)
$170

A brass charcoal iron, lacking wooden handle, with cold tip and spring-hinged lid, circa 1900.
(Auction Team Köln) $66

A charcoal iron, richly decorated with dragon closure and American handle, circa 1870.
(Auction Team Köln) $69

Geneva Hand Fluter, a small American pleating iron, 14cm. long.
(Auction Team Köln)
$186

American Hand Fluter, a hinged heatable pleating machine by North Bros. Mfg. Co., Philadelphia, 17cm. long, circa 1880.
(Auction Team Köln)
$186

Westphalian Oxtongue iron, with asbestos heating mantel in the interior and porcelain handle, 19cm. long, circa 1870.
(Auction Team Köln)
$254

A Staffordshire enamel snuff box of rectangular shape and with turquoise ground, the cover painted with a lady and gentleman in the park of a country house, 7.5cm.
(Phillips) $2,639

A Staffordshire scent bottle case, printed and colored with panels of figures in classical and rustic landscapes, 5.8cm.
(Phillips) $400

A Staffordshire enamel rectangular box, painted in colors with two lovers in elegant 18th century dress, 9cm.
(Phillips) $800

A fine enameled and gilt bowl, Jules Barbe, probably for Thomas Webb and Sons, Stourbridge, late 19th century, painted with large flowers against an acid-finished reserve, 8¼in. diameter.
(Sotheby's) $2,898

A Staffordshire enamel patch box of oval form, the cover painted in colors with a scene of a Punch and Judy puppet show, 4cm.
(Phillips) $447

A rare Staffordshire boar's head bonbonnière, the cover painted with a seated figure of Zephyrus, 6.5cm.
(Phillips) $2,880

A Staffordshire enamel snuff box, the cover painted with two couples at a card table, the inner cover with a lady on a bed eagerly awaiting the ministrations of a priest, 9cm.
(Phillips) $3,857

A small Staffordshire bullfinch bonbonnière with black head, red breast and gray and black plumage, 3.8cm.
(Phillips) $640

An English enamel circular snuff box painted on the cover with a standing figure of an old shepherd, 7cm. diameter.
(Phillips) $2,030

Les Cuisines Républicaine de 1795.96 ... &c., a printed fan, the leaf with an engraving of street vendors and their clients, French, 9¼in.
(Christie's) $547

The Illustrated Fan, a card brisé souvenir fan printed with ten views of Brighton, published by J. Newman & Co., 7½in., 1874.
(Christie's) $352

A fan, the black gauze leaf painted with circus scenes, signed *Donzel*, with ebony stick, the guardsticks carved with clowns with ivory heads and hands, 12½in., circa 1890.
(Christie's) $743

A fan, the silk leaf painted with an elegant family in a park, two portrait miniatures, and putti holding escutcheons with monograms *C.B.* or *G.B.*, 10in., circa 1775.
(Christie's) $2,542

A pierced ivory brisé fan, painted with a circular vignette of a scene from a novel, and carved with smaller vignettes, 9½in., English, circa 1790.
(Christie's) $1,564

An ivory brisé fan lacquered in various shades of gold with a vase of flowers and sprays of flowers, signed twice *SHOZAN* and *SHOKASAI*, 11in., Japanese, late 19th century.
(Christie's) $5,084

A fan, the leaf of Brussels lace, the mother of pearl sticks finely carved and pierced with trophies of love and an oval vignette of a lady playing the piano signed *J. Vaillan*, 11in., circa 1880.
(Christie's) $587

A Canton tortoiseshell brisé fan carved and pierced with figures and building, the guardsticks decorated with gilt metal filigree butterflies and waterlilies, 9½in., mid-19th century.
(Christie's) $1,212

Laurel and Hardy, signed album page by both Stan Laurel and Oliver Hardy, still contained in album.
(Vennett-Smith) $264

Al Jolson, signed color postcard to lower white border.
(Vennett-Smith) $120

Clark Gable, a good signature on reverse of Polurrain Hotel notepaper, also bearing one other signature.
(Vennett-Smith) $192

Alfred Hitchcock, a Paramount Pictures Inc. receipt signed by Alfred Hitchcock, and completed in his hand.
(Vennett-Smith) $400

Walt Disney, an excellent signed and inscribed 13.5 x 10.5 photograph inscribed to Gladys Cooper, showing Disney, full length stood on staircase, surrounded by the cast of 'The Happiest Millionaire.
(Vennett-Smith) $1,520

Charles Chaplin, signed document, one page, 26th May 1945, being Chaplin's Power of Attorney constituting and appointing United Artist's Corporation Ltd. to be his 'True and lawful attorney'.
(Vennett-Smith) $832

George Reeves, a good signed piece, over-mounted in blue beneath 9 x 7.25 reproduction photo of Reeves in costume as Superman.
(Vennett-Smith) $352

Marlene Dietrich, signed sepia postcard, with full vintage signature, partially signed in darker portion.
(Vennett-Smith) $80

Leslie Howard, signed 6.25 x 4.5 photograph, partially signed in darker portion.
(Vennett-Smith) $120

Rita Hayworth, signed album page, signature to the reverse just showing through. (Vennett-Smith) $72

Rita Hayworth, signed card, in **later years, overmounted in gray** and black beneath 12 x 9.5 reproduction photo. (Vennett-Smith) $72

Veronica Lake, signed album page, annotated and dated in ink in another hand, *Theatre Royal, Brighton 31–5–69.* (Vennett-Smith) $67

W. C. Fields, signed piece, laid down to album page and further laid down to larger page alongside. (Vennett-Smith) $208

Brigitte Bardot, signed 8 x 10, full length standing on steps, topless. (Vennett-Smith) $64

Grace Kelly, signed 6 x 4, as Princess, featuring an illustration of a postage stamp showing her portrait. (Vennett-Smith) $69

Romy Schneider, signed postcard to lower white border from 'Sissi'. (Vennett-Smith) $66

Ingrid Bergman, signed color 10.5 x 7.75, half length embracing three young children from 'The Inn of the Sixth Happiness'. (Vennett-Smith) $152

Humphrey Bogart, a large signed album page, attractively overmounted in green beneath a 7.5 x 9.5 reproduction photo of Bogart. (Vennett-Smith) $448

Boris Karloff, signed album page.
(Vennett-Smith) $128

Peter Sellers, signed and inscribed postcard to lower white border, surrounded by various caricatures.
(Vennett-Smith) $45

Elizabeth Taylor, signed album page, also signed by Eddie Fisher, annotated in ink in another hand to lower border.
(Vennett-Smith) $80

Richard Burton, signed theater program to front cover, 'King Henry IV' part one, at the Shakespeare Memorial Theatre, 1951.
(Vennett-Smith) $48

A letter and two signed photographs of Laurel and Hardy, 1940's/50's, comprising a letter in blue ink written by Stan Laurel on a sheet of *The Central Hotel Glasgow* headed paper, dated *11–3–52*.
(Sotheby's) $871

Charles Chaplin, signed document, one page, 26th May 1945, being Chaplin's Power of Attorney constituting and appointing United Artist's Corporation Ltd. to be his 'True and lawful attorney'.
(Vennett-Smith) $480

James Stewart, an original 7 x 10 sketch of 'Harvey', signed by James Stewart.
(Vennett-Smith) $80

Montgomery Clift, signed album page, *Monty Clift*, annotated in ink in another hand to lower border.
(Vennett-Smith) $160

Chico Marx, signed postcard to lower border, full length seated resting his head in his hands.
(Vennett-Smith) $120

Jayne Mansfield, signed album page, tape stain to left edge, not affecting signature, together with a separate album page signed by Mickey Hargitay.
(Vennett-Smith) $72

Hattie McDaniel, starred in 'Gone With The Wind', the first black actress to win an Academy Award.
(Vennett-Smith) $288

Clark Gable, signed album page, annotated in ink in another hand to lower border.
(Vennett-Smith) $208

Vivien Leigh, typed letter, 9th November 1966, to Albert Louwerens, thanking him for his charming birthday card.
(Vennett-Smith) $336

Leigh and Olivier, signed album page by both Vivien Leigh and Laurence Olivier individually.
(Vennett-Smith) $168

Mary Pickford, signed document, one page, 18th April 1956, being Mary Pickford's letter of resignation as a director of United Artists (Export) Limited.
(Vennett-Smith) $138

Marilyn Monroe, signed album page, *Marilyn Monroe Miller*, rare, annotated in ink in another hand.
(Vennett-Smith) $1,840

Richard Burton, signed postcard, Picturegoer No. W912.
(Vennett-Smith) $80

Laurel and Hardy, signed and inscribed sepia 7 x 5 by both Stan Laurel and Oliver Hardy individually.
(Vennett-Smith) $576

Romy Schneider, signed 7 x 5, early scarce, slight ink staining showing through to image from reverse.
(Vennett-Smith) $51

Maria Montez, signed and inscribed 8 x 10 photograph, full length standing, extremely rare in this form.
(Vennett-Smith) $280

Jayne Mansfield, signed 6 x 4, half length, small tear to left border, not affecting image or signature.
(Vennett-Smith) $115

Harpo Marx, signed sepia postcard, playing harp, slightly weaker ink signature and some damage to corners.
(Vennett-Smith) $128

Brigitte Bardot, signed color 8 x 10 photograph, full length naked, looking out of window, her back to the camera.
(Vennett-Smith) $48

Edward G. Robinson, signed postcard, portrait, partially signed in dark portion.
(Vennett-Smith) $40

Bette Davis, signed and inscribed vintage 8 x 10 photograph, in white ink.
(Vennett-Smith) $56

Sonja Henie, signed postcard, full length standing on ice from 'Lovely to Look At'.
(Vennett-Smith) $35

John Wayne, a good signed 8 x 10 photograph in cowboy attire, modern reproduction signed in later years.
(Vennett-Smith) $232

Groucho Marx, signed 8 x 10 photograph, with first name only, smoking cigar, signed in later years.
(Vennett-Smith) $144

Boris Karloff, signed and inscribed sepia 8 x 10 photograph, some corner creasing.
(Vennett-Smith) $208

Vivien Leigh, signed 6 x 4, half length, with advert to reverse for 'The Doctor's Dilemma', slight corner creasing.
(Vennett-Smith) $208

Noel Coward, signed 6 x 4 photograph, with advert to reverse for 'Blithe Spirit'.
(Vennett-Smith) $48

Marlon Brando, signed 8 x 10 photograph, half length holding cat from 'The Godfather', rare in this form.
(Vennett-Smith) $560

Marlene Dietrich, signed and inscribed sepia 7.5 x 9.5 photograph, with full vintage signature, 1943.
(Vennett-Smith) $48

Grace Kelly, signed 5.5 x 4 to lower white border, slightly weaker ink signature.
(Vennett-Smith) $82

Cecil B. de Mille, a good signed and inscribed 9.5 x 8 photograph looking directly into the camera.
(Vennett-Smith) $80

Orson Welles, signed sepia 7 x 5 photograph.
(Vennett-Smith) $136

A George II cast-iron and polished steel fire grate, the railed basket surmounted by elongated knopped urn finials, 37½in. wide.
(Christie's) $2,888

An Irish gun metal, polished steel and cast-iron register grate, the railed front with urn finials above a pierced frieze with engraved oval paterae and foliage, late 18th century, 36¼in. wide.
(Christie's) $4,235

A brass, steel and cast-iron fire grate, by Thomas Elsley, the railed serpentine front above a fret-pierced frieze with incised plaque, 19th century, 32in. wide.
(Christie's) $8,085

A polished steel, gun metal and cast-iron fire grate, the basket with Chinese style fret rails, the pierced frieze flanked by column uprights with shaped urn finials, late 18th/19th century, 28¼in. wide.
(Christie's) $3,080

A polished steel and cast-iron fire grate, of George III style, the railed serpentine basket above a frieze pierced and engraved with birds, urns and scrolling foliage, 19th century, 30in. wide.
(Christie's) $1,251

An alloy fire grate, the railed serpentine basket above a pierced and beaded frieze with engraved urns and swags, the square tapering uprights with urn finials, early 19th century, 37½in. wide.
(Christie's) $3,658

A brass, polished steel and cast-iron fire grate, the railed serpentine basket above a fret-pierced frieze, flanked by square tapering uprights with urn finials, 36in. wide.
(Christie's) $5,390

A cast-iron fire grate, the backplate decorated in relief with a flaming urn flanked by foliate scrolls, early 19th century, 36in. wide.
(Christie's) $1,059

A modern brass, steel and cast-iron fire grate, the railed serpentine basket above a pierced frieze centered by an oval patera, on a stepped square plinth, 30¼in. wide.
(Christie's) $674

A brass, polished steel and cast-iron fire grate, the railed serpentine basket above a fret-pierced frieze with applied oval paterae, 30¼in. wide.
(Christie's) $6,160

An oval brass-mounted, polished steel fire grate, of brazier form, the pierced basket on waisted socle, the stepped square plinth with lamb head masks, 29in. wide.
(Christie's) $5,775

A cast-iron and polished steel fire grate, the railed front above a fret-pierced frieze with stylized anthemion motifs, late 18th century, 28½in. wide.
(Christie's) $3,080

A late Victorian brass and steel grate of Adam style, with arched back cast with interlaced laurel swags above a half-fan medallion, the pierced bow-fronted basket filled with waved sunburst, late 19th century, 36in. wide.
(Christie's) $3,029

A George III steel firegrate of large size and serpentine form, the basket with three horizontal bars flanked by two columnar supports crowned by urn finials, later framing and backplate, 43in. wide.
(Christie's) $4,567

A brass, steel and cast-iron fire grate, the railed frieze flanked by bulbous knopped standards with urn finials, on square bases, with conforming central support, late 17th/early 18th century, 35in. wide.
(Christie's) $3,850

A brass, polished steel and cast-iron fire grate, the railed front above a pierced frieze with engraved birds, trees and foliage, 19th century, 27½in. wide.
(Christie's) $5,583

A brass-mounted cast-iron fire grate, of Louis XVI style, the pierced basket above a riband laurel leaf frieze, the cylindrical uprights with chased harebells and pineapple finials, 28in. wide.
(Christie's) $3,160

A polished steel and cast-iron fire grate, of Chippendale style, the railed serpentine front above a pierced and engraved frieze, on stepped plinths, 19th century, 29¼in. wide.
(Christie's) $3,658

A set of three steel fire irons, with knopped shafts, faceted pommels and pierced shovel, late 18th/early 19th century. (Christie's) $866

A pair of ormolu chenets, the uprights surmounted by heads of winged putti, with 'C' scroll terminals, with iron billet bars, 9in. wide. (Christie's) $963

A set of three George II brass fire irons, with knop shafts and loop terminals, early 18th century. (Christie's) $3,465

A set of Benham & Froud brass fire tools, comprising a poker, shovel and pair of tongs, ornately cast and with engraved decoration, 75.5cm. length of poker. (Christie's) $2,680

A French brass and wire mesh spark guard, of cartouche outline, on scroll supports, 29in. wide. (Christie's) $1,194

A fine shovel, coal tongs, and poker designed by C.F.A. Voysey and manufactured by Thomas Elsey and Co., circa 1898, patinated brass, 25^1/2in. long. (Sotheby's) $3,410

A set of three George IV steel fireirons each with octagonal shaped stepped finial and spirally-twisted shafts, 31in. long. (Christie's) $2,101

A pair of brass-mounted cast-iron fire dogs, of 'Haddon Hall' type, the uprights with pierced circular plaques with tulips and other flowers, 19th century, 12^3/4in. wide. (Christie's) $2,503

A set of three steel fire irons, with ball finials, knop shafts and pierced shovel, early 19th century. (Christie's) $924

A set of three steel fire irons, the faceted pommels with knopped finials, with pierced shovel, late 18th/early 19th century. (Christie's) $732

Pair of sunburst andirons, sun personified by smiling face surrounded by rays on shaped post and arched base, black finish, 16½in. high. (Skinner) $935

A set of three steel fire irons, with knopped shafts and pommels, with pierced shovel, late 18th century. (Christie's) $1,540

A Federal brass and marble firetool stand, American, early 19th century, with brass ball finial above a scrolled arm over a cylindrical shaft above a gridded marble base, 31½in. high. (Christie's) $1,100

A brass folding fan-shaped spark guard, 39½in. wide. (Christie's) $789

A Thornton & Downer set of polished steel fire irons, comprising poker, tongs, shovel and hearth brush on stand, 64.5cm. high. (Christie's) $1,627

A set of three Victorian steel and silvered brass fireirons in the Adam style, comprising a poker, pair of tongs and a shovel, circa 1880, 29½in. long. (Christie's) $1,471

A pair of Federal brass andirons with matching firetools, by John Molineux, Boston, Massachusetts, 1800–1810, each with bell finial above a faceted octagonal turning above a hexagonal plinth with spurred arched legs, 19½in. high. (Christie's) $6,820

A set of three steel fire irons, with engraved urn finials, knopped shafts, and shaped pierced shovel, late 18th century. (Christie's) $1,540

Federal carved mantel, possibly Salem, Massachusetts, circa 1800, 73¹/₂in. wide. (Skinner) $1,320

A white marble chimneypiece, in Louis XVI style, the breakfront shelf with a molded edge, above a paneled frieze carved with oak branches, late 19th/20th century, 57¹/₂in. wide. (Christie's) $9,240

An Art Deco macassar ebony and fruitwood fire surround, the top with curved overlapping sections forming a swag design, 162cm. wide. (Christie's) $957

American School, 19th/20th century, Owls and Ivy, a fireplace surround, unsigned, oil on three panels, assembled dimensions, 37 x 43in. (Skinner) $3,575

An early Victorian Mason's ironstone chimneypiece, gilt and green decorated overall with flowers on a cream ground, the serpentine shelf of three sections, 62in. wide. (Christie's) $5,775

A fine Federal carved and gessoed pine fireplace mantel, attributed to Robert Wellford, Philadelphia, circa 1805, painted white, overall width 6ft. 11in. (Sotheby's) $4,025

An Irish white marble chimneypiece, the rectangular shelf with a molded edge, above a fluted frieze with a central tablet carved with an urn and ribbon-tied swags, late 18th century, 69in. wide.
(Christie's) $10,588

A late Victorian plain walnut mantlepiece and overmantel, the mirror and scroll panel back with fluted pillars, 199cm. wide.
(Allen & Harris) $1,015

A George II white and gray-painted carved pine chimneypiece, the breakfront shelf with foliate-carved and blind-fret-molded edge, the shaped hearth surround carved with flowerheads, 74¹/₂in. wide.
(Christie's) $5,390

A pine and marble chimneypiece, of George III style, with a breakfront shelf with a molded edge, above a foliate-carved frieze, with verde antico marble ingrounds, the grate late 18th/19th century, the chimneypiece 32¹/₄in. wide.
(Christie's) $1,829

A portoro marble chimneypiece, of Louis XV style, the serpentine shelf with a molded edge, above a shaped paneled frieze centered by rocaille decoration, second half 19th century, 63³/₄in. wide.
(Christie's) $10,588

A gray-veined white marble chimneypiece, of Louis XV style, the serpentine shelf with a molded edge, above a shaped, paneled frieze centered by a seashell and foliate decoration, late 19th century, 54¹/₂in. wide.
(Christie's) $6,160

An Empire style gilt-metal-mounted mahogany
fireplace and matching over-mantel mirror, the
mirror with molded cornice and frieze with
central female mask, 63in. wide.
(Christie's) $1,996

A white-painted, parcel-gilt carved wood
chimneypiece, in the Kentian style, the
breakfront shelf with an elaborately carved edge,
above a frieze, centered by a mask, 66¼in. wide.
(Christie's) $8,663

A George II carved pine chimneypiece, with an
inverted breakfront shelf with egg-and-dart
molded edge, the frieze centered by two eagle
heads and scrolling foliage, 67in. wide.
(Christie's) $13,943

A carved statuary marble chimneypiece, the
breakfront shelf with a molded, acanthus-carved
edge, the frieze centered by a mask flanked by
drapery swags, 78in. wide.
(Christie's) $53,900

An early Victorian chinoiserie decorated
Mason's ironstone chimneypiece, polychrome
and gilt-decorated overall on a blue ground, with
shaped inset panels of flower and pavilion
landscapes, 62¾in. wide.
(Christie's) $17,325

An Irish George III statuary marble and
scagliola chimneypiece, in the manner of Pietro
Bossi, the breakfront shelf above a frieze
decorated with ribbon-tied trophies, late 18th
century, 73¾in. wide.
(Christie's) $50,050

A Hardy, 'Perfect', 4in., alloy fly reel, smooth brass foot, turk's head locking nut above brass strap and tension adjuster. (Christie's) $397

A fine Bambridge, Maker, Eton-on-Thames, oak oblong fly-tying cabinet, the hinged lid with concealed compartment to the underside. (Christie's) $2,936

A Hardy, The 'Silex' No. 2., 6in., sea-fishing reel, smooth brass foot, ivorine brake lever. (Christie's) $863

A Farlow, 3³/₄in., brass fly reel, raised check housing, crank winding arm, ivory handle. (Christie's) $449

A Hardy, japanned metal oblong fly box, the hinged lid enclosing four lift-out trays, containing a collection of approximately 225 graduated salmon flies. (Christie's) $691

A Hardy, 'Perfect', 1896 pattern, 2¹/₂in., brass fly reel, smooth brass foot, brass strap above tension adjuster. (Christie's) $2,418

A Hardy, 'Perfect', 4in., brass-faced, alloy fly reel, smooth alloy foot, brass strap above tension adjuster, ivorine handle. (Christie's) $656

A stuffed and mounted brown trout, naturalistic setting, incorporating cast of flies, inscribed, *Brown Trout, Weight 5¹/₂lbs, Caught on the Bob-Fly*, 28in. wide. (Christie's) $345

A Farlow, 5in., brass fly reel, raised check housing, the crank winding arm with folding ivory handle and cut-away rim. (Christie's) $656

BEDS

A North Swedish carved cradle, the gadrooned sides painted with diamonds, the ends with polychrome fleur de lys and the date *1849*, 87cm. long.
(Auktionsverket) $497

An oak single bed, the paneled headboard carved with lozenges enclosing stylized flowerheads, partly 17th century, 42in. wide.
(Christie's) $2,087

A Charles X elmwood and fruitwood inlaid lit en bateau, the curved ends with scroll terminals, 218cm. long.
(Finarte) $5,338

A Federal carved mahogany four-post bedstead, American, probably Salem, Massachusetts, 19th century, the feet with foliate caps, 80in. long.
(Sotheby's) $2,750

An early 19th century North Italian walnut cradle, the rectangular body with folding ebonized hood bands, on gadrooned vase-shaped ends, 4ft. 1in. long.
(Phillips) $1,416

A carved mahogany four poster bed, the tester supported by floral-carved cluster column and octagonal supports with **paneled square section legs, 55in. wide.**
(Christie's) $1,848

A rare red-painted cherrywood and pine, child's bedstead, American, first half 19th century, has full set of cotton crocheted hangings, width 36in.
(Sotheby's) $2,990

A Federal turned curly maple four-post bedstead, American, circa 1815, having an arched tester, 6ft. 7in. long.
(Sotheby's) $4,675

A rare heart-decorated chestnut and cherrywood child's cradle on stand, Pennsylvania, 1780–1800, on an arched base joined by a double medial transverse, length 39in.
(Sotheby's) $5,750

BEDS

A late Federal mahogany child's crib with tester, American, first half 19th century, with a serpentine tester, width 48½in.
(Sotheby's) $2,990

A French calamander and ebonized daybed with dual scroll ends and splayed bracket feet, complete with mattress, 86in. wide.
(Christie's) $1,287

A Federal birchwood and maple four-post bedstead, New England, circa 1810, on tapered feet, with tester.
(Sotheby's) $5,750

A fine Federal carved mahogany bedstead, Philadelphia, circa 1800, having a shaped headboard, 7ft. long.
(Sotheby's) $16,500

An American 'Aesthetic' Movement double bed, in the manner of the Herter Brothers, New York, circa 1880, the headboard with a carved pierced, gilt and ebonized cresting, 5ft. wide.
(Sotheby's) $3,154

Antique American Sheraton field bed in cherry, rebuilt with new rails and replaced headboard and canopy.
(Eldred's) $2,420

A George III mahogany cot, with a fluted top domed hood, zinc liner for flowers, on rockers.
(Woolley & Wallis) $505

A mahogany four-post bed with pale green-painted arched canopy and two reeded baluster columns, part early 19th century, 58in. wide.
(Christie's) $5,328

An 18th century oak cradle with hinged canopy, baluster-turned finials and fielded panels to the sides, 33½in. long.
(Bearne's) $1,639

BOOKCASES

An attractive mahogany serpentine front bookcase in the Georgian style, with fret carved broken swan neck pediment, 6ft. 11in. wide.
(Spencer's) $4,101

An early 19th century mahogany veneered open bookcase, the figured shaped and banded raised back with a central anthemion motif and fan corners, 6ft. 6in. wide.
(Woolley & Wallis)

$3,136

A late Victorian walnut library bookcase, the molded cornice above three glazed doors, on plinth, 151cm. wide.
(Allen & Harris) $759

A George III mahogany breakfront bookcase attributed to Thomas Chippendale with gothic dentiled broken pediment and interwoven blind-fret cornice above four ogee-arched gothic glazed doors, 84in. wide.
(Christie's) $80,784

A Georgian mahogany open bookcase fitted with two graduated and adjustable shelves, containing two drawers below, on ring-turned tapering legs, 2ft. 8in. wide.
(Phillips) $4,248

A modern pine bookcase, of George III style, with breakfront stiff leaf egg-and-dart and dentil-molded cornice above a fluted frieze (parts of carving 18th century), 90in. wide.
(Christie's) $6,160

An early 19th century figured walnut and ebonized bookcase, the stepped molded dentil carved cornice over frieze inlaid with heart motifs and husks, 4ft. 9in. wide.
(Spencer's) $3,800

A late George III mahogany breakfront library bookcase, the upper part with a molded cornice and four pointed gothic arched astragal glazed doors enclosing shelves, 8ft. 6in. wide.
(Phillips) $11,505

A Scottish oak bookcase, in two parts, rectangular overhung top above glazed folding cupboard doors, enclosing adjustable shelves, 128cm. wide.
(Christie's) $1,487

BOOKCASES

A 'gothic' oak secrétaire library bookcase, the molded cornice carved with repeating quatrefoils, 85¹/₂in. wide.
(Bearne's) $1,073

A Regency rosewood standing bookcase with two central doors applied with reeded moldings, flanked by open shelving, 30in. high by 73¹/₄in. wide.
(Bearne's) $1,677

A mid-Victorian burr walnut breakfront library bookcase with four arched glazed doors, on a plinth base, 99in. wide.
(Bearne's) $17,135

A George III satinwood open bookshelf inlaid with amaranth lines, the three-quarter galleried superstructure above two shallow and two deep shelves and a mahogany-lined drawer, with carrying-handles to each side, 38¹/₂in. wide.
(Christie's) $11,781

A George II mahogany or possibly 'red walnut' breakfront library bookcase, the lower part with six drawers flanked on each side by a cupboard with simulated triple drawer fronts, 8ft. 4in. wide.
(Phillips) $11,885

One of a pair of Regency mahogany standing bookcases, each with waved superstructure with reeded edge, on turned tapering toupie feet, one with both back legs replaced, 26in. wide.
(Christie's)
(Two) $11,781

An Edwardian inlaid mahogany bookcase in the George III manner, with satinwood crossbanding and boxwood and ebony stringing throughout, 41¹/₂in. wide.
(Bearne's) $2,980

A very fine Federal inlaid mahogany breakfront bookcase, Salem, Massachusetts, circa 1800, in two parts, on tapering legs, 5ft. 7³/₄in. wide.
(Sotheby's) $126,500

A 19th century purple ebony bookcase with two part glazed doors beneath a molded pediment, 115cm. wide.
(Finarte) $4,270

BUREAUX

A Venetian giltwood and lacquered bureau on stand, the flap and frieze painted in the arte povera style with genre scenes, on slender cabriole legs, 18th century, 110cm. wide.
(Finarte) $19,241

An early 19th century Dutch mahogany and marquetry bombé cylinder bureau all over inlaid with flower stems and sprays within scrolling strapwork borders, 4ft. 5in. wide.
(Phillips) $9,735

A South German walnut and inlaid bureau, 18th century, with three drawers in the serpentine frieze and above a slope front inlaid with rectangular panel, 49in. wide.
(Lawrence Fine Art) $4,805

A Chippendale carved mahogany serpentine slant-front desk, Massachusetts, circa 1770, the rectagular hinged lid carved with a concave fan flanked by two convex fans, 40in. wide.
(Sotheby's) $7,150

An early George III oak bureau with fall enclosing fitted interior including secret drawer above two short and two long drawers on bracket feet, 41in. wide.
(Christie's) $1,294

A Chippendale carved walnut slant-front desk, Pennsylvania, circa 1770, the hinged lid opening to an interior fitted with shell-carved, blocked and serpentine small drawers, 38³/₄in. wide.
(Sotheby's) $3,575

A George III mahogany bureau with hinged rectangular slope enclosing a fitted interior above four long graduated drawers, on bracket feet, 42in. wide.
(Christie's) $2,875

A George III mahogany bureau, with slope front enclosing fitted interior, on bracket feet, 91.5cm. wide.
(Allen & Harris) $1,107

Antique American Chippendale slant-lid desk in pine, twelve-drawer interior over three long drawers, 39¹/₂in. wide.
(Eldred's) $1,045

BUREAUX

A Dutch walnut and marquetry bureau inlaid throughout with medallions, baskets of flowers, foliage and swags, 38in. wide.
(Bearne's) **$4,172**

A 19th century French lady's bureau, of Louis XV design in kingwood with marquetry panels of flowers, scrollwork and trellis, 2ft. 9in. wide.
(Russell Baldwin & Bright)
$1,504

A George III oak bureau, the sloping flap crossbanded in walnut enclosing an interior of four drawers, pigeonholes and a well, 3ft. 1in. wide.
(Phillips) **$2,520**

A George III mahogany bureau, the sloping crossbanded flap enclosing an interior of pigeonholes and six drawers around a cupboard, 3ft. 1in. wide.
(Phillips) **$1,350**

An early 18th century walnut and featherbanded bureau, the rectangular top with a sloping flap enclosing a cupboard, flanked by pillar drawers, on later bracket feet, 3ft. 1in. wide.
(Phillips) **$3,240**

A 19th century mahogany and later inlaid bureau, banded with satinwood, boxwood and ebonized lines, the sloping flap with a shell and fan spandrels, 3ft. 4in. wide.
(Phillips) **$2,340**

A George III mahogany bureau with hinged fall enclosing fitted interior above four graduated drawers, on bracket feet, 35½in. wide.
(Christie's) **$2,402**

A George III mahogany bureau with sloping fall enclosing fitted interior of shelves and drawers around a central inlaid door, on later ogee bracket feet, 47½in. wide.
(Christie's) **$1,663**

A George III mahogany and later inlaid bureau, with classical urn inlaid fall enclosing fitted interior, on bracket feet, 28in. wide.
(Christie's) **$1,584**

BUREAUX

Chippendale maple and tiger maple slant lid desk, New England, circa 1780, 40in. wide. (Skinner) $4,675

A Chippendale mahogany slant-front desk, New England, 1760–1790, the thumb-molded slant lid opening to a fitted interior of short drawers over valanced pigeonholes, 41in. wide. (Christie's) $3,080

Chippendale mahogany ox bow slant lid desk, Massachusetts, circa 1780, 42in. wide. (Skinner) $2,750

A Chippendale figured walnut slant-front desk, Pennsylvania, circa 1765, the hinged lid opening to interior fitted with small drawers over valanced pigeon holes, 38¹/₂in. wide. (Sotheby's) $7,150

A Chippendale carved cherrywood slant-front desk, probably Woodbury, Connecticut, 1760–1780, the rectangular thumbmolded slant lid opening to a fitted interior with eight pigeonholes above eight short drawers, on straight bracket feet, 41in. wide. (Christie's) $3,300

A Chippendale maple slant-front desk, Eastern Connecticut, 1760–1780, the rectangular top above the hinged lid opening to a fitted interior of a pinwheel carved prospect door, 33in. wide. (Christie's) $3,520

A Chippendale walnut slant-front desk, Pennsylvania, probably Delaware River Valley, circa 1770, on ogee bracket feet, 38in. wide. (Sotheby's) $6,050

Chippendale walnut slant lid desk, Pennsylvania, circa 1770, 38in. wide. (Skinner) $3,630

A Chippendale curly maple and cherrywood slant front desk, New England, circa 1770, on bracket feet, 36in. wide. (Sotheby's) $4,675

BUREAUX

A George III mahogany bureau with sloping flap enclosing small drawers and pigeon holes, on shaped bracket feet, 36in. wide.
(Bearne's) $3,000

William and Mary burled walnut veneer slant lid desk, Boston area, 1710–30, interior with end blocked serpentine small drawers and valanced compartments, 38¾in. wide.
(Skinner) $12,100

David W. Kendall designed oak slant lid desk, Grand Rapids, Michigan, circa 1900, Phoenix Furniture Co., 38in. wide.
(Skinner) $825

A mid-Georgian green and gilt-lacquer bureau-on-stand, the top and sloping flap and sides decorated with chinoiserie scenes enclosing a fitted interior with a well, 35in. wide.
(Christie's) $2,844

A Chippendale carved cherrywood slant-front desk, Connecticut, 1760–1780, with rectangular top above a **rectangular thumbmolded lid** opening to a fitted interior with six pigeonholes above four short and two long drawers, 37in. wide.
(Christie's) $4,180

A mid-18th century oak bureau, the sloping flap enclosing a cupboard, drawers and pigeon holes, on shaped bracket feet, 38in. wide.
(Bearne's) $1,271

A George III mahogany bureau, the molded rectangular fall flap above four long graduated drawers on bracket feet, 39in. wide.
(Christie's) $1,636

Queen Anne maple slant lid desk/dressing table, New England, circa 1760, 35¼in. wide.
(Skinner) $9,350

A George III mahogany bureau, with hinged fall enclosing fitted interior, above four graduated drawers, on bracket feet, 36in. wide.
(Christie's) $4,428

BUREAU BOOKCASES

An attractive Edwardian
Sheraton Revival bureau
bookcase for a child, the upper
section with shallow stepped
molded cornice, 2ft. 2in. wide.
(Spencer's)   **$1,178**

A mid 18th century Austrian
fruitwood inlaid bureau cabinet
on bun feet, 106cm. wide.
(Finarte)   **$4,982**

A George III mahogany bureau
bookcase with a pair of thirteen-
pane glazed doors, sloping flap
enclosing a cupboard, drawers
and pigeon holes, on bracket
feet, 44in. wide.
(Bearne's)   **$4,766**

A George II figured walnut
veneered bureau bookcase, the
top with cavetto molded frieze,
on fret bracket feet, 3ft. 2in.
wide.
(Woolley & Wallis)

                             $8,400

An 18th century Dutch walnut
bombé miniature bureau
cabinet, in two sections,
crossbanded in oak, the arched
molded domed cornice with
domed sides above a mirror
panel door, 1ft. 5in. wide.
(Phillips)   **$4,165**

An early 18th century oak
bureau cabinet, the upper
section with two fielded panel
doors, the fall front enclosing a
stepped interior with a well,
37in. wide.
(Bearne's)   **$3,354**

A German serpentine fronted
walnut bureau cabinet, the top
section with a central door
flanked by ten drawers, on bun
feet, 18th century.
(Herholdt Jensen)

                             $7,124

The Samuel Morris
Chippendale mahogany desk-
and-bookcase, Philadelphia,
1760–1780, in two sections, on
ogee bracket feet, 42¼in. wide.
(Christie's)   **$14,300**

A Federal walnut desk-and-
book-case, probably Virginia,
1790–1810, the lower section
with line inlaid slant lid opening
to a fitted interior, 38¾in. wide.
(Christie's)   **$7,150**

BUREAU BOOKCASES

An 18th century walnut and ebony banded bureau bookcase, the upper section having two arched mirrored doors, on scroll feet, Lombardy, 114cm. wide.
(Finarte) $67,699

A Queen Anne inlaid walnut desk-and-bookcase, Boston, Massachusetts, 1725–1735, on incised bun feet, 37$\frac{1}{2}$in. wide.
(Christie's) $82,500

An early 18th century burr walnut bureau bookcase of bombé outline, the upper part with broken arch pediment above two incised glass mirrors, Lombardy, 123cm. wide.
(Finarte) $64,049

A walnut and burr walnut bureau-cabinet with ogee-molded cornice centered by a parquetry starburst above a pair of shaped arched doors with beveled mirror-plates, 38$\frac{1}{2}$in. wide.
(Christie's) $9,095

A George I walnut, crossbanded and feather strung bureau cabinet of small size, the upper part with a molded cornice and fitted with adjustable shelves, the lower centered by a recessed arch, inlaid sunburst, on bracket feet, 2ft. 9in. wide.
(Phillips) $31,860

A late 18th century Ligurian palisander veneer bureau bookcase, the lower section comprising two herringbone banded drawers, the upper section with two glazed doors, 126cm. wide.
(Finarte) $41,432

A fine George I walnut and burr-walnut bureau cabinet, the upper part with a broken arched pedimented cornice centered with a giltwood figure of Atlas, on bracket feet, 3ft. 4in. wide.
(Phillips) $96,688

A mid-Georgian mahogany bureau, the broken pediment cornice with later turned vases above and a pair of mirror-glazed arched doors, on bracket feet, 38in. wide.
(Christie's) $5,855

A fine 18th century Venetian walnut bureau cabinet, the base with a sloping flap, enclosing an interior of pigeonholes and two drawers around a cupboard, 3ft. 1in. wide.
(Phillips) $41,650

253

CABINETS

An Egyptian Revival mahogany cabinet, enclosed by a pair of glazed doors flanked by ebonized figures of Sekhmet, 47in. wide.
(Lawrence) $7,462

A walnut marquetry side cabinet, possibly London, circa 1860, with an ogee mirrored door flanked by arched glazed doors inlaid with foliate marquetry, 5ft. 11in. wide.
(Sotheby's) $5,115

German metal liquor cabinet, circa 1910, conforming tray on overhanging top with handles, single door with green wavy glass and attached grill, $21^{1}/_{2}$in. wide.
(Skinner) $440

A walnut cabinet, circa 1880, with three long and two short drawers, the top decorated with a Tunbridgeware panel of Hever Castle, 20in. high.
(Sotheby's) $1,961

A black and gilt lacquer cabinet, the front fitted with doors and with engraved brass hinges and lock plate, 18th century European, possibly Irish, 38in. wide.
(Christie's) $3,011

A satinwood collectors' cabinet, probably London, circa 1860, the pair of paneled cupboard doors open to reveal ten graduated drawers, with key, 67cm. wide.
(Sotheby's) $3,921

A black japanned, gilt chinoiserie and brass-mounted decorated cabinet on later stand decorated overall with figures and pagodas in foliate landscapes, early 18th century.
(Christie's) $3,217

A Victorian walnut-veneered side cabinet of breakfront 'D'-shaped form with amboyna banding, boxwood and ebony stringing, on a plinth with bun feet, $58^{1}/_{2}$in. wide.
(Bearne's) $4,589

A mid-Victorian giltmetal mounted walnut, harewood and purple-heart dwarf side cabinet with central oval porcelain plaque flanked by female gilt mounts, 33in. wide.
(Christie's) $2,359

CABINETS

A Victorian walnut and boxwood lined pedestal cabinet, the molded rectangular top above an inlaid frieze fitted with a glazed door enclosing a velvet lined interior, 29¾in. wide.
(Christie's) $808

A Victorian burr walnut ebonized boxwood and harewood inlaid side cabinet, the rectangular D-shaped top, above a gilt metal mounted frieze, 78in. wide.
(Christie's) $17,710

A mahogany and black bean paneled cabinet on chest designed by Betty Joel, in two parts, with a pair of inlaid cupboard doors enclosing adjustable shelf, January 1937, 60cm. wide.
(Christie's) $1,340

A late Victorian ebonized and amboyna large salon cabinet, the stepped superstructure with balustraded frieze over a horizontal rectangular miror plate, 6ft. 1in. wide.
(Spencer's) $3,150

A carved wooden wall cabinet, the design attributed to the Workshop of Princess Tenichef in Talachkino, the rectangular overhanging top above two doors carved with the characters 'Tsar Saltan Saltanivich' and 'Solovei the Robber', 40cm. wide.
(Christie's) $670

A J. P. White inlaid dwarf cabinet designed by M. H. Baillie-Scott, the cupboard door with pewter and fruitwood inlay of a stylized flower, flanked on one side by an open recess, circa 1904, 51cm. wide.
(Christie's) $1,148

A Regency rosewood side cabinet, the upper section with plain frieze applied with a gilt metal spray of flowers and leaves, 5ft. 9in. high.
(Spencer's) $1,650

French Restoration mahogany and mahogany veneer marble top console cabinet, probably New York, circa 1820, 42in. wide.
(Skinner) $1,870

A Chinese export black and gilt lacquer cabinet-on-stand, the rectangular top above a pair of doors enclosing nine variously-sized drawers, early 18th century, 41in. wide.
(Christie's) $3,045

CABINETS

An inlaid walnut cabinet, circa 1850, the serpentine lower part with inset oval leather panel, a drawer and cabriole legs, 3ft. 2in. wide.
(Sotheby's) $4,262

A late Victorian satinwood and marquetry bowfronted side cabinet by Edwards & Roberts, the shaped rectangular top crossbanded with rosewood and inlaid with a central fan medallion, on molded plinth and turned tapering toupie feet, 79^{1}/$_4$in. wide.
(Christie's) $7,253

A walnut and marquetry cabinet on stand, inlaid with 17th century Augsburg marquetry panels of stylized architectural and foliate landscapes, 3ft. 4in. wide.
(Phillips) $4,248

A satinwood, rosewood and parcel-gilt breakfront side cabinet, the top crossbanded with rosewood and with two curved sides above a pair of paneled doors filled with brass grille and backed with pleated silk, basically late 18th century, 42^{1}/$_4$in. wide.
(Christie's) $10,940

A Regency rosewood side cabinet, surmounted by a grey veined marble top enclosed by a pair of pleated silk grille doors, 3ft. 7in. wide.
(Phillips) $2,478

An ormolu-mounted kingwood and parquetry side cabinet of Louis XV style, with eared serpentine-shaped breche violette marble top above a frieze drawer, late 19th/20th century, 48^{1}/$_2$in. wide.
(Christie's) $9,498

A black and gold japanned chinoiserie double dome cabinet, the concave molded cornice with gilt finials above a pair of doors with pierced brass lock plates and hinges, parts 18th century, 4ft. 1in. wide.
(Phillips) $11,505

A small marquetry side cabinet, London, circa 1855, in the contemporary French manner, the breakfront 'D' shape door inlaid with foliage, 4ft. 3in. wide.
(Sotheby's) $3,154

A Regency rosewood dwarf side cabinet inlaid with boxwood lines, the frieze with marquetry panels above a pair of grille doors, backed by pleated silk, 2ft. 4in. wide.
(Phillips) $3,540

An ormolu-mounted rosewood, simulated rosewood and parcel-gilt inverted-breakfront side cabinet with shaped channeled rectangular white marble top, part early 19th century, 72¹/₄in. wide.
(Christie's) $12,370

A Lamb of Manchester walnut carved side cabinet, the design attributed to Bruce J. Talbert, overall with ebonized details, on four turned and carved legs supporting a platform shelf, 100cm. wide.
(Christie's) $4,785

A fine marquetry side cabinet, attributed to Cremer of Paris, circa 1860, with two mirrored doors flanking a pair of doors inlaid with musical trophies, 7ft. wide.
(Sotheby's) $13,640

One of a pair of ormolu-mounted, pietra dura and ebonized cabinets, each with a rectangular verde antico marble top, above an egg-and-dart molding, the frieze with an acanthus and flower stem cast mount, 19th century, 44³/₄in. wide. (Two)
(Christie's) $18,997

A pair of Chinese export brass-mounted red and gilt-lacquer cabinets-on-stands decorated overall with chinoiserie landscapes, each with rectangular top above a pair of doors enclosing seven variously-sized decorated drawers, 22in. wide.
(Christie's) $10,940

A walnut and marquetry cabinet-on-stand inlaid overall with stylized foliate scrolls, the later rectangular cavetto cornice above a long convex-fronted frieze drawer, basically late 17th century, 48in. wide.
(Christie's) $3,848

A George III satinwood and floral marquetry side cabinet of semi-elliptical form, the top banded with rosewood and centered by a ribbon-tied floral spray of roses, narcissi and other flowers, 26¹/₄in. wide.
(Christie's) $15,147

A George III satinwood and marquetry table cabinet, crossbanded in tulipwood and inlaid with fan spandrels, the top inlaid with a harewood medallion, 1ft. 4in. wide.
(Phillips) $1,593

A Japanese copper-mounted Lac Burgaute black lacquer cabinet-on-stand, decorated overall with flowering trees, the foliate legs headed by putti clasping flowers and joined by an X-shaped stretcher centered by a flowerhead, 32¹/₄in. wide.
(Christie's) $8,415

CABINETS

A 19th century oak tobacco cabinet, the center section recessed with two baluster pyramids, the lower section with a door, on bun feet.
(Herholdt Jensen) $567

A birch, amaranth, maple and rosewood veneer bureau with inlaid design of foliate swags and urns, applied with gilt bronze scrollwork, by Georg Haupt, Stockholm, late 18th century, 107cm. wide.
(Auktionsverket)
$74,290

One of a pair of black painted late 18th century Piedmontese corner cabinets, the edges outlined in gilt with a Greek key pattern border, on bracket feet.
(Finarte) (Two) $4,625

A Queen Anne style cream lacquered and gilt chinoiserie decorated brass-mounted cabinet on silvered stand, on cabriole legs headed by Indian masks, 33in. wide.
(Christie's) $1,740

A boulle and ormolu mounted French side cabinet, of arc en arbelette form with marble top, 19th century, 117cm. wide.
(Herholdt Jensen) $940

One of a pair of 19th century French 'Boulle' credenzas in ebonized wood with copper banding and ormolu mounting, the top in white marble, 89cm. wide.
(Finarte) (Two) $3,701

A late 17th century credenza, the rectangular top with projecting corners, on toupie feet, Lombardy, 142cm. wide.
(Finarte) $9,252

An impressive early Victorian mahogany bookcase, the upper section with swept molded cornice over four sets of shelves, 4ft. 8in. wide.
(Spencer's) $5,445

A 19th century French ebonized and ormolu mounted credenza, the front inlaid with quatrefoil motifs in mother of pearl, with white marble top, 134cm. wide.
(Finarte) $3,701

CANTERBURYS

A 19th century mahogany four division canterbury, fitted with a drawer on square legs with brass cappings and castors.
(Phillips) $1,710

A mid-Victorian walnut three section canterbury with pierced fret-carved divisions and frieze drawer, on turned tapering legs, 21½in. wide.
(Christie's) $1,586

A Regency rosewood canterbury with four sections within slatted sides, on ring-turned legs with brass castors, 18¼in. wide.
(Bearne's) $2,682

A Victorian walnut music canterbury, by Gillows, the rectangular galleried shelf with rounded corners, supported on turned uprights, with a paneled base and two open compartments, second half 19th century, 25¼in. wide.
(Christie's) $2,245

A Regency mahogany canterbury, the rectangular rail top with turned finials and two divisions and with turned corner supports, 18¼in. wide.
(Christie's) $3,782

A mid Victorian walnut library buffet and canterbury combined, carried on turned legs with brass castors, 42in. wide.
(Locke & England) $1,440

A rare Federal mahogany canterbury, Boston or New York, circa 1815, the four turned uprights centering scrolled transverses, 20in. wide.
(Sotheby's) $3,025

An Edwardian mahogany five division canterbury with boxwood and bone inlaid mask shell and scrolling foliage decorations to the front and rear, 21½in. wide.
(Christie's) $1,686

A Regency rosewood canterbury with four lyre-shaped divisions, on turned legs with brass castors, 22¼in. wide.
(Bearne's) $1,192

DINING CHAIRS

One of a set of six Regency style mahogany dining chairs with scalloped decorated scrolling top rails, the drop-in seats on saber front legs.
(Lawrence Fine Art)
(Six) **$1,571**

Two of a set of twelve George I style mahogany dining chairs including two open armchairs on shell headed cabriole legs.
(Christie's)
(Twelve) **$5,434**

One of a set of six Victorian rosewood chairs, each with a dished top rail above stylized scroll splat, lift-off seat and turned front supports.
(Lawrence Fine Art)
(Six) **$1,848**

One of a matched set of six ash and fruitwood 'ear' spindle back rush seat chairs, early 19th century, North West Region, attributed to Lancashire or Cheshire.
(Lawrence Fine Art)
(Six) **$1,700**

Two of a set of five early 19th century Provincial mahogany dining chairs, the shield shaped backs in the Hepplewhite manner.
(Phillips) (Five) **$1,440**

A William and Mary banister-back side chair, New England, 1730–50, on cylindrical and ring-turned front legs that extend above the seat, 41$\frac{1}{2}$in. high.
(Christie's) **$330**

One of a set of six Regency mahogany dining chairs, the reeded frames with scrollover finials, and saber front supports.
(Lawrence Fine Art)
(Six) **$2,680**

A set of four Regency mahogany dining chairs, including an elbow chair, the curved, **paneled top rails scrolled at** each end above carved tablet crossbars.
(Phillips) **$810**

One of a pair of antique American 'birdcage' Windsor side chairs in pine and maple with bamboo turnings, 33in. high.
(Eldred's) (Two) **$193**

DINING CHAIRS

One of a set of nine early Victorian mahogany dining chairs with solid curved top rails, lift-off seats and lobed front supports.
(Lawrence Fine Art)
(Nine)　　$1,940

Two of a set of four George III mahogany dining chairs, the oval backs carved and pierced with floret filled wheel splats.
(Phillips)　(Four)　　$900

One of a set of five late 18th/early 19th century Dutch carved elm dining chairs, the oval backs with riband crestings and pierced splats.
(Phillips)　(Five)　　$1,682

One of a matched set of six ash spindle back rush seat chairs, each with double-row of baluster shape spindles, rush seats and turned underframes, North West Region, attributed to Lancashire or Cheshire.
(Lawrence Fine Art)
(Six)　　$1,478

Two of a set of eight Regency period mahogany dining chairs, the backs with oval paterae to the horizontal rails.
(Woolley & Wallis)
(Eight)　　$2,682

One of a set of seven Windsor scroll back small chairs, including one with arms, in beech, fruitwood and elm, each with triple baluster spindles, 19th century.
(Lawrence Fine Art)
(Seven)　　$2,125

One of a pair of Dutch walnut and marquetry chairs, the high curved backs with shell carved cresting rails, inlaid with birds and flowers, early 18th century.
(Lawrence Fine Art)
(Two)　　$2,772

Two of a set of four Dutch beechwood, mahogany and marquetry side chairs on saber legs.
(Christie's)
(Four)　　$1,986

One of a set of six Regency mahogany dining chairs, each with curved bar top rail, on molded saber legs.
(Christie's)
(Six)　　$3,024

DINING CHAIRS

One of a set of twelve mahogany hall chairs by Seddon, Sons & Shackleton, the molded oval backs painted with the crest of Richard Hall Clarke.
(Bearne's)
(Twelve) $40,595

Two of a set of six George II mahogany dining chairs, each with a paper-scroll serpentine toprail.
(Bearne's) (Six) $8,100

One of a pair of oak side chairs, designed by Peter Behrens, the slightly tapering backs with broad central splats flanked by three intersecting cross bars, on waisted square section legs, 100cm. high.
(Christie's) (Two) $5,742

One of a set of four George IV rosewood dining-chairs, each with curved scrolled rectangular toprail above a pierced lotus-carved foliate splat centered by a horizontal bar mounted by three balls.
(Christie's)
(Four) $5,363

Two of a set of ten mahogany dining chairs, including two armchairs, of George III design, each with an arched molded and yoked toprail.
(Christie's)
(Ten) $23,418

A Chippendale walnut side-chair, Philadelphia or Pennsylvania, 1740–1760, the incised serpentine crest flanked by shaped ears above a solid vase-shaped splat over a trapezoidal slip-seat, 39¹/₂in. high.
(Christie's) $4,400

One of a pair of Regency mahogany hall chairs, each with shield-shaped back crowned by eagle-heads flanking a paper-scroll, with central oval sunken panel.
(Christie's)
(Two) $5,042

Two of a set of six early George III mahogany dining chairs, the waved pounced toprails carved with scallop shells and acanthus foliage and a pair of later date.
(Christie's)
(Six) $21,747

One of a set of twelve William IV rosewood and parcel-gilt dining-chairs each with arched waisted back, with flowerhead-centered tablet toprail flanked by leaf-carving.
(Christie's)
(Twelve) $13,943

A Federal mahogany Klismos chair, New York, 1790–1810, the carved tablet crest centering intertwined cornucopiae over a lyre splat flanked by scrolled and reeded stiles, 23¹/₂in. high. (Christie's) $5,280

A very fine pair of Queen Anne carved walnut balloon-seat side chairs, Newport, Rhode Island, circa 1755, on shell volute and bellflower-carved cabriole legs. (Sotheby's) $71,500

A rare William and Mary turned and joined walnut wainscot side chair, Southeastern Pennsylvania, 1700–30. (Sotheby's) $24,200

One of a set of thirteen George III dining-chairs, each with paneled curved toprail and trellis-filled splat, with bowed padded seat covered in beige cotton, on square tapering legs and spade feet. (Christie's)
     (Thirteen) $27,885

Two of a set of eight Regency Irish mahogany dining chairs, including two armchairs, each with a curved paneled and reeded top rail, on grooved saber legs. (Christie's)
     (Eight) $20,073

A Chippendale carved mahogany side-chair, Philadelphia, 1765–1785, with bead-molded shaped crestrail centering a carved pendent leaf flanked by carved scrolled ears above a pierced and scroll-carved splat over a trapezoidal slip seat, 38in. high. (Christie's) $6,050

One of a set of ten ebonized, parcel-gilt and red-painted dining-chairs including a pair of open armchairs and four Regency single chairs, each with scrolled bowed toprail. (Christie's) (Ten) $8,564

A fine and rare pair of Queen Anne carved mahogany side-chairs, Newport, Rhode Island, 1750–1770, each with shaped crest centering a carved shell above a vase-shaped splat flanked by tapering stiles over a balloon seat, 38³/₄in. high. (Christie's) $104,500

A Chippendale mahogany side-chair, Newport, Rhode Island, 1765–1785, the serpentine crest with central carving flanked by molded scrolled ears over a pierced interscrolling vase-shaped splat, 38in. high. (Christie's) $7,150

DINING CHAIRS

A good painted turned and carved maple side chair, Boston, Massachusetts, 1720–60, the C-scroll- and leaf-carved crest above a leather-covered splat.
(Sotheby's) $2,750

Two of a good set of ten mahogany dining chairs, in Hepplewhite style, on square **tapered molded legs with 'H'** stretchers.
(Woolley & Wallis)
(Ten) $6,384

One of six oak side chairs, with slat backs, on front square baluster legs with stretchers.
(Woolley & Wallis)
(Six) $533

A Chippendale carved mahogany side chair, Philadelphia, circa 1770, on cabriole legs ending on claw-and-ball feet.
(Sotheby's) $1,760

Two of a set of six George III style mahogany dining chairs, each with eared foliate scroll carved toprail and pierced interlaced vase splat above serpentine drop-in seat.
(Christie's)
(Six) $2,574

A rare ebonised oak 'ladder back' chair, designed by Charles Rennie Mackintosh for the Willow Tearooms, 1903.
(Christie's) $25,875

A Federal carved curly maple side chair, New York, early 19th **century, on saber legs ending in** carved paw feet.
(Sotheby's) $2,475

Two of a set of eight George III style mahogany dining chairs, with arched back and pierced splat carved with bellflowers and Prince-of-Wales feathers.
(Christie's)
(Eight) $3,646

A Queen Anne carved walnut side chair, Pennsylvania, circa 1760, on cabriole legs ending in pad feet.
(Sotheby's) $3,575

DINING CHAIRS

One of a set of six Regency mahogany dining chairs, the backs with scroll carved curved bar top rails with foliate brass inlay, on saber legs.
(Phillips) (Six) $2,700

Two of an attractive set of four Regency beech stained as rosewood salon chairs, with rope twist carved slightly arched cresting rails.
(Spencer's) (Four) $722

One of a pair of Dutch walnut and marquetry dining chairs with scroll arched backs and a vase-shaped splat.
(Phillips)(Two) $1,770

An 18th century mahogany library steps chair, the seat on square legs with a pull out step and bracketed stretchers.
(Woolley & Wallis)
$1,669

A pair of important oak arm chairs designed by C. F. A. Voysey, each with a slatted back rest with tapering square section supports, carved arms, above rush seats with shaped apron.
(Christie's) $34,452

One of a pair of laminated walnut side chairs by Thonet, each with curved bar toprail, pierced splat, caned seat and incurved legs, 19th century.
(Christie's)
(Two) $1,072

One of a pair of George II walnut side or dining chairs with gadrooned scroll crestings and rosette terminal top rails having pierced interlaced vase splats.
(Phillips)(Two) $2,301

Two of a set of eight painted and decorated rush-seat dining chairs, New York State or New England, circa 1820.
(Sotheby's)
(Eight) $2,750

One of a pair of Edwardian mahogany salon chairs, each with boxwood and bone inlaid foliate scrolling toprail and splat with waisted back.
(Christie's)
(Two) $1,289

265

EASY CHAIRS

Gustav Stickley slant arm Morris chair, no. 369, circa 1904, adjustable back with five horizontal back slats, held with round pegs.
(Skinner) $5,500

A George III mahogany hall-porter's chair, the arched, deeply-curved padded canopy back covered in close-nailed pale brown striped horsehair.
(Christie's) $1,427

A rare tubular rocking chair, attributed to R. W. Winfield, London, circa 1860, the gilt-brass framework carved with flowerheads, now button-upholstered.
(Sotheby's) $3,069

A Victorian tub bergère by Lenygon & Morant, on turned tapering legs and casters, with its chintz loose cover with exotic birds and flowers on an ivory ground.
(Christie's) $3,235

A George IV brass-inlaid rosewood bergère with rectangular padded back, scrolled arms and padded squab cushion, the padded seat covered in close-nailed pale brown material.
(Christie's) $4,948

One of a pair of Louis XV walnut fauteuils, each with padded cartouche-shaped back, arms and serpentine seat, on cabriole legs headed by flowerheads.
(Christie's)
(Two) $8,882

A Morris and Company ebonized oak reclining chair, after a design by Philip Webb, circa 1870, with bobbin turned legs and stretchers.
(Sotheby's) $2,302

A mahogany bergère with swiveling action, the curved padded back and circular seat upholstered in close-nailed tan suede, 19th century.
(Christie's) $3,572

A George III mahogany library open armchair with slightly arched rectangular padded back, arms and seat covered in brown suede.
(Christie's) $3,218

266

EASY CHAIRS

Chippendale mahogany easy chair, Newport, Rhode Island, 1770–90, 44¹/₂in. high.
(Skinner)   **$11,000**

J. M. Young & Sons Morris chair, no. 284, circa 1915, five horizontal back slats on hinged back with adjustable bar.
(Skinner)   **$935**

One of a pair of Italian gray painted throne chairs, each with an arched tapered back and seat upholstered in tasseled pink velvet, 19th century.
(Christie's)
                 (Two) $1,388

A George II mahogany wing armchair, the rectangular padded back, outscrolled arms and rounded rectangular seat covered in close-nailed green velvet, on cabriole legs and pad feet.
(Christie's)   **$3,148**

An Irish mahogany wing armchair, the padded back, outward-scrolling arms and seat covered in floral needlework, and an oak footstool, on scrolled feet.
(Christie's)   **$2,574**

A William IV mahogany library bergère, with scroll-topped rectangular back with channeled scrolled and leaf-carved sides, the padded back, sides and squab cushion covered in black leather.
(Christie's)   **$2,789**

A George III mahogany wing armchair with rectangular padded back, shaped scrolling sides and seat covered in close-nailed red leather, on chamfered square legs.
(Christie's)   **$4,897**

A George IV mahogany caned bergère, the rectangular back and sides with squab cushions covered in florally-patterned red silk damask.
(Christie's)   **$2,521**

One of a pair of late Victorian oak and floral upholstered easy armchairs, each with button upholstered outswept back and arms.
(Christie's)
                 (Two) $3,861

A Liberty & Co. throne armchair, circa 1900, oak, leather back panel and seat cushion, 44in. high.
(Sotheby's) $2,898

Two of a set of four 17th century armchairs with scrolling arms and turned legs joined by upper and lower stretchers, North Italian.
(Finarte) (Four)
          $17,079

A George III giltwood armchair in the manner of John Linnell, the frame carved with entrelac, supported by foliate-enriched and spirally-carved stiles.
(Christie's) $1,903

A Queen Anne walnut armchair with arched padded back and swollen shaped padded seat upholstered in associated mid-18th century floral crewel-work on an ivory ground.
(Christie's) $20,196

One of a pair of Anglo-Indian rosewood open armchairs, each with shaped toprail carved with anthemion lunettes, the tapering rectangular padded back, arm-rests and drop-in seat upholstered in green and white floral material, second quarter 19th century.
(Christie's) (Two) $2,855

A carved walnut armchair, circa 1850, the back with an arched padded panel above a carved armorial, with padded serpentine seat and the legs with lion heads and paw feet.
(Sotheby's) $3,921

A George IV mahogany adjustable open armchair by Robert Daws, with rectangular padded back, lotus-enriched scrolled arms and seat covered in close-nailed green leather.
(Christie's) $3,616

An unusual English walnut armchair, circa 1860, the padded arched back on a pair of massive wing-like scrolls, on down-curved legs with hoof-like feet.
(Sotheby's) $4,092

A George II mahogany armchair with slightly-arched padded wing-back, outscrolled arms and seat covered in pink velvet, on cabriole legs headed by an acanthus-carved cabochon.
(Christie's) $5,673

A George IV mahogany library
bergère with later adjustable
reading-slope, the reeded
scrolling top rail above a caned
rectangular back, seat and sides
with green velvet squab
cushions.
(Christie's) $10,467

One of a pair of William IV
library bergères, each with
dished deeply-curved padded
back, sides and seat covered in
crimson velvet, on turned
tapering legs and brass caps.
(Christie's) (Two) $7,722

A pair of Egyptian Revival
parcel-gilt walnut armchairs,
circa 1880, almost certainly
retailed by Christopher
Dresser's 'Art Furnishers
Alliance'.
(Sotheby's) $23,870

A Regency brass-mounted
ebonized and parcel-gilt
bergère, the padded scroll back,
sides and squab cushions
covered in green and white
floral cotton, on paneled saber
legs and brass paw feet.
(Christie's) $5,386

A Regency mahogany library
bergère with caned scrolled
back and sides, buttoned green-
leather covered drop-in seat and
close-nailed padded arms above
a paneled frieze on tapering
channeled saber legs.
(Christie's) $5,891

One of a pair of Regency
bamboo bergères, each with
deeply curved arched pierced
back filled with vertical rails
and pierced fretwork, with
squab cushion covered in green
silk.
(Christie's) $12,012

An early George III giltwood
open armchair in the manner of
John Cobb, the arched
cartouche-shaped gadrooned
back, scrolled arms and
serpentine padded seat covered
in associated petit point
needlework.
(Christie's) $6,732

A Queen Anne walnut easy-
chair, Rhode Island, 1740–1760,
the arched crest flanked by
shaped wings, on cabriole legs
with disk feet, joined by block
and arrow-turned H-stretchers,
46in. high.
(Christie's) $8,800

One of a set of four George III
giltwood open armchairs, each
with oval padded back, armrests
and seat upholstered in peach
silk, the frame with guilloche
molding.
(Christie's)
(Four) $25,245

A French giltwood throne armchair, Paris, circa 1910, a copy of Napoléon I's throne, the circular padded back carved with laurel, the padded arms with ball finials.
(Sotheby's) $3,498

A George I walnut armchair, the upholstered rectangular back, outscrolled arms and seat covered in gros and petit point needlework.
(Lawrence) $2,950

A fine Queen Anne leather-upholstered turned walnut and maple wing armchair, Boston, Massachusetts, circa 1760.
(Sotheby's) $68,750

A late 17th century carved walnut open armchair, the acanthus carved undulating arms with flowerhead terminals, on turned arm supports.
(Phillips) $3,894

A pair of Victorian mahogany elbow chairs, the high waisted backs with 'paper-scroll' crestings, scroll arms and scroll front supports.
(Lawrence Fine Art) $1,386

A 19th century satinwood and inlaid bergère, the panel top rail with husk garland inlay and cane back, sides and seat on square tapering legs.
(Phillips) $1,080

A fine and rare Queen Anne carved walnut balloon-seat wing armchair, Newport, Rhode Island, circa 1750.
(Sotheby's) $8,800

Rare early Morris chair, 20th century, in oak with cabinet drawers, Dutch carving of scenes, made in Holland, Michigan, 46in. wide.
(Eldred's) $853

A Federal inlaid mahogany wing armchair, the back with arched cresting, shaped wings and outward-scrolling arms.
(Sotheby's) $2,475

EASY CHAIRS

An early George III mahogany wing armchair, with stuffover shaped undulating back, outscrolled padded arm supports and seat with a cushion.
(Phillips) $5,823

One of a pair of walnut open armchairs with solid toprails and scrolling sides, upholstered in close-nailed hide, on saber legs, possibly German, circa 1830, 30in. high.
(Christie's)
(Two) $4,349

A Louis XV carved beechwood fauteuil, the cartouche-shaped upholstered panel back with a floral cresting, on cabriole legs, bearing the stamp *I. NADAL.*
(Phillips) $1,558

A William and Mary stained wing armchair, English, 18th century, ring-turned legs with scrolled Spanish feet joined by a molded X-stretcher, 32in. wide.
(Christie's) $7,700

A pair of mahogany library armchairs of mid-Georgian design, each with a tapestry back and seat, on square molded legs, joined by an H-stretcher.
(Christie's) $4,684

One of a pair of William & Mary side chairs, each with padded rectangular back and seat covered in red silk damask and hung with tasseled borders, on boldly-scrolling cabriole legs.
(Christie's)
(Two) $2,099

A Regency simulated rosewood bergère chair with a rectangular cane filled back, the ring-turned spreading arm supports on turned legs, castors.
(Phillips) $1,080

One of an unusual set of four Continental ebonized hardwood open armchairs, each with high triple leaf carved arched cresting rail.
(Spencer's)
(Four) $4,900

A Louis XVI carved beechwood fauteuil with a tapered upholstered panel back, padded scroll arm supports and stuffover bowed seat.
(Phillips) $708

271

ELBOW CHAIRS

Scandinavian modern walnut folding chair, mid twentieth century, organic design frame with adjustable seat.
(Skinner) $440

Painted William and Mary bannister back armchair, New England, 18th century, 50¼in. high.
(Skinner) $4,675

Gustav Stickley rocker, no. 317, circa 1904, straight crest rail over five vertical slats, flat arms with front corbels, red decal.
(Skinner) $550

A George III mahogany open armchair with bowed rectangular seat covered in yellow silk damask, the waved toprail carved with a central anthemion and flanked by husk swags.
(Christie's) $1,224

A painted comb-back Windsor rocking chair, 19th century, the stepped crestrail above five spindles over seven bamboo-turned spindles flanked by scroll arms, 42½in. high.
(Christie's) $1,540

One of a pair of Regency simulated bamboo bergères, each with caned back, sides and seat, on turned tapering legs joined by an H-shaped stretcher, decoration refreshed.
(Christie's)
    (Two) $9,761

One of a pair of Heal & Sons oak open arm chairs, each turned base with curved and vertical back rails, with linking spheres, above rush seat, circa 1915.
(Christie's) (Two) $861

Sack-back knuckle arm Windsor chair, New England, circa 1780, with old red varnish, 28in. high.
(Skinner) $3,850

Harden & Co. armchair, circa 1910, wide straight crest rail over three vertical back slats, flat arms over three wide vertical slats.
(Skinner) $385

ELBOW CHAIRS

Sack-back knuckle arm Windsor chair, New England, circa 1780.
(Skinner) $990

Gustav Stickley armchair, no. 366, circa 1907, straight crest rail over three vertical slats, flat arms with front corbels, 26in. wide.
(Skinner) $330

A George III mahogany ladderback open armchair with four pierced foliate-carved serpentine crossbars.
(Bearne's) $1,236

A George III mahogany ladder back armchair with pierced waved back, padded needlework seat and square chamfered legs joined by stretchers.
(Christie's) $772

An oak settle after the design by M. H. Baillie-Scott, rectangular paneled back inlaid with pewter, ebonized and fruitwood roundels, 136.5cm. wide.
(Christie's) $2,488

One of a set of six Morris & Co. ebonized Sussex open armchairs each back with four horizontal turned rails and spindles, on turned tapering legs with double stretchers.
(Christie's)
(Six) $2,488

A George III mahogany ladderback open armchair, the gadrooned back with four pierced serpentine crossbars.
(Bearne's) $1,130

Pilgrim oak and maple turned armchair, probably Massachusetts, circa 1700, 43$\frac{1}{2}$in. high.
(Skinner) $1,540

A George III mahogany open armchair, the shield-shaped back centered by a beaded circular medallion enclosing the Prince-of-Wales' feathers.
(Christie's) $2,284

Gustav Stickley V-back rocker, circa 1902, original leather upholstery with black finish tacks, red decal, 26in. wide. (Skinner) $880

Walnut child's chair, Scandinavia, early 20th century, tenon and peg construction, unsigned, 36⁵/₈in. high. (Skinner) $165

L. & J. G. Stickley Morris chair, circa 1910, original medium finish and box spring, Handcraft decal, 29¹/₄in. wide. (Skinner) $3,520

Victorian carved walnut and oak corner chair, the cresting rail profusely carved with bell flower and foliage. (G. A. Key) $471

Alvar Aalto designed Paimio chair, circa 1932, birch plywood seat suspended within a continuous laminated wood frame, unsigned, 24¹/₂in. wide. (Skinner) $3,300

A walnut child's armchair, with arched back, serpentine splat padded seat and cabriole legs, mid 19th century. (Christie's) $704

A late Stuart walnut armchair, carved cherubs supporting a crown to the cresting rail and front stretcher, with caned panels to the back and seat. (Russell Baldwin & Bright) $2,106

A Régence carved beechwood fauteuil, with cartouche cane back and rocaille scroll cresting with trailing flowers, on cabriole legs and scroll feet. (Phillips) $1,682

A Victorian oak armchair, in French caquetoire style, with narrow gothic pierced back outswept arms above wedge shaped seat. (Russell Baldwin & Bright) $382

One of a set of eight French style salon chairs with carved hoop formed back rails, late 19th century period.
(G. A. Key)
(Eight) $1,492

A Regency rosewood library chair with bow back, twisted stick back on turned front and rear splay supports.
(Russell Baldwin & Bright)
      $1,143

One of a set of seven Regency mahogany dining chairs, with outscrolled bar top-rails, on **channeled saber legs.**
(Christie's)
(Seven) $1,584

Rare Gustav Stickley inlaid armchair, circa 1903, designed by Harvey Ellis, unconventional inlay design of copper, pewter and varying woods, 22³/₄in. wide.
(Skinner) $33,000

A painted and turned maple double-back conversation 'Courting' chair, New England, 1780–1810, painted brown with yellow highlights, length 43in.
(Sotheby's) $7,475

A turned maple rush-seat corner chair, New England, 1720–60, the U-shaped back with scrolled handholds above a rush-seat.
(Sotheby's) $3,450

A George III elm corner armchair, the curved and shaped toprail with twin pierced waisted splats, panel seat, on **square chamfered and molded** supports.
(Russell Baldwin & Bright)
      $893

A fine and rare William and Mary turned and joined walnut Wainscot armchair, southeastern Pennsylvania, 1720–40, on vase- and block-turned legs.
(Sotheby's) $11,500

A Queen Anne carved walnut balloon-seat corner chair, Newport, Rhode Island, 1740–65, the U-shaped back ending in scrolled handholds.
(Sotheby's) $16,100

ELBOW CHAIRS

A rare turned and painted maple rush-seat child's high chair, New England, early 18th century, on turned legs joined by stretchers.
(Sotheby's) $2,475

An oak Turner's chair with bobbin and baluster turnings and squab seat, legs re-toed, late 17th/early 18th century.
(Christie's) $941

A George III mahogany child's chair, the molded shield shaped back and pierced splat inlaid with a ribbon suspended medallion.
(Lawrence) $2,169

A Windsor red-painted comb-back armchair, Connecticut, 19th century, on four splayed ring and baluster-turned legs joined by an H-stretcher, 42in. high.
(Christie's) $8,800

Two of a set of four Eastlake Victorian parlor chairs in walnut, one gentleman's chair and three lady's chairs, all with arms.
(Eldred's)   (Four) $660

Antique child's rabbit-ear high chair painted black and red.
(Eldred's) $303

A George III mahogany spindle back desk chair, decorated with paterae, garya husks and foliate molding with a curved toprail and arm supports.
(Phillips) $2,655

A Regency painted elbow chair, the horizontally railed back with arched and pierced top rail and 'X'-crossbar.
(Phillips) $720

One of a pair of George III mahogany elbow chairs, with loop backs, pierced and fluted splats, on square, tapering and chamfered legs joined by stretchers.
(Phillips)   (Two) $900

ELBOW CHAIRS

A carved, turned and partially black-painted maple banister-back rush-seat armchair, New England, circa 1720.
(Sotheby's) $1,540

A mid-Georgian elm armchair with waved toprail and solid **paneled back, on square tapering legs with paneled sides** and back.
(Christie's) $669

One of two similar Venetian-style 18th century walnut armchairs, on cabriole legs with scroll feet and wavy stretchers.
(Woolley & Wallis)
(Two) $5,544

An attractive mahogany open armchair in the George II style, the serpentine cresting rail with acanthus and husk carved tracery, pierced interlaced 'C' scroll and strapwork baluster splat.
(Spencer's) $1,041

An unusual pair of branch-form laurel 'Centennial' armchairs, signed by *W. L. Carter*, Marietta, Pennsylvania, circa 1876.
(Sotheby's) $7,700

An oak Wainscot elbow chair, the back carved with a cresting of two birds flanking a corn sheaf above an arched panel containing a figure of Justice, 17th century, 47in. high.
(Lawrence Fine Art)
                    $14,784

A Regency painted open armchair, the back with curved top rail, and lion head tablet **centered crossbar, the carved** tapering seat with buttoned squab cushion.
(Phillips) $630

A Georgian bergère armchair, the mahogany frame with reeded top rail, supported upon fluted tapering legs ending in brass castors.
(Spencer's) $1,980

One of a pair of of Regency mahogany elbow chairs, the reeded frames with solid curved cresting rails above X shape splats.
(Lawrence Fine Art)
(Two) $2,125

FURNITURE

A William and Mary walnut oyster veneered and acacia banded chest, the rectangular molded top with geometric panels, on later bracket feet, 3ft. 1in. wide.
(Phillips) $6,018

A William and Mary grain-painted blanket-chest, Connecticut, 1725–1735, the case with applied molding with two sham and two long drawers, 41½in. wide.
(Christie's) $3,300

A Charles II oyster walnut and floral marquetry chest of drawers, the top inlaid with birds and a flower filled urn, 36½in. wide.
(Lawrence) $15,617

A good Federal satinwood-inlaid mahogany bow-front chest of drawers, New England, circa 1800, with four cock-beaded and graduated long drawers, 40in. wide.
(Sotheby's) $3,575

A walnut and feather-banded chest with rectangular molded top above five drawers, on bracket feet, 28½in. wide.
(Christie's) $1,983

A Chippendale mahogany serpentine-front chest of drawers, Massachusetts, circa 1770, on ogee bracket feet, 40½in. wide.
(Sotheby's) $6,050

A William and Mary pine chest-of-drawers, with two short drawers over three long drawers above a base molding, on ball feet, 40in. wide.
(Christie's) $4,180

A Chippendale carved walnut chest of drawers, Pennsylvania, circa 1780, with four graduated molded long drawers, quarter-columns flanking, on ogee bracket feet, 35in. wide.
(Sotheby's) $11,000

A rare William and Mary walnut chest of drawers, Pennsylvania, probably Chester County, early 18th century, the molded base continuing to ball feet, 41¾in. wide.
(Sotheby's) $8,250

FURNITURE

A George III small mahogany bow-front chest of three long graduated drawers surmounted by a slide, on bracket feet, 37in. wide. (Lawrence Fine Art)
$3,142

A mahogany and oak Wellington chest-cabinet with **molded cornice, glazed door,** two drawers and two dummy drawers, on plinth base, 28in. wide.
(Christie's) $892

A late George III mahogany bow front chest, the boxwood strung caddy top above four graduated long drawers on splayed legs, 3ft. 1in. wide.
(Phillips)   **$1,482**

A Georgian mahogany serpentine front chest with **rosewood molded crossbanded** top with boxwood lines, containing four long drawers between reeded stiles, on swept bracket feet, 3ft. 1in. wide. (Phillips) $5,664

Eastlake lock-side six-drawer bureau, late 19th century, in walnut veneers, 36in. wide.
(Eldred's) $770

Antique American Sheraton four-drawer chest in cherry, scrolled splashguard, turned and ribbed legs, brass knobs, 43in. wide.
(Eldred's)   **$1,210**

A Federal inlaid walnut serpentine-front chest of drawers, Maryland, circa 1800, with four beaded and graduated long drawers outlined with stringing, 41½in. wide.
(Sotheby's)   **$9,350**

American Sheraton four-drawer chest, 19th century, in maple with mahogany drawer fronts, wooden pulls, probably of Maine origin, 43½in. wide.
(Eldred's) $550

A Hepplewhite period mahogany veneered serpentine front chest, on bracket feet, 3ft. 8in. wide.
(Woolley & Wallis)
$3,546

A George III mahogany chest, **the molded rectangular top** above four graduated long drawers on shaped bracket feet, 2ft. 10in. wide.
(Phillips) $1,350

A Chippendale applewood serpentine-front chest of drawers, Massachusetts, circa 1785, the oblong top with incised edge, 39in. wide.
(Sotheby's) $4,950

A George II mahogany chest of small size, the rectangular **molded top fitted with a slide** and containing four graduated long drawers, on later bracket feet, 2ft. 6in. wide.
(Phillips) $3,540

A **Federal** grain-painted pine bow-front chest-of-drawers, New England, probably Massachusetts, circa 1810, the oblong top above a case with four graduated long drawers, 40in. wide.
(Sotheby's) $1,870

A mid-19th century German oak tall chest, the six long drawers inlaid in contra and premier partie with grotesque animal heads and scrolling foliage on bracket feet.
(Phillips) $1,080

A George III mahogany and inlaid serpentine chest, with satinwood crossbanding and fan inlay spandrels, heightened in harewood, the top with a central oval fan medallion, 3ft. 6½in. wide.
(Phillips) $3,363

A late 18th century mahogany serpentine chest, with a brushing slide, on bracket feet, 3ft. 6in. wide.
(Woolley & Wallis) $2,682

A burr walnut and feather banded bachelor's chest, the hinged rectangular top above four graduated long drawers on bracket feet, 2ft. 1in. wide.
(Phillips) $3,960

A William III oyster yewwood and walnut veneered chest, on later bracket feet, 3ft. 1½in. wide.
(Woolley & Wallis) $5,712

A walnut chest, the rectangular mahogany top above three short and three long feather strung drawers on bracket feet, part early 18th century, 3ft. 6in. wide.
(Phillips) $1,080

A George III mahogany bachelor's chest, the rectangular fold-over top with draw-out lopers, and with four long graduated drawers below, 2ft. 5in. wide.
(Spencer's) $2,450

A Dutch walnut small bombé chest of four drawers with waved top and projecting angles, on carved paw feet, 18th century, 35in. wide.
(Lawrence Fine Art) $2,495

A small George III mahogany chest, having brass swan neck handles, beneath a brushing slide, on bracket feet, 32in. wide.
(Woolley & Wallis) $2,862

A George III mahogany chest, surmounted by a George II mahogany specimen cabinet, the latter with a pair of fielded panel doors enclosing twenty-four drawers, 2ft. 7in. wide.
(Phillips) $990

A George III mahogany chest with molded rectangular top, two short and three graduated long drawers, on bracket feet, 37 1/2in. wide.
(Christie's) $2,342

An 18th century German oyster veneered and floral marquetry chest, on turned feet, 38in. wide, plate glass top.
(Woolley & Wallis) $4,536

An attractive mahogany serpentine front chest in the Georgian style, the top with thumb molded edge, 2ft. 11in. wide.
(Spencer's) $1,715

A George III small mahogany chest of four graduated drawers surmounted by a slide with molded top and base and on bracket feet, 33 1/2in. wide.
(Lawrence Fine Art) $1,848

A good Chippendale mahogany serpentine-front chest of drawers, Massachusetts, circa **1780, the molded base** continuing to ball and claw feet, 38³/₄in. wide.
(Sotheby's) $10,450

A mahogany and ormolu mounted chest, with rectangular marble top above a frieze drawer and three large drawers under, first half 19th century, 14cm. wide.
(Finarte) $3,701

A Federal curly maple-inlaid birchwood chest of drawers, New England, circa 1820, the rectangular top above four cockbeaded graduated drawers, width 41in.
(Sotheby's) $2,645

A Chippendale walnut chest of drawers, Lancaster County, Pennsylvania, circa 1785, the **rectangular thumb-molded top** above three short and three long graduated molded drawers, 42in. wide.
(Sotheby's) $4,125

An ebony-veneered Wellington chest by Edwards & Roberts, circa 1870, in the form of a semanier with seven graduated drawers held by a locking flap, 2ft. 4in. wide.
(Sotheby's) $2,557

A William and Mary red-painted chestnut and pine chest-of-drawers, Eastern Connecticut, 1725–1735, the rectangular top with molded edge, on turned feet, 39¹/₂in. wide.
(Christie's) $12,100

A George I walnut, fruitwood and pine chest with banded top above two short and three long drawers, 37¹/₄in. wide.
(Christie's) $1,460

An 18th century walnut veneered chest of drawers, of serpentine form with three drawers, 122cm. wide, Ferrara.
(Finarte) $14,923

An early 18th century walnut and boxwood strung chest, the crossbanded top decorated with geometric inlay, on bun feet, 3ft. 2in. wide.
(Phillips) $4,165

A fine Federal inlaid mahogany chest of drawers, Boston area, Massachusetts, circa 1805, the shaped skirt continuing to reeded legs, on brass casters, 41in. wide.
(Sotheby's) $8,800

A George III mahogany serpentine chest, the eared top crossbanded in kingwood, above three graduated long drawers and on splayed bracket feet, 43³/₄in. wide.
(Christie's) $5,247

An 18th century Danish walnut crossbanded and parcel gilt serpentine chest with simulated black marble top and incised gesso frieze, 2ft. 7in. wide.
(Phillips) $7,080

An English oak and fruitwood chest of drawers, the rectangular top above a **molded channeled cornice and four variously-sized paneled** long drawers each simulated as two drawers, late 17th century, 42in. wide.
(Christie's) $3,148

A Queen Anne oyster-veneered walnut chest crossbanded and inlaid overall with geometric patterns, the rectangular top above two short and three graduated long drawers, on later bun feet, 38in. wide.
(Christie's) $16,616

A very fine Federal flame birch and ivory-inlaid mahogany bow-front chest of drawers, Portsmouth, New Hampshire, circa 1805, 41¹/₄in. wide.
(Sotheby's) $28,600

A William and Mary red and black-painted chest-of-drawers decorated with geometric **moldings in imitation of pairs of short drawers, on turned feet,** 39in. wide.
(Christie's) $9,900

A 19th century camphorwood **campaign chest with ebonized** stringing, two deep drawers above three long drawers and on turned feet, 37³/₄in. wide.
(Bearne's) $1,341

A fine Queen Anne mahogany block-front chest of drawers, Boston, Massachusetts, circa **1765,** the molded base with shaped pendant continuing to bracket feet, width 35¹/₂in.
(Sotheby's) $60,250

CHESTS ON CHESTS

A George II walnut-veneered tallboy, the cavetto cornice above two short and six graduated long drawers and on bracket feet, 42½in. wide.
(Bearne's) $4,766

A George III mahogany chest on chest with a concave cornice above three short and three long drawers flanked by fluted canted angles, 41in. wide.
(Lawrence Fine Art) $2,033

A George III mahogany and crossbanded tallboy chest, the upper part with a molded cornice, two short and three long graduated drawers, 3ft. 4in. wide.
(Phillips) $1,800

A George I walnut and crossbanded tallboy chest with a molded cornice and fitted with three short and six long drawers, on later bracket feet, 3ft. 5in. wide.
(Phillips) $3,540

A George III mahogany tallboy, the upper section with rectangular key pattern-carved molded cornice above two short and three graduated long drawers between canted fluted angles, 43in. wide.
(Christie's) $6,006

A Chippendale carved cherrywood chest-on-chest on frame, Connecticut, probably Woodbury, circa 1770, on C-scroll carved frontal cabriole legs, 39¾in. wide.
(Sotheby's) $10,450

A George I walnut and featherbanded chest on chest, with molded cornice above three short and three long drawers, with a brushing slide, 40in. wide.
(Christie's) $6,930

A George III mahogany tallboy chest with dentil molded cornice and blind fret frieze, on bracket feet, 44in. wide.
(Christie's) $2,930

A George III mahogany tallboy, the upper part with a dentil molded cornice, the frieze and canted angles decorated with blind fretwork, 3ft. 7in. wide.
(Phillips) $8,181

CHESTS ON CHESTS

A fine Chippendale carved mahogany block-front bonnet-top chest-on-chest, Boston, Massachusetts, circa 1770, 42in. wide.
(Sotheby's) $52,250

A George III Welsh walnut and oak tallboy, the later molded cornice above three short and three long graduated drawers, flanked to each side by fluted angles, 42¼in. wide.
(Christie's) $3,425

The Samuel Morris Chippendale carved mahogany chest-on-chest, Philadelphia, 1760–1780, in three sections, on ogee bracket feet, 95½in. high, 43½in. wide.
(Christie's) $74,800

An important Federal carved and figured mahogany serpentine-front chest-on-chest, the carving attributed to Samuel McIntire, Salem, Massachusetts, circa 1795, 45¼in. wide.
(Sotheby's) $363,000

A small George II fruitwood tallboy, with pierced shaped fret brass plate handles and escutcheons, on bracket feet, 3ft. 3in. wide.
(Woolley & Wallis) $1,908

An early Georgian walnut tallboy, featherbanded overall, the upper section with rectangular cavetto cornice above two short and three graduated long drawers, 40½in. wide.
(Christie's) $4,934

A fine Chippendale carved mahogany scroll-top chest-on-chest, Philadelphia, circa 1770, in three parts, on a molded base and ogee bracket feet, 47in. wide.
(Sotheby's) $13,200

A George II walnut tallboy, the lower part with a brushing slide above three long drawers, on bracket feet, 41in. wide.
(Lawrence) $10,585

Chippendale cherry bonnet top chest-on-chest, probably Connecticut, circa 1770, 38½in. wide.
(Skinner) $6,600

CHESTS ON STANDS

A very good Queen Anne maple bonnet-top highboy, Rhode Island, circa 1765, the shaped skirt continuing to removable cabriole legs, 38¹/₂in. wide.
(Sotheby's) $7,150

An 18th century walnut veneered chest, the base with a shaped frieze and three drawers.
(Woolley & Wallis) $1,463

A Chippendale cherrywood high chest-of-drawers, probably New London County, Connecticut, 1760–1780, in two sections, on cabriole legs with pad feet, 82¹/₄in. high, 38³/₄in. wide.
(Christie's) $66,000

A George I walnut chest on later stand with overall scroll inlaid crossbanding, with two short and three long drawers, the stand with three drawers about an arched apron, 38in. wide.
(Christie's) $3,371

A William and Mary walnut oyster veneered and marquetry chest on stand, having oak veneered sides, on later turned legs, stretchers and bun feet, 3ft. 1in. wide.
(Phillips) $4,602

A Chippendale carved walnut high chest-of-drawers, Salem, Massachusetts, 1760–1780, on cabriole legs with pad-and-disk feet, 84in. high, 40in. wide.
(Christie's) $60,500

A very fine Queen Anne burl-walnut veneered and maple diminutive flat-top highboy, Boston, Massachusetts, circa 1740, 37¹/₂in. wide.
(Sotheby's) $30,800

A good Queen Anne figured walnut flat-top highboy, Pennsylvania, circa 1760, in two parts, the upper section with molded cornice above five short and three long molded graduated drawers, 44¹/₂in. wide.
(Sotheby's) $46,200

A Queen Anne walnut high chest-of-drawers, in two sections, the lower section with two short drawers above one long drawer over a scalloped apron and cabriole legs, 40in. wide.
(Christie's) $3,520

A Queen Anne style walnut chest on stand, of shaped bow front form, on cabriole supports with shell carved knees and pad feet, 3ft. wide.
(Russell Baldwin & Bright) $2,588

A walnut and feather-banded chest-on-stand with molded cornice, three short and three long drawers between reeded canted angles, early 18th century, 43in. wide.
(Christie's) $1,716

An early 18th century walnut, burr elm veneered featherstrung chest on stand, the base with a long drawer and shaped apron, on cabriole legs, pad feet, 3ft. 2in. wide.
(Phillips) $3,540

A Queen Anne tiger maple high chest-of-drawers, New Hampshire, Dunlap School, 1740–1770, the upper case with molded cornice above three thumbmolded short drawers over four draguated thumbmolded long drawers, 40¼in. wide.
(Christie's) $24,200

A William and Mary black-painted high chest-of-drawers, Pennsylvania, 1720–1740, the upper section with rectangular molded cornice over two short drawers and three graduated long drawers, 39in. wide.
(Christie's) $15,400

A Queen Anne walnut chest-on-stand, feather-banded overall, the upper section with rectangular molded cornice above three short and three graduated long drawers, 41in. wide.
(Christie's) $6,996

A Queen Anne walnut and feather-banded chest-on-stand with molded cornice above three short and three graduated long drawers, 44in. wide.
(Christie's) $5,577

A William & Mary burr elm chest-on-stand crossbanded overall in walnut, the quarter-veneered rectangular top inset with an oval, above two drawers, 40½in. wide.
(Christie's) $6,303

A Queen Anne tiger maple high chest of drawers, North Shore, Massachusetts, 1740–1760, in two sections, on cabriole legs with pad feet, 38in. wide.
(Christie's) $7,150

CHIFFONIERS

Fine early Victorian figured
walnut small chiffonier, the
back mirror decorated with
applied fruit and leaf carving,
3ft. 9in. wide.
(G. A. Key) $787

A Regency brass-inlaid
rosewood side cabinet, 45in.
wide.
(Christie's) $10,276

Early 19th century rosewood
chiffonier, with fielded panels
and applied scrolls to the side
pilasters, 3ft. 6in. wide.
(G. A. Key) $2,268

A Regency ormolu-mounted and
brass-inlaid rosewood chiffonier
inlaid overall with foliate-scroll
angles, the superstructure with
three-quarter galleried
rectangular top on turned
supports, 39in. wide.
(Christie's) $6,090

A George IV brass-mounted
rosewood chiffonier with
mirror-backed two-tier
superstructure, the upper level
edged with bead-and-reel and
with three-quarter pierced
scrolled gallery, on ribbed bun
feet, 60in. wide.
(Christie's) $5,792

A Regency mahogany and
ebonized secrétaire à abattant
with inverted breakfront top
above a flowerhead-mounted
frieze with mahogany-lined
drawers and a paneled fall-
front with green leather-lined
writing-surface, 36¼in. wide.
(Christie's) $7,574

A Regency mahogany
secrétaire-chiffonier, the
associated two-tier
superstructure of pedimented
form with brass-supports above
a sliding mahogany-lined fitted
drawer, 52½in. high.
(Christie's) $2,521

A William IV rosewood corner
chiffonnier with spindle turned
shelved gallery, 46in. wide.
(Christie's) $4,159

A Regency simulated rosewood
and brass inlaid secrétaire
chiffonier, with shelved superstructure and drop-front
drawer, 36in. wide.
(Christie's) $2,508

COMMODE CHESTS

An 18th century crossbanded Dutch mahogany and later marquetry bombé chest, the serpentine top with central musical trophy and others to the corners, 4ft. 4¹/₂in. wide. (Phillips) $6,248

A Louis XV kingwood and ormolu mounted bombé commode en tombeau, by B. Péridiez, quarter veneered and crossbanded with ormolu mounts, 4ft. 10in. wide. (Phillips) $14,875

A Louis XV purplewood, tulipwood and marquetry bombé commode, the projecting angles with 'C'-scrolls and flowerheads leading to lion paw feet, 4ft. 5in. wide. (Phillips) $9,223

A 19th century North Italian walnut, fruitwood and ivory marquetry bombé commode, inlaid with hunting scenes between canted angles, on splayed legs, 2ft. 10in. wide. (Phillips) $4,602

One of a pair of George III ormolu-mounted rosewood, mahogany and floral marquetry bombé commodes, attributed to Pierre Langlois Junior, each with serpentine eared top crossbanded in rosewood and centered by a ribbon-tied floral spray flanked by two butterflies, 36¹/₄in. wide. (Christie's)   (Two) $114,444

A George III mahogany, satinwood and painted commode crossbanded and inlaid overall with boxwood lines, the D-shaped top inlaid with geometric patterns above a pair of doors, 47³/₄in. wide. (Christie's) $21,450

A Dutch walnut and marquetry bombé commode inlaid throughout with vases of flowers, birds, insects and foliage, on scroll feet, 33³/₄in. wide, mid-18th century. (Bearne's) $7,413

A George III mahogany commode of serpentine form, the eared quarter-veneered top above four graduated long drawers, the top drawer fitted with a ratcheted baize-lined writing-slide, 52¹/₂in. wide. (Christie's) $10,435

A Louis XV style gilt metal mounted marquetry bombé commode with mottled red marble top on splayed legs, with gilt clasps and sabots, 28in. wide. (Christie's) $2,299

COMMODE CHESTS

A North Italian walnut, olivewood and checker-strung commode, with rounded rectangular banded top above two short and two long drawers, late 18th century, 50in. wide.
(Christie's) $4,125

A good French marble-topped marquetry commode, by Paul Sormani of Paris, circa 1890, in Louis XV/XVI Transitional style, with molded mottled rust and beige marble top, 146cm. wide.
(Sotheby's) $11,369

A fine George III mahogany serpentine commode, in the French taste and in the manner of Thomas Chippendale, with a molded overhanging top, 4ft. 4½in. wide.
(Phillips) $32,725

A late 18th century Baltic mahogany commode of small size, the rectangular top above a frieze drawer applied with a band of raised dots interspersed with foliate clasps, 2ft. 10in. wide.
(Phillips) $2,975

A Dutch mahogany and marquetry commode inlaid throughout with fan medallions and stringing, on a plinth base, 39in. wide, early/mid-19th century.
(Bearne's) $2,383

A Continental Empire style small mahogany commode, the top drawer flanked by two carved gilt eagles, the lower drawer with recessed arch, on lion's claw feet, 19th century, 34½in. wide.
(Lawrence Fine Art) $1,663

A South German cherrywood, walnut and inlaid reversed breakfront commode, 18th/19th century, 47½in. wide.
(Lawrence Fine Art) $4,250

A French rosewood-veneered petite commode, circa 1910, in Louis XV/XVI Transitional manner, the pierced heart-shaped galley with marble top, 79cm. high.
(Sotheby's) $3,673

A late 18th century Italian fruitwood commode, the rectangular quarter veneered top above four long graduated drawers, on square tapering legs, 3ft. 11in. wide.
(Phillips) $5,841

COMMODE CHESTS

An Italian painted pine and marblised commode of canted outline, with two drawers on shallow bracket feet, 43¹/₂in. wide.
(Christie's) $2,284

An Italian walnut, marquetry and parquetry commode, the crossbanded top set with a roundel within scrolling foliage, 47¹/₂in. wide, late 18th century.
(Bearne's) $15,532

A mid-Victorian satinwood, giltwood and decorated serpentine commode, the top painted with a vase issuing flowers and suspending floral garlands, 53in. wide.
(Christie's) $29,040

A thuya, mahogany, satinwood and decorated semi-elliptical commode, the radiating top with a border painted with classical altars, probably 18th century, 41¹/₂in. wide.
(Christie's) $2,798

A French Provincial 18th century petit commode, with molded marble top, on slender cabriole legs, 21¹/₂in. wide.
(Woolley & Wallis)
                    $2,688

A French ormolu-mounted kingwood and parquetry commode with rounded rectangular inverted breakfront black and white marble top, on cabriole legs and ormolu sabots, late 19th/20th century, 49in. wide.
(Christie's) $2,245

An Italian walnut and marquetry dwarf commode, inlaid overall with geometric lines and feather-banding, mid 18th century, 21¹/₂in. wide.
(Christie's) $2,359

A George III mahogany serpentine commode with eared rectangular top above a slide and four graduated long drawers, on ogee bracket feet, 45¹/₂in. wide.
(Christie's) $4,547

An 18th century palisander veneered and fruitwood inlaid commode, the top in gray marble, on outswept legs with gilt sabots, Genoa, 121cm. wide.
(Finarte) $81,950

One of a pair of English painted satinwood bedside tables, 20th century, in the Georgian manner, 41cm. wide. (Sotheby's)

(Two) $4,515

A pair of 19th century walnut veneered Lombard bedside tables, with colored fruitwood inlay of female heads within ornate palm leaf borders, 88cm. wide. (Finarte) $3,914

An Empire mahogany table de chevet, the square gray marble top above a drawer, a hinged fall front door and a further cupboard under, 1ft. 1in. square. (Phillips) $1,151

A pair of tulipwood, walnut and marquetry brass-mounted tables de nuit of Transitional style, crossbanded overall with green-stained beechwood, each with key-pattern gallery, 19th century, 22in. wide. (Christie's) $49,742

A set of George III mahogany bed-steps with three-quarter galleried columnar top step above tambour shutter slide, the sliding middle step with hinged lid enclosing a fitted interior with later removable lid and white porcelain pot, 18in. wide. (Christie's) $1,903

A George III mahogany bedside commode, the rounded rectangular galleried top above a pair of cupboard doors, 21in. wide. (Christie's) $4,485

A 19th century cherrywood veneer commode, in the form of an octagonal marble topped column upon a square base, on ebonized bun feet, 113cm. high. (Finarte) $1,708

Pair of Venetian rococo painted bedside cabinets, mid 18th century, 18½in. wide. (Skinner) $9,900

An Italian walnut and parquetry bedside commode inlaid overall with geometric banding, on square tapering legs, late 18th/early 19th century, 18in. wide. (Christie's) $6,040

A George III mahogany bedside commode, the shaped tray top above a pair of doors and an adapted drawer below on square molded legs, 1ft. 11in. wide.
(Phillips) $684

Georgian mahogany commode with rising top, two door front and fitted interior, 2ft. wide.
(G. A. Key) $337

A George III mahogany serpentine-fronted bedside cabinet with shaped tray top, tambour shutters, 23¹/₂in. wide.
(Bearne's) $2,458

One of a pair of Continental bedside cupboards, probably French, third quarter 20th century, in Louis XV manner, 38cm. deep.
(Sotheby's)
(Two) $4,515

A pair of George III mahogany pot cupboards, the tray tops with pierced handles fitted with sliding cupboard doors, on molded square legs, 2ft. 2in. wide.
(Phillips) $10,115

A North Italian walnut and marquetry bedside cupboard, on associated square channeled legs with block feet, parts late 18th century, 16in. wide.
(Christie's) $3,339

A George III mahogany night commode, the pull out pot holder with a brass swan neck handle, and serpentine edge to square pull out legs, 20in. wide.
(Woolley & Wallis)
$2,051

A George III mahogany bedside cupboard, the rectangular top with a shaped gallery and side hand grips, 17in. wide.
(Woolley & Wallis)
$1,590

An Irish mahogany bedside commode with waved gallery and pierced frieze above a drawer, a door and a sliding base, retaining ceramic pot, 17in. wide.
(Christie's) $1,004

CORNER CUPBOARDS

A Dutch painted corner cupboard, the top with two shelves above a bowed door depicting a Dutch admiral and a naval engagement, late 18th century, 14in. wide.
(Christie's) $920

Federal walnut inlaid corner cupboard, South Eastern U.S., 90¾in. high.
(Skinner) $3,025

A mid 18th century Continental kingwood and walnut serpentine corner cupboard of arc en arbelette outline enclosed by a pair of parquetry doors, 1ft. 10in., German or Scandinavian.
(Phillips) $1,947

A late George III mahogany corner display cabinet with a pair of geometrical astragal glazed doors and a further pair of panel doors below, 43in. wide.
(Christie's) $1,672

A Louis XV period fruitwood, purpleheart and ormolu mounted encoignure, in the style of Adrian Delorme, on shaped bracket feet, 2ft. 6½in. wide.
(Phillips) $3,540

An 18th century oak upright corner cabinet, the dentil molded cornice above a pair of fielded panel doors enclosing three serpentine shelves, on bracket feet, 3ft. 5in. wide.
(Phillips) $2,880

A late George III mahogany and line-inlaid corner cupboard with molded cornice and pair of paneled doors, on shaped bracket feet, 45in. wide.
(Christie's) $2,033

A George III mahogany veneered bow front corner cupboard, the molded cornice above a banded frieze, 28in. wide.
(Woolley & Wallis) $1,674

A rare yellow-painted pine 'turkey-breast' corner cupboard, Middle Atlantic States, circa 1780, on a molded and dentil-carved base, 56in. wide.
(Sotheby's) $8,800

CORNER CUPBOARDS

A late 19th century mahogany standing corner cupboard, in the Sheraton Revival style with marquetry inlay, 31in. wide. (Woolley & Wallis)
$3,975

Late Federal two-part cherry corner cupboard, probably North Carolina, circa 1800, 46in. high. (Skinner)
$4,950

Pine barrel-back cupboard, New England, late 18th century, 35in. wide. (Skinner)
$1,650

A Federal walnut corner cupboard, Pennsylvania or Middle Atlantic States, circa 1810, the molded and reeded cornice above a pair of glazed hinged doors, 51³/₄in. wide. (Sotheby's)
$5,225

A George II red walnut corner cupboard, the hinged triangular top above a pair of paneled doors enclosing a serpentine-fronted shelf, on block feet, 25¹/₂in. wide. (Christie's)
$2,449

A Federal cherrywood corner cupboard, American, probably New England, first quarter 19th century, the shaped skirt continuing to bracket feet, 42¹/₂in. wide. (Sotheby's)
$6,600

A Federal painted pine corner cupboard, New England, 19th century, in two parts, on bracket feet, painted in an overall mustard ground with green detailing, 39¹/₂in. wide. (Christie's)
$68,200

A good Federal pine corner cupboard, American, probably Delaware River Valley, first quarter 19th century, 52¹/₄in. wide. (Sotheby's)
$5,500

A Chippendale painted and carved pine corner cupboard, New Jersey, 1750–1770, the elaborately molded cornice above two fielded panels, 51in. wide. (Christie's)
$5,500

CORNER CUPBOARDS

A Biedermeier mahogany corner cabinet, with a drawer over a door flanked by carved spiral and turned columns, 157cm. high.
(Herholdt Jensen) $774

A George III mahogany standing corner cupboard with **molded cornice and blind fret** carved frieze, on bracket feet, 49in. wide.
(Christie's) $3,297

A 19th century flame mahogany corner cupboard, with galleried top, the beaded door with drawer under, 131cm. high.
(Finarte) $1,423

A birchwood corner vitrine, with two three paned glazed **doors beneath a curved molded** pediment, two small and two large cupboards under, German, early 19th century, 238cm. high.
(Kunsthaus am Museum) $5,573

A pair of Dutch tulipwood, amaranth-banded and marquetry corner cupboards, each with mottled red marble top, early 19th century, each 26in. wide.
(Christie's) $3,267

A Dutch black lacquer and painted bowfront corner cupboard fitted with a pair of paneled cupboard doors decorated with a panel of a king seated on his throne, 47$\frac{1}{2}$in. high.
(Christie's) $1,180

A Louis XV rosewood, tulipwood and marquetry encoignure, the gray molded Brescia marble top above a door inlaid with a spray of flowers, 2ft. wide.
(Phillips) $2,380

A Dutch mahogany and floral marquetry corner cupboard, the breakfront top above a pair of doors, 19th century, 24in. wide.
(Christie's) $1,543

A George II mahogany standing corner cupboard with galleried triangular top above a fielded paneled central door enclosing a shelf, 22in. wide.
(Christie's) $5,253

CUPBOARDS

An 18th century polychrome painted small commode with galleried top, on narrow cabriole legs, Genoa, 47cm. wide.
(Finarte) **$10,853**

An oak and elm dresser base, with rectangular top above two frieze drawers and pair of paneled doors, late 18th century, 55in. wide.
(Christie's) **$895**

A carved and painted pine 'Tramp art' wall cupboard, American, circa 1930, decorated with layered chip-carved hearts and diamonds, 34in. high.
(Sotheby's) **$1,265**

An oak buffet, the rectangular top above a molded frieze fitted with two paneled doors applied with winged portrait masks, partly 18th century, 47in.
(Christie's) **$2,904**

A Hälsingland cupboard, polychrome painted with flower sprays and trailing on a dark blue ground, the upper and lower section each with a single cupboard door, 110cm. wide.
(Auktionsverket) **$6,124**

An oak and walnut food cupboard fitted with a pierced and carved rectangular paneled cupboard door, 17th century, 36in. wide.
(Christie's) **$3,267**

A green painted hanging cupboard with polychrome decoration, the arched pediment with a carved bird in relief, signed with initials and dated *1854*, 97cm. high.
(Auktionsverket) **$1,406**

A cupboard with drawer and doors, Cambridge, Massachusetts, 1680–1700, in two parts, the upper section with projecting cornice and dentil frieze mounted with corbels, 48⁷/₈in. wide.
(Christie's) **$68,500**

A late Victorian walnut hall cupboard, the molded and dentiled cornice above two turned baluster columns, on bulbous supports, 30in. wide.
(Christie's) **$1,540**

An antique oak court cupboard in the mid 18th century style, the recessed upper portion having three 'cupid's bow' paneled doors, 4ft. 8in. wide. (Russell Baldwin & Bright) **$4,844**

A late 18th century Dutch mahogany buffet, the interior with four fall flap shelves and pewter bowl, the base with two drawers above tambour doors, 3ft. 11in. wide. (Phillips) **$2,301**

18th century oak two tier cupboard with baluster turned supports with turned finials, 21in. wide. (G. A. Key) **$421**

A William and Mary carved cherrywood kas, Hudson River Valley, early 18th century, on turned feet, 6ft. 1in. wide. (Sotheby's) **$6,600**

A red-painted pine cupboard, New England, 19th century, with molded cornice above a canted bookcase cupboard with open arched top enclosing two shelves, 77½in. high. (Christie's) **$4,180**

Antique American Empire server in pine, one molded drawer over two cupboard doors flanked by turned columns, 32in. wide. (Eldred's) **$440**

A Federal blue-painted cupboard, New England, late 18th/early 19th century, with **deeply molded rectangular cornice over a fielded paneled cupboard door**, 40½in. wide. (Christie's) **$7,150**

An oak court cupboard, with molded cornice above frieze dated *1690 R.H.*, late 17th century, 54in. wide. (Christie's) **$2,992**

Antique American two-part step-back kitchen cupboard in **pine, molded cornice, glazed and mullioned doors**, late 18th century, 50in. wide. (Eldred's) **$3,300**

An 18th century oak cupboard, with a molded cornice above a pair of fielded arched panel doors, the lower part with fielded panels and two drawers below, 4ft. 2in. wide.
(Phillips) $1,440

A good painted and decorated pine hanging wall cupboard, Pennsylvania, circa 1780, the molded cornice above a hinged glazed door opening to shelves, width 31in.
(Sotheby's) $5,750

A Continental oak cupboard, on sleigh supports, late 17th/early 18th century, probably North European, 41½in. wide.
(Christie's) $2,508

A Chippendale walnut step-back cupboard, Pennsylvania, 1750–1800, the rectangular top with overhanging molded cornice above five vertical beaded tongue-and-groove backboards, 61in. wide.
(Christie's) $15,400

An oak press cupboard in three sections, with molded rectangular cornice on column supports, above two paneled doors flanking a portico, on stile feet, the feet and back replaced, 17th century and later, 53in. wide.
(Christie's) $3,848

A late 18th century Dutch kingwood side cupboard inlaid with boxwood and ebonized lines, with a cavetto molded cornice above a pair of paneled doors, with splayed legs, 5ft. 5in. wide.
(Phillips) $4,602

A Biedermeier mahogany and boxwood strung pedestal cupboard with molded cornice and frieze drawer, mid 19th century, 26in. wide.
(Christie's) $1,254

An oak aumbry, the front with two doors pierced with roundels, flanked by pierced panels, 44¾in. wide, part 16th/17th century.
(Bearne's) $4,619

A rare antique primitive cupboard, hewn from elm trunk with plank front and door, 4ft. x 2ft.
(Russell Baldwin & Bright)
                             $3,035

DAVENPORTS

A late Victorian burr walnut davenport, with pierced gallery and leather lined sloping lid enclosing a fitted interior, 22in. wide.
(Christie's) $1,766

A mahogany davenport, Victorian, circa 1870, the wide sliding writing slope with an interior lined with marbled paper, 71cm. wide.
(Sotheby's) $1,935

A Victorian walnut davenport, the baluster turned gallery above a hinged leather-lined writing slope, on turned baluster supports, 23¹/₂in. wide.
(Christie's) $3,811

A mid-Victorian walnut piano-davenport, with rising superstructure, fitted with drawers and pigeon holes, foliate scroll supports and turned feet, 28in. wide.
(Christie's) $3,118

A Regency gilt brass-mounted mahogany davenport with three-quarter galleried swivel-action top centered by a berried lotus-leaf cast handle, above a hinged writing-slope with inset green leather writing-surface, 15¹/₄in. wide.
(Christie's) $6,996

19th century mahogany davenport, the rising top, leather inset, reveals a drawer interior, with contemporary cabriole front supports, 22in. wide.
(G. A. Key) $878

A rosewood-veneered davenport, early Victorian, circa 1850, with a pen drawer on the right, 61cm. wide.
(Sotheby's) $1,564

A late Victorian brass-mounted sycamore davenport with three-quarter brass gallery and leather-lined fall, 21in. wide.
(Christie's) $2,904

A walnut davenport, Victorian, circa 1860, in well figured wood, the hinged top with pull-out writing drawer, 58.5cm. wide.
(Sotheby's) $3,343

A late Victorian oak davenport, with three-quarter galleried hinged top enclosing a stationery cupboard, above four drawers to one side, 21in. wide.
(Christie's) $962

Victorian walnut davenport with satinwood crossbandings, the rear has a stationery section, with four squat feet supporting, 1ft. 9in. wide.
(G. A. Key) $1,639

A mid-Victorian burr-walnut davenport, with three-quarter gallery above hinged superstructure, on bun feet, 21in. wide.
(Christie's) $1,461

A Victorian burr walnut-veneered davenport, the rising stationery compartment with fret-carved front and hinged top, the projecting piano front enclosing an adjustable writing slide, 22^{1}/$_{2}$in. wide.
(Bearne's) $3,618

A good mahogany davenport with three-quarter brass gallery, leather inset sliding slope enclosing an interior with three small drawers, 19th century, 20in. wide.
(Lawrence Fine Art) $1,626

A Victorian walnut davenport, the superstructure with rectangular top and small drawers flanked by pigeon holes enclosed by a pair of double mirror paneled doors, 1ft. 9in. wide.
(Spencer's) $1,311

A Victorian burr walnut-veneered davenport with amboyna banding and boxwood stringing throughout, the raised stationery compartment above a sloping flap, 22in. wide.
(Bearne's) $3,001

A Victorian figured walnut piano top harlequin davenport, the rising superstructure with rectangular hinged cover opening to reveal stationery slides, 1ft. 11in. wide.
(Spencer's) $3,150

A George IV rosewood davenport, with three-quarter pierced brass gallery above hinged leather-lined fall enclosing fitted interior, 24in. wide.
(Christie's) $3,300

DISPLAY CABINETS

An unusual Continental painted display cabinet, probably German, circa 1880, of architectural form imitating the English Adam manner, 100cm. wide.
(Sotheby's) $4,722

A good French gilt-bronze-mounted kingwood display table, Napoléon III, by Raulin of Paris, circa 1870, 61cm. wide.
(Sotheby's) $8,395

A Dutch marquetry display cabinet, fitted with two glazed doors, the bombé base with angled sides, fitted with two long drawers, on scroll feet, 56in. wide.
(Christie's) $8,698

A good rosewood and kingwood-veneered side cabinet, circa 1850, the arched mirror back with a glazed door, flanked by open shelves with gilt-bronze mounts throughout, 4ft. 2³/₄in. wide.
(Sotheby's) $4,603

A French kingwood vitrine, Paris, circa 1900, in Transitional manner, with three shaped glazed doors and side, 175cm. wide.
(Sotheby's) $19,239

A good French rosewood and amboyna breakfront secrétaire display cabinet, Napoléon III, by Grohé of Paris, circa 1860, 120cm. wide.
(Sotheby's) $5,247

One of a pair of French 'Vernis Martin' display cabinets, circa 1900, in Louis XV manner, with arched serpentine glazed doors and sides, 53cm. wide.
(Sotheby's) $8,745

An English painted satinwood display cabinet, Edwardian, circa 1910, of classical breakfront form, the whole painted with foliage and scènes galantes, 6ft. 4¹/₂in. wide.
(Sotheby's) $7,161

One of a pair of English ebony-veneered display cabinets, circa 1860, each with a glazed door and sides divided by brass fluted quadrant columns.
(Sotheby's)
(Two) $4,774

DISPLAY CABINETS

One of a pair of French mahogany display cabinets, by Peneland of Paris, circa 1890, in Louis XVI manner, with white marble tops, 66cm. wide.
(Sotheby's)
(Two) $6,996

An Edwardian mahogany and marquetry display cabinet, with molded cornice above swag-hung frieze, 45in. wide.
(Christie's) $1,494

A small French marquetry vitrine, circa 1880, of serpentine outline with brown marble top above glazed door and sides, 154cm. high.
(Sotheby's) $3,498

A good French gilt-bronze-mounted vitrine, Paris, circa 1900, of serpentine form, veneered in kingwood with shaped top, central door and six cabriole legs, 148cm. wide.
(Sotheby's) $13,642

A pair of mahogany and brass-mounted display cabinets, each with glazed door and canted glazed sides, 21in. wide.
(Christie's) $2,970

A fine English inlaid satinwood display cabinet, circa 1895, in George III manner, with pair of serpentine glazed doors and serpentine canted glazed sides, 5ft. wide.
(Sotheby's) $10,230

An unusual satinbirch display cabinet, attributed to Gillows of Lancaster, circa 1870, the glazed upper parts supporting Ionic columns, 3ft. 7³/₄in. wide.
(Sotheby's) $3,751

A Victorian Aesthetic Movement amboyna and ebonized wood salon display cabinet, 1343, 39in. wide.
(Tennants) $1,782

A fine George III mahogany corner display cabinet, the pierced foliate swan neck pediment over glazed doors with panel astragals, 55³/₄in. wide.
(Tennants) $14,580

An attractive late Victorian mahogany salon cabinet, the arched canopied superstructure with foliate carved cresting, 4ft. 1in. wide.
(Spencer's) $1,185

An ormolu-mounted giltwood vitrine table, with a hinged serpentine top inset with a **beveled glazed panel and velvet-lined interior**, late 19th/early 20th century, 31in. wide.
(Christie's) $1,554

An Egyptian carved wood and mother-of-pearl inlaid corner display cabinet inset with mashrabya panels, 35^1/2in. wide.
(Bearne's) $1,447

A 19th century Dutch mahogany **vitrine, the molded arched cornice with ribbon carved plinths above a pair of glazed doors with velvet lined interior,** on claw and ball feet, 5ft. 5in. wide.
(Phillips) $4,680

An attractive Edwardian mahogany bow front salon cabinet, the broken arch superstructure inlaid with laurel leaves, scrolling acanthus leaves **and flowerheads in colored woods and ivory,** 3ft. 8in. wide.
(Spencer's) $1,419

An Aesthetic Movement gilded, **ebonized and glazed cabinet, the designed attributed to Dr. Christopher Dresser, the rectangular superstructure with molded cornice with oriental style pierced finials and brackets,** 96.5cm. wide.
(Christie's) $4,211

A cherrywood vitrine, with **ebonized stringing and inlay,** circa 1925, 109cm. wide.
(Arnold) $1,588

An Edwardian mahogany break bow front salon cabinet, the broken arched pediment surmounted by pierced ribbon and husk carved cresting, 3ft. 8in. wide.
(Spencer's) $1,488

A French giltmetal mounted mahogany vitrine with veined red marble top and pierced gallery above foliate scroll frieze, 27in. wide.
(Christie's) $1,386

DISPLAY CABINETS

An Edwardian mahogany and satinwood banded breakfront display cabinet, with pair of central geometrically astragal glazed doors, 57in. wide.
(Christie's) $2,381

Edwardian mahogany display table, with beveled glazed side panels all round, molded friezes, 21in. wide.
(G. A. Key) $787

Sheraton Revival period mahogany display cabinet, bow fronted lead glazed door, 27in. wide.
(G. A. Key) $721

A rosewood and gilt-metal mounted serpentine vitrine enclosed by a pair of glazed doors with arched Vernis Martin panels of cherubs below, 47in. wide.
(Christie's) $2,926

An Italian painted cabinet, the scrolling pediment with a carved rococo spray of foliage, 5ft. 3in. wide.
(Woolley & Wallis)
                   $4,102

An Art Nouveau mahogany display cabinet and cupboard, the lower section with glazed side and front panels flanking a central part glazed door, 94cm. wide.
(Arnold) $1,700

19th century French kingwood vitrine, the base painted with Vernis Martin panels of landscapes and figures, the whole cabinet surmounted with ormolu embellishments, 25in. wide.
(G. A. Key) $2,425

An attractive Edwardian satinwood salon cabinet by Edwards & Roberts, with broken swan neck pediment, 3ft. 11in. wide.
(Spencer's) $15,400

An Art Nouveau marquetry and carved vitrine, the overhanging rectangular top surmounted by a shaped panel with carved floral decoration, on shaped square section legs, 67cm. wide.
(Christie's) $1,148

DRESSERS

An oak open low dresser with two plank top and ogee molded frieze above three drawers, late 17th century, 69½in. wide. (Lawrence Fine Art)

$4,805

A George III oak dresser, the lower part with simulated short drawers, the frieze with three short drawers, 55in. wide. (Lawrence)

$5,206

A late George III low oak dresser with single plank top above three frieze drawers with mahogany crossbandings, waved apron and square supports, 69¼in. wide. (Lawrence Fine Art)

$4,250

An oak dresser with shelved superstructure containing four small drawers, the base with two drawers and central paneled door, 57in. wide. (Christie's)

$1,848

An oak dresser designed by Sidney Barnsley, the shaped superstructure with open grid-work back, supporting two open shelves, on shaped bracket feet, 140.8cm. wide. (Christie's)

$17,226

An Arts and Crafts dresser, attributed to the Guild of Handicraft, circa 1900, stained oak, leaded glass, beaten copper, brass, 77in. high. (Sotheby's)

$5,115

Late 18th century oak Welsh dresser with three drawers in line and three smaller drawers beneath, 5ft. 3in. wide. (G. A. Key)

$2,980

An early George III oak dresser and rack with molded cornice above open shelves, on style feet, the rack possibly associated, 63½in. wide. (Christie's)

$3,135

A George III oak dresser and associated rack, with molded cornice and open shelves, 65½in. wide. (Christie's)

$2,442

DRESSERS

An oak dresser with associated stained pine rack, with molded cornice and open shelves, parts early 18th century, 58½in. wide.
(Christie's) **$2,279**

An oak dresser, the molded rectangular top above a frieze drawer and an arched paneled cupboard door, basically 18th century, 74in. wide.
(Christie's) **$5,082**

An early Victorian oak dresser, with molded cornice and central plate rack flanked by glazed cupboards, 64in. wide.
(Christie's) **$1,791**

An early Georgian oak enclosed dresser with associated rack, the base fitted with three drawers flanked by cupboards, on block feet, 69in. wide.
(Christie's) **$2,587**

A George III oak dresser, the associated superstructure with rectangular cornice and plain frieze above three open shelves, the base with rectangular top above three frieze drawers, 61in. wide.
(Christie's) **$5,597**

An 18th century oak dresser, the delft rack with ogee molded cornice over four open shelves flanked by small shelves, 6ft. 4in. wide.
(Spencer's) **$3,950**

A George III oak and mahogany inlaid dresser with later plate-rack, the molded cornice above three open shelves, 66½in. wide.
(Christie's) **$3,085**

A Victorian oak kitchen dresser, the molded fluted cornice centered by a stylized shell, on a molded plinth, 114in. wide.
(Christie's) **$2,904**

A late 18th century oak Welsh dresser, the front square legs partly reeded to a shaped front pot board, 5ft. 10in. wide.
(Woolley & Wallis) **$4,611**

307

KNEEHOLE DESKS

An attractive serpentine front pedestal desk, the rectangular top with molded edge, inset with gilt tooled green skiver, 6ft. 1in. wide.
(Spencer's) **$1,155**

A late Victorian mahogany roll top pedestal desk, with galleried top and paneled fall enclosing a fitted interior, 54in. wide.
(Christie's) **$2,464**

A mahogany, boxwood lined and satinwood crossbanded twin pedestal partner's desk of George III design, with nine variously sized drawers, on bracket feet, 58in. wide.
(Christie's) **$3,080**

A late George II mahogany kneehole desk, the rectangular molded top above a long frieze drawer, apron drawer and recessed cupboard, bracket feet, 3ft. 1in. wide.
(Phillips) **$2,478**

A golden roll top desk with cherrywood inlay, the ends embellished with carved leaf decoration, by Schrenk & Co., Connecticut, bearing patent date 1888, 60in. wide.
(Schrager Auction Galleries) **$5,700**

A Queen Anne walnut and featherbanded kneehole desk, fitted with a frieze drawer and six short drawers about an arched recess, on later bun feet, 3ft. wide.
(Phillips) **$4,248**

An Edwardian mahogany and marquetry kidney-shaped writing desk, on short square tapered legs with socket feet, 4ft. wide.
(Woolley & Wallis) **$5,040**

Roll-top desk, early 20th century, in oak with fitted interior, six drawers, paneled ends, 41in. wide.
(Eldred's) **$440**

A George III mahogany 'Harlequin' kneehole desk, the hinged top opening to reveal rising compartments with drawers and pigeonholes, on a plinth base, 3ft. 9in. wide.
(Phillips) **$8,181**

KNEEHOLE DESKS

A mahogany partner's desk, the rectangular top inset with leather, the frieze fitted with three drawers with blind fretwork decoration, 64in. wide.
(Christie's) $3,513

A mahogany partner's desk, the rectangular leather-lined top with gadrooned edge, on shell-headed cabriole legs and claw and ball feet, late 19th/20th century, 60½in. wide.
(Christie's) $2,888

A 19th century mahogany twin pedestal partners' desk, having insert leather top and fitted drawers with brushing slides under, 62in. wide.
(Locke & England)
                      $3,906

A German walnut and burr walnut-veneered kneehole desk of inverted serpentine form and with cast brass mounts throughout, 40½in. wide, late 19th century.
(Bearne's) $1,271

A Chippendale mahogany block-front kneehole-bureau, Boston, 1760–1780, the rectangular top with blocked front and molded edge over a conforming case fitted with a long drawer over a short scalloped valance drawer and recessed kneehole, 36½in. wide.
(Christie's) $88,000

A William III style kneehole desk, veneered in burr walnut and banded, on bun feet, 33in. wide.
(Woolley & Wallis)
                      $1,669

Arts and Crafts oak partner's desk, circa 1910, rectangular top over central drawer and kneehole flanked by cabinet door and bank of three short drawers, 54in. wide.
(Skinner) $770

A George II padouk and sabicu kneehole desk possibly by John Channon, with breakfront rectangular top above a central frieze drawer, on bulbous acanthus-scrolled feet, 55in. wide.
(Christie's) $117,810

A 19th century central European birchwood writing desk, the raised back section with galleried top, the lyre shaped pedestals on turned feet, 134cm. wide.
(Finarte) $6,405

KNEEHOLE DESKS

A Regency mahogany partner's library table, with rectangular leather-lined top, above cupboards to each end and brass grille doors with upholstered panels, on plinth bases, 84in. wide.
(Christie's) $30,800

A mahogany library pedestal desk, the molded recangular green leather-lined top with concave frieze with a drawer to each end, the pedestals with acanthus-carved volute-angles and a pair of paneled doors to each end, 89¹/₂in. wide.
(Christie's) $12,370

A George III mahogany pedestal partner's slat desk with molded rectangular top, inset with green leather, each side with one long and two short frieze drawers above a pair of pedestals, 55¹/₂in. wide.
(Christie's) $10,494

A George I walnut and feather-banded kneehole desk, with rectangular quarter-veneered top, above a frieze drawer and three drawers either side of the kneehole, on later bracket feet, 33¹/₂in. wide.
(Christie's) $8,663

A mid-Victorian burr-walnut kidney-shaped desk with inset gilt-tooled brown leather writing-surface above one long and two short mahogany-lined frieze drawers, the concave kneehole flanked by two convex-fronted pedestals, 52in. wide.
(Christie's) $38,709

A Chippendale block-front kneehole-desk, Massachusetts, 1760–1780, the rectangular top with molded edge and blocked front over a conforming case fitted with a long drawer over a short scalloped valance drawer and recessed kneehole backed by a fan-carved door, 35in. wide.
(Christie's) $33,000

A George II mahogany or possibly 'red walnut' kneehole desk, the molded edge with re-entrant rounded corners containing a long frieze, on ogee bracket feet, 2ft. 6in. wide.
(Phillips) $6,694

A George II mahogany kneehole desk, the rounded rectangular top with molded edge and re-entrant corners above a frieze drawer, 30¹/₄in. wide.
(Christie's) $8,151

A William and Mary stained burr kneehole desk with molded rectangular part-hinged top crossbanded with geometric walnut borders, enclosing a green baize-lined fitted interior of three short and two long drawers, 43in. wide.
(Christie's) $4,373

LINEN PRESSES

A late Georgian mahogany linen press, the wide cornice above a pair of crossbanded doors enclosing slides, 216cm. wide.
(Allen & Harris) $1,199

A late George III mahogany linen press with molded and crossbanded cornice above a pair of crossbanded oval paneled doors, 50in. wide.
(Christie's) $3,142

A George III mahogany clothes-press with molded cornice above a pair of oval paneled doors, the base with two short and two graduated drawers, 52½in. wide.
(Christie's) $3,178

A Federal mahogany linen press, New York, circa 1820, the removable projecting cornice above a pair of hinged paneled doors, 54in. wide.
(Sotheby's) $4,400

A Marsh & Jones inlaid linen press, the design attributed to Charles Bevan, scalloped and molded cornice above a pair of cupboard doors with various wood inlay, 123.5cm. wide.
(Christie's) $4,211

A George III mahogany linen press with molded cornice and pair of paneled doors above two short and two long drawers, on bracket feet, 50¼in. wide.
(Christie's) $2,145

A Chippendale walnut linen-press, Pennsylvania, 1760–1790, the upper part with molded rectangular cornice above a molded frieze and a pair of cupboard doors with inset shaped panels, on bracket feet, 47½in. wide.
(Christie's) $10,450

A George III mahogany clothes-press, the upper section with rectangular cavetto cornice above a pair of paneled doors enclosing five blue paper-lined slides, 49½in. wide.
(Christie's) $4,934

A mid-Victorian bird's-eye maple and mahogany clothes-press by C. Hindley and Sons, the rectangular eared top above a molded cornice and paneled frieze flanked by flowerheads, 65in. wide.
(Christie's) $4,719

LOWBOYS

A Queen Anne inlaid and carved cherrywood lowboy, Connecticut, probably Coastal Area, circa 1785, on cabriole legs ending in raised pad feet, 34¼in. wide.
(Sotheby's) $8,800

An 18th century Dutch walnut, mahogany and marquetry lowboy, the shaped top with projecting corners inlaid with a bird perched upon an urn of flowers, 2ft. 8in. wide.
(Phillips) $5,310

A good George II 'red walnut' lowboy, the rectangular molded top with re-entrant corners, on cabriole legs with pad feet, 2ft. 6in. wide.
(Phillips) $9,223

A very fine Chippendale carved mahogany lowboy, Philadelphia, circa 1770, the shaped skirt continuing to shell-carved cabriole legs ending in claw-and-ball feet, 36⅞in. wide.
(Sotheby's) $104,500

A late 18th century Dutch walnut, crossbanded featherstrung and marquetry lowboy in the William and Mary style, on polygonal tapered legs, united by fret scroll stretchers, 2ft. 11in. top.
(Phillips) $6,195

A fine Queen Anne carved walnut lowboy, Philadelphia, circa 1750, the skirt centering a carved shell and continuing to shell-carved cabriole legs, 33½in. wide.
(Sotheby's) $16,500

An early 18th century oak lowboy, having fitted single long drawer, on cabriole legs and pad feet.
(Locke & England) $880

A Queen Anne japanned, carved walnut and pine lowboy, Massachusetts, circa 1765, the japanning first quarter 19th century, 34in. wide.
(Sotheby's) $6,050

An oak lowboy, the rectangular top with re-entrant corners, on cabriole legs and pad feet, mid 18th century, 29in. wide.
(Christie's) $873

LOWBOYS

An 18th century oak lowboy fitted with three drawers with shaped apron, on four square chamfered legs with reeded edges, 2ft. 7in. wide. (Russell Baldwin & Bright) **$1,408**

18th century oak three drawer lowboy, each drawer with crossbanded detail, standing on four tapering legs, 2ft. 6in. wide. (G. A. Key) **$417**

A fine Queen Anne walnut lowboy, New York, 1730–60, the incised cyma-shaped skirt continuing to faceted cabriole legs, width 36¼in. (Sotheby's) **$18,400**

A Chippendale carved walnut lowboy, Pennsylvania, circa 1770, having shell-carved cabriole legs ending in claw-and-ball feet. (Sotheby's) **$12,100**

A Chippendale walnut lowboy, Pennsylvania, circa 1765, the rectangular molded top with notched front corners above four molded drawers, width 36¾in. (Sotheby's) **$12,650**

A Queen Anne burr walnut and fruitwood lowboy, the rectangular quarter veneered top with cusped corners above a long drawer and two short drawers flanking a false drawer in the shaped apron, 2ft. 6in. wide. (Phillips) **$5,664**

A Chippendale carved mahogany lowboy, signed *Wallace Nutting*, early 20th century, in the Philadelphia manner, width 36½in. (Sotheby's) **$3,163**

A fine and rare Chippendale carved and figured cherrywood lowboy, New York, 1750–65, 30¼in. wide. (Sotheby's) **$18,400**

A fine Chippendale mahogany lowboy, Pennsylvania or New Jersey, circa 1765, the shaped skirt continuing to cabriole legs, 34¼in. wide. (Sotheby's) **$27,500**

SCREENS

Early 19th century figured walnut framed tapestry fire screen with carved detail and dual formed feet.
(G. A. Key) $566

A Louis XVI five leaf screen, of green lacquered wood, painted with musical trophies on a yellow ground, each leaf 49cm. wide.
(Finarte) $9,252

Three panel floor screen, poplar panels decorated with pyrographic and polychrome poppies, 48^{1}/$_2$in. wide.
(Skinner) $770

A Dutch gilt-leather decorated six-leaf screen, each leaf painted in the manner of Nicolas Lancret with courting couples, late 18th/early 19th century, each leaf 96^{1}/$_2$ x 21^{3}/$_4$in.
(Christie's) $7,461

A mahogany pole-screen, the rectangular banner with an 18th century petit point wool needlework panel of flowers beneath a pierced acanthus-scroll cresting, 57in. high.
(Christie's) $2,311

A Chinese coromandel lacquer six-leaf screen, decorated overall with cranes, mandarins, ducks and other birds, late 18th/early 19th century, each leaf 67^{1}/$_4$ x 16in.
(Christie's) $2,760

A Dutch painted leather four-leaf screen decorated overall with exotic birds perched amidst branches, in a nailed border, 19th century, each leaf 84 x 24in.
(Christie's) $4,934

Japanese ivory table screen, approximately 7in. high, finely inlaid on one side in the Shibayama style, lacquered with stylized clouds, unsigned, late 19th century.
(G. A. Key) $1,287

A Japanese carved wood and Shibayama two-fold screen, the gold lacquered panels inlaid in mother-of-pearl and hardstone with peacocks and flowering shrubs, 11^{1}/$_2$in. high.
(Bearne's) $2,118

SCREENS

Early 19th century rosewood fire screen with rising center panel of a woolwork floral tapestry, 21in. wide.
(G. A. Key) $343

A painted eight-leaf 18th century screen decorated with Chinese wallpaper panels painted with exotic birds and butterflies among bamboo shoots, flowering shrubs and rockwork, each leaf 105 x 20in.
(Christie's) $4,948

An early Victorian walnut firescreen, the central glazed section with a display of exotic stuffed birds, 46in. high.
(Bearne's) $825

A four-fold transfer printed screen, designed by Piero Fornasetti, one side polycrome decorated with birds in an ornate aviary, 136.6cm. high.
(Christie's) $11,484

A six leaf coromandel lacquer screen, the top with a wide border of Buddhist emblems, Chinese, circa 1700, 7ft. high.
(Schrager Auction Galleries) $4,000

'The Four Seasons', a four panel screen, circa 1900, incised and polychrome stained wood, the reverse decorated with stylized flowers, 5ft. 11in. high.
(Sotheby's) $2,728

A French mahogany and gilt-metal-mounted three-fold screen, each panel with beveled astragal glazed upper section, 19½in. wide.
(Christie's) $1,669

English six-panel paper floor screen, 19th century, decorated with maps, each panel 81½in. high.
(Skinner) $2,200

Fine Victorian rosewood framed fire screen, the glazed center panel depicting cavalier figures in an interior.
(G. A. Key) $666

A mahogany and line inlaid secrétaire bookcase with molded cornice and pair of arched astragal doors, on bracket feet, 40in. wide.
(Christie's) $2,359

Antique American Sheraton secretary in pine, molded cornice, two glazed doors, writing surface lifts for storage under.
(Eldred's) $550

Eastlake two-part cylinder front secretary in walnut with figured walnut veneers, the lower section with paneled cylinder lid, fitted interior, 39in. wide.
(Eldred's) $1,210

A Federal mahogany and birch veneer secretary, New Hampshire, 1800–1820, the upper section with shaped pediment centering three finials above a coved cornice over double cupboard doors with patterned glazing, on ring-turned and tapering reeded legs, 42in. wide.
(Christie's) $8,800

A George IV mahogany breakfront secrétaire-bookcase with molded cornice centered by a stylized anthemion with acanthus-carved scrolled volutes above a pair of glazed doors, on plinth base, 85³/₄in. wide.
(Christie's) $14,306

A mahogany secrétaire-bookcase crossbanded overall with tulipwood, the upper section with molded rectangular cornice above a pair of hinged glazed doors with a lozenge within an oval glazing pattern and enclosing three adjustable shelves, 39¹/₄in. wide.
(Christie's) $6,996

A Regency mahogany and line inlaid secrétaire bookcase with simulated dentil-molded cornice above a pair of astragal glazed doors, on bracket feet, 52in. wide.
(Christie's) $4,719

An unusual double secrétaire bookcase, London, circa 1840, with six arched glazed doors above conforming cupboard doors, either side with the unusual feature of a baize-lined fitted secrétaire writing drawer, 9ft. 10¹/₂in. wide.
(Sotheby's) $8,184

A fine and rare Federal diminutive satinwood-inlaid mahogany cylinder-front secretary/bookcase, Philadelphia or Baltimore, circa 1805, supported on line-inlaid square tapering legs, 36in. wide.
(Sotheby's) $79,750

SECRETAIRE BOOKCASES

A Federal inlaid mahogany and eglomise gentleman's desk-and-bookcase, Salem, Massachusetts, 1790–1810, in two sections, on cylindrical tapering legs, 61¼in. wide.
(Christie's) $4,950

Federal tiger maple desk/bookcase, New England, circa 1820, 39½in. wide.
(Skinner) $3,960

A George III 'plum pudding' mahogany secrétaire breakfront library bookcase, the key-pattern cornice with fret-carved swan-neck pediment, 81in. wide.
(Bearne's) $12,002

An early 19th century mahogany secrétaire bookcase, the upper section with molded cornice and two glazed doors with pointed arch astragals, on splayed bracket feet, 49½in. wide.
(Bearne's) $1,853

A George IV mahogany breakfront secrétaire library bookcase with molded cornice, four thirteen-pane astragal-glazed doors, and on a plinth, 89in. wide.
(Bearne's) $7,060

A George III mahogany secrétaire cabinet in three parts, the upper section with a bead, fluted and molded cornice above a pair of doors centered with oval astragals, 3ft. 7in. wide.
(Phillips) $3,600

A mahogany and inlaid secrétaire bookcase, the molded cornice above two glazed paneled doors enclosing shelves, on bracket feet, early 19th century, 37in. wide.
(Christie's) $5,155

An early 19th century mahogany secrétaire cabinet, inlaid with boxwood and ebony lines, the associated upper part with a molded cornice above a pair of geometrically glazed doors, 3ft. 5in. wide.
(Phillips) $1,710

A late Georgian mahogany secrétaire bookcase, the secrétaire drawer enclosing fitted drawers and pigeon-holes, supported upon turned tapering legs, 3ft. 11in. wide.
(Spencer's) $4,125

SECRETAIRES

A small French kingwood veneered secrétaire writing desk, Paris, circa 1890, in Louis XV/XVI Transitional manner, 52cm. wide.
(Sotheby's) $5,422

A 17th century Lombard walnut veneered secrétaire, the fall front revealing six small drawers with six fielded drawers under, on bracket feet, 140cm. wide.
(Finarte) $18,172

A Queen Anne walnut burr veneered, crossbanded and featherstrung secrétaire cabinet, the upper part with fitted interior, on bracket feet, 3ft. 8in. wide.
(Phillips) $8,496

A late 18th century German walnut, fruitwood and marquetry secrétaire, the fall with a cartouche panel of flowers and foliage within interlaced strapwork, on bracket feet, 3ft. 11in. wide.
(Phillips) $4,463

A George IV rosewood secrétaire cabinet, with rectangular molded top above hinged fall enclosing fitted interior, 48in. wide.
(Christie's) $2,109

A George III satinwood and marquetry secrétaire crossbanded in tulipwood and amaranth, the rectangular top above a fall-front inlaid with swagged drapery and a medallion of a musician, 35$^{1/4}$in. wide.
(Christie's) $7,871

A Regency rosewood chiffonier, the frieze decorated with brass molded lozenges, paterae and laurel wreaths with a pair of brass trellis doors, 2ft. 9in. wide.
(Phillips) $4,425

A Regency rosewood secrétaire breakfront cabinet, the top crossbanded with tulipwood and kingwood, the frieze with a fall front secrétaire drawer, 4ft. 6in. wide.
(Phillips) $4,602

A Dutch mahogany and marquetry secrétaire à abattant, with overall floral, urn and ribbon-tied drapery decoration, 38in. wide.
(Christie's) $2,109

SECRETAIRES

An Empire flame mahogany and ormolu secrétaire à abattant, with rectangular white marble top, the fall front carved with cornucopia, 81.5cm. wide.
(Finarte) $21,350

A Louis XVI lacquered secrétaire à abattant, decorated in gold and red with chinoiserie motifs, with cavetto cornice in pink marble, 84cm. wide.
(Finarte) $25,620

A late 18th century walnut veneered secrétaire richly inlaid and banded, with gray marble pediment and on pyramid feet, Lombardy, 90cm. wide.
(Finarte) $32,561

A Biedermeier satin-birch secrétaire, with stepped molded cornice above frieze drawer and hinged fall enclosing fitted interior, mid 19th century, 39¹/₂in. wide.
(Christie's) $4,217

A Regency mahogany secrétaire in the manner of Gillows of Lancaster, with three-quarter galleried inverted-breakfront superstructure supported by twin foliate-scrolled and anthemion-carved volutes, 44¹/₄in. wide.
(Christie's) $6,296

One of a pair of Empire mahogany and ormolu secrétaires with molded cornice and drawer over two pairs of doors, 111cm. wide.
(Finarte)
(Two) $24,909

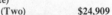

A Charles X burr elm secrétaire à abattant, inlaid with fruitwood, and with gray marble top, on ebonized square feet, 103cm. wide.
(Finarte) $11,386

A Beidermeier walnut secrétaire chest, with rectangular molded top and fall front drawer below with galleried sides, central European, 52in. wide.
(Christie's) $1,485

A cream lacquered and painted secrétaire à abattant, painted with ornate floral borders and scenes galantes, on cabriole legs, Piedmont, second half 18th century, 123.5cm. wide.
(Finarte) $28,466

SECRETAIRES

Antique American Sheraton blind-front secretary in mahogany, bonnet top, two paneled doors in upper section, rope-turned legs, 37½in. wide.
(Eldred's) $1,320

A mahogany breakfront secrétaire cabinet, the rectangular recessed top with ribbon and flowerhead border above central frieze drawer, late 18th century, 73in. wide.
(Christie's) $1,663

A Charles X ormolu-mounted secrétaire à abattant with frieze drawer and hinged fall, enclosing fitted interior, 42in. wide.
(Christie's) $3,432

A Biedermeier birchwood and ebonized secrétaire, the stepped pediment with a drawer above a long frieze drawer and fall flap inlaid with lozenge panels, on square tapering legs, 3ft. 3in. wide.
(Phillips) $3,540

A George III mahogany secrétaire-chest, the rectangular galleried top above a secrétaire drawer, enclosing a green leather writing-surface, on later bracket feet, 29¼in. wide.
(Christie's) $2,521

A 19th century French kingwood purpleheart banded and strung escritoire with a variegated rouge marble top, fitted with a central dummy drawer front fall enclosing a fitted interior, 2ft. 11in. wide.
(Phillips) $3,540

A German Empire style mahogany and gilt-metal mounted secrétaire à abattant, the long frieze drawer with central anthemion motif, 19th century, 37in. wide.
(Lawrence Fine Art)
                             $4,435

An early 19th century German walnut escritoire à abattant, the rectangular top with a molded frieze drawer above a hinged flap enclosing a carved fitted interior, on shortened carved feet, 3ft. 10in. wide.
(Phillips) $2,700

A French Empire mahogany secrétaire à abattant with later molded top above an overhanging frieze drawer, the baize-lined fall-flap enclosing an architectural mirror back interior, 35½in. wide.
(Christie's) $1,673

SECRETAIRES

A French Empire mahogany secrétaire à abattant, applied with gilt bronze foliate motifs and figures, 31¹/₂in. wide. (Bearne's) **$2,756**

An early 19th century Austrian walnut secrétaire, the fall front concealing pigeon hole and five drawers, with three long drawers under, on gilt claw front feet, 133cm. wide. (Finarte) **$2,847**

An early 19th century Austrian flame mahogany secrétaire à abattant, the upper part with arched molded pediment above a central drawer, on block feet, 111cm. wide. (Finarte) **$7,828**

A George III satinwood secrétaire-chest, inlaid overall with ebonized lines, with molded rounded rectangular top above a fitted secrétaire drawer with marquetry paterae to the corners, 28¹/₂in. wide. (Christie's) **$3,647**

A George III mahogany secrétaire chest with rectangular molded top above hinged fall faced as two drawers enclosing fitted interior, 41¹/₂in. wide. (Christie's) **$1,496**

A late 18th century Dutch secrétaire à abattant, veneered in a variety of exotic woods, on square tapering feet, 3ft. 1in. wide. (Woolley & Wallis) **$9,381**

A Louis Phillipe mahogany secrétaire à abattant, with rounded rectangular black marble top, frieze drawer and fall front, 37¹/₂in. wide. (Christie's) **$3,344**

An early 18th century walnut-veneered secrétaire by John Coxed, with feather banding throughout, on bracket feet, 43¹/₂in. wide. (Bearne's) **$17,650**

A Louis XVI walnut secrétaire à abattant, the fall front concealing six small drawers and pigeonholes, with black veined marble top. (Galerie Moderne) **$4,409**

SETTEES & COUCHES

A turned Windsor settee, American, 1785–1810, the U-shaped back above twenty-nine bulbous spindles, length 6ft. 4¹/₂in.
(Sotheby's) $5,463

A classical carved mahogany sofa, Boston, Massachusetts, circa 1820, the scrolled crest above swan's head-carved arm supports, length 7ft. 1in.
(Sotheby's) $2,875

A Chippendale style three piece mahogany framed lounge suite, with surface fretted frieze, carved mask and scroll decoration on cabriole legs with claw and ball feet.
(Russell Baldwin & Bright) $1,821

L. & J. G. Stickley Onondega Shops settle, circa 1902, molded crest rail over thirteen canted vertical slats, original medium finish, unsigned, 76¹/₄in. wide.
(Skinner) $4,510

A Biedermeier satin-ash sofa, with undulating back, scroll ends and padded seat on outswept legs with scroll feet, second quarter 19th century, possibly Scandinavian, 92in. wide.
(Christie's) $2,541

A walnut three-seat settle with rectangular leather-covered back and padded seat on turned baluster supports and bun feet, 69in. wide.
(Christie's) $6,534

A late Victorian painted satinwood sofa, the rectangular top with central tablet of putti above scroll arms, 75in. wide.
(Christie's) $1,740

An Empire mahogany sofa with out scrolled, flat topped mahogany arms and on splayed legs, 19th century.
(Herholdt Jensen) $630

SETTEES & COUCHES

A carved fruitwood Biedermeier sofa with
serpentine back and outward scrolled end
supports, 203cm. wide
(Arnold) $1,470

A fine and rare classical brass-inlaid mahogany
sofa, attributed to Joseph Barry, Philadelphia,
circa 1820, on brass-inlaid saber-legs ending in
sleeping lion's head-cast brass caps, length 7ft.
2in.
(Sotheby's) $18,400

A Regency mahogany chaise longue frame, with
scroll ends, channeled seat rail and reeded saber
legs, 73in. wide.
(Christie's) $2,722

A giltwood sofa with curved back, guilloche and
floral-carved frame, serpentine seat and cabriole
legs, 81in. wide.
(Christie's) $1,558

A mahogany Empire-style sofa with curved
scrolling arms, 19th century
(Herholdt Jensen) $806

An Italian walnut chaise longue, with cream
floral upholstery, on outswept legs with scroll
feet, mid 19th century, attributed to Luigi
Bruscelli, 67in. high.
(Christie's) $1,996

An American mahogany scroll end sofa, the back
with ribbon-tied laurel-leaf toprail, the scroll end
with eagle's head terminals, mid 19th century,
possibly Philadelphia, 81in. wide.
(Christie's) $2,178

Arts and Crafts settle, circa 1910, crest rail over
ten canted vertical back slats, unsigned, 83in.
wide.
(Skinner) $1,210

SETTEES & COUCHES

A George IV cream-painted and parcel-gilt sofa, the out-scrolled back, arms and bowed seat upholstered in pink floral repp, on ring-turned fluted tapering feet, 79in. wide.
(Christie's) $836

One of a pair of early Victorian giltwood sofas, each with a rectangular back and low scroll arms upholstered in striped damask, on turned fluted tapering legs, 73in. wide.
(Christie's)   (Two) $2,509

A George III Irish hump-back sofa, on four blind-fretwork square legs with pierced brackets, 73in. wide.
(Christie's) $18,400

An attractive Victorian rosewood framed settee, the rectangular padded back with foliate carved cushion molded cresting rail.
(Spencer's) $1,072

A fine classical diminutive carved mahogany recamier, probably by Charles White, Philadelphia, circa 1825, on acanthus-carved legs ending in animal paw feet, 65½in. long.
(Sotheby's) $3,575

A fine Federal mahogany sofa, attributed to Slover and Taylor, New York, circa 1815, on reeded square tapering legs ending in spade feet, 6ft. 6½in. long.
(Sotheby's) $8,800

A good Federal carved mahogany sofa, Philadelphia, circa 1815, the crest carved with drapery swags, tassels and flowerheads on a punchwork ground, 6ft. 4in. long.
(Sotheby's) $5,225

A good Federal carved mahogany sofa, New York, circa 1810, the crest carved with three rectangular reeded panels flanked by reeded downcurving arms, 6ft. 6in. long.
(Sotheby's) $4,400

SETTEES & COUCHES

A classical carved mahogany sofa, New York, circa 1825, the columnar crest with scrolled leaf-carved terminals above scrolled arms, 7ft. 9in. long.
(Sotheby's) $2,200

A mahogany triple chair back settee, in the manner of Butler, in 18th century Irish style with scroll leaf carved arms, on four carved short cabriole legs with claw and ball feet, 69¼in. wide.
(Christie's) $3,011

A Regency mahogany sofa, the rectangular padded back, outscrolled arms and squab cushion covered in pale cream and green floral silk, 64in. wide.
(Christie's) $3,425

A Chippendale carved mahogany camel-back sofa, late 18th century, on molded square tapering legs joined by a recessed stretcher, 7ft. 6in. wide.
(Sotheby's) $3,300

A very fine Federal carved mahogany saber-leg sofa, attributed to Duncan Phyfe, New York, circa 1810, the reeded seat rail on volute-carved and reeded saber legs, 7ft. 6in. long.
(Sotheby's) $24,200

A George III hump-back sofa with scroll arms, on a mahogany frame with four grooved square legs joined by stretchers and on brass barrel casters, 72½in. wide.
(Christie's) $10,036

A giltwood canape with a deeply curved padded back, sides, arm-rests and bowed seat covered in golden floral material, the back headed by a foliate clasp, on turned tapering fluted legs headed by flowerheads, 54½in. wide.
(Christie's) $1,382

A Federal inlaid mahogany settee, circa 1800, the back with four rectangular crests above an upholstered back rest and arms, 5ft. 11½in. wide.
(Sotheby's) $3,850

Arts and Crafts couch, circa 1910, square legs
with wide cushion rail over elongated corbels,
retail label, 74in. long.
(Skinner) $330

A George III mahogany settee with arched
padded back and seat upholstered in yellow
floral damask, with channeled scrolling padded
arms above channeled tapering cabriole legs
headed by stylized shells and foliage, 75in. wide.
(Christie's) $11,781

A walnut double-chair-back settee of George II
style, with waved toprail and vase-shaped splats,
the arms with ferocious lion-mask terminals, on
cabriole legs headed by lion-masks and rings,
63in. wide.   (Christie's) $3,498

Bruno Mathesson working armchair and
footstool, circa 1941, laminated bentwood and
solid wood with attached arms and webbed
fabric upholstery.
(Skinner) $990

A William IV mahogany hall seat in the style of
George Bullock, the pediment-shaped back
centered by a scroll with anthemia-shaped and
carved ends, 60in. wide.
(Christie's) $2,941

A fine Chippendale mahogany sofa,
Philadelphia, 1765–1785, with serpentine arched
and canted back flanked by downward sloping
and outward flaring scrolled arms above a
straight seatrail, 98in. wide.
(Christie's) $19,800

One of a pair of George III green-painted garden
benches attributed to the Yealmpton chair-
makers, each with waved serpentine toprail
above a pierced strigil splat centered by an
interwoven oval panel, 53³/₄in. wide.
(Christie's) $13,464

A George III white-painted and parcel-gilt sofa,
on turned tapering fluted legs headed by lotus-
leaf and flowerheads, on turned feet, 72in. wide.
(Christie's) $3,806

A carved mahogany Gothic Revival bench, 1820–1840, the angled over-upholstered seat with carved seatrails centering a quatrefoil, centering a faceted lancet-carved leg, 65in. wide.
(Christie's) $1,540

A 19th century Goanese teak-framed sofa carved with repeating flower-heads and scrolling acanthus, 92¹/₂in. wide.
(Bearne's) $688

A French beech settee, the outscrolled buttoned end and bowed cushioned seat upholstered in calico, the waved seat rail and cabriole legs carved with flowers and foliage, late 19th century, 70in. wide.   (Christie's) $1,586

Arts and Crafts settle, circa 1910, wide crest rail over nine canted vertical back slats and three vertical slats at each side, 65in. wide.
(Skinner) $1,760

A settee with inlaid mahogany surround, designed by Maria Philipp and Professor Alfred Grenander, the top section with central rectangular mirror, flanked by two narrow shelved compartments, 251cm. wide.
(Christie's) $12,441

A mahogany settee with rounded rectangular padded back, seat and arms upholstered in green velvet, the scrolled arm-terminals profusely carved with foliate swags on a pounced ground above acanthus-carved eared cabriole legs, constructed using 18th century pieces, 48in. wide.   (Christie's) $5,247

A Chippendale mahogany sofa, Philadelphia, 1770–1790, the canted back with serpentine crest flanked by down-sloping outward scrolling arms above a serpentine seatrail, 85¹/₂in. wide.
(Christie's) $38,500

L. & J. G. Stickley settle, no. 281, circa 1910, molded crest rail over sixteen vertical back slats, five vertical side slats, spring cushion seat, Handcraft decal, 76in. wide.
(Skinner) $3,850

SETTEES & COUCHES

A three piece suite in the Hepplewhite style, the mahogany frame with reeded top rails, supported upon cabriole legs carved with stylized foliage.
(Spencer's) $3,465

Victorian grape-carved upholstered loveseat in walnut with cabriole legs, sea green velvet upholstery, 51in. wide. (Eldred's) $248

A Federal mahogany and birchwood settee, New England, probably Massachusetts, early 19th century, on frontal ring-turned tapering legs, 6ft. 4in. long. (Sotheby's) $17,600

An early 19th century carved giltwood sofa in the Louis XV manner, the buttoned back serpentine seat and squab cushion upholstered and piped in pale green silk with scrolled arm terminals, on cabriole legs, 6ft. 6in. wide.
(Phillips) $2,478

A mahogany sofa with padded arched back and sides with roundel arm terminals, 18th century, 73in. wide. (Christie's) $1,568

A very fine Chippendale carved mahogany sofa, Philadelphia, circa 1770, having an arched back, flanked by dramatically out-scrolled and sloped arms, 7ft. 6in. wide.
(Sotheby's) $36,300

A Regency mahogany and gilt brass surmounted day bed with an upholstered panel scroll end, on slight saber legs within stiff foliate gaiters, brass cappings and castors. (Phillips) $1,505

A Federal mahogany sofa, possibly Baltimore, 1790–1810, on square tapering legs with green-painted flower and trailing vine decoration, joined by medial and rear stretchers, 92³/₄in. wide.
(Christie's) $19,800

SETTEES & COUCHES

A Dutch mahogany and floral marquetry scroll end sofa with undulated back and padded seat on splay legs, mid 19th century, 79in. wide. (Christie's) $2,299

An Italian stained beechwood canape, the undulating back with channeled surround, mid-18th century, stenciled indistinctly *Coleman...?*, 75in. wide. (Christie's) $2,822

A Genoese giltwood canape, the waved serpentine molded top-rail centered by a floral cartouche within a stylized C-scroll flanked by eared C-scrolls to the frame, mid-19th century, repairs to both arms, 84in. wide. (Christie's) $1,554

An oak settle, the arched top rail carved with portrait masks and panels of stylized vine leaves, above four foliate carved panels, one bearing the initials *TM* and the date *1708*, early 18th century, 76³/₄in. wide. (Christie's) $1,444

An early Victorian rosewood chaise longue with foliate scroll carved end and button upholstered back on turned lappeted legs, 71in. wide. (Christie's) $1,512

An early Victorian giltwood settee, the rectangular padded back, arms and serpentine seat covered in crimson floral damask, the waved top-rail elaborately carved with trailing foliage and centered by a floral rosette within a stylized C-scroll cartouche, 75in. wide. (Christie's) $5,328

An Edwardian mahogany chair back settee in the Hepplewhite style, with undulating triple shield back, raised upon square tapering supports tied by plain stretchers. (Spencer's) $867

A fine Federal carved mahogany sofa, New York or Philadelphia, circa 1810, the paneled crest carved with drapery swags and tassels centering a reserve carved with a bow with arrows, 6ft. 6in. wide. (Sotheby's) $9,350

329

SIDEBOARDS

Gustav Stickley oak sideboard, no. 814, circa 1904, open plate rack, three central drawers flanked by two cabinet doors over long drawer, 56in. wide. (Skinner) $2,970

A George III inlaid mahogany bowfront sideboard with overall boxwood lines and rosewood bands, on square tapering legs with spade feet, 60in. wide. (Christie's) $3,217

L. & J. G. Stickley sideboard, no. 735, circa 1910, plate rail on overhanging top, central stacked short drawers flanked by cabinet doors above single long drawer, 56in. wide. (Skinner) $2,420

An Arts and Crafts sideboard, circa 1900, dark stained oak, copper, 74in. high. (Sotheby's) $1,057

An inlaid mahogany demi-lune dwarf sideboard, with boxwood and ebony lines, on square tapering legs with spade feet, early 19th century, 48in. wide. (Christie's) $10,010

Classical revival mahogany and mahogany and wavy birch veneer inlaid carved sideboard, Massachusetts, circa 1825, 46¹/₂in. wide. (Skinner) $1,430

A good Federal bird's eye maple and mahogany inlaid cherrywood small sideboard, New England, probably Connecticut, circa 1815, 46in. wide. (Sotheby's) $5,225

A Federal inlaid mahogany sideboard, Massachusetts, 1800–1815, the rectangular top with outset rounded corners and edge inlaid with light and dark wood checkered and chevron banding, on turned feet, 51in. wide. (Christie's) $6,050

An ebony, purplewood and holly-inlaid pollard oak sideboard, by Marsh and Jones, to a design by Charles Bevan, circa 1870, the upper section with mirror. (Sotheby's) $6,138

SIDEBOARDS

Federal cherry inlaid sideboard,
Southern New England, 1790–
1810, 72in. wide.
(Skinner) $13,200

Federal mahogany and veneer
sideboard, Massachusetts, circa
1815, 55in. wide.
(Skinner) $3,575

Federal mahogany inlaid
sideboard, New York, circa
1790, 72in. wide.
(Skinner) $4,400

A Morris & Co. ebonized
sideboard designed by Philip
Webb, the carved and molded
canopied superstructure
mounted with a single molded
shelf supported on turned
columns, 1863, 157cm. wide.
(Christie's) $3,828

Edward Wormley designed
'Janus' sideboard and
superstructure, 1957, for
Dunbar Furniture Corp., black
faux marble drop-in top over
four cabinet doors, 66in. wide.
(Skinner) $3,025

An inlaid oak sideboard
designed by J. P. Seddon, the
castellated rectangular mirrored
superstructure ornately carved,
molded and inlaid, with two
tiled friezes, on molded plinth
base, circa 1870, 197cm. wide.
(Christie's) $10,527

Lifetime Furniture buffet, no.
5272, circa 1910, three short
drawers over single long drawer
with cabinet doors below, brass
hardware.
(Skinner) $825

A small George III mahogany
veneered serpentine front
sideboard with shell marquetry
inlay, the square tapering legs
on socket feet, 4ft. 6in. wide.
(Woolley & Wallis)
                             $6,290

An Art Nouveau sideboard by
Johnson & Appleyard, the
upper section with railed gallery
and repoussé copper panels
depicting stylized trees and
fruit, 6ft. wide.
(Spencer's) $1,567

SIDEBOARDS

A George III elliptical mahogany sideboard, the top with feather stringing to the edge, on shell inlaid square tapering legs, 5ft. wide.
(Woolley & Wallis)
$4,733

Antique server or sideboard in pine with two paneled doors, 52in. wide.
(Eldred's)
$440

A George III mahogany breakfront sideboard inlaid with ebonized lines, the frieze with a drawer above an arched apron flanked by a cupboard and a deep drawer, 5ft. wide.
(Phillips)
$2,880

A fine early Victorian sideboard in oak, carved oval panels of dead game, lion mask capitals, pendants and friezes of flowers and scrolled leafage, 7ft. 4in. wide.
(Russell Baldwin & Bright)
$2,256

A George III mahogany and ebonized sideboard, the bowfronted top with central frieze drawer above a fluted band, flanked to the left by a fitted cellaret drawer simulated as two drawers, 54¼in. wide.
(Christie's)
$7,993

A George II mahogany bowfront sideboard with tulipwood crossbanding and inlaid with boxwood lines, on square tapering legs and spade feet, 3ft. 5in. wide.
(Phillips)
$4,956

A William IV mahogany sideboard, the scroll-capped shaped panel back above a shaped front base, 198cm. wide.
(Allen & Harris)
$2,306

A fine and rare Federal inlaid mahogany diminutive sideboard, Philadelphia, circa 1800, the oblong top with projecting center section, width 54½in.
(Sotheby's)
$34,500

Quaint Furniture mirrored sideboard, circa 1910, gallery top over mirror flanked by arched corbels, 48in. wide.
(Skinner)
$1,100

STANDS

A late 17th century Flemish giltwood stand, the foliate carved frieze above a pierced fascia carved with strapwork, flowerheads and an urn, 2ft. 2in. wide.
(Phillips) $1,562

A pair of gilt-metal and pink-onyx-mounted Sèvres-pattern pedestals in the form of Corinthian columns, the dark-blue grounds painted by B. Guérin in a pale palette with lovers in pastoral landscapes, late 19th century, 43¼in. high.
(Christie's) $16,406

A large majolica bear stick stand, William Brownfield and Sons, circa 1885, naturalistically modeled, the creature standing erect on a rocky base, 34in. high.
(Sotheby's) $3,751

A very fine and rare Chippendale cherrywood scalloped-top candlestand with drawer, attributed to the Chapin family, East Windsor or Hartford, Connecticut, circa 1785.
(Sotheby's) $66,000

A set of Regency bedsteps, both treads with inset green leather surface, on columnar supports and turned tapering legs, 12¼in. and 18in. high.
(Christie's) $1,786

One of a pair of ormolu-mounted ebonized stands, each of square tapering form, with a molded rectangular top, centered by a female mask within an inset pierced scroll panel, late 19th century, 25½in. wide. (Christie's)
(Two) $6,044

A mahogany drum bookstand, the circular top with later brass gallery above four piers in the form of simulated bookspines and four shelves, the Regency base with a gadrooned turned baluster shaft, 23½in. diameter.
(Christie's) $6,090

A pair of walnut torchères, each with hexagonal galleried mahogany top, on spirally-twisted central support and tripod base, part late 17th century, 40in. high.
(Christie's) $1,312

A Regency rosewood double-sided jardinière with reeded rectangular top centered by a removable oval panel enclosing an associated green-painted removable metal tray, on turned tapering feet, 26¼in. wide.
(Christie's) $4,712

STANDS

A late 18th century Dutch mahogany tea comfort, the cylindrical body with a brass liner, the sides carved with trailing flower stems, 10in. diameter.
(Phillips) $1,593

A George II mahogany reading stand, the rectangular ratchet adjustable hinged top with a rising bookcase and two drawers to each side of the frieze, 2ft. 4in. wide.
(Phillips) $3,186

A metal transfer printed umbrella stand, designed by Piero Fornasetti, the beige ground decorated with polychrome walking sticks, crops, umbrellas and golf clubs, 57cm. wide.
(Christie's) $689

Set of Italian baroque walnut library steps, late 18th century, 41in. high.
(Skinner) $3,850

A pair of early 20th century cutlery urns on pedestals, in the manner of Robert Adam, the urns carved in high relief with ram masks and husk pendants, 65in. high.
(Tennants) $4,145

An important oak billiards scoreboard designed by Sir Edwin Lutyens, for Marshcourt, Stockbridge, Hampshire, the central rectangular blackboard flanked by slides with various mother-of-pearl inlaid disks and markers, 112.5cm. wide.
(Christie's) $4,976

A rectangular black marble and boulle work pedestal, the marble top supported by a tapering shaft decorated with ebony and brass boulle work panels and repeating ormolu borders, 19th century, 48³/₈in. high.
(Christie's) $1,525

Edwardian mahogany plant stand with slatted detail, on circular base with ball feet, 15in. wide.
(G. A. Key) $494

A maple stand, on a shaped joined trestle base, painted green, 24in. high.
(Christie's) $1,210

An early Victorian mahogany folio stand, the two slatted sides hinged on to a central baluster and opening to form a table, 30in. wide.
(Bearne's) $3,707

Roycroft 'Little Journeys' bookrack, circa 1910, rectangular overhanging top, two lower shelves with keyed tenons through vertical side slats, 26¼in. wide.
(Skinner) $468

An early Victorian mahogany duet music stand, the hinged lyre shaped easel on a ratchet with adjustable brass twist stem candle brackets.
(Woolley & Wallis) $2,220

A rare and important Momoyama period christian folding missal stand (shokendai), decorated in aogai and hiramakie with a central sunburst halo containing the monogram of the Society of Jesus IHS, late 16th/early 17th century, 36cm. high.
(Christie's) $112,948

A pair of George III mahogany urns-on-stands, with ring-turned flaming finials, the shaped bodies carved with swags of husks and bands of overlapping foliage, 66in. high.
(Christie's) $11,709

A Federal carved mahogany two drawer stand, Salem, Massachusetts, 1790–1810, the rectangular top with outset rounded corners decorated with molded roundels over a conforming case fitted with two cockbeaded frieze drawers, 19½in. wide.
(Christie's) $4,400

An early Victorian mahogany two-tier buffet with channeled standard uprights with scroll brackets, on dual bun feet, 36in. wide.
(Christie's) $1,179

A Louis XVI fruitwood, mahogany and marquetry music stand, stamped *Canabas and Jme*, 2ft. 4in. high.
(Phillips) $2,083

A George III circular mahogany jardinière with a shallow everted rim and fluted frieze, 18in. diameter.
(Lawrence) $2,603

STOOLS

A Belgian ormolu-mounted mahogany stool by Warnie of Bruxelles, the dished padded seat and out-leaning arms covered in florally patterned white and yellow striped silk, late 19th century, 34¹/₂in. wide.
(Christie's) $3,146

A George IV mahogany window-seat, the demi-patera carved frieze mounted with ball finials, 42in. wide.
(Christie's) $6,555

One of a pair of Biedermeier birch stools, each with rectangular padded seat covered in black horsehair, first half 19th century, 23¹/₂in. wide.
(Christie's)
             (Two) $5,345

One of a set of four walnut and oak back stools, the rectangular leather-covered backs above similar seats fastened by brass studs, late 17th century.
(Christie's)
             (Four) $2,359

A pair of early George III mahogany stools, each with dished scroll-end seats on four grooved swept supports, 23¹/₂in. wide, circa 1760.
(Tennants) $17,820

An ebonized and gilt oak circular piano stool, by Lamb of Manchester, circa 1880, the upholstered screw top, above a waisted tripod base.
(Sotheby's) $647

A walnut stool with padded oval seat covered in close-cut floral velvet on a green ground, 21in. wide.
(Christie's) $3,450

A Regency mahogany adjustable foot-stool with beaded horizontal plain frieze and close-nailed tan-leather hinged seat with tablet splat, on saber legs, 16¹/₄in. wide.
(Christie's) $1,261

An Irish mahogany stool of Chippendale style, the rectangular seat upholstered in floral needlework on a yellow ground, with cabriole legs and claw feet, 27¹/₂in. wide.
(Christie's) $4,015

STOOLS

A Regency gilded-mahogany stool, the rectangular seat with padded squab cushion between scrolled horizontally-fluted padded end supports, 50in. wide.
(Christie's) $58,350

A Regency ebonized and parcel-gilt window seat, the padded seat and scrolled arms covered in buttoned pale yellow silk, the channeled frame with flowerhead terminals and on saber legs with shell spandrels, 46in. wide.
(Christie's) $5,049

An unusual painted pine patriotic footstool, Henry G. Perry, New York, circa 1875, painted with a waving American flag with gilt finial, length 18½in.
(Sotheby's) $4,600

An Italian walnut X-framed stool by V. Aimoni, with foliate-carved baluster-turned arms supported by grotesque figures, 33in. wide.
(Christie's) $8,020

A pair of Royal English giltwood stools, from Buckingham Palace, Victorian, circa 1850, 17in. wide.
(Sotheby's) $5,845

A Regency mahogany child's exercise-horse with bellow rectangular seat upholstered in close-nailed red leather, 17in. wide.
(Christie's) $1,470

A George I oval mahogany stool, on cabriole legs headed by a scallop shell and bell husk, on pad feet, 21¼in. wide.
(Christie's) $2,968

A George III mahogany library stool, the rectangular solid saddle pierced with gothic cusps and confronting scrolls, 1ft. 6in. high.
(Phillips) $1,451

A mahogany stool with needlework-covered seat, on cabriole legs joined by stretchers, 22½in. wide.
(Christie's) $4,485

STOOLS

A Regency mahogany hall bench, in the manner of Charles H. Tatham, the rectangular incised seat with hump ends applied with roundels, 4ft. wide.
(Phillips) $2,825

A good antique carved giltwood window seat, the high scrolled ends with flat facings, with horizontal fluting above plain seat, 4ft. 2in. wide.
(Russell Baldwin & Bright) $9,310

An unusual upholstered hooked rug footstool, New England, circa 1850, on turned maple 'turnip' feet, length 28½in.
(Sotheby's) $1,093

A gilded walnut stool, the rounded rectangular padded seat covered in rose and laurel needlework, on acanthus-enriched carved cabriole legs and claw-and-ball feet, 18½in. wide.
(Christie's) $2,941

A set of George III mahogany metamorphic library steps folding into a stool with padded rectangular green leather seat and hinged top opening to reveal a step with square legs, 18½in. wide.
(Christie's) $5,247

An oak and walnut stool, in the Carolean style, with a stuffover seat, on cabriole legs joined by pierced stretchers with cherubs supporting a crown.
(Phillips) $900

L. & J. G. Stickley footstool, circa 1918, original spring cushion and upholstery, medium finish, 20in. wide.
(Skinner) $467

A fancy-painted and decorated footstool, New England, first quarter 19th century, the bowed rectangular top centering a rush seat, on turned cylindrical legs joined by ring and block stretchers, 15¼in. long.
(Christie's) $3,520

Victorian mahogany framed and brown hide covered stool, the frame of 'X' form.
(G. A. Key) $360

STOOLS

A George III carved and decorated window seat, the seat with a cushion and a fluted frieze on turned fluted tapering legs.
(Phillips) $3,868

An antique carved dressing stool in the Louis XV style having floral petit point upholstered seat on six scroll carved supports, 3ft. 6in. wide.
(Russell Baldwin & Bright) $1,125

A George III mahogany-framed window seat with raised over-scrolled sides, on molded square tapering legs with spade feet, 50in. wide.
(Bearne's) $2,295

An oak joint stool, the seat with a molded edge, on ring-turned supports joined by stretchers, part 17th century.
(Phillips) $684

A pair of Victorian stools, with rectangular stuffed over seats, the serpentine frames on cabriole legs, 19in. wide.
(Woolley & Wallis)
$2,352

Late 19th century mahogany framed revolving piano stool, supported by four fluted turned legs.
(G. A. Key) $493

Victorian rosewood stool of tapering step and waisted form with green velvet top and cabriole formed front legs.
(G. A. Key) $366

George III mahogany stool, the upholstered top supported on four cabriole legs with 'C' scrolled shoulders and club feet, mid 18th century.
(G. A. Key) $1,490

A late 17th/early 18th century Italian walnut and marquetry prie dieu, fitted with a frieze drawer and enclosed by a panel door below, on bracket feet, 2ft. 2in. wide.
(Phillips) $2,478

SUITES

A French tapestry upholstered salon suite, circa 1900, of generous proportions comprising a settee and four armchairs, the gilt wood frames elaborately carved with foliage acanthus, the settee 158cm. wide.
(Sotheby's) $21,863

Cloud back suite, 1930s, comprising settee, three armchairs, two footstools, figured veneer, simulated leopard skin upholstery.
(Sotheby's) $7,128

A suite of Empire giltwood seat furniture in the manner of Pierre-Gaston Brion comprising: four fauteuils and eight chairs, with rectangular padded backs and upholstered seats covered in yellow-ground gros and petit-point needlework with vases of flowers.
(Christie's) $31,977

A French Aubusson-upholstered salon suite, Paris, circa 1880, in Louis XVI style, comprising four armchairs, a pair of bergères and a settee, the settee 187cm. long.
(Sotheby's) $45,474

Desk, dressing table and bookcase, circa 1910, mahogany inlaid with fruitwoods, glass, bronze, desk, 49¹/₄in. wide.
(Sotheby's) $9,801

A suite of Louis XVI white-painted seat-furniture by Martin Jullien comprising: a set of four fauteuils, and a pair of bergères en suite with squab and baluster cushions.
(Christie's) $83,495

SUITES

A mahogany sofa and five chairs, the backs carved with stylized palm motifs, on saber legs, second half 19th century, sofa 179cm. wide.
(Finarte) $4,410

A carved walnut 'parlor suite', circa 1865, comprising a 'Grandfather' chair, a 'Grandmother' chair, four side chairs and a chaise longue, all with carved cabriole legs on brown ceramic castors.
(Sotheby's) $7,161

An attractive late Victorian/Edwardian rosewood part salon suite, comprising a set of four single chairs, and a pair of nursing chairs with upholstered cresting rails.
(Spencer's) $1,232

A Regency suite of seat furniture previously black and gilt by John Gee, comprising: a pair of open armchairs and a settee, the overscrolled backs with caned top panels, lower crossbars and cane filled seats on ring turned legs.
(Phillips) $3,186

An Ico Parisi three-piece suite, comprising a chaise-longue and two armchairs, each of curvilinear form, upholstered in dark blue and ivory, on short tapering cylindrical legs, with swivel feet.
(Christie's) $1,531

An Art Deco macassar ebony bedroom suite, comprising: a double bed, two similarly decorated bedside cabinets, and a large wardrobe with central mirrored door flanked by two other doors, concealing adjustable shelving.
(Christie's) $2,488

BREAKFAST TABLES

A coromandel breakfast table, William IV, circa 1830, the circular hinged top with a crossbanded border, 4ft. diameter.
(Sotheby's) $3,018

A Regency rosewood breakfast table, with rounded rectangular banded tip-up top, 60¼in. wide.
(Christie's) $4,297

A Regency rosewood and brass inlaid breakfast table, the circular tip-up top with foliate scroll border above trefoil shaft, 52in. diameter.
(Christie's) $7,326

A George III mahogany breakfast-table with oval tilt-top crossbanded overall upon a turned tapering columnar quadripartite base, 54in. long.
(Christie's) $3,105

A Regency mahogany breakfast-table with rounded rectangular tilt-top, on turned shaft and reeded downswept legs with brass caps, 64in. wide.
(Christie's) $7,762

A Regency oval mahogany breakfast table with banded tip-up top above a turned columnar stem and downswept tripod base, 63in. wide.
(Christie's) $4,061

A mahogany breakfast table, George IV, circa 1820, the hinged top with round corners on a ringed pillar, a platform and four saber legs.
(Sotheby's) $6,900

A George III mahogany and plum-pudding breakfast-table, on turned fluted spreading base and quadripartite base with fluted downswept square tapering legs and brass caps, 42in. diameter.
(Christie's) $16,176

A George III mahogany breakfast-table, with oval top on turned spreading shaft and channeled downswept legs and brass caps, probably adapted from a section of a dining table, 71¼in. wide.
(Christie's) $11,798

BREAKFAST TABLES

A good English satinwood breakfast table, early Victorian, circa 1840, the octagonal tip-top on a square column, 4ft. 1/2in. wide.
(Sotheby's) $5,245

A George III mahogany oval breakfast-table with molded tilt-top crossbanded overall and inlaid with boxwood and ebonized lines, 52³/₄in. wide.
(Christie's) $6,900

A Scottish rosewood and marquetry breakfast table, Victorian, by Deans of Melrose, circa 1845, 4ft. 5in. wide.
(Sotheby's) $5,135

A George IV rosewood breakfast table, the rounded rectangular tilt-top crossbanded with thuyawood, on a part spirally-twisted and reeded turned shaft, 60¹/₄in. wide.
(Christie's) $3,905

A George III mahogany breakfast-table, with associated rounded rectangular twin-flap top above a double-ended frieze drawer, on a concave-fronted platform, octagonal legs and rounded block feet, 41in. wide.
(Christie's) $4,897

A Regency mahogany breakfast-table the rounded rectangular tilt-top crossbanded with rosewood, satinwood, boxwood and ebonized borders, 53in. wide.
(Christie's) $3,450

A walnut circular breakfast or library table, by Howard of Berners Street, London, circa 1860, on tripod support overlaid with gilt bronze acanthus, 4ft. 6in. diameter.
(Sotheby's) $10,230

A Regency mahogany breakfast-table, the oval tilt-top crossbanded and inlaid with boxwood and ebonized lines, late 19th century, 54³/₄in. wide.
(Christie's) $4,500

A Regency giltmetal-mounted rosewood and parcel-gilt breakfast-table, the circular tilt-top banded in satinwood and on turned spreading shaft with gadrooned base, 50³/₄in. diameter.
(Christie's) $6,646

CARD & TEA TABLES

An Edwardian envelope card table in mahogany, having satinwood banding and ebony stringing to the quartered top, 1ft. 11in. square.
(Russell Baldwin & Bright)
$2,265

A Federal carved mahogany card table, New York, circa 1810, on four waterleaf-carved uprights, length 36in.
(Sotheby's) $4,600

A George II mahogany tea table, on lappeted turned tapering legs with pad feet, 29in. wide.
(Christie's) $1,266

A half-round mahogany card table inlaid with boxwood lines, on square tapering legs headed by oval fan medallions, late 18th century and later, 3ft. 2in. wide.
(Phillips) $2,340

Sheraton Revival period mahogany fold top card table, the top inlaid with musical instruments and music and satinwood crossbanded, 1ft. 8in. wide.
(G. A. Key) $432

A mahogany card table with rectangular hinged top on foliate scroll carved cabriole legs with claw and ball feet, second-quarter 18th century, restored, 33in. wide.
(Christie's) $1,359

A good Federal inlaid mahogany serpentine card table, attributed to Bryant & Loud, Boston, Massachusetts, circa 1815, the shaped top with lunette-inlaid edge, 35¼in. wide.
(Sotheby's) $2,750

A Victorian figured walnut card table, raised upon a formal strapwork foliate carved inverted baluster pillar and cabriole quadruped support, 3ft. 1in. wide.
(Spencer's) $1,501

A mid 18th century mahogany demi-lune tea table, the double hinged top enclosing an open compartment, on cabriole legs and claw and ball feet, 2ft. 8in. wide.
(Phillips) $1,682

CARD & TEA TABLES

An early Georgian burr-walnut card table, the crossbanded eared rectangular top enclosing counter-wells, on claw-and-ball feet, 33¼in. wide.
(Christie's) $3,011

A classical carved mahogany swivel-top card table, American, New York or Philadelphia, circa 1820, the oblong crossbanded top with canted corners, width 37¼in.
(Sotheby's) $9,775

An early George III mahogany concertina-action tea table, on molded square legs with pierced acanthus brackets, 36in. wide.
(Bearne's) $4,470

A William IV mahogany 'D'-shaped card table, the turned shaft with leaf carving on a quadripartite platform with outscrolled carved feet, 3ft. wide.
(Phillips) $1,476

A Regency rosewood card table with reeded paneled and roundel decorated frieze on U-shaped support, 26in. wide.
(Christie's) $1,150

An early Victorian mahogany 'D'-shaped card table, the turned column on a quatdripartite platform with gadrooned bun feet, 3ft. wide.
(Phillips) $1,044

An early 19th century Dutch mahogany and floral marquetry triangular card table, on fluted tapering legs with block feet, 19th century, 2ft. 6in. square.
(Phillips) $1,593

A Regency rosewood and simulated rosewood and brass strung card table, on dual turned columns, platform and on scroll headed splayed legs, 3ft. wide.
(Phillips) $2,124

A George III mahogany and satinwood crossbanded 'D'-shaped card table inlaid with boxwood and ebonized lines, on square gaitered legs, 3ft. wide.
(Phillips) $1,800

CARD & TEA TABLES

A Regency rosewood card-table, the canted hinged green baize-lined rectangular top crossbanded in satinwood, above a frieze inlaid with lozenges centered by anthemia, 36in. wide.
(Christie's) $2,093

A late Victorian rosewood and marquetry envelope card table, with overall foliate-scroll decoration, 21½in. wide.
(Christie's) $1,757

A Regency rosewood tea table, the 'D' shaped fold-over swivel top over a plain frieze, raised upon a 'U' shaped support, 3ft. wide.
(Spencer's) $1,419

A Victorian burr walnut-veneered card table with shaped oval fold-over top, and on four splayed legs carved with fruit and flowers, 40½in. wide.
(Bearne's) $1,730

A fine Federal carved mahogany swivel-top card table, New York, circa 1810, on waterleaf-carved reeded and ring-turned legs, 36¾in. wide.
(Sotheby's) $2,475

A Federal carved mahogany card-table, Philadelphia, 1810–1820, the bow-shaped front with reeded edges folding above a conforming crossbanded apron, above a tripod base with three acanthus and molded cabriole trick legs, 36in. wide.
(Christie's) $1,540

A George II red walnut card table, with a well to the paneled frieze, on cabriole legs with pointed pad feet, 33in. wide.
(Lawrence) $1,822

A George III mahogany card table, the divided hinged rectangular top with satinwood ovals and crossbanding, on tapering square legs with brass castors, 18½in. wide.
(Bearne's) $4,060

A mid-Georgian Irish mahogany card table, the deep shaped apron carved with a shell and foliage on a punched ground, 35in. wide.
(Lawrence) $2,863

CARD & TEA TABLES

An early Victorian mahogany card table, raised upon a foliate sheathed cylindrical pillar issuing from a shaped rectangular plinth, 3ft. wide. (Spencer's) **$1,155**

A Victorian walnut card table by Johnstone & Jeanes, raised upon fluted and semi-melon fluted baluster turned double pillar end standards, 3ft. 1in. wide. (Spencer's) **$1,567**

Federal mahogany inlaid card table, probably Massachusetts, circa 1790, 36in. wide. (Skinner) **$6,050**

An early George III mahogany triple top tea cum card table, the card section with dished counter wells, 33in. wide. (Lawrence) **$2,603**

A Federal inlaid mahogany card table, Massachusetts, 1790–1810, the D-shaped hinged top with inset rounded corners, the edge with crossbanding and line inlay folding above a conforming line-inlaid apron, 35¼in. wide. (Christie's) **$3,850**

A mahogany combined bonheur du jour and tea/card table, with triple fold-over top and rising back section, 18th century, 29in. wide. (Christie's) **$2,015**

A George III mahogany folding card table with concertina action, on capped tapering legs and pad feet, 34½in. wide. (Christie's) **$2,676**

A small Queen Anne walnut card table, the semi-circular cross and feather banded top lined with petit point needlework, 24in. wide. (Lawrence) **$6,073**

A George III mahogany small card table, the rounded rectangular green baize-lined top above a frieze drawer, on lappeted club legs and pad feet, 32in. wide. (Christie's) **$2,101**

CENTER TABLES

A French marble-topped serpentine giltwood center table, Paris, circa 1885, with inset brèche-violette marble, the top 140 x 80cm.
(Sotheby's) $9,620

A William IV mahogany center table, the molded rectangular top crossbanded with maple on lyre-shaped end-supports carved with lotus leaves, 60in. wide.
(Christie's) $13,943

A good French marquetry center table, Napoléon III, circa 1860, on fluted tapering legs, 136cm. wide.
(Sotheby's) $7,346

A Continental marquetry center table, Swiss or Austrian, circa 1860, the top etched and inlaid with hunting scenes and a man defending himself from an eagle, 92cm. diameter.
(Sotheby's) $4,373

A giltwood center table, in the Louis XVI style, with a breche violette marble rectangular top, the frieze centered by an Apollo sunburst mask, flanked by panels of scrolling foliage, the tapering fluted legs each with a Corinthian capital, second half 19th century, 38½in. wide.
(Christie's) $3,454

A good English and Italian pietra dura center table, the Derbyshire top with a Florentine base, circa 1860, 85cm. diameter.
(Sotheby's) $16,616

A 19th century Sorrento walnut and marquetry center table, by Luigi Garguilo, inlaid with classical figures after the Antique, 2ft. 5in. wide.
(Phillips) $23,010

A fine Italian micro-mosaic and giltwood circular center table, Rome, circa 1860, 88cm. diameter.
(Sotheby's) $36,729

An impressive bronze center table, the design after the Antique, and possibly by Gottfried Semper, circa 1860, the circular marble top on three lion monopodia, 3ft. 5in. high.
(Sotheby's) $35,805

CENTER TABLES

A French marquetry and parquetry serpentine center table, Napoléon III, Paris, circa 1860, on cabriole legs, 130cm. wide.
(Sotheby's) $4,722

A fine French circular gilt-bronze jardinière table, Napoléon III, cast by Ferdinand Barbedienne, Paris, circa 1860, 86cm. high.
(Sotheby's) $15,391

A French circular ormolu-mounted kingwood and marquetry table, Paris, circa 1890, in flower-inlaid quarter-veneered wood, 77cm. diameter.
(Sotheby's) $4,373

A Gothic Revival oak center table, New York, second quarter 19th century, the octagonal top with green baize lining and molded edge above a conforming frieze with ebonized molding above an octagonal pedestal carved with ogee arches, 48¹/₂in. wide.
(Christie's) $9,900

A rare Queen Anne carved walnut slab-table, Philadelphia, 1730–1750, the rectangular thumbmolded marble top above a conforming walnut apron with shaped multiple lobed skirt, 36¹/₂in. wide.
(Christie's) $462,000

A bronzed and ebonized center table with associated circular painted marble top decorated with figures on rocks in a Mediterranean coastal scene within a border of oak leaves and acorns on a black ground, 19th century, 33¹/₄in. diameter.
(Christie's) $4,719

An unusual German oval porcelain mounted elm center table, circa 1850, the top with one hexagonal and six circular Sèvres-style plaques, top 129 x 94cm.
(Sotheby's) $3,498

A Chinese export black and gilt lacquer center table, the circular tilt-top decorated with a chinoiserie battle scene within a foliate border with mythical monsters, first half 19th century, 36in. diameter.
(Christie's) $4,719

An unusual North Italian burr walnut table, inlaid all over with fruitwood marquetry, with serpentine molded border, 117cm. diameter, 19th century.
(Finarte) $28,466

CENTER TABLES

A George IV mahogany center
table with wide crossbanding to
the circular tip-up top, on four
hipped reeded splayed legs,
49½in. diameter.
(Bearne's) $4,413

A South German walnut and
marquetry center table, the
rectangular top with rounded
corners inlaid with figures in
various country pursuits within
strapwork borders, 19th
century, 59in. wide.
(Christie's) $3,003

A Victorian amboyna inlaid and
brass mounted center table, the
oval quarter veneered surface
widely banded in walnut and
kingwood, 54in. wide.
(Tennants) $3,070

A Regency mahogany center
table, the circular top inset with
a slab of pink mottled Verona
marble, on part-fluted baluster
shaft, 32½in. diameter.
(Christie's) $1,087

A mid-Victorian walnut and
marquetry center table in the
style of Edward Holmes
Baldock, the circular top
centered by a floral circle and
inlaid overall with flowers and
foliage scrolls, 53¼in. diameter.
(Christie's) $7,771

An early 19th century
mahogany table, the top of green
marble, on turned central
column and concave triform
base, 112.5cm. diameter.
(Finarte) $3,416

A circular maplewood and oak
center table, circa 1850, with a
strapwork-filled purple-heart
roundel and crossbanding, and
the leaf-carved baluster on three
carved scroll legs, 4ft. 4in.
diameter.
(Sotheby's) $3,410

An Edwardian giltwood and
painted center table, the pale
hexagonal top painted with a
roundel of hop pickers, 56in.
wide.
(Lawrence) $5,900

A Victorian mahogany center
table, the molded foliate carved
and fluted baluster shaft
supporting four scrolled
columns, stretching to foliate
carved scrolled toes, 37in. wide.
(Christie's) $1,540

CENTER TABLES

A fruitwood center table now with frieze drawer, the rectangular top with shaped friezes on tapering fluted legs, early 19th century, 43in. wide. (Christie's) $991

A Victorian mahogany shaped oval center table, on lobed carved pedestal with four leaf carved scroll supports, 131 x 79cm. (Allen & Harris) $1,328

A Victorian carved oak center table, the rectangular top with deeply molded and carved edge above leafage carved frieze, one side with drawer, 4ft. 6in. x 3ft. (Russell Baldwin & Bright) $1,330

A 19th century walnut and marquetry center table, with geometric fruitwood inlay, on a turned baluster column and quadripartite base, 89cm. diameter, Sorrento. (Finarte) $1,423

A colored glass mosaic center table, the circular top inset with a star motif to the center within geometric designs and a guilloche band, the molded ebonized edge with a brass band, 19th century, 44in. diameter. (Christie's) $3,108

A burr walnut and ormolu mounted center table, with white marble top, on concave triangular column and paw feet, 118cm. diameter, early 19th century. (Finarte) $7,116

A George IV rosewood center table with a reeded rim, on concave triangular platform base with grooved knob terminals, on fluted bun feet, 51in. diameter. (Christie's) $2,509

A center table with agate top of irregular outline on base formed of antler horns, 25in. wide. (Christie's) $1,814

A Victorian center table, veneered in faded amboyna, on inlaid splayed legs with brass casters, 3ft. 6in. wide. (Woolley & Wallis) $3,339

CONSOLE TABLES

One of a pair of Louis XV giltwood console tables each with serpentine-molded brown breccia marble top above a pierced frieze with central scallop shell, 46¼in. wide.
(Christie's)
(Two) $30,200

One of a set of four Continental parcel gilt corner console tables, probably French, circa 1880, in Louis XV/XVI Transitional manner, 75cm. wide.
(Sotheby's)
(Four) $7,346

A George III sycamore, burr, yew-wood and crossbanded pier table, in the manner of William Moore of Dublin, the elliptical top radially veneered with central fan lunette and fan segments, 4ft. 1in. wide.
(Phillips) $10,413

One of a pair of Louis XVI ormolu-mounted white-painted and parcel-gilt corner consoles each with eared bowed honey alabaster top, 36in. wide.
(Christie's)
(Two) $35,530

A pine console table with portor rectangular marble top above a Vitruvian scroll frieze supported upon a splayed eagle resting on a rockwork base, 29½in. wide.
(Christie's) $4,686

One of a pair of mahogany and giltwood console tables, each with rectangular top above a deep paneled frieze with entrelac and rosette beneath lotus-leaf, late 18th/early 19th century, 27in. wide.
(Christie's)
(Two) $10,098

An Empire white painted console table, with rectangular white marble top, the front supports carved with gilt female terms, 137.5cm. wide.
(Finarte) $8,895

A late 17th/early 18th century carved giltwood console table, the legs and stretchers heavily carved with foliate and shell motifs, with yellow marble top, Neapolitan.
(Finarte) $9,620

A rare French 'Boulle' pier table, Louis-Philippe, Paris, circa 1845, the inverted breakfront frieze above four square tapering legs, 113cm. wide.
(Sotheby's) $5,422

CONSOLE TABLES

An 18th century Italian baroque giltwood console table with a later rectangular Siena mottled marble veneered top, 5ft. 3in. wide.
(Phillips) $5,653

A George II carved giltwood 'eagle' console base, in the form of a four winged bird, one claw resting on an orb, 3ft. 7in. wide.
(Phillips) $6,018

One of a pair of Bolognese giltwood console tables each with later serpentine green marble top above a molded frieze and pierced apron, mid-18th century, 68in. wide.
(Christie's)
(Two) $35,530

One of a pair of ormolu and verde antico console tables, each with molded rectangular top above a plain frieze mounted at each end with a patera, possibly North European, 35¹/₂in. wide.
(Christie's)
(Two) $14,212

A Louis XVI brass-inlaid mahogany console desserte with rectangular gray marble top with pierced three-quarter gallery, on later toupie feet, 34¹/₄in. wide.
(Christie's) $4,619

A marble top pier table, attributed to Charles-Honore Lannuier, New York, 1819, the rectangular white marble top with canted corners above a conforming frame centering applied ormolu trophies and foliage, 43in. wide.
(Christie's) $12,100

A Swedish giltwood console table attributed to Burchardt Precht with molded rectangular green and white Swedish Tolmards granite top, early 18th century, 39³/₄in. wide.
(Christie's) $35,530

A George III giltwood console table in the manner of Thomas Johnson, the top of arc en arbelette outline with a later marble slab, 2ft. 6in. wide.
(Phillips) $9,669

An early Louis XV oak console table, with later-rounded-rectangular mottled red-marble top, 34in. wide.
(Christie's) $4,620

DINING TABLES

An Arts and Crafts oak dining
table, rectangular paneled top
above shaped frieze and four
square section chamfered legs,
137.5cm. wide.
(Christie's) $1,914

A William IV mahogany
extending dining table, on a
concave square tapering pillar
issuing from a concave square
platform and shell carved
stylized claw feet, 9ft. 11in. long
extended.
(Spencer's) $2,185

An oak extending dining table
designed by Arthur Romney
Green, with carved scalloped
details, on four hexagonal
carved legs supporting platform
shelf, on X-shaped stretcher,
187cm. wide (extended).
(Christie's) $3,062

A large William IV rosewood
veneered loo table, the triform
base on knurled toes with tulip
scrolls, 4ft. 5in. diameter.
(Woolley & Wallis)
    $1,987

An early Victorian burr walnut
and walnut dining-table by
Gillows, the circular top with
plain frieze and on part-
gadrooned turned spreading
fluted legs, 60in. diameter.
(Christie's) $36,465

A rosewood veneered loo table,
the grained base with a turned
stem and three splay legs with
shaped knees, 4ft. diameter.
(Woolley & Wallis)
    $1,590

A Louis XIV walnut refectory
table, the detachable
rectangular top pegged and
fitting onto a cross frame, on
ring-turned columns with bun
feet, 1.1m. x 89cm.
(Phillips) $2,301

Federal walnut inlaid banquet
table, probably Virginia, circa
1800, 92in. wide open.
(Skinner) $2,640

Gustav Stickley dining table, no.
632, circa 1904, overhanging
round top with apron on five
square tapering legs, 49in.
diameter.
(Skinner) $2,420

DINING TABLES

A Charles I oak draw leaf refectory table, the rectangular framed top with retractable ends on ring turned spreading column legs joined by stretchers, 4ft. 8in. long.
(Phillips) $3,240

A Victorian burr-walnut loo table, shaped oval tip-up top on a bulbous pillar with triple curved supports, 57in. wide.
(Lawrence Fine Art)
                              $1,515

A small early 17th century oak refectory table, the rectangular plank top above an arcaded front frieze, on baluster turned legs joined by stretchers, 7ft. 2in. long.
(Phillips) $8,100

An early Victorian mahogany drum top library table, the circular leatherette inset top above four frieze drawers on a turned spreading shaft, 3ft. 6in. diameter.
(Phillips) $2,880

A George IV loo table, the circular tilt top veneered in figured rosewood, with a band of brass marquetry and a gadroon edge, 4ft. 2in. diameter.
(Woolley & Wallis)
                              $5,995

A mid-Victorian burr-walnut loo table with oval quarter-veneered tip-up top and cabochon carved baluster shaft, 39in. wide.
(Christie's) $1,091

An early Victorian mahogany extending dining table with rounded rectangular top on turned tapered legs, 127in. extended.
(Christie's) $2,926

A Victorian mahogany extending dining table, the two central baluster supports each with two splayed scroll-carved legs, 94in. wide.
(Bearne's) $3,442

A mahogany circular extending dining table with foliate carved and ribbon-twist frieze, on foliate carved turned legs, 120in. wide.
(Christie's) $2,788

DINING TABLES

A good Victorian rosewood dining table with quatrefoil shaped top, 59 x 43in.
(G. E. Sworder) **$1,869**

Regency mahogany extending dining table on tapering spiral turned legs with brass terminals, 48 x 88in.
(Ewbank) **$5,338**

A Regency rosewood and parcel-gilt center table, the circular tilt-top on bold acanthus-carved turned shaft, 53$\frac{1}{2}$in. diameter.
(Christie's) **$14,662**

An extending dining table, with rounded rectangular top on foliate-headed line-inlaid baluster-turned legs with brass cappings and castors, 201$\frac{1}{2}$in. wide extended.
(Christie's) **$6,000**

A mid-Victorian rosewood, mahogany and marquetry dining table, the circular tip-up top with central radially-veneered circular panel, 52in. diameter.
(Christie's) **$3,750**

A 19th century mahogany 7 leaf extending table, the central standard in the form of columns on a quadripartite base and paw feet, 153cm. diameter unextended, each leaf 30.5cm.
(Finarte) **$7,828**

A South German burr walnut veneered table on gadrooned baluster column and tripartite base, 115cm. diameter.
(Kunsthaus am Museum) **$2,786**

A William and Mary turned walnut and yellow pine gateleg dining table, American, probably Southern, 1720–50, width extended 51in.
(Sotheby's) **$9,200**

Regency rosewood round dining table on turned gadrooned central pillar and platform base with lion's paw feet, 53in. diameter.
(Ewbank) **$3,140**

DRESSING TABLES

A George III mahogany kidney-shaped dressing table crossbanded overall and with a central frieze drawer, on square tapering legs, 42½in. wide. (Christie's) $6,037

An Empire mahogany and ormolu mounted dressing table, with arched swing frame plate on columns with urn finials, 2ft. 2in. wide. (Phillips) $2,231

A fine George III mahogany Rudd's dressing chest, with a molded edge centered by a fitted drawer, having carrying handles to the sides, on bracket feet, 3ft. 6in. wide. (Phillips) $8,925

An Anglo-Chinese white-metal-mounted padouk dressing-table with part-hinged tripartite serpentine top banded in ebony and with boxwood stringing, enclosing a central mirrored section within an ebony frame, mid-18th century, 33in. wide. (Christie's) $14,306

A Queen Anne maple dressing table, Massachusetts, 1740–1760, the rectangular top with thumbmolded edges above a conforming case fitted with one long thumbmolded drawer above three short thumbmolded drawers, 33½in. wide. (Christie's) $8,250

A Louis XV ormolu-mounted mahogany and tulipwood poudreuse by Roger Vandercruse Lacroix (RVLC), the banded waved eared rectangular tripartite top inlaid à quatre faces with key-pattern corners, 36¼in. wide. (Christie's) $13,464

A George III ormolu-mounted rosewood, sycamore and marquetry serpentine dressing-table attributed to Mayhew & Ince, 33in. wide. (Christie's) $53,856

An Edwardian satinwood, crossbanded and decorated bowfront lady's dressing table, painted with floral and drapery swags and sprays, 1ft. 10in. wide. (Phillips) $2,400

The Samuel Morris Chippendale carved mahogany dressing table, Philadelphia, 1760–1780, on shell-carved cabriole legs with ball-and claw feet, 36in. wide. (Christie's) $28,600

DRESSING TABLES

A classical mahogany dressing table with mirror, attributed to the workshop of Duncan Phyfe & Sons, New York, circa 1845, 47⅞in. wide.
(Sotheby's) $7,700

Queen Anne cherry base to high chest of drawers, New England, circa 1770, 37in. wide.
(Skinner) $1,540

A Federal mahogany dressing table with mirror, Philadelphia, circa 1825, surmounted by spirally turned uprights centering a rectangular mirror, width 37in.
(Sotheby's) $805

A Queen Anne oak dressing table, England, circa 1725, the rectangular molded top above a conforming case with a central long drawer flanked by two short drawers, 31in. wide.
(Christie's) $1,870

A Regency mahogany dressing-table by Gillows of Lancaster, the rounded rectangular three quarter-galleried top above a mahogany-lined paneled frieze drawer, on gadrooned turned tapering legs and toupie feet, 27in. wide.
(Christie's) $3,235

A walnut and marquetry dressing table with triple hinged top with central floral ribbon-twist inlay enclosing compartments and a mirror, 31½in. wide.
(Christie's) $1,190

A Chippendale carved mahogany dressing table, Philadelphia, circa 1770, the rectangular thumb-molded top above one long and three short molded drawers, 35in. wide.
(Sotheby's) $20,900

An ivory inlaid macassar ebony veneered dressing table, inlaid overall with ivory stringing, long rectangular mirror swiveled on square-section supports, circa 1930, 121cm. wide.
(Christie's) $1,148

A Chippendale mahogany dressing table, Philadelphia, 1760–1780, on four cabriole legs, the knees shell-carved, with claw-and-ball feet, 36½in. wide.
(Christie's) $7,700

DRESSING TABLES

A Federal carved mahogany dressing table with mirror, New York, circa 1815, the rectangular mirror plate pivoting between two scrolled supports, 36½in. wide.
(Sotheby's) $3,300

A Regency Irish mahogany double-fronted dressing table with a rectangular recessed top with rope-twist rim above five drawers surrounding an arched kneehole, 54in. wide.
(Christie's) $3,680

A Federal mahogany dressing chest with mirror, labeled *Michael Allison*, New York, circa 1821, the oblong top surmounted by two scrolled supports centering a rectangular mirror, width 38⅛in.
(Sotheby's) $2,875

A Queen Anne carved walnut dressing-table, Salem, Massachusetts, 1725–1760, the rectangular top with cupid's bow corners above a conforming case with a long drawer over a pair of short drawers, on cabriole legs with pad feet, 34½in. wide.
(Christie's) $4,950

A George III mahogany dressing table, the divided hinged rectangular top enclosing a fitted interior with adjustable mirror, with block feet and leather castors.
(Bearne's) $5,472

A Louis XVI-style mahogany and marquetry dressing table applied throughout with gilt brass mounts, the hinged rectangular top with projecting corners and inlaid with musical trophies, 26in. wide.
(Bearne's) $2,383

Federal mahogany dressing table, New England, circa 1825, 33in. wide.
(Skinner) $605

A 19th century mahogany dressing table, with white marble top above frieze drawer, on turned legs, 114cm. wide.
(Finarte) $3,202

A Louis XV cherrywood toilet table, the molded top opening to reveal a mirror and various compartments, 65cm. wide.
(Finarte) $9,252

DRESSING TABLES

A small kingwood veneered necéssaire, possibly English, circa 1900, various hallmarked silver gilt fittings, 82.5cm. high.
(Sotheby's) $4,198

A French gilt-bronze mounted dressing table, by Krieger of Paris, circa 1900, 110cm. wide, fitted for electricity.
(Sotheby's) $6,020

A German ormolu-mounted burr elm, burr thuya and mahogany dressing-table of Empire style, early 19th century, 40³/₄in. wide.
(Christie's) $6,200

A Louis XVI mahogany dressing table with molded rounded rectangular hinged top with mirror on the reverse, the interior with later marble base, 32¹/₂in. wide.
(Christie's) $3,553

A fine and rare Queen Anne mahogany block-front kneehole dressing table, Boston, Massachusetts, circa 1760, on scroll-cut bracket feet, width 36in.
(Sotheby's) $90,500

A William and Mary black-painted pine and maple dressing-table with baluster and trumpet-turned legs joined by flat serpentine X-stretchers, 32¹/₂in. wide.
(Christie's) $9,350

An inlaid toilet table attributed to Luigi Gargiulo, the surface with a mythological scene within a foliate border, Sorrento, 1840, 72cm. wide.
(Finarte) $14,584

A North Italian walnut crossbanded and strung bombé kneehole dressing table of serpentine form, on cabriole legs, 3ft. 6in. wide.
(Phillips) $4,602

An Arts and Crafts dressing table, circa 1900, oak, copper handles, lockplates and repoussé panels, 4ft. wide.
(Sotheby's) $1,477

DROP LEAF TABLES

A William and Mary maple gate-leg table, New England, 1700–1730, with rectangular top and two hinged rectangular leaves, 36in. wide open. (Christie's) $4,600

A classical carved and inlaid mahogany breakfast table, attributed to Duncan Phyfe, New York, 1805–1815, 49¹/₂in. wide open. (Christie's) $5,750

19th century mahogany Sutherland table on a central reeded pillar and quadruped base with matching supports, 32in. wide. (Ewbank) $740

A fine and rare French marquetry occasional or Sutherland table, attributed to Joseph Cremer, Napoléon III, Paris, circa 1855, 103cm. wide open. (Sotheby's) $51,359

A very fine and rare Queen Anne maple 'butterfly' tavern table, New England, 1730–60, the oblong top with two hinged D-shaped leaves, width extended 37¹/₄in. (Sotheby's) $9,350

A William and Mary gumwood trestle drop-leaf table, New York, 1720–1735, the oval top with hinged drop leaves above baluster and ring-turned legs, 33³/₄in. wide. (Christie's) $20,900

A Queen Anne mahogany drop-leaf table, Rhode Island or Pennsylvania, 1740–1760, the hinged oval top with D-shaped drop-leaves, 43³/₄in. open. (Christie's) $8,000

A burr-walnut Sutherland table, Victorian, circa 1850, with shaped oval top, 117cm. open. (Sotheby's) $1,495

A Queen Anne mahogany drop-leaf table, Salem or Boston, Massachusetts, 1740–1760, with two rounded drop leaves, 30¹/₂in. wide. (Christie's) $36,800

DROP LEAF TABLES

A George II mahogany oval dining table, with two gate flaps raised on four pied-de-biche supports with scroll eared tops, 150cm. wide.
(Allen & Harris) $2,844

A Federal red-painted maple and pine drop-leaf harvest table, American, first half 19th century, painted red, length 6ft.
(Sotheby's) $4,600

Antique American Sheraton drop leaf table in cherry, one drawer in apron, turned legs, top open, 42 x 48in.
(Eldred's) $330

A Queen Anne maple drop-leaf dining table, New England, circa 1775, the cyma-shaped skirt continuing to cabriole legs ending in pad feet, length 53in.
(Sotheby's) $2,990

A fine Queen Anne mahogany drop-leaf dining table, Goddard-Townsend School, Newport, Rhode Island, 1740–60, on turned tapered legs ending in pad feet, width extended 48¹/₄in.
(Sotheby's) $4,950

A mahogany drop-leaf table with rounded rectangular twin-flap top above a plain frieze with ogee-shaped apron, on later cabriole legs headed by acanthus knees, part 18th century, 38¹/₂in. wide.
(Christie's) $787

A Federal painted birchwood drop-leaf dining table, New England, circa 1810, on square tapering legs, the base painted red, length 39¹/₂in.
(Sotheby's) $1,495

An oak drop-leaf table, designed by Henry Woodyer, circa 1860, in 18th-century manner, but with stylized medieval detail, 2ft. 11¹/₂in. wide.
(Sotheby's) $1,705

A good Chippendale walnut drop-leaf breakfast table, Boston, Massachusetts, circa 1760, the oblong top with two hinged D-shaped leaves, 35³/₄in. long.
(Sotheby's) $3,300

DROP LEAF TABLES

A good Queen Anne maple drop leaf dining table, Rhode Island, circa 1765, on angular cabriole legs ending in pad feet, width extended 52½in.
(Sotheby's) $3,335

An early 19th century Dutch inlaid mahogany drop leaf dining table, raised upon turned and tapering fly leg supports with foliate inlay, 3ft. 7in. wide.
(Spencer's) $1,422

Queen Anne cherry dining table, New England, circa 1760, 53in. wide open.
(Skinner) $7,150

A well-figured walnut Sutherland table, possibly London, circa 1860, the oval hinged top with twist turned supports, the trestle legs with ceramic castors, 3ft. 4in. wide.
(Sotheby's) $1,875

Gustav Stickley round drop leaf table, circa 1912, demi-lune drop leaves, paper label, 32in. long.
(Skinner) $1,430

A Queen Anne walnut drop-leaf table, Pennsylvania, 1740–1760, the oval top with two drop leaves above a shaped skirt, on cabriole legs with slipper feet, 65½in. wide.
(Christie's) $9,350

Queen Anne mahogany dining table, Rhode Island, circa 1770, 46½in. wide open.
(Skinner) $5,500

A George II mahogany drop-leaf table, the oval top on turned legs with club feet, 3ft. 11in. long.
(Phillips) $900

Chippendale walnut dining table, Pennsylvania, 1770–90, with two end thumb-molded drawers, 49¼in. wide.
(Skinner) $4,290

365

DRUM TABLES

A Regency mahogany drum top table, on turned column and quadruped splayed legs with foliate carved ornament, 4ft. diameter.
(Phillips) $5,950

A George III mahogany rent table, on a cupboard base enclosed by a panel door, on a plinth base, 3ft. 7in. diameter.
(Phillips) $5,653

A George III circular mahogany drum table with inset gray tooled leather top, with four reeded splay legs, 42in. diameter.
(Anderson & Garland)
$4,213

A Regency mahogany drum top library table, on a baluster turned column and quadruped reeded splayed legs, brass cappings and castors, 3ft. 1in. diameter.
(Phillips) $5,058

A Regency mahogany library table with circular green leather-lined top above a paneled frieze with eleven mahogany-lined segmental drawers, on turned spreading shaft and quadripartite base, 54½in. diameter.
(Christie's) $8,151

A George III mahogany drum table, the circular top with inset green leather above two long and two short drawers lettered *B/R/M/L* and four simulated drawers, 40¾in. diameter.
(Christie's) $12,623

A Regency maplewood drum table inlaid with ebonized lines, the circular green leather inset top above eight frieze drawers, 2ft. 8in. diameter.
(Phillips) $5,250

A Regency mahogany library drum table, the circular leather inset top above four frieze drawers, 3ft. 5in. diameter.
(Phillips) $4,500

A Regency mahogany and yew-wood drum table, the circular banded top centered by a circle, the frieze with two cedar-lined drawers, 30in. diameter.
(Christie's) $9,000

DUMB WAITERS

A mid-Georgian mahogany three-tier dumb waiter with ring-turned baluster shaft, **arched base and pad molded feet, 47in. high.**
(Christie's) $1,505

A George III mahogany two-tier dumb waiter, the circular hinged tiers on downswept legs with brass caps and castors, 2ft. 8in. high.
(Phillips) $1,487

A George II mahogany three-tier dumb waiter, each circular shelf on baluster-turned shaft and chamfered tripod base and pointed pad feet, 43¹/₂in. high.
(Christie's) $3,848

A Regency mahogany triple folding three-tier dumb waiter with hinged tops, on column and tripod splayed legs.
(Phillips) $2,655

A pair of mahogany and brass-mounted two tier dumb waiters, each circular tier with pierced Greek key gallery, each 22½in. diameter.
(Christie's) $2,418

A George III mahogany dumb waiter of good color, with three dished circular tiers, 40in. high.
(Bonhams) $4,500

A mahogany three-tiered dumb-waiter with circular dished tiers on laurel-carved baluster shaft and downswept legs carved with acanthus, 18th century, 26in. diameter.
(Christie's) $3,362

One of a pair of brass-mounted mahogany dumb-waiters, on turned spreading shaft and tripod base with channeled downswept legs, block feet and casters, 45¹/₂in. high.
(Christie's) $9,257

A George III mahogany two-tier folding dumb-waiter, each double-hinged tier with rounded rectangular swiveling support, on turned urn-shaped shaft, 23in. wide.
(Christie's) $1,219

GATELEG TABLES

An oak gateleg table, the oval drop leaf top on chamfered legs with stretchers, 4ft. 7in. x 6ft. (Woolley & Wallis)

$3,330

A William and Mary maple gate-leg dining-table, probably Massachusetts, 1730–1745, with oval drop-leaf top above an apron with single end drawer, 45¹/₂in. deep.
(Christie's)

$6,050

An early George III mahogany gateleg table with an oval top, on cabriole legs with scrolled knees with pony's hoof feet, 44in. wide.
(Lawrence)

$3,037

George III mahogany spider-leg table, last quarter 18th century, the rectangular top with drop leaves, length open 29¹/₂in.
(Butterfield & Butterfield)

$3,500

An early 18th century Chinese export lacquer triple top games table top, on an English black japanned turned gateleg frame, 32in. wide.
(Lawrence)

$1,562

A late 17th century oak gateleg table with oval top, frieze drawer, the baluster legs joined by square stretchers, 28¹/₄in. high.
(Bearne's)

$671

A rare William and Mary walnut large gateleg table, Pennsylvania or Middle Atlantic States, early 18th century, on baluster-and ring-turned supports.
(Sotheby's)

$2,475

Ernest W. Gimson, folding table, 1907, walnut, 36¹/₄in. wide.
(Sotheby's)

$3,386

William and Mary walnut gateleg table, New York or Pennsylvania, 18th century, the oval top with two drop leaves, 5ft. 1in. wide.
(Butterfield & Butterfield)

$9,000

GATELEG TABLES

Fine quality antique oak gate leg dining table with end drawer, standing on baluster legs, approximately 4ft. 3in. wide.
(G. A. Key) $708

An early George III mahogany gate-leg dining table with D-shaped flaps on six chamfered block legs, 58in. long.
(Hy. Duke & Son) $1,080

A William and Mary maple butterfly gate-leg table, New England, 1730–1750, on double baluster-turned legs joined by a box stretcher and with butterfly wing supports, 46in. wide.
(Christie's) $19,800

A rare William and Mary turned walnut gateleg dining table, American, probably New York, circa 1720, on block-turned legs joined by blocked stretchers, width 54in.
(Sotheby's) $10,350

A George III mahogany spider gateleg table, the rectangular twin flap top on ring turned legs joined by turned stretchers, 2ft. 3in. wide.
(Phillips) $1,770

Drop leaf maple and pine trestle base table, New England, 18th century, refinished, 37½in. open.
(Skinner) $2,970

A Charles II oak gateleg table, the oval hinged top on bobbin turned legs joined by rectangular stretchers, 4ft. 1in. x 3ft. 9in.
(Phillips) $900

William and Mary walnut and maple gateleg table, New England, 18th century, the oval top with two drop leaves above a frieze with one short drawer, 48in. wide.
(Butterfield & Butterfield) $7,000

An oak gateleg table, the oval hinged top on turned legs joined by stretchers, basically early 18th century, 4ft. 4in. x 3ft. 11in.
(Phillips) $630

LARGE TABLES

An Edwardian mahogany extending dining table
with rounded rectangular top on foliate-headed
cabriole legs, 152in. wide extended.
(Christie's) $3,872

A Regency mahogany patent extending dining
table, the hinged 'D'-shaped reeded top with two
extra leaves, on concertina action turned and
ribbed legs, 6ft. 11in. long.
(Phillips) $6,195

A George IV mahogany extending dining table
with D shape pedestal ends, each on three saber
shape leaf capped supports, 126in. long.
(Lawrence Fine Art) $4,990

A late Federal mahogany three-part dining table,
New York, circa 1820, on ring and spirally
turned legs on brass casters, length 9ft. 6in.
(Sotheby's) $6,038

A William IV mahogany and brass mounted
extending dining table with concertina action,
the D end folding over and extending to take
three additional leaves, 132in. long.
(Lawrence Fine Art) $9,240

A William and Mary oak and pine stretcher-base
table with molded edge over four block and
baluster-turned supports, on baluster feet joined
by molded box stretchers, 67³/₄in. long.
(Christie's) $3,080

An oak refectory table, the rectangular support
above a channeled frieze and on baluster-turned
legs joined by plain stretchers, part 17th century,
116in. long.
(Christie's) $5,247

An early 19th century mahogany twin-pedestal
dining table, on ring-turned knopped column
and quadruped splayed reeded legs terminating
in paw feet and castors, 6ft. 6in. extended.
(Phillips) $8,925

LARGE TABLES

An early 19th century mahogany twin pillar dining table with a molded edge on ring-turned columns and reeded splayed quadruped supports, 6ft. 2in. long.
(Phillips) $4,248

An oak refectory table with rectangular plank top, on turned legs joined by stretchers, basically late 17th century, 119in. long.
(Christie's) $5,855

A Charles I oak refectory table, with a rectangular plank top, the front with an interlaced lunette carved frieze on ring turned barrel shaped legs, 11ft. long.
(Phillips) $8,640

An early 19th century mahogany D-end dining table with reeded edge to the top, on tapering legs with ebonized ring-turned details, 108in. long.
(Bearne's) $5,295

A French Provincial walnut center table, the rounded rectangular top with central star inlay above waved scroll frieze, late 18th century, 76in. wide.
(Christie's) $3,520

A fine Federal mahogany three-part dining table, American, probably Boston, circa 1810, on turned and reeded tapering legs ending in ball feet, length extended 13ft. 3$\frac{1}{2}$in.
(Sotheby's) $7,700

A classical mahogany three-pedestal dining table, American, circa 1825, comprising a rectangular center section and two D-shaped end sections, length approximately 15ft. 7in.
(Sotheby's) $13,800

A classical mahogany two-part dining table, 19th century, comprising two end sections above an inlaid frieze with removable leaf, length extended 68$\frac{1}{2}$in.
(Sotheby's) $4,675

A mid-Victorian polished granite occasional table with circular segmentally-inlaid specimen marble top edged with polished slate, on a baluster shaft, 20³/₄in. diameter.
(Christie's) $8,404

A rare Queen Anne cherrywood slate-top mixing table, Pennsylvania, 1730–1750, on tapering cylindrical legs with pad feet, 26¹/₄in. wide.
(Christie's) $15,400

A Regency rosewood and brass mounted octagonal wine table, on foliate reeded column circular trefoil base with ball ornament, with scroll feet, 1ft. 3¹/₂in. wide.
(Phillips) $3,540

An Empire mahogany and brass inlaid and mounted bouillotte table with pierced galleried breche d'Alep marble circular top fitted with slides and drawers, 2ft. 1¹/₂in. diameter.
(Phillips) $3,363

A 19th century Belgian black and micro mosaic round table top, the center with Pliny's doves within a lapis band, surrounded by panels with Roman scenes, 75cm. diameter.
(Finarte) $39,906

A rare William and Mary painted and turned cherrywood stretcher table, New York or Connecticut, 1710–50, painted gray over red, length 21³/₄in.
(Sotheby's) $13,800

An early 19th century decorated occasional table, the top depicting a seascape with rounded corners, the frieze with classical grisaille figures, 2ft. 7in. high.
(Phillips) $2,655

A William and Mary cherrywood slate-top table, the rectangular top with inset slate panel above an elaborately scalloped apron, 25in. wide.
(Christie's) $6,050

A painted papier mâché tripod table, circa 1840, the circular tip-top with a monk surveying the day's game, entitled *Bolton Abbey*, 62cm. diameter.
(Sotheby's) $8,525

A fine George III sabicu envelope-top tripod table, the cross-banded harewood-veneered top set with a yewwood circular reserve centered by a sunburst motif, 28in. high. (Bearne's) $75,895

A mid 19th century walnut veneered table, richly inlaid with fruitwood and mother of pearl, on a carved column and four carved legs ending on paw feet, Umbrian, 82cm. high. (Finarte) $13,539

A fine George III painted and parcel-gilt specimen marble top occasional table, in the manner of Robert Adam, the circular top veneered with a trompe l'oeil design, 2ft. 4in. high. (Phillips) $7,735

A walnut and palisander veneered circular table, inlaid with fruitwood, the central medallion flanked by female figures in regional costumes, Piedmont, mid 19th century, 102cm. diameter. (Finarte) $8,141

A George III mahogany architect's table, the rounded rectangular hinged rising top with re-entrant corners and spring-loaded book-support, with two hinged brass candle-slides, on canted square legs and scrolled-carved block feet, 37¾in. wide. (Christie's) $6,122

A George III mahogany tripod table, the galleried hexagonal tilt-top with egg-and-dart edge and on birdcage support and turned spreading shaft with cabriole legs and lion-mask feet, 26in. wide. (Christie's) $6,395

A George III mahogany piecrust tripod table, with later scallop-edged circular top above a bird-cage support on turned spreading urn-shaped shaft, 26in. diameter. (Christie's) $6,732

A very fine and rare early Chippendale carved mahogany piecrust tilt-top tea table, Philadelphia, circa 1745, height 27in. (Sotheby's) $43,125

A Regency rosewood circular specimen marble top occasional table with beaded ornament, the top inset with a specimen marble panel including lapis, porphery, malachite and portor, 2ft. 7in. high. (Phillips) $7,438

A mahogany tripod stand with associated dished circular top on a spirally-twisted spreading urn-shaped stem, on cabriole legs and pointed pad feet, 22in. high.
(Christie's) $4,187

An early Victorian mahogany marble-specimen center table, the circular top with various marbles including verde antico and Siena, 27in. wide.
(Christie's) $3,300

Chippendale cherry and pine carved tea table, Woodbury, Connecticut, circa 1780, 35½in. diameter.
(Skinner) $550

A late George III rosewood occasional-table inlaid overall with boxwood and geometric banding, the crossbanded canted rectangular top above a frieze drawer inlaid with key-pattern, 26in. wide.
(Christie's) $5,148

Arts and Crafts oak occasional table, circa 1915, round top with square tapering legs and rectangular medial shelf held at either end with ball topped pins, 34in. diameter.
(Skinner) $1,100

An oak inlaid two-tiered occasional table, supported on four shaped legs each decorated with a band of checkered ebonized and fruitwood inlay, 56.5cm. high.
(Christie's) $766

A Regency ormolu-mounted and ebony-inlaid mahogany tripod table, the circular top banded with ebonized lines, on turned stop-reeded spreading shaft, 23¾in. diameter.
(Christie's) $2,093

A George II mahogany tripod table, the circular dished tilt-top on bird-cage support and spirally-fluted baluster shaft, the downswept legs carved with acanthus, 29½in. diameter.
(Christie's) $18,233

A George III mahogany occasional table, the circular tilt top on a spiral twist stem to three cabriole legs, on club feet, 18in.
(Woolley & Wallis) $2,775

A mahogany tripod table, the circular tilt-top with piecrust edge and on spirally-channeled baluster shaft, downswept legs and pad feet, 23¹/₂in. diameter. (Christie's) $3,432

Lifetime Furniture end table, no. 996, circa 1910, hexagonal top on three legs with elongated arched corbels, and low triangular shelf, 23in. wide. (Skinner) $715

A mid-18th century mahogany tripod table, the later tip-up top with gadrooned and foliate-carved piecrust edge, 28¹/₂in. diameter. (Bearne's) $883

A 'Two-All' burr olive ash and hickory table, by John Makepeace, square overhung top over two shelves, each inset with a burr olive panel supporting two leather-lined drawers, 64.5cm. wide. (Christie's) $3,445

A Regency mahogany teapoy, on baluster shaft and ribbed splayed tripartite base with roundel caps, the sides with lion mask and ring handles, 16¹/₂in. wide. (Christie's) $836

A George III mahogany urn-table with square galleried top above a plain frieze with candle-slide, on canted square legs headed by pierced fretwork angles, on block feet, 11³/₄in. square. (Christie's) $2,836

A mahogany tripod table, the shaped square top with a spindle gallery on an associated bird-cage support above a baluster-shaped acanthus carved stem, 23in. wide. (Christie's) $5,709

Gustav Stickley table, no. 441, circa 1903, round overhanging top with apron, on square post legs, arched, stacked cross-stretchers and central round pin, 36in. diameter. (Skinner) $880

A George III mahogany tripod table, the circular tilt-top on bird-cage support, the turned columnar spreading shaft on cabriole legs and rounded pad feet, 34in. diameter. (Christie's) $1,903

PEMBROKE TABLES

A George III painted satinwood oval Pembroke table, with overall rosewood bands and boxwood and ebony lines, 39in. wide.
(Christie's) **$7,260**

A mahogany Pembroke table, George IV, circa 1820, with round corners, a drawer at each end, 96cm. open.
(Sotheby's) **$1,759**

A fine Federal inlaid mahogany Pembroke table, Newport, Rhode Island, circa 1800, the oblong top with hinged D-shaped leaves, width extended 38½in.
(Sotheby's) **$37,375**

A George III satinwood decorated and tulipwood crossbanded oval Pembroke table, the radially veneered top with a central guilloché and paterae roundel with vine leaf border, 3ft. 5in. overall extended.
(Phillips) **$6,195**

One of a pair of George III mahogany serpentine Pembroke tables, each with crossbanded twin-flap top inlaid with ebonized and boxwood lines above a mahogany-lined frieze drawer and a simulated frieze drawer to the reverse, 39½in. wide.
(Christie's)
(Two) **$21,879**

One of a matched pair of Regency mahogany and ebonized Pembroke-tables, each with rounded rectangular twin-flap top above a paneled frieze with a blue paper-lined drawer, 28in. high.
(Christie's)
(Two) **$6,996**

A George III plum-pudding mahogany Pembroke table, the serpentine twin-flap top crossbanded and inlaid with a geometric line, 37in. wide.
(Christie's) **$6,248**

A George III mahogany butterfly Pembroke table, after designs by Chippendale, of rich color with a deep grain, 2ft. 4in. high.
(John Nicholson) **$5,400**

A George III mahogany Pembroke-table, the serpentine twin-flap top above a waved frieze with a drawer to one end and a dummy drawer to the other, 32¼in. wide.
(Christie's) **$3,362**

PEMBROKE TABLES

A George III green and polychrome-painted wood and papier-mâché Pembroke table, the panels possibly by Henry Clay, 32¼in. wide. (Christie's) **$5,049**

A mahogany Pembroke work table, William IV, 1834, stamped *Thomas Bartram, 1834*, with crossbanded top, 67cm. open. (Sotheby's) **$2,700**

A very fine Federal satinwood-inlaid mahogany Pembroke table, Baltimore, Maryland, circa 1795, on inlaid square tapering legs ending in brass caps, width extended 41¼in. (Sotheby's) **$24,150**

An inlaid mahogany Pembroke table, Baltimore, Maryland, 1790–1810, the line-inlaid oval top with drop leaves above a conforming apron with line inlay flanked by inlaid paterae on ring-and-flower and line-inlaid square tapering legs, 41½in. wide. (Christie's) **$19,800**

A George III painted satinwood Pembroke table, inlaid overall with ebonized lines and banded in tulipwood, the rounded rectangular twin-flap top with central oval mahogany panel painted with a fruit basket flanked by foliate scrolls, 42¾in. wide. (Christie's) **$22,523**

A George III satinwood Pembroke table, the tripartite oval top with two hinged flaps, banded overall with tulipwood and rosewood above a mahogany-lined frieze drawer and simulated frieze drawer to the reverse, 45in. wide. (Christie's) **$7,612**

A George III satinwood and mahogany Pembroke table, decorated with fruiting floral trails, the rectangular twin-flap top crossbanded and inlaid with a central oval panel, 39¾in. wide. (Christie's) **$8,366**

A mahogany 'Spider-leg' Pembroke table, English, late 18th century, with oblong top and slender turned legs and stretchers. (Sotheby's) **$2,155**

A late George III plum-pudding mahogany, rosewood crossbanded and marquetry Pembroke games table, 39in. extended. (Christie's) **$7,425**

SIDE TABLES

An Italian giltwood side table, the rectangular top above a paneled frieze carved with foliate scrolls within lotus-leaf borders and centered by vestal masks, late 18th century, 60in. wide.
(Christie's) $4,974

A Louis XV walnut side table with serpentine rectangular variegated red languedoc molded marble top above a waved pierced paneled frieze, 47in. wide.
(Christie's) $40,859

A satinwood and marquetry side table crossbanded overall in kingwood and inlaid with ribbon-tied husk swags, the demi-lune top centered by a half-fan medallion, 50in. wide.
(Christie's) $6,303

A Florentine serpentine specimen marble table top with a central verde antico oval medallion flanked by radiating Siena, portor, jasper and specimen marble wedges within a black marble border, third quarter 18th century, 35½in. wide.
(Christie's) $4,686

A Regency mahogany side table, in the manner of Gillows, with a rectangular top and rounded corners, on projecting reeded tapered legs with turned feet, 3ft. 3in. wide.
(Phillips) $3,009

A Regency mahogany side table attributed to Thomas Chippendale Junior, with rectangular white marble top above a paneled frieze supported by Egyptian caryatids above turned tapering reeded columns and human feet, 33½in. wide.
(Christie's) $13,464

A George III mahogany marquetry and parquetry side table, on stop-fluted square tapering legs and blocks inset with painted roundels, above shaped feet, 47in. wide.
(Christie's) $8,415

A good French marble-topped giltwood serpentine side table, Paris, circa 1880, in Louis XV style, with a later molded mottled purple green and white marble top, 141cm. wide.
(Sotheby's) $6,296

A Régence giltwood side table with later rectangular alabaster top with black marble border, on angled scrolled legs headed by scallop shells, 44in. wide.
(Christie's) $17,765

SIDE TABLES

A giltwood side table with later simulated verde antico scagliola top above a boldly scrolled pierced acanthus-carved frieze centered by a Vesta head, on naturalistic scrolled legs headed by bold eagles, 61½in. wide. (Christie's) $12,441

A George II mahogany side table, the rounded rectangular top above a plain frieze centered by a pendant boss, on cabriole legs headed by scallop shells and on paw feet, 54in. wide. (Christie's) $4,934

An Italian giltwood side table with later veined rectangular white marble top, on cabriole legs carved with trailing foliage, rockwork and C-scrolls, 62in. wide. (Christie's) $6,218

A George III satinwood and inlaid pier table of small size, the top of bowed and broken outline crossbanded in tulipwood and harewood, 3ft. wide. (Phillips) $4,463

An Italian red-painted and parcel-gilt side table with serpentine molded top above a pierced frieze with scrolling foliage and confronting C-scrolls, mid-18th century, 44in. wide. (Christie's) $2,487

One of a pair of gilt lead-mounted satinwood, marble and simulated tortoiseshell side tables of George III style, on square tapering legs and tapering block feet, 32½in. wide. (Christie's)
(Two) $15,620

A satinwood D-shaped side table, the radiating top centered by a stylized fan medallion terminated by bell husks, the mahogany-banded edge with stylized flowerhead and oval running motif, 52¼in. wide. (Christie's) $12,623

An early George III mahogany serving table, the frieze carved with blind fretwork, on pierced fretwork and ring-turned legs with spade feet, 62in. wide. (Christie's) $15,891

A George III mahogany serpentine serving-table, the shaped rectangular top above a paneled frieze and central baize-lined fitted frieze drawer divided by marquetry panels of flowers in an urn, 69¾in. wide. (Christie's) $13,464

SIDE TABLES

A rare Federal carved mahogany marble-top two-drawer server, New York, circa 1815, on acanthus-carved ring-turned legs, 29¼in. wide.
(Sotheby's) $4,950

One of a pair of George III mahogany side tables with D-shaped tops, the friezes carved with classical urns and ribbon-tied swags of berried foliage, 45¾in. wide.
(Christie's)
(Two) $3,011

A Federal cherrywood and curly maple single-drawer side table, probably New England, circa 1800, on square tapering legs, 21in. wide.
(Sotheby's) $990

A Dutch oak side table, with two drawers on cabriole supports and pointed pad feet, 19th century, 21in. wide.
(Christie's) $674

A good Federal mahogany three-drawer serving table, New York, dated 1816, on frontal reeded supports joined by a shaped medial shelf, 36½in. wide.
(Sotheby's) $5,500

Lifetime Furniture buffet server, circa 1915, plate rail on overhanging rectangular top, single long drawer with brass pulls, 39in. wide.
(Skinner) $495

An oak side table, the **rectangular** top with a single drawer, on baluster turned legs joined by an 'X'-stretcher, bun feet, 2ft. 6in. wide.
(Phillips) $1,044

A fine Federal mahogany two-drawer side table, New York, circa 1810, on reeded tapering legs ending in ebonized vase and ball feet, 20½in. wide.
(Sotheby's) $4,125

A Victorian gilt-metal mounted walnut and marquetry side table, the serpentine top inlaid with a foliate marquetry in fruitwoods, 30in. wide.
(Christie's) $1,295

SIDE TABLES

A William and Mary giltwood side table with later inset green-painted white marble top above a pierced vigorous acanthus-carved frieze centered by putti, 46in. wide.
(Christie's) $3,218

A walnut side table, the rectangular top on shell carved cabriole legs with pad feet, 5ft. 1in. wide.
(Phillips) $3,060

A giltwood and gesso side table, the rectangular verde antico marble top with moulded edge, the frieze with an arcaded foliate molding and Vitruvian scroll, early 20th century, 72in. wide.
(Christie's) $3,799

A George II oak side table with rectangular tray top, serpentine underframe and on cabriole legs with hoof feet, 31in. wide.
(Bearne's) $1,024

A Federal cherrywood single-drawer side table, American, probably New England, first quarter 19th century, 19in. wide.
(Sotheby's) $1,430

A George III mahogany side table with a deep frieze carved with blind fretwork, on square chamfered legs with similar fretwork, 38¹/₂in. wide.
(Christie's) $4,684

A Louis XIV oak side table, the flowerhead-and-trellis apron and sides carved with a palmette and scrolling acanthus, 37in. wide.
(Bearne's) $1,271

A George III mahogany serpentine side table, with boxwood stringing and a single frieze drawer with pressed brass oakleaf and acorn handles, 40in. wide.
(Christie's) $1,338

A George III mahogany side table, the rounded rectangular top with molded edge above two long drawers and on club legs and pad feet, 31¹/₂in. wide.
(Christie's) $2,099

SOFA TABLES

An Anglo-Chinese padoukwood double-sided twin-flap sofa table, the rectangular twin-flap top crossbanded with satinwood and inlaid with ebony and boxwood lines, 19th century, 59in. wide.
(Christie's) $4,897

A Regency gilt-brass mounted mahogany sofa table with rounded rectangular twin-flap top inlaid with boxwood lines and crossbanded with rosewood, 60½in. wide.
(Christie's) $7,029

A Regency brass-inlaid and giltmetal-mounted rosewood sofa table with rounded rectangular twin-flap top, the paneled frieze with two mahogany-lined drawers to the front, 58¼in. wide.
(Christie's) $9,896

A Regency ebony-inlaid amboyna sofa table with rounded rectangular twin-flap top inlaid with ebonized lines above two mahogany-lined frieze drawers, 60in. wide.
(Christie's) $7,498

A Regency ebony and brass-inlaid specimen wood and parquetry pedestal sofa table, on turned quadripartite baluster-supports and a concave-sided platform centered by a lotus-leaf finial, 63½in. wide.
(Christie's) $26,928

A Regency mahogany and ebony-inlaid sofa table, with line and stellar banded top, two Greek key-decorated frieze drawers and opposing dummy drawers, 59½in. extended.
(Christie's)   £5,060 $7,590

A Regency rosewood sofa table, on standard ends joined by an arched stretcher with dual downswept legs, paw cappings and castors, 4ft. 11in. x 1ft. 1in.
(Phillips) $4,760

A late George III mahogany sofa table of rounded rectangular form with reeded edge, 61¼in. wide extended.
(Tennants) $3,726

A Regency mahogany sofa table inlaid with boxwood lines and geometric shapes, the rounded rectangular twin flap top containing two drawers, 4ft. 11in. x 1ft. 11in.
(Phillips) $5,653

A Regency rosewood tric-trac sofa table with chamfered twin-flap rectangular top, 52in. wide. (Christie's) $3,795

A William IV rosewood games table, the rectangular top with central detachable panel inlaid with chess board, 45in. wide. (Christie's) $3,256

A George II mahogany Harlequin tea, card and writing-table with rounded rectangular triple-flap top enclosing a tea-table, 32in. wide. (Christie's) $7,762

A William IV brown oak work-table with twin-flap rounded rectangular top above a mahogany-lined beaded paneled frieze drawer, on downswept legs and foliate feet, 31³/₄in. wide. (Christie's) $4,686

A fine Regency mahogany, ebonized and parcel gilt library and games table, by John Maclean, on curved 'X'-frame end supports, 2ft. 9in. x 1ft. 7in. (Phillips) $53,550

A Regency mahogany work-table inlaid with ebony lines, the canted rectangular hinged top enclosing a fitted interior with lift-out section comprising four satinwood lidded corner compartments, 16¹/₂in. wide. (Christie's) $2,311

An amboyna and rosewood-veneered work table by Alphonse Tahan, on cabriole legs applied with gilt brass acanthus mounts, 24³/₄in. wide. (Bearne's) $4,023

A painted satinwood work-table crossbanded with rosewood, with hinged octagonal top painted with roses suspending leaves and bellhusk chains, 16¹/₂in. wide. (Christie's) $2,178

A satinwood marquetry work table, circa 1870, the hinged lid with brass-molded border and a roundel of musical trophies, 1ft. 10¹/₂in. wide. (Sotheby's) $5,626

A Federal brass-mounted and inlaid mahogany two-drawer work table, Philadelphia, circa 1810, with ring-turned three-quarter-round columns at each corner, width 20in.
(Sotheby's) $3,738

A George IV maple, grained and ebonized work-table, the rectangular twin-flap top banded in mahogany above three mahogany-lined drawers, on bobbin-turned tapering legs with brass caps, 37³/₄in. wide.
(Christie's) $4,187

A William IV rosewood combined games and work table, on standard end supports joined by a ring turned stretcher with bar bases and bun feet, 1ft. 9in. wide.
(Phillips) $2,070

A rosewood lady's sewing, writing, reading and painting table, circa 1840, inlaid with a star and with Vandyck borders, 31in. high.
(Sotheby's) $2,728

A 19th century Dutch mahogany marquetry and strung demi-lune games table, the frieze enclosed by two tambour shades, on square tapered fluted legs, 2ft. 5in. wide.
(Phillips) $2,478

Federal mahogany veneer carved astragal-end work table, New York, circa 1815, the hinged top above a fitted interior, 26¹/₂in. wide.
(Skinner) $1,760

A Federal mahogany two-drawer work table, Boston, Massachusetts, circa 1810, the rectangular top above a case with two drawers, 21in. wide.
(Sotheby's) $3,850

An early Victorian ebony and ivory games-table with hinged chamfered molded square top with an ebony border inset with a printed and pencil-drawn checker-board, 29in. high.
(Christie's) $3,323

A classical carved mahogany worktable, New York, 1815–1825, the rectangular top above conforming case with two graduated drawers on reeded tapering legs, 21in. wide.
(Christie's) $3,520

A Victorian figured walnut games table, with hinged swivel action to reveal an inlaid draughts board and backgammon, 35³/₄in. wide. (Tennants) $2,106

Shaker cherry and pine work table, possibly New York State, mid 19th century, 36¹/₄in. wide. (Skinner) $3,850

A mid-19th century mother-of-pearl inlaid ebonized work table, the sarcophagus body decorated throughout with floral sprays and gilt foliage, 23¹/₂in. wide. (Bearne's) $441

An Anglo Indian rosewood work table, the rectangular top with lotus-carved edge above scroll brackets and fitted frieze drawer, mid 19th century, 30in. wide. (Christie's) $1,386

A George III mahogany games-table, inlaid overall with boxwood and ebonized lines, the sliding reversable featherbanded top lined with a chessboard and trellis-pattern leather, 40³/₄in. wide. (Christie's) $13,118

An early Victorian rosewood work table with rectangular wavy galleried top, two frieze drawers and turned foliate-carved and fluted column supports, 28in. wide. (Christie's) $2,217

A late Regency rosewood combined games and reading table, the rounded rectangular top divided into two, 35in. wide, circa 1830. (Tennants) $3,402

An unusual Regency mahogany gaming table, the rounded rectangular top inlaid with geometric panels, concentric circles and flowerheads in colored woods, 3ft. 8in. wide. (Spencer's) $1,735

A late George III mahogany work-table inlaid overall with boxwood lines, the canted rctangular top crossbanded in satinwood, 22in. wide. (Christie's) $2,101

A Regency mahogany library table, with a crossbanded leather tooled top, the frieze with a pair of drawers to either side, 4ft. wide.
(Phillips) $4,165

A rare 'boulle' and tortoiseshell writing desk, by Collinson & Lock, circa 1890, in the French Louis XIV manner, on eight square tapering legs, the whole inlaid with brass and pewter foliage, 3ft. 11in. wide.
(Sotheby's) $4,262

A William IV mahogany writing-table, the rounded rectangular top with hinged sliding red leather-lined central section, the paneled frieze with two mahogany-lined drawers to each end, 61in. wide.
(Christie's) $12,370

A Louis XV ormolu mounted kingwood, tulipwood, purpleheart marquetry mechanical table à ecrire, by Jean Francois Oeben, 2ft. 10in. x 1ft. 5in. top.
(Phillips) $71,400

A Bruce Talbert gothic bureau manufactured by Holland & Son, circa 1865, oak with traces of gilding, 64^{1}/$_{2}$in. high.
(Sotheby's) $4,774

A George III mahogany chamber writing-table in the manner of Gillows, the rounded rectangular top with inset hinged section enclosing three compartments and a pen slide, 36in. wide.
(Christie's) $5,042

A Regency rosewood and brass inlaid library table, on concave shaped standard end supports, united by a ring-turned stretcher with outswept legs, 4ft. wide.
(Phillips) $11,505

An ormolu-mounted kingwood and parquetry bureau plat, by François Linke, the serpentine top inset with tooled red leather skiver and banded with a gilt-metal molded edge, the wavy frieze centered by a female mask head within a foliate scroll surround, late 19th/20th century, 56^{1}/$_{4}$in. wide.
(Christie's) $18,997

A solid satinwood simulated bamboo writing table, by Howard & Sons, circa 1875, with shaped rectangular green leather-lined top, 3ft. 10^{1}/$_{2}$in. wide.
(Sotheby's) $2,302

WRITING TABLES & DESKS

A George III rosewood box-on-writing-stand, the coffered top centered by a mahogany panel and inlaid with geometric banding, repair to stretcher, 15¼in. wide.
(Christie's) $2,361

A Regency mahogany writing-table with rounded rectangular black leather-lined top, above three frieze drawers to each side, on fluted turned tapering legs and brass caps, 53in. wide.
(Christie's) $11,418

A George III mahogany reading-table with molded rectangular adjustable hinged top and fitted reading-stop above two short and one long mahogany-lined fitted frieze drawer, 28in. wide.
(Christie's) $9,257

A French ormolu-mounted kingwood and marquetry bonheur du jour in the manner of Topino, inlaid overall with a pictoral marquetry including a flower-filled vase, an inkstand and quiver, books and a teapot, second half 19th century, 26½in. wide.
(Christie's) $2,936

A Regency mahogany small writing-table, the rounded rectangular green leather-lined top with brass molded rim and pierced three-quarter gallery, 30¼in. wide.
(Christie's) $5,883

A George III satinwood writing-table, the twin-flap hinged top banded in amaranth and each flap centered by an oval thuyawood medallion, 36¼in. wide.
(Christie's) $5,328

A late George III mahogany writing table in the manner of Gillows, the rounded rectangular leather inset top above two frieze drawers, on turned reeded legs, 4ft. wide.
(Phillips) $5,310

A George III Irish mahogany two-handled metamorphic writing table, with a leather inset top opening to form library steps, 28in. wide.
(Christie's) $20,073

A late George III mahogany and ebony strung library table, the leather tooled top with rounded ends and a ratcheted adjustable top, 3ft. 6in. wide.
(Phillips) $3,717

WRITING TABLES & DESKS

A mahogany writing table, the rectangular top with fan inlay and satinwood stringing, on square capped turned legs, 3ft. 4in. wide.
(Woolley & Wallis) $1,773

A painted satinwood and rosewood banded Carlton House desk, on square tapering legs, modern, 56in. wide.
(Christie's) $4,224

A small walnut writing or center table, circa 1860, on trefoil supports, joined by an unusual hipped stretcher, 3ft. 4¹/₂in. wide.
(Sotheby's) $3,921

A George III mahogany bonheur du jour, the breakfront superstructure with four doors above a central drawer, on square tapering legs joined by a concave lower platform, 2ft. 8in. wide.
(Phillips) $2,478

L. & J. G. Stickley desk and chair, no. 611 and 1313, circa 1910, flat top desk with central letter compartments flanked by single small drawers.
(Skinner) $1,100

A walnut patent desk, inset with a decorated cast iron letter box inscribed *Manufactured By Wooton Desk Manufacturing Company, Indianapolis, W S Wooton's Patent October 6th 1874*, 3ft. 7in. wide.
(Spencer's) $4,200

A Louis XVI style mahogany cylinder bureau, the cylinder enclosing a fitted interior and a green leather lined pull out slide, 49in. wide.
(Lawrence) $3,818

Quaint Furniture oak desk, circa 1910, single drawer flanked by side bookshelves over two vertical side slats, 40in. wide.
(Skinner) $247

An unusual oval amboyna writing table, circa 1850, in the French Louis XV manner, quarter-banded in tulipwood and with a curved brass gallery, 4ft. wide.
(Sotheby's) $7,672

WRITING TABLES & DESKS

Edwardian mahogany and satinwood crossbanded Carlton House desk, 4ft. 6in. wide, bearing *Maple & Co.* stamp.
(Lawrences) $4,906

A fine and rare Federal mahogany writing table, Philadelphia, circa 1805, the rectangular top with a raised shelf on each end, width 5ft. 2in.
(Sotheby's) $9,775

A Victorian walnut kidney-shaped writing table with inset top, fitted with two frieze drawers on cheval frame with turned stretcher, 4ft. wide.
(Russell Baldwin & Bright) $2,464

L. & J. G. Stickley library table, no. 520, circa 1910, overhanging rectangular top, single drawer with copper hardware elongated corbels inside each leg with medial shelf, 36in. wide.
(Skinner) $715

Victorian cylinder-front writing desk in walnut, fitted cubbyhole interior over four drawers, 34in. wide.
(Eldred's) $550

Gustav Stickley table desk, similar to no. 430, circa 1903, central drawer flanked by small stacked double side drawers, 36in. wide.
(Skinner) $660

Gustav Stickley writing desk, no. 518, circa 1903, gallery top, paneled back and sides, drop front with recessed central panel, iron hardware, 26in. wide.
(Skinner) $1,650

A mid 19th century mahogany cylinder desk, having satinwood stringing and crossbanding, fitted pierced gilt-metal gallery over three frieze drawers, 4ft. 8in. wide.
(Russell Baldwin & Bright) $4,820

A George III mahogany bowfronted bonheur du jour, the superstructure with a quarter ledge back containing six drawers, on square tapering legs, 2ft. wide.
(Phillips) $3,717

A French marquetry Boulle and ebonized wood serpentine bureau plat, Napoléon III, Paris, circa 1850, 150cm. wide.
(Sotheby's) $9,095

A good French marquetry center or writing table, Louis Philippe/Napoléon III, by Gros of Paris, circa 1850, 133cm. wide.
(Sotheby's) $8,395

A French 'Boulle' bureau mazarin, Napoléon III, Paris, circa 1870, in Louis XIV style, the rectangular top with three drawers in each pedestal, 156cm. wide.
(Sotheby's) $20,988

An 18th century Austrian walnut veneered writing desk, inlaid with fruitwood, the raised back with six drawers flanking a central cupboard, on six legs joined by stretchers, 62cm. wide.
(Finarte) $12,115

A Louis XV style burr-walnut and mahogany bonheur du jour, the raised back having pierced gilt metal gallery over central doors inset with oval floral-painted Sèvres type porcelain panel, 2ft. 9in. wide.
(Russell Baldwin & Bright)
                             $2,560

A fine and rare Federal mahogany lift-top writing table with drawer, labelled *John T. Dolan*, New York, circa 1805, on reeded tapering legs ending in vase-form feet on brass casters, width 33in.
(Sotheby's) $17,250

Late 18th century walnut veneered writing desk with one long frieze drawer and two small drawers under, on square tapering legs, Emilian, 99cm. wide.
(Finarte) $11,193

An Edwardian satinwood, rosewood-banded and line-inlaid Carlton House desk, the leather-lined top with galleried superstructure, 52½in. wide.
(Christie's) $16,167

A mid 18th century walnut writing desk with poplar wood inlay and ivory banding, on gold edged cabriole legs, Modena, 117cm. wide
(Finarte) $67,699

WRITING TABLES & DESKS

An Edwardian mahogany and satinwood banded kidney shaped writing desk, on square tapering legs, 42½in. wide. (Christie's) **$5,128**

A late Victorian mahogany partners library table with rounded rectangular leather lined top, 67in. wide. (Christie's) **$2,198**

A tortoiseshell veneered and ormolu mounted writing desk, with three frieze drawers, on ormolu mounted cabriole legs, French, 19th century. (Finarte) **$3,255**

A 19th century mahogany roll top desk opening to reveal an arrangement of drawers and pigeonholes with architectural centre piece, on bracket feet. (Herholdt Jensen) **$3,020**

A Quebec pine slope front desk in the George III style, the hinged top opening upwards above a pair of molded doors with raised panels, on bracket feet, original blue green paintwork, 36in. wide. (Fraser-Pinney) **$5,876**

An early 18th century Piedmontese thuya wood veneered writing desk, on square tapering legs joined by X-stretchers, 103cm. wide. (Finarte) **$17,103**

A 19th century palisander writing desk, the raised back with two doors flanked by four small drawers, on slender cabriole legs, 110cm. wide. (Finarte) **$1,992**

A 19th century German mahogany veneer roll top desk, with fall front drawer over, a long drawer and two doors under, on ball feet, 110cm. wide. (Kunsthaus am Museum) **$1,487**

A mahogany and ormolu mounted writing table with blue leather skiver over one frieze drawer, on turned legs, 19th century, 99cm. wide. (Finarte) **$7,116**

TRUNKS & COFFERS

An Italian walnut cassone, the body elaborately carved with scrolling strapwork motifs around a central cabochon cartouche, part late 16th/early 17th century, 51¹/₂in. wide.
(Christie's) $4,264

A George III oak mule chest, the shallow box top with two dummy drawers above two short and one long drawer, raised on ogee bracket feet, 4ft. 11in. wide.
(Russell Baldwin & Bright)
                    $1,285

A punch-decorated six-board pine blanket chest decorated with hearts and geometric designs, on bracket feet, 50in. wide.
(Christie's) $1,650

A Punjabi oak coffer with hinged rectangular top, the trelliswork front on square supports and wheels, 19th century, 62in. wide.
(Christie's) $1,361

A Venetian cedarwood and penwork coffer with rectangular hinged top enclosing a part-fitted interior decorated with courtly figures in a landscape, 17th century, 27¹/₂in. wide.
(Christie's) $2,309

Grain painted salmon red maple and pine blanket chest, probably Massachusetts, circa 1750, 41³/₄in. wide.
(Skinner) $1,540

A good painted and decorated pine blanket chest, Pennsylvania, circa 1805, the rectangular hinged lid opening to a well, length 51in.
(Sotheby's) $8,050

Paint decorated poplar blanket box, probably Pennsylvania or Ohio, early 19th century, 35¹/₂in. wide.
(Skinner) $7,700

An unusual painted and decorated pine dome-top trunk, Worcester, Massachusetts, circa 1830, with hinged lid opening to a deep well, length 24in.
(Sotheby's) $7,475

392

TRUNKS & COFFERS

An Italian walnut cassone, the paneled frieze carved with playful putti baiting a lion flanked by a pair of scrolling cartouches within studded pilaster strips, 19th century, 72in. wide.
(Christie's) $5,685

A cherrywood and pine dough box on stand, Pennsylvania, first half 19th century, the rectangular removable top above a well, length 48in.
(Sotheby's) $1,035

A late 17th century iron bound strong box, the front with a false lock and two hasps, a camouflaged locking device in the lid, 34cm. wide.
(Auktionsverket) $2,152

An ormolu-mounted walnut, kingwood, fruitwood and parquetry coffer, inlaid overall with cube decoration, probably German, mid-19th century, 18in. wide.
(Christie's) $3,731

A Goanese hardwood and ivory inlaid box on later stand, inlaid with flowering prunus, late 17th/early 18th century, 21in. wide.
(Christie's) $4,435

A Chinese Export red and gilt-japanned coffer-on-stand decorated overall with courtly figures in an extensive watery landscape, late 18th/early 19th century, 39in. wide.
(Christie's) $3,553

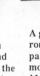

An 18th century walnut veneered and burr walnut inlaid coffer, the domed top inlaid with putti holding a crown monogram *ASR* and the date *1768*, Saxony, 124cm. wide.
(Kunsthaus am Museum) $4,024

A 17th century rectangular strongbox, iron banded with criss-cross pattern within and without, with two orifices in the base for floor attachment, 66cm. wide.
(Duran) $1,217

A green painted oak trunk with rounded top and banded in iron, painted with garlands and monogram *CPL 1839 den 13ten May*, 123cm. wide.
(Kunsthaus am Museum) $929

TRUNKS & COFFERS

A William and Mary walnut blanket chest, Pennsylvania, early 18th entury, the molded hinged lid opening to an interior with till with hinged cover, 47¹/₂in. wide.
(Sotheby's) **$2,420**

A south German walnut coffer, with hinged lid enclosing a fitted interior, on later bun feet, late 18th century, 38in. wide.
(Christie's) **$1,077**

A Chippendale pine blanket chest, Pennsylvania, 19th century, the rectangular overhanging top with conforming dove-tailed case, 47³/₄in. wide.
(Christie's) **$440**

Antique American lift-top blanket chest in pine under old red stain, shaped apron, bracket base, 42in. wide.
(Eldred's) **$358**

An Afro-American painted and decorated yellow pine slave's trunk, Southern, 19th century, the rectangular hinged lid opening to a divided well, 24in. wide.
(Sotheby's) **$1,870**

Salmon grain painted pine blanket chest, New England, late 18th century, 42in. wide.
(Skinner) **$1,650**

A painted and punch decorated six-board pine chest, New London, Connecticut, 1700–1730, with rectangular hinged lid above a case with two rows of intersecting punchwork semi-circles, 31¹/₂in. wide.
(Christie's) **$15,400**

A painted trunk, probably Pennsylvania, late 18th/early 19th century, the hinged rectangular top with thumbmolded edge lifting to an open compartment lined with portions of Claypoole's Advertiser, 1793 (Philadelphia), 38¹/₄in. wide.
(Christie's) **$800**

A painted and decorated dower chest, Pennsylvania, circa 1787, the hinged rectangular top with applied molded trim decorated with three painted floral panels, 48³/₄in. wide.
(Christie's) **$6,600**

TRUNKS & COFFERS

A Flemish oak and fruitwood coffer with later quadruple paneled top, the front with triple-arched panels inlaid with vases of flowers, mid-17th century, 55in. wide.
(Christie's) **$3,011**

Chippendale walnut inlaid dower chest, Pennsylvania, circa 1774, 49in. wide.
(Skinner) **$1,540**

A James I oak coffer, the frieze carved with a compressed guilloche design above three arcaded panels, inlaid uprights and on stile feet, 65¹/₂in. wide.
(Bearne's) **$2,118**

Grain painted pine blanket chest, New England, circa 1820, 37¹/₂in. wide.
(Skinner) **$1,540**

Country Federal grain and putty decorated blanket chest, Central Massachusetts, circa 1820, 38in. wide.
(Skinner) **$4,290**

Queen Anne pine blanket chest, Massachusetts, circa 1740, with old red paint, 36in. wide.
(Skinner) **$1,980**

A painted blanket chest, 19th century, flanked on either side by painted, decorated and braided cloth pulls with hand mounts, probably International Order of Odd-Fellows, 36in. wide.
(Christie's) **$1,870**

A Chippendale mahogany blanket chest, labeled by William Savery (1721–1787), Philadelphia, circa 1760, the hinged rectangular molded top above a compartment fitted with a till and two secret short drawers, 48in. wide.
(Christie's) **$4,180**

A 17th century Singhalese hardwood and ebony chest applied with massive brass carrying handles with pierced backplates, 59in. wide.
(Bearne's) **$1,589**

WARDROBES & ARMOIRES

Victorian mahogany wardrobe, having a center mirrored door flanked by single doors to either side, 5ft. wide.
(G. A. Key) $343

A late 18th century Wesphalian oak armoire with molded rectangular cornice above two carved fielded doors and two drawers, monogramed in pewter *ICF 1776*, 174cm. wide.
(Kunsthaus am Museum)

$3,095

A stained wardrobe designed by M. H. Baillie-Scott, with carved decoration and green staining, 103.7cm. wide.
(Christie's) $700

A pine Gothic Revival wardrobe inset with quatrefoils above a pair of pointed arched doors, late 19th century, probably French, 71in. wide.
(Christie's) $1,313

A pair of Biedermeier walnut armoires each with a molded cornice and enclosed by a pair of panel doors on block feet, 3ft. 9in. wide.
(Phillips) $1,980

A polychrome painted Scandinavian wardrobe, with **molded rectangular cornice** above a single door painted with flower sprays, on bun feet, 114cm. wide.
(Auktionsverket) $5,130

A fine classical gilt-stenciled mahogany wardrobe, New York, possibly by Joseph Meeks and Sons, circa 1820, with stylized carved paw feet, 54¹/₂in. wide.
(Sotheby's) $10,450

A late 18th century French oak armoire, the molded cornice above a frieze carved with a leaf spray and a pair of doors with shaped fielded panels below, 5ft. wide.
(Phillips) $900

An 18th century Dutch mahogany and floral marquetry **armoire, with molded** undulating pediment, on splayed claw and ball feet, 165cm. wide.
(Finarte) $7,828

WARDROBES & ARMOIRES

A French Provincial walnut and fruitwood armoire with a drawer below and waved apron on cabriole legs, late 18th/early 19th century, 65in. wide. (Christie's) $1,936

A Charles X burr elm wardrobe, with foliate fruitwood inlay, **with molded pediment and** single mirrored door, 86.5cm. wide. (Finarte) $4,270

One of a pair of 19th century Austrian walnut and beech armoires stamped *Jacob & Joseph Kohn*, 45¹/₂in. wide. (Bearne's)
(Two) $3,129

A 19th century armoire with **molded arched cornice over** two conforming arched doors painted with drapery and urns and inscribed *M A D 1813*, Scandinavian, 128cm. wide. (Auktionsverket) $6,619

An important oak wardrobe, by Anthony Salvin, circa 1835, the cornice and four arched doors incised with vases of flowers, acorns, roses and foliage, the lower panels with figures, 8ft. 9in. wide. (Sotheby's) $6,479

A German armoire, in pine and other softwoods, with a projecting cornice, a frieze inlaid with geometric panels and above two doors decorated in Renaissance style, 18th/19th century, 74in. wide. (Lawrence Fine Art)
$2,957

An early 19th century German walnut armoire, the molded cornice with a pair of shaped panel doors on block feet, 6ft. 3in. wide. (Phillips) $828

Wardrobe closet, 19th century, **in pine with paneled door and** drawer in base, 52in. wide. (Eldred's) $209

A Flemish oak armoire with a molded cornice, fluted and flower head-carved frieze, 61in. wide, part late 17th century. (Bearne's) $2,756

FURNITURE

Shaker pine painted wash stand, circa 1850, retains original chrome yellow wash, 45¼in. wide.
(Skinner) **$6,050**

Victorian mahogany shaving stand, the oval mirror supported on cradle support to a circular centre.
(G. A. Key) **$588**

Grain painted chamber stand, New England, circa 1830, 39in. wide.
(Skinner) **$413**

A late Federal curly maple single-drawer washstand, Pennsylvania or Middle Atlantic States, circa 1825, 21¼in. wide.
(Sotheby's) **$2,415**

A George III mahogany gentleman's washstand, the tulipwood crossbanded divided top enclosing a ratchet adjustable mirror and six lidded compartments, 2ft. 5in. wide.
(Phillips) **$1,530**

A Federal inlaid mahogany corner washstand, New England, 1790–1810, the shaped splashboards with shelf above a convex top fitted with three holes for basin and dishes, 18¾in. wide.
(Christie's) **$1,150**

A very fine Federal bird's eye maple veneered mahogany corner basin stand, Boston, Massachusetts, circa 1805, height 40½in.
(Sotheby's) **$6,325**

Painted decorated washstand, probably England, 19th century, 35in. wide.
(Skinner) **$1,000**

A Louis XVI mahogany washstand by Joseph Gengenbach dit Canabas with twin-flap rectangular top enclosing an inset white marble wash surface, 31in. wide.
(Christie's) **$7,461**

WHATNOTS

A rosewood whatnot, early Victorian, circa 1840, with three tiers, spiral-twist pillars and a drawer, 33cm. square.
(Sotheby's) $1,196

An oval mahogany and brass three-tier whatnot, Victorian, circa 1880, 69cm. wide.
(Sotheby's) $1,288

A rosewood whatnot, George IV, circa 1825, with four tiers, the top one hinged and the lowest with a drawer, 51cm. wide.
(Sotheby's) $1,932

A good walnut three-tier table, Victorian, circa 1850, with fret-pierced end panels and down-curved legs, 67cm. wide.
(Sotheby's) $1,021

A pair of mid-Victorian ormolu-mounted burr walnut, amaranth and trellis-pattern parquetry three-tier whatnots by Gillows, 20in. wide.
(Christie's) $27,600

A serpentine mahogany three-tier whatnot, early Victorian, circa 1840, on turned pillars, 64cm. wide.
(Sotheby's) $1,671

A Victorian rosewood canterbury/whatnot, the rectangular top with four baluster finials to the corners, 1ft. 11in. wide.
(Spencer's) $1,050

A William IV mahogany five-tier whatnot, with baluster and bobbin-turned uprights, 20½in. wide.
(Christie's) $1,815

An ebonized and parcel-gilt mahogany whatnot, by Gillows of Lancaster, circa 1875, the two shelves above a drawer.
(Sotheby's) $852

WHATNOTS

A rare Federal mahogany etagère, probably Boston, circa 1820, having three tiers, each centered by ring-turned supports.
(Sotheby's) $2,310

A late Victorian walnut three-tier buffet with pierced fret carved gallery on scroll and spiral twist uprights, 45in. wide.
(Christie's) $1,613

Victorian walnut graduated four tier rectangular whatnot, each tier with shaped front detail, 19in. wide.
(G. A. Key) $280

A George III mahogany corner whatnot with three reeded bowfronted graduated tiers, each reeded support crowned by an urn-finial with radially-carved spandrels and paterae, 26¼in. wide.
(Christie's) $17,859

A pair of 19th century mahogany and ormolu mounted three-tier corner étagères in the Louis XVI style with gray marble tops, 3ft. high.
(Phillips) $6,372

Victorian walnut four tier corner whatnot, inlaid with marquetry scrolled designs and having drop fronts with marquetry detail.
(G. A. Key) $723

A George IV mahogany whatnot, the four rectangular tiers supported on baluster turned columns with acorn finials, on turned legs, castors, 2ft. wide.
(Phillips) $1,440

An oak Gothic Reform etagère, in the manner of Charles Bevan for Marsh and Jones, circa 1870, with three shelves on trestle supports stenciled with gothic devices, 2ft. ½in. wide.
(Sotheby's) $1,364

A Regency simulated rosewood whatnot, the four tiers supported upon knopped turned columns with pyramidal finials, on turned legs and castors, 1ft. 8in. wide.
(Phillips) $1,260

WHATNOTS

A mahogany four-tier whatnot, with graduated rectangular shelves on turned supports and above one drawer, on brass caps, 18¼in. wide.
(Christie's) $4,897

A mid Victorian burr-walnut three-tier whatnot, each cartouche-shaped tier joined by spiral-twist uprights and pierced splats to the sides, 32in. wide.
(Christie's) $833

A George III mahogany two-tier whatnot, the reeded rectangular top with two shelves and double-X latticework sides, 13in. wide.
(Christie's) $2,941

Early 19th century mahogany three tier square whatnot, turned baluster columns and conial finials, 16in. square.
(G. A. Key) $1,006

A pair of gilt-lacquered brass-mounted three-tier mahogany whatnots each with ball finials to the corners, 19th century, 15in. wide.
(Christie's) $12,075

Victorian figured walnut three tier whatnot, the top tier with a pierced gallery and shaped finials, 2ft. wide.
(G. A. Key) $1,371

A George IV mahogany whatnot, the four tiers on ring turned columns with an apron drawer on turned legs, 1ft. 8in. wide.
(Phillips) $1,800

Victorian mahogany three tier side whatnot, the bottom and middle tiers supported by swan neck designs, 2ft. 11in. wide.
(G. A. Key) $2,129

A mid-Victorian mahogany whatnot with five graduated tiers, turned uprights and drawer, on turned legs, 24in. wide.
(Christie's) $3,326

401

Georgian mahogany and brass bound wine cooler of oval form, measuring 2ft. x 1ft. 6in.
(G. A. Key) $1,788

A Regency mahogany and brass mounted wine cooler of sarcophagus design, in the manner of Thomas Hope, the beveled domed hinged top with cavetto frieze, 2ft. 7in. wide.
(Phillips) $8,628

An early Victorian sarcophagus shaped wine cooler with raised hinged lid, lead-lined interior and paneled sides, 32in. wide.
(Christie's) $1,056

A George III brass-bound mahogany wine-cooler, the hinged octagonal top enclosing a lead-lined fitted interior, the stand with blind fretwork frieze, 29^{1}/$_{4}$in. high.
(Christie's) $3,498

A pair of George II brass-bound mahogany oval wine-coolers on George III octagonal stands, each with removable beaten-tin lining and tapering oval body mounted with lion-mask handles, 28in. wide.
(Christie's) $13,464

A George III mahogany cellaret with octagonal hinged top enclosing a lead-lined interior, the frieze inlaid with a rounded rectangular panel, the tapering octagonal body inlaid with ovals, 19^{1}/$_{2}$in. wide.
(Christie's) $18,513

A late George III mahogany and brass-bound wine cooler on later stand, the domed lid with later finial, 24in. wide.
(Christie's) $1,547

An early Victorian mahogany sarcophagus wine cooler, the raised hinged lid with fruit and acanthus cresting, on paw feet, 27^{1}/$_{2}$in. wide.
(Christie's) $2,957

A late 18th century octagonal wine cooler, in exotic hardwoods, brass bound with side handles, 20in. wide.
(Woolley & Wallis) $1,669

A Victorian mahogany sarcophagus shaped wine cooler, the hinged rectangular lid carved with a panel of foliage, the foliate carved frieze above tapering sides, 25in. wide. (Christie's) $1,001

A William IV brown oak wine cooler with hinged stepped oval top with lotus-leaf molding, on stepped oval base, with anti-friction casters, 38¼in. wide. (Christie's) $8,580

An early Victorian mahogany sarcophagus wine cooler, the hinged top surmounted by bunches of grapes and enclosing a zinc-lined fitted interior, 33½in. wide. (Bearne's) $1,447

An attractive George III mahogany wine cooler, the hinged cover with molded edge, bound with brass, 1ft. 7in. wide. (Spencer's) $4,785

A George III mahogany and brass banded oval vine cooler, on stand with brass carrying handles and lined interior, 2ft. 3in. wide. (Phillips) $3,363

A George III brass-bound mahogany wine-cooler with oval hinged top enclosing a lead-lined fitted interior with slightly tapering sides with ring-handles, 26¾in. wide. (Christie's) $5,253

A Regency mahogany and ebonized wine-cooler, on a part-reeded lotus-leaf carved turned shaft and concave-sided canted rectangular platform base and bronzed scroll feet, 30in. wide. (Christie's) $8,415

A William IV rosewood sarcophagus wine cooler with acanthus carved hinged lid, fitted interior and reeded corner ornament on paw feet, 26½in. wide. (Christie's) $2,508

A Regency mahogany sarcophagus cellaret on stand, the architecturally molded tapering body with gilt brass lion mask and ring handles and on lion paw feet, 20in. wide. (Bearne's) $5,472

A green-painted cast-iron garden chair, the curved back with foliate scrolls and upturned handles, with pierced oval seat, late 19th century.
(Christie's) $815

A Venetian Istrian stone well head, with a square molded cornice with rope-twist band, the circular body carved with four acanthus scrolls, probably 14th/15th century, 56in. wide.
(Christie's) $38,830

A large carved stone figure of Nelson, by Robert Forrest, depicted standing, in military uniform and with his cloak draped over his shoulders, circa 1836, 88in. high.
(Christie's) $29,123

A pair of carved sandstone urns, each with an everted egg-and-dart molded rim, with a gadrooned body on a circular fluted spreading foot, late 18th/early 19th century, 30in. diameter.
(Christie's) $6,213

A George III lead cistern, of rectangular form, the paneled front centered with the initial *P*, with two cherub mask heads, dated *1781*, 40in. wide.
(Christie's) $4,660

The Hampton Court Moor by John Van Nost, kneeling and supporting a Portland stone salver with a bronze sundial, wearing a feathered skirt, his hands held above his head, the Moor circa 1701, the dial early 18th century, the figure: 41³/₄in. high.
(Christie's) $55,770

A lead cherub sundial pedestal, shown holding a cornucopia in his right hand and supporting a circular stone platform, 41³/₄in. high.
(Christie's) $1,942

One of a set of four lead urns, each with a foliate-cast molded rim, the body cast with a seam to each side, and with two scrolled dragon head handles, mid-18th century, 23¼in. wide.
(Christie's)
(Four) $6,795

A Scottish stone sundial, surmounted by a spherical finial, the four sides with arched pediments, each with a carved dial and a bronze gnomon, early 18th century, 66in. high.
(Christie's) $12,620

A modern lead fountain group of a swan and putto, the swan with outstretched wings and head held high, the boy at his side looking up, 49¼in. high. (Christie's) $8,154

One of a pair of carved Portland stone salamanders, each beast shown seated, wearing a collar and engulfed by 'flames', 18th century, 24in. wide. (Christie's)
(Two) $8,737

A lead figure of a shepherdess, after John Cheere, shown holding a staff in her left hand, a lamb supported by her right hand, late 19th/20th century, 48in. high. (Christie's) $9,319

One of a pair of Doulton stoneware gate pier eagles, each with outstretched wings, on rockwork square bases, late 19th/early 20th century, 38½in. high. (Christie's)
(Two) $6,795

A carved stone royal coat of arms of Edward VII, with lion and unicorn supporters, within an arched frame, 50in. wide. (Christie's) $1,844

One of a pair of lead vases, each of hexagonal form, the waisted body cast in high relief and with a drilled background, the six sides each with an oval cartouche above a stylized twin-handled flower-filled vase, first half 18th century, 23in. wide. (Christie's)
(Two) $27,181

An Italian carved white marble wall fountain, the body decorated with acanthus leaf and centered by a grotesque mask fitted with a spout, first half 18th century, 40¼in. high. (Christie's) $6,213

One of a pair of stone jardinières, each of square tapering form, the paneled sides each with fluted and arcaded decoration and paneled center, 19th century, 18½in. square. (Christie's)
(Two) $4,077

An Italian carved Verona marble wall fountain, the rectangular bowl with tapering upright and lion mask fountain head, late 19th/20th century, 69in. high. (Christie's) $6,213

A large lead figure of a nymph, attributed to John Cheere, emblematic of Spring, depicted bare-breasted, flowers in her hair and a basket of flowers in her right hand, 18th century, 59in. high.
(Christie's) $29,123

A pair of white marble brackets and a matching armorial tablet, the brackets each elaborately carved overall with acanthus, second half 19th century, the brackets: 8¼in. wide.
(Christie's) $3,850

One of a pair of carved white marble urns, each with a molded overhanging rim, the body with drapery suspended between four mask heads, 19th century, 34in. diameter.
(Christie's)
(Two) $8,737

A bronze fountain figure of a winged putto carrying a duck, the putto striding forward, on associated circular bronze base with Sabatino de Angelis foundry mark, late 19th century, 21⅝in. high.
(Christie's) $1,445

A pair of English lead urns, each with the handles, rim, lower body and foot elaborately cast with acanthus leaf decoration, 18th century, 29in. high.
(Christie's) $25,240

An Italian carved white marble font, the frieze carved with a Bacchic scene of festive cherubs, above a central shaft with central caryatid carving above a fluted baluster, 19th century, 42¾in. high.
(Christie's) $9,319

A carved white marble figure of Pan, the satyr depicted grimacing, clutching his pipes and a bunch of roses to his chest, his hair entwined with grapevines, second half 19th century, 41½in. high.
(Christie's) $6,213

A matching pair of Italian marble urns, after the Medici and Borghese vases, each of campana form, intricately carved overall, first half 19th century, 19½in. high.
(Christie's) $53,900

One of a set of four lead urns, each with bulbous upper section decorated with alternating gadrooning and acanthus leaves, the body with four masks above drapery swags, 18th century, 20in. high.
(Christie's)
(Four) $8,154

A Victorian white marble group of Diana, by John Thomas, her hair tied in a chignon and with a crescent moon at her brow, a seated grayhound at her feet, circa 1854, 74¹/₂in. high.
(Christie's) **$26,210**

A pair of lead sphinxes, possibly depicting Madame du Barry and Madame de Pompadour, each seated on their haunches, with their front legs crossed, early 20th century, 36in. wide.
(Christie's) **$9,319**

One of a pair of carved red sandstone lions, each sitting back on its haunches and with its paws held before it, 18th/19th century, 34in. high.
(Christie's)
(Two) **$5,048**

A Scottish carved stone sundial pedestal, the circular top with a gadrooned edge and molded support, above an octagonal faceted shoulder with the compass points, late 18th century, 52in. high.
(Christie's) **$3,495**

A pair of modern lead grayhounds, each shown standing and looking forward, on rectangular stone bases, 36in. wide.
(Christie's) **$4,271**

A rare terracotta sundial, designed by Archibald Knox, supported on octagonal pedestal cast with leaves and Runic knots, designed and manufactured by Liberty & Co., 3ft. 8in. high.
(Sotheby's) **$1,705**

A rare terracotta garden urn on stand, designed by Archibald Knox, the circular bowl with four outset handles divided by stylized foliage, 3ft. high.
(Sotheby's) **$1,023**

A pair of lead urns, the upper part of the body decorated with vine, above a frieze of classical figures, late 19th/early 20th century, 30in. high.
(Christie's) **$6,795**

A Victorian stoneware heraldic griffin, seated on his haunches and supporting a shield with his forelegs, on a square stepped base, 42¹/₂in. high.
(Christie's) **$5,825**

A marble bench, the arched back centered by a mask, flanked with a cornucopia of fruit to each side, above arabesque foliate scrolls, 18th century, 63in. wide.
(Christie's) $9,708

A white marble statue of Cleopatra, signed *Clerici Roma 1804*, 81cm. wide.
(Finarte) $17,791

An Italian carved pink Verona marble rectangular trough, the sides with Bacchic reliefs of grapevine and winged putti filling a vat with grapes, 19th century, 88½in. wide.
(Christie's) $21,357

An attractive pair of sandstone garden figures of pixies, each seated cross-legged, eating an apple, 21in. high.
(Spencer's) $1,138

One of a set of three wrought-iron gates, each with a scrolled pediment with central arrow surmount, the frame with central scrolled panel, 74in. high.
(Christie's)
(Three) $3,106

Two lead cherubs, each with one arm raised, on square stone bases, first half 18th century, 33in. high.
(Christie's) $4,854

A marble and mosaic bench, the rectangular top inlaid with geometric tessuto fragments, on solid lion's claw monopodia base, 39in. wide.
(Christie's) $5,855

A mid 19th century marble sculpture of Flora, 108cm. high.
(Finarte) $4,413

A St. Annes marble oval cistern, the waisted body on conforming spreading foot, 18th century, 27½in. wide.
(Christie's) $5,436

A Coade stone royal coat of arms, with lion and unicorn supporters, centered by a crown with the heraldic device below, 70½in. wide.
(Christie's) $33,006

Cast iron garden ornament in the form of a Newfoundland dog, America, mid 19th century, 52in. long.
(Skinner) $24,200

A glazed composition stone group of a lion attacking a kid, after Oscar Waldmann, the lion lying down, snarling, with his right paw clutching the kid, inscribed *O. WALDMANN/ CR(?)ES Emile Muller*, late 19th/ 20th century, 70in. wide.
(Christie's) $6,160

A pair of English lead figures, attributed to John Cheere, emblematic of Summer and Autumn, Ceres representing Summer, Bacchus representing Autumn, mid 18th century, 53¾in. high.
(Christie's) $50,479

A stone figure of St. George, after Donatello, the saint standing with feet apart, his left hand holding his shield before him, 24½in. high.
(Christie's) $673

A pair of carved sandstone gate pier finials of heraldic beasts, each sitting on its haunches, its tongue protruding, holding a blank cartouche before it, 19th century, 40in. high.
(Christie's) $2,912

One of a set of three modern lead jardinières, the paneled sides cast in high relief with ogee molding, a ship, dolphins and foliate festoons, 31in. square.
(Christie's)
       (Three) $5,825

A 19th century white marble sculpture of Michelangelo's Moses, 102cm.
(Finarte) $11,031

A rectangular lead cistern, the front with the date *1709*, above a panel centered with the initials *R.D.*, early 18th century, 65¾in. wide.
(Christie's) $6,989

A 'Talbot' hot plate by Fletcher Russell & Co., with front tap rail for two burners and turnover grill, circa 1897. (Christie's) $427

A blue enamel French table gas cooker 'Le Standard No 3' by Et. Brachet & Richard with drop-down door with porcelain handle, circa 1900. (Christie's) $169

A 'Puritan' No 502 double hot plate by the Florence Co., Florence Mass, USA, with front tap rail with two brass lever taps, circa 1890. (Christie's) $116

A 'Eureka' No 405 gas cooker by John Wright & Co., with front tap rail for two rack-type boiling burners and grill, 21¹/₂in. high, circa 1907. (Christie's) $622

A rare circular gas cooker by Hare & Co., with single wrought-iron boiling ring on top and another in oven base, 38in. high. (Christie's) $1,778

A New World Junior gas cooker by Davis & Co. under Radiation Patents with front tap rail with four brass lever taps feeding three Rado burners. (Christie's) $249

A No 552 gas cooker by John Wright & Co., with loose white enamel crown plate and cast iron sides to oven, circa 1910. (Christie's) $249

A 'Kater' cooker on stand by The British Gas Appliance Co., with three brass taps feeding the side boiling ring, circa 1907. (Christie's) $169

A grey enamel No 1 'Bungalow' cooker on cast iron stand by The Elmscott Foundry Co. Ltd, Warwick with blank cast iron sides and back, circa 1912. (Christie's) $53

GAS APPLIANCES

A small Uno gas coffee roaster with wooden base.
(Christie's) $213

An amber enamel French table gas cooker 'Le Vatel' type 400 by Lilor Paris, with six brass taps to feed oven burner, circa 1915.
(Christie's) $1,333

A rare No 1 gas griller by T. Redamyne & Co, Sheffield with single pierced bar type burner, and drop down door.
(Christie's) $213

A rare gas range (Model 140. New pattern) by Richmond & Co., Warrington & London, with original copper hot water urn and gas attachment.
(Christie's) $1,778

The 'Great Duck' portable deflector cooker, of sheet steel with four cast iron cabriole feet, thre boiling rings fed from one large ring burner, 32^1/$_2$in. wide, circa 1915.
(Christie's) $249

A 'Cheerful' gas fire and boiling stove by John Wright & Co., Birmingham, with wrought-iron boiling ring on top.
(Christie's) $160

A Main cooker No 52, with side tap rail and four brass-handled taps, feeding four boiling rings, circa 1890.
(Christie's) $178

A 'Metropolitan' No 211 double gas range, by the Davis Gas Stove Co., 200/210 Camberwell Road, London SE, with front tap rail, eight taps and cast plate rack.
(Christie's) $338

A 'Davis Wee Cooker' by the Davis Gas Stove Co., Metropolitan Works 200/210, Camberwell Road, London SE, with front tap rail, circa 1898.
(Christie's) $1,067

ASHTRAYS

Steuben glass ashtray with
applied handle, 7in. diameter.
(Eldred's) $100

A pair of Almaric Walter pâte-
de-verre ashtrays modeled by
Henri Bergé, 12cm. diameter.
(Christie's) $3,010

'Clos Sainte-Odile', a Lalique
frosted and polished ashtray of
circular design, 11cm. high.
(Christie's) $803

BASKETS

Victorian glass basket,
attributed to Stevens &
Williams, opaque opal glass
cased to raspberry pink, applied
with amber leaves and fruits,
11in. high.
(Skinner) $660

Escalier de Cristal ormolu
basket, attributed to Baccarat,
stylized trees and floral enamel
decorated on clear bowl
mounted with gilt metal double
dragon handle, 6³/₄in. high.
(Skinner) $660

A Venetian latticinio small
bucket in vetro a retorti, the
body of compressed baluster
form supported on a merese
above a spreading conical foot,
late 16th century, 12.5cm. high.
(Christie's) $1,993

19th century cranberry glass to
opalescent white glass bride's
basket, set in white metal frame,
6in. wide.
(Du Mouchelles) $100

Steven & Williams Victorian
glass basket, applied crimped
amber glass rim and handles on
transparent blue folded
pedestaled bowl, 6in. high.
(Skinner Inc.) $260

A Venetian bucket or aspersory,
the compressed baluster sides
with two bands of molded
double-ribs, second half of the
16th century, 18.5cm. high.
(Christie's) $3,654

BEAKERS

Blown three-mould flip glass, colorless, pontil scar, 4³/₄in., New England, 1825–40. (Skinner) $82

Blown three-mold flip glass, colorless, pontil scar, 5³/₈in., New England, 1825–40. (Skinner) $132

A Biedermeier beaker, engraved with a spray of roses, carnation and other flowers, 12cm. (Phillips) **$1,100**

One of a group of four green glass Roman beakers, with a thick band of trail around the upper body, 3¹/₂in. high, circa 4th century A.D. (Bonhams) (Four) $406

A lithyalin green tinted remembrance beaker from the workshop of Friedrich Egermann, of faceted, waisted form, 11cm. (Phillips) $900

Engraved flip glass, engraved with wavy lines and geometrics, 5³/₄in. high, Northern Europe, late 18th/early 19th century. (Skinner) $137

A German glass beaker, dated *1722*, enameled in colors with a horse seller leading a pack of horses, 5¹/₂in. high. (Bonhams) $1,500

A topographical flared tumbler engraved with a view of Alnwick Castle, named on a matt band, circa 1830, 11.5cm. high. (Christie's) $446

A German flared beaker enameled in colors with The King of Sweden on horseback, late 19th century, 5³/₄in. high. (Christie's) $581

BOTTLES

Drakes/Plantation/Bitters figural bottle, cabin shape, rare variant with 'St.' missing, 9⁷/₈in. high, America, 1870–80. (Skinner) $302

Early free-blown bottle, very bubbly green, crudely applied lip-pontil scar, 9⁵/₈in., New England, 1790–1830. (Skinner) $143

An opalescent glass bottle of upright rectangular shape, painted with a basket of flowers in colors on each side, 11cm. (Phillips) $609

Drakes Plantation labelled bitters bottle, light honey amber with full back label, 10in., America, 1860–70. (Skinner) $253

Emile Gallé Islamic style enameled bottle, squared transparent oval-form decorated overall with colorful enameled foliate devices, 6¹/₄in. high. (Skinner) $7,150

'Arabian Bitters' bottle, unlisted, 'An old and Reliable Tonic', 9⁵/₈in., America, 1870's. (Skinner) $330

A turquoise squared glass bottle with thick disc rim and wide strap handle, Roman, 2nd century A.D., 8¹/₂in. (Bonhams) $898

Early spirits bottle, half size, olive green, 5in. high, probably England, 1710–25. (Skinner) $550

Free blown storage jar, straight sided, greenish aqua, rolled lip-pontil scar, 9in. high, America, 1840–60. (Skinner) $93

Cathedral pickle bottle, square, forest green shading, rolled lip-iron pontil, 8⁷/₈in., America, 1850–65.
(Skinner) **$715**

Large chestnut bottle, wavy glass, olive green, applied lip-pontil scar, 11⁷/₈in., New England, 1800–30.
(Skinner) **$302**

Poison bottle, skull figural poison bottle, cobalt blue, 4³/₈in. high, late 19th century.
(Skinner) **$440**

Swirled rib globular bottle, twenty-four ribs, aqua, 7⁵/₈in. high, Midwest America, 1820–50.
(Skinner) **$357**

'Dr. Phelps Arcanum Genuine' medicine bottle, hexagonal, deep red amber with green tint, 8in. high, New England, 1830–45.
(Skinner) **$12,100**

Hayward hand grenade fire extinguisher bottle, with contents, deep blue, 6in. high, late 19th century.
(Skinner) **$192**

A late 18th century clear glass bottle of flat oval shape, engraved on one side with the initials *SPC* within floral garlands, 11cm.
(Phillips) **$650**

Early utilitarian bottle, cylinder, crude flattened string lip, deep olive green, 8¹/₂in. high, New England, 1820–40.
(Skinner) **$330**

Blown three-mold cologne, sapphire blue, no stopper, pontil scar, 6in., New England, 1825–40.
(Skinner) **$192**

BOTTLES

Keystone/Bitters figural bitters bottle, barrel shape, amber, 10in. high, America, 1870–80.
(Skinner) $467

'Dingens Napoleon Cocktail Bitters' bottle, banjo shape, green, 10¹/₂in., America, 1860–65.
(Skinner) $9,900

National Bitters, ear of corn figural, amber, 12¹/₂in. high, America, 1870–80.
(Skinner) $220

Large case gin bottle, deep olive green, crude applied lip-pontil scar, 13¹/₄in., 1780–1840.
(Skinner) $467

Early octagonal snuff bottle, unusual shape, deep green, flaring lip-pontil scar, 3³/₄in., New England, 1800–30.
(Skinner) $385

'Dr. J. Walkers/Vinegar Bitters' bottle, 95% of label intact, cylinder, aqua, 8¹/₄in., 1880–90.
(Skinner) $110

'Greeleys Bourbon/Bitters' bottle, barrel shaped, medium olive green, 9¹/₄in. high, America, 1860–70.
(Skinner) $825

An early sealed 'shaft and globe' wine-bottle of green tint, circa 1670, 19.5cm. high.
(Christie's) $7,711

Pillar molded bar bottle, eight vertical base ribs, light electric blue, 11¹/₈in. high, possibly Pittsburgh area glasshouse, 1840–60.
(Skinner) $550

René Lalique Madagascar bowl, opalescent white-blue centerbowl with twelve press molded monkey faces in extreme high relief, 13in. diameter. (Skinner) $6,875

Durand Art Glass peacock feather centerbowl, broad flared trumpet-form of brilliant ruby color with pink and white pulled feather motif on bowl and foot, 14in. diameter. (Skinner) $880

An Orrefors blue tinted glass bowl with wavy rim, the exterior intaglio-molded with turtles, 1950, 30cm. diameter. (Christie's) $301

An Art Nouveau acid-etched and carved cameo bowl, in gilt metal wirework stand, 17cm. diameter. (Christie's) $368

A pair of early Victorian red glass bowls on stands of boat shape with bracket cut and cusped edges, 11¼in. wide. (Tennants) $891

Mt. Washington Napoli compôte, colorless glass bowl, handpainted on exterior with pink water lilies against green background, 11in. high. (Skinner) $468

Early engraved compôte, bowl engraved with wreaths and tassels, 8¼in. high, New England, 1825–35. (Skinner) $1,320

Early engraved bowl, hexagonal with leaf and grape etching, colorless, 6¼in. high, New England, circa 1850. (Skinner) $467

Steuben Rosaline bowl, flared pink jade color with applied alabaster foot, 12in. diameter. (Skinner) $358

BOWLS

Bowl, 1927–1930, pâte de verre, impressed Decorchement seal, 2¹/₂in. high.
(Sotheby's) $3,208

Threaded Lutz-type bowl, bands of pink threading around ruffled rim, 12in. wide, probably Boston & Sandwich Glassworks, 1870–85.
(Skinner) $385

René Lalique, bowl, 'Perruches', after 1931, opalescent glass, 9³/₄in. diameter.
(Sotheby's) $2,317

René Lalique, bowl, 'Calypso', after 1930, opalescent glass, 11³/₄in. diameter.
(Sotheby's) $3,920

An Almaric Walter pâte de verre bowl modeled by Henri Bergé, the mottled yellow body decorated in relief with three yellow snails amongst green foliage, 4¹/₄in. diameter.
(Christie's) $5,621

René Lalique, bowl, 'Gui No. 1, after 1921, opalescent glass, 9¹/₂in. diameter.
(Sotheby's) $356

A cut deep bowl, the polygonal sides with horizontal prisms beneath a fluted dentil rim, circa 1820, 20.5cm. diameter.
(Christie's) $1,028

Early free blown wine glass, applied foot, very bubbly aqua with white wisps running throughout, 4in., America, 1820–40.
(Skinner) $192

Grooved Bigler bowl, very rare, deep blue purple, 3in. high, New England, 1840–50.
(Skinner) $550

BOWLS

A Gallé acid-etched, wheel-carved and martelé-ware cameo bowl, of compressed globular form, 9cm. high.
(Christie's) $1,137

Loop patterned pressed bowl, canary, 8¹/₂in. wide, New England, 1840–60.
(Skinner) $495

Charles Schneider/Le Verre Français, stylized flower two handled bowl, 1920s, 5in. wide.
(Sotheby's) $1,069

René Lalique, bowl, 'Poissons No. 2', after 1921, opalescent glass, 9¹/₂in. diameter.
(Sotheby's) $463

An Irish cut circular bowl, the sides with panels of exaggerated step-cutting beneath a fan-cut rim, circa 1830, probably Waterford, 25.5cm. diameter.
(Christie's) $770

René Lalique, bowl, 'Lys', after 1924, opalescent glass, 9¹/₄in. diameter.
(Sotheby's) $570

Free blown punch bowl, unusual size, with folded rim, colorless, 8³/₄in. high, New England, 1830–40.
(Skinner) $275

Afers Swedish crystal bowl, Ernest Gordon studio work with internal rows of circles in square frames, 6³/₄in. diameter.
(Skinner) $550

An Irish cut 'kettle-drum' bowl, the border with panels of diamonds divided by bands of vertical and diagonal flutes, circa 1800, 21.5cm. diameter.
(Christie's) $685

CANDLESTICKS

Early pressed candlestick, wafer attachment, colorless, probably New England, 1845–60.
(Skinner) $467

A fine pair of Regency cut-glass two-branch candelabra, each with faceted spherical finials and thistle cut nozzles, 19in. high.
(Bearne's) $3,354

A glass candlestick with a cylindrical sconce above a square tapered stem and ringed domed foot, 7³/₄in. high.
(Christie's) $835

Pair of dolphin candlesticks, wafer attachments, electric blue sockets, 10¹/₄in., Sandwich Glassworks, 1845–70.
(Skinner) $2,200

A Regency lacquered gilt-brass mahogany candlestick with glass storm-shade with molded tapering circular bowl, on turned spreading socle and concave-sided fluted paneled hexagonal plinth base, 17¹/₂in. high.
(Christie's) $2,693

A rare pair of George III cut-glass candlesticks, each with two tiers of prismatic drops, on 'Bristol' blue glass cylindrical plinths, 12in. high.
(Bearne's) $12,708

Tiffany gold iridescent Art glass candlestick vase with ribbed twist stem, marked on base, *LCT*, 5¹/₄in. high.
(Eldred's) $440

Pair of early pattern molded candlesticks, with domed radial molding, colorless lead glass, 6¹/₈in. high, England, 1715–30.
(Skinner) $550

One of a pair of pressed candlesticks, deep amethyst, 9¹/₈in. high, New England Glass Co., 1840–50.
(Skinner) (Two) $550

DECANTERS

A clear glass decanter and stopper engraved with flowering branches and tulips and a band of stylized foliage, 9¼in. high.
(Christie's) $3,300

A green glass and electroplate decanter in the form of a walrus, the head with bone tusks, 14in. long.
(Christie's) $977

Swirled Art glass decanter, blown crystal with alternating green and colorless spiral design, 11in. high.
(Skinner) $165

An engraved magnum decanter for claret of club shape, named within a quatrefoil cartouche, circa 1780, 31.5cm. high.
(Christie's) $1,627

A pair of Continental decanters and silver-gilt stand, French, early 19th century, the central extension of twisted vine motif, with blue glass decanters decorated with twisted vine gold leaf decoration, maker's mark *LB*, 28cm. high.
(Lawrence) $3,323

Steuben gold Aurene six-piece cordial set, rare cylindrical decanter set within round tray-holder with four matching conical glasses, 8in. high.
(Skinner) $2,860

An engraved 'rock crystal' decanter and stopper, possibly John Orchard, Stevens and Williams, Stourbridge, circa 1895, the sides deeply engraved and cut with scrolls, 13⅝in. high.
(Sotheby's) $3,069

A pair of magnificent magnum cut decanters and stoppers, printed in colored enamels with figures symbolic of Asia and Africa, 35cm., probably Irish.
(Phillips) $15,200

An unusual silver mounted decanter with spherical stopper, Birmingham, 1913–14, 28.5cm. high.
(Finarte) $856

DISHES

Bonbonnière and cover, circa 1910, etched and enameled glass, with cameo mark *Daum Nancy*, 5¼in. diameter.
(Sotheby's) $1,247

A pair of cut oval two-handled deep dishes, the flared sides with horizontal prisms beneath dentil rims, circa 1815, 20.5cm. wide.
(Christie's) $942

Early multi-colored dish and under plate, clambroth melon-shaped hobnailed body and cover, 5¾in. high, possibly New England, mid 19th century.
(Skinner) $770

René Lalique, dish, 'Poissons No. 1', after 1931, opalescent glass, 12¼in. diameter.
(Sotheby's) $463

Ribbon edge compôte, wafer attachment, amethyst, 8in. high, New England, 1840–60.
(Skinner) $8,800

René Lalique, dish, 'Volubilis'. after 1921, amber glass, 8½in. diameter.
(Sotheby's) $392

A J. Couper & Sons Clutha dish, circular with pulled and undulated rim and shallow well, green tinted glass with milky-white and red striations, 22.5cm. wide.
(Christie's) $1,244

Blown three-mold hat whimsey, deep sapphire blue, pontil scar, 2¼in., New England, 1825–40.
(Skinner) $825

René Lalique, plate, 'Sirene', after 1920, opalescent glass, 14½in. diameter.
(Sotheby's) $5,346

DISHES

An Irish cut oval turnover center-dish, the bowl with a band of facet ornament, circa 1800, 35cm. wide.
(Christie's) $2,742

A pair of large cut glass cylindrical two-handled coolers and liners, circa 1820, 26cm. wide.
(Christie's) $11,138

One of a pair of cut small deep circular two-handled dishes, the flared sides with allover horizontal prisms beneath dentil rims, circa 1815, 16cm. wide.
(Christie's) (Two) $942

René Lalique, dish, 'Martigues', after 1920, opalescent glass, 14¼in. diameter.
(Sotheby's) $2,317

A Spanish tazza of straw tint, the shallow tray supported on a slender hollow stem with a shoulder knop, 18th century, perhaps Andalusia, 13.5cm. high.
(Christie's) $747

A large Venetian latticinio circular dish in vetro a reticello, the depressed center rising to a point and with a folded rim, 17th century, 46.5cm. diameter.
(Christie's) $23,254

A Venetian enameled armorial low tazza, the shallow tray enameled in iron-red, blue and ocher with a coat-of-arms with pendant scrolling tendrils, early 16th century, 23cm. diameter.
(Christie's) $18,271

A French 'Gorge de Pigeon' ormolu-mounted two-handled tazza with everted rim, supported on a knopped spreading stem and square foot, circa 1835, 21cm. wide.
(Christie's) $2,492

A large Venetian radially ribbed dish, the depressed center rising to a point and with a shaped folded rim, circa 1700, 50cm. diameter.
(Christie's) $4,651

DRINKING GLASSES

An opaque-twist toastmaster's firing-glass, the deceptive bowl with a band of diagonal tool marks, on a terraced foot, circa 1765, 10.5cm. high. (Christie's) $830

An opaque-twist ratafia-glass, the slender round funnel bowl with hammered flutes to the lower part, circa 1765, 18.5cm. high. (Christie's) $1,163

A Jacobite dram-glass, the bell bowl engraved with a six-petaled rose, a bud and a half-opened bud, circa 1745, 9.5cm. high. (Christie's) $1,578

A color-twist firing-glass, the stem with an opaque gauze core entwined by a pair of translucent green and a pair of opaque spiral threads, circa 1770, 11cm. high. (Christie's) $2,824

A Venetian drinking-glass, the radially ribbed small bowl with a wide everted rim supported on a merese, early 17th century, 12cm. high. (Christie's) $2,824

An engraved rummer attributed to William Absolon, the pointed funnel bowl decorated with a wheat-sheaf within a circular cartouche, early 19th century, 14.5cm. high. (Christie's) $747

An airtwist cider-glass, the generous round funnel bowl engraved with a meandering band of apples among foliage, circa 1750, 18.5cm. high. (Christie's) $2,492

An airtwist firing-glass with a bell bowl, the stem filled with spiral threads above a thick foot, circa 1750, 10cm. high. (Christie's) $532

A diamond-engraved ale-glass, decorated with two peacocks perched among scattered stylized flowerheads and foliage, circa 1695, 12.5cm. high. (Christie's) $3,322

A pedestal-stemmed sweetmeat-glass, the round funnel bowl with saucer-topped rim and molded with vertical ribs, circa 1740, 15.5cm. high. (Christie's) $532

A balustroid champagne glass with a double-ogee bowl, the ·stem with a beaded knop between two plain sections above a domed foot, circa 1730, 12cm. high. (Christie's) $432

An opaque-twist molded champagne or sweetmeat-glass, the double-ogee bowl with an everted rim and molded allover with honeycomb ornament, circa 1760, 17cm. high. (Christie's) $1,495

An opaque-twist ale-flute, molded with vertical ribs, the stem with a gauze core within two spiral threads, circa 1770, 20cm. high. (Christie's) $581

A Venetian drinking-glass, the shallow bowl supported on a wrythen-molded slender tapering stem, late 16th/early 17th century, 14.5cm. diameter. (Christie's) $2,990

An ale glass, the bowl engraved with hops and barley, on double opaque slightly tapered stem, 18th century. (Woolley & Wallis) $333

A baluster toastmaster's glass, the deceptive straight-sided funnel bowl supported on an inverted baluster stem enclosing an elongated tear, circa 1710, 11.5cm. high. (Christie's) $581

An engraved airtwist ale-flute, the slender funnel bowl engraved with two ears of barley flanked by insects, circa 1750, 22cm. high. (Christie's) $747

A balustroid molded champagne-glass, the double-ogee bowl with everted rim molded with allover honeycomb ornament, circa 1735, 15.5cm. high. (Christie's) $598

FLASKS

'Success To The Railroad' historical flask, deep green, pint, Keene Marlboro St. Glassworks, New Hampshire, circa 1830. (Skinner) $187

A molded-blown yellow-brown glass grape flask, Roman circa 1st century A.D., 5¼in. (Bonhams) $1,224

Pitkin-type flask, thirty-six ribs broken swirl, light olive green, half pint, 5½in. high, New England, 1790–1830. (Skinner) $220

Eagle 'Willington/Glass Co.' historical flask, sloping collar, smooth base, medium blue-green, pint, Willington Glass Works, 1860's. (Skinner) $357

Pitkin-type flask, thirty ribs, broken swirl, greenish aqua, half post, sheared lip-pontil scar, 6¼in., Midwest America, 1810–40. (Skinner) $302

Masonic historical flask, light olive amber, sheared lip pontil scar, half-pint, Coventry Glassworks, Coventry, Connecticut, 1815–30. (Skinner) $5,170

Washington-Taylor historical flask, sloping collar with bevel-smooth base, lime yellow, Dyottville Glassworks, 1850–65. (Skinner) $495

A Netherlands turquoise globular flask, the lower part molded with 'nipt diamond waies', late 17th century, 24.5cm. high. (Christie's) $7,475

Eagle 'Willington Glass Co.' historical flask, deep golden amber, half pint, Willington Glassworks, 1850's. (Skinner) $121

FLASKS

Franklin-Dyott portrait flask, aqua, quart, Kensington Glassworks, Philadelphia, 1826–28.
(Skinner) $247

Washington eagle portrait flask, aqua, sheared lip-pontil scar, pint, Kensington Glassworks, Philadelphia, 1826–30.
(Skinner) $220

Washington eagle portrait flask, aqua, sheared lip-pontil scar, quart, possibly Baltimore Glassworks, 1836–50.
(Skinner) $77

Grotesque head men arguing pictorial flask, aqua, sheared lip-pontil scar, possibly Continental Europe, early 19th century.
(Skinner) $385

Bohemian black glass moon flask decorated with polychrome flowers, birds and white jewel work, 15in. tall.
(G. A. Key) $96

Pitkin-type flask, broken swirl, deep golden amber, sheared lip-pontil scar, half-pint, $6^5/8$in. high, Midwest America, 1790–1830.
(Skinner) $495

Eagle masonic historical flask, aqua, sheared lip-pontil scar, pint, Kensington Glassworks, Philadelphia, 1822–25.
(Skinner) $143

A Netherlands cobalt-blue globular flask, the body molded with vertical flutes, with shallow kick-in base, late 17th century, 26.5cm. high.
(Christie's) $1,246

Pattern molded flask, eighteen vertical ribs, light aqua, $6^1/2$in. high, Midwest America, 1820–50.
(Skinner) $165

427

GOBLETS

A heavy baluster goblet, set on an inverted baluster stem enclosing a large tear above a folded conical foot, circa 1700, 19cm. high.
(Christie's) $747

Early engraved goblet, golden amber with animals and wavy lines and initials *FR*, 5¼in. high, Bohemia, 1840–60.
(Skinner) $302

A baluster goblet with a bell bowl, the solid lower part enclosing a tear, above a domed and folded foot, circa 1720, 18cm. high.
(Christie's) $532

The Bacchus goblet, engraved and polished with a youthful Bacchus holding a bunch of grapes and seated astride a wine-cask, 1740–1750, 28cm. high.
(Christie's) $16,610

A Bohemian dated enameled goblet, the slender bell bowl enameled in shades of light and dark-blue, brown, yellow and white with a Biblical scene, 1575, 14cm. high.
(Christie's) $27,416

A large composite-stemmed goblet with a bucket bowl, the stem with a columnar section filled with airtwist spiral threads, circa 1750, 22.5cm. high.
(Christie's) $1,329

A Venetian goblet, the shallow widely flared bowl supported on a merese above a slender hollow tapering oviform stem, 17th century, 16cm. high.
(Christie's) $3,986

A Wiener Werkstätte enameled and engraved glass goblet, manufactured by Moser, Karlsbad, the slightly flared cylindrical cup on a bell-shaped foot, 18.5cm. high.
(Christie's) $1,818

An engraved baluster goblet, the slender bell bowl with a border of flower-sprays pendant from shell ornament, 1720, 18cm. high.
(Christie's) $598

GOBLETS

A baluster goblet, the bell bowl supported on a triple annulated knop, on a conical foot, circa 1730, 16cm. high.
(Christie's) $465

A Jacobite armorial airtwist goblet, the funnel bowl engraved and polished with a coat-of-arms, mid-18th century, 18.5cm. high.
(Christie's) $7,711

A Varnish & Co. double walled goblet in blue glass over silver, with bell bowl above a faceted knop, 20.2cm. high.
(Phillips) $160

A tall 'Façon de Venise' goblet with a widely flared bowl, the stem formed as three hollow inverted baluster knops divided by mereses, 17th century, Liège, 25cm. high.
(Christie's) $5,814

A Jacobite portrait airtwist goblet, the funnel bowl with a bust portrait of Prince Charles Edward within a circular double-line cartouche inscribed above *Audentior ibo*, circa 1750, 16.5cm. high.
(Christie's) $6,976

A 'Façon de Venise' goblet of straw tint, the deep round funnel bowl supported on a hollow ball knop, second quarter of the 17th century, 17cm. high.
(Christie's) $2,325

A Dutch-engraved light-baluster goblet, the bell bowl with swags of fruit and flowers pendant from the rims, mid-18th century, 18cm. high.
(Christie's) $698

A Venetian ring-goblet with a model of a turquoise bird perched in the center of the oval compressed bowl, 17th century, 13.5cm. high.
(Christie's) $2,399

A Saxon engraved goblet, the round funnel bowl decorated in Tief and Mattschnitt with a multitude of animals, circa 1730, probably Dresden, 25cm. high.
(Christie's) $9,136

A finely engraved English clear glass claret jug of baluster shape, engraved with birds perched on branches, 30cm. high.
(Phillips) $800

A cut and stained-amber ewer of tapering oviform with a scroll handle, cut with three rows of sunburst medallions, circa 1830, 24.5cm. high.
(Christie's) $1,113

An attractively engraved English clear glass claret jug, engraved with a swan on a pond flanked by trees and foliage, 26.5cm., possibly Richardson.
(Phillips) $480

An engraved topographical jug, possibly J. B. Millar, John Ford and Co., Edinburgh, circa 1865, engraved with titled views of Holyrood Palace, Calton Hill and Edinburgh Castle, 9in. high.
(Sotheby's) $2,216

Mt. Washington Royal Flemish pitcher, bulbous-form with molded raised fishnet design handpainted with seashells, marine plants and two realistic fish, 8in. high.
(Skinner) $1,100

A fine engraved armorial claret ewer, possibly John Baird Glassworks, Glasgow, circa 1860, finely engraved possibly by Henry Keller, with a Grecian warrior and chariot, 9⅝in. high.
(Sotheby's) $2,131

An English gilt-metal mounted blue glass parrot claret jug, complete with stopper, 11¾in. high.
(Christie's) $864

Lacy creamer, colorless, 4¼in., New England, 1830–50.
(Skinner) $247

A cut glass ruby-stained claret ewer, circa 1865, the ovoid body cut overall with large diamonds, the shoulder and slender neck with printies, 11¾in. high.
(Sotheby's) $1,620

JUGS & PITCHERS

A Victorian silver-mounted cut-glass claret jug, 11in. high, John Grinsell and Sons, London 1897. (Bearne's) $1,103

A silver mounted claret jug by Heath and Middleton, London, the globular body with wrythen ornament, 1889–90, 22cm. high. (Finarte) $605

'Griffith Hyatt & Co/Baltimore' handled jug, deep golden amber, 7¼in., America, 1840–60. (Skinner) $412

A good early Victorian claret jug, engraved with an oasis depicting two camels, one recumbent under a palm tree and an Arab kneeling beside his tent, 31cm. high. (Spencer's) $320

Antique amberina water pitcher with applied ribbed amber handle, New England, circa 1860, 8¹/8in. high. (Eldred's) $193

A fine silver-mounted cameo claret ewer, probably Thomas Webb and Sons, circa 1884, the deep amber-tinted glass overlaid in opaque-white and carved with dahlias, a raspberry and insects, 10³/8in. high. (Sotheby's) $5,115

A Bohemian enameled green-ground slender oviform ewer and stopper, decorated in the Persian taste in bright colors with stylized foliage, circa 1890, 46cm. high. (Christie's) $1,661

Fleur de lys pitcher, circa 1895, etched glass, heightened with gilding, with gilt mark *Daum Nancy*, 7¹/2in. high. (Sotheby's) $927

A Victorian claret jug, the ovoid glass body finely engraved with daisies and leafy stems, Sheffield 1900. (Russell Baldwin & Bright) $940

MISCELLANEOUS

European Art Glass candleholder, gilt metal tripod frame with opal glass bell shade decorated in gold and blue pulled feather design, 11in. high. (Skinner) $220

A pair of mid-Victorian red overlay table lusters of trumpet shape pendant with facet cut drops, 9^1/8in. high. (Tennants) $729

Mount Washington glass jewelry box with stippled green glaze and floral decoration, 3^1/2in. high. (Eldred's) $121

Almaric Walter pâte-de-vere figural seal, signed by H. Mercier, full bodied animal perched on simulated rock pedestal, 6^1/4in. high. (Skinner) $1,870

A novelty pair of cranberry glass honey pots as bees, with cranberry glass bodies, by Mappin & Webb, 15.5cm. long overall. (Spencer's) $480

An oval pâte sur pâte plaque by Frederick Rhead, signed, decorated with a young maiden holding a basket of fruit and dressed in a diaphanous costume, 27cm. (Phillips) $3,248

'Suzanne au Bain', a Lalique opalescent figure, molded as a nude maiden poised on one leg, her arms outstretched supporting a drape, 22.5cm. high. (Christie's) $10,527

A pair of Victorian mushroom opaque glass lusters, the cylindrical bowls printed in colors with eight oval panels enclosing female heads, on a gilt decorated ground, 33cm. high. (Spencer's) $354

A Stourbridge glass millefiori inkwell with stopper, the canes arranged in concentric rows including four showing the date *1848*, 4^1/2in. diameter. (Russell Baldwin & Bright) $526

Mount Washington glass biscuit jar with raised and painted floral design, silver plated cover and swing handle, 8in. high.
(Eldred's) $138

A German Milchglas teapot and cover of globular shape, and a teabowl and saucer en suite.
(Phillips) $352

A pair of St. Louis crown door-handles with metal mounts, the red and green twisted ribbon alternating with entwined latticinio thread, mid-19th century, 5.5cm. diameter.
(Christie's) $1,080

A St. Louis macedoine wafer-stand, the rim to the ogee bowl applied with a cobalt-blue twisted ribbon entwined with white latticinio thread, mid-19th century, 7.5cm. diameter.
(Christie's) $997

An attractive pair of Victorian ruby glass lusters, painted in polychrome enamels with a continuous band of flowers and leaves, on baluster stems, 38cm. high.
(Spencer's) $643

A 19th century ormolu mounted glass centerpiece, the flared dish on dragon supports, 17cm. high.
(Finarte) $1,280

Finely made hourglass, wooden frame with turned posts, 9in. high.
(Eldred's) $303

A Richardson's water-set, comprising a baluster water-jug with loop handle and two goblets, circa 1848, the jug 20.5cm. high.
(Christie's) $1,885

An unusual Varnish & Co. ring stand with ruby glass over the silver, and tall pointed spire, 13cm. high.
(Phillips) $672

PAPER WEIGHTS

A Clichy pansy weight, the flower with two large mauve petals and three smaller yellow petals, mid-19th century, 6.5cm. diameter.
(Christie's) $2,492

A Baccarat dated close millefiori paperweight with dated cane *B 1846*, 7.5cm.
(Phillips) $2,080

A very rare St. Louis panelled carpet ground millefiori paperweight, with a central blue and white cluster of canes from which radiate six triangular-shaped panels, 6.5cm.
(Phillips) $10,150

A large Clichy garland paperweight with translucent green ground, the trefoil garland of alternate pink and white canes interspersed with white canes, 8cm.
(Phillips) $832

An unusual sulphide obelisk paperweight with a sulphide head and shoulders bust depicting Napoleon full face and Wellington from the side views, 10.5cm.
(Phillips) $650

A Baccarat butterfly and clematis weight, the insect with transparent purple body and marbled wings hovering over a white double-clematis, mid-19th century, 6.5cm. diameter.
(Christie's) $3,654

A St. Louis sulphide portrait paperweight in clear glass set with a profile to sinister, titled *L. Napoleon*, 7.5cm.
(Phillips) $448

A Clichy colour ground paperweight, with central rose within concentric millefiori canes in red, white and pink, 7.5cm. diameter.
(Spencer's) $1,286

A St. Louis vegetable paperweight with two parsnips, two beetroot and two radishes, 6.5cm.
(Phillips) $672

PAPER WEIGHTS

A Baccarat strawberry weight, the two realistic ripe fruit pendant from a green stalk, on a star-cut base, mid-19th century, 7.2cm. diameter.
(Christie's) $2,824

A Clichy red-ground patterned concentric millefiori weight, the central white star set within two circles of canes, mid-19th century, 6.8cm. diameter.
(Christie's) $747

An interesting American rose paperweight in clear glass, set with a thin multi-petaled pink rose with yellow center, 8.5cm., possibly Mount Washington.
(Phillips) $1,920

A Baccarat red-ground patterned millefiori weight, the central pink, blue and white setup within a circle of pink-centered white star canes, mid-19th century, 7cm. diameter.
(Christie's) $3,986

A New England free-blown pear weight, the naturally modeled pear in shades of pink and yellow resting on a clear glass circular base, circa 1870, 7cm. diameter.
(Christie's) $747

A St. Louis faceted garlanded camomile weight, the flower with numerous pink feathery petals about a pale-blue and white center, mid-19th century, 7cm. diameter.
(Christie's) $1,080

A good Paul Ysart paperweight, signed *PY*, with a brightly colored dragonfly with yellow wings and green body, 8cm.
(Phillips) $704

A Baccarat sulphide portrait paperwight with a nearly full face portrait of Czar Nicholas I of Russia, 8cm.
(Phillips) $800

A Baccarat garland weight with translucent strawberry-red ground, with a white stardust cane in the center, 8.2cm.
(Phillips) $640

435

A Baccarat faceted red
'Thousand-petaled' rose weight,
the flower with numerous dark-
red petals, mid-19th century,
7cm. diameter.
(Christie's) $4,798

A St. Louis pink dahlia weight,
the flower with four rows of
pink petals, mid-19th century,
7.6cm. diameter.
(Christie's) $2,056

A Clichy carpet-ground initial
weight with the letters *R D*
formed from pink-centered
white canes, mid-19th century,
8.3cm. diameter.
(Christie's) $2,228

A Baccarat pink 'thousand-
petaled' rose weight, the flower
with numerous overlapping
pale-pink petals surrounded by
five green leaves, mid-19th
century, 7.2cm. diameter.
(Christie's) $3,654

A St. Louis faceted close
concentric millefiori mushroom
weight, the tuft with four circles
of canes in salmon-pink, dark-
blue, white and pale-green about
a central blue whorl, mid-19th
century, 7.8cm. diameter.
(Christie's) $2,658

A Clichy moss-ground scattered
millefiori weight, the central
pink and green rose surrounded
by scattered brightly colored
canes including a pink rose,
mid-19th century, 6.6cm.
diameter.
(Christie's) $9,634

A Baccarat garlanded yellow
buttercup weight, the flower
with two rows of recessed yellow
petals about a yellow-centered
white star cane, mid-19th
century, 7.8cm. diameter.
(Christie's) $6,640

A Baccarat white bell-flower
weight, the three white bell-like
flowers pendent from a single
green stalk, mid-19th century,
6.8cm. diameter.
(Christie's) $4,455

A Clichy flat bouquet weight,
the central pink flower with ten
ribbed petals about a red, green
and pale-yellow center and
flanked by two pink buds, mid-
19th century, 7.8cm. diameter.
(Christie's) $14,119

PAPER WEIGHTS

A St. Louis pink dahlia weight, the flower with three rows of deep-pink lightly ribbed petals about a yellow-dotted red center, mid-19th century, 7.2cm. diameter.
(Christie's) $1,284

A Baccarat faceted garlanded two-flower weight, the large white double-clematis with twelve ribbed petals, mid-19th century, 7cm. diameter.
(Christie's) $857

A Clichy flower weight, the daisy-like flower with radiating white petals tipped in pale-yellow about a red, white and pale-yellow center, mid-19th century, 7.5cm. diameter.
(Christie's) $9,424

A Baccarat flat bouquet weight, the central pink 'thousand-petaled' rose surrounded by a cobalt-blue and white primrose, a pansy of conventional type, a yellow wheatflower and dark-blue and red buds, mid-19th century, 7.8cm. diameter.
(Christie's) $9,970

A Clichy double-overlay close concentric millefiori mushroom weight, the tuft with five circles of canes in shades of moss-green, white, dark-blue and including five pink roses, mid-19th century, 7cm. diameter.
(Christie's) $6,976

A St. Louis green carpet-ground concentric millefiori weight, the central silhouette of a devil within a circle of white and dark-blue canes surrounded by five silhouettes, mid-19th century, 6.8cm. diameter.
(Christie's) $6,976

A St. Louis faceted upright bouquet weight, edged with green leaves and including a large white flower with yellow 'match head' center, mid-19th century, 7.5cm. diameter.
(Christie's) $4,983

A Clichy sulphide garlanded swirl weight, the sulphide portrait of the young Queen Victoria in profile to the left, mid-19th century, 7.8cm. diameter.
(Christie's) $1,113

A Clichy flower weight, the daisy-like flower with radiating purple petals tipped in pale-yellow about a blue and pale-yellow center, mid-19th century, 7.4cm. diameter.
(Christie's) $6,976

SHADES

Leaded glass poppy border hanging shade, fitted with three-socket ceiling mount, shade diameter 22in.
(Skinner) $1,045

A Daum Art Deco frosted glass plafonnier, of inverted mushroom form, the exterior with acid-textured surface, 46cm. diameter.
(Christie's) $752

One of three leaded colored glass light shades in 1920's style. (Woolley & Wallis)
(Three) $512

Bigelow Kennard leaded shade, diminutive brickwork dome shade composed of matching pearl pink slag glass segments, 12^{1}/$_{4}$in. diameter.
(Skinner) $770

Leaded glass hanging dome shade, green slag segments arranged above broad border of ducks in flight, 25in. diameter.
(Skinner) $660

Hanging paneled lamp shade attributed to Miller Glass Co., eight caramel slag curved panels over red slag border panels, 18in high.
(Skinner) $303

Two Tiffany Aladdin shades, conical cased glass lamp shades with vertically striped iridescent decoration, one amber, one blue, 7^{1}/$_{4}$in. diameter.
(Skinner) $2,310

Handel bent panel hanging shade, caramel slag curved glass segments bordered by orange shaded crescents, 17^{1}/$_{2}$in. diameter.
(Skinner) $880

Hanging slag glass lamp, six shaped caramel slag glass panels framed by hammered brass straps with riveted decorations, 24^{1}/$_{2}$in. diameter.
(Skinner) $880

Leaded glass Victorian hanging lamp shade, crown cap above shaped dome with wide border of pink rose blossoms and red cherries, 14in. high.
(Skinner) $440

A Daum Nancy etched and enameled lamp shade, the clear glass overlaid with brown and green, 25cm. wide.
(Bonhams) $2,099

STAINED GLASS

Pair of Prairie School design windows, rectangular-form, geometric design with clear and caramel slag glass, 39in. high. (Skinner) $1,210

Leaded glass scenic window, multicolored and textured glass segments arranged to depict pink dogwood trees above iris blossoms, 5ft. 8in. x 6ft. 11in. (Skinner) $6,050

Scenic leaded glass window, multicolored segments arranged as a Tiffany wisteria landscape copy, 48¼in. wide. (Skinner) $2,530

A stained glass panel in the manner of Hans Holbein of 'John Poynes', 13½ x 10in. (Hy. Duke & Son) $930

A late 19th century stained glass panel in two sections, decorated with a feeding heron standing on a pond, 88cm. x 1.22m. (Phillips) $2,250

'St. Peter', a stained glass panel by Harry Clarke, of the winged youthful St. Peter wearing a miter, and holding symbolic keys and book, polychrome, framed, 129 x 72cm. (Christie's) $2,680

A leaded glass window, designed by Frank Lloyd Wright, for the J. J. Walser House, Chicago, Illinois, circa 1903, 164.5 x 74cm. (Christie's) $5,175

Three panel leaded glass window, scene of woodland stream, framed in iron, unsigned, overall 95in. high. (Skinner) $4,675

A leaded glass window, designed by Marion Mahoney, for the Gerald Mahoney House, Ekhardt Indiana, circa 1905, 119.5 x 72cm. (Christie's) $1,897

VASES

Argy-Rousseau pâte de verre crab vase, decorated by three black and green crabs with pincer claws and red eyes, 5¹/₂in. high.
(Skinner) $5,500

Daum cameo glass flying bat vase, extraordinary trefoil bowl form of mottled yellow, brown, red amber mixture, 6³/₄in. high.
(Skinner) $5,390

A cameo glass vase, Thomas Webb & Sons, circa 1888, the lime green body carved in opaque white with sprays of flowers and leaves, 6³/₄in. high.
(Sotheby's) $4,433

A three-colour cameo vase, Thomas Webb and Sons, circa 1885, the yellow glass overlaid in pink and opaque white and carved with a spray of flowers and leaves, 6¹/₈in. high.
(Sotheby's) $4,092

A very fine pair of blown and engraved ruby glass vases: The President's House, Washington, and Battle Monument, Baltimore, Bohemian, circa 1860, 14in. high.
(Sotheby's) $29,700

'Bacchantes', a Lalique opalescent and gray-stained vase, molded with a frieze of dancing maidens, with wheel-carved signature *R. Lalique, France*, 24.3cm. high.
(Christie's) $11,484

A clear glass cylinder vase with raven decoration in blue and black, signed *Orrefors, Sweden, Ariel No. 209* (1939), 21.5cm. high.
(Auktionsverket) $16,660

'Orléans', a Lalique blue vase, molded with a band of flowers of leafy stems, with engraved signature *R. Lalique*, 20cm. high.
(Christie's) $5,742

A cameo glass vase, Thomas Webb & Sons, circa 1885, the red glass overlaid in opaque white and carved with cyclamen sprays, 4³/₄in. high.
(Sotheby's) $1,364

VASES

'Aras', a Lalique purple vase, with short tapering neck, molded with exotic birds amid berry-laden thorny branches, 22.5cm. high.
(Christie's) $28,710

'Camouflage Form', a glass vase form by Pauline Solven, decorated with linear, spot and ring designs, amber, purple, blue, pale green, red and red ocher, 16.7cm. high.
(Christie's) $957

'Formose', a Lalique green vase, spherical with short cylindrical neck, molded with gold fish, 17cm. high.
(Christie's) $2,603

René Lalique Avallon vase, frosted flared bowl with birds in cherry tree molded in high relief, 6in. high.
(Skinner) $605

Tiffany favrile engraved vase, gold iridescent angular form with wheel engraved Art Deco design, 18in. high.
(Skinner) $3,960

'Bacchantes', a Lalique amber vase, molded with a frieze of dancing naked maidens, with acid-stamped signature, 24.5cm. high.
(Christie's) $28,710

Webb gem cameo tricolor passion flower vase, brilliant blue layered in amethyst and overlaid with white, 7¹/₂in. high.
(Skinner) $9,075

'Prunes', a Lalique opalescent vase, the base heavily molded with plums and leaves, with wheel carved signature *R. Lalique, France*, 17.3cm. high.
(Christie's) $4,211

A Thomas Webb & Sons engraved oviform vase decorated probably by William Fritsche in an intaglio technique, circa 1900, 30.5cm. high.
(Christie's) $3,322

VASES

A Varnish & Co. double walled vase in deep amethyst glass over silver, of trumpet shape, 23.2cm. high.
(Phillips) $672

René Lalique Camaret vase, frosted molded sphere with four rows of blown-out fish, traces of blue wash, 5¼in. high.
(Skinner) $1,650

Amethyst glass vase with floral Sterling silver overlay, polished pontil, 10in. high.
(Eldred's) $264

Venini Pezzato vase, designed by Fulvio Bianconi, flared large trumpet-form composed of fused glass patchwork squares, 9¼in. high.
(Skinner) $5,500

Loetz Art Glass handled vase, brilliant emerald green jardinière-form with three gold iridescent oil spot handles, 5½in. high.
(Skinner) $550

Art Glass vase with enameled scenery, possible Val St. Lambert attribution, most unusual textured polychrome depiction of Medieval knight on horseback, 11in. high.
(Skinner) $880

René Domremy Thistle vase, broad frosted molded oval-form with double rows of thistle blossoms and spiked leaves, 8½in. high.
(Skinner) $1,540

Webb cameo glass Pluvia portrait vase, by George Woodall, slender cylindrical amethyst-raisin colored vase overlaid in stark white, 7¼in. high.
(Skinner) $24,200

Loetz silvered and enameled vase, ruffled brilliant green body with maroon-red swirling inclusions, enamel decorated with foliate and insect designs, 7in. high.
(Skinner) $495

VASES

Mt. Washington peachblow vase, flattened flared and crimped extended rim on oval body of matt finish dusty pink shaded to blue-white, 4¼in. high.
(Skinner) $3,300

English intaglio cut glass vase, attributed to Stevens & Williams, sapphire blue cased to opal white squat bowl with ruffled crimped rim, 7½in. diameter.
(Skinner) $440

Tiffany cameo glass vase, iridescent golden amber baluster body with green inclusions wheel-cut as broad naturalistic leaves, 8⅝in. high.
(Skinner) $3,025

European silver overlay lapis stone glass vase, cobalt blue body with simulated mineral deposits overlaid with swirling silver decoration, 7½in. high.
(Skinner) $440

Steuben blue Cintra vase, flared and ruffled blossom-rim on acid finished body of colorless glass, 8in. high.
(Skinner) $2,420

René Lalique Palestre vase, frosted colorless ovoid vessel with press molded frieze of ten naked male athletes in various interactive poses, 16in. high.
(Skinner) $30,800

Gallé tri-color cameo glass vase, mottled green and yellow oval vessel layered orange, tan and brown, 6in. high.
(Skinner) $2,090

An iridescent glass shell vase, attributed to Loetz, frilled rim conch shell on a frilled foot, 16.4cm. high.
(Bonhams) $1,130

A Wiener Werkstätte black glass vase, with molded foliate design, with acid-stamped WW monogram, 19.8cm. high.
(Christie's) $612

VASES

A Daum acid-etched and enamel painted vase, the mottled white ground polychrome enameled with an extensive wooded landscape, 38.5cm. high.
(Christie's) $4,211

'Dahlia', a Lalique enameled and amber-stained vase, molded with large overlapping flowers and black enameled centers, with molded signature
R. Lalique, 12.5cm. high.
(Christie's) $1,148

A fine two-handled ruby-stained vase and cover, possibly Daniel Pearce, the mounts dated *1867*, with panels of scroll and vacant neo-Baroque oval cartouches, 15^{1}/$_{8}$in. high.
(Sotheby's) $6,308

Loetz 'Octopus' air trap vase, Federzeichnung design of quatrefoil rim on cased oval body of shaded browns with trapped air design outlined and enhanced by gold enameling, 6^{3}/$_{4}$in. high.
(Skinner) $1,870

A Lalique bucket-shaped vase molded with six birds perched among berry-laden branches, incised *R. Lalique*, 5^{3}/$_{4}$in. high.
(Christie's) $1,505

Legras enameled snow scene vase, misshapen oval vessel completely enamel painted with tall trees arising from snow covered ground, 15^{3}/$_{4}$in. high.
(Skinner) $990

Tiffany Tel el Amarna gold vase, heavy walled amber body with elongated cased brown collar decorated by alternating green and gold zig-zag medial design, 5^{1}/$_{2}$in. high.
(Skinner) $3,300

Lalique Druides opalescent vase, molded sphere with blown out berry clusters and cross stem configurations decorated by strong green wash, 7in. high.
(Skinner) $1,320

Webb ivory cameo glass vase, designed attributed to George Woodall, sepia-stained simulated ivory decorated by three overlapping medallions, 8^{1}/$_{4}$in. high.
(Skinner) $3,850

VASES

Monumental cut glass vase, American brilliant period, flared cylindrical parasol stand/ vase with alternating hobstar and cane panels, 26in. high.
(Skinner) $5,775

A good heraldic 'vase parlant', circa 1890, the underside with engraved mark *E Gallé Nancy*, 8in. high.
(Sotheby's) $12,830

Double gourd vase with mount, circa 1900, iridescent glass, silver colored metal, *Loetz Austria*, 11in. high.
(Sotheby's) $12,118

A glass and brass vase, the design attributed to Josef Hoffmann, blue tinted vase of flared baluster form with scalloped design, on a flared brass foot, 23.5cm. high.
(Christie's) $1,115

Loetz Austrian Art Glass vase, design attributed to Michael Powolny, flared rim on elongated hipped form, 9¹/₂in. high.
(Skinner) $1,100

A Wiener Werkstätte enamel painted vase, manufactured by Moser, Karlsbad, decorated in blue, yellow, white and black with scalloped designs, Czechoslovakia, 24cm. high.
(Christie's) $1,053

Tiffany Tel el Amarna green vase, brilliant green cased to opal white oval body with black glass shoulder decorated by green ribbon pulled over iridescent silver-blue controled swirls, 8¹/₂in. high.
(Skinner) $4,950

Wasps and spider's web leaf form vase, circa 1910, etched and enameled glass, with gilt mark *Daum Nancy*, 8¹/₄in. high.
(Sotheby's) $4,990

Tiffany silver mounted cameo cut vase, colorless oval body with amethyst and green glass pads wheel cut and carved as grape clusters, 14¹/₂in. high.
(Skinner) $5,500

WINE GLASSES

A Jacobite plain-stemmed wine-glass, the funnel bowl engraved with a rose and bud, on a conical foot, circa 1750, 16cm. high.
(Christie's) $1,885

A Jacobite airtwist wine-glass of drawn-trumpet shape, engraved with a rose, bud and half-opened bud, circa 1750, 15.5cm. high.
(Christie's) $1,113

A baluster wine-glass, the bell bowl supported on a seven-ringed annulated knop stem, circa 1715, 15.5cm. high.
(Christie's) $1,028

A Duke of Cumberland portrait glass of drawn-trumpet shap, engraved with a bust portrait of the Duke to sinister wearing the Garter Star, circa 1745, 16cm. high.
(Christie's) $10,281

An opaque-twist 'Privateer' glass, the bucket bowl engraved with a sailing ship and inscribed above *Succefs to the EAGLE FRIGATE John Knill Commander*, circa 1760, 16.5cm. high.
(Christie's) $8,225

A Williamite portrait opaque-twist wine-glass, engraved with a portrait of William III in profile to the right within the inscription *THE IMMORTAL MEMORY*, 18th century, 15cm. high.
(Christie's) $5,980

A Jacobite crested light-baluster wine-glass, the funnel bowl engraved with a seven-petaled rose and a bud, circa 1755, 16cm. high.
(Christie's) $3,084

An engraved airtwist wine-glass of drawn-trumpet shape, the bowl decorated with Bacchus holding a goblet and flask seated on a barrel, circa 1750, 17cm. high.
(Christie's) $864

A Jacobite portrait airtwist wine-glass, the funnel bowl with a bust portrait of The Young Pretender, circa 1750, 15cm. high.
(Christie's) $5,483

WINE GLASSES

A plain-stemmed cordial-glass with a pan-topped bowl, on a domed foot, mid-18th century, 15.5cm. high.
(Christie's) $770

An engraved airtwist wine-glass, the bowl engraved with a spray of honeysuckle, circa 1750, 15.5cm. high.
(Christie's) $651

A composite-stemmed wine-flute with a slender bell bowl, the stem filled with airtwist spirals, circa 1750, 21cm. high.
(Christie's) $942

A color-twist wine-glass with a bell bowl, the stem with shoulder, waist and basal knops and enclosing an opaque laminated corkscrew core, circa 1765, 16.5cm. high.
(Christie's) $2,159

A color-twist wine-glass, the stem with a twisted opaque ribbon core within two corkscrew spirals with translucent red inner edges, circa 1765, 14.5cm. high.
(Christie's) $1,661

A color-twist wine-glass, the stem with an opaque gauze corkscrew core entwined by two translucent dark-red spiral threads, circa 1765, 14.5cm. high.
(Christie's) $2,159

An engraved opaque-twist ratafia-glass, the slender funnel bowl with hammered flutes, on a conical foot, circa 1765, 18.5cm. high.
(Christie's) $1,456

A Jacobite wine-glass, the bell-shaped bowl engraved with a portrait medallion of Prince Charles Edward Stuart, 4¼in. high.
(Christie's) $2,541

An engraved drawn airtwist wine-glass, engraved with a border of flowering swags and pendent grapes, circa 1750, 17cm. high.
(Christie's) $651

WINE GLASSES

A small opaque-twist wine-glass with an ogee bowl, the stem with a laminated corkscrew core within a pair of flat ribbon spirals, circa 1765, 12cm. high. (Christie's) $316

A Jacobite wine-glass, the bowl engraved with a pendant spray of two acorns, on a conical foot, mid-18th century, 16.5cm. high. (Christie's) $1,827

A Beilby opaque-twist wine-glass, the bell bowl enameled in white with a border of fruiting-vine beneath a gilt rim, circa 1770, 17cm. high. (Christie's) $1,578

An engraved opaque-twist wine-glass, the round funnel bowl inscribed *THE UNION CLUB* within tied sprays of thistle, rose and shamrock, circa 1820, 15cm. high. (Christie's) $664

A Jacobite airtwist wine-glass, the pan-topped round funnel bowl engraved with a border including honeysuckle, a rose and a carnation amongst fruiting-vine, circa 1750, 15.5cm. high. (Christie's) $631

A pedestal-stemmed wine-glass, the thistle-shaped bowl supported on an octagonally molded tapering stem enclosing an elongated tear, circa 1730, 15.5cm. high. (Christie's) $498

A Jacobite light-baluster wine-glass, the bell bowl with a seven-petaled rose and a bud, the reverse with a butterfly, circa 1745, 16.5cm. high. (Christie's) $747

A Beilby enameled opaque-twist wine-glass, the stem with a gauze core within four spiral threads, on a conical foot, circa 1770, 14.5cm. high. (Christie's) $997

A Jacobite balustroid wine-glass, the drawn-trumpet bowl engraved with a six-petaled rose, and a bud and a butterfly, circa 1750, 17.5cm. high. (Christie's) $830

A Beilby opaque-twist wine-glass, **the funnel bowl enameled in white** with a border of fruiting-vine, circa 1770, 15.5cm. high. (Christie's) $1,495

A Jacobite mercury-twist wine-glass of drawn-trumpet shape, the bowl engraved with a six-petaled rose and a bud, circa 1750, 15.5cm. high. (Christie's) $1,495

A baluster wine-glass with a bell bowl, supported on a cushion knop above a beaded knop, on a domed foot, circa 1720, 16.5cm. high. (Christie's) $664

A toastmaster's opaque-twist wine-glass, the stem with a gauze core within two spiral threads above a heavy foot, circa 1770, 14.5cm. high. (Christie's) $864

A baluster wine-glass, the bell bowl supported on a triple annulated knop above an inverted baluster section, circa 1720, 16cm. high. (Christie's) $532

An opaque-twist toastmaster's glass, the deceptive ogee bowl with wrythen-molded lower part, on a conical foot, circa 1765, 14cm. high. (Christie's) $1,329

A composite-stemmed wine-glass of drawn shape with a tulip bowl, the stem filled with airtwist spirals, circa 1750, 15cm. high. (Christie's) $465

An engraved composite-stemmed wine-glass, the round funnel bowl engraved with a border of fruiting-vine, circa 1740, 17cm. high. (Christie's) $914

A quadruple-knopped engraved opaque-twist wine-glass, the bell bowl with fruiting-vine and a bird in flight, circa 1765, 17cm. high. (Christie's) $1,246

449

A James Beveridge (Isle of Wight) putter, circa 1890, with head possibly of rockwood, original hickory shaft. (Sotheby's) $1,104

A carved and painted wood advertising figure of a golfer, wearing a beret, with brown pullover and trousers, 40in. high. (Christie's) $2,310

A long nosed mid spoon by Tom Morris, circa 1885, with golden beech head and hickory shaft, shaft 41in. long. (Sotheby's) $4,036

A fine Simplex cross headed long spoon, circa 1900, with hickory shaft, hardwood head with shaped iron sole plate, 44$^{1}/_{2}$in. high. (Sotheby's) $1,805

North Berwick golf, lithographic poster, backed onto linen, 48$^{1}/_{2}$ x 39in. (Sotheby's) $3,186

A Crolf patent hammer head putter/lofter, circa 1910, similar to Dalrymple patent, of aluminium alloy. (Sotheby's) $1,912

A McEwan long spoon, circa 1885, with beech head and original hickory shaft stamped *McEwan*. (Sotheby's) $2,124

A rare early golf club carrying case, patented 1892, designed to be carried by hand with an iron spike built into the base in order to keep the bag upright when stuck in the ground. (Sotheby's) $807

A patent driver, maker unknown, with huge persimmon head drilled through the center with a 2in. diameter hole, 48$^{1}/_{2}$in. long. (Sotheby's) $1,274

A scared-head long-nosed driver by McEwan, the sole with rams horn inset, the grip lacking, circa 1870.
(Christie's) $3,502

One dozen unused 'Cestrian' gutty balls, circa 1898, made by the Telegraph Manufacturing Co Ltd Helsby, Cheshire.
(Sotheby's) $5,735

A scared-head long-nosed playclub by John Allan of Prestwick, the head stamped *J. Allan*, circa 1870.
(Christie's) $4,816

A Lamb of Loanhead patent adjustable golf club, circa 1928, the iron adjusting for left and right hand use.
(Sotheby's) $1,487

A Forgan hand hammered gutta percha golf ball, late 19th century, together with an original sepia photograph of the Forgan shop facade with staff, circa 1908.
(Sotheby's) $2,336

An unusual mid-iron with pierced and sparred face, the hosel stamped *W. Wilson, Maker, St. Andrews*.
(Christie's) $6,567

An early very heavy rut iron, circa 1830, blacksmith made, ash shaft, with 5 inch hosel.
(Sotheby's) $1,168

A very rare Honourable Company of Edinburgh Golfers membership certificate, 1784, Scottish, 10¼ x 14¼in.
(Sotheby's) $19,116

A mammoth niblick by Cochrane of Edinburgh, the back stamped *Fort Mason, Piccadilly, London*.
(Christie's) $1,313

GOLFING ITEMS

A fine unused silver score book, circa 1906, hallmarked Birmingham 1906, originally belonging to Harry Vardon, 4½ x 2½in.
(Sotheby's) $2,974

A spelter caddy matchstriker, 1920s, in tones of green and brown and brown, striker made as a club removable from its golf bag, 8in. high.
(Sotheby's) $637

J. H. Taylor's own Braid Mills putter, circa 1908, with hickory shaft, and J. H. Taylor's personal stamp to sole.
(Sotheby's) $3,823

Hilton (H.H.), The Royal and Ancient Game of Golf, with half title, numbered *239/900*, morocco bound.
(Sotheby's) $1,529

A Doulton Lambeth stoneware golfing jug, English, circa 1905, relief molded with three reserves showing lost ball, putting and driving scenes, 7½in. high.
(Sotheby's) $1,381

Kerr (John), The Golf Book of East Lothian, 1896, small paper edition, numbered *353/500*, and signed in ink by the author.
(Sotheby's) $850

Samaden, lithographic poster for the Swiss resort, backed onto linen, 38½ x 25in.
(Sotheby's) $2,655

Grant (J. P), The Banff Golf Club Bazaar, Edinburgh, 1895, paper cover faded, slightly torn and stained, the spine distressed and mended with sellotape.
(Sotheby's) $1,274

Mont Revard, lithographic poster, backed onto linen, 39 x 24in.
(Sotheby's) $1,274

GOLFING ITEMS

A model of The Dunlop Caddy, carved and painted wood standing figure inscribed on the reverse *To Bobbly Locke, with best wishes from Roy Trickett*, 6¼in. high.
(Christie's) $430

The Phoenix Open, 1948, winner's medal, a silvered metal medal of American Indian design.
(Christie's) $790

A long nosed spoon by Tom Morris, circa 1885, with markedly curved face and hickory shaft, shaft 43½in. long.
(Sotheby's) $6,797

A Royal Doulton Kingsware pottery tobacco jar, modeled with numerous golfing figures after Charles Crombie, 6½in. high.
(Christie's) $660

A Slazenger B51 golf ball, inscribed *Bobby Locke, 1957*, the fruitwood stand inscribed *ball used by Bobby Locke in the final round at the British Open Championship at St. Andrews 1957 to give a record score of 279.*
(Christie's) $3,960

The Stag Tournament, 1951, a plated two-handled prize cup, inscribed *Stag 1000 Golf Tournament*, 15in. high.
(Christie's) $910

The Open Championship, 1957, a gold prize medal inscribed *Open Golf Championship 1957*, the reverse inscribed *Winner A. D. Locke, July*, 1⅝in. diameter.
(Christie's) $31,350

Henry Mayo Bateman (1887–1970), 'The Man who coughed at the 18th Hole', signed lower left *H. M. Bateman*, pen and ink, 9½ x 13in.
(Christie's) $5,610

The Open Championship, 1952, a gold prize medal inscribed *Open Golf Championship, 1952*, the reverse inscribed *Winner, July*, 1⅝in. diameter.
(Christie's) $21,450

A metal golf ball marking machine, stamped *Chamber's patent No. 18712–10*, on shaped rectangular base.
(Christie's) $700

A Ryder Cup medal of 1947 won by Reg Horne, of round form, recto with gilt relief image of the trophy cup, 1¹/₂in.
(Sotheby's) $595

A silver plated golfing inkwell, English, circa 1890, rectangular tray with pen well, 11in. wide.
(Sotheby's) $1,317

Harry Vardon, a photographic print, published by the Swan Electric Engraving Company, signed by Vardon to lower right in pencil, unframed, 19 x 12¹/₂in.
(Sotheby's) $1,168

Three boxes of the "Colonel" patented "Blue Ring" cardboard tees.
(Christie's) $985

A framed photograph of Alex Herd, James Braid, J. H. Taylor and Harry Vardon, by J. Fairweather, St. Andrews, 21 x 18¹/₂in.
(Christie's) $1,970

A bronze figure of Harry Vardon by Hal Ludlow for Elkington and Co., 9¹/₂in. high, on a rectangular ebonized plinth.
(Christie's) $6,129

A brass gutty golf ball mold for the "Trophy" dimple pattern golf ball, stamped *John White and Co., Edinburgh*, 3in. diameter.
(Christie's) $1,489

A Penfold man with pipe, 20th century, plaster figure, 20in. high.
(Sotheby's) $935

Eight gutta percha golf balls, various dates, together with two rubber-cored balls in a box reading *Kempstall 'Arlington'*, 1902.
(Sotheby's) $1,062

A composite set of six silver golf buttons by Villiers & Jackson, inscribed *Brough Golf Club*, 42 grammes total.
(Spencer's) $312

An Art Deco golfing desk piece, 1938, on onyx, with silver colored golfer having driven, and a chrome barometer, 1938, 5³/₄in. high.
(Sotheby's) $637

Balfour (James), Reminiscences of Golf on St Andrews Links, 1887, printed by David Douglas, Edinburgh.
(Sotheby's) $2,974

A 'Colonel' patent golf ball box, and three bramble pattern gutty floating golf balls.
(Christie's) $1,138

A large lithographic portrait of Tom Morris, circa 1870, shown three quarter length in check jacket, cap, a golf club under his arm, 26³/₄ x 20in.
(Sotheby's) $956

An interesting silver pocket golf score keeper, American, 1930s, inscribed to the back with initials *G.B.S.*, 3¹/₂in. high.
(Sotheby's) $807

A bronze bramble golf ball mold, circa 1905, size 27, with unusual opening mechanism.
(Sotheby's) $1,381

A 'He played Penfold' plaster advertising figure, 20th century, shown with his hands in the pockets of his gray plus fours, 20in. high.
(Sotheby's) $425

A J. Gourlay feathery golf ball, circa 1835, diameter approximately 1⁵/₈in., excellent condition.
(Sotheby's) $10,195

A fine early blacksmith made general iron, Scottish, early 18th century, with curved cut off blade and 5¹/₂ inch hosel.
(Sotheby's) $178,415

A smooth gutta golf ball, circa 1850.
(Christie's) $3,283

A rare Coste Jeu de Mail hardwood iron-bound club, French, mid 18th century.
(Sotheby's) $20,178

A blacksmith made track iron with well dished and hand hammered face, the hickory shaft with crossed threadleather grip, circa 1790.
(Christie's) $41,591

A Sir W. H. Dalrymple hammer cross head patent golf club, circa 1892, patent 16148/1892.
(Sotheby's) $4,673

A very large feather golf ball, early 19th century, together with an Ocobo mesh pattern gutty stamped *27* inscribed *1900* in ink.
(Sotheby's) $4,036

An interesting 'hoe' design putter, circa 1900, with shortened hickory shaft stamped *R Forgan & Son St Andrews.*
(Sotheby's) $2,974

United States Golf Association 'Open Championship' gold medal, 1898, won by Fred Herd (1874–1954), at the Myopia Hunt Club.
(Sotheby's) $31,860

A long nosed putter by David Strath, circa 1875, with beech head and hickory shaft.
(Sotheby's) $5,310

Urquhart patent adjustable iron, circa 1905, the head stamped *Mitchell Manchester*, with hickory shaft and contemporary grip.
(Sotheby's) $2,018

A long nosed short spoon by Tom Morris, circa 1885, with golden beech head and hickory shaft, both stamped *Luffness 2*, shaft 38¹/₂in. long.
(Sotheby's) $2,761

A fine unused hand-hammered gutta golf ball by Andrew Patrick of Leven, the ball stamped *A. Patrick 27 1/2*, circa 1860.
(Christie's) $15,323

A fine boxed putting set, circa 1900, including four brass center balance putters with hickory shafts, 42¹/₄in. long.
(Sotheby's) $3,398

A red-painted feather-filled golf ball, maker unknown, circa 1840.
(Christie's) $5,254

A red playing coat with blue serge cuffs and collar, the brass buttons engraved *L.G.C.*, for Leicestershire Golf Club, circa 1890.
(Christie's) $1,861

A scared-head long-nosed baffing spoon by McEwan, the sole with rams horn inset, the grip lacking, circa 1870.
(Christie's) $6,129

A Doulton Burslem wall plaque, painted in blues and whites with a panel of a golfer and his caddy, 14in. diameter.
(Christie's) $7,005

The Thief of Bagdad, United Artists, 1924, one-sheet, paper backed, 41 x 27in.
(Christie's) $30,800

King Kong RKO, 1933, original French poster, linen backed, 63 x 47in.
(Christie's) $14,300

Tarzan of the Apes, First National, 1918, one-sheet, linen backed, 41 x 27in.
(Christie's) $30,800

The Hunchback of Notre Dame, RKO, 1939, three-sheet, linen backed, 81 x 41in.
(Christie's) $5,280

The Painted Veil, MGM, 1934, six-sheet, linen backed, 81 x 81in.
(Christie's) $11,000

The Maltese Falcon, Warner Brothers, 1941, three-sheet, linen backed, 81 x 41in.
(Christie's) $4,950

Love Before Breakfast, Universal, 1936, one-sheet, linen backed, 41 x 27in.
(Christie's) $5,500

Jean Harlow, MGM, circa 1933, special promotional poster, unfolded, 28 x 22in.
(Christie's) $1,650

The Perils of Pauline, Eclectic Film, 1914, one-sheet, linen backed, 41 x 27in.
(Christie's) $6,600

Mammy, Warner Brothers, 1930, window card, backed on board, unfolded, 22 x 14in.
(Christie's) $770

Casablanca, Warner Brothers, 1946, original French poster, linen backed, 63 x 47in.
(Christie's) $19,800

Jailhouse Rock, MGM, 1957, one-sheet, linen backed, 41 x 27in.
(Christie's) $1,320

Star of Midnight, RKO, 1935, three-sheet, linen backed, 81 x 41in.
(Christie's) $13,200

The Wizard of Oz, MGM, 1939, half-sheet, unfolded, paper backed, 22 x 28in.
(Christie's) $19,800

The Kid, First National, 1921, three-sheet, linen backed, 81 x 41in.
(Christie's) $6,600

Tobacco Road, 20th Century Fox, 1941, one-sheet, paper backed, 41 x 27in.
(Christie's) $825

Cabaret, Allied Artists, 1972, original Polish poster, unfolded, 33 x 23in.
(Christie's) $495

Queen Christina, MGM, 1934, one-sheet, linen backed, 41 x 27in.
(Christie's) $5,280

The Canary Murder Case,
Paramount, 1929, one-sheet,
paper backed, 41 x 27in.
(Christie's) $28,600

Adventures of Captain Marvel,
Republic, 1941, six-sheet, linen
backed, 81 x 81in.
(Christie's) $4,620

The Sin of Nora Moran,
Majestic Pictures, 1933, one-
sheet, linen backed, 41 x 27in.
(Christie's) $19,800

The Worst Woman in Paris?,
Fox, 1933, one-sheet, linen
backed, 41 x 27in.
(Christie's) $550

The Walking Dead, Warner
Brothers, 1936, six-sheet, linen
backed, 81 x 81in.
(Christie's) $28,600

The White Sister, Metro, 1923,
three-sheet, linen backed, 81 x
41in.
(Christie's) $8,250

Bad Girl, Fox, 1931, one-sheet,
linen backed, 41 x 27in.
(Christie's) $2,420

The Walking Dead, Warner
Brothers, 1936, half-sheet,
unfolded 22 x 28in.
(Christie's) $3,520

The Border Wireless, Artcraft,
1918, one-sheet, linen backed, 41
x 27in.
(Christie's) $3,740

Every Day's a Holiday,
Paramount, 1938, one-sheet,
linen backed, 41 x 27in.
(Christie's) $2,200

Uncle Tom's Cabin, Universal,
1927, six-sheet, linen backed, 81
x 81in.
(Christie's) $4,950

Bordertown, Warner Brothers,
1934, one-sheet, paper backed,
41 x 27in.
(Christie's) $8,800

Johanna Enlists, Artcraft, 1918,
one-sheet, linen backed, 41 x
27in.
(Christie's) $4,180

Things to Come, United Artists,
1936, six-sheet, linen backed, 81
x 81in.
(Christie's) $22,000

Captain Blood, Warner
Brothers, 1935, one-sheet, 41 x
27in.
(Christie's) $6,820

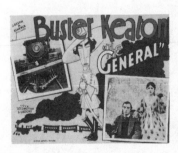

The 39 Steps, Gaumont British,
1935, one-sheet, paper backed,
41 x 27in.
(Christie's) $14,300

The General, United Artists,
1926, half-sheet, unfolded, 22 x
28in.
(Christie's) $13,200

The Painted Lady, Fox, 1924,
one-sheet, linen backed, 41 x
27in.
(Christie's) $5,720

The Bank, Essanay, 1915, one-sheet, paper backed, 41 x 27in.
(Christie's) $16,675

Creature from the Black Lagoon, Universal, 1954, three-sheet, linen backed, 81 x 41in.
(Christie's) $8,625

Snow White and the Seven Dwarfs, RKO, 1937, one-sheet, linen backed, 41 x 27in.
(Christie's) $12,650

Son of Frankenstein, Universal, 1939, one-sheet, linen backed, 41 x 27in.
(Christie's) $20,125

Lloyd's of London, 20th Century Fox, 1936, six-sheet, linen backed, 81 x 81in.
(Christie's) $7,590

Flash Gordon's Trip to Mars, Universal, 1938, one-sheet, linen backed, 41 x 27in.
(Christie's) $7,820

The Cactus Kid, Columbia, 1930, one-sheet, linen backed, 41 x 27in.
(Christie's) $29,900

La Belle et la Bête, Paulve, 1946, original French poster, linen backed, 63 x 94in.
(Christie's) $9,200

The Devil is a Woman, Paramount, 1935, one-sheet, unfolded, 41 x 27in.
(Christie's) $13,800

Gilda, Columbia, 1946, one-sheet, linen backed, 41 x 27in.
(Christie's) $7,700

Dumbo, Disney, 1941, three-sheet, linen backed, 81 x 41in.
(Christie's) $19,800

Five and Ten, MGM, 1931, one-sheet, linen backed, 41 x 27in.
(Christie's) $2,200

A Night at the Opera, MGM, 1935, one-sheet, linen backed, 41 x 27in.
(Christie's) $7,700

The Devil is a Woman, Paramount, 1935, one-sheet, unfolded, 41 x 27in.
(Christie's) $46,200

The Lady Vanishes, Gaumont British, 1938, one-sheet, linen backed, 41 x 27in.
(Christie's) $9,350

The Seven Year Itch, 20th Century Fox, 1955, three-sheet, linen backed, 81 x 41in.
(Christie's) $2,750

The Prisoner of Zenda, United Artists, 1937, one-sheet, linen backed, 41 x 27in.
(Christie's) $5,500

She Done Him Wrong, Paramount, 1933, three-sheet, linen backed, 81 x 41in.
(Christie's) $4,620

Godzilla, Toho, 1956, Italian poster, linen backed, 55 x 39in. (Christie's) $1,320

Frankenstein, Universal, 1931, original Spanish poster, unfolded, 41 x 27in. (Christie's) $11,000

Cimarron, RKO, 1931, one-sheet, linen backed, 41 x 27in. (Christie's) $16,500

Son of Frankenstein, Universal, 1939, three-sheet, linen backed, 81 x 41in. (Christie's) $11,000

Citizen Kane, RKO, 1941, six-sheet, linen backed, 81 x 81in. (Christie's) $22,000

The Informer, RKO, 1935, three-sheet, linen backed, 81 x 41in. (Christie's) $14,300

Sadie Thompson, United Artists, 1928, one-sheet, linen backed, 41 x 27in. (Christie's) $5,280

Attack of the 50 ft. Woman, Allied Artists, 1958, one-sheet, linen backed, 41 x 27in. (Christie's) $2,090

Laughing Sinners, MGM, 1931, one-sheet, linen backed, 41 x 27in. (Christie's) $1,320

Joan of Arc, RKO, 1948, one-sheet, linen backed, 41 x 27in.
(Christie's) $770

Metropolis, Paramount, 1927, window card, unfolded, 22 x 14in.
(Christie's) $26,400

Pinocchio, Disney, 1940, one-sheet, linen backed, 41 x 27in.
(Christie's) $6,050

G-Men, First National, 1935, three-sheet, linen backed, 81 x 41in.
(Christie's) $18,700

The Girl from 10th Avenue, First National, 1935, half-sheet, unfolded, 22 x 28in.
(Christie's) $17,600

The Vanishing American, Paramount, 1926, three-sheet, linen backed, 81 x 41in.
(Christie's) $5,280

The Circus, United Artists, 1928, one-sheet, linen backed, 41 x 27in.
(Christie's) $18,700

The Ghost of Frankenstein, Universal, 1942, one-sheet, linen backed, 41 x 27in.
(Christie's) $10,450

The Girl from Missouri, MGM, 1934, one-sheet, paper backed, 41 x 27in.
(Christie's) $6,600

An 18th century Greek icon of the Mother of God enthroned, 21¹/₂ x 17in.
(Christie's) $2,233

A 19th century icon of the Mother of God of Smolensk, 13¹/₂ x 11in.
(Christie's) $893

A 19th century icon of the Mother of God of Unexpected Joy, 14 x 11¹/₂in.
(Christie's) $893

A 19th century icon of the Mother of God Kazanskaya, the parcel gilt oklad with river and seed pearls, 12¹/₂ x 10¹/₄in.
(Christie's) $5,136

A Greek triptych icon, the Mother of God flanked by Angels, with Sts. Nicholas, George, Dimitrios and Spiridon?, 15 x 15in.
(Christie's) $5,806

A 19th century icon of Sts. John the Forerunner and Anna, the Old Testament Trinity above, 12 x 10in.
(Christie's) $938

A 19th century icon of St. John in Silence, with the Guardian Angel and St. Paul on the borders, 12¹/₄ x 10¹/₂in.
(Christie's) $1,340

An 18th century icon of the Hodigitria Mother of God, the Christ Child with His fingers raised in Benediction, 20 x 16³/₄in.
(Christie's) $5,583

A 19th century icon of the Mother of God of Kazan, overlaid with a gilt metal and jeweled oklad, 21 x 16¹/₂in.
(Christie's) $3,573

A 17th century icon of St. John the Forerunner, holding the Chalice, 11½ x 9½in.
(Christie's) $4,466

A Monastic School icon of St. Nicholas the Miracle Worker, 21 x 17¼in.
(Christie's) $1,228

A 19th century icon of Christ Pantocrator, the Saviour holding the Gospels, 14 x 12¼in.
(Christie's) $670

A Monastic School icon of the Deisis, with Sts. James and Irena on the borders, 17½ x 14in.
(Christie's) $2,010

A Greek triptych icon, the Mother of God flanked by Saints, 13 x 15½in. extended.
(Christie's) $2,680

An 18th century icon of the New Testament Trinity, flanked by the Mother of God and St. John the Forerunner, 12½ x 11in.
(Christie's) $2,233

A 19th century icon of the Mother of God of Kazan, with the Guardian Angel and St. Evdokia on the borders, 17¼ x 15½in.
(Christie's) $2,345

A 19th century icon of the Deisis, Christ Pantocrator flanked by the intercessionary figures of the Mother of God and St. John the Forerunner, 24½ x 17½in.
(Christie's) $1,786

A 19th century icon of the Crucifixion, with inset brass Cross, with figures and Seraphim surrounding, 14 x 12in.
(Christie's) $670

A 1960s Cartier cluster brooch, with rose coral and pavé cut diamond spheres, diamonds 5.5ct.
(Finarte) $5,267

A 1950s gold bow brooch with a central emerald surrounded by small diamonds, diamonds 0.6ct.
(Finarte) $2,106

A 1940s gold brooch, modeled as two daisies and gold leaves, one flower having the pistils of rubies the other of sapphires, both centering diamonds.
(Finarte) $2,040

A 1940s two colored gold clip brooch in the form of a flower, the petals edged with diamonds and the center of six diamonds centering a ruby, the stem of square cut rubies.
(Finarte) $4,759

Bicoloured gold pendant earrings comprised of oval rings set with pavé cut brilliants and emeralds suspended from a chased gold ring, diamonds 4.5ct.
(Finarte) $6,719

A yellow and white metal brooch by Arthur and Georgina Gaskin set with opals and green paste, with two opal drops, marked *G*.
(Christie's) $1,340

A 1940s rhodium plated gold bow clip brooch, with a central flower set with pavé cut diamonds, with a larger central diamond.
(Finarte) $6,789

A gold brooch in the form of the bust of an Oriental, his hat set with bands of diamonds, 1ct.
(Finarte) $711

A platinum ring set with an octagonal Colombian emerald, flanked by three graduated baguette diamonds, emerald 11.1ct.
(Finarte) $82,755

A 1940s gold brooch by Trabert & Hoeffer, Mauboussin, as two crossed swirls fringed by cabochon sapphires and pavé cut diamonds.
(Finarte) $7,462

A 1950s bracelet comprised of fifteen strands of satin gold.
(Finarte) $1,430

A satin gold leaf brooch with the veins in white gold and diamonds, 7ct.
(Finarte) $1,805

A 1950s clip brooch in the form of an owl in gold and enamel, the eyes of imitation emeralds, signed Corletto.
(Finarte) $2,407

A pair of pendant earrings, comprised of two heart shapes set with pavé cut diamonds, onyx and two cabochon sapphires, 5.60ct.
(Finarte) $4,890

A 1940s gold and white gold brooch in the form of a spray of berries, the fruit comprised of clusters of imitation cabochon rubies and onyx.
(Finarte) $1,505

A clip brooch in the form of a mandolin player, of gold and quartz, with jadeite hat and mandolin.
(Finarte) $904

A late 19th century oval clasp, the central square cut emerald surrounded by alternating bands of smaller emeralds and rose diamonds, emeralds 22ct.
(Finarte) $6,019

A clip brooch in the form of an amethyst basket holding flowers in gold with colored enamel petals.
(Finarte) $1,505

Fine 18ct. gold large center sapphire and twelve diamond surround cluster ring.
(G. A. Key) $2,826

A W. H. Haseler, Liberty silver and enamel waist clasp designed by Jessie M. King, each circular openwork section of stylized birds in flight and floral motifs, Birmingham hallmarks for 1906.
(Christie's) $3,637

A leafage spray brooch set with approximately forty-five diamonds and six sapphires.
(Russell Baldwin & Bright)
$4,640

A pendant set with large circular peridot surrounded by eight small diamonds with diamond-set bow above.
(Russell Baldwin & Bright)
$1,520

A pair of horn hair ornaments by Fred T. Partridge, set with moonstones and detailed with white metal.
(Christie's) $1,914

A yellow and silver pendant on a chain by Joseph A. Hodel, wirework foliate design set with a black opal, baroque pearls and two modeled and cast yellow metal maidens.
(Christie's) $3,062

Art Art Nouveau gilt metal buckle designed by Prince Bojidar Karageorgevitch, cast in an openwork design of entwined sweet peas, stamped maker's mark.
(Christie's) $345

A Victorian gold stiff hinged bangle, the upper section centered by a circular boss engraved with strapwork and set with five pearls.
(Spencer's) $1,094

A white and yellow metal mounted cloisonné enamel pendant by Harold Stabler, designed by Phoebe Stabler, of a cherub with a rose, signed with initials and dated *1914*.
(Christie's) $861

A gold vari-gem butterfly brooch, the body with ruby set eyes and four graduated half pearls, the wings illusion set with small rosecut diamonds. (Spencer's) **$918**

A gold, diamond and seed pearl bar brooch, with two swallows divided by seed pearls, cased. (Allen & Harris) **$446**

A Guild of Handicraft white metal and enamel waist clasp designed by C. R. Ashbee, each circular piece with pierced floral decoration and set with turquoises. (Christie's) **$1,436**

A horn hair comb by Fred T. Partridge set with baroque pearls in white metal, formed as an umbellifer. (Christie's) **$1,340**

A Liberty & Co. silver and enamel waist clasp designed by Jessie M. King, circular openwork decoration of stylized flowers and birds with blue-green enamel details, Birmingham hallmarks for 1906. (Christie's) **$2,871**

A Liberty & Co. Glasgow style silver and enamel waist buckle with openwork decoration of stylized foliage with enamel details, with Birmingham hallmarks for 1902. (Christie's) **$1,531**

A Victorian pendant/brooch, open back collet set with a large faceted oval citrine, the scroll surround set with faceted garnets. (Spencer's) **$741**

A jade bangle of mottled green mutton fat jade, 56mm. inside diameter, 76mm. diameter overall. (Bearne's) **$3,874**

A Guild of Handicraft white metal brooch designed by C. R. Ashbee, in the form of a winged insect with an articulated body. (Christie's) **$1,436**

'Medusa', a yellow metal, ivory and enamel brooch by George Hunt of the head of Medusa, set with opals and pendent pearls.
(Christie's) $3,828

A Victorian turquoise and half-pearl brooch, designed as two birds and a ribbon bow motif supporting a heart shaped pendant, on a fine safety chain with bird motif pin.
(Lawrence) $525

An Edwardian enamel and diamond brooch, decorated with green and pink guilloche enamel, claw-set at the center with a circular-cut diamond.
(Lawrence) $507

A platinum, pearl and diamond circular brooch of open cagework design with central single pearl.
(Bearne's) $1,788

An enamel pendant designed by Sir Frank Brangwyn for La Maison de l'Art Nouveau, Paris, circular with three knots, set with green and mottled white enamel.
(Christie's) $3,828

A white metal brooch by Henry Wilson, domed seven-sided form of cast stemwork with a central flowerhead with pale turquoise enamel detail.
(Christie's) $498

A 1950s French Boucheron gold clip brooch as a feather, studded with sapphires, rubies, emeralds and diamonds, in original box.
(Finarte) $6,783

A Victorian diamond brooch, for Queen Victoria's Jubilee, 1837–1887, designed as a coronet within a border of sunburst rays, pavé-set throughout with rose-cut diamonds.
(Lawrence) $665

A Guild of Handicraft white and yellow metal brooch designed by C. R. Ashbee, in the form of a 'crowned' cockerel, set with blister pearl, pearls, sapphires, tourmalines and moonstones.
(Christie's) $13,398

Early 20th century gold and green enamel brooch in the form of a four leaved clover, with central diamond.
(Finarte) $1,632

Early 20th century 14ct. gold and enamel brooch in the form of two leaves, one set with a small diamond, a flower and buds of pearls.
(Finarte) $884

A yellow metal, enamel and rock crystal brooch by Henry Wilson or Henry G. Murphy, the outer ring with geometric green, black, red and blue enamel decoration.
(Christie's) $2,871

A Guild of Handicraft silver brooch designed by C. R. Ashbee in the form of a peacock, detailed and set with enamel, abalone and a ruby, with London hallmarks for 1907.
(Christie's) $2,871

A gold 'slave' bracelet with grooves edged in white gold and diamonds.
(Finarte) $5,098

A late 19th century gold, silver, ruby and diamond double heart brooch.
(Bearne's) $1,713

Yellow gold ring with oval motif in peridots and navette cut green toumalines, with diamonds around the center stone.
(Finarte) $646

'Tristan and Isolde', a white metal and enamel belt buckle designed by Alexander Fisher, set with opals, and repoussé inscription *Tristan Isolde*, the oval polychrome enamel panels depicting scenes from the legend, dated 1896, 19.2cm. long.
(Christie's) $6,890

An 18ct. gold, ruby and diamond brooch in the form of a chick with fluffed up feathers and ruby and diamond cluster eye, signed *Kutchinsky*.
(Bearne's) $894

14ct. gold ring with cut coral insert and lateral bands of white gold set with diamonds.
(Finarte) $408

A gold and enamel brooch in the form of a small dog, with two diamonds for the eyes.
(Finarte) $1,107

A yellow metal and 'émail aux paillons' bracelet designed by James Cromer Watt formed as a snake, of blue-green enamel, set with opal.
(Christie's) $3,828

A gold clip brooch as the bust of a Moor, with ebony face and set with rose diamonds and rubies, his turban surmounted by a diamond.
(Finarte) $6,457

Grape cluster gold earrings, the grapes of ruby and onyx spheres, the stems of onyx and pavé cut diamonds.
(Finarte) $2,257

A 1950s gold bracelet in the form of a belt, the buckle and loop set with diamonds.
(Finarte) $3,762

A gold ring set with an oval quartz within a chased foliate border.
(Finarte) $827

Large gold brooch in the form of a snake, set with round and oval cabochon rubies, with 9ct. gold chain for adapting as a necklace.
(Finarte) $3,399

A 14ct. gold and white gold brooch as a seated cat, the body set with pavé cut turquoises, the face with rubies and small diamonds.
(Finarte) $2,056

A late 19th century gold, opal, ruby and diamond crescent bar brooch with graduated oval opals and rose diamonds.
(Bearne's) $894

A gold clip brooch as a crab, the body of malachite and the eyes set with two diamonds.
(Finarte) $1,147

A late 19th century silver and gold brooch as three interlaced rings set with diamonds and emeralds.
(Finarte) $26,513

A gold and citrine brooch, circa 1840, designed as a lozenge-shape of pierced foliate motif, the center collet-set with an oval shaped citrine.
(Lawrence) $979

A 1930s double clip platinum brooch of stylized form, set with diamonds and baguette and cabochon sapphires, diamonds 3.5ct.
(Finarte) $3,762

A gold slave bracelet with repoussé mythological scenes, the ends edged with sapphires and diamonds.
(Finarte) $1,343

A 1940s stylized and pierced shield shaped brooch, in bicolored gold set with cabochon and square cut rubies and diamonds.
(Finarte) $1,501

Green bakelite horse-head pin with metal pegged mane, 2^1/$_2$in. long.
(Eldred's) $61

A yellow metal and enamel ring by Fred T. Partridge set with five moonstones, signed *Partridge*.
(Christie's) $2,871

A Murrle Bennett Arts and Crafts style silver brooch, a faceted cabochon center on a beaten silver disc.
(Bonhams) $226

A silver and enamel dragonfly brooch, stamped *T.L.M.*
(Bonhams) $120

A Charles Horner silver brooch, of an amber faceted thistlehead with an entwined stem, stamped *C.H., Chester, 1911.*
(Bonhams) $258

A pair of shell cameo pendant earrings depicting Cupid and Psyche.
(Christie's) $1,361

A gold-mounted Swiss enamel brooch painted with two girls in Swiss regional costume, in foliate scroll mount, circa 1830.
(Christie's) $1,361

A pair of Swiss gold-mounted pendant earrings with porcelain portraits.
(Christie's) $2,904

A memorial locket decorated with blue enamel and diamonds, with hair arrangement inside, engraved *My Father's and Mother's hair*, 1837–1855.
(Christie's) $907

A portrait miniature of a dog, mounted as a brooch.
(Christie's) $871

A Murrle Bennett gold and turquoise brooch,the oval turquoise cabochon in a delicate leaf framework.
(Bonhams) $388

A Momoyama period domed coffer decorated in gold hiramakie and inlaid in mother-of-pearl with panels of birds among tachibana, late 16th century, 79cm. wide.
(Christie's) $53,152

A fine early Edo period Export coffer with coved cover and a samegawa-togidashi ground bordered with bands of scrolling foliage and stylized tessen, early 17th century, 132cm. long with gilt stand.
(Christie's) $116,270

A fine lacquer box and cover decorated in gold, black and silver iroe hiramakie, takamakie, hirame, heidatsu on a nashiji ground, late 18th/early 19th century, 37.5 x 26.5 x 27.4cm.
(Christie's) $22,425

A large gyobu ground three-case inro with a silver-rimmed oval kinji panel on each side decorated in Shibayama inlay, 19th century.
(Christie's) $6,644

A kinji ground suzuribako with silver rims decorated in gold hiramakie with a profusion of chrysanthemums issuing from behind a brushwood fence, 19th century, 26cm. long.
(Christie's) $17,250

A koban-shaped gyobu-nashiji two-case inro, each side with a silver-rimmed kinji panel finely decorated in Shibayama style, signed *Gyokuhosai*, 19th century.
(Christie's) $7,475

A lacquer box and cover, decorated in silver and gold hiramakie, on a nashiji ground with aoi mon interspersed among a geometric design, late 18th/early 19th century, 21.3cm. wide.
(Christie's) $6,000

Japanese lacquer kimono boxes, 18in. high, black lacquer ground with hand painted gold motif of leaves and mon.
(Du Mouchelles) $1,500

A fine kojubako, the two tiers and cover decorated on a gyobu ground with raised panels representing framed paintings, 19th century, 12.4cm. wide.
(Christie's) $8,305

LAMPS

Cut glass table lamp, American brilliant period, double star, hobstar and fan patterns with peaked dome shade, 30in. high. (Skinner) **$1,210**

Handel paneled table lamp, six panel amber slag glass shade with brickwork grid above green and red repeating border design, 23in. high. (Skinner) **$825**

Tiffany three-light lily lamp, floriform bronze base with three stem arms above ribbed cup platform base, 16in. high. (Skinner) **$990**

Handel reverse painted scenic reading lamp, dome glass shade with unusual moonlit riverside scene, signed on rim *Handel 6963*, 23in. high. (Skinner) **$3,520**

Tiffany lotus leaf lamp, flared Oriental parasol shade of green and white favrile glass segments arranged with raised leaded ribbing, 22in. high. (Skinner) **$40,700**

Tiffany gilt bronze desk lamp, simple banded dome shade raised on three arm spider above cushion base with five ball feet, 7¼in. high. (Skinner) **$1,430**

Leaded glass table lamp, blue and green rippled glass segments in progressive arrangement, mounted on elaborate acanthus decorated base, 16in. diameter. (Skinner) **$770**

A painted bronze, spelter and blue glass table lamp by Limousin, in the form of four elephants facing outward from a central square column, 15¾in. high. (Christie's) **$1,066**

Bradley & Hubbard paneled table lamp, dome shade composed of six bent panels of closely ribbed glass decorated with painted urns and floral arrangements, 24in. high. (Skinner) **$825**

Cowan Pottery Art Deco lamp base, of blue and green high glazed stylized orchard motif, mounted with heavy and elaborate silvered metal lamp fittings, 25in. high.
(Skinner) $468

Dirk Van Erp copper and mica table lamp, circa 1911, vented cap on conical shade of four mica panels, separated by riveted hammered columns, 16¹/₂in. high.
(Skinner) $22,000

One of a pair of English brass colza-oil lamps, each with acanthus-cast urn-shaped reservoir with gadrooned edge and domed finial, second quarter 19th century, 21in. high.
(Christie's) $4,622

Tiffany red azalea adjustable lamp, hipped dome shade of red and green favrile glass segments arranged as blossoms on leafy branches, 20in. diameter.
(Skinner) $77,000

Two pewter chamber lamps, *S. Rusts Patent New York*, 19th century, 8⁵/₈in. high.
(Skinner) $522

Victorian bent panel table lamp, elaborate floral decorated metal shade and base frames for green-amber slag glass curved panels, 19in. diameter.
(Skinner) $715

Paneled slag glass and brass lamp, angular flared shade of green and white glass behind pierced brass framework with repeating spade and loop design, 25in. high.
(Skinner) $495

Dirk Van Erp copper and mica table lamp, circa 1909, raised cap over conical shade of four mica panels separated by riveted hammered columns, 19¹/₂in. high.
(Skinner) $4,400

An early brass table lamp designed by Robert Weir Schultz, with bird finial, the domed shade with pierced foliate decoration with birds, fitted for electricity, 45cm. high.
(Christie's) $6,316

Fern lamp, circa 1900, cameo glass, the shade and base with cameo mark *Gallé*, 15in. high.
(Sotheby's) $8,910

Emile Gallé, swallow landscape lamp, circa 1900, cameo glass, bronze, 13½in. high.
(Sotheby's) $20,995

Desny, adjustable table lamp, 1930s, nickel plated metal, 8¼in. high.
(Sotheby's) $1,604

Winter landscape lamp, circa 1900, internally decorated glass, with enameled mark *Daum Nancy A.R.*, 14¼in. high.
(Sotheby's) $11,048

René Lalique, pair of lamps, 'Grand Depot', after 1928, frosted glass and nickel plated metal, 19¾in. high.
(Sotheby's) $11,097

A stoneware oil lamp by Mark V. Marshall, the ovoid body and oil reserve incised with panels of mythic beasts beneath imps, 25in. high.
(Christie's) $2,471

A Lalique frosted glass illuminated table ornament, cataloged 'Oiseau de Feu', total weight 47cm.
(Bearne's) $27,000

René Lalique, lamp, 'Suzanne', after 1925, 11in. high overall.
(Sotheby's) $12,474

Emile Gallé, cherry blossom and humming bird lamp, circa 1900, cameo glass, bronze, 10¼in. high.
(Sotheby's) $27,384

Stylized flower lamp, 1920s, pâte de verre, wrought iron, marked *G. Argy-Rousseau*, 13in. high.
(Sotheby's) $37,422

A pair of French porcelain-mounted oil lamps, Napóléon III, Paris, circa 1870, fitted for electricity, 57cm. high overall.
(Sotheby's) $4,198

Daum, Dutch winter landscape lamp, circa 1900, internally decorated etched and enameled glass, 14in. high.
(Sotheby's) $16,431

Emile Gallé, peony lamp, circa 1900, carved cameo glass, fire polished, bronze, 11¾in. high.
(Sotheby's) $6,937

One of a pair of mahogany wall-lanterns, each with broken pediment centered by an ivory acorn finial above a mirror-backed body with three glazed panels, 12in. wide.
(Christie's) $4,202

Chrysanthemum lamp, circa 1900, cameo glass, bronze, the shade and base with cameo mark *Gallé*, 11¼in. high.
(Sotheby's) $19,602

Emile Gallé, trumpet flower lamp, circa 1900, cameo glass, bronze, 22in. high.
(Sotheby's) $20,082

A pair of Empire ormolu and bronze lamps in the form of Atheniennes, each with later vertical shaft and white pleated silk shades, possibly Austrian, 34in. high.
(Christie's) $35,530

A Daum acid-etched cameo table lamp, the patinated cast-iron trefoil column with triple scrolled base, 51cm. high.
(Christie's) $5,016

Victorian table lamp, attributed to Bradley & Hubbard, flower-form lights centering amber glass bud vase, 21in. high.
(Skinner) $220

Emile Gallé, dragonfly veilleuse, circa 1900, cameo glass, patinated metal, 6³/₄in. high.
(Sotheby's) $10,223

Handel scenic landscape lamp, dome shade reverse painted with strong sunset forest scene, 21in. high.
(Skinner) $2,970

Handel reverse painted bird lamp, 7120 dome shade with four exotic birds of paradise in multicolored leafy foliage, 23in. high.
(Skinner) $13,200

Pair of French mantel lamps with Muller shades, silvered metal reticulated stick-shaft torchère forms with amethyst, pink, green and white mottled glass shades, 15¹/₂in. high.
(Skinner) $1,320

Arts and Crafts oak table lamp, hexagonal base with open lattice work, oil lamp insert under hexagonal lamp shade, unsigned, 23in. high.
(Skinner) $385

Decorative Mickey Mouse child's lamp, circa 1955, 42cm. high.
(Auction Team Köln)
                             $232

Tiffany favrile glass table lamp, brilliant green damascene dome shade cased to opal with gold iridescent wavy surface decoration, 17¹/₂in. high.
(Skinner) $5,610

Table lamp, 19th century, font with painted floral decoration, matching shade, original burner, 21in. high.
(Eldred's) $358

Tiffany pansy table lamp, colorful leaded favrile glass segments arranged as four repeating clusters, 23in. high. (Skinner) **$11,000**

Bradley & Hubbard brass and iron table lamp with repoussé decoration, reverse-painted glass shade, 22in. high. (Eldred's) **$248**

Tiffany zodiac turtleback desk lamp, very heavy dark bronze adjustable shade, 14¹/₂in. high. (Skinner) **$4,290**

Leaded glass table lamp, attributed to Suess Ornamental Glass Co., Chicago, broad parasol dome with wide yellow, red and pink stylized tulip blossom decorative border, 26in. diameter. (Skinner) **$2,420**

A pair of Hurricane table lamps, the baluster-shaped storm shades raised on pineapple stems, on blue and white 'jasper-ware type' drums, 46.5cm. high. (Phillips) **$797**

Bigelow Kennard leaded table lamp, domed shade of white-amber glass segments arranged in repeating border belt of subtle yellow variations, mounted on elegant bronze base, 16in. diameter. (Skinner) **$3,080**

Art Nouveau spelter figure table lamp in the form of a female artist, signed at base, *Ch Perron*, verde antico base, 26in. high. (G. A. Key) **$414**

A Muller Frères yellow and brown cameo glass mushroom lampshade, depicting an Arab leading a camel beneath palm trees, 47cm. high overall. (Spencer's) **$3,155**

An unusual pierced tin hanging lantern, American, probably Pennsylvania, late 19th century, the cylindrical form with hinged door and conical top, 16in. high. (Sotheby's) **$1,100**

A pair of gilt-bronze mounted
Chinese porcelain lamps,
mounted in Paris, circa 1880,
80cm. high.
(Sotheby's) $4,373

One of a pair of ormolu-
mounted Samson and hard-
paste porcelain lamps each with
square spreading ivory silk
shade, 21in. high.
(Christie's)
          (Two) $7,994

A pair of French red marble
lamps, Napoléon III, Paris, circa
1870, each in the form of a
classical urn, 97cm. high overall.
(Sotheby's) $4,198

A Daum carved and acid-etched
double-overlay table lamp, with
three-branch wrought iron
mounts, the base of baluster
form on flared circular foot,
30cm. high.
(Christie's) $5,742

A pair of French gilt-bronze
lamps, Paris, circa 1895, in the
Art Nouveau influenced Louis
XV manner, 66cm. high overall.
(Sotheby's) $2,099

A Daum acid-etched and enamel
painted winter landscape table
lamp, with three-branch
wrought-iron mount, the slightly
flared cylindrical base on wide
circular foot, 33.5cm. high.
(Christie's) $7,656

A Benson copper and brass
table lamp, on flared brass
tripod foot with heart feet,
57cm. high.
(Christie's) $869

A Clarice Cliff lamp base, of
ovoid form molded in relief
with a young girl in swimming
costume riding a water buffalo,
21cm. high.
(Christie's) $217

A Chinese cloisonné lamp with
white pleated silk shade and
baluster-shaped body, the
cloisonné late 17th/early 18th
century, 25$^{1}/_{2}$in. wide.
(Christie's) $5,329

Tiffany bronze and favrile glass oil lamp, broad gourd-form opal glass shade with gold iridescent combed surface, shade diameter 9¹/₂in.
(Skinner) **$2,860**

Tiffany seven light lily lamp, gold iridescent eight-rib lily blossom shades marked *L.C.T.*, 22in. high.
(Skinner) **$1,870**

Tiffany nautilus desk lamp, early shell-form shade of green leaded glass segments, 14in. high.
(Skinner) **$4,290**

Pairpoint etched glass dragon lamp, cased red to white closed top shade with etched and gold enameled dragon decoration, 18in. high.
(Skinner) **$770**

Tiffany counterbalance desk lamp, brilliant iridescence on cased gold and amber wave design damascene shade signed *L.C.T.*, shade diameter 7in.
(Skinner) **$3,190**

Handel handpainted dragon lamp, closed top dome shade with colorful Oriental dragon motif on interior with outside gold accents, 22in. high.
(Skinner) **$880**

Handel Arts and Crafts slag glass desk lamp, three caramel slag glass panels under hammered metal strap and floral framing, 16in. high.
(Skinner) **$660**

Tiffany bronze and favrile glass double student lamp, green and iridescent gold damascene ribbed glass shades lined in opal white, total height 30in.
(Skinner) **$11,000**

Jefferson Art Deco table lamp, reverse painted glass shade with four repeating elements of **stylized double blossom motif,** 22in. high.
(Skinner) **$990**

A 19th century white marble bust of Michelangelo, 55cm. high.
(Finarte) $2,491

A carved white marble relief, depicting Christ kneeling within a pointed arch, His arms outstretched, inscribed *HOMO DEUS CHRISTUS PONTIFEX*, circa 1942, 17³/₄in. wide.
(Christie's) $1,320

A 19th century Japanese marble okimono of a young woman spinning silk, signed on base *Rysukeda*, circa 1850.
(Duran) $2,106

A white marble bust of the Apollo Belvedere, after the Antique, by Cesare Lapini, his cloak held with a morse on his right shoulder, circa 1889, 30¹/₂in. high.
(Christie's) $4,813

A pair of 19th century French pentallic marble and ormolu mounted vases and covers, on square marble feet with applied foliate spandrels, 54cm. high.
(Phillips) $5,653

An Italian white marble jardinière, after the Antique Albani cinerary urn, of octagonal form, each side carved in relief with a winged dancing putto, 19th century, 18¹/₈ x 17⁷/₈in.
(Christie's) $3,388

An English white marble group of Diana the Huntress, after the Antique, the goddess striding forward, a leaping stag beside her, 19th century, 30¹/₂in. high.
(Christie's) $1,925

A French white marble group of a shepherd and shepherdess, by L. Charles Fremont, the couple shown seated on a tree trunk, second half 19th century, 36¹/₄in. high.
(Christie's) $9,936

A 19th century carved white marble bust of Napoleon, after Canova, the Emperor dressed al'antica, 1.23m. high.
(Phillips) $5,355

MARBLE

A fine carved white marble figure of a girl by Affortunato Gory, Paris, the semi nude girl standing in exotic pose, 40in. high.
(Bearne's) $5,119

A rectangular English marble relief of a winged maiden in a horse-drawn chariot, the chariot followed by two winged putti, late 18th/early 19th century, 27in. wide.
(Christie's) $1,733

A marble bust of a girl in Art Nouveau style, circa 1900, 56cm. high.
(Arnold) $963

An English white marble figure of Antinous, after the Antique, shown standing and wearing an Egyptian headdress and kilt, first half 19th century, 30³/₄in. high.
(Christie's) $4,235

A pair of English white marble busts of Wellington and Blucher, by Peter Turnerelli, both generals in military uniform and wearing numerous medals, early 19th century, 29¹/₄in. high.
(Christie's) $17,325

A Greek white marble figure of Aphrodite, by Georgios Vroutos, her gown draped over her right arm, her left hand holding the apple, late 19th century, 31in. high.
(Christie's) $9,498

A Greek white marble figure of Apollo, by Georgios Vroutos, a lyre in his left hand and a quill in his right, a cloak draped over his shoulders, late 19th century, 31in. high.
(Christie's) $9,498

A circular marble table top, including numerous marble types, in a radiating geometric pattern, 19th century, 27in. diameter.
(Christie's) $3,850

A large Italian black marble vase, mid 20th century, flecked with white marble, 75cm. high.
(Sotheby's) $2,624

A Gem roller organ with twenty-note mechanism in gilt stenciled ebonized case and six 'cobs'.
(Christie's) $753

A small Mikiphone Pocket Phonograph, pocket gramophone with original pick up.
(Auction Team Köln) $1,350

An Edison Spring Motor phonograph, now with Bettini type 'C' reproducer and recorder, japanned 'funnel' horn with fixed elbow, and light oak case with lid.
(Christie's) $3,871

An Ideal Blaupunkt Type 2 GD music cabinet with built in Schaub radio, direct current receiver and converter, in mainly original condition, circa 1933.
(Auction Team Köln) $386

Coinola Mod. CJX electric piano with xylophone, coin operated, with decorative Jugendstil glass front, with folding seat and three rolls, 1916.
(Auction Team Köln) $8,489

A Kalliope No. 42 musical box for 25cm. discs, with 42-tone comb with four disks, with original hand crank and dealer's label *A. Brandenburger, Berlin*, circa 1900.
(Auction Team Köln) $578

The Wonder Portable Chiftophone, portable gramophone, with flat pick up and turntable, circa 1920.
(Auction Team Köln) $170

Le Concert Automatique Français, a coin operated standard gramophone for Pathé vertical disks, with large 13-section blue and gold flower horn, circa 1910.
(Auction Team Köln) $2,161

A rosewood musical tea caddy, English/Swiss, circa 1840, the hinged lid containing musical movement and opening to reveal two tea compartments, 12in. wide.
(Sotheby's) $781

A Gramophone Co. Pigmy Grand hornless gramophone with Exhibition soundbox on detachable gooseneck tone-arm, mahogany case with internal horn, 1909 HMV transfer. (Christie's) $430

A bakelite designer Philips record player, circa 1955. (Auction Team Köln) $109

A 27-inch Regina table disk musical box, with twin combs in mahogany case with concertina-action folding top, 34½in. wide. (Christie's) $17,204

A Schaub Supraphon 52 music center with ultra short wave function, record player, magnetic tape recorder and two tapes, in working order, 1951. (Auction Team Köln) $695

An Electrola Re-entrant tone-chamber gramophone (HMV Model 193) in oak case with 34 quadruple-spring motor and oxidized 5a soundboxes and fittings, 44½in. high, 1928–30. (Christie's) $3,656

A 'bells, drum and castanets in sight' cylinder musical box, Swiss, circa 1880, playing six airs, accompanied by snare drum, six saucer bells and castanets, 20in. wide. (Sotheby's) $2,603

An HMV Junior Monarch gramophone with Exhibition soundbox, single 1¼-inch spring motor, fluted oak horn and oak case dated *December 1911*. (Christie's) $3,011

A Lochmann Original Mod. 60d table musical box for 39cm. tin discs with complete 120-tone double comb and speed regulator, with 25 disks, with original crank, circa 1905. (Auction Team Köln) $1,929

A Gramophone & Typewriter Ltd Melba gramophone with G & T Exhibition soundbox on gooseneck tone-arm ebonized case with embossed brass lunettes of a female head in scrolling Art Nouveau surround. (Christie's) $8,172

A mandoline eight-air musical box, with zither attachment and inlaid lid, 22½in. wide. (Christie's) **$1,183**

A Gramophone Company coin-operated gramophone with Clark-Johnson soundbox, wood traveling arm and rectangular oak case with coin mechanism, 1898–9. (Christie's) **$7,326**

An Edison red Gem phonograph, Model D, with K reproducer, maroon Fireside horn, crane and thirty-four wax amberols. (Christie's) **$1,547**

An E.M.G. Mark IX hand made gramophone with double-spring Paillard motor. (Christie's) **$2,605**

An 11⅞-inch Symphonion longcase clock with twin combs, two-train clock and walnut case with applied turned and carved moldings and finials, 78½in. high. (Christie's) **$15,053**

An Edison Fireside phonograph, Model A, with K reproducer and No. 10 black Cygnet horn, and approximately forty cylinders, mainly two-minute. (Christie's) **$1,384**

An HMV Model 1 automatic gramophone, with Florentine bronze fittings including No. 16 soundbox, 42in. wide, circa 1929. (Christie's) **$1,954**

A musical box playing eight airs accompanied by six bells with gilt automaton mandarin strikers, in case with inlaid front and lid, 22in. wide. (Christie's) **$3,441**

A Nicol Frères walnut cased 'Penny in slot' polyphon, playing 20in. diameter disks, on baluster turned feet, 27in. wide. (Spencer's) **$3,465**

A Stroviol, four-string model, with main and auxiliary aluminium horns, in case. (Christie's) $1,140

A mandolin musical box by P.V.F., playing six airs (teeth grouped in fours), in feather-banded bird's eye maple case, 19½in. wide.
(Christie's) $1,465

A 'Fortissimo comb' musical box by B. A. Bremond, playing twelve mainly operatic airs, accompanied by nine optional bells with bee strikers, 29¾in. wide.
(Christie's) $3,582

A Symphonion 19⅛-inch upright disk musical box with diametric combs, coin mechanism, oak motor cover with Riley, Birmingham transfer, 52⅜in. high.
(Christie's) $3,093

A 19⅝-inch upright Polyphon disc musical box with two combs, coin mechanism and dark stained case with glazed door, 75½in. high.
(Christie's) $7,326

A Regina musical disc player, playing 15½in. discs, A. Wolff, New York, contained in a blond oak case, together with fifteen discs contained in a beech case.
(Spencer's) $1,402

An HMV Model VIIA mahogany horn gramophone (HFM) with triple-spring motor, rocking turntable, 21¾in. diameter horn, circa 1913.
(Christie's) $1,791

A rare musical necessaire, the sur-plateau movement with two-sets of seventeen separate teeth, four-wing governor and male winding key, 5¼in. wide, circa 1810.
(Christie's) $6,186

'Symphonia' roll organ, early 20th century, by Wilcox & White Organ Co. of Meriden, oak case with simulated inlay, 18in. wide.
(Eldred's) $358

A musical clock base, Swiss, circa 1830, the 8in. cylinder playing four operatic airs on sectional comb in rosewood veneered oval base.
(Sotheby's) **$1,996**

A German Mammut coin operated gramophone, lacking horn and needing restoration, in richly carved and decorated wooden housing, circa 1910.
(Auction Team Köln)
$772

Tin toy portable gramophone by Gebr. Bing, 1925.
(Auction Team Köln)
$170

A Lochmann's original 48D 11 inch disk musical box, German, circa 1905, the double comb periphery drive movement contained in walnut case, together with thirteen discs, 17in. wide.
(Sotheby's) **$1,475**

A Bremond 'hidden drum and bells' cylinder musical box, Swiss, circa 1880, playing eight airs as listed on tune sheet, 19in. wide.
(Sotheby's) **$1,648**

A 15½-inch Polyphon disc musical box, German, circa 1900, with twin comb movement in walnut case with carved and molded decorations, together with approximately twenty five disks.
(Sotheby's) **$3,210**

The Trade Mark Gramophone, with label of the Gramophone & Typewriter Ltd., London, the first gramophone to carry the world renowned HMV logo with Nipper the dog, 1898.
(Auction Team Köln)
$3,473

A 11⅛-inch Polyphon disc musical box, German, circa 1910, with single comb and top-wind motor in walnut veneered case with print applied to lid interior, 13½in. wide.
(Sotheby's) **$694**

A Carette cylinder gramophone by Georg Carette, Nürnberg, with red base decorated in relief with flower and bird motifs and a 7-section blue and gold horn, circa 1910.
(Auction Team Köln)
$926

A musical Christmas tree stand, perhaps by Eckardt, Stuttgart, with rotating cast iron, decorated tree holder, playing four melodies on two cylinders, in working order, circa 1890. (Auction Team Köln)

$578

Trombino, a rare plated tin 18 tone mechanical trumpet by M. Winkler & Co., Munich, with four paper rolls, circa 1900. (Auction Team Köln)

$1,775

A tin toy Electric Phonograph Mod. 777 gramophone by the Lindstrom Corp., Bridgeport, CT, 110v, red and green with bright children's decoration, circa 1955. (Auction Team Köln)

$254

A 'hidden drum and bells' cylinder musical box, Swiss, 1880's, playing eight airs with optional drum and bells accompaniment, 23¹/₂in. wide. (Sotheby's) $1,648

An American Peerless electric piano, coin operated, with 44-note pneumatics, by Roth & Engelhardt, St. Johnsville, NY, for 21.2cm. wide continuous rolls (two supplied), 1898. (Auction Team Köln)

$9,259

A Dawkins/AMI Rivenc mandoline cylinder musical box, Swiss, circa 1880, playing six airs, as listed on colored lithographic tune sheet, 24in. wide. (Sotheby's) $2,169

A Berlin double flute player organ with wooden cylinders, in walnut case with palisander inlay, playing eight Berlin melodies, circa 1950. (Auction Team Köln)

$7,716

An HMV Model VIIa mahogany horn gramophone, English, circa 1912, with triple spring motor, 12 inch rocking turntable, the horn 21¹/₂in. diameter. (Sotheby's) $1,735

A 15¹/₂-inch Polyphon disc musical box, German, circa 1900, the periphery driven disc playing on two combs, with approximately eight metal disks, 36in. high. (Sotheby's) $1,735

A Deccalian bijou grand gramophone with Decca New Crescendo soundbox, simulated wood 'Dulciflex' in lid and walnut case, 33in. high, circa 1922.
(Christie's) $1,183

A German Ariston 24 tone musical box for flat disks, circa 1890, with twenty 33cm. diameter disks.
(Auktionsverket) $132

A 19⁵/₈-inch upright Polyphon disc musical box with double combs, coin-slot mechanism and drawer, in typical case with pediment and glazed door, 51in. high.
(Christie's) $5,698

An His Master's Voice Model 510 Lumière pleated diaphragm gramophone, in quarter-veneered mahogany cabinet, 43in. high, 1924–5.
(Christie's) $2,930

A fruitwood music box, Pennsylvania, 1780–1810, of rectangular form with hinged lid opening to a printed paper-lined interior fitted with works, length 15¹/₂in.
(Sotheby's) $2,415

A Swiss 'Celestial Voice' cylinder musical box No. 10011, the 16in. cylinder playing ten airs on two combs and with sixteen key organ attachment (possibly not working), 27¹/₂in. wide.
(Bearne's) $4,060

A Klingsor gramophone with Klingsor soundbox and walnut case with hinged flap to turntable compartment, 34¹/₂in. high, circa 1910.
(Christie's) $1,398

19th century national music box, playing six tunes with ratchet wind mechanism, in decorative mahogany box.
(G. A. Key) $504

A rare Gramophone Grand cabinet gramophone with G & T Exhibition soundbox on gooseneck tone-arm, 45in. high, 1907–8.
(Christie's) $2,043

A miniature painted pine document-box, the rectangular top lifting above a conforming case over a shaped apron, on bracket feet.
(Christie's) $462

A George II mahogany miniature tripod table, the circular snap top on an urn-shaped shaft on tripod legs, 9in. wide.
(Phillips) $863

A George III mahogany miniature chest, the rectangular top banded with ebonized and boxwood lines, above four short and two graduated long drawers, 16³/₄in. wide.
(Christie's) $1,224

A mahogany miniature bureau inlaid with boxwood lines, the sloping fall with oval fan inlay and conforming spandrels enclosing an interior of four drawers and pigeonholes, 11in. wide. (Phillips) $1,339

A miniature William and Mary dower-chest, New England, 1710–1725, on four ball and baluster-turned feet, 12¹/₄in. wide.
(Christie's) $4,620

A Regency mahogany miniature chest, with ebonized stringing, on later ogee bracket feet, 1ft. 1in. wide.
(Phillips) $625

A 19th century Dutch walnut and checker strung miniature cabinet with a pair of doors enclosing two short and one long drawer with three drawers below, 1ft. 11in. wide.
(Phillips) $1,593

A Victorian mahogany miniature sample dining-table, the molded extending rectangular top above four bulbous baluster legs with a patent-brass mechanical extending action, fully extended: 13¹/₄in. wide.
(Christie's) $4,832

A late Regency mahogany miniature linen press, the plain rectangular top above a pair of paneled doors enclosing four slides, on bracket feet, 1ft. 1in. wide.
(Phillips) $864

A George II giltwood mirror with oval plate within a gadrooned frame carved with scrolling oak leaves and acanthus, 50¹/₂ x 30in.
(Christie's) $6,996

An unusual 19th century rolled-paperwork mirror frame of arched form, 39in. high.
(Bearne's) $4,321

A good classical giltwood four-light convex wall mirror, first quarter 19th century, surmounted by a wingspread eagle on a rock work support, 44in. high.
(Sotheby's) $8,800

A fine and large Queen Anne inlaid and parcel-gilt walnut wall mirror, 18th century, the shaped crest centering a finial in the form of a pierced flower-filled basket, 6ft. 3¹/₄in. high.
(Sotheby's) $8,250

A Regency pollard oak, oak and ebony swing frame toilet mirror, attributable stylistically to George Bullock, 2ft. 5in. wide.
(Phillips) $1,487

A fine Federal inlaid and parcel gilt mahogany wall mirror, New York, circa 1795, surmounted by an urn with spray of flowers and wheat ears, height 53¹/₄in.
(Sotheby's) $24,150

An early George II giltwood mirror, the later rectangular beveled plate within a strapwork molded surround, the frame carved with egg and dart, 4ft. 10in. x 2ft. 8in.
(Phillips) $5,653

A French ormolu, silvered bronze and Limoges enamel mirror, in the Renaissance style, by F. Barbedienne, the octagonal plate with beveled edges within a cushion-shaped frame, second half 19th century, 42in. wide.
(Christie's) $22,451

A gilt-gesso mirror with rectagular beveled plate, the frame carved with acanthus scrolls on a pounced ground, with broken pediment cresting centered by an acanthus scroll, 40 x 23in.
(Christie's) $3,148

MIRRORS

A gilt girandole mirror, American, 1820–1830, surmounted by an ebonized eagle on a rocky plinth flanked by acanthus leaves, the coved mirror frame hung with spherules, 30¼in. high.
(Christie's) $15,400

A George III giltwood mirror with later shaped and divided plate, the shaped rectangular frame carved with stylized scrolling foliage, rockwork and upspringing acanthus, 51 x 28½in.
(Christie's) $26,928

A Wiener Werkstätte giltwood mirror, the design attributed to Josef Hoffmann, the outer edge decorated with linen-fold molding, the inner with eight stylized flowerheads, 30.5cm. diameter.
(Christie's) $1,723

One of a pair of verre eglomisé tortoiseshell and parcel-gilt mirrors, each with rectangular plate in a molded frame, the border decorated with figures and animals, 60¾ x 28½in.
(Christie's) $16,830

A Wiener Werkstätte giltwood mirror, designed by Dagobert Peche, decorated with overlapping stylized leaf design, 48 x 46.6cm.
(Christie's) $18,183

A George I gilt-gesso mirror with beveled shaped rectangular plate in a concave-fronted frame carved with strapwork on a pounced ground, with shaped arched cresting centered by a satyr-mask and flanked by scrolls, 52 x 31½in.
(Christie's) $12,593

A giltwood and verre eglomisé mirror, the later rectangular plate between fluted pilasters with stiff-leaf capitals flanking a panel of ribbon-tied floral swags with eagle cresting, 60¼in. high.
(Christie's) $3,029

One of a pair of giltwood oval mirrors, each with later oval plate within a husk molded pierced rockwork frame, crested by a confronting C-scroll and acanthus carved cresting, 50½ x 51½in.
(Christie's)
(Two) $7,574

One of a pair of Scottish George III giltwood mirrors, each with arched beveled rectangular plate in a rockwork-encrusted scroll frame and mirrored border, 85 x 48in.
(Christie's)
(Two) $49,478

Fine Queen Anne style gilt mirror with Prince of Wales and shell decoration, 26 x 55in. (Eldred's) $715

Over-mantel mirror, 19th century, painted green, three panels with griffin and acanthus leaf design, possibly Italian, 59¼in. wide. (Eldred's) $660

Antique Chippendale mirror in mahogany with gilt phoenix and bezel, 20 x 32in. (Eldred's) $330

An early 18th century gilt and gesso mirror, the later arched rectangular plate within a flowerhead and salmon spawn molded front, 3ft. 3in. x 1ft. 9in. (Phillips) $1,239

An early Victorian giltwood overmantel mirror by William Thrale Wright, the central rectangular plate flanked by shaped plates and divided by entwined foliate bars, 78½ x 66in. (Christie's) $2,099

A mid-19th century gilt brass-framed looking glass of arched rectangular form, the reeded frame applied with swags of fruiting vines and flowers, 39in. high. (Bearne's) $1,412

A George II mahogany and parcel gilt mirror, the shaped rectangular plate within a gilt slip molded frame, fret carved borders and pierced bird cresting, 2ft. 5in. high. (Phillips) $540

A Federal carved ebonized mahogany dressing glass with drawers, Boston, Massachusetts, circa 1820, the mirror plate pivoting between reeded and scrolled uprights, 20¾in. wide. (Sotheby's) $1,100

A Queen Anne inlaid and parcel-gilt walnut wall mirror, early 18th century, having a scroll-cut cresting centering a pierced gilded shell, 39¼in. high. (Sotheby's) $14,300

MIRRORS

A Chippendale carved and parcel-gilt mahogany wall mirror, late 18th century, having a swan's-neck cresting ending in flowerheads, 5ft. 1¼in. high.
(Sotheby's) **$9,350**

An Edwardian mahogany toilet mirror with shield-shaped plate and scrolling frame inlaid with paterae, on arched feet, 22in. wide.
(Christie's) **$753**

A walnut parquetry and giltwood toilet-mirror, with later adjustable shaped arched mirror-plate within a beveled giltwood mirrored border crowned by a flaming finial, 18in. wide.
(Christie's) **$4,187**

A George II walnut veneered mirror, the beveled rectangular plate to a leaf carved gilded border, 29½in x 4ft. 9in., circa 1735.
(Woolley & Wallis) **$5,724**

An early Victorian white painted overmantel mirror with rectangular plate and reeded slip within a foliate carved surround, 54½in. wide.
(Christie's) **$832**

An early 19th century Irish ebonized and parcel gilt mirror, the oval plate within a molded and glass studded frame, 2ft. 5in. high.
(Phillips) **$936**

A giltwood mirror with rectangular plate with molded frame carved with flowerheads, on a part-star pounced ground, 50 x 38in.
(Christie's) **$1,304**

A Regency mahogany toilet mirror with rectangular plate and reeded uprights, the bowed hinged base enclosing a fitted interior, 22in. wide.
(Christie's) **$836**

A late Victorian silver framed easel backed mirror by William Comyns, London 1897, 46 x 39cm. overall dimensions.
(Spencer's) **$935**

A Regency giltwood, composition and ebonized mirror with circular convex plate, with reeded slip, the cushion frame decorated with lotus leaves and lozenges, 37 x 23in.
(Christie's) $1,786

An Italian carved giltwood rococo frame mirror, the shaped plate with a scroll spray border, floral open spray surmount, 3ft. x 3ft. 2in.
(Woolley & Wallis) $666

A Queen Anne pier glass, the two beveled glass plates within a parcel gilt walnut molded cross-grain frame, 56¹/₂in. high.
(Bearne's) $7,413

An early Georgian walnut and parcel-gilt toilet-mirror, the later rectangular plate in a molded foliate surround between channeled supports, 18in. wide.
(Christie's) $1,609

A rare parcel-gilt and carved walnut mirror, designed by Alfred Stevens, the divided plates etched with foliage within an egg and dart molding, 5ft. 9¹/₄in. high.
(Sotheby's) $8,525

A George II walnut toilet-mirror, the rectangular plate in molded frame with inner gilt molding flanked by plain supports with acorn finials, 17in. wide.
(Christie's) $1,576

An Empire giltwood mirror, American, 1820–1840, the molded rectangular frame with carved applied foliate spandrels containing a two-part rectangular mirror plate, 55¹/₂in. high.
(Christie's) $2,420

A William and Mary oyster-veneered ebonized and marquetry cushion frame mirror with rectangular plate and foliate scroll surround, 41¹/₂in. high.
(Christie's) $5,577

A Chippendale carved giltwood and mahogany mirror, American, late 18th century, the giltwood swan's-neck pediment centering a carved gilt phoenix above a shaped rectangular frame, 21¹/₂in. wide.
(Christie's) $4,620

Classical giltwood looking glass, America, circa 1830, 39½in. high.
(Skinner) $660

Limbert hall mirror, no. 22, circa 1910, oak frame with slats at each side of mirror, seven copper hooks, branded mark, 23½in. high.
(Skinner) $990

A George IV mahogany cheval mirror with rectangular glass plate, ring-turned baluster support with urn finials and on splayed legs, 65in. high.
(Bearne's) $1,059

A George II walnut and parcel-gilt mirror with rectangular beveled plate in a foliate frame and rectangular eared surround below a swan-neck cresting, 49½ x 32in.
(Christie's) $3,362

A George III mahogany toilet-mirror with oval plate in a plain surround and eared supports, the serpentine base with a single mahogany-lined frieze drawer, on shaped bracket feet, 17¾in. wide.
(Christie's) $1,522

A Regency gray-painted and parcel-gilt mirror by Robert Cribb and Son, with rectangular plate flanked by twin-fluted columns with leafy capitals and divided by stars, 64½ x 38½in.
(Christie's) $5,148

A George III giltwood girandole, with oval plate in a pierced scrolling foliate frame, the pierced cresting with stylized acanthus-enriched confronting C-scrolls, 26½ x 15in.
(Christie's) $4,377

A George III mahogany toilet-mirror with later shield-shaped plate in a plain surround and on scroll supports, back feet replaced, 17in. wide.
(Christie's) $1,237

A Regency circular convex wall mirror, surmounted by an eagle flanked by dolphins and with a seahorse and acanthus apron below, 41 x 23½in.
(Bearne's) $1,730

A Directoire ebony and brass-inlaid mahogany cheval glass with rectangular plate, the inverted breakfront molded cornice inlaid with Greek-key, possibly German, 41¼in. wide.
(Christie's) $6,218

Modern hallmarked silver mounted dressing table mirror with oval glass, easel back, London assay.
(G. A. Key) $52

An early 18th century walnut veneered toilet mirror with arched fret cornice, on bracket feet, 15¼in.
(Woolley & Wallis) $605

An Italian giltwood mirror with later rectangular plate within a pierced molded frame elaborately carved with stylized foliage and C-scrolls, German, 48 x 30in.
(Christie's) $5,685

A pair of giltwood girandoles of George III style, with oval plates and beaded fluted frames, with triple branches and conforming pierced scrolling aprons, 50 x 23½in.
(Christie's) $2,509

An early 19th century giltwood overmantel, the pediment applied with palm leaves above a panel with two affronted griffins, 137cm. wide.
(Finarte) $6,414

A Flemish parcel-gilt carved-wood overmantel mirror, circa 1880, in Renaissance manner, with a rectangular beveled plate, 148cm. wide.
(Sotheby's) $2,624

A rare small French parcel-gilt-bronze dressing mirror, Louis-Philippe/Napoléon III, by Giroux of Paris, circa 1845, 1ft. 10in. high.
(Sotheby's) $6,996

A pewter mirror frame by Helen Muir-Wood, rectangular, repoussé decoration of stylized thistles, 65.8 x 44.5cm.
(Christie's) $766

A fine George III carved and giltwood oval wall mirror, surmounted by a basket of flowers, 47³/₄in. high, circa 1760. (Tennants) $8,100

A Regency ivory-mounted and inlaid mahogany dressing mirror with drawers, first quarter 19th century, on turned ivory feet, width 20¹/₄in. (Sotheby's) $1,035

A Regency walnut framed cheval mirror, with hinged oblong mirror, scroll swan neck supports, 2ft. 2in. wide. (Russell Baldwin & Bright) $1,018

A George I walnut and parcel gilt mirror, the arched rectangular divided plate cut with a flower spray and within a molded frame, 4ft. 8in. high. (Phillips) $900

A pair of 18th century rectangular giltwood mirrors, with the carved figures of a hunter and his dog above, the other with a horse, 121cm. high, Venetian. (Finarte) $22,773

Queen Anne walnut and gilt looking glass, probably England, circa 1750, 48in. high. (Skinner) $2,200

A large Italian mirror, Lombardy, in 17th century manner, the broadly canted rectangular frame applied with gilt-bronze repoussé masks and foliage, 186 x 145cm. (Sotheby's) $36,729

A rare Federal inlaid mahogany miniature shaving mirror, probably New York, 19th century, with a shield-shaped mirror plate, height 9in. (Sotheby's) $1,380

A mirror frame by Comyns & Sons, London 1894/5, molded in high relief around a heart shaped glass, 31cm. high. (Finarte) $1,069

A 2in. scale model of a Shand Manson Horse Drawn Fire Appliance of circa 1894 built by B. Hatswell, 13³/₄ x 22¹/₂in. (Christie's) $3,476

A well engineered model of a single cylinder pear crank water pumping engine built by H. Beech, 12 x 6⁵/₈in. (Christie's) $826

A well engineered 2in. scale single cylinder, single speed, three shaft general purpose traction engine 'Claire', 20¹/₂ x 30in. (Christie's) $2,824

A fine early 20th century live steam stationary steam set with brass labels inscribed *T R Barker Alpha Bristol and Babcock and Wilcox Boilermakers*, 22 x 21in. (Christie's) $2,607

A fine and unusual late 19th century brass model condensing twin cylinder vertical blowing engine, one frame engraved *M Noton, maker, Salford, 1874*, 16¹/₂ x 12³/₄in. (Christie's) $5,214

A Bing 'Phoenix' spirit fired model traction engine, German, circa 1906, with 3 inch cast flywheel and four road wheels hand painted in red and cream, 8¹/₂in. long. (Sotheby's) $607

Märklin steam engine with vertical brass boiler and open housing on red cast iron base, having spirit burner, 34cm. high, circa 1925. (Auction Team Köln) $424

A finely engineered exhibition standard 1/12th scale model of a single cylinder 10 NHP high pressure pendulous engine designed by Dr. E. Alban circa 1838, 16 x 15³/₄in. (Christie's) $4,345

A small Carette stationary steam plant, circa 1915, with horizontal brass boiler, complete with water gauge glass, 10¹/₄in. wide. (Sotheby's) $625

Cased painted model of the steam yacht 'Vamoose' 1891, America, early 20th century, 51in. long.
(Skinner) $1,650

An early 20th century model of a British passenger liner, painted in black and red, in glass and mahogany case, 116cm. long.
(Auktionsverket) $2,862

Early 20th century cased model of the clipper ship, 'Sea Witch' of New York, case 38in. long.
(Eldred's) $1,265

A late 19th/early 20th century hand built model of a Norfolk wherry, of traditional construction and painting, overall length 28$^{1}/_{2}$in.
(Bearne's) $894

Carved and painted shadow box of three-masted ship, America, late 19th/early 20th century, 21$^{1}/_{2}$ x 32in.
(Skinner) $1,650

Cased painted model of the ship 'Sovereign of the Seas', America, early 20th century, fully rigged, case 29 x 11 x 20$^{1}/_{2}$in.
(Skinner) $935

A 19th century display model of the steam sailing ship 'Alexandria', the well detailed model with three masts and twin funnels, 34$^{1}/_{2}$in. wide.
(Bearne's) $670

A Märklin hand painted clockwork cruise liner, the top masts with American flags and Swedish flags fore and aft, circa 1910, 41cm. long.
(Auktionsverket) $6,404

MODEL SHIPS

A carved and painted wood ship model,
American, late 19th/early 20th century, carved in
the full round, the three-master fully rigged,
flying the American flag, 29½in. long.
(Sotheby's) $1,980

Cased model of the turn-of-the-century paddle
steamer, 'Martha's Vineyard', a popular steamer
for years traveling between the New England
coast and the islands of Nantucket and Martha's
Vineyard, 43½in. long.
(Eldred's) $1,650

Cased plank on frame model of the Constitution,
America, 20th century, fully rigged, 46in. high.
(Skinner) $13,200

The Dutch fishing vessel, 'Maria', known as an
'Ever', this was the most widespread type of
German sailboat in the 19th century, case 33in.
wide.
(Eldred's) $660

Painted pond model of a three masted schooner,
American, late 19th century, with lead keel, 42in.
long.
(Skinner) $1,430

Cased plank-on-frame model of a brig, America,
early 20th century, 21in. high.
(Skinner) $1,320

Cased painted wood model of the 'Flying Cloud' of Boston, America, 20th century, bearing label *by E. F. Tanner*, fully rigged, 29in. high. (Skinner) $3,190

A Napoleonic Prisoner-of-War bone model of an 84-gun ship-of-the-line, with planked solid hull with horn strakes, 26in. long x 17in. high. (Lawrence Fine Art) $16,632

Cased model of the whale ship 'Two Brothers', America, 20th century, plank on frame model, hull copper-sheathed from water line down, painted above, 58 x 78in. (Skinner) $14,300

Finely executed plank-on-frame model of a shore launched whaleboat, the floor of the model has gratings, compartments, floorboards, and equipment, case 29in. wide. (Eldred's) $1,320

Cased wood model of the sail and steam brig 'Caledonia', late 19th century, with carved figurehead, brass fittings, fully rigged, case 32 x 13 x 23in. (Skinner) $4,125

Planked model of the American steam tugboat, 'Seguin', the hull is painted black and red, with the deckhouse and wheelhouse left natural, case with inlaid rope-style banding, case 43¹/₂in. long. (Eldred's) $1,430

A Bing for Bassett-Lowke gauge 'I' 4–4–2
clockwork locomotive, German, circa 1920,
together with a Carette tender.
(Sotheby's) $815

A Bing for Bassett-Lowke electric 4–4–2 gauge I
precursor tank locomotive, German, circa 1911,
finished in L&NWR livery.
(Sotheby's) $625

The London Midland and Scottish Railway Class
4P Stanier 2–6–4 side tank locomotive No. 2603,
by Bassett-Lowke Ltd, circa 1947.
(Christie's) $2,323

Carved and painted engine and tender on tracks,
America, late 19th/early 20th century, bearing
the name *Cornwall*, 40in. long.
(Skinner) $1,100

The Great Western Railway King Class
locomotive and tender No. 6005 King George II,
circa 1950, by V. Hunt for Bassett-Lowke Ltd.
(Christie's) $3,291

The Great Western Railway Castle locomotive
and tender No. 5072 'Hurricane' in near mint
original condition, by V. Hunt for Bassett-Lowke
Ltd, circa 1950.
(Christie's) $2,130

A well engineered 5in. gauge model of the British
Railways (ex Great Western Railway) 1500 class
0–6–0 pannier tank No. 1500 built by L. W.
Richards, 14 x 35in.
(Christie's) $3,485

A gauge 'I' Märklin 'Great Bear' spirit fired 4–
6–2 locomotive, German, circa 1909, finished in
Great Western green with black and gold lining.
(Sotheby's) $1,301

A Carette gauge 'I' 0–6–2 clockwork tank
locomotive, German, circa 1910, finished in GNR
apple green livery.
(Sotheby's) $1,076

The London and North Éastern Railway 2–8–2
locomotive and tender No. 2001 'Cock O' The
North', circa 1938, by Mills Brothers Ltd.
(Christie's) $2,710

The Caledonian Railway McIntosh 4–4–0
locomotive and tender No. 140 in original blue
livery, by Bond's o' Euston Road, circa 1938.
(Christie's) $774

The London Midland and Scottish Railway
(ex L & NWR) large boiler Claughton Class
locomotive and tender No. 5919 'Lord Kitchener'
originally by Leeds Model Coy, circa 1938.
(Christie's) $1,258

A finely detailed exhibition standard 5in. gauge
model of the Great Western Railway Armstrong
4–4–0 locomotive and tender No. 16 'Brunel'
built by J. F. Bowman, 14 x 61½in.
(Christie's) $7,357

A rare Trix 'Portable' set, in original fitted
wooden case with special inserts, comprising
operating mineral train and operating mineral
conveyor, 21in. long.
(Christie's) $985

A model steam locomotive, 3½in. gauge of
LNER Pacific 'Great Northern', 4:6:2, working
model with tender in green livery.
(Russell Baldwin & Bright) $3,392

The London and North Eastern Railway Class
A1 locomotive and tender No. 4472 by Bassett-
Lowke Ltd, circa 1936, with added detail by
C. Littledale.
(Christie's) $1,549

The London Midland and Scottish Railway
Duchess Class locomotive and tender No. 6232
by Bassett-Lowke Ltd, circa 1947.
(Christie's) $4,259

The London Midland and Scottish Railway Class
7P locomotove and tender No. 6201 'Princess
Elizabeth', by Mills Brothers Ltd, circa 1938.
(Christie's) $1,839

A cornet by Kohler, London, in brass with three patent piston action rotary valves, in the original box.
(Christie's) $3,482

A portable three-octave harmonium by Debain, with burr-walnut case, ormolu mounts and gilt tripod base, 23in. wide.
(Christie's) $977

A double action pedal harp by Sebastien Erard, decorated in gilt and black with classical motifs and figures.
(Christie's) $1,973

Rare Martin Bros. five-string banjo, Dobson patent, patent dates of *1867* and *1873*, unfretted, 35in. long.
(Eldred's) $396

A Victorian rosewood two octave and straight strung upright miniature pianoforte, in the manner of John Broadwood & Sons, on turned chamfered legs, 1ft. 1in. wide.
(Phillips) $1,116

A Manuel Contreras guitar, circa 1970, the back and ribs of rosewood, the front of cedar, the length of back 19in., in a case.
(Christie's) $987

A gold lacquered alto saxophone engraved *The Regent, The British Band Co. Ltd.*, in fitted case.
(Christie's) $696

A Tonsyreno 46-note player organ with ten stops and knee-swells, in walnut case with fretted front, 50in. wide.
(Christie's) $1,183

A set of bagpipes of Hutcheon of Edinburgh, circa 1920, with later Kintail pipe chanter and bag.
(Christie's) $696

OPTICAL INSTRUMENTS

A cardboard-body hand-cranked An Excursion Around the World panorama with opening side doors.
(Christie's) $1,577

A rare leather magnifying glass, hand stitched frame with tapered handle (glass cracked), 17th century, 3³/₈in. long.
(Christie's) $1,511

A black-painted metal conical polyrama panoptique viewer with hinged top and back sections, 6in. high.
(Christie's) $2,452

W. Butcher & Sons, Blackheath, a wood-body Reflectoscope lantern viewer with 3¹/₄ inch diameter viewing lens.
(Christie's) $388

A cardboard-body The Cinématograph-Toy with five picture strips, metal hand-crank and marble weight, in original box.
(Christie's) $457

A mahogany body Kinora viewer with metal eyeshade, hand-crank mechanism and fourteen reels.
(Christie's) $1,059

A 9 inch diameter Le Praxinoscope with candle holder, later shade and six picture strips, on a wood base.
(Christie's) $971

Ernst Planck, Germany, hot-air powered child's praxinoscope with spirit burner, condensing piston, connecting pulleys and six-inch diameter mirrored drum.
(Christie's) $6,657

A wood-body patent reflecting stereoscope with screw focusing eyepiece section, hinged lid with label *Chappuis' patent*.
(Christie's) $1,314

An Avanti Laterna Magica/ Liesegang slide projector, with original components in portable case, circa 1910.
(Auction Team Köln)

$247

A nickel-body Votra stereo viewer.
(Christie's)

$782

A magic mirror gramophone zoetrope attachment, American, 1950's, by the Morgan Development Laboratories Inc., 4in. high.
(Sotheby's)

$868

A metal-body Cinematographe Lumiere projector marked *J. Carpentier, Paris* with hand-crank, brass bound lens with rack and pinion focusing, a spare lens and flange.
(Christie's)

$5,405

A coin operated musical clock and stereo viewer by Henri Vidoudez, St. Croix, the walnut table viewer with Swiss cylinder music works and 57-tone comb, 50cm. high, circa 1900.
(Auction Team Köln)

$5,787

A pair of metal-body Improved Phantasmagoria magic lanterns each with $3\frac{1}{2}$ inch condensing lenses, Carpenter & Westley, 24 Regent St, London.
(Christie's)

$2,233

A hand-held stereoscope with dividing eyepieces, hinged lid and inset maker's label *London Stereoscopic Company, 313 Oxford St.*
(Christie's)

$229

A mahogany and brass biunial magic lantern with brass bound lens section, a pair of three-draw rack and pinion focusing lenses.
(Christie's)

$5,583

A Brewster-pattern hand-held stereoscope with painted floral decoration, green painted pattern and gilt design.
(Christie's)

$1,040

A mahogany and brass-fitted Merito Optical lantern with red-leather bellows, brass bound lens, metal chimney, electric illuminant and plate *Thornton-Pickard Merito Optical Lantern*. (Christie's) **$212**

London Stereoscopic Co, 12-inch diameter Wheel of Life zoetrope on a turned wood stand and with twelve picture strips. (Christie's) **$631**

A wood-body stereoscopic Kromaz color viewer with brass fittings, stereoscopic slide holder, inset label *Barnard & Gowenlock's Kromax*. (Christie's) **$963**

An Ernst Plank Laterna Magica projector for 90mm. slides, lacking burner, with original case and four slides, circa 1890, 35cm. high. (Auction Team Köln) **$170**

A 7¹/₂ x 5¹/₄ inch five-part peep view, the front section printed in German, French and English. (Christie's) **$1,675**

A phenakistiscope part-set comprising five 7 inch diameter double-sided slotted disc, in maker's marbled folder. (Christie's) **$790**

A cardboard-body New Jewel kaleidoscope with turned wood eyepiece, rotating brass section, on a decorative metal stand. (Christie's) **$1,051**

A mahogany and brass-fitted biunial lantern with chimney, condensing lenses, shutter, a pair of brass bound lenses. (Christie's) **$2,495**

Gaumont, Paris, a metal-body table-top automatic 45 x 107mm. stereoscope with dividing eyepieces and internal slide magazine. (Christie's) **$312**

A Swedish Art Deco pewter bowl, attributed to Gullsmeds Aktie Bolaggt, supported on four ribbed feet and stepped circular foot, 22cm. diameter. (Christie's) **$268**

A rococo style two-handled oval bombé pewter soup tureen and cover, monogrammed and dated for 1761, 34cm. high. (Auktionsverket) **$579**

Orivit Art Nouveau pewter centerpiece, Germany, circa 1900, tall cut-glass liner in a round handled pewter bowl, 8^{1}/$_4$in. diameter. (Skinner) **$495**

One of a pair of Osiris pewter five-branch candelabra, designed by Friedrich Adler, the waisted, knopped and tapering stems supporting four sinuous branches with drip pans and sockets, 40.7cm. high. (Christie's) (Two) **$2,871**

A pair of W.M.F. silvered pewter twin-handled vases, cast in relief each side with an Art Nouveau maiden, 36.5cm. high. (Christie's) **$2,508**

A Continental pewter coffeepot, late 18th century, Dutch or German, marked *Blocktin*, the hinged domed cover with baluster finial, 11^{1}/$_2$in. high. (Christie's) **$825**

A pear shaped pewter coffee urn on three legs with bun feet, having domed cover and two scrolled handles, German, late 18th century, 53cm. high. (Kunsthaus am Museum) **$1,549**

Possibly Archibald Knox for Liberty & Co., biscuit box and cover, designed 1903, pewter and enamel, 4^{1}/$_2$in. square. (Sotheby's) **$499**

A Kayzerzinn pewter chalice, with three stag skulls each with full antlers curving up and around the tapering cylindrical bowl, 36cm. high. (Christie's) **$284**

Pewter quart mug, Samuel Hamlin (1767–1801), Hartford, Middletown, Connecticut and Providence, Rhode Island, 5⁷/₈in. high.
(Skinner) $605

Kayserzinn Art Nouveau pewter dish, Germany, circa 1897, designed by Hugo Leven, covered dish raised on tapered feet with sculpted foliate design, 9¹/₂in. long.
(Skinner) $413

A 'Tudric' pewter tankard with hinged cover, the design attributed to Archibald Knox, 21cm. high.
(Christie's) $334

A W.M.F. electroplated pewter table mirror, with ridged and open border, on bracket feet, supported by a hinged strut, with engraved monogram *BL*, 53cm. wide.
(Christie's) $1,244

A W.M.F. electroplated pewter ewer and basin, with repoussé decoration of two profiles of young maidens and stylized flowers, the basin with everted rim, 45cm. high.
(Christie's) $1,340

An American pewter flat-top tankard, Henry Will, New York, circa 1775, the body with shaped handle with bud terminal, on a stepped molded foot, height 7in.
(Sotheby's) $3,450

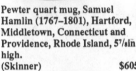

A pewter dome-top tankard by Frederick Bassett, New York City, 1761–1780 and 1785–1799, the dome-top with a crenellated lip and a scrolling thumbpiece, 7¹/₂in. high.
(Christie's) $24,200

A rare pewter covered flagon, touchmark of Thomas D. and Sherman Boardman, Hartford, Connecticut, 1810–30, 13³/₄in. high.
(Sotheby's) $2,420

A Loetz pewter mounted vase, the yellow glass decorated with iridescent purple wavy lines and pink ovals, with two-handled pewter mounts, 17cm. high.
(Christie's) $1,818

David Octavius Hill and Robert Adamson, Three Newhaven Fisherwomen, mid 1840s, calotype, 7³/₄ x 5¹/₂in.
(Christie's) $2,302

Bill Brandt, 'Religious Demonstration, Epsom Derby Day', 1930s, gelatin silver print, 6¹/₂ x 8³/₈in.
(Christie's) $1,240

Herbert List (1903–1975), Headstand, London, 1936, printed circa 1950, gelatin silver print, 11¹/₂ x 9in.
(Christie's) $2,125

Alexander Rodchenko, 'Solntsepoklonniki, 1933' [Sun Worshippers], gelatin silver print, 22³/₄ x 14⁷/₈in., signed, titled (twice) and dated in pencil.
(Christie's) $13,282

Man Ray, 'Rrose Sélavy' [Marcel Duchamp], 1921, printed circa 1936–40, gelatin silver print, 8³/₄ x 7in., photographer's ink credit stamp, *8 rue Val de Grâce*, on verso.
(Christie's) $11,083

Norman Parkinson, 'Changing of the Guard', late 1970s, gelatin silver print, image size 14 x 11¹/₂in., signed in ink on recto, mounted on card.
(Christie's) $1,430

Man Ray (1890–1976), Untitled (spherical light objects), 1926, Rayograph, 9³/₄ x 7⁵/₈in., signed and dated *Man Ray '26* in pencil on image.
(Christie's) $39,325

David Octavius Hill and Robert Adamson, Mr Finlay the deer stalker, mid 1840s, calotype, 8 x 5³/₄in.
(Christie's) $4,959

Alexander Rodchenko, 'Kulaki, 1928' [Kulaks], gelatin silver print on textured paper, 11³/₈ x 9¹/₁₆in., titled and dated in pencil.
(Christie's) $14,168

Ida Kar, Stanley Spencer, 1954, gloss gelatin silver print, 11³/₄ x 9in., signed in white crayon.
(Christie's) $496

Cecil Beaton, 'Tallulah Bankhead', 1930 printed 1960s, gelatin silver print, 15 x 16³/₄in.
(Christie's) $973

Bill Brandt, 'Homes fit for Heroes', 1930s, gloss gelatin silver print, 9 x 7⁵/₈in.
(Christie's) $1,771

Alexander Rodchenko, 'Pionerka, 1930' [Pioneer], possibly printed 1940s-early 50s, gelatin silver print, 17⁷/₁₆ x 13⁹/₁₆in., signed, titled and dated in pencil.
(Christie's) $15,939

Alexander Rodchenko, 'Otriad pionerov Akademii kom-vospitaniia, 1925', gloss gelatin silver print, 11⁵/₁₆ x 9³/₁₆in., photographer's ink credit stamp *Foto A. M. Rodchenko* with title and date in pencil on verso.
(Christie's) $1,698

Anon, Tintern Abbey detail, [1850s], salt print, 7⁵/₈ x 6in., possibly an early view by Roger Fenton.
(Christie's) $531

Weegee (1899–1968), Arrest, 1940s, gelatin silver print, image size 13¹/₂ x 10⁵/₈in., photographer's ink credit stamp.
(Christie's) $1,771

A ninth-plate daguerreotype, hand-tinted and gilt highlights, arched top gilt surround, in folding morocco case.
(Christie's) $145

Rudolf Koppitz (1884–1936), Bewegungsstudie [study of movement], 1926, gelatin silver print, 10³/₄ x 8in., matted, signed in pencil on mount.
(Christie's) $30,107

PHOTOGRAPHS

Ivan Shagin, 'Final Fashizma 1945', [The End of Fascism], gloss gelatin silver print, 16³/₄ x 20³/₄in., titled, signed and dated in pencil and with other annotations in ink on verso. (Christie's) $2,145

Irving Penn (b. 1917), Opticians window, New York, 1939 printed later, gelatin silver print, 13 x 9¹/₂in., signed, stamped, matted, framed. (Christie's) $3,933

Norman Parkinson (1913–90), British Airways Electra, n.d. circa 1937, gelatin silver print, 12 x 16¹/₂in., matted, framed. (Christie's) $2,860

Alexander Rodchenko, 'Pozharnaia lestnista, 1927' [Fire Escape], gelatin silver print, 11⁷/₁₆ x 9¹/₈in., signed, titled, dated and inscribed *niz* [bottom] in pencil with collection stamp of Rodchenko and Stepanova on verso. (Christie's) $80,438

Diane Arbus (1923–1971), Teenage couple on Hudson Street, N.Y.C., 1963 printed later, gelatin silver print, image size 15 x 14³/₄in., stamped *A Diane Arbus Photograph*, signed *Doon Arbus*. (Christie's) $1,430

Alexander Rodchenko, 'E. I. Shub. (kinorezhisser) 1928' [E. I. Shub (film director)], gelatin silver print, 15³/₈ x 11¹¹/₁₆in., signed, titled and dated in pencil and with collection stamp of Rodchenko and Stepanova on verso. (Christie's) $13,406

Ivan Shagin, 'I. V. Stalin, 1935', gelatin silver print, 23 x 16³/₈in., signed, titled, dated in pencil and with Novosty press agency stamp on verso. (Christie's) $1,073

Robert Mapplethorpe (1946–89), Chest, 1987, selenium-toned gelatin silver print, 19¹/₂ x 23¹/₄in., signed, stamped and numbered on verso. (Christie's) $5,720

Cecil Beaton (1904–80), Nancy Cunard, 1927 printed 1960s, gelatin silver print, 17⁷/₈ x 14¹/₄in., mounted on card, signed in pencil on mount. (Christie's) $1,108

Julia Margaret Cameron (1815–79), 'The Passing of Arthur', 1874 and 'Childhood of St. John the Baptist', 1872, two albumen prints, 13³/₄ x 10in. and 14¹/₄ x 10¹/₂in.
(Christie's) $1,251

Alexander Rodchenko, 'Kolonna Dinamo, 1928' [Dynamo's Formation], gelatin silver print, 11 x 16¹/₁₆in., signed, titled and dated in pencil and with collection stamp of Rodchenko and Stepanova on verso.
(Christie's) $21,450

Alexander Rodchenko, 'V. V. Maiakovskii, 1926', gelatin silver print, 16¹/₂ x 11¹/₂in., signed, titled and dated in pencil and with collection stamp of Rodchenko and Stepanova on verso.
(Christie's) $19,663

Anon, Turkoman gentleman with tall hat, circa 1850, quarter-plate daguerreotype, black and tortoiseshell-effect octagonal glass surround with gilt edges, paper-taped.
(Christie's) $1,430

Alexander Rodchenko, 'Pioner', [Pioneer], n.d. [circa 1930–31], gloss gelatin silver print, 4⁷/₈ x 5in., photographer's ink credit stamp *Foto A. M. Rodchenko* with title in pencil and collection stamp of Rodchenko and Stepanova on verso.
(Christie's) $28,600

Alexander Rodchenko, 'Devushka leikoi, 1934' [Girl with Leica], warm-toned gelatin silver print, 15³/₄ x 11⁷/₁₆in., signed, titled and dated (1932 changed to 1934).
(Christie's) $187,688

Frank A. Reinhart, 'Blackhorse', 'Three Fingers', 'Yellow Feather' and 'Bony tela and Hattie Tom', 1898–1900, four platinum prints, each approx. 9¹/₈ x 7¹/₈in., signed.
(Christie's) $1,788

Alexander Rodchenko, 'Na Krasnoi Ploshchadi Zariadiia, 1938' [In line on Red Square], warm-toned gelatin silver print, 11¹/₂ x 14⁷/₈in., contemporary retouching, photographer's monogram on recto.
(Christie's) $5,005

Alvin Langdon Coburn (1882–1966), 'Vortograph', 1917, gelatin silver print, 10⁷/₈ x 8in., mounted on card, signed in pencil on recto.
(Christie's) $121,550

A walnut spinet by Joannes Johnston, the case inlaid with harewood lines, fitted with a hinged rectangular top enclosing a keyboard with carved ivory keys, inscribed *Joannes Johnston, Edinburgi fecit*, circa 1800, 75in. long.
(Christie's) $10,890

An ormolu-mounted kingwood and tulipwood crossbanded grand piano, by Erard Paris, the case banded with ormolu and raised on three legs with scroll feet and lyre-shaped pedal bracket, late 19th/20th century, 60in. wide.
(Christie's) $39,744

A rare Great Exhibition walnut and painted glass piano, by Dimoline of Bristol, circa 1851, with a glass panel painted with Arcadian scenes of gondoliers and an extensive landscape, 4ft. 10³/₄in. wide.
(Sotheby's) $4,433

A late 18th century mahogany square piano by Haxby, York, the case feather banded, ivory and ebony keys, satinwood board inscribed *Haxby, York 1788*, 60¹/₂in. wide.
(Tennants) $2,916

A Bechstein boudoir grand pianoforte, 88-note overstrung, A1 frame, in rosewood case with twinned squared tapering frame, 5ft. 10in. long, 4ft. 11in. wide.
(Russell Baldwin & Bright) $4,687

Steinway, a model K overstrung, underdamped upright piano in a rosewood case with satinwood and tulipwood crossbanding.
(Christie's) $6,907

A pair of South German 18th century baroque sculptures, lacking arms, on wooden plinths, total height 191cm. (Arnold) $5,669

A plaster panel by G. A. Williams, mounted in an oak frame, relief decoration of a central figure of the Christ Child, flanked by praying Saints. (Christie's) $2,010

A pair of English painted plaster figures, London, circa 1900, each boy with bare feet, one wearing a fez, 1ft. 9¹/₂in. high. (Sotheby's) $1,748

A patinated plaster bust of William Shakespeare, the playwright's head turned slightly to sinister, his cloak draped about his shoulders, on integrally cast circular socle, 27³/₄in. high. (Christie's) $732

A pair of George IV plaster wall brackets in the manner of Thomas Hopper, each supported by winged chimera with acanthus-cast tails, 17in. high. (Christie's) $1,903

A French Art Deco plaster urn, on pedestal foot, the body with diagonal flutes, incised *acrapole*, 49cm. high. (Christie's) $502

Two Continental painted plaster boys, possibly Austrian, circa 1900, one smiling holding a basket, the other playing a banjo, 2ft. 2in. high. (Sotheby's) $3,845

Large painted plaster figure of a blackamoor by Picard of Paris, well modeled and featured, 5ft. high. (G. A. Key) $677

A pair of 18th century South German polychrome angels, 80cm. high. (Arnold) $5,102

Andreas Mussard, a gentleman, wearing blue coat with gold buttons, signed on the reverse and dated *1750*, oval, 2in. high. (Bonhams) **$1,177**

J. Borsyni, a gentleman, wearing a brown coat with black collar, signed indistinctly, gilt-metal frame, oval, 2¹/₂in. high. (Bonhams) **$785**

William Thicke, a gentleman, wearing a mole colored coat, gold frame, the reverse with plaited hair, oval, 2³/₄in. high. (Bonhams) **$1,884**

Flemish School, circa 1600/05, a fine portrait of Emperor Matthias (1557–1619), wearing a gold embroidered black doublet, and lace ruff, on vellum, oval, 2¹/₈in. high. (Bonhams) **$53,380**

French School, circa 1790, a lady, wearing a yellow stole and white dress decorated with flowers, gilt-metal mount, circular, 3in. diameter. (Bonhams) **$911**

English School, circa 1820, a double-sided miniature of a gentleman: one side depicts him wearing a scarlet uniform, the other side shows him wearing a blue coat, oval, 2³/₄in. high. (Bonhams) **$597**

Josué Dollfus, a gentleman, with dark hair and beard, wearing a black coat, signed on the obverse and dated *1836*, oval, 3⁷/₈in. high. (Bonhams) **$1,099**

Ozias Humphry, a young boy, wearing green coat and waistcoat, his right hand tucked into his waistcoat, oval, 1¹/₂in. high. (Bonhams) **$785**

French School, circa 1805, a lady, wearing décolleté green dress with lace inset and necklace with gold bordered black jewel, oval, 2¹/₂in. high. (Bonhams) **$628**

George Engleheart, an officer, wearing scarlet uniform with **buff colored facings and silver** epaulettes, oval, 2in. high.
(Bonhams) $4,082

George Engleheart, a gentleman, wearing brown coat, white waistcoat and tied white cravat, oval, 2¼in. high.
(Bonhams) $1,256

Harry Edridge, a lady, wearing a black shawl and white dress, white headgear, oval, 2¾in. high.
(Bonhams) $1,287

Thomas Roth, an officer, wearing scarlet uniform with **blue facings and silver** epaulettes, signed on the obverse and dated *1804*, oval, 2¾in. high.
(Bonhams) $942

Richard Cosway, R.A., a gentleman, believed to be a self-portrait, gilt-metal mount with glazed reverse, circular, 1⅝in. diameter.
(Bonhams) $1,727

James Warren Childe, an officer of the Lancers Regiment, wearing blue uniform with gold epaulettes and gold collar, signed on the obverse, oval, 4¾in. high.
(Bonhams) $1,334

Attributed to Henry Bone, a gentleman, wearing a lilac-**colored coat, yellow waistcoat** and lace cravat, oval, 2¼in. high.
(Bonhams) $471

Attributed to Alexander Gallaway, a lady, half length, facing left, in mourning dress, signed with initials *A.R.G.* and dated *1800*, oval, 2½in. high.
(Bonhams) $502

Joseph Daniel, a fine portrait of a gentleman, wearing blue coat, gilt-metal mount, the reverse with plaited hair, oval, 2⅞in. high.
(Bonhams) $1,884

English School, 18th century, Oliver Cromwell, on card, turned gilt-wood frame, the reverse with the hand inscription *This belongs to my son Tom*, 3in. high.
(Bonhams) $1,176

A miniature of a young lady in eighteenth century costume, in the manner of Greuze, 2¹/₄in. high.
(Tennants) $486

A late 18th century miniature portrait in the manner of Henry Edridge, head and shoulder study of fashionably dressed youth.
(Locke & England) $469

James Tassie, William Murray, 1st Earl of Mansfield, bust length, in profile to the right, signed and dated *1779*, 3¹/₄in. high.
(Bonhams) $1,764

William Wood, a fine pair of portraits of a lady and gentleman believed to be of the Arbathnot family, the former signed on the reverse, 3¹/₈in. high.
(Bonhams) $5,880

Attributed to James Nixon, A.R.A., James Ray, aged 23, wearing a gold-bordered green coat and matching waistcoat, gold frame with the sitter's name engraved on the reverse, 1¹/₂in. high.
(Bonhams) $745

Frederick Buck, an infantry officer, in scarlet uniform of the 82nd Regiment or Prince of Wales' Volunteers, the reverse with lock of hair tied with seed pearls and gold wire, 2³/₈in. high.
(Bonhams) $686

Thomas Heathfield Carrick, an interesting portrait of a gentleman holding a magnifying glass, he wears a black coat, jacket and white shirt, wood frame, 3³/₄in. high.
(Bonhams) $862

Ludwig (Louis) Schmidt, Captain Godfrey Charles Morgan, wearing the white uniform of the 17th Lancers Regiment, signed on the obverse and dated *1812*, oval, 3³/₄in. high.
(Bonhams) $706

English School, circa 1745, Prince James Francis Edward Stuart, facing left in armor and a sash of the Order of the Garter, oval, 1³/₈in. high.
(Christie's) $2,541

John Barry, a charming double portrait of Eliza and Sarah Bird, wearing white tunics, gilt-metal frame, with plaited hair reverse, 3¹/₄in. high.
(Bonhams) $3,724

Scottish School, circa 1745, Prince James Francis Edward Stuart, facing left in armor and sash of the Order of the Garter, oval, 2⁵/₈in. high.
(Christie's) $5,445

Josef Heigel, Lady George William Russell, holding a book, wearing green dress with lace cuff and ruff, rectangular, 6³/₄in. high.
(Bonhams) $7,850

Nicholas Hilliard (1547–1619), a superb miniature of a man clasping a hand from a cloud, possibly Lord Thomas Howard, on vellum, gilt-metal frame, oval, 2³/₈in. high.
(Christie's) $266,250

Miss Charlotte Jones, a lady, dressed in Turkish costume, seated before a curtain background, playing a guitar, rectangular, 5¹/₂in. high.
(Bonhams) $1,020

Attributed to Pierre Marie Gault de St. Germain, a gentleman, head and shoulders, en grisaille with brown tones simulating cameo, 1795, 4in. high.
(Bonhams) $745

Charles Jenour, Henry Christopher Metcalfe (1822–1881), aged 8, wearing a blue tunic trimmed with black ribbon over white pantaloons, rectangular, about 9in. high.
(Bonhams) $1,256

J. R. Galland, a delightful portrait of a young boy holding a stick and pug dog kneeling in a landscape setting, signed on the obverse and dated 1804, 4³/₄in. high.
(Bonhams) $2,940

Charles Shirreff, a naval officer, bust length, facing right, wearing a gold bordered blue uniform with gold buttons, in fitted fishskin case, 2³/₄in. high. (Bonhams) $1,274

Attributed to Sampson Towgood Roche, a lady, wearing a blue dress with frilled white border, gold bracelet clasp frame, 1³/₄in. high. (Bonhams) $823

Circle of John Bogle, a gentleman, wearing a blue coat with gold buttons and white facings, monogram *MM* on plaited hair, oval, 1¹/₂in. high. (Bonhams) $942

John Thomas Barber Beaumont, an officer, in scarlet uniform with blue facings, signed with monogram, gold frame with lock of hair tied with wire on the reverse, 2³/₄in. high. (Bonhams) $1,470

Vittorio Amidio, a fine portrait of Ducci Di Milorja, in navy blue cloak, light blue dress with frilled white border, oil on copper, indistinctly inscribed on reverse, 2⁵/₈in. high. (Bonhams) $1,764

German School, circa 1750, a fine portrait of a lady, wearing an ermine bordered blue cloak and gold figured white dress, on vellum, silver-gilt frame, 1¹/₂in. high. (Bonhams) $1,078

Samuel Shelley, a fine portrait of a gentleman, wearing a blue coat with silver colored buttons and black collar, signed on the reverse, 3in. high. (Bonhams) $1,764

Gervase Spencer, bust length portrait of a young cleric with powdered wig, initialed and dated *1757*, ivory, 3.5 x 3cm. (Spencer's) $883

French School, early 19th century, after Jean Baptiste Greuze, a young lady, holding two white doves in a basket, 2³/₄in. high. (Bonhams) $882

Thomas Hazlehurst, a lady, wearing a white dress with frilled collar, signed with initials on the obverse, gold frame with blue glass reverse, 2⁵/₈in. high. (Bonhams) $1,411

Christian Friedrich Zincke, a young lady, wearing a pink cloak, and white dress trimmed with matching pink ribbon at her corsage, enamel, 1⁷/₈in. high. (Bonhams) $2,352

François Xavier Vispré, a lady, wearing a blue dress, the lace collar decorated with matching bow, signed with initials and dated *1761*, 1¹/₂in. high. (Bonhams) $490

Attributed to Gideon or George Slous, a gentleman, wearing a blue coat, the reverse with the initial R of seed pearls on a lock of hair tied with gold wire, 2¹/₂in. high. (Bonhams) $588

School of Jean Baptiste Isabey, Emperor Napoleon I, wearing the uniform of the Chasseurs-à-Cheval de la Garde, gilt-metal mount engraved with stars set in maple wood frame, 4³/₈in. high. (Bonhams) $1,568

Attributed to William Hamlet the Younger, an officer, believed to be the Duke of Wellington, colored silhouette on card, gilt-mounted rectangular black wood frame, 2³/₄in. high. (Bonhams) $372

William Egley, a lady, wearing a lilac colored dress and long gold chain, a tortoiseshell comb in her brown hair, 2⁵/₈in. high. (Bonhams) $882

Attributed to Nicholas Dixon, Sir Thomas Allin (1612–85), a naval commander, wearing armor and lace jabot, oval, 3¹/₈in. high. (Bonhams) $1,413

N. Freese, a lady, wearing a décolleté white dress with lace border, her brown hair upswept, gold frame, 2⁷/₈in. high. (Bonhams) $1,176

N. Currier (Publisher), 'The road, – winter',
hand colored lithograph, a fine, fresh
impression, with touches of gum arabic, on stone
by Otto Knirsch, 1853, 17¹/₂ x 26¹/₄in.
(Sotheby's) $34,500

Currier and Ives (Publishers), 'A midnight race
on the Mississippi', hand colored lithograph,
after the sketch by H. D. Manning, on stone by
Frances F. Palmer, 1860, 18 x 27⁷/₈in.
(Sotheby's) $4,600

George Caleb Bingham (after), 'Stump
speaking', engraving, mezzotint and roulette, by
Louis-Adolphe Gautier, published by Fishel,
Adler & Schwartz, New York, 1856, 22¹/₄ x
30¹/₈in.
(Sotheby's) $3,738

Henry A. Papprill, 'New York, taken from the
north west angle of Fort Columbus, Governor's
Island', hand colored aquatint, 1844, published
by Henry J. Megarey, New York, image 16⁵/₈ x
26³/₄in.
(Sotheby's) $5,175

William Sharp, 'Opening bud; Opening flower;
Intermediate state of bloom; and Complete
bloom', four chromolithographs, from John
Frisk Allen's Victoria Regia, or The Great Water
Lily of America, Boston, Dutton and Wentworth,
1854, 14⁵/₈ x 20⁵/₈in. (Sotheby's) $5,175

Sigismond Himely, 'New York', hand colored
engraving, after the painting by Heine, published
by Goupil & Co., New York, Paris, London,
Berlin, and W. Schaus, New York, 1851, plate
28⁷/₈ x 43in.
(Sotheby's) $6,900

John James Audubon (after), 'Polar bear', hand colored lithograph, with touches of gum arabic, a fine, fresh impression by J. T. Bowen, Philadelphia, 1846, 21¹/₂ x 27¹/₈in.
(Sotheby's) $3,910

Currier and Ives (Publishers), 'The champion pacer Johnson', chromolithograph, with gum arabic, J. Cameron in the stone, 1884, 18¹/₈ x 27in.
(Sotheby's) $1,380

Currier and Ives (Publishers), 'The life of a hunter, 'A tight fix', hand colored lithograph, a very fine impression of this rare lithograph, with touches of gum arabic, after the painting by A. F. Tait, 1861, 18¹/₂ x 27in.
(Sotheby's) $63,000

N. Currier (Publisher), 'Catching a trout, 'We hab you now, sar', hand colored lithograph with touches of gum arabic, after the painting by A. F. Tait, lith. by N. Currier, 1854, 18¹/₈ x 25⁵/₈in.
(Sotheby's) $7,475

E. Walker, 'Sleigh scene, Toronto Bay, Canada West', lithograph, printed with tint stone and with touches of hand coloring, after the painting by J. T. Downman, printed by Day & Son, published by Ackermann & Co., London 1853, 20⁵/₈ x 30¹/₂in.   (Christie's) $6,325

Sigismond Himely, 'Vue de New York, Prise de Weahawk', a view of New York taken from Veahawk', hand colored aquatint, with touches of gum arabic, circa 1834, image 12³/₄ x 17¹/₂in.
(Sotheby's) $8,050

Masonic jacquard coverlet, dated *July 4, 1827*, corner block inscribed *Agriculture Independence*, 78 x 96in.
(Skinner) $715

An Arts and Crafts bedcover, circa 1895, velvet, 10ft. 6in. long.
(Sotheby's) $1,193

A fine pieced, applique and reverse applique cotton quilt, probably Baltimore, mid 19th century, composed of brilliantly colored red, yellow, green and blue cotton patches, approximately 72 x 72in.
(Sotheby's) $4,400

A pieced and appliqued cotton quilted coverlet, Ohio, mid-19th century, worked in green, red, pink, yellow and orange in a Rose of Sharon variation, 82 x 82in.
(Christie's) $1,760

Printed cotton centennial exposition tied quilt, 1876, 86 x 82in.
(Skinner) $495

Antique appliqued quilt with red, yellow and green floral and swag design, 77 x 81in.
(Eldred's) $275

A patchwork commemorative quilt, composed of various sprigged, floral and plain cottons, arranged in a series of frames, 76 x 88in., circa 1810.
(Christie's) $1,177

A fine and rare pieced, appliqued and reverse applique cotton and velvet flower basket quilt, probably Pennsylvania, mid-19th century, approximately 104 x 112in.
(Sotheby's) $6,613

A pieced cotton quilted coverlet, American, circa 1880, worked in the Thousand Triangles pattern with blue, red, brown, yellow and green calicos decorated with chevron-stitching, with blue calico binding, 73 x 77in.
(Christie's) $990

A pieced and appliqued cotton coverlet top, American, circa 1845, comprised of multiple calico fabrics and chintz, bears ink inscribed cloth label *This quilt is to be given to Mary Steel McCullock it was made in 1845 by her Grandmother Mrs. Mary Foulke*, 148 x 108in.
(Christie's) $1,320

A fine pieced cotton Amish quilt, probably Lancaster County, Pennsylvania, circa 1930, composed of brilliantly colored plum, navy blue and forest green patches, 80 x 82in.
(Sotheby's) $7,150

A very fine pieced calico and chintz Star of Bethlehem quilt, probably Pennsylvania, mid-19th century, approximately 116 x 114in.
(Sotheby's) $7,130

A pieced and appliqued cotton iris quilt, made by Caroline C. Drake, American, dated *1939*, composed of dark and light lavender, yellow and green patches arranged in sprays of irises, approximately 88 x 80in.
(Sotheby's)   **$1,320**

A pieced cotton quilted coverlet, American, circa 1850, worked in red, brown, and blue calico and blue floral chintz, the central blue floral-printed diamond surrounded by four chintz corner blocks, 107 x 109¹/₂in.
(Christie's)   **$880**

A pieced cotton quilted coverlet, Pennsylvania, circa 1880, worked in the Log Cabin Barn Raising pattern with white, red, green, blue, brown, and yellow calicos, surrounded by a blue calico border, 80 x 84in.
(Christie's)   **$550**

An unusual pieced calico odd-fellows quilt top, New York or New Jersey, late 19th century, composed of brightly colored red, green, yellow and blue printed and solid calico patches, approximately 104 x 92in.
(Sotheby's)   **$2,640**

A pieced cotton quilted coverlet, American, circa 1880, worked in the Baby Blocks pattern in brown, red, and blue calico, with a blue binding, 76 x 96in.
(Christie's)   **$462**

An unusual pieced and appliqued American flag quilt, probably Virginia, circa 1920, composed of red, white and blue stars and stripes, approximately 84 x 72in.
(Sotheby's)   **$4,400**

A pieced cotton quilted coverlet, American, circa 1880, worked in green, red and gold diamond-quilted cotton in the Joseph's Coat pattern, with a red binding, 72 x 74in.
(Christie's) $880

A pieced cotton presentation album quilt, Massachusetts, dated 1859, worked in brown, red and green calico blocks with ink inscriptions of children's names and ages, 82 x 84in.
(Christie's) $990

A pieced and appliqued cotton quilted sampler coverlet, American, circa 1880, the central square with a red, green, and yellow tulip and posy medallion surrounded by a variety of designs in the same cottons, 76 x 83in.
(Christie's) $880

A pieced cotton quilted coverlet, American, circa 1880, worked in the Thousand Triangles pattern with brown, red, yellow, green, blue, purple and white calicos, with a blue calico binding, 74 x 76in.
(Christie's) $605

A very unusual pieced cotton and broderie perse Star of Bethlehem quilt, Southern, probably Alabama, early 19th century, arranged in the Star of Bethlehem pattern, 112 x 107in.
(Sotheby's) $7,150

A pieced and appliqued cotton quilted coverlet, American, signed *Louise Bryan*, dated *1933*, worked in blue, green, orange and purple calico, 86 x 68in.
(Christie's) $495

A pieced and appliqued cotton quilted coverlet, American, circa 1830, the broderie perse center block with an exotic bird perched atop a Tree of Life on a white double diamond quilted ground framed by a blue chintz sashing, 110 x 108in.
(Christie's) $9,900

An Amish pieced wool and cotton quilted coverlet, Lancaster County, Pennsylvania, circa 1910, worked in purple, cranberry, blue, pink, green, red and black wool in the Sunshine and Shadow pattern, 70 x 76in.
(Christie's) $6,600

A pieced and appliqued cotton quilted coverlet, American, circa 1850, worked in red, green, and yellow calico in the Spice Rose pattern on a white cotton ribbed quilted ground surrounded by a continuous rose and bud vine decorated with red birds, 72 x 85in.
(Christie's) $3,850

An Amish pieced wool and cotton embroidered and quilted coverlet, Topeka, Indiana, dated 1899, worked in black, blue, purple, tan, brown, and cranberry wool and cotton, embroidered *May 10, 1899, Lizzie, From a Friend, Mrs. I.J.H., Think of me, Ida, Remember Me, Lizzie, Forget me not, Katie, Your Cousin, Mirna*, 66 x 76in.
(Christie's) $7,700

A pieced and appliqued cotton quilted coverlet, American, circa 1880, worked in green and yellow calico and red cotton on an elaborately floral and Princess Feather-stitched white cotton ground, 87 x 86in.
(Christie's) $3,080

A pieced wool and cotton quilted coverlet, American, circa 1880, worked in numerous fabrics of blue, red, green, orange, purple, brown, and black in the Tumbling Block design, 84 x 84in.
(Christie's) $1,100

A pieced, appliqued and embroidered silk and velvet contained crazy quilt, American, circa 1890, worked in multicolored silk and velvet fabrics in the Contained Crazy pattern framed by multicolored embroidery and decorated with a variety of designs, 67 x 69in.
(Christie's) $11,000

An Amish pieced cotton quilted coverlet, Ohio, dated 1916, initialed *BM* and dated *1916*, worked in thirty blocks of the Ohio Star pattern with pieced blue stars on black flower-stitched blocks on a copper spade-quilted ground, 77 x 67in.
(Christie's) $4,950

An Amish pieced wool and cotton quilted coverlet, Lancaster County, Pennsylvania, circa 1920, worked in the Diamond-in-the-Square pattern, the central blue diamond embellished with elaborate tulip-quilting framed by burgundy sashing with blue corner blocks, 77 x 75in.
(Christie's) $3,850

An Amish pieced wool and cotton quilted coverlet, Lancaster County, Pennsylvania, circa 1930, worked in purple and mint wool in the sawtooth Diamond-in-the-Square pattern, the mint sawtooth diamond and sashing with scrolling Princess Feather vine and grapevine-quilting, 78 x 78in.
(Christie's) $1,650

An Amish pieced cotton and wool quilted and embroidered coverlet, Indiana, circa 1930, worked in brown, blue, gray, pink, black, petal, green, and tan wool and cotton with numerous blocks of pieced stripes, 85 x 86in.
(Christie's) $1,540

An Amish pieced wool and cotton quilted coverlet, Lancaster County, Pennsylvania, circa 1925, worked in sixteen blocks of the Double Nine Patch pattern in peach, rust, green, lilac, mint, and blue diamond-quilted wool, 83 x 82in.
(Christie's) $3,520

An Isaria Type RL in original condition, lacking valves, with RTV stamp for 1924. (Auction Team Köln) $3,396

An Adler Royal horn speaker with built in wooden horn, centrifugal casting system, circa 1926, with Magnavox Type 2 Model B horn speaker, circa 1923. (Auction Team Köln) (Two) $386

A Siemens Riesenskala single screen straight receiver with special coil-variable capacitor arrangement, lacking tuning band, circa 1931. (Auction Team Köln) $501

A Telefunken 127 WLK single screen receiver with short wave, some parts replaced, 1933. (Auction Team Köln) $101

A Telefunken 31W radio with horn speaker, alternating current receiver, lacks key, 1929–30. (Auction Team Köln) $849

A Telefunken superhet receiver with wooden housing, export model, lacks backplate, circa 1935. (Auction Team Köln) $85

A detector receiver with distributor box and headset, original Daki crystal, circa 1925. (Auction Team Köln) $309

A Nora bakelite free oscillator loudspeaker, circa 1930. (Auction Team Köln) $232

A Howe Radio Receiver detector/receiver, circa 1925, rare as patent only applied for and never granted. (Auction Team Köln) $232

A Talisman 308V radio with U-21 valve facing and designer bakelite casing by Tesla, circa 1948.
(Auction Team Köln)
$263

A Braun Radio TS2 in working order, wooden case.
(Auction Team Köln) $58

A Telefunken 121 W single screen radio with large dial and decorative tin housing, circa 1931.
(Auction Team Köln)
$200

A Kleinempfanger 'People's Set' receiver in upright black bakelite case, 15¼in. high, circa 1933.
(Christie's) $301

An Ekco Type AD65 AC/DC mains receiver in circular brown bakelite case with semi-circular dial, 15½in. diameter.
(Christie's) $301

A Ferguson Type 501 AC receiver in upright wooden case, 18in. high.
(Christie's) $151

A Philco Model 38–60 3-valve upright receiver in walnut veneered plywood cabinet, 17in. high.
(Christie's) $323

An early mains Kolsterbrandes Pup radio, with free oscillator loudspeaker, circa 1931.
(Auction Team Köln) $123

A Philips 'Superinductance' Model 830A 4-valve receiver with illuminated dial, in 'Arbolite' case with simulated walnut finish, 19¼in. high, 1932.
(Christie's) $516

A Fada 'Streamliner' Model 115 receiver in bright yellow bakelite case with bright red bakelite handle, 10¹/₂in. long, 1941.
(Christie's) $454

An early portable battery television, the Symphonic Mini TV Model TPS 5050, Japanese, circa 1965.
(Auction Team Köln) $123

A Fada Model 252 receiver in bright yellow bakelite case with bright red bakelite tuning scale surround and turning knobs, 10¹/₂in. long, 1946.
(Christie's) $454

An Ekco Type A22 AC mains receiver in circular black bakelite case with circular dial, 13¹/₄in. diameter, 1945.
(Christie's) $488

A Sachsenwerk Rembrandt FE 852D TV set, with round 31cm. diameter picture tubes, mass produced after the war in the DDR, circa 1955.
(Auction Team Köln) $232

An Ekco Type AD75 AC mains receiver in circular brown bakelite case with ³/₄-circle speaker and small semi-circular dial below, 14¹/₂in. diameter.
(Christie's) $488

A Fernseh GmbH TV monitor, an early studio piece dating from the early years of German television, circa 1958.
(Auction Team Köln) $170

A lacquered iron table speaker, signed *Sterling*, London 1920s, 29cm. high.
(Auktionsverket) $265

An Awa Radiolette 'Fisk' Model 32 receiver in upright brown bakelite case of Art Deco design, circa 1930.
(Christie's) $454

A Nomura battery-operated lithographed tinplate Mobile Space TV unit and trailer, with mystery action, in original box, 11in. long.
(Christie's) $1,742

A Kosuge battery-operated (by remote control) High Wheel Robot, finished in metallic blue, 10¹/₂in. long, 1960's.
(Christie's) $255

A Yonezawa 'Cragstan's talking robot', Japanese, early 1960's, finished in red with silver face and arms, in maker's box, 10³/₄in. high.
(Sotheby's) $347

SH, battery operated radar-scope space scout, tin-plate and plastic, with flashing light and chest T.V. image, 9¹/₂in., boxed.
(Bonhams) $98

A Nomura 'Robby' mechanized robot, Japanese, 1950's, the black body with perspex dome to head covering mechanism, in original box, 12¹/₂in. high.
(Sotheby's) $1,735

A Masudaya battery-operated lithographed tinplate Target robot, red target on chest causing evasive action, 1950's, 15in. high.
(Christie's) $1,549

An Asakusa Thunder robot, Japanese, 1960's, finished in brown, with plastic sleeves and hands, 11¹/₄in. high.
(Sotheby's) $1,215

A rare Nomura tinplate battery operated 'Robby Space Patrol', with mystery action, clear plastic dome and light dishes, 1950's, 12¹/₂in. long.
(Christie's) $2,323

Horikawa Toys, 'Attacking Martian', a printed and painted tinplate robot, battery operated with moveable legs, boxed, circa 1960, 11¹/₄in. high.
(Bonhams) $375

A set of five Elvis Presley 'Sun' singles, one side of each 45 with tape damage to label, other side good and disks in excellent condition.
(Sotheby's) $2,178

George Harrison's fur coat by Mary Quant, 1966, in black Mongolian lamb, with designer's label inside, this was worn by George at his wedding to Patti, who wore a Quant coat of red fox.
(Sotheby's) $15,246

The Cavern Club sign, hardboard, the design painted in orange, black, white, red, blue and gray, 35¹/₂ x 95in.
(Sotheby's) $16,988

A promotional coat for Elvis Presley's film 'Girls! Girls! Girls!', 1962, in herringbone-weave, off-white cotton, belt marked at back *A Hal Wallis Production*.
(Sotheby's) $6,970

A handwritten memo by Brian Epstein regarding the Beatles' meeting with Elvis Presley, August, 1965, on hotel notepaper, addressed to his P.A., Wendy Hanson, in blue ballpoint, each sheet 10¹/₂ x 7¹/₂in.
(Sotheby's) $5,227

John Lennon's handwritten lyrics for 'A day in the life', 1967, in black felt-tip and blue ballpoint pens, the reverse with the lyrics in neater form, 10¹/₂ x 7³/₄in.
(Sotheby's) $95,832

A signed Beatles' concert programme, March, 1963, the front cover signed in blue ink or black ballpoint, also signed inside by Ricky Fenton and The Apaches.
(Sotheby's) $1,851

A customised B.E.A. flight bag, 1964, black canvas with white lettering, 'President Hotel Hong Kong, sticker to one side, 9¹/₂ x 13³/₄in.
(Sotheby's) $2,287

A Beatles' bass drumskin, circa 1965, the Ludwig Weathermaster skin with handpainted black lettering, mounted, framed and glazed, 29 x 28¹/₂in.
(Sotheby's) $22,651

A signed Australian tour program, 1964, the center black and white group portrait signed in black ballpoint pen.
(Sotheby's) $1,851

'Mersey Beat', vol. 1, no. 13, January, 1962, eight pages, 12¹/₂ x 9³/₄in., very good condition.
(Sotheby's) $3,267

Paul McCartney's handwritten lyrics for 'She's leaving home', 1967, in blue and black ink, the reverse with a conceptual sketch in blue ballpoint of the cover of 'Sgt. Pepper', the sheet 10 x 8in.
(Sotheby's) $89,298

A scarce set of six record company advertising posters, English, circa 1963, the Beatles' example printed in orange, blue and black on white, the others for Cilla Black, Gerry and The Pacemakers, Billy J. Kramer and The Dakotas, The Hollies and The Swinging Blue Jeans, 33 x 20in.
(Sotheby's) $6,098

John Lennon's handwritten lyrics for 'Because', 1969, in blue felt-tip pen with pencil and ballpoint annotations, on the back of a copy of a letter addressed to the Beatles from John L. Eastman, dated *July 8, 1969.*
(Sotheby's) $16,335

Madonna's gold basque by Jean Paul Gaultier, in gold lamé with zipper front, laced paneling, designer's label inscribed *Madonna*, flesh-colored elasticated lining, showing evidence of much wear.
(Sotheby's) $19,602

A signed copy of 'Love me do', 1962, the red label signed by all four Beatles in blue ball-point pen, poor contrast to Ringo's signature.
(Sotheby's) $1,307

A T.W.A. Beatles' U.S. tour flight bag, red plastic with zipper and adjustable shoulder-strap, white lettering pocket with I.D. card marked *Malcolm F. Evans*, 12in. high.
(Sotheby's) $3,485

A signed copy of the album 'A hard day's night', 1964, the back cover signed by all four Beatles in blue ballpoint and with dedications *To Karen and Kim.*
(Sotheby's) $2,614

Buddy Holly, a good signed album page, also signed by the Crickets, Joe Mauldin and Jerry Allison.
(Vennett-Smith) $808

Mick Jagger, signed 8 x 10, full length in recent years.
(Vennett-Smith) $99

The Rolling Stones, signed album page by all five individually, Mick Jagger, Brian Jones, Bill Wyman, Keith Richards and Charlie Watts.
(Vennett-Smith) $320

Paul McCartney, signed 6 x 4 postcard, half length standing by microphone, also with facsimile signature.
(Vennett-Smith) $72

John Lennon, signed album record sleeve, ' Hard Day's Night', being a compilation of songs from the Beatles film.
(Vennett-Smith) $280

The Beatles, signed piece by all four individually, John Lennon and George Harrison in red ink and Paul McCartney and Ringo Starr in blue ink.
(Vennett-Smith) $800

Paul McCartney, signature and inscription on sheet of Associated British-Pathe Ltd. headed notepaper, 4th April 1966.
(Vennett-Smith) $160

The advertising sign from the Casbah Coffee Club, circa 1960, thin metal, colored red and black on a white ground, 30 x 39in.
(Sotheby's) $27,225

The Monkees, signed color 8 x 10 photograph by Davy Jones, Peter Tork, Mickey Dolenz and Michael Nesmith.
(Vennett-Smith) $112

Brian Epstein, signed album page, annotated in ink in another hand.
(Vennett-Smith) $104

Bruce Springsteen, signed color 10.75 x 7.25 magazine photo, full length performing on stage with guitar.
(Vennett-Smith) $64

Abba, signed 6 x 4 photograph by all four individually, in red ink, full length standing in a row, surface crease.
(Vennett-Smith) $80

Bill Haley, signed and inscribed postcard, to lower white border, half length in profile, playing guitar.
(Vennett-Smith) $192

A BEA flight brochure page signed by the Beatles, 1964, signed in black ball-point pen on one side printed in black on red, $7^{1}/_{2}$ x $6^{1}/_{2}$in.
(Sotheby's) $1,220

Buddy Holly, a rare set of unpublished handwritten lyrics by Buddy Holly, on one side of a sheet of pale pink notepaper, the lyrics beginning *Heart break tomorrow* and ending *Let's be happy tonite.*
(Vennett-Smith) $880

Madonna, signed 8 x 10 photograph, half length in 'Vogue' dance pose.
(Vennett-Smith) $144

Prince, signed 8 x 10 photograph, composite style featuring two images of Prince in concert, probably during the Purple Rain Tour.
(Vennett-Smith) $160

Roy Orbison, signed postcard, signed in very dark portion.
(Vennett-Smith) $128

Jimi Hendrix, two unpublished photographs, 1967, each black and white print with corresponding negative, to be sold with copyright.
(Sotheby's) $1,416

Bob Dylan's jacket by 'Nudies of Hollywood', 1976, black wool gaberdine with red, blue and white silk lining, decorated with hand-sewn rhinestones, size 40Regular.
(Sotheby's) $13,068

Signatures of The Doors, on three separate pieces of paper, mounted in glazed frame with sleeve for the album 'The Doors'.
(Sotheby's) $1,960

A 'Triple-platinum' award for the album 'Kick' by INXS, British, 1989, presented to Bill Leabody for sales of more than 900,000 copies.
(Sotheby's) $1,307

A signed Led Zeppelin tour sweatshirt, 1980, from their 'Over Europe' tour, signed by all four in black felt-tip pen, gray, printed in red and black.
(Sotheby's) $915

An advertising poster for Jerry Lee Lewis at the Tower Ballroom, New Brighton, May, 1962, printed in black and bright red on white, 30 x 20in.
(Sotheby's) $1,481

Peter McKenna: Buddy Holly, 1984, pencil, signed, 11 x 8in., this portrait appears on the sleeve for MCA Records' 'Buddy Holly Series'.
(Sotheby's) $697

A signed 'Silver' award for the album 'Trick of the Tail' by Genesis, British, 1976, presented to Phil Collins for sales in the UK in excess of £75,000.
(Sotheby's) $697

Johnny Rotten's handwritten lyrics for 'Problems' from the album 'Never Mind the Bollocks Here's the Sex Pistols', 1977.
(Sotheby's) $2,396

A postcard signed by the Beatles, circa 1967, the colour card of the Great Danes Hotel, Hollingbourne, Kent, signed on the reverse in blue and black ballpoint pens, 3¹/₂ x 5¹/₂in.
(Sotheby's) $1,089

A signed cigarette case, English, circa 1964, in leather with metal edging, the interior signed by all four Beatles and Neil Aspinall, with dedication by George, 8 x 4³/₄in.
(Sotheby's) $3,703

A letter from John Lennon to his father, 1968, in black ink on wood-effect paper, addressed to Freddie & Pauline, 10 x 7¹/₂in.
(Sotheby's) $2,287

One of Freddie Mercury's leotards, 1970's, in three-color stretch polyester, together with a magazine, 'Freddie Mercury: The Legend Lives On', Nowscreen Ltd., 1992.
(Sotheby's) $10,454

Bryan Adams' giant 'Bucking Bronco' guitar from the video of 'Can't stop this thing we started', 1991, Stratocaster-style in sunburst finish, realistically modeled complete with srings, lead and strap.
(Sotheby's) $13,068

Annie Lennox's stage costume from the 'Free Nelson Mandela' concert, Wembley, 1988, the two-piece, black leather outfit decorated with studs and buttons.
(Sotheby's) $10,454

An early Beatles' concert poster, English, 1962, printed in red and green on white, 30 x 20in.
(Sotheby's) $8,276

A proof of the sleeve for the unreleased Beatles' album, 'Sessions', black and white, with Catalogue number SWAV-12373.
(Sotheby's) $1,133

Cher's Tour bathrobe, 1990, in white cotton toweling, left breast embroidered with 'Heart of Stone' logo and Cher Tour 1990.
(Sotheby's) $697

Freddie Mercury, a black wet-look two-piece stage suit, with maker's printed label *Fred Spurr* stitched inside, worn by Freddie Mercury on stage, circa 1979.
(Christie's) $5,174

The Beatles, a Parlophone Records publicity card, signed on the front by each member of the group in different inks.
(Christie's) $1,380

Eric Clapton, a pair of turquoise leather stage-shoes by Terry de Havillard, London, decorated with navy and white appliquéd leather and gilt-metal western-style buckles.
(Christie's) $2,156

David Bowie, a color poster, Glamour, by Edward Bell, signed and inscribed *To Dave, with best wishes, Bowie 82*, 31 x 24in. framed.
(Christie's) $862

The Rolling Stones, an album, The Rolling Stones, 1964, signed on the back cover by all five members of the group including Brian Jones.
(Christie's) $755

Madonna, a crucifix pendant inlaid with black composition material, and a letter of authenticity from choreographer Brad Jeffries to whom Madonna gave the crucifix.
(Christie's) $8,193

John Lennon, a presentation 'Gold' disk, Imagine, the album mounted above a reduction of the cover and a plaque bearing the R.I.A.A. Certified Sales Award.
(Christie's) $5,174

Jim Morrison, An American Prayer, self-published, limited edition book, 1970, sm.8vo. signed and inscribed on title page *For Donald Vetters, J. Morrison.*
(Christie's) $3,018

The Beatles, an early machine-print photograph, signed by each member of the group in blue biro, 11 x 8¼in.
(Christie's) $1,725

The Rolling Stones, a rare
German tour poster *Die Beat-
Sensation 1967, Die härteste
Band der Welt, The Rolling
Stones...*, 23¹/₈ x 32⁷/₈in.
(Christie's) $5,606

Prince, a black trilby of pure
wool, and a letter of authenticity
from Appolonia Kotero, Prince's
co-star in the film Purple Rain,
stating that she *... received this
black felt hat from Prince while
we were working on the film...*
(Christie's) $1,035

Elvis Presley, a single sleeve,
Love Letters, RCA Records,
1966, signed and inscribed *Best
Wishes, Elvis Presley* in black
felt pen.
(Christie's) $690

John Lennon, a rare autograph
letter, signed [n.d. but
September 1st, 1967] Kenwood,
Cavendish Rd, St Georges Hill,
Colesbridge, Surrey to a pupil of
Lennon's former school Quarry
Bank High School.
(Christie's) $6,037

The Beatles, an album, Please
Please Me, 1963, signed on the
front cover by all four members
of the group and inscribed by
each *love from.*
(Christie's) $2,156

Paul McCartney and John
Lennon, a patterned burgundy,
white, yellow, green and gray,
knitted sleeveless jumper with
maker's woven label, *John Weitz
Designs.*
(Christie's) $2,048

Jim Morrison, a machine print
photograph of Jim Morrison,
signed and inscribed *to Sandy +
Mike cheers, Morrison the Doors
(thanks for everything)*, 10 x
7³/₄in.
(Christie's) $1,509

The Rolling Stones, a long
sleeved t-shirt of black jersey,
appliquéd with an alternative
version of the Rolling Stones
mouth logo worked in pastes
and diamanté.
(Christie's) $539

A piece of paper signed by
Buddy Holly in pencil in
common mount with an E.P.,
Rave On, Coral Records, 1958,
signed by Joe Mauldin and
Jerry Alison, 12 x 9in.
(Christie's) $755

Afshar rug, South Persia, last quarter 19th century, 5ft. 7in. x 3ft. 10in.
(Skinner) $440

'Two grey hills' Navajo indian rug, 2ft. 6in. x 4ft. 2in.
(Eldred's) $468

Oriental rug: Kazak, 2ft. 9in. x 4ft. 6in., prayer design on a red field, ivory mihrab.
(Eldred's) $495

A Caucasian Chondzoresk, with three octagonal medallions worked in tones of blue, green, ivory and red within triple border, second half 19th century, 220 x 122cm.
(Finarte) $6,105

An antique Kashgai rug, South Persia, the ivory field decorated with large characteristic 'mother & child' botehs, 6ft. 2in. x 4ft. 10in.
(Phillips) $974

An antique Kashgai rug, South West Persia, the indigo field enclosing a light green central medallion, surrounded by floral scrolls within copper-red spandrels, 6ft. 1in. x 4ft. 9in.
(Phillips) $4,956

A Karaja runner, indigo field closely filled with a variety of medallions in ivory, green, beige and brick, 12ft. 9in. x 3ft. 5in.
(Woolley & Wallis) $397

A Saruk rug, the dark blue field woven all over with flowerheads, around a central ivory stepped floral medallion with pendants, 82 x 51in.
(Christie's) $1,347

Oriental rug: Heriz, 8ft. 4in. x 12ft. 1in., with central medallion, good pile, some moth damage.
(Eldred's) $4,840

Star Ushak carpet, Turkey, late 16th/early 17th century, 11ft. 1in. x 6ft. 2in.
(Phillips) $35,700

A Chondzoresk Kazak rug, brick field with pale green center, 7ft. 10in. x 4ft. 2in.
(Woolley & Wallis) $3,276

Arabesque Ushak or 'Lotto' rug, Turkey, early 16th century, 6ft. 10in. x 4ft.
(Phillips) $26,775

A Bakshaigh carpet from northern Persia, the field dominated by a large lozenge with a heavily stylized Tree of Life pattern, second half 19th century, 420 x 335cm.
(Finarte) $12,888

An antique Yuruk Kellei, Eastern Anatolia, the copper-red field covered with multi-colored polygons within an indigo border, 8ft. 2in. x 4ft. 10in.
(Phillips) $2,832

A Chinese Ningxia carpet, the central medallion of classic stylized dragon motifs picked out in ivory on a plain blue ground, second half 19th century, 355 x 278cm.
(Finarte) $5,766

An antique Kazak rug, the field with four rectangular medallions containing serrated floral motif, 6ft. 5in. x 3ft. 9in.
(Christie's) $1,221

Oriental rug: Heriz, 7ft. 7in. x 10ft. 10in., central medallion on a rust field with floral and geometric design elements, areas of slight wear.
(Eldred's) $2,640

An antique Qashqai rug, the indigo field with diagonal rows of stylized lozenges, 6ft. 5in. x 3ft. 9in.
(Christie's) $2,768

An antique Chelaberd rug, South Caucasus, the rose-red field decorated with two large characteristic sunburst medallions, 7ft. 5in. x 4ft. 6in.
(Phillips) $7,965

A machine tufted woollen carpet, rectangular, brown and gray ground with green and gray abstract foliate design, circa 1935, 282 x 180cm.
(Christie's) $766

An antique Kazak rug, South West Caucasus, the ocher yellow field with hooked motifs around a keyhole medallion, 6ft. 1in. x 3ft. 2in.
(Phillips) $2,655

A fine Shirvan rug, indigo field with two rows of octagons in indigo, brick and ivory divided by rectangular plaques extending out of the field, 6ft. 4in. x 4ft. 2in.
(Woolley & Wallis)
$1,850

Art Deco wool rug, repeating clamshell design in shades of green, 143in. long.
(Skinner) $1,100

A Lesghi rug, North East Caucasus, the field in copper-red and indigo with stylized octagonal motifs around three characteristic star medallions, 5ft. 4in. x 3ft. 5in.
(Phillips) $2,655

An antique Marasali prayer rug, Shirvan, East Caucasus, the yellow mihrab filled with an all over trellis containing stylized floral motifs, 4ft. 7in. x 3ft. 7in.
(Phillips) $2,655

A Kurdish long rug, the deep indigo field filled with large typical medallions, quartered in various colors surrounded by small floral motifs, 9ft. 11in. x 5ft. 1in.
(Woolley & Wallis) $740

A Bijar Kelim, the beige field with ivory jewel pendant medallion, arrowhead and flèche-type motifs in the field, 5ft. 8in. x 3ft. 8in.
(Woolley & Wallis) $389

RUGS

A fine antique Perepidil rug, North East Caucasus, the indigo field decorated in characteristic fashion with ram's horn motifs, 6ft. 2in. x 4ft. 4in.
(Phillips)   **$4,956**

Pictorial hooked rug, America, late 19th century, depicting a trout, worked in shades of purple, blue, cream, green, brown, beige and red, 18$^{1}/_{2}$ x 32in.
(Skinner)   **$468**

Penny table rug, America, late 19th/early 20th century, wool appliqués in shades of red, yellow, orange, green, blue, tan and brown, 61in. long.
(Skinner)   **$825**

A Lambalo-Kazak, South West Caucasus, the sky blue field with three lozenge medallions in indigo, ivory and rose-red, 7ft. 3in. x 5ft. 8in.
(Phillips)   **$4,425**

A Kuba Konagkend long rug, the narrow indigo panel with all over ivory trellised skeletal motifs with flowerheads and other motifs within, late 19th century, 7ft. 3in. x 3ft. 2in.
(Woolley & Wallis)   **$1,850**

A fine Shirvan rug, the indigo field with a central row of ivory skeletal medallions enclosing tarantula motifs and linked with pale green winged medallions, 5ft. 6in. x 4ft. 2in.
(Woolley & Wallis)   **$1,332**

An Abadeh rug, the ivory field closely filled with zil-i-sultan design, the indigo vases each with a large floral arrangement and flanked by pairs of birds, 7ft. 1in. x 4ft. 10in.
(Woolley & Wallis)   **$1,443**

An antique Chinese saddle rug, late 18th/early 19th century, the golden brown field decorated with small stylized tree motifs around two circular ornaments, 4ft. 1in. x 2ft.
(Phillips)   **$673**

Kurd-Bidjar rug, Northwest Persia, late 19th/early 20th century, the navy blue Herati decorated hexagonal medallion with large sky blue 'anchor' pendants, 7ft. x 4ft. 4in.
(Skinner)   **$1,430**

An antique Bergama rug, West Anatolia, the copper red field with a characteristic central rectangular panel, 6ft. 1in. x 4ft. 11in.
(Phillips) $5,950

An antique Yomut Okbash, West Turkestan, the copper-red ground decorated with characteristic tree design, 1ft. 10in. x 2ft. 2in.
(Phillips) $1,274

A fine Khamseh rug, stepped edge indigo field with all over large light red medallions, 6ft. x 4ft. 4in.
(Woolley & Wallis) $1,113

A Kazak rug, the tomato field woven with a blue lobed medallion set with 'serpents', the blue spandrels with plants, 7ft. x 5ft. 3in.
(Lawrence Fine Art) $702

Cloudband Karabagh rug, South Caucasus, late 19th/early 20th century, two and a half large red and sky blue hexagonal medallions, 9ft. 7in. x 4ft. 4in.
(Skinner) $770

An American floral hooked rug, probably New England, early 19th century, worked in bright tones of red, blue, green, beige and brown shirred fabric, approximately 49 x 62in.
(Sotheby's) $7,425

A Persian carpet, possibly Kashan, the dark blue field woven all over with lobed medallions and foliate tendrils, 12ft. 6in. x 10ft.
(Lawrence Fine Art) $6,283

Yomud Ensi, West Turkestan, early 20th century, the quartered garden plan of small midnight blue plants on the aubergine field, 5ft. x 4ft. 10in.
(Skinner) $413

An antique Salor Chuval, West Turkestan, late 18th/early 19th century, this rare Turkoman artefact was acquired in Central Asia before 1920, 2ft. 7in. x 4ft. 8in.
(Phillips) $11,505

Melas prayer rug, Southwest Anatolia, late 19th century, the small red and gold diamond medallion rests on a rust field, 6ft. 2in. x 4ft. 8in.
(Skinner) $660

An antique Mudjur prayer rug, the apple-green mihrab decorated by a central stylized floral stem in flame-red, 5ft. 9in. x 3ft. 11in.
(Phillips) $2,083

A Heriz carpet, North West Persia, the copper-red field with a design of large palmettes and feathered leaves and vines, 11ft. 11in. x 7ft. 10in.
(Phillips) $1,947

An antique Perepidil rug, North East Caucasus, the indigo field decorated with characteristic ram's horn motifs, palmettes and stylized griffins, 7ft. 5in. x 4ft. 9inn.
(Phillips) $2,478

An antique Tekke rug, West Turkestan, the madder red field enclosing a characteristic pattern of linked guls, within a border decorated with typical geometric motifs, 4ft. 6in. x 3ft. 6in.
(Phillips) $1,416

Yomud Ensi, West Turkestan, late 19th century, the quartered aubergine-brown field inset with staggered rows of bracket motifs in red, midnight blue, gold and blue-green, 5ft. 8in. x 4ft. 7in.
(Skinner) $825

An Oushak rug, possibly 17th century, the light yellow ground covered by reciprocal and serrated leaf forms surrounded by a wide border of light chestnut red.
(Christie's) $13,200

An antique Kashgai rug, South West Persia, the indigo field with large flowering shrubs around a square center panel, 7ft. 2in. 5ft. 9in.
(Phillips) $1,062

A Sarouk rug, the cream field woven with flowering tendrils, blue spandrels, the dark blue main border with a palmette meander, 6ft. 6in. x 4ft. 7in.
(Lawrence Fine Art) $3,326

Needlework sampler, *Abigail E. Read*, New England, circa 1820, worked with silk threads in shades of blue, green, pink, yellow, coral, cream and black on linen ground, framed, 17³/₄ x 17¹/₂in.
(Skinner) $5,500

Needlework sampler, *Louisa Perkins at Miss Williams School, Boston, June 18th, 1817*, bands of alphabet and verse over inscription, 14 x 12¹/₂in.
(Skinner) $440

Needlework sampler, *Elizabeth A. Goshen's work*, Chester County, Pennsylvania, circa 1825, worked with silk threads in shades of blue, green, yellow, cream, peach on a natural linen, 23¹/₂ x 27¹/₂in.
(Skinner) $8,800

A fine needlework sampler: signed *Harriet Weiser*, probably Reading, Pennsylvania, dated *1830*, executed in a variety of blue, green, yellow, pink, and brown stitches, 26¹/₄ x 17³/₄in.
(Sotheby's) $11,000

A sampler by Stwart *(sic)* Kerr worked in red, green and pink wools with alphabets and stylized bands, 22 x 10in., Scottish, 18th century.
(Christie's) $726

A needlework sampler, anonymous, probably Pennsylvania, mid-19th century, with the figure of a shepherd and a lady flanking a large brown and white cow, 17 x 17in.
(Sotheby's) $2,310

Needlework sampler, *Wrought by Charlotte Chapin in the 12th year of her age 1842*, Massachusetts, worked in silk threads, 18¹/₄ x 15¹/₄in.
(Skinner) $1,540

Needlework sampler, *Lydia Ashleys sampler, aged eleven years, worked September 1798*, Massachusetts, worked in silk threads in shades of pink, green, yellow and burnt umber, framed, 10 x 7in.
(Skinner) $1,045

Framed antique sampler with alphabet, verse, flowers and animals, by Sarah Baker, 1795, 12¹/₂ x 10¹/₂in.
(Eldred's) $770

A sampler, by Christian Mackenzie, 1830, with a verse *Why should we start*, also with trailing floral patterns and spot motifs of trees and plants above a large house, 17 x 13in.
(Christie's) $1,456

A needlework sampler, Hannah Parry, 1828, Pennsylvania, worked in green, brown, yellow, red, blue and black silk threads, with a central medallion inscribed *Hannah Parry's in the tenth year of her age 1828*, 21 x 13¹/4in.
(Christie's) $2,420

A fine and rare needlework sampler, Elizabeth Beale, probably Pennsylvania, dated *1832*, worked in a variety of pale pink, yellow, green and blue silk stitches, 21¹/2 x 23¹/2in.
(Sotheby's) $15,525

A fine needlework sampler: Mary Clothilda Dare, Chester County, Pennsylvania, dated *1837*, executed in a variety of pink, blue, yellow, green, white and red silk stitches, 25⁵/8 x 23¹/2in.
(Sotheby's) $22,000

A long sampler worked in colored silks, with spot motifs, with borders of Tudor roses and sprays of flowers, 34 x 8¹/2in.
(Christie's) $2,722

A fine needlework sampler, signed Hannah McCriller, Canterbury, New Hampshire, dated 1795, worked in a variety of green, blue, pink, white and black silk stitches, 17³/4 x 17in.
(Sotheby's) $2,760

A needlework sampler, signed *Elisabeth Landis*, Pennsylvania, dated *1831*, worked in a variety of red, lavender, yellow and green, 15³/4 x 15³/4in.
(Sotheby's) $1,150

A good early Victorian child's needlework sampler worked with a verse, buildings, sportsmen, birds, butterflies and trees by Martha Bitterson, aged 9, and dated *1845*, 16¹/2 x 17¹/2in.
(Bearne's) $1,412

Needlework sampler, *Polly Wilde Sampler Wrought in Salem, June 1796* and further inscribed *Maffachufetts State Salem*, 13³/4 x 12¹/2in.
(Skinner) $8,800

A cristallo ceramie scent bottle with a head and shoulders profile portrait of a Roman with wavy hair, 8cm.
(Phillips) $609

A Victorian cut glass egg shape scent bottle, the silver gilt cover, maker Samson Morden London 1885, cased.
(Woolley & Wallis) $775

An early French clear glass scent bottle of flattened pear shape, mold-blown with the Royal fleur-de-lys on one side and three hearts on the reverse within leaf scrolls.
(Phillips) $812

A blue overlay double-ended scent bottle in clear glass, cut with rows of panels with blue dentate motifs, 14cm.
(Phillips) $325

A French gilt-metal mounted kingwood and crossbanded scent casket, by Tahan, Paris, the base with a quarter veneered hinged top and parquetry sides, late 19th century.
(Christie's) $553

A Böttger Hausmalerei chinoiserie scent-bottle of pilgrim-flask form applied with Frauenköpf masks, painted in the Augsburg workshop of Sabina Auffenwerth, circa 1725, 8cm. high.
(Christie's) $4,435

An attractive silver mounted clear glass scent bottle, of globular form with diamond and slice cut decoration, by Levy & Saloman, 12.5cm. high.
(Spencer's) $318

A ceramic scent bottle, Chelsea Pottery, designed as a kneeling young woman and a peacock, silver colored metal mount, 7cm.
(Lawrence) $262

A façon de Venise scent bottle of flattened pear shape and in clear glass trailed with bands of white festooning, 9.5cm.
(Phillips) $223

An Italian millefiori scent bottle of diskoid shape, both sides with a cane of a bearded Persian, the ground with a sprinkling of aventurine, metal cover and chain, 6.5cm.
(Phillips) $650

English cameo dolphin perfume, attributed to Webb, undulating yellow body overlaid in white, cameo cut and carved as the swimming fish, 4¹/₄in. long.
(Skinner) $4,950

A clear glass scent bottle of oval shape with hinged repoussé cover and silver plaque on the front engraved with a love-bird in an everlasting knot, 10cm.
(Phillips) $183

A three-colour cameo scent flask, probably Thomas Webb and Sons, circa 1890, the light blue glass overlaid in white and lilac and carved with flowers and leaves, 2¹/₂in. high.
(Sotheby's) $818

Pair of French porcelain scent decanters, decorated in the Imari style, each with an umbrella shaped stopper, 9in. overall.
(G. A. Key) $489

A Pellatt and Green 'cristallo ceramie' ovoid scent bottle and stopper, set with a sulphide of Cupid leaning on a pillar above the inscription *Garde a vous*, 7.5cm.
(Phillips) $1,056

Extremely fine French glass dressing table scent decanter and stopper, signed *E Galle Nancy*, 6¹/₂in. overall.
(G. A. Key) $667

A silver mounted glass perfume flask by the Goldsmiths and Silversmiths Co., 1918/9, the silver top incised with stylized garlands, 12.5cm. high.
(Finarte) $428

French porcelain set of three scent bottles and stoppers, decorated with floral swags, gilt brass holder, 6in. high.
(G. A. Key) $255

A rare brass circumferentor signed *G. ADAMS*, with four detachable sighting vanes, twin rotating verniers, compass box divided 10°–360°, late 18th century, 14½in. wide.
(Christie's)   **$1,648**

An oxidised brass universal equinoctial brass dial, engraved on the hour ring *W.&.S JONES*, with spring loaded gnomon, mid 19th century, 5⅜in. wide.
(Christie's)   **$1,403**

An early 19th-century lacquered brass and mahogany vacuum pump, with double rack action, and a rare pear-shaped endiometer.
(Christie's)   **$1,786**

A lacquered brass universal equinoctial compass dial, engraved on the hour ring *Troughton & Simms*, in fitted mahogany case, 19th century, 6in. wide.
(Christie's)   **$833**

A Hamilton Model 22 deckwatch, 21 jeweled lever movement, matt silver dial signed *HAMILTON, LANCASTER, P.A., U.S.A.*, 8in. wide.
(Christie's)   **$672**

An exceptionally rare 19th-century oxidized, lacquered brass and silvered equatorial/azimuth sextant, signed on the latitude ring *Patent Applied for by Wm. A. Burt*, 12⅝in. high.
(Christie's)   **$14,707**

A plaster phrenological head, the cranium incised and marked out in black lines, 19th century, 6¼in. high.
(Christie's)   **$139**

A rare lacquered brass railroad surveying compass, the silvered compass dial signed *W. & L. E. Gurley, Troy, N.Y.*, and further engraved *Jas, W. Queen & Co., Agents, Philada, and New York*, 16½in. wide.
(Christie's)   **$882**

A silver plated resonator ear trumpet, signed *F C Rein & Son*, with decorative engraving, fretwork funnel cover, and bone earpiece, circa 1865, 7½in. high.
(Christie's)   **$1,128**

A 19th-century surveying compass, the silvered dial signed *W. & L. E. Gurley, Troy, N.Y.,* the blued-iron needle with jeweled pivot and clamp.
(Christie's) **$1,156**

A 'Dr Butcher's' bone saw signed *Perry Greenwich*, with cross hatched ebony pistol grip handle, the wrought iron frame with central adjustment screw, 12³/₄in. wide.
(Christie's) **$121**

A rare early 19th-century lacquered brass transit telescopic surveyor's compass, the telescope with bubble level and cross wire adjustors, 10in. wide.
(Christie's) **$1,786**

A French two-day marine chronometer, the silvered dial signed *E. DELEPINE No. 1693 A ST NICOLAS, PRÈS DIEPPE,* external brass drop handles, the whole in outer guard box, 6³/₄in. square.
(Christie's) **$4,412**

A rare early 19th-century miniature equatorial surveying telescope, signed on the base plate W & S Jones, the telescope with twin pin-hole sights and draw-tube focusing, 9¹/₂in. high.
(Christie's) **$4,622**

A mid 19th-century lacquered brass compound monocular microscope, sgned on the Y-shaped base *A. ROSS, LONDON,* in a mahogany case with six graduated drawers, 20⁵/₈in. high.
(Christie's) **$4,202**

A late 19th-century brass transit telescope, by Troughton & Simms, the 1³/₄ inch diameter telescope with lens hood and dust cap, 20¹/₄in. wide.
(Christie's) **$1,891**

A porcelain phrenological bust with impressed mark by *F Bridges Phrenologist*, the cranium outlined in black, 19th century, 5⁷/₈in. high.
(Christie's) **$781**

A fine lacquered brass transit theodolite, signed *Thomas Jones Charing Cross London*, the telescope with right angle eyepiece on sliding plate, early 19th century, 17¹/₄in. high.
(Christie's) **$9,544**

A Millionaire calculator by Hans W. Egli, with brass bed, facility for addition, subtracting, division and multiplication, 25¹/₂in. wide.
(Christie's) $1,079

A Curta Type 1 calculator, sectioned for display with separate components, in fitted green case, by Contina, Liechtenstein.
(Christie's) $1,187

A brass sundial cast in relief with a medieval scene of Saints, under Romanesque arches, the dial with hour scale, late 19th century, 13¹/₂in. high.
(Christie's) $302

A rare male contraceptive device, of animal membrane, with erotic illustration, indistinct inscription, with silk tie, mid 19th century, 8³/₄in. long.
(Christie's) $3,818

An 18th-century lodestone, with brass mounts and suspension ring, in fishskin case, 2in. high.
(Christie's) $2,311

A rare male contraceptive device, of animal membrane, with erotic illustration, indistinct inscription, with silk tie, mid 19th century, 8¹/₂in. long.
(Christie's) $5,206

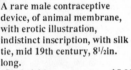

A Regency turned mahogany and engraved brass terrestrial globe, English, dated *1833*, on ring-turned legs joined by turned stretchers, height 15in.
(Sotheby's) $1,610

A 19th-century lacquered brass grain balance, stamped on the measuring arm *H. Kohlbusch 59 Nassailsiny* in fitted mahogany case, 14¹/₄in. wide.
(Christie's) $420

A 20th century two-day marine chronometer, by Thomas Mercer, movement with Earnshaw spring detent escapement, helical spring and bi-metallic balance.
(Bonhams) $856

An oxidized and lacquered brass aneroid barometer signed *J. Goldschmid a Zurich*, with internal scale, 6in. wide.
(Christie's) $756

A part surgeon's amputation set, signed *LAUNDY*, with a small bone saw, in fitted velvet lined mahogany case (large bone saw missing) circa 1800, 16¼in. wide.
(Christie's) $1,187

A lacquered brass barograph, unsigned, with recording drum, key, mechanism, ink bottle and ink needle, 14¾in. wide.
(Christie's) $1,079

A brass miner's dial signed *Stanley Gt. Turnstile Holburn London*, with gimballed ring, two folding sighting vanes, 12¼in. wide, 19th century.
(Christie's) $518

A late 19th-century mahogany slide cabinet of 24 drawers, containing a large collection of professional and amateur slide preparations by various preparers, 24in. high.
(Christie's) $1,891

An 18th-century brass surveying level, signed on the limb *Baddely Albrighton*, the telescope with dust slides and bubble level, 19½in. wide.
(Christie's) $1,008

A Victorian black-painted terrestrial globe on stand, A. H. Andrews Co., Chicago, second half 19th century, 34¾in. high.
(Sotheby's) $1,650

A Thatcher's rotary calculator by Keuffel & Esser, New York, with instructions on baseboard and mahogany case, 24in. wide.
(Christie's) $1,036

A late 18th-century German fruitwood diptych dial, with printed and colored paper plates, the cover with table of latitudes signed *Er. Chr. Stockert*, 4½in. long.
(Christie's) $630

A late 18th-century mining compass, unsigned, the mahogany frame incorporating the compass with silvered dial, 13¹/₄in. high.
(Christie's) **$756**

Cased ebony and brass octant, English, 19th century, by Spencer, Browning and Co.
(Eldred's) **$440**

A gimballed azimuth compass, the 7 inch compass with silvered quadrantly divided reversed engraved outer ring signed *J. SPEYER AMSTERDAM*, 12in. square.
(Christie's) **$1,261**

An 18th century boxwood nocturnal, with heart pierced shaped handle, index arm and rotating disc stamped with lunar and solar scales, 10in. high.
(Spencer's) **$2,730**

A set of Victorian blond oak jockey scales, the seat with **square paneled back,** downward outward scroll open arms on a rectangular base, 3ft. 2in. wide.
(Spencer's) **$726**

An early 19th century brass portable sundial, mounted on a walnut quadrant, the turned stem to a molded circular base.
(Woolley & Wallis) **$5,910**

A late 18th-century 'Culpeper'-type brass microscope, unsigned, with draw tube focusing for a numbered set of five objectives, 16¹/₂in. high.
(Christie's) **$1,576**

A 19th-century lacquered brass, three-draw 1¹/₂ inch telescope, signed *Dollond*, with ebonized outer body tube and folding tripod stand, 10¹/₂in. wide.
(Christie's) **$966**

A 19th-century brass gyroscope, of large size on turned pillar support and iron base, 21in. high.
(Christie's) **$798**

A 3 inch reflecting telescope, signed on the back plate *JAMES SHORT LONDON*, on alt-azimuth mounting with column support, with inswept cabriole legs, 21in. wide.
(Christie's) **$3,362**

An articulated human skeleton (dismantled) in carrying case with trade label *Established A.D. 1815, Millikin & Lawley*, 22in. wide.
(Christie's) **$191**

A fine lacquered brass monocular microscope, signed *Smith & Beck*, with rack and pinion focusing, triple nosepiece, square mechanical stage, and plano-concave mirror.
(Christie's) **$1,041**

A late 19th-century Wheatstone-pattern telegraph receiver, the lacquered brass mechanism mounted on a mahogany base, 12½in. wide.
(Christie's) **$945**

A late 17th/18th century white-metal astrological volvelle, unsigned, with punched numerals for the calendar scale and engraved representations for the constellations, 7¼in. diameter.
(Christie's) **$164**

An oxidized and lacquered brass 'Hendersons' rapid traverser, by E. T. Newton & Son, with 10 inch diameter, in fitted mahogany case with maker's trade label inside lid, 12in. wide.
(Christie's) **$882**

An 18th-century brass pair of gunner's calipers, signed on one arm *G. Adams London*, with scales for Brafs Guns, Iron Guns, and other scales, 12in. long.
(Christie's) **$1,576**

An early 19th-century lacquered brass 'Cary'-type pocket botanical microscope, unsigned, the rectangular pillar with rack and pinion focusing, 5½in. wide.
(Christie's) **$672**

A 19th-century brass surveying level, signed on the dial *W. J. Young Maker Philadelphia*, the silvered scale divided in four quadrants, 14⅝in. wide.
(Christie's) **$735**

A South German polished steel door lock and key, shooting one bolt, embellished with engraved foliage and applied rosettes, 17th/18th century, 10³/₄in. wide.
(Christie's) $1,636

A silver sick syphon with makers mark for *T&E Phipps London 1802* (George III), with perforated foot, with screw head attachment, 5¹/₈in. long.
(Christie's) $382

A pair of George IV, mother-of-pearl and steel razors, signed *LAMPREY 28 DAME ST*, the mother-of-pearl guards engraved with crown and *GR IV*.
(Christie's) $121

A brass binnacle and compass signed *Cornelius Knudsen, Copenhagen*, the compass signed *AB Lyth, Stockholm*, 19th century, 140cm. high.
(Auktionsverket) $1,189

An Irish brass-mounted rosewood door lock plate, late 18th century, and another similar, 15in. wide.
(Christie's) $1,540

A fine lacquered brass binocular microscope signed *C. BAKER*, the body tubes with rack and pinion eyepiece focusing, in fitted mahogany case, with a substantial collection of accessories.
(Christie's) $6,247

A rare 17th century solar quadrant of polygonal form, the vertical lid with hour rings.
(Duran) $2,106

A lacquered brass barograph/barometer, unsigned, with recording drum, key, mechanism, ink bottle, ink needle, and circular weather indicator, 14¹/₄in. wide.
(Christie's) $1,735

A rare male contraceptive device, of animal membrane, with erotic illustration, indistinct inscription, with silk tie, mid 19th century, 8¹/₂in. long.
(Christie's) $3,818

A Dutch de Elsevier globe, by Dr. G. J. Dozy, Rotterdam, manufactured on a similar principle to the Betts portable globe, 30in. long.
(Christie's) $588

A rare field surgeon's amputation saw with folding horn handle and blade guard, circa 1780, 17¼in.
(Christie's) $521

A South German polished steel door lock and key, shooting one bolt, engraved with scrolls and grotesque beasts, 17th/18th century, 12½in. wide.
(Christie's) $1,733

A set of lithotomy instruments, some signed *STODART*, in velvet lined mahogany case, 16¾in. wide, mid-19th century.
(Christie's) $1,187

A pair of Regency brass-bound mahogany globes by J. W. Cary, on turned baluster stem and downswept tripod base with spade feet, brass caps and casters, 45in. high, overall.
(Christie's) $19,355

Victorian brass strut back table thermometer with brass cherub mounted top, 12in. high.
(G. A. Key) $159

Vintage oak cased Continental wall telephone.
(G. A. Key) $101

An early 19th century terrestrial globe, marked *Newtons Terrestrial Globe, Discovery*, mahogany mounted with brass meridian ring, 31cm. diameter.
(Auktionsverket) $1,784

A brass ship's chronometer in walnut case, signed *Charles Frodsham, London No. 3337*, circa 1862.
(Auktionsverket) $1,083

An 18th-century compound monocular microscope, signed on the body tube *B. Martin*, the Y-shaped stand in pyramid-shaped mahogany case, 14in. high.
(Christie's) $2,521

An 18th-century brass 'Butterfield'-type octagonal compass dial, signed *N. BION A-PARIS*, engraved on the underside with the latitudes of twenty-four continental cities and towns, 3¼in. long.
(Christie's) $1,366

A 19th-century lacquered brass inverted microscope, signed *NACHET a Paris*, with circular stage, in case, 10in. high.
(Christie's) $3,572

An 18th-century 'Augsburg'-pattern gilt-brass universal equinoctial compass dial, signed on the base of the compass box *And. Vogler*, 2³⁄₈in. wide.
(Christie's) $1,261

A rare plaster demonstration model of a womb with internal foetus, indistinctly signed and dated *ANZ – Doctr Fecit anno 1875*, probably French, 6½ x 5in.
(Christie's) $1,128

An instructional globe, unsigned, dated *1910*, the horizon ring with zodiac, time and calendar scales on plinth base, 10½in. diameter.
(Christie's) $798

C. Smith, Smiths terrestrial globe, a rare 12 inch diameter terrestrial table globe, with twelve colored paper gores, showing the voyages of Capt. Gore and Capt. Cook.
(Christie's) $2,426

A lacquered brass enema signed *MAYER & MELTZER*, with double nozzle and release mechanism, in fitted velvet lined case, 11⁹⁄₁₀in. wide.
(Christie's) $416

A 19th-century surveyor's compass, signed on the silvered dial *W. & L. E. Gurley, Troy, N.Y.*, the blued-iron needle with jeweled cap and pivot, 6½in. high.
(Christie's) $546

A late 19th-century lacquered brass compound monocular universal microscope, signed on the body tube *A Microscope Achromatique Universal de Charles Chevalier, Imperieur Opticien, Palais Royal, Paris.*
(Christie's) **$2,311**

A World War I field surgeon's instruments case, signed *Meyer & Meltzer London*, in velvet lined brass bound mahogany case, with protective metal casing, 17½in. wide.
(Christie's) **$1,215**

A rare equinoctial sundial signed *PHILIPS' SUN-DIAL*, with paper card dial, in paper card carrying box, 8¾in. high.
(Christie's) **$729**

A late 17th-century brass perpetual calendar, unsigned, inscribed *Allgemeiner und Imer Werender Calender*, 2in. diameter.
(Christie's) **$882**

A 19th-century oxidized and lacquered brass surveyor's transit theodolite, signed on the silvered compass dial *W. & L. E. Gurley, Troy, N.Y.*, 13½in. high.
(Christie's) **$840**

A mid 18th-century Dutch brass circumferentor, signed and dated *J.v. Wyk, Amsterd. 1759.*, 12⅛in. diameter.
(Christie's) **$1,576**

A 19th-century mining tacheometer, by E T Newton & Son, Camborne, Cornwall, with trough compass and staff mounting, overall height 12¾in.
(Christie's) **$546**

A 19th-century lacquered brass surveyor's cross, signed on the silvered compass dial *W & T Gilbert London*, in mahogany case, 4¾in. wide.
(Christie's) **$840**

An early 19th-century brass universal equinoctial ring dial, unsigned, the meridian ring with sliding suspension ring, 4¼in. diameter.
(Christie's) **$1,723**

A brass theodolite by Alexis Wery, Liège, using the Lenoir system, circa 1880.
(Auction Team Köln)
$695

Galileo aluminum opera glasses with enameled decoration of dogs playing, circa 1875, marked *Iris, Paris*.
(Auction Team Köln) $131

A Karl Krause board cutter for coarser book binding board with manual drive and a rare corner cutter, cut width 70cm.
(Auction Team Köln)
$695

A J. R. Delius sterilizing chamber, with copper boiler on iron legs, with Bunsen burner, circa 1910.
(Auction Team Köln)
$346

A hearing aid with copper resonance box and brass tube, circa 1900.
(Auction Team Köln)
$386

A Loewe 3 NFB valve, filament in order, otherwise untested, with copy of the British patent for Dr. Siegmund Loewe, dated *19.12.1928*, 1929.
(Auction Team Köln)
$186

An English Hearson's Patent Biological Incubator, for the culture of micro-organisms, with gas heating regulator.
(Auction Team Köln)
$293

An early wood and brass polarimeter by Griffin & Sons of London, on cast iron tripod stand with wooden shaft, circa 1860.
(Auction Team Köln)
$216

A mechanical Brandt Automatic Cashier money changer with full keyboard, 1921.
(Auction Team Köln)
$170

French mother of pearl and
brass deluxe opera glasses, circa
1870.
(Auction Team Köln) $131

Railway steam valve with brass
bell, on wooden base, circa 1920.
(Auction Team Köln) $69

Plated cast-iron Enterprise
Colonial ware shop scales, with
four weights, circa 1920.
(Auction Team Köln) $69

A de Maelzel metronome by
Seth Thomas Clocks,
Thomastown CT, in mahogany
casing and with spring wound
drive.
(Auction Team Köln) $93

A brass theodolite by Cary of
London with silver scale,
compass and two vials, on ebony
base, circa 1830.
(Auction Team Köln)
                        $1,698

A Curta Type II four-function
sliding cylinder calculator, the
smallest ever built, by Curt
Herzstark, 1948.
(Auction Team Köln)
                        $540

A Swift & Son, London, brass
compound microscope, with
double objective revolver with
original ⅙ and 1in. optics,
boxed, circa 1900.
(Auction Team Köln)
                        $386

US patent model A. C. Carey
knitting machine, a
demonstration model for the
patent application of 18.4.1865,
with copy of the patent.
(Auction Team Köln)
                        $463

Wooden aneroid wall barometer
with two-color ceramic dial and
carved and turned housing,
bears initials *J.C.*, circa 1880,
35cm. high.
(Auction Team Köln) $117

A late 18th-century lacquered brass 2 inch reflecting telescope, signed on the back plate *Made by GEO ADAMS*, the leather covered 15in. long body tube, with speculum mirrors.
(Christie's) $3,152

An exhibition multi-blade pocket knife with ninety-six blades and mother-of-pearl scales, marked *Hoffritz N.Y. Germany* and *Stainless*, 4³/₄in. long (folded).
(Christie's) $2,603

A silver plated 'London dome' ear trumpet signed *F.C. Rein & Son Patenteed*, with decorative engraving, and bone earpiece, circa 1865, 6¹/₂in. high.
(Christie's) $781

An oxidized brass transit, signed on the silvered compass dial *W. & L. E. Gurley, Troy, N.Y.*, and further engraved *F W Lincoln Jr. & Co., Agents, Boston, Mass.*, in fitted mahogany case, 13¹/₂in. wide.
(Christie's) $1,051

An early 19th-century lacquered brass 4³/₄ inch reflecting telescope, unsigned, the 30³/₄in. long body tube with speculum mirrors and screw-rod focusing, 33³/₄in. wide.
(Christie's) $3,992

A set of drawing instruments with trade label *W. & S. Jones Optician*, with bone rectangular protractor, dividers, protractor, parallel rule and other instruments in fitted fishskin case, early 19th century, 6³/₄in. high.
(Christie's) $278

A 19th-century two-day marine chronometer, the top-plate of the movement signed *Poole, LONDON 803*, the silvered dial signed *A. Bruce, MANCHESTER 803*, 6¹/₄in. square.
(Christie's) $3,152

A wood-body hand-cranked projection shutter with applied paper labels *Cinématographe. Fabrication Française Déposé E.V.L. Déposé.*
(Christie's) $701

A late 19th century phrenological porcelain bust signed *PHRENOLOGY BY L. N. FOWLER*, the cranium divided in areas controlling emotion, 11³/₄in. high.
(Christie's) $2,776

Whale's tooth, 19th century, with 20th century engraved decoration of a ship approaching a lighthouse, 7in. long.
(Eldred's) $330

Fine whale's tooth, 19th century, one side depicts a whale hunt with a whale destroying a whale boat over a whale and harpoons, 5³/₄in. long.
(Eldred's) $3,190

Whale's tooth, 19th century, one side with 20th century decoration of a full-rigged ship.
(Eldred's) $165

Scrimshaw busk, America, late 19th century, engraved with figure of Columbia, reverse initialed *FS*, 12¹/₂in. long.
(Skinner) $440

Pair of polychrome engraved whale's teeth, 19th century, each decorated with square-rigged ships under full sail, 4¹/₄in. high.
(Skinner) $3,740

Scrimshaw busk, America, 19th century, engraved with rising sun, mourning scene, bird and primrose, 13¹/₄in. long.
(Skinner) $467

A fine engraved sperm whale tooth, early 19th century, engraved on one side with a bust portrait of Washington, the reverse with a bust portrait of Lafayette, 5¹/₂in. high.
(Sotheby's) $1,320

Undecorated whale's tooth, 19th century, polished, 6in. long.
(Eldred's) $99

A fine engraved scrimshaw sperm whale's tooth, American, 19th century, the broad-sided tooth engraved with a depiction of a harbor and townscape, height 7¹/₄in.
(Sotheby's) $2,070

SEWING MACHINES

An American Willcox and Gibbs chain stitch machine with unusual manual drive, circa 1872.
(Auction Team Köln) $117

An American Fairy/Madame Demorest running stitch machine with table clamp, circa 1863.
(Auction Team Köln) $2,700

An American New England chain stitch machine, with fine gold and foliate decoration, circa 1880.
(Auction Team Köln) $216

An Original Express sewing machine by Guhl and Harbeck, Hamburg, circa 1890.
(Auction Team Köln) $89

German Casige No. 205 collapsible child's sewing machine, circa 1953, very rare.
(Auction Team Köln) $232

A New Avona oscillating shuttle machine by the New Home Sewing Machine Co., Orange, MA, USA, circa 1900.
(Auction Team Köln) $186

An American Wilson chain stitch machine, with unusual second thread holder welded on, circa 1870.
(Auction Team Köln) $1,040

An American Grover & Baker double chain stitch grip machine, on turned wooden stand, 1872.
(Auction Team Köln) $2,470

An American Monitor chain stitch machine, finely decorated and on paw feet, circa 1864.
(Auction Team Köln) $926

US patent model Singer
buttonhole machine, lacking
patent details, circa 1880.
(Auction Team Köln)
$772

Home Companion Ideal
oscillating shuttle machine,
ornately decorated, in original
wooden case, 1890.
(Auction Team Köln) $139

An American Shaw & Clark
chain stitch machine, with
closed tower, circa 1864.
(Auction Team Köln)
$2,315

A Hurtu Mod. A, French frame
machine with gilt decoration, on
a wooden plinth, circa 1890.
(Auction Team Köln)
$216

The Muller No. 6 child's chain
stitch sewing machine, lacking
loop drive, circa 1910.
(Auction Team Köln)
$309

A Jones transverse shuttle
machine, with shuttle but
lacking handle, circa 1880.
(Auction Team Köln) $139

US patent model John W.
Lufkin buttonhole sewing
machine, for the US patent no.
242. 462 of 7 June 1881, with all
relevant documentation.
(Auction Team Köln)
$1,698

US patent model R. H. St. John,
prototype for the patent
application no. 219.780 of 16
September 1879, complete with
copy patent, on original wooden
base.
(Auction Team Köln)
$386

La Voyageuse No. 5, a French
ring spool machine by D. Bacle,
Paris, possibly produced by
Clemens Müller, Dresden, circa
1890.
(Auction Team Köln)
$386

Nicolae Ceaucescu, signed **color 5.5 x 8.75 photograph, to** lower white border. (Vennett-Smith) $112

Sir Winston S. Churchill, an excellent signed 7 x 9.5 photograph, with full signature, a slightly shaky example signed in later years. (Vennett-Smith) $1,400

Andy Warhol, signed 8 x 10 to white border, half length. (Vennett-Smith) $224

Mother Teresa, signed 8 x 10 photograph, half length standing with hands clasped together praying. (Vennett-Smith) $88

An unusual 8.5 x 6.5 press photo of a policeman, Jack Gardner, full length walking towards the camera, signed at the base of the photo by Sir Winston S. Churchill and Clement R. Attlee. (Vennett-Smith) $480

Mikhail Gorbachev, signed 8 x 10 photograph, also signed by Brian Mulroney, showing both Gorbachev and Mulroney stood amongst other World Leaders. (Vennett-Smith) $384

Dame Margot Fonteyn, signed postcard, full-length dancing, on point. (Vennett-Smith) $48

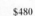

Jim Henson, signed 8 x 10 photograph, also signed by co-creator of the Muppets Frank Oz. (Vennett-Smith) $208

John Philip Sousa, signed sepia postcard with additional two bars from 'The Diplomat', 1908. (Vennett-Smith) $272

Richard Strauss, a fine signed postcard to lower white border, half-length seated writing at desk.
(Vennett-Smith) $496

J. Ramsay MacDonald, British Prime Minister, a good signed 12.5 x 10 photograph, full length standing in front of desk, sending New Year's greetings, 1933–34.
(Vennett-Smith) $120

General Francisco Franco, signed postcard, in uniform, rare.
(Vennett-Smith) $272

Harry Houdini, a signed and inscribed 10 x 8 photograph, the lengthy inscription reading *To my red Pal of Twenty years Dr. R. B. Lothian.*
(Vennett-Smith) $648

Muhammed Ali, signed color 8 x 10 photograph, full length in ring standing over Sonny Liston.
(Vennett-Smith) $120

Maria Callas, an early signed and inscribed 9.5 x 7 photograph, looking downwards and holding her hands to her face, Buenos Aires, 1949.
(Vennett-Smith) $288

Anna Pavlova, signed postcard, full length, standing on point.
(Vennett-Smith) $168

King Edward VIII, a fine signed photograph 5.25 x 7.5 to lower white border, as Prince of Wales, three quarter length standing in uniform, 1922.
(Vennett-Smith) $560

Neil Armstrong, signed 8 x 10 photograph, half length in spacesuit, in profile.
(Vennett-Smith) $208

David Lloyd George, signed
5 x 3¹/₂in., in later years.
(T. Vennett-Smith) $52

Jascha Heifetz, an 8 x 5¹/₂in.
card featuring a photo of Heifetz
playing the violin, dated *1935*.
(T. Vennett-Smith) $148

Vaclav Havel, President of
Czechoslovakia, signed color
7 x 5in.
(T. Vennett-Smith) $67

King Edward VIII, a fine signed
11.5 x 14.5, 'Edward R.I.', as
King, three quarter length in
ceremonial uniform, 1936.
(Vennett-Smith) $640

Franz Lehar, a good signed
postcard, featuring oval image
of Lehar with printed musical
quotation from 'The Merry
Widow', 13th May 1909.
(Vennett-Smith) $224

Ayatollah Khomeini, signed
color 5 x 3¹/₂in., one of the
rarest 20th century political
autographs.
(T. Vennett-Smith) $533

Sir Winston S. Churchill, a good
early signed 6 x 3.5 photograph
to mount, full signature, half
length standing, wearing a
bowtie.

Charlie Chase, American
comedian, a good signed and
inscribed sepia 10¹/₂ x 14in.
(T. Vennett-Smith) $133

Babe Ruth, a rare early signed
6³/₄ x 4³/₄in. book photo, showing
Ruth, full-length in action pose,
1927.
(T. Vennett-Smith) $888

(Vennett-Smith) $832

Augustin Edouart, dated *1840*, silhouette portrait of Stephen Matlack and his dog, 'Rush', free cut black paper mounted on a wash ground, 9³/₄ x 7³/₄in. (Sotheby's) **$2,990**

William James Hubard (1807–1862), free cut black paper silhouette with bronzing mounted on white paper with wash, 12 x 19in. (Sotheby's) **$3,220**

Double watercolor and paper portrait silhouette, The Surrender at Yorktown, early 19th century, 6¹/₂ x 8¹/₂in. (Butterfield & Butterfield) **$2,500**

Royal Victoria Gallery, Sir John Henry and Lady Scourfield, silhouettes cut-out on card with details painted in gold, 10³/₄in. high. (Bonhams) **$941**

Pair of framed 19th century silhouettes depicting black men, by Beaumont, one signed, 11 x 8¹/₂in. (Eldred's) **$303**

John Field, one of a pair of silhouettes of John Stonor (1771–1846) and his wife Helen (née Chadwick) (1773–1852), bronzed silhouettes, painted on plaster, 3¹/₈in. high. (Bonhams)(Two) **$1,078**

Augustin Edouart, Colonel Robert Samuel Hustler, silhouette cut-out on card, signed on obverse and dated *1833*, sepia and pencil background, 11in. high. (Bonhams) **$1,019**

Augustin Edouart (1789–1861), a full-length group; Monsieur Iaac, Monsieur Edmond Jagot, holding a whip and his grandmother Madame Catherine Hyn, rectangular, 9³/₄in. high. (Christie's) **$1,262**

Attributed to George Crowhurst, circa 1830, one of a pair of full length silhouettes of Mr. and Mrs. Mutrie, painted on card, the details with gold and red, 10in. high. (Bonhams) (Two) **$490**

SILVER

George IV silver cake basket, John Edward Terry, London, 1823–24, approximately 34 troy oz.
(Skinner) $1,540

A good late Victorian basket by William Comyns, of bombé flared quatrefoil form, raised upon an elaborately cast and pierced foliate and knurl foot, London 1888, 1492 grammes, 38cm. wide.
(Spencer's) $2,640

A good late George III basket, London 1808, maker's mark either *H.S.* or *S.H.*, 1083 grammes, 31cm. wide.
(Spencer's) $1,290

A large George II circular bread basket, the spreading foot chased with a band of acanthus leaves, by Louis Laroche, 1733, 12¼in. diameter, 79oz.
(Christie's) $65,626

A fine pair of oval boat shape sugar baskets, makers Samuel Roberts Jr, George Cadman & Co., Sheffield 1798, together with a pair of ladles, maker Richard Crossley, London 1794, 14½oz.
(Woolley & Wallis) $1,853

A German oval basket with swing handle and oak leaf border, on oval base with four paw and ball feet, date for 1833, 1130gr.
(Kunsthaus am Museum) $1,610

A good early Victorian silver gilt basket by Robert Hennell, of shaped oval form with openwork overhead swing handle, London 1858, 1052 grammes, 36cm. wide.
(Spencer's) $1,693

A 19th century German silver basket, the sides of leaves, terminating in external hanging spheres, with spiral border and filigree handle, 845gr.
(Duran) $937

A George III oval cake basket, the body with fruiting vine and wheatear decoration, spiral swing handle, London 1762, maker A.S., 33oz.
(Russell Baldwin & Bright) $1,120

BEAKERS

A silver beaker, maker's mark of Nicholas Geoffroy, Newport, Rhode Island, 1795–1817, 2⁷⁄₈in. high, 3oz.
(Christie's) $550

A Continental late 19th century tapering circular beaker on spherical feet and with a molded rim, London 1885, 3¹⁄₂in., 5.75oz.
(Christie's) $246

A silver beaker, maker's mark of Jesse Churchill, Boston, circa 1800, 3³⁄₄in. high, 6oz.
(Christie's) $660

An early Provincial silver beaker of waisted circular form having gilt interior, the exterior having scroll engraved frieze, bears initials C, T.E. and E.H. and bearing date 1579, 3¹⁄₂in. high.
(Russell Baldwin & Bright)
                    $1,379

A German parcel-gilt cage-work beaker and cover, by Frederick Klemm, Dresden, circa 1640, 7¹⁄₂in. high, 731gr.
(Christie's) $62,172

A silver beaker of historical interest, maker's mark of Churchill & Treadwell, Boston, 1805–1813, 3¹⁄₂in. high, 4oz. 10dwt.
(Christie's) $4,400

A plain beaker by Jens Bierring (1762–1801), engraved with three cartouches with laurel leaves, initials and date 1798, Danish, 11cm. high, 180gr.
(Herholdt Jensen) $862

A Continental late 19th century tapering circular beaker, depicting the Philosopher Diogenes and Alexander the Great, Berthold Muller, 5¹⁄₂in., 8.75oz.
(Christie's) $930

An 18th century German white metal beaker, engraved with two bands of strapwork on a matt ground, engraved *Joachim Blecken 1752 8th September*, 8.5cm. high.
(Spencer's) $1,440

BOWLS

Kirk repoussé Sterling fruit bowl, 1903–24, chased floral design, monogrammed, 9⁵/₈in. diameter, approximately 24 troy oz.
(Skinner) $935

Tiffany Sterling footed bowl, circa 1860, approximately 30 troy oz.
(Skinner) $1,870

A Hukin and Heath oval plated fruit bowl with waved rim, the foot applied with flowers, buds and foliage, 38cm. diameter.
(Christie's) $334

An American silver punch bowl, William Gale & Son, New York, 1852, the hemispherical bowl chased with rococo ornament, 63oz., diameter 13¹/₄in.
(Sotheby's) $2,990

A Genoese sugar bowl and cover, the oval body chased with laurel leaves, on paw feet, circa 1790, 12cm. high, 270gr.
(Finarte) $6,050

An Edward VII circular rose bowl, 26cm. diameter, W. H. Sparrow, Birmingham 1907, together with a metal grille and ebonized wood plinth, 33.2oz. weight of silver.
(Bearne's) $1,073

A late Victorian low pedestal bowl, the everted scroll crimped rim over a band of scrolling acanthus leaves, Sheffield 1898, 712 grams, 25cm. diameter.
(Spencer's) $832

Victorian plated rose bowl with rope decorated border, chased center with cupid and dome foot.
(G. A. Key) $165

A C. R. Ashbee hammered silver bowl, with pierced design of stylized fruit-laden branches, stamped C R A with London hallmarks for 1899, 430 grams.
(Christie's) $2,105

BOWLS

A rare and large American silver two-handled bowl, Cornelius Vander Burgh, New York, circa 1690, 19oz. 3dwt., length over handles 12¼in.
(Sotheby's) $233,500

A Tiffany white metal footed bowl, one side cast in relief with a scene of a rabbit being pulled along in a straw basket by a duck, 13.5cm. diameter.
(Christie's) $752

A G. L. Connell Ltd. silver bowl, applied with exaggerated angular handles and leafage, on flared bracket feet, London hallmarks for 1903, 36.5cm. wide, 2804 grams.
(Christie's) $5,742

An A. E. Jones hammered silver rose-bowl, with everted rim decorated with a repoussé frieze of Tudor Roses amid foliage, mounted in wooden plinth, 1909, 22.7cm. diameter, 990 grams.
(Christie's) $2,871

An Edwardian silver-gilt and cut-glass rose bowl, the circular lobed cut-glass body with foliate decoration, by William Comyns, 1904, 15cm.
(Lawrence) $1,959

A Georg Jensen footed bowl, with openwork leaf and berry stem, on flared circular foot, with stamped maker's mark for 1925–32, 11cm. high, 305 grams.
(Christie's) $4,211

A late Victorian pedestal bowl by Walker and Hall, with ribbon tied swags of flowers on a fluted pedestal and domed foot, Sheffield 1898, 1139 grams, 26cm. diameter.
(Spencer's) $1,580

An American silver octagonal punch bowl and ladle, Tiffany & Co., New York, 20th century, matching ladle, 162oz., length over handles 16½in.
(Sotheby's) $8,338

An American silver bowl, George Ridout, New York, circa 1750, with flared rim and molded foot, 16oz. 15dwt., diameter at rim 7⅛in.
(Sotheby's) $16,100

BOXES

A French silver box and cover, the hinged cover chased, engraved and repoussé with an inn interior with figures, London 1897, 399 grammes, 15.5cm. wide.
(Spencer's) $640

An attractive and unusual French white metal spice box, the centrally hinged cover engraved with a crest, and enclosing a cylindrical nutmeg grater/box with a circular knop, 11cm. wide.
(Spencer's) $1,147

An Omar Ramsden silver mounted shagreen box, inscribed *Omar Ramsden me fecit* with maker's marks and London hallmarks for 1930, 13cm. wide, 390 grams gross.
(Christie's) $4,211

A Continental oval box, possibly Dutch 19th century, the hinged cover and sides decorated with repoussé classical figures and foliate scrolls, 1889, Chester, 9cm.
(Lawrence) $787

A late Victorian wafer box, of fluted rectangular form, centrally hinged and opening to reveal two pierced liners with wreath cast handles, 24cm. high.
(Spencer's) $424

A Ramsden and Carr box, 1910, silver and enamel, maker's mark, London, and inscribed on the underside *Omar Ramsden et Alwyn Carr Me Fecervnt*, 4in. high.
(Sotheby's) $1,364

A silver box by Joachim Henrich Dysterdijk decorated in relief with a woman playing a spinet and a listening man, 1760, 145gr.
(Herholdt Jensen) $862

A Continental trinket box, French, mid-19th century, shaped rectangular with repoussé scroll and cherub decoration, import marks, 1896 by E.T.B., 9cm.
(Lawrence) $507

An Edwardian silver mounted ring box with velvet padded hinged cover and apricot silk and velvet fitted interior, Birmingham 1908, 10cm. wide.
(Spencer's) $160

One of a pair of six branch candelabra with spiral foliate decoration, on fluted circular bases, 59cm. high, 5000gr.
(Finarte) (Two) $4,070

Pair of Art Nouveau candelabra, silvered metal with stylized arms supporting candle nozzles, impressed marks, 12¼in. high.
(Skinner) $605

Fine late Victorian silver five light candelabrum in Adam style having a beaded sloped stepped square base, Sheffield 1896, 20in. tall.
(G. A. Key) $2,520

One of a pair of Victorian silver-gilt candelabra, four-light, the circular base with foliate repoussé decoration, by John Bodman Carrington, 1898, 44cm., 168oz.
(Lawrence)
(Two) $7,871

A pair of Sheffield plate three-light candelabra, each on circular base with tapering stem, vase-shaped sconces, circa 1820, 22in. high.
(Christie's) $2,813

A Harold Stabler silver twin-branch candelabrum, tall ovoid fluted and faceted stem with similarly faceted curved branches, stamped facsimile signature *Harold Stabler*, 1935, 29cm. high, 569 grams.
(Christie's) $1,531

An Edwardian four branch five light table candelabrum, with detachable square sconces, Sheffield 1906, by Martin Hall and Co., 56cm. high overall.
(Spencer's) $2,016

A pair of three light candelabra by Giovanni Casolla, Naples, the stems as female figures holding aloft the branches, circa 1830, 66.5cm. high, 7830gr.
(Finarte) $24,229

A large nine-branch candelabra by the Barnards, London, circa 1835, on trifid base decorated with cartouches incised with different scenes, 94cm., 14,400gr.
(Finarte) $16,391

CANDLESTICKS

A good pair of late George III candlesticks by John Parsons & Co., on swept circular bases stamped with fluting, Sheffield 1792, 29cm. high.
(Spencer's) **$1,558**

A pair of Edwardian dwarf candlesticks on scroll-decorated rounded square bases applied with scroll feet, Thomas Law, Sheffield 1902, 4³/₄in. high.
(Christie's) **$553**

A fine and attractive pair of early George III cluster column candlesticks by Ebenezer Coker, London 1768, 31.5cm. high.
(Spencer's) **$2,103**

John Cafe, a George II cast taperstick, the spool shape holder with a detachable nozzle, 5¹/₈in. high, London 1752, 4¹/₂oz.
(Woolley & Wallis) **$1,023**

A set of four table candlesticks, in the Louis XV manner, each on a shaped circular base with shell and scroll borders, 10¹/₂in. high.
(Christie's) **$1,996**

An Edwardian Corinthian column electric table lamp base, the foliate capital on fluted column and swept square base, Sheffield 1908, 38cm. high.
(Spencer's) **$1,271**

A pair of Victorian candlesticks, on square shaped bases with foliate swag motif, and corinthian capitals, by H.E., Sheffield 1898, 23cm., loaded.
(Lawrence) **$670**

A pair of George V silver mounted oak barley twist candlesticks by Albert Edward Jones, with planished silver cylindrical sockets, Birmingham 1920, 21.5cm. high.
(Spencer's) **$371**

Pair of Victorian pillar candlesticks in the Adam style having garland, ribbon and ram's head molded decoration, London 1892, 12in. high.
(Russell Baldwin & Bright) **$1,663**

CANDLESTICKS

A pair of reproduction cast candlesticks in the William III manner, by Carrington & Co., weight 24oz., 6¼in. high. (Christie's) **$1,180**

A good pair of late George III telescopic candlesticks by Alexander Goodman and Co., Sheffield 1797, 16cm. high. (Spencer's) **$1,152**

A pair of James Dixon & Sons silver candlesticks, the concave drip pans with everted rim and cylindrical detachable candleholder, 1907, 22cm. high, 780 grams gross. (Christie's) **$2,297**

An almost matching pair of early George II small candlesticks, the cylindrical sockets issuing from inverted octagonal baluster stems, London 1732, by James Gould, 794 grams total, 16.5cm. high. (Spencer's) **$2,804**

A pair of Georg Jensen candlesticks, with slightly flared sockets, decorated with four pendent buds with berries, on broad circular feet, with stamped maker's marks for 1925–32, 10.2cm. high, 315 grams. (Christie's) **$4,594**

An unusual pair of George V candlesticks, richly chased and engraved with scrolling foliage and enclosing a vacant cartouche, raised upon three openwork supports, London 1920, 464 grams total. (Spencer's) **$494**

A pair of late 18th century candlesticks, the lightly channeled stems with slight spiral swirl, stamped with two crowns, Milan, 19cm. high, 700gr. (Finarte) **$4,410**

Pair of Russian silver gilt and enamel candlesticks, Moscow, late 19th century, approximately 25 troy oz. (Skinner) **$1,870**

A pair of late Victorian table candlesticks in the George III manner, decorated with neo-classical urns and trailing oak leaves, by L. A. West, 1898, 12in. high. (Christie's) **$1,815**

CASTERS

A George I baluster sugar caster on a rising circular foot, with a molded body band and rim, Charles Adam, London 1714, 6in., 6.25oz.
(Christie's) $1,049

A George I plain baluster caster on a rising foot, John Elston Jnr., Exeter 1726, 6¼in., 5.75oz.
(Christie's) $735

Early George III embossed silver caster of baluster form, wrythen finial to lid, London 1767.
(G. A. Key) $280

A Victorian spiral-fluted and foliate-chased inverted pear-shaped pedestal caster with baluster finial, London 1894, 7½in.
(Christie's) $377

A set of three George III baluster casters, the wrythen pierced high covers with urn shaped finials, London 1778, 337 grammes total.
(Spencer's) $1,172

A silver caster, maker's mark of Eleazer Baker, Ashford, Connecticut, circa 1785, 5¼in. high, 3oz. 10dwt.
(Christie's) $3,850

An early George III inverted pear-shaped caster on a rising circular foot, Samuel Wood, London 1761, 6¾in., 6oz.
(Christie's) $655

A pair of George II plain vase-shaped casters, each on spreading circular foot and with pierced detachable domed cover with baluster finial, by John Whyte, 1732, 6½in. high, 19oz.
(Christie's) $3,167

An Art Deco tapering circular sugar caster applied with a stylized shell frieze, H W, Sheffield 1934, 6½in.
(Christie's) $237

CENTERPIECES

A late Victorian centerpiece formed as a horse beneath an oak tree, on rockwork base with presentation shield plaque dated *1899*, 12in. high.
(Christie's) $1,361

A George IV table centerpiece on a fluted rising waisted circular base, Rebecca Emes and Edward Barnard, London 1824, 16in., 134oz.
(Christie's) $7,043

A trumpet-shaped table centerpiece on a rising circular foot, M. Beaver Ltd., London 1913, 12¾in., 38.25oz.
(Christie's) $1,478

A Victorian silver-gilt four-light candelabrum centerpiece, by Edward Barnard & Sons, 1846, 27½in. high, 195oz.
(Christie's) $8,635

Richard Sibley II, a fine pair of Victorian tazzas, pierced fret, interspersed with bright cutting, 9in. diameter, London 1870, 46½oz.
(Woolley & Wallis) $3,335

An early George V centerpiece, the central flute trumpet shaped posy vase with undulating rim, Chester 1919, maker's mark *C & S*, 39cm. high.
(Spencer's) $511

A table centerpiece on open work scrolling foliate feet and with presentation inscription, Cooper Brothers and Sons Ltd., Sheffield 1918, 16½in., 93oz.
(Christie's) $3,552

A good late Victorian table centerpiece by Messrs. Hancock, supported on the outstretched arms and head of a nude, London 1886, 1950 grams, 33cm. high.
(Spencer's) $3,115

Sorley silver épergne, Glasgow, central vase with four curved arms and attached collar suspending trumpet-shaped vases, 14in. high.
(Skinner) $275

CHAMBERSTICKS

A George II plain chamber candlestick with vase-shaped socket and scroll handle, engraved crest and motto, by James Ker, Edinburgh, circa 1740, weight 8oz.
(Christie's) $1,996

A Swedish shaped circular chamber candlestick with foliate and flute-decorated campana-shaped socket, 5³/₄in.
(Christie's) $1,187

One of a pair of German 19th century circular traveling candlesticks with detachable waisted sockets, 4¹/₄in. high.
(Christie's) (Two) $1,800

A pair of George III large chamber candlesticks, each with telescopic cylindrical stem and shell-capped reeded scroll handle, by Crispin Fuller, 1817, 8¹/₄in. diameter, 37oz.
(Christie's) $2,763

Part of a set of four square chamber candlesticks with wire-work superstructures to hold storm shades, 5³/₄in. overall.
(Christie's) (Four) $776

A pair of George III gadrooned rounded oblong chamber candlesticks, Thomas and Daniel Leader, Sheffield 1810, 6in., 22oz.
(Christie's) $1,342

A George II chamber candlestick and snuffer of circular form engraved with crest and monogram, London 1751, 8oz.
(Russell Baldwin & Bright) $650

An unusual George IV silver-gilt chamber candlestick, the base formed as oak leaves and with twig handle and detachable acorn and oak leaf socket, by Paul Storr, 1828, 4³/₄in. wide, 7oz.
(Christie's) $2,932

A George III chamberstick, with reed rim, vase shape sconce, detachable nozzle and conical extinguisher, by Peter and Anne Bateman, 1797, 14cm.
(Lawrence) $630

CIGAR BOXES

A cigar and cigarette box, engine turned, the twin lidded compartments cedar lined, 9in., makers The Goldsmiths & Silversmiths Co., London 1927. (Woolley & Wallis) $926

A Cartier cigar box and cover, the exterior veneered in burr maple, the top set with a rectangular clock, 22.5cm. wide. (Christie's) $1,421

A Russian silver rectangular cigar box, the cover, sides and base engraved to simulate a wood grain finish, dated 1911, 15.7cm. long. (Bearne's) $1,275

CIGARETTE CASES

A Continental white metal cigarette case, of rounded square form, engraved with a dachshund, stamped *800 F.S.*, 9 x 7.5cm. (Spencer's) $194

An Art Deco engine-turned square novelty cigarette box, Asprey & Co. Ltd., London 1926, 6½in. wide. (Christie's) $582

A Russian silver niello cigarette case, shaped rectangular, maker's mark *G.K.*, Gustav Klingert, 1896, Moscow, 8.5 x 7.5cm. (Lawrence Fine Art) $613

A good Irish Arts & Crafts cigarette box, with cut card type hinges, raised upon four peg feet, Dublin 1906, by West & Sons, 19cm. wide. (Spencer's) $389

A cigarette case and lighter given to Sam K. Winston by Marlene Dietrich, French, 1931, in silver- and gold-colored metal, black enamel outer with red, black and white rectangles/ squares. (Sotheby's) $4,356

A Victorian part spiral-fluted and foliate-stamped oblong cedar-lined double cigarette box, John Bodman Carrington, London 1894, 7¾in. (Christie's) $1,019

CLARET JUGS

A Victorian claret jug, the baluster body on a circular pedestal foot, maker's mark *R.B.*, Sheffield 1856, 34cm., 36oz.
(Lawrence Fine Art) **$1,226**

A pair of Victorian silver-gilt mounted clear glass claret jugs, each on circular slightly spreading foot, by John Figg, 1865, 16$\frac{1}{2}$in. high.
(Christie's) **$9,677**

A Victorian star-cut globular clear glass claret jug, with a scroll handle, W. and G. Sissons, Sheffield 1870, 9$\frac{3}{4}$in.
(Christie's) **$1,651**

An Edwardian silver mounted claret jug, the silver mount chased and repoussé with an Art Nouveau maiden's head and Bacchus mask surrounded by fruiting vines, London 1907, 27.5cm. high.
(Spencer's) **$1,165**

A Frederick Elkington silver barrel-shaped claret jug designed by Dr. Christopher Dresser, London 1866, 17.5cm. high, 20.25oz.
(Christie's) **$1,672**

A late Victorian silver mounted clear glass claret jug by Martin Hall and Co., the clear glass globular body with star and diamond cut decoration, Sheffield 1890, 21.5cm. high.
(Spencer's) **$777**

A late Victorian clear glass claret jug, of baluster form with diamond facet cut decoration, Birmingham 1893, by Heath & Middleton, 20cm. high.
(Spencer's) **$516**

A pair of Victorian pear-shaped claret jugs, by Stephen Smith and William Nicholson, 1858 and 1859, 13$\frac{1}{2}$in. high, 71oz.
(Christie's) **$3,799**

A German tapering cut glass claret jug with plain mount, and slightly-domed hinged cover, 14$\frac{1}{4}$in.
(Christie's) **$1,008**

COASTERS

A set of four Regency part-fluted and gadrooned molded circular wine coasters, William Elliot, London 1814, 6¹/₄in.
(Christie's) $3,267

A pair of silver wine coasters, maker's mark of Gale & Willis, New York, 1859, with turned wood bases, 5¹/₈in. diameter.
(Christie's) $2,750

A set of four Regency Sheffield plate decanter stands, the turned wood bases with crested bosses.
(Woolley & Wallis) $660

A pair of William IV wine coasters, each with plain base and cast trailing vine border, by Benjamin Smith, 1831.
(Christie's) $9,315

A set of four George IV silver gilt molded circular wine coasters chased with eagles, flowers and scrolling foliage, William Elliot, London 1822, 6¹/₂in.
'Christie's) $4,366

A pair of George III wine coasters, plain circular with gadroon rims, by Rebecca Emes and Edward Barnard I, 1810, 15cm.
(Lawrence Fine Art) $2,540

A pair of George III decanter stands, the pierced fretwork sides with applied paterae linked swags, London 1775.
(Woolley & Wallis) $1,650

A pair of Victorian wine coasters, scroll pierced sides and with floral mounts, by Robinson, Edkins and Aston, Birmingham, 1839, 16cm.
(Phillips) $1,914

A pair of George IV coasters, plain circular with gadroon rim, wooden bases, engraved with crest, by John Russell, 1822, 15cm.
(Lawrence) $1,609

COFFEE POTS

A pear shaped coffee pot by
Eliza Godfrey, London with
richly chased rocaille
decoration, 27.5cm. high,
1040gr., 1758/9.
(Finarte) $2,352

A coffee pot by Emanuele
Caber, Milan 1812–50, of ovoid
shape, the elongated spout
ending in a bird's beak, the lid
with swan finial, 37cm. high,
1130gr.
(Finarte) $7,462

A mid 18th century Viennese
pear shaped coffee pot, the
handle and finial of ebonized
wood, 23cm. high, 500gr.
(Finarte) $2,134

A George III plain baluster
coffee pot on a spreading foot,
with a leaf-capped and flute-
chased rising curved spout,
Samuel Wood, London 1763,
10$^{1}/_{4}$in., 25oz. gross.
(Christie's) $2,763

Coffee pot attributed to Gaetano
Pane, of ovoid shape on three
claw feet, the spout ending in a
canine head, first half 19th
century, Neapolitan area,
31.5cm. high, 1190gr.
(Finarte) $4,070

An American silver coffee pot,
J. E. Caldwell, Philadelphia,
circa 1850–60, derived from
German 18th century rococo,
51oz. 10dwt., height 13$^{1}/_{2}$in.
(Sotheby's) $1,265

A Victorian plain baluster coffee
pot in the 18th century taste,
with a foliate-chased rising
curved spout, Messrs. Barnard,
London 1840, 9in., 14$^{3}/_{4}$oz.
(Christie's) $1,209

A George III coffee pot, of
slender baluster form, repoussé
with ribbon tied drapes centered
by rosette medallions, London
1776, 751 grammes gross.
(Spencer's) $1,803

An oviform coffee pot on a
circular foot, the spout ending in
an eagle's head, the cover with
pineapple finial, Novara, 1824,
31cm. high, 700gr.
(Finarte) $3,914

COFFEE POTS

A small cylindrical coffee pot, decorated in relief with chinoiserie motifs and with a Fo dog finial, London 1850, 16.5cm. high.
(Finarte) $997

A spiral fluted, pear shaped coffee pot with ebony side handle, Turin, second half 18th century, 22cm. high, 800gr.
(Finarte) $20,638

A Genoese oviform coffee pot of three claw feet, the spout ending in a dog's head, the cover with pineapple finial, 25cm. high, 550gr., marks for 1824.
(Finarte) $2,134

A George III coffee pot of plain baluster form on beaded circular base, the hinged cover with acorn finial, Newcastle 1784, 25oz., 11½in., makers Langlands and Robertson.
(Russell Baldwin & Bright) $1,695

A George II silver coffee pot, Newcastle, 1744, maker's mark of Isaac Cookson, the hinged stepped domed cover with urn finial, 9in. high, gross weight 18oz. 10dwt.
(Christie's) $7,150

A silver coffee pot by Joyce R. Himsworth, the tapering cylindrical body applied with bands of plaited rope decoration and wirework motifs, Sheffield hallmarks for 1926, 23cm. high, 840 grams gross.
(Christie's) $1,436

A coffee pot by Giuseppe Giovara, Turin, incised with monogram within a cartouche, the lid with fruit finial, 19th century, 24cm. high, 680gr.
(Finarte) $2,170

E. E. J. & W. Barnard, a naturalistic coffee pot, melon paneled, with foliage entwined root spout and handle, 8½in., London 1841, 25oz.
(Woolley & Wallis) $1,287

A pear shaped coffee pot with broadly reeded body, second half 19th century, Novara, signed with monogram WB, 27.5cm. high, 1000gr.
(Finarte) $2,988

CREAM JUGS

A George III gadrooned and gilt-lined molded shaped oblong cream jug, London 1810, 5¹/₂in.
(Christie's) $200

A silver cream jug, maker's mark of Elias Pelletreau, Southampton, New York, circa 1775, 5³/₈in. high, 5oz. 10dwt.
(Christie's) $4,400

Victorian silver cream jug of paneled baluster form chased and embossed with flowers, Birmingham 1864.
(G. A. Key) $158

A silver cream jug, maker's mark of Daniel Rogers, Ipswich, Massachusetts, circa 1780, 4¹/₄in. high, 4oz. 10dwt.
(Christie's) $1,540

A Victorian gilt-lined vase-shaped cream jug on a foliate and bead decorated rising circular foot, George Adams, London 1861, 5¹/₄in., 9oz.
(Christie's) $592

A novelty cream jug formed as a milk churn with cast handle formed as a cat, by George Angell, 1867, weight 5oz., 4¹/₂in. high.
(Christie's) $5,082

A silver cream jug, maker's mark of William Seal, Philadelphia, circa 1815, 6¹/₈in. high, 8oz. 10dwt.
(Christie's) $770

A Victorian slender baluster cream jug, H. & H. Lias, London 1863, 5¹/₄in., 4.75oz.
(Christie's) $315

A silver cream jug, maker's mark of Samuel Tingley, New York, circa 1775, 5³/₈in. high, 5oz.
(Christie's) $2,420

CRUETS

A George II oil and vinegar cruet on scroll and shell supports, Samuel Wood, London 1747, 12.75oz.
(Christie's) $787

A Victorian novelty cruet on an oval ebonized wood base applied: 'Just Out', Robert Hennell, London 1872.
(Christie's) $621

A George III gadrooned and foliate-pierced cinquefoil cruet, Jabez Daniell and James Mince, London 1767, 21oz.
(Christie's) $875

A George IV cruet and stand, fitted with four cut glass vinaigrette bottles, a mustard jar and two pepperette bottles, one mustard spoon, by Jonathan Hayne, 1822.
(Lawrence) $1,137

A Regency part-fluted rounded square eight-bottle cruet on scrolling foliate feet, Thomas Robins, London 1814, 8³/₄in., 35oz.
(Christie's) $1,098

An attractive George III eight piece cruet and stand, with cast beaded borders enclosing rosette pierced bands and a solid band bright cut engraved with swags of flowers, fruit and pendant husks, London 1787, 18.5cm. wide.
(Spencer's) $1,942

A silver cruet stand, maker's mark of Matthew Pettit, New York, circa 1811, 9¹/₈in. long, weighable silver 25oz. 10dwt.
(Christie's) $2,640

A George III Irish Provincial wire-work shaped oval six-cup egg cruet, Carden Terry and Jane Williams, Cork, probably circa 1810, 7¹/₂in., 9.25oz.
(Christie's) $397

Fine Victorian silver cruet stand, oval shaped with bombé fronted base, containing seven original bottles, London 1850 by G. Angell.
(G. A. Key) $1,777

Silver caudle cup, Jeremiah Dummer, Boston, (1645–1718), engraved *N^{S}M* at base and marked *I.D.* in heart cartouche, approx. wt. 6 troy oz.
(Skinner)   **$2,090**

John S. Hunt, a fine Victorian stag's head stirrup cup, with gilt interior, 6in., London 1846, 19oz.
(Woolley & Wallis)   **$6,762**

A late Victorian two handled cup by J. Wakley & F. C. Wheeler, the semi-wrythen fluted lobed cup chased and repoussé with winged cherub masks and foliage, London 1896, 294 grams, 17cm. wide.
(Spencer's)   **$416**

An Irish two handled Challenge Cup and cover, the cylindrical body on a circular pedestal foot, engraved with a coat of arms, by Charles Lamb, Dublin 1920, 55oz.
(Lawrence)   **$1,084**

Silver presentation cup, Nicholas J. Bogert (fl. 1801–1830), New York City, the octagonal body engraved *This Goblet was Presented to the Guards by 1st Lieut. W. Bruen as a Prize to be shot for Jan 8th 1845*, 4in. high, 6 troy oz.
(Skinner)   **$1,045**

Silver presentation cup, dated *1842*, Oscar T. H. Dibble, Savannah, Georgia, the cylindrical body engraved *Presented by Savannah Rifle Club*, 3^1/$_2$in. high.
(Skinner)   **$660**

An American silver octagonal standing cup, Hyde & Goodrich, New Orleans, circa 1849, chased with a lake view with swans and sail boat, 5oz. 10dwt., height 7^1/$_2$in.
(Sotheby's)   **$4,888**

A William IV fox head stirrup cup by Benjamin Smith, with chased and repoussé features, London 1835, 202 grams, 11cm. long.
(Spencer's)   **$4,236**

A late Victorian trophy cup, engraved with a fern wreath enclosing a vacant panel, raised upon a single blade knop stem and swept circular foot, London 1879, 229 grams, 20cm. high.
(Spencer's)   **$141**

DISHES

Sterling silver open vegetable dish by Durgin, applied floral border, monogrammed, 13³/₄in. wide, 16.8 troy oz.
(Eldred's) $220

An Edwardian two handled dish of rounded rectangular form with scroll handles, the border pierced with scrolling foliage, London 1902, 465 grams, 30cm. wide.
(Spencer's) $460

A Guild of Handicraft electroplated serving dish and cover, with complex intertwining wirework handle, 14cm. high.
(Christie's) $536

A fine pair of Victorian oval dessert dishes, the sides with repoussé fruit and foliage, 12¹/₄in. across handles, maker William Evans, London 1878, 39oz.
(Woolley & Wallis) $2,722

A pair of George III gadrooned shell butter dishes on triple periwinkle feet, Rebecca Emes and Edward Barnard, London 1810, 5¹/₂in., 9¹/₄oz.
(Christie's) $1,382

An attractive pair of early George V boat shaped bon bon dishes by Hamilton and Inches, Edinburgh 1910, 330 grams total, 13.5cm. wide.
(Spencer's) $416

A Continental sweetmeat dish, Dutch, 18th century, on an oval pedestal foot with similar lobed decoration, scrolled handles, import marks 1889, Chester, 21cm.
(Lawrence) $455

A Japanese pierced silver dish mounted with a central Shibayama panel, signed, decorated with a vase of flowers on a table, 12¹/₄in. diameter.
(Bearne's) $2,383

A late Victorian small tazza, of circular form with crimped rim, richly repoussé with pineapples, fruits and acanthus leaves, London 1894, 19cm. diameter.
(Spencer's) $441

FLATWARE

An attractive Russian plique à jour sifter spoon, the circular bowl centered by a flowerhead, with wire work stem and triple flower finial, 15cm. long.
(Spencer's) $494

An American silver soup ladle, Christian Wiltberger, Philadelphia, circa 1790, pointed end with wrigglework borders, 5oz. 10dwt., length 14¹/₂in.
(Sotheby's) $920

A giant pair of silver-mounted carved ivory and steel carvers, the mounts T. Rodgers, Sheffield, 1827, the ivory handles carved with busts of George Washington, the American Eagle and Seal, length of knife 37¹/₄in.
(Sotheby's) $14,950

An attractive pair of early George V fish servers, with foliate pierced and engraved blade and tine, ivory handles with fluted silver pistol grips, Sheffield 1911.
(Spencer's) $274

A set of thread edge Old English pattern cutlery, makers Thomas Alfred & Walter Brinsley Slater, London 1895/96, 85oz., sixty pieces.
(Woolley & Wallis)   £1,500 $2,779

An oak canteen of cutlery, London 1929, viz: 24 table forks, 24 dessert forks, 24 dessert spoons, 18 table spoons, 2 sauce ladles, 11 teaspoons.
(Russell Baldwin & Bright)   £2,700 $4,320

Five piece Victorian carving set, the bone handles richly decorated with plated mounts, in original oak box.
(G. A. Key) $193

A 72 piece canteen of cutlery by Johann Jakob Kirstein, Strasbourg 1785–93, the knives with mother of pearl handles, in original case.
(Auktionsverket) $22,876

FLATWARE

An American silver flatware set, Tiffany & Co., New York, circa 1890, chrysanthemum pattern, 196oz. 10dwt. weighable, 176 pieces.
(Sotheby's) $15,870

An extremely rare American silver two prong dognose fork, John Noyes, Boston, circa 1700–1710, the terminal engraved with initials *HA*, 1oz. 8dwts., 7³/₈in. long.
(Sotheby's) $28,600

An American silver wine syphon, Baldwin Gardiner, Philadelphia or New York, circa 1820–30, of typical hooped form, 6oz. 10dwt. gross, length 15in.
(Sotheby's)   £757 $1,150

A silver cheese scoop, maker's mark of A. E. Warner, Baltimore, 1823, 9³/₈in. long, 3oz.
(Christie's)   £871 $1,320

An American silver flatware set, Tiffany & Co., New York, 20th century, Faneuil pattern, monogrammed, 151oz. excluding knives, 124 pieces.
(Sotheby's) $3,565

An early Victorian fiddle pattern fish slice, with fish and seaweed pierced and engraved blade, London 1843, maker's mark *RW*, 164 grams.
(Spencer's) $156

A Guild of Handicraft silver jam spoon, designed by C. R. Ashbee, set with turquoise, engraved *Lorna*, 1904, 50 grams gross.
(Christie's) $287

A good and attractive pair of late Victorian fish servers, the silver elliptical shaped blades centrally engraved with a fishing rod, net, creel and fish, Sheffield 1877, maker's mark *HA*.
(Spencer's) $544

A Viners Studio fifty-one-piece stainless steel flatware service designed by Professor Gerald Benney, the handles with textured surface decoration.
(Christie's) $651

GOBLETS

Dutch silver goblet, Dordrecht, 17th century, chased with floral scrolls, 3³/₄in. high, approximately 3¹/₂ troy oz.
(Skinner) **$440**

A pair of George III campana-shaped goblets with reeded lower bodies on plain spreading bases, 6¹/₂in. high, John Edwards, London 1808, 22.7oz.
(Bearne's) **$1,341**

A George III goblet, cylindrical body with half fluted decoration, on circular pedestal foot, by Samuel Hennell, 1816, 16.5cm., 11oz.
(Lawrence Fine Art) **$561**

A Norwegian goblet, on octagonal foot and with cylindrical stem chased and engraved with scallop shells and stylized foliage, by Johannes Johannesen Reimers, Bergen, circa 1680, 4in. high.
(Christie's) **$3,871**

Victorian silver presentation goblet, foliate engraved, beaded circular foot, London 1875, 7¹/₂in. tall, 8oz.
(G. A. Key) **$105**

A mid Victorian small goblet by Roberts & Briggs, the baluster bowl repoussé with lozenge shaped panels on a matt ground, London 1865, 150 grams, 13cm. high.
(Spencer's) **$318**

A pair of George III gilt-lined goblets on beaded rising circular bases, Hester Bateman, London 1779, 6¹/₂in., 14.25oz.
(Christie's) **$1,390**

Austrian silver chalice, circa 1910, raised repeating geometric and medallion pattern on cup, trumpet base with raised repeating pyramid pattern, 7⁷/₈in. high.
(Skinner) **$193**

William Grundy, a good pair of ovoid goblets, gilt lined with flared feet, 6¹/₄in., London 1776, 17oz.
(Woolley & Wallis) **$2,038**

A George III inkstand, with gadroon rim, central taper holder and two cut glass silver mounted bottles, by Henry Nutting, 1811, 25cm., weighable silver 15^1/$_2$oz.
(Lawrence)　　　　$2,309

A Venetian desk set on serpentine molded oval tray on paw feet, two inkpots and covers a bell shaped pen holder, 1100gr., second half 18th century.
(Finarte)　　　　$4,982

Boat shaped silver ink well with single faceted glass bottle, having a hinged silver lid with gadrooned edge, Sheffield 1906.
(G. A. Key)　　　　$284

A Victorian ink stand, with inscription and oil lantern with snake motif handle, by Edward & John Barnard, 1858, 26cm., 33oz.
(Lawrence)　　　　$1,487

A good George VI silver mounted heavy clear glass inkwell, the silver mount with hinged and swiveling watch cover, Birmingham 1945, possibly by J. Grinsell & Sons, 11.5cm. square.
(Spencer's)　　　　$928

An inkstand by Antonio Maria Legnani, Milan, with ovoid pen holder surmounted by a figure of Mercury in the center, 520gr., circa 1820.
(Finarte)　　　　$5,130

An early 19th century inkstand with octagonal dishes in pierced silver coasters, the lids with pierced foliate decoration, on ball feet, Messina, 1180gr.
(Finarte)　　　　$357

A Victorian ink stand, with pierced scrolled border to three sides, and two pierced divisions with two silver mounted cut glass bottles, by William & John Barnard, 1890, weighable silver 16oz.
(Lawrence)　　　　$1,312

A Victorian shaped oblong large inkstand on scrolling feet, Elkington and Co., Birmingham 1893, 14^1/$_4$in., 48.25oz. free.
(Christie's)　　　　$3,145

JUGS

A Victorian lidded beer jug, the sides embossed with foliage scrolls, maker Robert Harper, 11in., London 1864, 37oz. (Woolley & Wallis)   **$1,945**

A fine Victorian Scottish jug, the frosted neck embossed with grape vines and a branch handle, 14in. high, maker J. Murray 1858, 35oz. (Woolley & Wallis)
                    $2,871

An early Scottish plain baluster-shaped jug on spreading rim foot, by Robert Keay of Perth, hallmark *Edinburgh, 1847*, weight 32oz., 11in. high. (Christie's)   **$3,993**

A Victorian beaded and fluted tapering oval gilt-lined milk jug, Henry Holland, London 1874, 4^{1}/2in., 7.25oz. (Christie's)   **$359**

A rare Elizabeth I silver-gilt mounted tiger-ware jug, winged demi-cherub thumbpiece, 1561, maker's mark *GW*, 6^{1}/2in. high. (Christie's)   **$19,860**

An Edward VII large beer jug with reed strap handle, London 1903, 24oz., maker Goldsmith & Co., London. (Russell Baldwin & Bright)
                    $709

E. E. J. & W. Barnard, a naturalistic milk jug, melon paneled with foliage entwined root spout, rim and handle, London 1837, 7^{1}/2oz. (Woolley & Wallis)   **$627**

A rare silver toby jug, maker's mark of A. E. Warner, Baltimore, 1840–1860, realistically formed as a man in contemporary dress, 14oz. (Christie's)   **$16,500**

A George II pear shaped beer jug with cast scroll handle and lip, maker Fuller White, London 1753, 23oz., 8^{1}/4in. high. (Tennants)   **$3,888**

MISCELLANEOUS SILVER

A late Victorian pierced and waisted dish ring in the Irish 18th century taste, Wakelin and Wheeler, London 1896, 8¼in., 12.25oz.
(Christie's) $660

A silver saucepan, maker's mark of Abraham Carlile, Philadelphia, 1791–1794, overall length 8¾in., gross weight 12oz.
(Christie's) $4,400

A late Victorian jewelry casket by William Comyns, of swept rectangular form, the cover and sides stamped with the cherub choir, London 1898, 20.5cm. wide.
(Spencer's) $777

A William Hutton & Sons silver picture frame, with pierced and repoussé stylized floral decoration with blue green enamel details, London hallmarks for 1904, 25.7cm. high, 330 grams gross.
(Christie's) $2,105

A pair of fine George IV silver-gilt double wine decanter trolleys, by Benjamin Smith, 1827, each stamped *LEWIS ST JAMES'S STREET*, 19½in. long, gross 226oz.
(Christie's) $39,721

An Art Nouveau shaped rectangular silver-mounted photograph frame, the mount stamped with flowers, foliage and a winged maiden, Birmingham 1907, 22cm. high.
(Christie's) $368

A William Hutton Art Nouveau silver frame, stamped in relief with entrelac medallions, Birmingham 1906, 18.5cm. high.
(Christie's) $702

A silver gilt ewer and basin, by Johann Alois Seethaler, Augsburg, 1799, the ovoid jug applied with lyre and mythological ornament, total weight 2080gr.
(Finarte) $11,758

A William Hutton & Sons silver and enamel photograph frame, with applied decoration of stylized honesty on a panel of blue and green enamel, 1903, 30.5cm. high, 520 grams gross.
(Christie's) $2,871

MISCELLANEOUS SILVER

An early George V silver pear shaped scent flask by Albert Edward Jones, Birmingham 1910, 9cm. high.
(Spencer's) $120

An early Victorian castle top aide-mémoire, with ivory slips for each day bar Sunday, by Nathaniel Mills, Birmingham, 1844.
(Phillips) $1,079

A fine cast table bell, having a cherub handle, the interior and clapper gilded, 6in., maker Henry Bourne, London 1901, 13oz.
(Woolley & Wallis) $891

An American silver-plated tilt-top tea table, Tiffany & Co., New York, circa 1893, length of top 28¹/₂in.
(Sotheby's) $29,900

A pair of silver-gilt Queen Anne brushes, each baluster shaped handle engraved with a crest, maker's mark only, Benjamin Payne, 10cm.
(Lawrence) $4,285

An early 19th century French baluster form censer with repoussé and chased decoration of rosettes and acanthus leaves and flame finial, by A. Renauld, Paris, 30cm. high, 670gr.
(Kunsthaus am Museum)
                          $1,487

A Continental silver bottle and stopper, decorated with cameo heads and swags, false gadroons around the base, 8.2cm.
(Phillips) $650

An attractive Arts & Crafts christening set, with blue and turquoise enameled decoration of seed pods and sinuous tendrils, Sheffield 1906, by Richard Richardson.
(Spencer's) $224

A 19th century silver mounted ram's horn tobacco mull, the lid with the badge and inscription *The Royal Scots*.
(Finarte) $926

MISCELLANEOUS SILVER

George III oval silver pap boat with reeded edge and off set pourer, London 1798 by Andrew Fogelberg.
(G. A. Key) $227

Elkington & Co. a cast table bell, the handle a putto playing a tambourine.
(Woolley & Wallis) $363

Fine Victorian silver presentation trowel bearing an inscription dated *1894*, carved ivory handle, Sheffield 1893.
(G. A. Key) $256

An unusual George V cake stand, of three tiers with scroll supports, Sheffield 1910, makers mark *R.R.*, 764 grams, 43cm. high.
(Spencer's) $459

Georgian Irish silver egg cups in circular hallmarked silver stand plus six spoons, 24oz. total.
(G. A. Key) $772

A set of six Georgian 'picture-back' silver teaspoons in case, London, mid-18th century, maker's mark *WT*, possibly for William Trenholme, height of case 6³/₈in., 1oz. 10dwt.
(Christie's) $4,400

A baroque oval flask by Johan Daniel Planitz, 9.5cm. high, 110gr.
(Herholdt Jensen) $1,079

A very fine and attractive early George V five piece tortoiseshell and silver dressing table set, Birmingham 1914, 39.5cm. wide.
(Spencer's) $800

Good cased four piece silver and tortoiseshell backed dressing table set, Birmingham 1924.
(G. A. Key) $358

MUGS & CANNS

An 18th century Irish gilt-lined tapering mug with molded rim, 3¹/₂in., 9oz.
(Christie's) $490

Rare solid silver shaving mug, circular shaped on a stepped base with beaded edges, Birmingham 1905, 3¹/₂in. tall, 6oz.
(G. A. Key) $405

Joseph Angell, a George IV mug, campana shape repoussé with dancing maidens, London 1830, 8³/₄oz.
(Woolley & Wallis) $676

A George III baluster pint mug with leaf-capped double scroll handle, W.T., London 1776, 5¹/₂in., 12.75oz.
(Christie's) $1,011

A William IV campana shaped christening mug monogrammed and with acanthus decorated lower body, 11cm. high, Charles Fox, London 1836, 7oz.
(Bearne's) $387

A silver child's cann, maker's mark of Ebenezer Moulton, Boston, circa 1790, 3in. high, 2oz. 10dwt.
(Christie's) $2,860

A rare silver cann, maker's mark of Charles Oliver Bruff, New York, circa 1770, 4³/₈in. high, 9oz.
(Christie's) $8,250

A silver cann, maker's mark of William Taylor, Philadelphia, circa 1775, 5¹/₄in. high, 11oz.
(Christie's) $2,200

An American silver small cann, Edmund Milne, Philadelphia, circa 1770, with leaf-capped double-scroll handle, 9oz., height 4¹/₂in.
(Sotheby's) $2,990

MUSTARDS

A Victorian gilt-lined baluster mustard pot on applied Chinaman and shell feet, William Cooper, London 1851, 4¼in., 8oz.
(Christie's) $1,442

A silver mustard pot and spoon, maker's mark of Eoff & Shepherd, for Ball, Black & Co., New York, circa 1840, 4oz. 10dwt.
(Christie's) $385

A Victorian gilt-lined compressed pear-shaped mustard pot on figural scroll feet, John S. Hunt, London 1851.
(Christie's) $984

A Victorian gilt-lined pear-shaped mustard pot on floral and foliate feet, Henry Holland, London 1852, 3½in.
(Christie's) $645

A Victorian drum mustard pot with green glass liner with star-cut base, Reily and Storer, London 1847, 3¼in.
(Christie's) $679

A Victorian novelty mustard pot modeled as a swing-handled cauldron, with a blue glass liner, Henry Stockwell, London 1859, 4in. overall.
(Christie's) $1,018

Fine large George Fox silver mustard of circular shape with blue glass liner, the body embossed with flowers and leaves, London 1827.
(G. A. Key) $605

A George IV gilt-lined part-fluted compressed vase-shaped mustard pot on a spreading circular foot, Philip Rundell, London 1822, 3¾in., 9.25oz.
(Christie's) $1,782

A Victorian novelty spool-shaped mustard pot modeled from woven wire and with ropework borders and scroll handle, B. & C. or B. & G., Birmingham 1858, 3in.
(Christie's) $1,493

607

PITCHERS & EWERS

Bailey & Kitchen coin silver water pitcher, monogram, approximately 38 troy oz. (Skinner) **$825**

A silver covered pitcher, maker's mark of Bassett and Warford, Albany, New York, 1800–1805, 13³/₈in. high, 36oz. (Christie's) **$8,250**

Italian silver ewer, 20th century, helmet form with relief vine design, 9¹/₄in. high, approximately 16 troy oz. (Skinner) **$1,045**

Georg Jensen Sterling water pitcher, 1922, marks of Copenhagen, Jensen, London import mark of 1922, 9in. high, approximately 18 troy oz. (Skinner) **$1,980**

An American silver and other metals 'Japanese style' water pitcher, Tiffany & Co., New York, circa 1875–80, 26oz. 15dwt. gross, height 7³/₄in. (Sotheby's) **$42,550**

An American silver ewer, Bailey & Co., Philadelphia, circa 1850, chased with chinoiserie buildings, a boat and birds, 64oz. 10dwt., height 19in. (Sotheby's) **$5,750**

Sterling silver water pitcher by Durgin, pedestal base, circa 1913, monogrammed, 28.4 troy oz. (Eldred's) **$468**

Whiting Sterling and mixed metal water pitcher, 1881, bird and floral decoration, 8¹/₂in. high, approximately 33 troy oz. (Skinner) **$4,125**

A Victorian Cellini pattern hot water ewer, 30cm. high, Stephen Smith, London 1880, 28.5oz. (Bearne's) **$1,192**

PLATES

Set of eight J. E. Caldwell Sterling dinner plates, reticulated borders and engraved interiors, 12in., approximately 204 troy oz. (Skinner) $6,050

Set of five Black, Starr & Frost Sterling plates, neoclassical design, approximately 107 troy oz. (Skinner) $1,210

A set of twelve George III dinner plates, by Thomas and Joseph Guest and Joseph Craddock, 1810, 9³/₄in. diameter, 220oz. (Christie's) $12,089

PORRINGERS

A silver porringer, maker's mark of Thauvet Besley, New York, circa 1740, 7⁷/₈in. long, 8oz. 10dwt. (Christie's) $2,860

A Queen Anne part spiral-fluted two-handled tapering circular porringer, maker's initials possibly T.E., London 1704, 8.25oz. (Christie's) $1,774

A silver porringer, maker's mark of Charles Le Roux, New York, circa 1740, 7⁵/₈in. long, 8oz. (Christie's) $2,200

Fine George II silver two handled porringer with fluted decoration to base, marked for London 1755, maker Henry Brind, 5in. tall, 16oz. (G. A. Key) $1,512

An American silver porringer, Edward Webb, Boston, circa 1700, of typical form with double arch handle, 5oz. 10dwt., 4³/₄in. diameter. (Sotheby's) $11,550

A William III part-fluted tapering circular porringer on a gadrooned spreading circular foot, London 1699, Britannia Standard, 8in. overall, 13oz. (Christie's) $1,442

SALTS & PEPPERS

A set of four Arts and Crafts oblong salt cellars of shallow boat-shaped form, on four shaped bracket supports, by Omar Ramsden, 1932, 2¾in. wide.
(Christie's)   **$1,271**

Pair of George III boat shaped silver pedestal salts, gilt lined, London 1796 by Henry Chawner and John Emes.
(G. A. Key)   **$310**

Four plated nautilus shaped salts, complete with spoons in original case, marked *E. Sanderson, London*, late 19th century.
(G. A. Key)   **$118**

Heavy pair of late Victorian cast silver salt frames of ornate pierced and draped design, complete with blue glass liners, Sheffield 1892, 5oz. free.
(G. A. Key)   **$403**

A good pair of early Victorian large salts by Henry Wilkinson & Co., of octagonal form, pierced and engraved with lobed oval panels enclosing leaves, Sheffield 1841.
(Spencer's)   **$335**

A good pair of George II salts, on cast knurled appliques, scroll legs to hoof feet, maker Henry Herbert, London 1738, 10oz.
(Woolley & Wallis)   **$577**

A set of four George II salts, on spreading molded foot, maker probably I. Wood, London 1759, 12½oz.
(Woolley & Wallis)
                    $2,779

An Edwardian novelty pepperette as a golf ball, on a swept circular foot supported by three curved arms, 40 grams, 7.5cm. high
(Spencer's)   **$53**

Set of six Georg Jensen Sterling salts and spoons, Acorn pattern, approximately 5 troy oz.
(Skinner)   **$880**

SAUCE BOATS

One of a pair of George III sauce boats on shell and hoof feet, maker's initials *W.F.*, London 1766, 7¹/₂in., 18.50oz. (Christie's)
(Two) $1,205

George II silver sauce boat with bold card cut rim, flying scrolled handle, standing on three animal feet, London 1737. (G. A. Key) $653

A silver-gilt mounted agate sauceboat, Charles Rawlings & William Summers, London, 1848, the handle formed as a wriggling snake, 6¹/₄in. long. (Sotheby's) $1,364

A pair of George II sauce boats on shell and scroll feet, S. Herbert & Co., London 1751, 6³/₄in., 16.25oz. (Christie's) $1,297

A pair of silver sauce boats, maker's mark of Marquand & Co., New York, 1833–1839, 9¹/₂in. long, 34oz. (Christie's) $3,080

A pair of George II large sauce boats on shell and scroll feet, Thomas Whipham, London 1749, 8¹/₂in., 32oz. (Christie's) $2,595

A pair of plain helmet-shaped sauce boats, each on rectangular base with reeded borders and scroll handles, by Hawkesworth Eyre & Co. Ltd., 1911, weight 20oz. (Christie's) $1,180

A pair of George II large gadrooned sauce boats on knurled scroll and shell feet, George Metheun, London 1751, 8³/₄in., 28.75oz. (Christie's) $2,688

A pair of silver sauce boats, maker's mark of Joseph Anthony, Jr., Philadelphia, circa 1785, 7¹/₂in. long, 28oz. 10dwt. (Christie's) $20,900

TANKARDS

A George II tankard, with thumbpiece and domed cover engraved with coat of arms within a rococo cartouche, by John Macbride, 1747, 18cm., 29oz.
(Lawrence) $3,148

A George II quart lidded tankard, on a spreading molded foot, 8in., makers William Shaw II and William Priest London 1753, 25oz.
(Woolley & Wallis) $2,310

A George I tapering cylindrical lidded quart tankard on a skirted foot, Richard Green, London 1715, Britannia Standard, 6³/₄in., 23³/₄oz.
(Christie's) $2,418

An early George III quart lidded tankard, the baluster body with a girdle molding, 7¹/₂in. high, makers Thomas Cooke II and Richard Gurney, London 1760, 23¹/₂oz.
(Woolley & Wallis) $2,392

An Augsburg tankard on three ball feet, densely chased in repoussé with scenes of children playing, late 17th/early 18th century, 15.5cm. high, 450gr.
(Finarte) $2,988

A fine silver tankard, maker's mark of John Moulinar, New York, circa 1750, applied with a band of cut-card leaves above the molded foot rim, 7¹/₄in. long, 35oz.
(Christie's) $38,500

A silver tankard, maker's mark of William Cowell, Sr. or Jr., Boston, 1725–1740, the scroll handle with molded drop, 7⁷/₈in. high, 29oz.
(Christie's) $7,700

George II silver tankard, J. Kentenber, London, 1759, with later chased scrolls, approximately 24 troy oz.
(Skinner) $2,090

An American silver small tankard, Benjamin Burt, Boston, circa 1799, of typical New England form, 18oz. 10dwt., height 7⁷/₈in.
(Sotheby's) $10,350

A fine silver tankard, maker's mark of Myer Myers, New York, circa 1760, with double scroll handle, 6⅞in. high, 31oz.
(Christie's)　　　**$24,200**

A Swedish gilt-lined lidded tankard in the 17th century taste, on ball feet, 8½in.
(Christie's)　　　**$1,477**

Scandinavian white metal tankard, decorated with mask mounts and embossed band of fruit and foliage, 44oz. (of white metal).
(G. A. Key)　　　**$371**

An American silver tankard, maker's mark of George Hanners, Boston, circa 1720, the tubular scroll handle with molded top and terminating in a George I coin, 7¾in. high, 23oz. 10dwt.
(Christie's)　　　**$10,450**

A George II lidded tankard of plain tapering shape with angular ring, maker Samuel Wood, London 1750, 7½in., 30oz.
(Tennants)　　　**$2,106**

A late George II tankard by William Shaw and William Priest, the hinged stepped domed cover with volute thumb piece, London 1757, 731 grams.
(Spencer's)　　　**$1,953**

An early George III tankard by W & J Priest, of single girdled tapering cylindrical form, London 1772, 846 grams, 19.5cm. high overall.
(Spencer's)　　　**$1,322**

A Queen Anne small tapering tankard with scroll handle and spreading foot, maker Thomas Holland, London 1709, 6oz., 3½in. high.
(Tennants)　　　**$1,053**

A late Victorian early Georgian style tankard, of single girdled baluster form, London 1823, maker's mark *H.S.*, 915 grams, 20cm. high.
(Spencer's)　　　**$1,064**

TEA & COFFEE SETS

A superb composite late George III four piece tea service by Edward Farrell, richly cast, repoussé and engraved with scenes after Tenier, London 1819/21, 6681 grams total gross.
(Spencer's)   **$8,472**

A fine five piece tea and coffee service, in Regency style, makers The Goldsmiths and Silversmiths Co., London 1905, 116¹/₂oz.
(Woolley & Wallis)   **$2,475**

A composite late Victorian morning tea service, the upper sections chased and repoussé with flowerheads, acanthus leaves and scrolls beneath everted crimped borders, London 1893/4, 499 grams total gross.
(Spencer's)   **$582**

A George IV three piece tea service by Charles Fox, of squat globular form with everted stiff leaf cast borders, richly chased with flowerheads and leaves, London 1827, 1453 grams total gross.
(Spencer's)   **$1,893**

A silver four-piece tea and coffee set, Elkington & Co., Birmingham, 1861, the decagonal bodies linear engraved with geometric motifs, the coffee pot further engraved with armorials, 84oz., 17dwt. all in.
(Sotheby's)   **$4,603**

A fine George IV three piece tea service, chased and repoussé with a band of fruit and flowers enclosing two rococo cartouches engraved with a crest and motto *Libertas et Plenitas*, London 1823, by William Hattersley or William Hewit.
(Spencer's)   **$2,118**

A composite Victorian four piece tea and coffee service, of lobed baluster form bright cut engraved with scrolls, London 1877 by Steven Smith, 2311 grams total gross.
(Spencer's)   **$2,338**

A good and attractive early Victorian four piece tea and coffee service by Richard Pearce and George Burrows, London 1840, 2189 grams total gross.
(Spencer's)   **$3,225**

TEA & COFFEE SETS

A Boulenger electroplated four-piece tea and coffee service, of fan-shaped design with similarly decorated handles and finials, 16.8cm. high.
(Christie's) $1,340

An attractive composite George V three piece boat shaped tea service, with swept shoulders and bobbin cast borders, Sheffield 1923/4, 1024 grams total gross.
(Spencer's) $806

A Victorian four piece tea and coffee service, the pear shaped paneled body repoussé with foliage and scrolls, makers Josiah Williams & Co., 1878, 72oz.
(Woolley & Wallis) $2,805

A good late George V four piece tea service, Sheffield 1934, by Mappin & Webb, 1177 grams total gross, and a matching circular tray.
(Spencer's) $3,120

A composite three piece tea service, of squat globular form, comprising teapot (Dublin 1827 by Edward Power); two handled sugar basin and milk jug (London 1910 by The Goldsmiths and Silversmiths Co), 1837 grams total gross.
(Spencer's) $1,853

A late George III four piece tea service by Dorothy Langlands, of lobed rounded rectangular baluster form, with prickwork engraved leaf and rosette band, Newcastle 1803/4, 1513 grams total.
(Spencer's) $1,412

A Victorian three piece tea service, circular with raised floral and wreath frosted panels, all on cast decorative panel feet, circa 1860.
(Woolley & Wallis) $315

Thomas Bradbury & Sons, a four piece tea and coffee service, the octagonal pear shaped bodies with girdle moldings, London 1911, 67^{1}/$_{2}$oz. all in.
(Woolley & Wallis) $1,519

TEA & COFFEE SETS

Mexican Sterling five-piece tea and coffee
service, Taxco, approximately 105 troy oz.
(Skinner) **$825**

A five piece Art Deco coffee service with handles
in Macassar ebony, 5500gr.
(Galerie Moderne) **$2,572**

Gorham Sterling six-piece tea and coffee service,
circa 1870, approximately 146 troy oz.
(Skinner) **$3,630**

Simons Brothers Sterling five-piece tea and
coffee service, approximately 96 troy oz.
(Skinner) **$1,540**

Tea service by Wm. Wilson & Son, Philadelphia,
comprising tea and hot water pots, sugar basin,
milk jug and sweetmeat dish, the pots with
swirled baluster finials, 2190gr., 19th/20th
century.
(Finarte) **$1,995**

Indian silver six-piece tea and coffee service,
each repoussé with scrolling vines,
approximately 175 troy oz.
(Skinner) **$1,650**

Lino Sabattini for Christofle, five piece tea and
coffee service, 'Como', 1960, electroplated metal,
cane covered handles, 5⁵/₈in. height of teapot.
(Sotheby's) **$4,633**

American coin silver tea set, early 19th century,
with chased C-scrolls, impressed *N.A. Freeman*,
approximately 68 troy oz.
(Skinner) **$1,870**

SILVER

Edward VII assembled silver four-piece tea and
coffee service, each London, maker E.Bs.Ld.,
approximately 73 troy oz.
(Skinner)   **$1,100**

An American silver three piece tea set, Charles
Louis Boehme, Baltimore, circa 1804, 40oz.
gross, height of teapot 6³/₄in.
(Sotheby's)   **$4,888**

An early 19th century three-piece circular tea
service, with chased foliate and scroll decoration
above reeded girdles, Joseph and John Angel,
London 1835, 1836 and 1839, 33.9oz.
(Bearne's)   **$745**

A composite late Victorian/Edwardian three
piece tea service by W & G Sissons, comprising
teapot with prow and hinged domed cover, with
ebony handle, two handled sugar basin and milk
jug, London 1899/1901, 1126 grams total gross.
(Spencer's)   **$953**

An American silver assembled four piece tea set,
Ball, Tompkins & Black, Ball, Black & Co., New
York, circa 1840 and 1850, 85oz. 10dwt., height
of teapot 10³/₄in.
(Sotheby's)   **$1,380**

Four-piece handmade Sterling silver demitasse
set by Ivar Petersen of New York City, weight
includes ivory handle on coffee pot, 79.2 troy oz.
(Eldred's)   **$1,980**

An American silver four piece tea and coffee set,
Ball, Black & Co., New York, circa 1870, 97oz.
10dwt., height of coffee pot 11¹/₂in.
(Sotheby's)   **$2,185**

An Art Deco tea service comprising two teapots,
a sugar basin and a milk jug, the squat bodies
with gadrooned ornament, 890gr.
(Finarte)   **$1,463**

TEA CADDIES

A George III oval engraved tea caddy with swags and crested motifs, maker J. Hampston and J. Prince, York, circa 1790, 5¹/₂in. long.
(Tennants) $4,050

A pair of George III vase-shaped tea caddies, the detachable covers with urn-shaped finials, 6¹/₂in. high, Peter Gillois, London 1777, 14.8oz.
(Bearne's) $2,086

A silver tea caddy, maker's mark of Eoff & Shepherd, for Ball, Black & Co., New York, circa 1855, 5¹/₄in. long, 13oz. 10dwt.
(Christie's) $1,540

A late Victorian fluted bombé-shaped molded oval tea caddy on leaf-capped stylized paw feet, T R and Co., Sheffield 1897, 3³/₄in., 8oz.
(Christie's) $484

A pair of silver-gilt tea caddies, rectangular, die-struck, with amorini and leafage, by Gorham, circa 1890, 14.5cm., 18oz.
(Phillips) $1,328

A pair of George III octagonal tea caddies, by James Phipps, 1775, contained in contemporary gilt painted lacquer case, 4in. high, gross 27oz.
(Christie's) $10,362

A George III fluted molded oval divided tea caddy on a reeded spreading foot, Charles Aldridge, London 1797, 7in., 16.75oz.
(Christie's) $1,399

A pair of George II tea caddies and sugar bowl, each on spreading molded base chased overall with flowers, foliage and scrolls, by Samuel Taylor, 1754, with shagreen casket, 12cm., 30oz.
(Lawrence) $4,810

A George V tea caddy, with gadroon edging and chased with foliate festoons, 13cm. high, London 1911, 11.5oz.
(Bearne's) $656

TEA KETTLES

A late 19th century spirit kettle, richly chased allover à rocaille, part ivory handle, Vienna, 34.5cm., 1710gr.
(Finarte)   **$2,352**

A teapot and burner, of squat baluster form with elaborate foliate repoussé decoration, signed *Schott*, 38cm. high, total weight 1770gr.
(Arnold)   **$1,813**

An American silver Japanese-style tea kettle on stand, Gorham Mfg. Co., Providence, RI, 1883, 57oz., height 12in.
(Sotheby's)   **$1,380**

A Victorian tea kettle on stand, complete with spirit burner, on reeded scroll supports and scallop feet, Sheffield 1900, 34oz. all in.
(Russell Baldwin & Bright)   **$667**

A kettle and stand, in a Queen Anne style, plain pear shaped body with domed cover and scrolled spout, by Charles Reynolds & Co. Ltd., 1926, 28cm., 65oz.
(Lawrence)   **$1,259**

A Scottish inverted pear-shaped tea kettle, stand and lamp, richly chased and embossed with fruiting vines, by Dougal Ged, Edinburgh, 1760, weight 78oz., 14^{1}/$_{2}$in. high.
(Christie's)   **$4,719**

An attractive Chinese white metal **tea kettle** on stand with burner, of baluster form repoussé with flowers on a matt ground, stamped *Shancha*.
(Spencer's)   **$677**

An imposing silver plate kettle on stand of later Georgian design with bright cut motifs, supported on Greek inspired base, 18in. high.
(Locke & England)   **$416**

A plated tea kettle with fluted decoration by Orvit AG, Cologne, with swing handle, circa 1905–10.
(Kunsthaus am Museum)   **$530**

TEAPOTS

Robert and Samuel Hennell, an oval boat shape teapot, with oval wood finial, London 1804, 20oz. (Woolley & Wallis) $577

A silver teapot, Boston, dated *1801*, the sides with panels of vertical flutes, 12in. long, 21oz. (Christie's) $3,300

George III silver teapot, Wm. Plummer, London, 1809, 5in. high, approximately 17 troy oz. (Skinner) $825

George III oval silver teapot of plain design, London 1790 by James Young, together with a contemporary plain oval stand, London 1791 by Elizabeth Jones.
(G. A. Key) $878

E. E. J. & W. Barnard, a naturalistic teapot, melon paneled with foliate entwined root spout and handle, London 1837, 24oz.
(Woolley & Wallis) $1,188

A Regency compressed circular teapot, embossed and chased with foliage, shells and scrolls to a scale ground, makers Rebecca Emes & Edward Barnard, London 1818, 24oz. all in.
(Woolley & Wallis) $704

A silver teapot, maker's mark of Gerardus Boyce, New York, circa 1830, 7⁷/₈in. high, gross weight 21oz.
(Christie's) $1,045

A silver teapot and caddy by Robert Hennell, London 1778–9 and 1783–4, the urn shaped bodies richly chased with foliate motifs and festoons, 21 and 21.5cm. high, 1450gr.
(Finarte) $6,414

German silver teapot, Seethaler, Augsburg, 1804, with eagle spout, approximately 15 troy oz.
(Skinner) $1,650

Emes & Barnard, a fine Regency compressed circular teapot, partly ribbed with a reeded band, London 1814, 25¹/₂oz.
(Woolley & Wallis) $815

Large Victorian circular silver teapot on cast four footed base, London 1840, 22oz.
(G. A. Key) $377

A George III oval teapot, the domed hinged cover with an oval ivory finial, makers Alice & George Burroughs, London 1804, 16¹/₂oz. all in.
(Woolley & Wallis) $630

TEAPOTS

A George III small oval teapot engraved with swags and crested cartouche, maker J. Hampston and J. Prince, York, circa 1790, 14oz., 8¹/₂in. long.
(Tennants) $2,835

Fine quality Queen Anne style silver teapot with domed lid and treen handle, London 1908, 25oz. all in.
(G. A. Key) $664

An attractive early George III teapot by Charles Wright, the plain lift off cover with ebony finial and with ebony handle, London 1775, 520 grams gross.
(Spencer's) $928

A Liberty & Co. silver teapot, Birmingham, 1900, designed by Archibald Knox, 4³/₄in. high, Birmingham, 1900.
(Bonhams) $1,495

A George III fluted oval straight-sided teapot with straight tapering spout and bright-cut foliage borders, by Charles Aldridge, 1792, with matching stand.
(Christie's) $6,171

A silver teapot, maker's mark of Elias Pelletreau, Southampton, New York, circa 1765, 9³/₄in. long, gross weight 19oz.
(Christie's) $12,100

An early Victorian teapot, chased and repoussé with flowerheads, acanthus leaves and rococo scrolls, with cast and applied flower knop, London 1853, maker's mark *W.M.*, 497 grams gross.
(Spencer's) $635

A Hukin & Heath electroplated teapot designed by Dr. Christopher Dresser, the circular cover with ebonized finial, stamped maker's marks, *Designed by Dr. C. Dresser*, 14.5cm. high.
(Christie's) $737

A teapot and stand en suite by Henry Chawner, London 1795/ 6, the undulating body with incised decoration and foliate cartouches, pot 17cm. high, 660gr. all in.
(Finarte) $1,995

A William IV teapot by Charles Fox, of melon fluted squat globular form, London 1831, 793 grams gross.
(Spencer's) $800

A fine silver teapot, maker's mark of Samuel Johnson, New York, circa 1765, 10in. long, gross weight 24oz. 10dwt.
(Christie's) $46,200

German-made silver teapot, 18th century, with floral engraving, French import marks, 5¹/₂in. high, 13 troy oz.
(Eldred's) $193

TOAST RACKS

A Hukin & Heath electroplate division letter rack, designed by Dr Christopher Dresser, 5in. high.
(Christie's) $675

A 6½in. golf club pattern seven-bar toast rack, with ball and ring carrying handle.
(Anderson & Garland)
                               $180

A Hukin & Heath electroplate division toast rack, the arched rectangular base surmounted by fixed rod and ball divisions, 12.5cm. high.
(Christie's) $301

An Edwardian novelty five bar toast rack by Heath & Middleton, the wire work rack forming the letters 'Toast', Birmingham 1906, 94 grams, 12.5cm. wide.
(Spencer's) $282

A Hukin & Heath electroplated toast rack designed by Dr. Christopher Dresser, the central support raised to a handle, stamped *H&H 2556* with dated lozenge for May 1881, 13cm. high.
(Christie's) $574

An electroplate toastrack designed by Dr. Christopher Dresser, the rectangular footed base surmounted by five rods on each side, 5¼in. high.
(Christie's) $5,420

A rare silver toast rack, maker's mark of A. E. Warner, Baltimore, 1818, 8¾in. long, 7oz. 10dwt.
(Christie's) $6,600

Large and heavy Victorian silver toast rack of seven hoop design, on four ball feet, London 1874, 9oz.
(G. A. Key) $217

A George III oval six-division toast rack, the base with reeded rim, London 1792, by Peter and Ann Bateman.
(Greenslade Hunt) $614

TRAYS & SALVERS

A large charger, possibly German in plated metal with a naval scene within an ornate foliate border, 19th century, 73.5cm. wide.
(Finarte) $1,960

Fine George II silver snuffers tray of waisted rectangular shape, London 1751, maker *I.P.*, 9oz.
(G. A. Key) $775

A large two handled tray, plain rectangular with reeded border and angular handles, 1925 by Charles Reynolds & Co. Ltd., 95cm., 119oz.
(Lawrence) $1,836

Sterling silver footed tray by Meriden Britannia Co., monogrammed, 9in. diameter, 7.6 troy oz.
(Eldred's) $83

A circular silver salver with finely molded edge punctuated with acanthus leaves in repoussé, and on four feet, 1040gr., probably Italian and late 18th century.
(Duran) $1,498

A George III circular salver, the raised molded border with leaf tied bead edge, 8in. diameter, maker Timothy Renou, London 1792, 13oz.
(Woolley & Wallis) $1,297

A salver, with a Chippendale style shaped rim, on three scrolled feet, engraved with crest to center, by S. Blanckensee & Son Ltd., 1939, 32cm., 26oz.
(Lawrence) $297

An American silver rectangular tray, Gorham Mfg. Co., Providence, RI, 1899, Martelé, .950 standard, 42oz. 10dwt., length 15in.
(Sotheby's) $6,325

An attractive early George III waiter by Hugh Mills, the piecrust border with escallop shell angles, London 1750, 281 grams.
(Spencer's) $451

A George III partly-fluted oval
soup tureen and cover, by Peter,
Ann and William Bateman,
1802, 15in. long, 90oz.
(Christie's) $9,498

A pair of Sheffield plate sauce
tureens, having detachable
liners, the covers with leaf shell
corners and detachable handles,
8¹/₂in., circa 1805.
(Woolley & Wallis) $704

An American silver circular
two-handled soup tureen and
cover, S. Kirk & Son, Baltimore,
circa 1860, 48oz. 10dwt., length
over handles 11⁵/₈in.
(Sotheby's) $2,760

A Regency partly-fluted oval
soup tureen and cover on richly
chased acanthus foliage and
scroll supports, by Paul Storr,
1811, weight 180oz., 18in. wide.
(Christie's) $30,855

A silver soup tureen and cover
of historical interest, maker's
mark of George B. Sharp for
Bailey & Co., Philadelphia, circa
1857, length over handles
15¹/₂in., 64oz. 10dwt.
(Christie's) $4,400

A George II two-handled oval
sauce tureen and cover,
Sebastian and James Crespell,
London 1768, 19.6oz.
(Bearne's) $1,311

A George III oval two-handled
soup tureen and cover, engraved
with inscription and coat-of-
arms, by Paul Storr, 1804, the
finial by Benjamin Smith, 17in.
long, 141oz.
(Christie's) $24,178

A pair of Victorian two-handled
melon-fluted soup tureens,
covers and liners, by Robert
Garrard, 1843, the base of each
tureen stamped GARRARDS
PANTON STREET LONDON,
14³/₄in. wide, 288oz.
(Christie's) $25,905

A silver covered sauce tureen,
maker's mark of Ball, Black &
Co., New York, circa 1860,
length over handles 8⁵/₈in., 27oz.
(Christie's) $1,210

URNS

An elegant early George V tea urn by J. Wilmot, of semi-ovoid form with high swept cylindrical lift-off cover, Birmingham 1910, 1458 grams total gross.
(Spencer's) $992

A Sheffield plate two-handled circular tea urn, on foliage and paw feet and shaped square base, circa 1815, 17in. high.
(Christie's) $1,361

A George III two-handled vase-shaped tea urn, on square base and four curved bracket feet, by John Scofield, 1785, 21½in. high, gross 110oz.
(Christie's) $2,763

A George III two-handled vase-shaped tea urn, on four ball feet and square base, the urn chased with drapery swags and foliage, by Thomas Heming, 1777, 20in. high, gross 102oz.
(Christie's) $3,519

An American silver tea urn, R. & W. Wilson, Philadelphia, circa 1840, of bulbous urn form with die-rolled borders of grapevine, 100oz., 15⅞in. high.
(Sotheby's) $6,600

George III silver two-handled urn, J. Robins, London, 1808–09, chased decoration, approximately 46 troy oz.
(Skinner) $1,980

A Victorian two-handled ovoid pedestal tea urn in the 18th century taste, Elkington & Co., 22¼in. overall.
(Christie's) $1,348

A 19th century Adam style tea urn, the square tiered platform base on four ball supports, 18in. high.
(Greenslade Hunt) $450

A silver covered sugar urn, maker's mark of Samuel Williamson, Philadelphia, circa 1800, 11¼in. high, 15oz.
(Christie's) $2,640

VASES

A quartz cup and cover, the vase shaped body collet-set with oval shaped faceted and cabochon amethyst, 25cm. high.
(Lawrence) $2,085

An attractive Edwardian pot pourri vase and cover, the high swept cover with flamiform finial and with foliate piercing, Chester 1909, 184 grams total, 14.5cm. high.
(Spencer's) $384

An Arts and Crafts silver vase in the form of a castellated turret, the body with hammered finish, Birmingham 1902, 16cm. high.
(Christie's) $334

An impressive W.M.F. two handled vase, the fascia depicting a maiden within entrelac and tendril borders, 50cm. high.
(Spencer's) $820

A pair of Viennese silver-mounted enamel vases, each painted overall with various allegorical scenes, the mounts enameled and set with masks, late 19th century, 12in. high.
(Bearne's) $6,178

An Arts and Crafts electroplate vase, of tapering cylindrical form on short cylindrical foot with scalloped border, 24.5cm. high.
(Christie's) $234

An attractive pot pourri vase and cover, the slightly domed cover pierced and engraved with foliage and with cast dove finial, London 1914, 181 grams.
(Spencer's) $240

A fine Edwardian replica of the Warwick vase by Elkington & Co Limited, the body chased and applied with masks, lion's pelts, foliage and trailing vines, Birmingham 1904, approximately 6000 grams.
(Spencer's) $8,825

Italian .800 fine silver vase by Buccellatti, 10in. high, 24.2 troy oz.
(Eldred's) $605

VESTA CASES

A late Victorian vesta case, with foliage engraving and a heart shaped vacant cartouche, maker P. & B., Birmingham 1898.
(Woolley & Wallis) $92

An unusual late 19th century American vesta case of rounded oblong form, stamped in low relief on one side with the portrait of a fat Japanese woman, 4 x 3cm., circa 1880, 0.5oz.
(Phillips) $131

A Victorian engine turned vesta case, the cartouche with initials and date, maker S. Blankenzee & Son, Birmingham 1883.
(Woolley & Wallis) $63

An Edwardian novelty vesta case, depicting four people motoring along a country road in a vintage car, 5 x 4cm., maker's mark RB^S, Chester, 1906, 1oz.
(Phillips) $502

An unusual Victorian novelty vesta case-cum-cigar cutter shaped like an artist's palette, by Alexander Jones, 1884, with incised registration number and retailer's mark of *Asprey & Sons 166 Bond St*, 1.5oz.
(Phillips) $731

A late Victorian 15ct. gold advertising vesta case of rounded oblong form, the cover decorated in polychrome enamel with a bottle and glass of 'Bass & C⁰ Pale Ale'.
(Phillips) $717

A late Victorian plain vesta case, inset one side with a compass, makers Collins & Cook, Chester 1900.
(Woolley & Wallis) $140

A late Victorian vesta case, with petal and flower overall design, maker Nathan and Hayes, Chester 1897.
(Woolley & Wallis) $69

An Edwardian rectangular vesta case, one side enameled with a wasp, Birmingham 1905.
(Christie's S. Ken) $500

627

A George IV vinaigrette, engine turned with reeded sides, 1¹/₂in., maker Clarke & Smith, Birmingham 1825.
(Woolley & Wallis) $148

A Regency purse vinaigrette, the gilt interior with pierced grille, 1in., maker Lea & Co., Birmingham 1818.
(Woolley & Wallis) $264

A good William IV vinaigrette, with pierced foliage engraved grille to the gilt interior, 1³/₈in., maker Gervase Wheeler, Birmingham 1834.
(Woolley & Wallis) $165

An early Victorian vinaigrette, the gilt interior with a foliage engraved pierced grille, 1¹/₂in., maker Edward Smith, Birmingham 1843.
(Woolley & Wallis) $157

A Victorian oblong vinaigrette, the gilt interior with a pierced foliage engraved grille, 2¹/₂in., maker Edward Smith, Birmingham 1859.
(Woolley & Wallis) $330

A William IV purse vinaigrette, the gilt interior with a pierced foliage grille, ⁹/₁₀in. high, maker Thomas Shaw, Birmingham 1835. (Woolley & Wallis) $231

A George III oblong vinaigrette, engraved on the cover with a woodsman in 18th century costume, by Matthew Linwood, Birmingham, 1809.
(Phillips) $359

An early Victorian oblong vinaigrette chased in low relief with Windsor Castle, with monogrammed cartouche, by Nathaniel Mills, Birmingham, 1838.
(Phillips) $825

An unusual George III vinaigrette, shaped and engraved with asymmetrical patches of hatching and pricked dots to simulate a tortoise shell, 2.5 x 2.5cm., by Matthew Linwood, Birmingham, 1815.
(Phillips) $430

A William IV book vinaigrette engraved with foliate scrolls, cover inscribed *J. Bonny* in a shaped cartouche, by Taylor & Perry, Birmingham, 1836.
(Phillips) $430

A good George IV silver-gilt vinaigrette, engine-turned base, heavily carved cover and thumbpiece, by Nathaniel Mills, Birmingham, 1826.
(Phillips) $592

A William IV silver-gilt vinaigrette, rectangular, engine-turned, carved thumbpiece, by Nathaniel Mills, Birmingham, 1835. (Phillips) $348

A George IV silver-gilt two-handled campana-shaped wine cooler, collar and liner, by Paul Storr 1825, 11¹/₂in. high, 157oz. (Christie's) $19,861

An Old Sheffield plate part-fluted and gadrooned campana-shaped wine cooler, 10¹/₄in. high. (Christie's) $612

A Victorian two-handled campana-shaped wine cooler, collar and liner, by James Garràrd, 1889, 10¹/₄in. high, 138oz. (Christie's) $17,250

A pair of Sheffield plate two-handled campana-shaped wine coolers, each on a spreading circular base with reeded, ring handles and gadrooned border, circa 1815, 10in. high. (Christie's) $5,808

A pair of Old Sheffield plate inverted pear-shaped wine coolers applied with shell, flute and foliate handles, 8¹/₂in. high. (Christie's) $1,860

A pair of old Sheffield plate wine coolers, with rounded shoulders and everted stamped and filled stiff leaf border with acanthus leaf sheathed reeded handles, 19.5cm. high. (Spencer's) $848

An American silver wine cooler, Gorham Mfg. Co., Providence, RI, 1906, derived from the Florentine pattern, 104oz., 12³/₈in. high. (Sotheby's) $7,150

A pair of George III two-handled vase-shaped wine coolers, each on spreading circular foot, by Samuel Hennell and John Terrey, 1814, each with copper liner, 8¹/₂in. high, 241oz. (Christie's) $17,595

A Victorian two-handled campana-shaped champagne cooler, the rockwork and scroll base on three shell and scroll feet, by John Hunt and Robert Roskell, 1865, 16¹/₂in. high, 214oz. (Christie's) $10,557

A George IV oblong gold snuff-box, engine-turned overall, the thumbpiece chased with flowers and shells, by John Nickolds, London, 1819–20, 2³/₈in. long. (Christie's) **$1,232**

French Samson enameled porcelain snuff box, the top decorated with lion and unicorn coat-of-arms, 3¹/₂in. long. (Eldred's) **$143**

A Louis XV oblong two-color gold snuff-box, engraved overall with panels of wavy basket-weave within waved scroll borders, George A Paris, Paris, 1752–53, 3in. long. (Christie's) **$5,806**

An early George III cartouche-shaped snuff box, the hinged cover richly chased with a classical scene, unmarked, circa 1760. (Christie's) **$399**

A Swiss oval gold enamel and diamond-set snuff-box, the cover with a portrait miniature of Napoleon I, maker's mark *SG*, 3¹/₂in. long. (Christie's) **$16,715**

An enamel snuff box, Staffordshire, late 18th century, modeled in the form of a spaniel recumbent upon a large pink cushion, 4.5cm. wide. (Lawrence Fine Art)

$1,086

A Continental gold and ivory snuff box, French, by Henry Allain, circa 1766, the cover and base with miniature painting of a rural scene, 6.5cm. (Lawrence) **$9,095**

An Austrian oblong snuff box, the hinged cover chased with a view of Vienna, on a matted ground, mid-19th century, 2³/₄in. wide. (Christie's) **$472**

A George II circular gold and enamel snuff-box, painted in soft blues and greens with figures in a rustic landscape, circa 1740, 1³/₄in. diameter. (Christie's) **$3,343**

A Swiss octagonal gold snuff-box, engraved with a classical allegory of music, by Georges Rémond et compagnie, Geneva, circa 1805, 3¼in.
(Christie's) $4,927

Victorian silver-mounted ram's horn snuff container, J. Aitchison, Edinburgh, second half 19th century, 11in. long.
(Skinner) $1,100

A Scottish cartouche-shaped silver and agate snuff-box, gilt interior, by Graham and Anderson, Edinburgh, 1834–35, 3⅝in. long.
(Christie's) $1,463

A fine Meissen chinoiserie snuff box of bombé section, painted in the manner of Christian Friedrich Herold, the top and sides with figures among tea tables, 6.7cm. wide.
(Phillips) $4,640

A Swiss oval enameled gold and jeweled snuff-box, overall enameled with panels of deep purple guilloché divided by opaque white enameled pelleted bands, maker's mark ES, 31in. long.
(Christie's) $13,724

A Swiss oval enameled gold and pearl-set snuff-box, enameled with panels of dark green guilloché with gilt patterned borders, probably François Joanin, circa 1800, 3⅜in. long.
(Christie's) $9,677

An oblong engine-turned gold snuff-box, the cover with a plaque engraved *KAMEHAMEHA IV*th*-TO-E. SHELLEY*, circa 1860, 3¼in. long.
(Christie's) $1,232

A Swiss oval two-color gold and enamel snuff-box engraved with engine-turned panels, maker's mark *FS*, 3⅜in. long.
(Christie's) $5,630

A papier-mâché snuff box, the cover painted with the sleeping figure of a gentleman about to receive an unpleasant surprise from three tree-climbing pranksters, circa 1820, 9cm.
(Phillips) $537

A pair of silver oval lens spectacles with segmental bridge, in fitted silver mounted tortoiseshell case, 5¹/₂in. long.
(Christie's) $243

A rare pair of 'Nuremburg' single wire round rim nose-spectacles, with 'Martins Margins' tortoiseshell visual inserts, frames 17th century, visuals later circa 1758.
(Christie's) $5,181

A rare pair of 'Nuremburg' single wire, round rim nose-spectacles, in flat-edged grooved copper wire with chamois leather fitted cover, German 17th century.
(Christie's) $8,203

A pair of iron Martins Margins, arched bridge, folding sides with large ring ends, inserted horn vissuals, 1 inch diameter lens, English circa 1760.
(Christie's) $604

A fine pair of 'Nuremburg' single wire round rim nose spectacles, in flat edged grooved copper wire, with *NUREMBURG* raised in relief on flat arched bridge, German, mid 17th century, 15mm. diameter lens.
(Christie's) $9,499

A pair of silver green tint D end spectacles, with segmental bridge, and folding sides with pad ends.
(Christie's) $260

A pair of 'Nuremburg' single wire round rim nose spectacles, with arched bridge in grooved copper wire, German, late 17th century, 4in. wide.
(Christie's) $864

A pair of silver round lens spectacles, arched bridge, in brown dyed shagreen case, late 18th century, 5¹/₈in. long.
(Christie's) $281

A rare pair of Chinese lacquered frame spectacles, brass cased folding bridge with clasp and ear threads, possibly 18th century, 4¹/₂in. wide.
(Christie's) $1,295

SPORTING ITEMS

Mike Tyson, signed color 8 x 10, photograph in bare chested pose.
(T. Vennett-Smith) $108

A Weinberger, The Backhand, signed and dated to base, *1912*, bronze figure, with dark patina, on rectangular base, 17³/₄in. high overall.
(Sotheby's) $2,336

American football, trade cards, B.G.C.C.I., 1955 N.F.L. players, some creasing and staining.
(T. Vennett-Smith) $116

A very rare patent model of a cricket bat, American, dated *1859*, the laminated wooden bat with cork interior, lettered *M. DOHERTY, BOSTON, MASS*, 7¹/₂in. high.
(Sotheby's) $425

A collection of six Jeu de Mail hardwood balls, French, mid 18th century.
(Sotheby's) $2,974

Bronze Award Plaque, 1900, by F. Vernon, winged Victory above a view of Paris, triumphant athlete on a podium die-stamped Concours Hippique, 57 x 39mm.
(Sothebys) $425

Jessie Owens, signed color trade card, featuring color caricature of Owens in racing pose.
(T. Vennett-Smith) $116

A signed cricket bat, 1928, by Pickersgill of Bradford, for a test match between England and West Indies at Headingley, 34¹/₄in. long.
(Sotheby's) $467

Muhammed Ali, signed color 8 x 10, full length in boxing pose.
(T. Vennett-Smith) $46

A punishment mask or scold's bridle, entirely of steel, composed of flat steel bars riveted together.
(Christie's) $1,361

A cast-iron royal coat of arms, the arms surmounted by a crown and flanked by a rampant lion and unicorn, banners with *DIEU ET MON DROIT* below, 27in. wide.
(Christie's) $4,660

A Victorian green-painted, cast iron umbrella and stick stand, the back cast with a central figure of a footballer holding a ball, 34in. high.
(Christie's) $777

A demonstration model Holland stove, 23cm. high, circa 1910.
(Auction Team Köln) $54

A cast-iron figure of a dog, probably American, late 19th century, with molded fur and curled tail, 24in. high.
(Sotheby's) $5,750

A cast-iron dog hitching post, American, late 19th century, the head of a dog in the full-round cast in two parts, 16¹/₂in. high.
(Sotheby's) $1,495

A pair of molded cast-iron owl andirons, American, 20th century, in the half-round, with cut-out round eyes, height 14in.
(Sotheby's) $4,888

A cast-iron and pine-plank 'Swan' bench, the swan supports centring five rectangular transverses, length 6ft. 1in.
(Sotheby's) $3,738

A pair of cast-iron horse's head hitching posts, American, 19th century, mounted on ovoid shaped ribbed columnar standards, height 15¹/₄in.
(Sotheby's) $1,840

A wrought-iron rack with set of four hanging utensils, possibly Pennsylvania, late 18th/19th century, overall height 27½in. (Sotheby's) **$1,840**

A painted cast-iron retriever dog garden figure, probably J. W. Fiske & Co., New York, third quarter 19th century, length 52in. (Sotheby's) **$9,200**

A fine and rare painted cast-iron Washington stove figure, Corona Stove Company, American, late 19th century, overall height 69in. (Sotheby's) **$14,950**

A pair of book ends in the style of Hagenauer, each in the form of a lacquered steel stylized figure of a horse, 16cm. high. (Christie's) **$334**

An unusual and rare painted pine and wrought iron 'bone shaker' bicycle, American, late 19th century, 65in. long. (Sotheby's) **$3,575**

An Aesthetic Movement cast iron stick stand by Thomas Jeckyll, painted white, cast in relief with sun, moon and cloud motifs, 82cm. high. (Christie's) **$635**

A pair of Thornton & Downer iron chamber sticks, with circular sconces and drip pans, engraved and stamped decoration, on scrolled feet, 23.2cm. high. (Christie's) **$383**

A green painted cast iron umbrella stand, attributed to Dr Christopher Dresser, with rectangular rail, 79cm. high. (Christie's) **$502**

A pair of cast-iron Hessian andirons, American, late 19th century, of typical form with striding figures. (Sotheby's) **$1,760**

A Gritzner sewing table set, cast iron with colored glass containers, inscriptions on lids, circa 1920.
(Auction Team Köln)
$254

Cast iron doorstop in the form of a terrier, good early paint, 10in. long.
(Eldred's)
$94

A pair of painted cast-iron dogs, American, 19th century, each full standing and life-size, with tails, raised on a plinth base, 49³/₄in. long.
(Sotheby's)
$4,950

A cast iron hitching post by O. Silberzahn Manufactory, Westbend, Wisconsin, 19th century, the cast horse's-head with wavy mane and molded features, retains traces of yellow polychrome, 14in. high.
(Christie's)
$880

A cast-iron fireback, with the Tudor rose on a shield flanked by a supporting lion and winged grayhound, and surmounted by a crown, inscribed *1571*, 27¹/₂in. wide.
(Christie's)
$866

One of a pair of Coalbrookdale white-painted cast-iron campana urns, decorated with scrolling flowerheads and foliage, with twin bacchic mask handles, 31in. high.
(Christie's)
(Two)
$3,011

Antique cast iron bank, a tumbling man, 9¹/₂in. high, paint faded and worn.
(Eldred's)
$303

A decorative cast-iron fireback, cast in relief with an armorial cartouche flanked by supporting lions, surmounted by a visored helmet and a third lion, 44in. wide.
(Christie's)
$1,425

A cast-iron umbrella stand, possibly Coalbrookdale, circa 1855, in the form of a dog begging with a whip in its mouth, 2ft. wide.
(Sotheby's)
$3,751

A wrought iron trivet, American, late 18th century, with strapwork and scrolled iron filigree within a pointed arch, on tripod legs, 12¹/₂in. long.
(Christie's) $770

A cast iron coal box with elegant relief decoration, circa 1880.
(Auction Team Köln) $109

A 'Naughty Nellie' bootpull, cast iron with gold varnish, circa 1910, 24cm. long.
(Auction Team Köln) $77

A decorative cast-iron fireback, decorated with two anchors interspersed with rosettes and fleur-de-lis, with rope-twist borders, 21in. wide.
(Christie's) $770

A Victorian cast iron whip stand, depicting a begging dog holding in his mouth his master's hunting whip, registration mark for 1880, 25in. overall.
(Woolley & Wallis) $1,388

A large decorative cast-iron fireback, the arched top surmounted by a seashell and supporting angels, the main panel decorated with a biblical scene in relief, 38in. wide.
(Christie's) $1,925

A Regency red-painted cast-iron lamp base, with a fluted circular shaft cast with outswept foliate scrolls, on shaped, square tapering base, 29in. wide.
(Christie's) $2,136

A decorative cast-iron fireback, with an arched top, decorated in relief with a mythological scene, surrounded by putti and fruiting foliage, 30¹/₂in. wide.
(Christie's) $1,251

19th century cast iron still bank, in the form of a monkey, 8in. high.
(Eldred's) $66

A Brussels tapestry woven in wools and silks depicting a scene from the triumphs of Petrarch, 10ft. 11in. x 14ft. 6in.
(Christie's) $8,882

A 17th century Aubusson tapestry of Judith with the head of Holofernes, within an ornate border with a cartouche of the Virgin and Child above, 315 x 306cm. (Finarte) $12,827

A Felletin chinoiserie tapestry woven in wools and silks with a pair of storks in a woody landscape with a palace and temples beyond, mid-18th century, 8ft. 10in. x 12ft.
(Christie's) $15,100

A tapestry woven in wools and silks in the Soho style of John Vanderbank, on a brown ground depicting courtly chinoiserie figures with a couple beneath a plumed canopy, 8ft. 10½in. x 7ft. (Christie's) $15,741

A Bruges tapestry woven in wools and silks depicting Astrology beside a celestial globe, flanked by a seated figure in Roman dress and a putto with an eagle, late 17th century, 12ft. 4in. x 11ft. 4in.
(Christie's) $33,753

A Brussels tapestry woven in silks and wools with Moses in a basket before Pharaoh's daughter, in an exotic wooded landscape with buildings beyond, early 18th century, 140 x 150in.
(Christie's) $21,747

A 19th century French Aubusson rug decorated allover with floral and foliate cartouches, 158 x 158cm.
(Finarte) $4,631

A Lille Teniers tapestry woven in verdure tones, blues and reds with rustic figures grouped in a clearing, one playing ninepins, early 18th century, 10ft. 6in. x 10ft.
(Christie's) $42,636

A Beauvais Teniers tapestry, woven in wools and silks, depicting a group of seated peasants playing musical instruments, 18th century, 8ft. 8³/₄in. x 4ft. 8in.
(Christie's) $15,988

A mid 18th century tapestry from the Royal Felletin factory of a landscape with buildings worked in browns, blues and ochers, 410 x 275cm.
(Finarte) $11,031

A 19th century French Aubusson rug, the central panel with a shield quartered on a blue ground, the border with laurel leaves and love knots, 372 x 352cm.
(Finarte) $11,402

A Brussels tapestry, woven in silks and wools with a battle scene in a pass, with a prophet and attendants on a rocky outcrop above, early 18th century, 140 x 151in.
(Christie's) $23,418

A honey golden plush covered teddy bear, with large clear and black glass eyes, large wide-apart ears, 18in. high.
(Christie's) $975

A pale golden plush covered teddy bear, with clear and black glass eyes, black stitched nose, smiling mouth and claws, 16in. high.
(Christie's) $412

A small Steiff white plush teddy bear, with brown glass eyes, beige stitched nose and mouth, 5in. high, circa 1910.
(Christie's) $758

A Steiff humped teddy bear with original gray eyes, long muzzle and covered in blond mohair, with growl and original pads, lacks button, circa 1925, 50cm. high.
(Auction Team Köln)
$1,080

A rare and early Steiff golden plush covered teddy bear, with black shoe-button eyes, pronounced snout, remains of sealing-wax nose, 19in. high, 1905.
(Christie's) $6,395

A rich golden plush covered teddy bear, with black boot button eyes, pronounced cut muzzle, black stitched nose, smiling mouth and claws, 13in. high.
(Christie's) $659

A rare 'Dicky' Steiff white plush covered teddy bear, with orange and black glass eyes, short plush covered muzzle, 12in. high, 1930.
(Christie's) $5,940

A Steiff dark cinnamon plush teddy bear, German, 1920's, with button in ear and remains of red label, together with a Steiff bear, German, circa 1960, 29in. high.
(Sotheby's) $3,498

A Steiff honey golden plush covered teddy bear, with black boot button eyes, black stitched mouth and claws, swivel head, elongated jointed limbs, 12in. high, 1908–10.
(Christie's) $1,980

A Schuco tumbling teddy bear, with pale golden plush covered metal face, body and limbs, 4¾in. high.
(Christie's) $634

A shaggy long haired golden plush covered teddy bear, with orange and black early plastic eyes, large pronounced snout, 19in. high.
(Christie's) $539

A Steiff dual plush petsy bear, German, circa 1928, with button in ear, blue glass eyes and center seam with blonde stitched snout, 16in. high.
(Sotheby's) $6,646

A Farnell golden plush covered teddy bear, with black glass eyes, pronounced clipped muzzle, black stitched nose with outer stitching extra long, black stitched inverted V mouth, 14in. high, circa 1915.
(Christie's) $1,648

A family of three Steiff silver plush teddy bears, German, circa 1908–15, each missing button, the two larger with brown stitched pointed snouts, the baby bear with white and black glass eyes, 12in., 10in., 3¼in. high.
(Sotheby's) $1,749

A Steiff golden plush covered teddy bear, with large black boot button eyes, pronounced snout, black stitched nose, 23½in. high, circa 1910.
(Christie's) $3,467

A Steiff apricot plush teddy bear, German, circa 1908, with button in ear, black stitched snout, black boot button eyes, excelsior stuffed and with swivel joints, 25in. high.
(Sotheby's) $3,673

A Gerbrüder Bing honey plush covered teddy bear, with black boot button eyes, pronounced snout, felt pads and pewter button attached to side of body, 14in. high, circa 1914.
(Christie's) $2,015

A large Steiff pale honey golden plush covered teddy bear, with large black boot button eyes, pronounced cut muzzle, black stitched nose, mouth and claws, 30in. high, circa 1910.
(Christie's) $6,930

A Syro-Hittite terracotta jar, the body decorated with multiple stylized figures, Syria, circa 2000–1500 B.C., 3³/₄in.
(Bonhams)   **$1,061**

A Wiener Werkstätte terracotta figure, of a polychrome glazed standing female, on an oval base with molded floral decoration, *Made in Austria*, 24.1cm. high.
(Christie's)   **$612**

A Hellenistic terracotta female head with an ornate crown of rosettes, circa 2nd-1st century B.C., 4in.
(Bonhams)   **$522**

A glazed terracotta oil jar, of baluster form, with two handles, and two others similar, 46in. high.
(Christie's)   **$2,718**

A Continental painted terracotta group of three boys, German, circa 1900, made in Germany, 11³/₄in. high.
(Sotheby's)   **$1,925**

An 18th century French terracotta portrait bust of a boy, his hair fastened en queue, signed *LP* on the reverse, 40cm. high.
(Phillips)   **$1,413**

A terracotta bas relief of St. Anthony of Padua with the Infant Christ and angels, attributed to Massimiliano Soldani Benzi, 34.5 x 25cm., late 17th/early 18th century.
(Finarte)   **$5,338**

A late 19th century Austrian painted terracotta model of a seated pug dog, with inset glass eyes, 11in. high.
(Christie's)   **$1,192**

A fine and rare modeled terra cotta newsboy architectural plaque, H. A. Lewis, South Boston, Massachusetts, 1883–1887, modeled in the half round with the figure of a running newsboy, 61in. wide.
(Sotheby's)   **$14,300**

A terracotta copy of the Sleeping satyr, called the Barberini Faun, probably 19th century, 90cm. high. (Kunsthaus am Museum) $6,811

A French terracotta roundel of the head of a Bacchante, cast from a model by Cesare Costantino Raimondo Céribelli, late 19th century, 11³/₄in. diameter. (Christie's) $1,159

George Goudray 'Les Nenuphars', painted terracotta bust of a girl in Art Nouveau style, with incised signature, 23in. high. (Lawrences) $1,728

A French terracotta bust of Diana, modeled and cast by Albert-Ernest Carrier-Belleuse, her head crowned by a crescent moon and star and star, signed *A. CARRIER*, second half 19th century, 24³/₄in. high without socle. (Christie's) $12,705

Two Liberty & Co. terracotta jardinières, designed by Mrs. F. G. Watts, after Archibald Knox. (Bonhams) $1,495

A Wiener Werkstätte terracotta bowl and cover, the circular cover surmounted by a stylized hunter and dog, covered in a running ink-blue glaze, with impressed *WW* monogram, 22.6cm. high. (Christie's) $804

'Lisetta', an Ernst Wahliss terracotta plaque molded in relief with a profile bust of a young woman surrounded by a garland of flowers, 41cm. high. (Christie's) $334

A Continental painted terracotta figure of a seated bulldog, naturalistically modeled with collar and glass eyes, 31cm. high. (Allen & Harris) $231

Portrait medallion of Benjamin Franklin, signed and dated *J. B. Nini 1770*, terracotta, 142mm. diameter. (Skinner) $825

A shield-shaped needlework purse, embroidered in colored silks and silver gilt threads, one side with a stag, the other with a unicorn, 4in. long, Continental, mid 18th century.
(Christie's) $1,123

A fine whitework picture depicting Judith presenting the head of Holofernes, embroidered with seed pearls, first half of 17th century, 5 x 3½in.
(Christie's) $8,277

An oval needlework picture, embroidered in colored silks, with a young girl holding a parrot and a bird cage, 13 x 12in., framed and glazed, early 18th century.
(Christie's) $1,123

Pieced worsted spread, America, 19th century, pink and olive patches arranged in a zig-zag pattern heightened with feather and parallel line quilting, 86 x 98in.
(Skinner) $935

A beadwork picture worked in many colored beads, with a lady and gentleman in a landscape, their hair of metal thread, 10 x 13in., English, mid 17th century.
(Christie's) $2,763

A shield shaped needlework purse of yellow silk, one side with the monogram CVI? possibly for the Emperor Charles VI, 4½in., Continental, circa 1740.
(Christie's) $1,468

Quilted chintz pocket, America, circa 1825, block printed plum tree and pheasant pattern in madder, blue and drab, 14in. long.
(Skinner) $880

A Shahsevan Sumak cradle, North Persia, each of the four sides comprising a central band in indigo blue, containing characteristic hexagonal motifs, 3ft. 2in. long.
(Phillips) $708

A rare needlework purse, with Tudor roses and thistles and fleurs-de-lys, crowns and crossed-swords and the initials *J.R.VIII*, very early 18th century.
(Christie's) $1,815

A Victorian beaded bag, with draw string top and tassel to the base, circa 1860.
(Woolley & Wallis) $134

A post war screen-printed linen panel by A. Fumeron, depicting a young girl playing a cello, 125 x 157cm.
(Christie's) $234

A needlework purse worked in green silk and gold thread in eye stitch with the initials *P.C.S.* and hearts, late 17th/early 18th century.
(Christie's) $998

A needlework picture, worked in colored silks and gilt threads, with the bust of Charles I within a raised work frame, 15 x 11in., English, late 17th century.
(Christie's) $2,649

Crewel embroidered linen pocket, America, late 18th century, worked in shades of yellow, green, blue and bound with variously printed cotton fabrics, 16¼in. long.
(Skinner) $990

Appliquéd and pieced table rug, England, initialed and dated *E.B. 1858* worked in red, blue, yellow, cream and brown wool patches, 66in. square.
(Skinner) $880

A rare early 18th century tapestry embroidery in the form of a card table top with projecting corner sections, 25 x 31in., glazed and framed.
(Locke & England) $3,440

A needlework picture, embroidered in colored silks, gilt and silver gilt threads, with a lady and gentleman standing in front of a castle, 7 x 10in., English, circa 1660.
(Christie's) $3,799

A petit point embroidered portrait of William and Mary, English, early 18th century, worked in predominantly blue and scarlet wools and silks, 14 x 10in.
(Sotheby's) $954

A RYNA 87 two slice folding toaster with original electric flex, unused, circa 1952. (Auction Team Köln)
$39

An Estate Electric Toaster No. 177, 4 slice toaster with simultaneous turning mechanism, 1925. (Auction Team Köln)
$208

A Meriden Mod. 60 decorative plated toaster with 2-slice tip mechanism, circa 1925. (Auction Team Köln)
$77

An early American Simplex T211 toaster with simple folding mechanism and heavy black enameled cast base, plated casing with wooden handle, 1909. (Auction Team Köln)
$131

An early American General Electric D12 ceramic toaster with two-sided toasting fork, white ceramic base with gold decoration, original flex with metal plug, circa 1910. (Auction Team Köln)
$772

An early Universal toaster No. E 945 by Landers, Frary & Clark, New Britain CT, with warming rack attachment, plated, circa 1918. (Auction Team Köln)
$169

A chromium Hotpoint Mod. 129 T41 2-slice toaster with simultaneous tip mechanism, by General Electric, Bridgeport CT, 1929. (Auction Team Köln)
$69

A Toastmaster Mod. 1B14 automatic pop-up toaster, a 2-slice chromium toaster with pop-up facility, 1941. (Auction Team Köln)
$61

A Hotpoint Model 115 T 1 plated toaster with two-sided tip mechanism, by the Edison Electric Appliance Co. Inc., New York, circa 1919. (Auction Team Köln)
$69

An Arnold army motorcyclist, lithographed tinplate, wind-up action with Firestone headlamp, lacking support, 1938–40. (Auction Team Köln) $432

A Märklin signalman with moving arm, 1940s, in original packing. (Auktionsverket) $727

A lithographed clockwork peacock, it moves slowly forward and lifts its tail feathers, 1920–30s, German, 25cm. long. (Auktionsverket) $410

A Linemar Karl Alfred lithographed clockwork Popeye figure, moves forward on rollerskates swinging its arms, 1950s. (Auktionsverket) $528

A carved and painted pine horse pull toy, probably American, late 19th century, the stylized figure of a dappled gray horse with real horsehair mane and tail, 28¹/₂in. wide. (Sotheby's) $1,760

A lithographed monkey drummer in red jacket and blue trousers, 1920s, German, total height 19.5cm. (Auktionsverket) $462

A Lehmann Skirolf 781, a lithographed skier with sticks, 1930–41, 19cm. high. (Auktionsverket) $2,391

A Lehmann Halloh 683 clockwork motorcyclist, with original box and instructions, 1910–20, 22cm. long. (Auktionsverket) $4,673

Folding iron doll's bed with canopy support, on castors, circa 1920. (Auction Team Köln) $139

TOYS

A Märklin first series clockwork battleship 'Chicago', German, circa 1905, with two large revolving turrets, 34¹/₂in. long.
(Sotheby's) $30,367

An Automobiles Geographical Ltd. Ranlite Austin saloon, English, 1930's, the bakelite body finished in green and black, in maker's box, 10¹/₂in. long.
(Sotheby's) $1,076

A Martin 'L' autopatte', French, circa 1910, the cart finished in blue with pink wheels and pushed by a crouching Negro, 6¹/₂in. long.
(Sotheby's) $521

A tinplate cooking range and accessories, German, circa 1900, the body finished in black with brass handrail and embossed brass doors, 11in. high.
(Sotheby's) $833

A Nomura 'Solar-X' battery powered space rocket, Japanese, circa 1960, in tinplate and plastic finished in silver, red and yellow, together with an S.H. Space Station.
(Sotheby's) $382

A Schuco panda, with black and white mohair-over-metal face, body and limbs, 3¹/₂in. high, circa 1950.
(Christie's) $257

A Lehmann 'Naughty boy' tinplate vis-à-vis, German, circa 1910, lithographed in cream with blue trim, the driver in brown the boy in blue, 5in. long.
(Sotheby's) $607

A painted wooded toy poultry shop, with colored flower transfer decoration and marble printed paper covered slab, 12in. wide, 1897.
(Christie's) $1,188

A Lehmann 'Masuyama' tinplate clockwork novelty toy, German, circa 1930, the figure with coolie hat and red trousers, 7in. long.
(Sotheby's) $1,180

TOYS

A painted wood Noah's Ark, with sliding side and animals including beavers and leopards, 21in. long, Sonneberg, second half of the 19th century.
(Christie's)   **$1,282**

A fine tinplate horse and gig toy, possibly Buchner, German, late 19th century, with well detailed composition top-hatted male driver, 12¼in. wide.
(Sotheby's)   **$1,996**

A rare Märklin clockwork painted camouflaged tinplate anti-aircraft half track, with steering and rubber front tires, circa 1938, 8in. long.
(Christie's)   **$348**

A Tipp & Co. tinplate fire station and engines, German, circa 1910, lithographed in orange and brown with figures of a petrol pump, ladder, post box and alarm bell, the station 10in. wide.
(Sotheby's)   **$1,735**

A Lehmann 'Oh my' tinplate mechanical dancer, German, circa 1925, the base lithographed in blue with red and white features, 10in. high.
(Sotheby's)   **$694**

A Bing tinplate garage and cars, German, 1920's, the double garage lithographed in gray and yellow with opening doors, the garage 8½in. wide.
(Sotheby's)   **$555**

A painted and carved wooden rocking horse, English, 1910, the well carved horse with remains of original paintwork, 52in. long.
(Sotheby's)   **$787**

A transfer-printed Waltershausen doll's house chiffonier, with four opening doors and a mirror, 4½in. high.
(Christie's)   **$356**

A tinplate motorcyclist, German, circa 1910, the cycle with good lithographed details, gyroscope mechanism, 7½in. long.
(Sotheby's)   **$3,991**

A Carette clockwork lithographed tinplate limousine, finished in red with white lining and gold detailing, circa 1913, 12¹/₂in. long.
(Christie's) $1,839

A Lehmann 'tut-tut' tinplate mechanical car, German, circa 1920, lithographed in cream and red, with handpainted driver.
(Sotheby's) $330

A fine Tippco painted and lithographed tinplate battery operated Mercedes 220S Convertible with composition driver and original trade label, 12¹/₂in. long.
(Christie's) $2,323

A Lehmann clockwork lithographed tinplate 'Adam' the porter with sack trolley and trunk.
(Christie's) $968

A rare Britains composition No. 43f Country Cottage with farmer, farmer's wife, villagers, poultry, pig, three trees, seat, circular flower bed and flowers, in original box.
(Christie's) $1,162

A Steiff 'Peter Rabbit' velveteen covered, with black boot button eyes backed with red felt, pink stitched nose and mouth, 8in. high, circa 1910.
(Christie's) $348

An Eberl clockwork lithographed tinplate 'Hipp-Hipp-Hurrah' yacht 'Maria', with sailor, fabric sails and lithographed deck detail, 1920's, 10in. long.
(Christie's) $620

A set of painted felt-headed dolls of Snow White and the Seven Dwarfs, Snow White in original yellow dress with blue velvet bodice and pink and blue cape, 17in. high, with Chad Valley label on foot.
(Christie's) $2,564

A German steam-jet powered painted tinplate two-tier carousel, fitted with seats and painted composition horses and figures, circa 1910, 15in. high.
(Christie's) $2,904

A Günthermann clockwork painted and lithographed tinplate closed four-seat tourer, with bellows action, circa 1908, 8½in. long.
(Christie's) $1,742

A Märklin painted tinplate swimming bath, with operating diving-board and ladder, circa 1900, 17in. long, 14½in. wide overall.
(Christie's) $871

A Nomura 'Atom' battery operated tinplate motorcycle and rider, Japanese, 1950's, lithographed in black with blue, cream and silver details, 12in. long.
(Sotheby's) $434

A Lehmann painted tinplate and fabric 'Dancing Sailor' with 'Brandenburg' cap tally, with swaying action, in original box.
(Christie's) $736

A Dean's Rag Book Company velveteen 'Dismal Desmond', in seated position with red felt tongue, 6in. high, 1926.
(Christie's) $293

A Linemar battery-operated fabric and lithographed tinplate Mickey the Magician with disappearing chicken, in original box, 10½in. high.
(Christie's) $736

A Distler lithographed tinplate fire station, with operating double doors linked to 'Fire!' indicator, 9in. long.
(Christie's) $465

A Louis Marx 'Marx Merrymakers' tinplate mouse band, English, circa 1935, the lithographed figures sitting on and around a piano, 9in. long, some rust.
(Sotheby's) $868

A rare Schuco clockwork tinplate and fabric two-wheel 210 mousecart with two mice, circa 1932, 4in. wide.
(Christie's) $542

A Louis Vuitton upright trunk covered in LV fabric and bound in brass, the lid opening to reveal a top compartment with tray, 25 x 16 x 45¹/₂in.
(Christie's) $8,516

Brass and wood bound Louis Vuitton trunk with fitted interior, 44¹/₂in. high.
(Eldred's) $2,750

A Louis Vuitton shoe case, covered in LV fabric and bound in leather and brass, divided into eight shoe compartments, 24 x 14 x 8in.
(Christie's) $1,553

A Louis Vuitton suitcase covered in LV fabric with travel stickers, bound in brass, the interior fitted with a tray, 24 x 15 x 8¹/₂in.
(Christie's) $595

A Louis Vuitton Jubilee wardrobe trunk, covered in LV fabric, bound in brass and wood, with key commemorating Louis Vuitton London's Jubilee 1885–1935, 22 x 22 x 44in.
(Christie's) $2,225

A brown pigskin leather dressing case with foul weather cover, the interior fitted with silver gilt (London 1929) mounted tortoiseshell topped flasks, hairbrushes and manicure set.
(Christie's) $869

A gentleman's green leather dressing case, completely fitted with four silver-topped (London 1907) flasks, 20 x 14 x 7in.
(Christie's) $750

A black leather Gladstone bag with side pocket, the interior lined in royal blue moiré silk and fitted with four silver topped flasks, Mappin & Webb 1938, 14 x 5¹/₂ x 10in.
(Christie's) $257

A brown crocodile leather dressing case, the interior completely lined in matching crocodile leather, 26 x 16 x 8in.
(Christie's) $525

Edwardian mahogany bordered tray with attached brass handles with marquetry motif to center, 20 x 13in.
(G. A. Key) **$119**

A Russian porcelain oval tray based on a design by Sergei V. Chekhonin with the silhouette in red of a sailor of the Baltic Fleet, circa 1921, 17³/₄in. wide.
(Christie's) **$2,225**

Cantonese enameled tray, depicting a village and shipping scene, circa 1750, approximately 12 x 8in.
(G. A. Key) **$596**

A Regency rectangular papier mâché tray by Clay, King St., Covent Garden, decorated in red, green and gold, 30 x 22in.
(Bearne's) **$2,471**

Fisher-Strand inlaid Art Nouveau tray, Germany, circa 1900, rectangular tray with bronze handles and brass stylized inlay, 13³/₄in. long.
(Skinner) **$330**

A 19th century rectangular papier mâché tray, heightened in gilt, the reverse stamped *MAPPLEBECK & LOWE*, 23³/₄in. wide.
(Christie's) **$433**

A late 18th/early 19th century oval tray, the burr yew plateau with satinwood fan patera and tulipwood crossbanded edge, 28¹/₄in. wide.
(Christie's) **$650**

A fine mahogany cutlery tray, possibly Thomas and/or John Seymour, Boston, Massachusetts, circa 1805, the sides with dividers cyma-shaped, width 10¹/₂in.
(Sotheby's) **$5,750**

A George III brass-bound mahogany oval tray with scrolled handles and gadrooned lip, previously with castors, the brass probably later, 27¹/₂ x 19³/₄in.
(Christie's) **$6,090**

A rosewood box, circa 1860, the top decorated with a floral panel depicting a lily and nasturtiums surrounded by a broad rose banding, 10½in. wide.
(Sotheby's) $682

A rosewood tea caddy, circa 1840, the hinged lid with a sycamore-reserved scene of Muckross Abbey, the three division interior lacking blending bowl, on bun feet, 12in. wide.
(Sotheby's) $682

A William IV rosewood tea caddy, circa 1830, the hinged lid with a maple panel of a spaniel, the interior with two divisions, 7in. wide.
(Sotheby's) $205

A bird's-eye maple jewel cabinet, circa 1850, the floral inlaid hinged lid above a fitted interior, on bun feet, 8¾in. wide.
(Sotheby's) $716

A fine coromandel box, circa 1870, the top with a fine inlaid view of Battle Abbey Gatehouse and floral bandings, 9½in. wide.
(Sotheby's) $2,216

An adjustable bookstand, circa 1860, veneered in stained ash on one face and rosewood on the back, incorporating two mosaic panels of flowers, 10in. wide.
(Sotheby's) $767

A stained ash box, circa 1870, the top decorated with a fine view of The Parade (Pantiles, Tunbridge Wells), 9½in. wide.
(Sotheby's) $2,131

A coromandel stationery box, circa 1850, the domed top with a scene of Tonbridge Abbey, the lined interior with divisions and concave sides, 9¾in. wide.
(Sotheby's) $938

A rosewood work box, circa 1850, inlaid throughout with floral borders, the lined interior with a removable tray, 12in. wide.
(Sotheby's) $938

A rosewood work box, circa 1840, the top decorated with a fine panel depicting the state apartments at Windsor Castle, 11½in. wide.
(Sotheby's) $2,557

A rosewood dressing table companion, circa 1850, the top fitted with compartments, three lidded and four with associated scent bottles, on bun feet, 12¾in. wide.
(Sotheby's) $2,046

A rosewood tea caddy of sarcophagus shape, circa 1845, the top inlaid with floral panel, floral and geometrical bandings, all sides with broad floral bandings, 12½in. wide.
(Sotheby's) $546

An unusual rosewood stationery box, circa 1845, the angled, hinged top inlaid with the Prince of Wales' feathers and royal supporters and *Ich Dien*, 8in. wide.
(Sotheby's) $1,500

A fine rosewood box, circa 1835, the top decorated with a panel depicting Eridge Castle in mosaic, 10in. wide.
(Sotheby's) $1,159

A coromandel tea caddy, circa 1850, of rectangular form, with a cube pattern top and floral mosaic inlaid sides, 5½in. wide.
(Sotheby's) $409

A coromandel jewel cabinet, circa 1860, the hinged top with a scene of Tonbridge Castle enclosing compartments, on bun feet, 10in. wide.
(Sotheby's) $818

A fine rosewood writing slope, circa 1860, the top inlaid with a panel depicting Hever Castle, with floral bandings and parquetry panel, 12in. wide.
(Sotheby's) $2,302

A fine rosewood tea caddy, circa 1860, the top inlaid with Battle Abbey Gatehouse flanked by oval medallions inlaid with geometrical designs, 14½in. wide.
(Sotheby's) $2,216

A rare three row American Hamilton Automatic under strike machine with short type bars, needs restoration, circa 1887.
(Auktion Team Köln)
$2,897

A Gramophone & Typewriter Ltd Lambert typewriter, with blue and gilt lining and oak case with accessories.
(Christie's) $659

A rare Diskret code typewriter with control arm and sliding second scale for printing coded texts, by Friedr. Rehmann, Karlsruhe, 1899.
(Auktion Team Köln)
$3,766

An American Postal No. 7 typewriter, produced only in limited numbers as a prototype, with wooden case and instructions, 1908.
(Auktion Team Köln)
$3,477

A Moya Visible No. 2 typewriter with oxidized top-plate and mahogany case.
(Christie's) $2,082

A Blickensderfer No. 7 typewriter with one typewheel, gilt finish to bright parts and bentwood cover.
(Christie's) $451

The Mignon AEG Model 4 German pointer typewriter with type cylinder, 1923.
(Auction Team Köln)
$186

An early Hammond typewriter, in oak case, 13$^{1}/_{2}$in. wide.
(Anderson & Garland)
$165

An Active typewriter with sliding typewheel, steel frame and leatherette case.
(Christie's) $521

Zinc and copper ox weather vane, America, mid 19th century, regilded, 34½in. long. (Skinner) **$3,850**

A painted sheet-iron weathervane, American, late 19th/early 20th century, in the form of a locomotive with conductor, 20in. high, 45½in. long. (Christie's) **$2,200**

Molded copper running horse weather vane, America, 19th century, fine verdigris surface, 31in. long. (Skinner) **$1,430**

Sheet metal weather vane in the form of a mariner with spy glass, America, 19th century, painted black. (Skinner) **$605**

Molded copper weather vane in the form of Henry Hudson's ship 'Half Moon', America, early 20th century, 44in. high. (Skinner) **$1,870**

Copper weathervane of a grass hopper, America, 20th century, verdigris surface, 35in. long. (Skinner) **$770**

A gilt copper weathervane cockerel, with elaborate tail, mounted on a wrought-iron stand (damages; bullet holes; gilding worn), 18th/19th century, 24in. wide. (Christie's) **$1,636**

Molded copper weather vane, America, early 20th century, in the form of a merino sheep, verdigris surface, 28½in. long. (Skinner) **$4,125**

A rare small molded and gilt zinc and copper rooster weathervane, J. Howard and Company, Bridgewater, Massachusetts, third quarter 19th century, 12½in. long. (Christie's) **$6,600**

A carved and painted pine flying Canada goose, possibly Maritime Provinces, early 20th century, in the style of Ira Hudson, length 40in.
(Sotheby's) $2,750

A fine and rare gilded copper peacock weathervane, attributed to A. L. Jewell, Waltham, Massachusetts, third quarter 19th century, the elegant swell-bodied figure of a stylized peacock with repoussé tail and wrought iron legs, 39in. long.
(Sotheby's) $9,350

A molded sheet copper flying dove weathervane, American, late 19th/early 20th century, the boxy stylized silhouette of a flying dove with wings raised and tail extended, overall length 22¹/₂in.
(Sotheby's) $770

A carved and painted pine and sheet-metal sailing ship weathervane, American, early 20th century, having a pine hull and pine masts, overall length 31in.
(Sotheby's) $990

An unusual molded and painted copper centaur weathervane, attributed to A. L. Jewell & Co., Waltham, Massachusetts, third quarter 19th century, the swell-bodied figure of a folky centaur with molded hair, aiming its bow and arrow, length 26in.
(Sotheby's) $16,500

A fine molded and gilded copper leaping stag weathervane, attributed to L. W. Cushing & Sons, Waltham, Massachusetts, third quarter 19th century, the swell-bodied stylized figure of a leaping stag with sheet copper antler and ears, length 38in.
(Sotheby's) $9,350

WEATHERVANES

An amusing carved and painted pine and sheet copper horned cow weathervane, American, late 19th/early 20th century, 33½in. long.
(Sotheby's) $2,530

An unusual molded and painted copper horse and sulky weathervane, probably New York, third quarter 19th century, repaired bullet holes, 45in. wide.
(Sotheby's) $11,000

A rare and important carved and gilded pine large rooster weathervane, Maine, late 18th century, the striking and impressive full-bodied figure with prominent comb, beak, wattle and strong feather and tail detail, 28in. high.
(Sotheby's) $66,000

An amusing painted sheet-metal rooster weathervane, American, early 20th century, the stylized folky figure of a swell-bodied rooster with applied sheet metal wings and shaped tail, overall length 42in.
(Sotheby's) $3,575

A molded copper and zinc ram weathervane, attributed to L. W. Cushing & Company, Waltham, Massachusetts, third quarter 19th century, length 34¼in.
(Sotheby's) $6,600

A small-scale molded and gilded copper standing horse weathervane, American, third quarter 19th century, covered in gilding, 20½in. long.
(Sotheby's) $1,100

A carved and painted wooden merganser decoy, New England, late 19th century, with groove-carved bill, glass eyes and tapering body, 17¹/₂in. long.
(Christie's) $990

A large carved-wood Royal coat of arms, circa 1900, carved and painted, 5ft. 11¹/₄in. wide.
(Sotheby's) $2,898

A carved and painted pine and tin touring car toy, American, early 20th century, 17¹/₂in. long.
(Sotheby's) $1,430

A late 17th or 18th century English turned lignum vitae cup, with reeded rim and central fillet on ribbed surbase and stem, 14cm. high.
(Phillips) $956

A painted pine parcheesi game board, American, 19th century, painted in tones of red, green and black, 19¹/₄ x 19¹/₄in.
(Sotheby's) $1,430

Carved and painted figure of a soldier, America, 19th century, painted blue, black, white, mustard and red, with articulated arms, 17in. high.
(Skinner) $8,250

Carved and painted kingfisher, America, late 19th century, 20in. high.
(Skinner) $825

A pair of Flemish carved oak putti, with short curling hair, some drapery around their hips, late 17th century, 21¹/₂in. high.
(Christie's) $2,310

Two wooden tankards, 18th century, each tapering cylindrical bound with hoops, the larger 9in. high.
(Christie's) $1,760

WOOD

A burlwood bowl, late 18th/ early 19th century, with lobed lip and molded upstanding handles, 17½in. long.
(Christie's) $1,760

A painted dummy board of 17th century style, depicting two young girls holding hands, on associated stained supports, 40½in. wide.
(Christie's) $2,932

A rare 17th century fruitwood oval snuff box and cover, carved with the Royal Coat of Arms and *C.R.* cypher, 11cm.
(Bearne's) $3,600

A carved walnut cartouche, surrounded by elaborate beaded scrolls and scrolling foliage, second half 17th century, 15½in. wide.
(Christie's) $770

A pair of 19th century Black Forest relief carved panels, carved with hunting trophies of dead game and weapons surrounded by branches and foliage, 34in. wide.
(Bearne's) $971

A carved walnut bull's-head, American, 19th century, with tapering horns, groove carved eyes, nostrils and mouth with carved applied ears, 11in. high.
(Christie's) $2,420

A carved, painted and gilded pine shaking hands sign, American, late 19th/early 20th century, 23½in. long.
(Sotheby's) $2,860

A fine carved, painted and gessoed American eagle, Wilhelm Schimmel, Cumberland Valley, Pennsylvania, circa 1880, wingspan 22½in.
(Sotheby's) $38,500

Reproduction carved and painted wood figure of a sailor holding a donation box, 57in. high.
(Eldred's) $715

WOOD

An unusual carved and painted pine and sheet-metal American eagle birdhouse, made by E. G. James, Mingo County, West Virginia, circa 1920, height 53in.
(Sotheby's) **$8,050**

An unusual carved and painted pine child's barber shop chair seat, American, late 19th/early 20th century, length 24in.
(Sotheby's) **$1,725**

A carved pine figure of a woman, American, 19th century, the stylized, worn three dimensional figure mounted on a rod in a black metal base, height 16¹/₄in.
(Sotheby's) **$748**

A good Norwegian burr-wood peg tankard, the cover, handle and feet carved with heraldic lions, late 18th/early 19th century, 9in. high.
(Bearne's) **$1,324**

An unusual painted pine checkerboard, American, late 19th century, the playing surface with brown and red squares within black and red borders, 15¹/₄ x 15¹/₄in.
(Sotheby's) **$1,725**

Gustav Stickley wastebasket, no. 94, circa 1910, thirteen vertical slats attached to interior iron rings, unsigned, 14in. high.
(Skinner) **$990**

A small carved and painted pine lady ship's figurehead, American, probably New England, circa 1860, height 23in.
(Sotheby's) **$4,313**

A green-painted wheelbarrow, the trapezoidal form with rounded sides, the outside painted with a running horse and *G.B. Tufts*, with tapering down-turned handle, chamfered tapering stops, and a central red painted front wheel, 51¹/₂in. long.
(Christie's) **$2,860**

A 16th century polychrome wood statue of the Virgin and Child, Spanish, 94cm. high.
(Duran) **$17,787**

INDEX

Abba 543
Absolon, William 424
Adam, Charles 586
Adams, Bryan 545
Adams, G. 558, 563, 570, 594
Adams, John 56
Adamson, Robert 516
Adventures of Captain Marvel 460
Advertising 16-19
Aeronautical Items 20-23
AFW 136
Aitchison, J. 631
AKPM 99
Alabaster 24
Alban, Dr. E. 504
Aldridge, Charles 618, 621
Alert Eagle Fire Society 26
Alexandria 505
Alfred, Thomas 598
Ali, Muhammed 575
Allain, Henry 630
Allan, John 451
Allen, John Frisk 528
Allied Artists 459, 464
Allison, Jerry 542, 547
Allison, Michael 361
American China 96, 97
American Machine Co. 227
Americana 25, 26
Amidio, Vittorio 526
Amusement Machines 27
Andrews, A.H. 561
Angel, Joseph & John 617
Angell, G. 594, 595
Angell, Joseph 606
Anthony, Joseph 611
Antiquities 28,29
ANZ 566
Arbus, Diane 518
Architectural Fittings 30, 31
Arita 98
Armand Marseille 219
Armour 32, 33
Arms and Armor 32-61
Armstrong, Neil 575
Aronsberg and Co. 71
Artcraft 460, 461
AS 578
Asahi Optical Co. 89
Ashbee, A.C.R. 580
Ashbee, C.R. 471-473
Ashtrays 412
Aspinall, Neil 545
Asprey & Co Ltd 589
ASR 393
Associated British-Pathe Ltd. 542
Attack of the 50ft. Woman 464
Attlee, Clement R. 574
Audubon, John James 529
Austin, W. 179
Autographed Documents 62-65
Automatons 66-69
Automobiles Geographical Ltd. 648

B. & C. 607
Babcock and Wilcox 504

Babe Ruth 576
Baccarat 434-437
Bachem Natter 22
Bachmann, E.W. 71
Bacle, D. 573
Bad Girl 460
Baddely Albrighton 561
Baggs, Arthur 97
Bagpipes 510
Bähr & Pröschild 221, 223
Bailey & Co. 608
Bailey & Kitchen 608
Baillie-Scott, M.H. 273, 396
Baird, John 430
Baker, C. 564
Baker, Eleazer 586
Baldock, Edward Holmes 352
Baldwyn, C.H.C. 177
Balfour, James 455
Ball Black & Co. 607, 617, 618
Ball, Tompkins & Black, Ball, Black & Co. 617
Bangles 470, 471
Banjo 510
Bank, The 462
Barbe, Jules 228
Barbedienne, Ferdinand 351
Bardot, Brigitte 231, 234
Barker Alpha Bristol 504
Barlow, Florence 125
Barnard & Gowenlock's 513
Barnard, E.E.J. & W. 593, 602, 620
Barnard, Edward 587, 591, 597, 620
Barnard, Messrs. 592
Barnards 583
Barnsley, Sidney 306
Barometers 70, 71
Barr, Flight & Barr 177
Barry, John 525
Barry, Joseph 323
Bartok, Bela 63
Barton, T. & Sons 205
Bartram and Co. 54
Bartram, Thomas 377
Baseball Machine 27
Baskets 72, 412, 578
Bassano 141
Bassett and Warford 608
Bassett, Frederick 515
Bassett-Lowke 508, 509
Bateman, H.M. 453
Bateman, Peter and Ann 588, 622
Bayreuth 136
BEA 540, 543
Beakers 28, 413, 579
Bean, J. 41
Beatles, The 540-543, 545-547
Beaton, Cecil 517, 518
Beaucort, Le Fleuron 207
Beaumont 577
Beaumont, John Thomas 526
Beaver, M. Ltd 587
Beck, R. and J. 87
Beds 244, 245
Beech, H. 504
Behrens, Peter 262

Bekking, J.A.M. 70
Bell, Edward 546
Belleek 105
Belton 218
Beney, Robt & Co. 92
Bennett, Murrle 476
Benney, Professor Gerald 599
Benson, W.A.S. 212
Bentley and Son. 52
Bergé, Henri 418
Bergman, Ingrid 231
Berlin 99
Berlin, Irving 62
Bernink, Jan 188
Berthon 69
Bertler & Eggert 190
Bertrand, Michel 67
Beslet, Thauvet 609
Best of Spirits 18
Bevan, Charles 330, 400
Beveridge, James 450
Bianconi, Fulvio 442
Bibendum 18
Biedermeier 137
Bierring, Jens 579
Bigelow Kennard 483
Bing 508, 649
Bingham, George Caleb 528
Bion, N. 566
Birks, Alboine 152
BL 515
Black, Cilla 541
Black, Starr & Frost 609
Blanckensee & Son Ltd 623
Blecken, Joachim 579
Blue John 73
Boardman, Sherman 515
Boardman, Thomas D. 515
Boch, Martin 94
Boehme, Charles Louis 617
Bogart, Humphrey 231
Bogert, Nicholas J. 596
Bogle, John 526
Bohemian 95
Bolaggt, Gullsmeds Aktie 514
Bolton Abbey 372
Bonds o' Euston Road 509
Bone, Henry 523
Bookcases 246, 247
Booth 34
Border Wireless, The 460
Bordertown 461
Borsyni, J. 522
Boston Oyster Company 25
Bottles 414-416
Boulton, Matthew 73
Bourne, Henry 604
Bow 100, 101
Bowen, J.T. 529
Bowie Knives 34, 35
Bowie, David 546
Bowls 28, 417-419, 580, 581
Bowman, J.F. 509
Boyce, Gerardus 620
Boyle, Gamble and Macfee 56
BR 195

Bracelets 469, 473-475
Brachet & Richard 410
Bracket Clocks 180, 181
Bradbury, Thomas & Sons 615
Bradley & Hubbard 478, 482, 483
Brand & Hine 191
Brando, Marlon 235
Brandt, Bill 516, 517
Brangwyn, Frank 472
Brannum 105
Breakfast Tables 344, 345
Breguet 208
Breitling Premier 211
Breker, Arno 76
Bremond, B.A. 491, 492
Brewer, Robert 121
Brewster 512
Bridges, F. 559
Brind, Henry 609
Brinsley, Walter 598
Bristol 116, 117
Bristol Bulldog 20
Britains 650
British Band Co Ltd., The 510
British China 102-105
British Gas Appliance Co., The 410
British Railways 508
Broad, John 124
Broadwood, John & Sons 510
Brokaw, Isaac 188
Bronze 74-77
Brooches 468-475
Brownfield, William & Sons 333
Browning, Robert 64
Bru Jeune 220, 223
Bruce, A. 570
Bruff, Charles Oliver 606
Bruno Schmidt 220
Bruscelli, Luigi 323
Bryant & Loud 346
Buchanan, James & Co. Ltd. 18
Buchanans Special Red Seal 18
Buchner 649
Buck, Frederick 524
Bucker Jungmann 23
Buckets 79
Buckingham, Jo. 180
Buckles 470, 471, 473
Buffalo 96
Bullock, George 80, 326, 496
Bureau Bookcases 252, 253
Bureaux 248-251
Burgh, Cornelius Vander 581
Burnside Rifle Co. 51
Burroughs, Alice and George 620
Burrows, George 614
Bursley Ware 102
Burt, Benjamin 612
Burt, Wm.. A. 558
Burton, J. 201
Burton, Richard 231, 233
Busch Light Beer 16
Bustelli, Franz Anton 135
Butcher, W. & Sons 511
Butler 325
Butler, Frank 125
Butter churner 224
Butter slicer 224

C & S 587
C,TE and EH 579
Cabaret 459
Caber, Emanuele 592
Cabinets 254-257
Cactus Kid, The 462
Caddies and Boxes 80-86
Cadman, George & Co.578
Cafaggiolo 140
Cafe, John 584
Cairelli, A 210
Caldwell, E.F. 195
Caldwell, J.E. 592, 609
Caledonia 507
Caledonian Railway, The 509
Callas, Maria 575
Cameras 87-91
Cameron, J. 529
Cameron, Julia Margaret 519
Campos, Foster, S. 202
Canabas and Jme 335
Canabas, Joseph Gengenback 398
Canary Murder Case, The 460
Candelabra 583
Candlesticks 420, 584, 585
Canon Camera Co. 88
Canterburys 259
Canton 106
Captain Blood 461
Car Mascots 92
Card and Tea Tables 346-349
Cardew , Michael178
Carette 508, 650
Carette, Georg 492
Carlile, Abraham 603
Carlton Ware 18, 19, 102
Carnegie, Andrew 65
Carousel Figures 93
Carpenter & Westley 512
Carpentier, J. 512
Carriage Clocks 182, 183
Carrick, Thomas Heathfield 524
Carrier, A. 643
Carrington & Co. 585
Carrington, John Bodman 583
Cartier 199, 208
Caruso, Enrico 65
Cary of London 569
Cary, J.W. 565
Casablanca 459
Casartelli, L. 71
Casbah Coffee Club 542
Cased Sets 36, 37
Casige 572
Casimir Bru 221
Casolla, Giovanni 583
Castelli 141
Castors 586
Catteau, Ch. 128
Catterfelder Puppenfabrik 218
Caughley 107
Cavern Club, The 540
CB 229
CCW 136
Ceaucescu, Nicolae 574
Center Tables 350-353
Centerpieces 587
CH 476

Ch Perron 483
Chadwick, Joseph 25
Chaffers 104
Chamberlain, Humphrey 177
Chamberlain, Neville 65, 104
Chambersticks 588
Chancellor & Son 196
Chandeliers 94, 95
Chandler, A. 203
Chapin 333
Chaplin, Charles 229, 232
Chapman, J.R. 194
Chariot 29
Charlotte Rhead
Chase, Charlie 576
Chawner, Henry 621
Cheere, John 405, 406, 409
Chelsea 108
Cheney, A.A. 203
Cheney, Benjamin 191
Cheney, Elisha 190
Cher 545
Chester Billings & Son 213
Chests of Drawers 278-283
Chests on Chests 284, 285
Chests on Stands 286, 287
Chiffoniers 288
Childe, James Warren 523
China 96-179
Chinese China 109-112
Chouffet, C.F. 17
Christ, D. 40
Churchill & Treadwell 579
Churchill, Jesse 579
Churchill, Winston 64, 574, 576
Cigar Boxes 589
Cigarette Cases 589
Cigarette dispenser 224
Cimarron 464
Cinématograph-Toy, The 511
Cinola Mod 488
Circus, The 465
Citizen Kane 464
Clapton, Eric 546
Claret Jugs 590
Clarice Cliff 113, 114, 484
Clark, Lynn 37
Clark, Nathan & Co. 97
Clarke & Smith 628
Clasps 469-471
Claypoole's Advertiser 394
Clerici Roma 408
Clichy 434-437
Cliff, Clarice 113, 484
Clift, Montgomery 232
Clinton and Russell 31
Clock Sets 184-186
Clocks & Watches 180-211
Coalport 104
Coasters 591
Coates, J.P. 17
Cobb, John 269
Coburn, Alvin Langdon 519
Coca Cola 17
Cochrane of Edinburgh 451
Cody, W.F. 64
Coffee grinder 224
Coffee Pots 592, 593

Coker, Ebenezer 584
Cole Brothers Circus 16
Collins, Phil 544
Collinson & Lock 386
Collot 130
Colman 19
Colts Pt. F.A. Mfg. Co. 36, 37
Columbia 462, 463
Commode Chests 289-291
Commodes & Potcupboards 292, 293
Comyns & Sons 503
Comyns, Wm 499, 578, 581, 603
Concert Automatique Français 488
Congreve, C. 34
Connell, A.G.L. Ltd 581
Console Tables 354, 355
Constitution 506
Contina 560
Contreras, Manuel 510
Cooke, Thomas 612
Cookson, Isaac 593
Cooper Brothers and Sons Ltd 587
Cooper, Susie 103
Cooper, William 607
Coper, Hans 115
Copper and Brass 212-215
Corgi Toys 17
Corner Cupboards 294-296
Cornet 510
Cornwall 508
Cortebert Watch Mfg. Co. 206
Costume 216, 217
Cosway, Richard 523
Couper, A.J. & Sons 422
Couturier, L. 71
Coventry Glassworks 426
Cowan Pottery 479
Coward, Noel 64
Coward, Noel 235
Cowell, William 612
Coxed, John 321
CPL 393
Craddock, Joseph 609
Craig, Burlon 97
Cream Jugs 594
Creature from Black Lagoon 462
Creil 127
Cremer, Joseph 363
Cribb, Robert and Son 501
Cricket, The 542
Crombie, Charles 453
Crosby & Vosburgh 202
Crowhurst, George 577
Crown Devon 103
Crown Ducal 104
Cruets 595
CS 56
Cupboards 297-299
Cups 596
Currier and Ives 528, 529
Currier, N. 528, 529
Curtis Owl 21
Curtis, Lemuel 203
Cushing, L.W. & Sons 658, 659

d'Honre, Narbon 132
Daggers 38, 39

Dakotas, The 541
Dalrymple, Sir W.H. 456
Danel et Cie 221
Daniel, Joseph 523
Daniell, Jabez 595
Daum 94
Daum Nancy 422, 431
Davenports 104, 300, 301
Davidson, N. 189
Davis & Co. 410
Davis Gas Stove Co. 411
Davis, Bette 234
Dawkins 493
Daws, Robert 268
Day & Son 529
De Morgan 119
de Havilland Mosquito 21
de Mille, Cecil B. 235
Dean's Rag Book Company 651
Deans of Melrose 345
Death of the Bear 166
Decamps 69
Decanters 421
Declaration of the Independence of the USA 26
Deccalian 494
Deckrullo 90
Delander 181
Delcroix 220
Delepine, E. 559
Delft 116-118
Delius, A.J.R. 568
Della Robbia 102, 103
Delorme, Adrian 294
Demuth, W. & Co. 16
Dent 189, 201
Dent, F. 181
Dentzel, Gustav & Co. 93
DEP 218, 222
Derby 120, 121
Devil is a Woman, The 462
Dewar, John & Sons Ltd 19
Diamond Tally-Ho 25
Dibble, Oscar T.H. 596
Dickens, Charles 62
Dietrich, Marlene 230, 235
Dimoline of Bristol 520
Dining Chairs 260-265
Dining Tables 356-358
Dirk Van Erp 479
Discovery 18
Dishes 422, 423, 597
Disney 64, 230, 463, 465
Display Cabinets 302-305
Distler 651
Dittrich, R. 99
Dixon, James & Sons 55, 585
Dixon, Nicholas 527
DL 104
Doccia 140
Doherty, M. 633
Dolenz, Mickey 542
Dollfus, Josué 522
Dollond 562
Dolls 218-223
Domestic Equipment 224-227
Doncaster Racecourse 20
Donitz, Karl 64

Donizetti, Gaetano 62
Donzel 229
Doors, The 544
Dorrel, Willm. 180
Dotty, G. 70
Douglas, Francis 86
Doulton 122-125
Downman, J.T. 529
Dozy, Dr. G.J. 565
Dresden 126
Dresser, Christopher 269, 304, 590, 621, 622
Dressers 306, 307
Dresses 217
Dressing Tables 359-362
Drinking Glasses 424, 425
Drop Leaf Tables 363-365
Drum Tables 366
Dubucand, Alfred 76
Duchamp, Marcel 516
Duke of Wellington 63
Dumb Waiters 367
Dumbo 463
Dummer, Jeremiah 596
Dunbar Furniture Corp 331
Dunhill 208
Durand Art 417
Durgin 597
Durrell, Frances 188
Durs Egg 41
Dyer, J. 72
Dylan, Bob 544
Dysterdijk, Joachim Henrich 582

E.Bs.Ld. 617
Earrings 474
Eastman Dry Plate & Film Co. 88
Eastman Kodak Co. 88, 89, 91
Eastman, John L. 541
Easy Chairs 266-271
EB 645
Eberl 650
Eckardt 493
Eclectic Film 458
ED 220
Edison 488, 490
Edo 58, 59
Edouart, Auguste 577
Edridge, Harry 523
Edwards & Roberts 256, 305
Egley, William 527
EGLG 182
Egli, Hans W. 560
Ehrhardt & Söhne Schwäbisch 199
Einstein, Albert 74
Eisenhower, Dwight, D. 63
Elbow Chairs 272-277
Electric Fire 224
Electric Phonograph 493
Electrola 489
Elgar, Edward Sir 65
Elgin 16
Elkington & Co. 77, 605, 614
Ellin, T. 34
Elliot, W., Ltd. 21
Elliot, William 591
Ellis, Harvey 275
Ellis, Henry 180

Elmscott Foundry Co. Ltd, The 410
Elsley, Thomas 236
Elston, John Jnr. 586
Emes, John 610
Emes, Rebecca 587, 591, 597,, 620
EMG 490
Empire 94
Enamel 228
Engleheart, George 523
Eoff & Shepherd 607, 618
Epstein, Brian 540, 543
Erard, Sebastien 510
Ermanox 90
ES 631
Essanay 462
Estate Electric Toaster 646
Esterlie, John 190
ETB 582
European China 127-129
Evans, Malcolm F. 541
Evans, William 597
Every Day's a Holiday 461
Ever Ready 16
Excursion Around the World 511
Eyre, Hawkesworth & Co. Ltd 611
Faenza 141
Fairbanks 212
Fairy/Madame Demorest 572
Falconnet 192
Fans 225, 229
Farmers Glory 18
Farnell 641
Farrell, Edward 614
Faveria, F. and Co. 71
Favrile, L.C.T. 478
Fayre Win 27
Fenton, Ricky and The Apaches 540
Fenton, Roger 517
Ferry, H. 41
FG 66
Field, John 577
Fields, W.C. 231
Figg, John 590
Film Star Autographs 230-235
Finnish Air Force 20
Firegrates 236, 237
Fireman, City of New York 26
Fireplace Furniture 238, 239
Fireplaces 240-242
First Flying Week in England 20
First National 458, 459, 465
Fishel, Adler & Schwartz 528
Fisher 34
Fisher, Alexander 473
Fisher, W.F. 70
Fishing Equipment 243
Five and Ten 463
Flash Gordon's Trip to Mars 462
Flasks 426, 427
Flatware 598, 599
Fletcher Russell & Co 410
Flight & Barr 177
Flint, William Russell 64
Flintlock Guns 40, 41
Flintlock Pistols 42, 43
Florence Co. 410
Flying Cloud 507
Fogelberg, Andrew 605

Fokker 22
Fonteyn, Dame Margot 574
Ford, Harrison 25
Ford, John & Co. 430
Forgan, R. & Son 456
Fornasetti 141
Fornasetti, Piero 315, 334
Forrest, Robert 404
Fortissimo Comb 491
Four Seasons, The 315
Fowler, L.N. 570
Fox 460, 461
Fox, Charles 187, 606, 614, 621
Fox, George 607
FR 428
Franco, General Francisco 575
Frankenstein 464
Franklin-Dyott 427
Fredjohns 205
Freeman, N.A. 616
Freese, N. 527
Fremont, Charles 486
French China 130-132
Freres, Wyss 206
Frères, Nicol 490
Fritsche, William 441
Frodsham, Charles 565
FS 631
Fuller, Crispin 588
Fumeron, A. 645
Furniture 244-401

G & T Exhibition 494
G-Men 465
Gable, Clark 230, 233
Gains, John 199
Gale & Willis 591
Gale, William & Son 580
Galland, J.R. 525
Gallaway, Alexander 523
Gallé, Emile 95, 131, 132, 414, 419,
445, 480, 481
Galteaux, N. 23
Garden Statuary and Furniture
404-409
Gardiner, Baldwin 599
Gardner 133
Gardner, Jack 574
Gargiulo, Luigi 362, 350
Garnier, Paul 182
Garrard, James 629
Gas Appliances 410, 411
Gaskin, Arthur and Georgina 468
Gateleg Tables 368, 369
Gault de St. Germain, Pierre 525
Gaultier, François 223
Gaultier, Jean Paul 541
Gaumont British 461, 463
Gautier, Louis-Adolphe 528
GB 229
GBS 455
Ged, Dougal 619
Gee, John 343
Gem 488, 490
General Electric 225, 646
General, The 461
Genesis 544
Geoffroy, Nicholas 579

George Jones 134
Gebrüder Bing 641
German China 135-137
Gerry and the Pacemakers 541
Ghost of Frankenstein, The 465
Gilbert Clock Co. 196
Gilbert, W. & T. 567
Gilda 463
Giles, James 176
Gillois, Peter 618
Gillows 259, 303, 319, 356, 360,
386, 387, 399
Gimson, Ernest W. 368
Giovara, Giuseppe 593
Girl from 10th Avenue, The 465
Girl from Missouri, The 465
Giroux 502
Glass 414-449
Gloster Gladiator 23
Gloster Meteor 22
Gloves 216
GNR 508
Goat, Ralph 181
Goblets 428, 429, 600
Goddard-Townsend School 364
Godfrey, Eliza 592
Godzilla 464
Goerz, C.P. 88
Goldscheider 127
Goldschmid, J. 561
Goldsmith & Co. 602
Goldsmith and Silversmiths Co.,
The 557,614
Golfing Items 450-457
Gone with the Wind 233
Goodman, Alexander and Co. 585
Gorbachev, Mikhail 574
Gordon, Ernest 419
Gorham 616, 618, 619, 623, 629
Goshu Ju Namitoshi 59
Gould, James 585
Goupil & Co. 528
Gourley, A.J. 456
Governor, The 27
Gowland, Jas 205
Gowns 216, 217
Graf Zeppelin, The 21, 23
Graham and Anderson 631
Grainger Lee & Co 176
Gramophone & Typewriter 489, 492
Gramophone Co. 489, 490
Gramophone 494, 512
Grant, J.P. 452
Grant, Ulysses S. 62
Gravel & Son 200
Gray's 102, 103
Great Bear 508
Great Northern 509
Great Western Railway, The 508
Greaves 34
Green, Arthur Romney 356
Green, Richard 612
Greenwich, Perry 559
Gregory, Albert 121
Grenander, Professor Alfred 327
Griffin & Son 568
Griffith Hyatt & Co. 431
Griffiths Camera Co. Ltd., The 90

Grinsell, John and Sons 431
Grohé 302
Grove, Geo. 215
Grover & Baker 572
Grueby 138
Gubelin, E. 183
Guerhard & Dihl 132
Guérin, B. 333
Guest, Thomas 609
Guhl and Harbeck 572
Guild of Handicraft 306, 597, 599
Guinness Toucan 19
Guitar 510
Günter Wulff Apparatebau 27
Günthermann 21,651
Gurley, W. & L.E. 558, 559, 566, 567, 570
Gurney, Richard 612
Gustavberg Argenta 127
GW 602
GWR 202, 203, 206

H & H 622
HA 599
Hagenauer 212
Hagiya Katsuhira 59
Haig, Douglas 65
Hair Comb 471
Hair Ornaments 470
Haley, Bill 543
Hall, J.H. 41
Hall, Martin & Co. 583, 590
Halstead, Rt. Evens 187
Hamada 139
Hamilton & Inches 597
Hamilton 208, 558
Hamlet, William 527
Hamlin, Samuel 515
Hammerstein, Oscar 65
Hampel 159
Hampston, J. 618,. 621
Hancock, Messrs 587
Handel 478, 482
Hanners, George 613
Hansa Brandenburg 20
Hanson, Wendy 540
Harden & Co. 272
Hare & Co. 410
Hare, George 87
Harlow, Jean 458
Harmonium 510
Harold, Christian Friedrich 631
Harp 510
Harper, Robert 602
Harrison, George 540, 542
Hart, William S. 62
Hartingue 205
Haseler, W.H. 470
Hatswell, B. 504
Hattersley, William 614
Haupt, Georg 176
Hausburg, F.L. 183
Havel, Vaclav 576
Havillard, Terry de 546
Haw Haw, Lord 103
Hawker Fury 22
Hawkesworth Eyre & Co. Ltd 611
Hawksley, G. and J.W. 55

Haxby 520
Hayes, Rutherford B. 64
Hayne, Jonathan 595
Hayworth, Rita 231
Hazlehurst, Thomas 527
HE 584
Heal & Sons 272
Hearst, William Randolph 63
Heater 224
Heath & Middleton 431, 590, 622
Heidoscop 91
Heifetz, Jascha 576
Heigel, Josef 525
Helfricht, Cuno 36
Helmets 44-47
Hendrix, Jimi 544
Henie, Donja 234
Hennell, Robert 578, 595, 620
Hennell, Robert and Samuel 620
Hennell, Samuel 629
Henri Alexandre Bébé Phénix 220
Henson, Jim 574
Herakles 29
Herbert & Co. 611
Herbert, Henry 610
Herculaneum 103
Herd, Fred 456
Herschell-Spillman Co. 93
Herter Brothers 245
Heubach Koppelsdorf 218
Hewell and James & Co. 200
Hewit, William 614
Hill, David Octavius 516
Hilliard, Nicholas 525
Himely, Sigismond 528
Himsworth, Joyce R. 593
Hindley, C. & Sons 311
Hirata Narusuke 59
His Master's Voice 494
Hitchcock, Alfred 230
HMV 489-491, 493
Höchst 136
Hocker, Jos. 187
Hodel, Joseph A. 470
Hoffmann, Josef 215, 445, 497
Hoffritz N.Y. 570
Holland & Son 386
Holland, Henry 602, 607
Holland, Thomas 613
Hollies, The 541
Holly, Buddy 542-544, 547
Hollywood Posters 458-465
Home Companion Ideal 573
Hon. Co. of Edinburgh Golfers 451
Hoops 216
Hoover, Herbert 63
Hope, Thomas 402
Horikawa 539
Horne, Reg. 454
Horner, Charles 476
Höroldt, J.G. 150
Horse 28
Hotpoint 646
Houdini, Harry 575
Howard & Sons 386
Howard of Berners Street 345
Howard, Charles 71
Howard, Leslie 320

HS 578, 613
Hubard, William James 577
Hubley 321
Hudson, Ira 658
Hukin & Heath 580, 622
Humbert, Jules-Eugène 164
Humphry, Ozias 522
Hunchback of Notre Dame 458
Hunt & Roskell 183
Hunt, George 472
Hunt, John 629
Hunt, John S. 596, 607
Hunt, V. 508
Hurricane 508
Hurtu 573
Hutcheon 500
Hutton, William & Sons 603
HW 586
Hyatt, Griffith & Co. 431
Hyde & Goodrich 596

ICF 396
Icons 466, 467
Ideal Blaupunkt 488
IDH 24
Imperial Airways 22
Imperial Chemical Industries 49
Independence Hose Co., The 26
Indiana Jones/Raiders/Lost Ark 25
Informer, The 464
Inkstands 601
INXS 544
IP 623
Ireland, Henry 187
Iris Paris 568
Irons 226, 227
Isabey, Jean Baptiste 527
Italian China 140, 141
Iwamoto Konkan 59

Jack, Archer 197
Jackets 216, 217
Jaeger, Ernst 78
Jagger, Mick 542
Jailhouse Rock 459
James, E.G. 662
Japanese China 142
Japy Freres 184, 195, 196
Jarvie 214
JC 569
Jenkins, J. 71
Jenour, Charles 525
Jensen, Dahl 129
Jensen, Georg 19, 581, 585, 608, 610
Jentzsch, Max and Meerz 27
Jewell, A.L. 658
Jewelry 468-476
Joan of Arc 465
Joanin, François 642
Joel, David 80
Johanna Enlists 461
John Baird Glassworks 430
Johnnie Walker Red Label 18
Johnson & Appleyard 331
Johnson, Samuel 621
Johnson, Thomas 355
Johnston, Joannes 520

Johnstone & Jeanes 349
Jolson, Al 230
Jones 483
Jones, Albert Edward 581, 584, 604
Jones, Brian 542
Jones, Davy 542
Jones, George 134
Jones, Miss Charlotte 525
Jones, Thomas 559
Jones, W. & S. 558-560
Jones, William 196
Jordan, Lucius 96
Jugs 602
Jugs and Pitchers 430, 431
Jullien, Martin 341
Jumeau 220, 221, 222, 223

Kaleidoscope 513
Kalliope 488
Kämmer & Reinhardt 220, 221
Kändler, J.J. 149, 150
Kar, Ida 517
Karageorgevitch, Prince Bojidar 470
Karloff, Boris 231, 235
Karlsbad, Moser 428
Karu 99
Keay, Robert 602
Keene Marlboro St. Glassworks 426, 427
Keller, Henry 430
Kelly, Grace 231, 235
Kendall, David W. 251
Kennedy, John and Robert 207
Kensington Glassworks 427
Kentenber, J. 612
Kentucky 26
Kerr, John 452
Kestner, A.J.D. 222
Ketland, T. and Co 40
Ketland, W. 40
Keuffel & Esser 561
Khomeini, Ayatollah 576
Kid, The 459
King George III 63, 64
King George V 62
King Kong 458
King William IV 65
King, Jessie M. 470, 471
Kinora Viewer 511
Kintail 510
Kirstein, Johann Jakob 598
Kishu Ju Teimei 59
Klemm, Frederick 579
Klimsch, Fritz 158
Klingsor 494
Kneehole Desks 308-310
Knight, Laura 65
Knirsch, Otto 528
Knox, Archibald 407, 514, 515, 621
Knox, Henry 26
Knudsen, Cornelius 564
Koch, Gabriele 212
Koehler Mfg. Co., 212
Kohler 510
Kohn, Jacob & Joseph 397
Komo Metal Paste 19
Koppitz, Rudolf 517

Kosuge 539
Kramer, Billy J. 541
Krause, Karl 568
Krause, R.M. 137
Krieger of Paris 362
Kunik, K. 18
Künnel 135
Kutchinsky 473

L & NWR 508, 509
L&Co 196
La Belle et la Bête 462, 463
Lacquer 477
Lacroix, Roger Vandercruse 359
Lady Vanishes, The 463
Lagarde 198
Lake, Veronica 231
Lalique René 92, 200, 417-419, 422, 440, 442, 444, 480
Lamb of Loanhead 451
Lamb, Charles 596
Lambert, Leopold 66, 67
Lambert, Val St. 442
Lambeth 116
Lamprey 564
Lamps 478-485
Lamson, E.G. and Co. 51
Lancaster, J. and Son 87
Lancret, Nicolas 314
Landers, Frary & Clark 646
Langlands and Robertson 593
Langlands, Dorothy 615
Langlois, Pierre Junior 289
Lannuier, Charles-Honore 355
Lantern 513
Lantern Clocks 187
Lanz, J.W. 132
Lapini, Cesare 486
Large Tables 370, 371
Laroche, Louis 578
Laughing Sinners 464
Laundy 561
Laurel and Hardy 230, 232, 233
Laurenzl 127
Law, Thomas 584
LB 421
LCT 420, 482
Le Roux, Charles 609
Le Roy e fil 185
Le Roy, Pierre 192
Lea & Co. 628
Leabody, Bill 544
Leach, Bernard 143
Leach, David 104
Leader, Thomas and Daniel 588
Led Zeppelin 544
Leeds Model Co. 509
Lehar, Franz 576
Lehmann 647-651
Lehmann Ikarus 21
Lehn, Joseph 79
Leica 87-89, 91
Leicestershire Golf Club 457
Leigh, Vivien 233, 235
Leman, H.E. 40
Lenci 219, 221
Lennon, John 540-542, 545-547
Lennox, Annie 545

Lenygon & Morant 266
Leroy, L. 197
Leslie & Price 180
Levi, S.J. & Co. 90
Levy & Saloman 556
Lewis, H.A. 642
Lewis, Jerry Lee 544
Lias, H. & H. 594
Liberty & Co. 154, 155, 268, 407, 471, 514, 621
Lichfield, Barry 189
Lifetime Furniture 331, 375, 380
Limehouse 104
Lincoln, F.W. 570
Linemar 651
Linen Presses 311
Lingard 35
Linke, François 386
Linnell, John 268
Linwood, Matthew 628
List, Herbert 516
Liston, Sonny 575
Littledale, C. 509
Liverpool 117 116, 144
Lloyd George, David 576
Lloyd's of London 462
LNER 509
Lochmann 489, 492
Locke, Bobby 453
Loetz 442
Loewe, Sr. Siegmund 568
London & North Eastern Rlwy 509
London Stereoscopic Co. 512, 513
Longcase Clocks 188-191
Longton Hall 145
Lord Kitchener 509
Louis, Joe 65
Louis-Philippe 354
Love Before Breakfast 458
Lowboys 312, 313
Lowestoft 105
Lowndes, Jonathan 181
LR 146, 147
Lucie Rie 146, 147
Lück, J.L.C. 171
Ludlow, Hal 454
Lufkin, John W. 573
Lutyens, Sir Edwin 334
Lux Clock Mfg. Co. 193

Macbride, John 612
MacDonald, William, P. 158
Macintyre, James & Co. 154, 155
MAD 397
Madonna 541, 543, 546
Magic Lanterns 512, 513
Magnifying Glass 511
Mahoney, Marion 439
Majestic Pictures 460
Makeig-Jones, Daisy 172, 173
Makepeace, John 375
Malcolm Forbes
Malkin, Samuel 170
Maltese Falcon, The 458
Mammy 459
Manning, H.D. 528
Mansfield, Jayne 233, 234
Mansion, Gabriel 206

Mantel Clocks 192-199
Manuel Contreras 510
Mappin & Webb 432, 615
Mapplethorpe, Robert 518
Marble 486, 487
Marc, Henri 195
March, Sydney 77
Marcuse, Rudolph 158
Margaine 182
Maria 506
Märklin 504, 505, 508, 647-651
Marquand & Co. 611
Marsh & Jones 311, 330, 400
Marshall, Mark V. 480
Marston, J., Thompson & Son 18
Martha's Vineyard 506
Martin Bros. 148, 510
Martin, B. 565
Martinware 148
Marx, Chico 232
Marx, Groucho 235
Marx, Harpo 234
Marx, Louis 651
Massachusetts Arms Co. 52
Masudaya 539
Mathesson, Bruno 326
Mauldin, Joe 542, 547
Maw 103
May, T. 206
Mayer & Meltzer 566, 567
McCartney, Paul 541, 542, 547
McDaniel, Hattie 232
McEwan 450, 451, 457
McKenna, Peter 544
Mecaflex 90
Meccano 21
Mechanical Music 488-494
Meeks, Joseph and Sons 396
Megarey, Henry J. 528
Meissen 149-151
Mene, P.J. 74-76
Mercer, Thomas 560
Mercier, H 432
Mercury, Freddie 545, 546
Meriden 646
Meriden Britannia Co. 623
Mersey Beat 541
Metheun, George 611
Metro 460, 463
Metropolis 465
MF 202
MGM 458, 459, 464, 465
Michelangelo 486
Michelin 18
Mickey Mouse 18, 64, 211, 482
Mikiphone Pocket Phonograph 488
Militaria 48, 49
Millar, J.B. 430
Millikin & Lawley 563
Mills Brothers Ltd 509
Mills Stars 27
Mills, Hugh 623
Mills, Nathaniel 604,628
Milne, Edmund 606
Mince, James 595
Minex 90
Miniature Furniture 495
Mino ju Nakanaga 58

Minton 152, 153
Mirrors 496-503
Miscellaneous 432, 433
Miscellaneous Silver 603-605
Mitchell Manchester 457
Mochaware 104
Model Ships 505-507
Model Trains 508, 509
Models 504
Molineux, John 239
Monitor 572
Monkees, The 542
Monocular 88
Monroe, Marilyn 233
Montelupo 140
Montez, Maria 234
Moorcroft, William 154, 155
Moore, William 354
Morant, George 80
Morgan Development Labs Inc. 512
Morris & Co 273
Morris, Benjamin 188
Morris, Tom 450, 453, 455, 457
Morrison, Jim 546, 547
Moser 445
Mother Goddess 29
Mother Teresa 574
Moulinar, John 612
Moulton, Ebenezer 606
Mouse trap 224
Mt. Washington 417, 430-433, 443
Mugs & Canns 606
Muhammed Ali 575
Muir-Wood, Helen 502
Muller 482, 483,573
Muller, Emile 409
Mummy 28
Murphy, Henry, G. 473
Murray, J. 602
Musical Clock 512
Musical Instruments 510
Mussard, Andreas 522
Mussolini 49
Mustards 607
Myers, Myer 613
Myopia Hunt Club 456

Nachet 566
Nancy Galle, E. 557
Neill, Robt 207
Nesmith, Michael 542
Ness, P.R.J. 208
Nestles Milk 19
New Avona 572
New England 572
New England Glass Co. 420
New Haven Conn. 51
New Home Sewing Machine 572
Newman J. & Co. 229
Newton & Co. 91
Newton, E.T. & Son 563, 567
Newtons Terrestrial Globe 565
Nguyen, Rosa 128
Nicholas, W. 191
Nicholson, William 590
Nickolds, John 630
Nicol Frères 490
Nielsen, Nicole & Co Ltd. 182

Night at the Opera 463
Nikon 88, 89, 91
Nippon Kogaku 89
Nixon, James 524
Noah's Ark 649
Nomura 648, 651, 539
Norris, George 180
North Bros. Mfg. Co 227
Noton, M. 504
Noyes, John 599
Nureyev and Fonteyn 63
Nutcracker 225

O'Casey, Sean 65
O'Neale, Jefferyes Hammett 177
Occasional Tables 372-375
Oeben, Jean François 386
Olivier, Laurence 233
Omega 27
Optical Instruments 511-513
Orbison, Roy 543
Orchard, John 421
Organ 510
Original Express 572
Orrefors 417
Orvit, A.G. 619
Owen, G 176
Owens, Jesse 633
Oxo 19

Painted Lady, The 461
Painted Veil, The 458
Pairpoint 96
Palmer, Frances F. 528
Pane, Gartano 592
Paper Weights 434-437
Papprill, Henry A. 528
Paramount 460-463, 465
Paris 131
Paris, Erard 520
Paris, George A 630
Paris, Lilor 411
Parker, W. 41
Parkinson, Norman 516, 518
Parsons, John & Co. 584
Partridge, Fred T. 470, 471, 475
Patrick, Andrew 457
Paulve 462
Pavlova, Anna 64, 575
Payne, Benjamin 604
Pearce, Daniel 444
Pearce, Henry 190
Pearce, Richard 614
Pearlware 156, 157
Pearson, John 214
Peche, Dagobert 497
Peerless 493
Pegg, W. 'Quaker' 121
Pellatt and Green 557
Pelletreau, Elias 594, 621
Pembroke Tables 376, 377
Pendants 468, 470-472
Peneland 303
Penn, Irving 518
Percolator 225
Percussion Carbines 50, 51
Percussion Revolvers 52, 53
Péridiez, B. 289

Perils of Pauline, The 458
Perron, Ch 483
Petersen, Ivar 617
Petit, Jacob 130
Pettit, Matthew 595
Pewter 514, 515
Pharoah Ptolemy 29
Phenakistiscope 513
Philipp, Maria 327
Philippe, Louis 354
Philippe, Patek 211
Philippe, Paul 78
Philips Sun-dial 567
Phillips 489
Phipps, James 618
Phipps, T. & E. 564
Phoenix Open, The 453
Photographs 516-519
Phyfe, Duncan 325, 360, 363
Pianoforte 510
Pianos 520
Picard of Paris 521
Pickford, Mary 233
Pinocchio 465
Pins 475
Pitchers & Ewers 608
Planck, Ernst 511
Planitz, Daniel 605
Plante, H.H. 198
Plaster 521
Plates 609
Plato Clock, The 192
Plummer, Wm. 620
Polyrama 511
Polyphon 491-494
Popeye 647
Porringers 609
Porthouse 209
Portrait Miniatures 522-527
Post, Wilhelmina 138
Potts 70
Pountney 102
Powder Flasks 54, 55
Power, Edward 615
Powolny, Michael 445
Prattware 157
Praxinoscopes 511
Precht, Burchardt 355
Presley, Elvis 540, 547
Preston, John Hardy 180
Priest, William 612, 613
Prince 543, 547
Prince, J. 618, 621
Prince Bojidar Karageorgevitch 470
Princess Elizabeth 509
Princess Tenichef 255
Prints 528, 529
Prisoner of Zenda, The 463
Probin 41
Projector 512
Propeller 21, 23
PVF 491
PY 435

Quaint Furniture 332
Quant, Mary 540
Queen Christina 459
Queen Elizabeth II 64

Queen Victoria 62
Queen, Jas, W. and Co 558
Quezal 94
Quilts 530-535

R & C 182, 193
Rabery & Delphieu 219
Radios & Televisions 538
Radios 536, 537
Ramsay MacDonald, J. 575
Ramsden, Omar 582, 610
Raulin 302
Rawlings, Charles 611
Ray, Man 516
RB 590
RD 409
Redamyne, T. & Co. 411
Reeves, George 230
Reflectoscope 511
Regent, The 510
Regina 489, 491
Reily and Storer 607
Rein, F.C. & Son 558, 570
Reinhart, Frank A. 519
Reldas, H. 171
Rémond, Georges 631
Renauld, A. 604
René Domremy Thistle 442
Renou, Timothy 66, 623
Republic 460
Requier a Lisieux 185
Revere, Paul 96
Reynolds, Charles & Co. 619, 623
Rhead, Charlotte 104
Rhead, Frederick 102, 432
Rhoads, G.W. 96
Richards, Henry 42
Richards, Keith 542
Richardson, Richard 604
Richmond & Co. 411
Richter, Otto 77
Ridout, George 705
Rie, Lucie 146, 147
Rings 468, 470, 473-475
RJWP 80
RKO 458, 459, 462, 464, 465
Roberts, Samuel Jnr. 578
Robertson, Hugh C. 97
Robes 216, 217
Robin Starch 18
Robins, Thomas 595
Robinson, Edkins and Aston 591
Robinson, Edward, G. 234
Robinson, Geo 207
Robinson, John 207
Robinson, Samuel 35
Robots 539
Roche, Sampson Towgood 526
Rock n Roll 540-547
Rockingham 157
Rodchenko, Alexander 516-519
Rodgers, T. 598
Rogers, Daniel 594
Rohmer 218
Rolex 210, 211
Rolleiflex 87, 91
Rolling Stones, The 542, 546, 547
Rookwood 158

Roop, Stanley 72
Rosenburg Juliana 127
Rosenthal 158
Roskell, Robert 629
Ross, A. 87, 559
Roth & Engelhardt 493
Roth, Thomas 523
Rothenbusch, Fred 158
Rotomat 27
Rotten, Johnny 544
Roullet et Decamps 66-69
Rowsewell, John 111
Royal Dux 159
Royal Porcelain Manufactory 136
RR 605
Rugs 548-553
Rundell, Philip 607
Ruskin 160
Russell, Fletcher & Co 410
Russell, Fletcher 140
Russell, Gordon 297
Russell, John 591
Russells Ltd 208
Rusts Patent 479
RVLC 359
RW 599
Rycutt, John 181
RYNA 646
Rysukeda 486

Sabattini, Lino 616
Sadie Thompson 464
Salts & Peppers 610
Salvin, Anthony 397
Samovar 225
Samplers 554, 555
Sampson 130
Samson Morden 556
Sanderson, E. 610
Satsuma 160-163
Sauce Boats 611
Savery, William 395
Saxophone 510
Scent Bottles 556, 557
Schaub Supraphon 489
Schaus, W. 528
Scheier 96
Schiaparelli 217
Schmidt, Ludwig 524
Schneider, Charles 419
Schneider, Romy 231, 234
Schott 619
Schrenk & Co. 308
Schuco 641, 648, 651
Schultz, Robert Weir 479
Schulz, Charles M. 65
Schwarzenegger, Arnold 25
Schweitzer, Albert 64
Scientific Instruments 558-570
Scott, John 181
Screen 314, 315
Scrimshaw 571
Sea Witch 62
Seal, William 594
Secretaire Bookcases 316, 317
Secretaires 318-321
Seddon, J.P. 331
Seddon, Sons & Shackleton 262

Seethaler, Johann Alois 603
Seger, Ernst 78
Seguin 507
Sellers, Peter 231
Selwood, William 187
Semper, Gottfried 350
Senior Service Cigarettes 19
Seth Thomas Clocks 569
Settees & Couches 322-329
Seven Year Itch, The 463
Sevres 77, 164, 165
Sewing Machines 572, 573
SFBJ 223
SH 57, 578, 630
Shackleton, Sir Ernest 63
Shades 438
Shagin, Ivan 518
Shanca 619
Shand Manson 504
Sharp, William 528
Shaw & Clark 573
Shaw, Thomas 628
Shaw, William 612, 613
Shelley, Samuel 526
Shirreff, Charles 526
Shoes 217
Shokasai 229
Short, James 563
Shozan 229
Shushin Saku 58
Sibley II, Richard 587
Sibley, Stephen 191
Sicilian 140
Sico 87
Side Tables 378-381
Sideboards 330-332
Siebe, Gorman & Co. 212
Signed Photographs 574-576
Silberzahn Manufactory 636
Silhouettes 577
Silvani 194
Silver 578-629
Simon & Halbig 69, 218, 219, 221, 222
Simons Brothers Sterling 616
Simplex 646
Sin of Nora Moran, The 460
Singer 573
Sissons, W. & G. 617
Sissons, W. & G. 590
Skeleton Clocks 201
Skyner John 190
Slide Projector 512
Sloane, Hans 108
Slous, G 527
Slover & Taylor 324
Smith & Beck 563
Smith and Co. 52
Smith and Wesson 53
Smith, Benjamin 591, 596, 603
Smith, C. 566
Smith, Edward 628
Smith, Jo. 70
Smith, Norman 96
Smith, Stephen 590, 608
Smith, Steven 614
Snow White and the Seven Dwarfs 462, 650

Snuff Boxes 630, 631
Society of The Cincinnati 26
Sofa Tables 382
Solven, Pauline 441
Sommer, August 77
Son of Frankenstein 462, 464
Sopwith Pup 20
Sormani, Paul 290
Sousa, John Philip 574
Sovereign of the Seas 505
Sparmann 23
Sparrow, W.H. 580
SPC 415
Spectacles 632
Spelzini, J. 70
Spencer, Edward 214
Spencer, Gervase 526
Spencer, Stanley 517
Speyer, J. 562
Spode 166
Sporting Items 633
Springsteen, Bruce 543
St Louis 434-437
St. John, R.H. 573
Stabler, Harold 470, 583
Stabler, Phoebe 470
Staffordshire 167-170
Stained Glass 439
Stands 333-335
Staniford, D. 26
Star of Midnight 459
Starr, Ringo 541, 542
Steel and Iron 634-637
Steiff 640, 641, 650
Stellmacher, Reissner 127
Stereo Mentor 90
Stereoscope 511-513
Steuben 94, 417, 421
Stevens & Williams 412, 443
Stewart, James 232
Stickley, Gustav 194, 213, 215, 266, 272-274, 330, 356, 365, 375, 389, 662
Stickley, L. & J.G. 274, 322, 327, 330, 338, 388
Stirn, C.P. 90
Stockert, Er. Chr. 561
Stockwell, Henry 607, 607
Stodart 565
Stools 336-339
Storr, Paul 588, 629
Strath, David 457
Strauss, Richard 65, 575
Stroviol 491
Suess Ornamental Glass Co. 483
Suit 216
Suites 340-343
Summers, William 611
Supermarine Spitfire 23
Susie Cooper Crown Works 103
Sutton, Thomas 87
Swift & Son 569
Swinging Blue Jeans, The 541
Swords 56, 57
Symphonion 490, 491

Tahan 556
Tait, A.F. 529

Talbert, Bruce 257, 386
Tankards 612, 613
Tanner, E.F. 507
Tapestries 638, 639
Tarzan of the Apes 458
Tassie, James 524
Tatham, Charles H. 338
Taylor & Perry 628
Taylor, Elizabeth 231
Taylor, J.H. 452
Taylor, Samuel 618
Taylor, W. Howson 160
Taylor, William 606
TE 609
Tea & Coffee Sets 614-617
Tea Caddies 618
Tea Kettles 619
Teapots 620, 621
Teco 96
Teddy Bears 640, 641
Telechrom 17
Telegraph Manufacturing Co 451
Telephones 224, 225
Terminator 185
Terracotta 642, 643
Terrey, John 629
Terry, Carden 595
Terry, Eli 204
Terry, John Edward 578
Textiles 644, 645
Thackeray, William Makepeace 62
Théroude 68
Thicke, William 522
Thief of Bagdad, The 458
Things to Come 461
Thistle, René Domremy 442
Thomas, John 407
Thomas, Seth 194
Thompson 35
Thonet 265
Thornton & Downer 239
Thornton-Pickard Co. 87, 91
Thuillier, A. 220
Thwaites 201
Ticka 89
Tickell, Geo. 70
Tiffany & Co. 76, 210, 445, 478, 479, 482, 483, 485, 580, 581, 581, 599, 604, 608
Tillotson 35
Tingley, Samuel 594
Tipp & Co. 649
Tippco 20, 650
TLM 476
TM 329
Toasters 646
Toastmaster 646
Toast Racks 622
TobaccoRoad 459
Toho 464
Tompion, Tho 180
Toohey, Sallie 158
Tork, Peter 542
Toys 647-651
TR and Co. 618
Trabert & Hoeffer 469
Trade Mark Gramophone, The 492

Travel Requisites 652
Trays & Salvers 623
Trays 653
Trenholme, William 605
Trickett, Roy 453
Tristan & Isolde 473
Trix 509
Trombino 493
Troughton & Simms 558, 559
Trunks & Coffers 392-395
Tsubas 58, 59
Tunbridgeware 654, 655
Tureens 624
Turner, Thackeray 102
Turnerelli, Peter 487
Turnstile, Stanley Gt. 561
Tuscan 140
Tutet, Edw. 204
TWA 541
20th Century Fox 459, 462, 463
Two Brothers 507
Typewriters 656
Tyson, Mike 633

Udet, Ernst 62
Uncle Tom's Cabin 461
United Artists 458, 461, 463-465
Universal 458, 461-465, 646
Universal Juwel 89
Urbino 140, 141
Urns 625

Vacheron & Constantin 211
Vaido 88
Vaillan, J. 229
Vamoose 505
Van Briggle 96, 97
Van Erp, Dirk 479
Van Nost, John 404
Vanishing American, The 465
Vann, D. 20
Vardon, Harry 452, 454
Varnish & Co. 429, 432, 442
Vases 440-445, 626
Veedol 22
Vesta Cases 627
Vichy, Gustave 66, 67
Vidoudez, Henri 512
Vienna 171
Villeroy & Boch 137
Villiers & Jackson 455
Vinaigrettes 628
Viner 193
Viners Studio 599
Vispré, François Xavier 527
Vogler, And. 566
Volkstedt 136
Von Star Amusement Co. 27
Votra Stereo Viewer 512
Voyageuse, La 573
Voyez, I 169
Voysey, C.F.A. 265
Vroutos, Georgios 487
Vyse, Charles 108

Wagner 99, 171
Wagstaff, William 152

Wain, Louis 103
Waistcoats 216, 217
Wakelin & Wheeler 603
Wakizashi 60, 61
Wakley, J. 596
Waldmann, Oscar 409
Walker & Hall 581
Walker, E. 529
Walking Dead, The 460
Wall Clocks 202-205
Wallis, Hall 540
Walton 102
Wardrobes and Armoires 396-397
Warhol, Andy 574
Warne, A.E. 602
Warner Brothers 458-461
Warner, A.E. 599, 622
Washington 26
Washington-Taylor 426
Washstands 398
Watches 206-209
Watcombe 105
Waterbury Clock Co 192
Watson, E. 180
Watt, James Cromer 474
Watts, Charlie 542
Watts, F.G. 643
Wayne, John 234
WB 593
Weathervanes 657-659
Webb, Edward 609
Webb, Philip 266, 331
Webb, Thomas & Son 228, 431,
    440, 441, 557
Webster, William 190, 200
Wedgwood 172, 173
Weegee 517
Welles, Orson 235
Wellford, Robert 240
Weltini 88
Wemyss 174
Wenz, A. 171
Wery, Alexis 568
West, L.A. 585
Western Electric Company 225
Westerwald 175
WF 611
Whatnots 400, 401
Wheeler, F.C. 596
Wheeler, Gervase 628
Whipham, Thomas 611
White Sister, The 460
White, Charles 324
White, Fuller 602
White, Geo 188
White, John and Co. 454
White,. A.J.P. 255
Whitehurst 202
Whiting Sterling 608
Whiting, Riley 189
Whyte, John 586
Wiener Werkstätte 443
Wilcox & White Organ Co. 491
Wileman, A. & Co. 102
Wilkinson, A.J. 104
Wilkinson, Henry & Co. 610
Will, Henry 515
Willard, Aaron 191

Willard, Benjamin 189
Willcox & Gibbs 572
Williams, Jane 595
Williams, Josiah, & Co. 615
Williams, Thos 36
Williamson, H.S. 20
Willington Glass Co. 426
Wilson 572
Wilson, Chas. & Sons 16
Wilson, Henry 472, 473
Wilson, W. 451
Wilson, Wm. & Son 616
Wiltberger, Christian 598
Winans, Walter 78
Wine Coolers 402, 403, 629
Wine Glasses 446-449
Winfield, R.W. 266
Wisbech, Alfred Heald 207
Wizard of Oz, The 459
WL 156
WM 621
WMF 514, 515
Wolff, A. 491
Wonder Portable Chiftophone 488
Wood 660-662
Wood, I. 610
Wood, Ralph 169-170
Wood, Robert 189
Wood, Samuel 586, 592, 595, 613
Wood, William 524
Woodall, George 442
Woodhead and Hartley 35
Woodyer, Henry 364
Woolf, Virginia 63
Worcester 176-179
Worden, Al 20
Work Box and Games Tables 383-
    385
Wormley, Edward 331
Worst Woman in Paris?, The 460
Wragg 35
Wright, Charles 621
Wright, Frank Lloyd 439
Wright, John & Co. 410, 411
Wright, William Thrale 498
Wrist Watches 210, 211
Writing Tables and Desks 386-391
WT 606
Wulff, Günter
WW 443
Wyk, J. 567
Wyman, Bill 542

Yankee Trade Stimulator 27
Yates and Son. 71
Yonezawa 539
Yoshu Matsuyama ju Shoami
    Hidetsugu 58
Young, J.M. & Sons 267
Young, James 620
Young, W.J. 563
Ysart, Paul 435

Zeiss 88-90
Zi Jin Shan 88
Zincke, Christian Friedrich 527
Zoetrope 513
Zurich 127